FERDYDURKE
PORNOGRAFIA
COSMOS

FERDYDURKE
PORNOGRAFIA
COSMOS

—— Three Novels by ——
WITOLD GOMBROWICZ

Grove Press, Inc., New York

First Edition 1978
First Printing 1978
ISBN: 0-394-17067-9
Grove Press ISBN: 0-8021-4210-9
Library of Congress Catalog Card Number: 78-55104

Library of Congress Cataloging in Publication Data

Gombrowicz, Witold.
    Three novels.

    CONTENTS: Ferdydurke.—Pornografia.—Cosmos.
    I.   Title.
PZ4.G6493Th   [PG7158.G669]   891.8'5'37   78-55104
ISBN 0-394-17067-9

Manufactured in the United States of America

Distributed by Random House, Inc., New York

GROVE PRESS, INC., 196 West Houston Street, New York, N.Y. 10014

FERDYDURKE

Translated by Eric Mosbacher

Contents

The History of Ferdydurke

1937 Publication in Warsaw. Literary sensation. Scandal. Controversy. Some critics predict an international career for the work.

1939 War, and invasion of Poland. *Ferdydurke* buried and forgotten. Gombrowicz arrives in Argentina.

1947 *Ferdydurke* published in Buenos Aires, translated into Spanish by the author in co-operation with a committee of South American writers under the aegis of the Cuban novelist Virgilio Piniera.

    Some years later Gombrowicz notes in his *Journal*: '*Ferdydurke* has been drowned in the sleep-walking immobility of South America.'

1957 Things begin to move at last. For the first ten years of the Communist régime in Poland Gombrowicz has been taboo and it has been forbidden to publish him, but now, after the events of October 1956, with Gomulka in the saddle, a little liberty is allowed.

    Ferdydurke is republished in Warsaw after twenty years. The Communists think they have let a canary out of its cage, but it turns out to be a wolf.

    The edition of 10,000 copies is sold out in a few days. Popularity? Success? Yes, such is sometimes the fate of books.... During the war years, under the Nazi occupation and after, under the Stalinist terror, *Ferdydurke*, i.e., the few pre-war copies that escaped destruction, never ceased to circulate from hand to hand. People, reading all this crazy stuff about people making faces, violation by the ears, tyranny of backside, said to themselves: Our situation precisely! For *Ferdydurke* contained, not only a premonition of existentialism, but an intuition of the deepest workings of totalitarianism. The novel becomes successful overnight. Its repressed popularity, long-suppressed laughter, burst out into the light of day.

Other works by Gombrowicz appear in Poland: *Transatlantic*, a novel; *Bakakai*, a volume of long short stories; *The Marriage*, a play; *Yvonne*, a comedy. They are warmly received by the press. Artur Sandauer, the best Polish critic, speaks on Warsaw radio of 'great literature', 'one of the greatest contemporary writers', and says: 'This writer is the pride of the nation'.

Works by Gombrowicz start appearing on the stage. *Yvonne* is a huge success in Warsaw; the critics compare it with Beckett and Ionesco. *The Marriage*, one of Gombrowicz's best works, is about to be produced at Cracow when . . .

1958 . . . a button is pressed, and Gombrowicz's name vanishes from publishers' lists, theatrical announcements and the press. It has been decided in high places that there has been too much Gombrowicz, and too much liberty in general. After that there is silence.

1959 But now the West starts taking an interest. When the French edition appears in Paris, François Bondy is the first to speak of the 'brilliant author of *Ferdydurke*, recently discovered by western Europe'. The French literary press, almost without exception, is enthusiastic. Mario Maurin in *Les Lettres Nouvelles* compares it to Sartre's *La Nausée*, the *Nouvelle Revue Française* speaks of a work 'of capital importance', and Jelenski of a 'strange masterpiece'.

★

Here, in conclusion, are two comments by Gombrowicz, the first an extract from his *Journal* and the second the concluding passage of his introduction to the Spanish edition of *Ferdydurke*:

I. What a bore is the everlasting question: What did you mean by *Ferdydurke*? Come, come, be more sensuous, less cerebral, start dancing with the book instead of asking for meanings. Why take so much interest in the skeleton if it's got a body? See rather whether it is capable of pleasing and is not devoid of grace and passion. . . .

II. . . . at worst the book will pass unnoticed, but friends and acquaintances when they meet me will certainly feel under an obligation to say to me the sort of thing that is always said when an author publishes a book. I should like to ask them to do nothing of the sort. No, let them say nothing, because, as a result of all sorts of falsifications, the social situation of the so-called 'artist' in our times has become so pretentious that whatever can be said in such circumstances sounds false, and the more sincerity and simplicity you put into your 'I enjoyed it enormously' or 'I like it very much indeed', the more shameful it is for him and for you. I therefore beg you to keep silent. Keep silent in hope of a better future. For the time being—if you wish to let me know that the book pleased you—when you see me simply touch your right ear. If you touch your left ear, I shall know that you didn't like it, and if you touch your nose it will mean that you are not sure . . . thus we shall avoid uncomfortable and even ridiculous situations and understand each other in silence. My greetings to all.

FERDYDURKE

1

Abduction

THAT Tuesday I awoke at the still and empty hour when the night is nearly over but there is still no sign of dawn. I lay in the dim light, while mortal fear lay heavy on my body and invaded my mind, and my mind in its turn lay heavy on my body; and the smallest particles of myself writhed in the appalling certainty that nothing would ever happen, nothing ever change, and that, whatever one did, nothing would ever come of it. The explanation of my terror was contained in the dream which had troubled me during the night and had ended by waking me.

What had I dreamt? By a regression of a kind that ought to be forbidden to nature, I had seen myself at the age of fifteen or sixteen, I had reverted to adolescence. Standing in the wind on a stone at the edge of a river, I had said something, heard myself saying something, heard my shrill, long-since-buried, adolescent voice, seen my excessively big hands and the immature nose on my soft, provisional, adolescent's face, felt the unprofitable content of that passing and intermediary phase of myself; and I had awoken between laughter and fear, for it had seemed to me that the adult, the thirty-year-old who I am today, was apeing and mocking the adolescent that I was then, while the adolescent was mocking the adult; and that each of my two selves was thus taking the rise out of the other. Hapless memory that forces on us knowledge of the paths that we followed in order to become what we are! Half-asleep, I even imagined that my body was not entirely homogeneous, and that parts of it were not yet mature, that my head was laughing at and mocking my thigh, that my thigh was making merry at my head, that my finger was ridiculing my heart and my heart my brain, while my eye made sport of my nose and my nose of my eye, all to the accompaniment of loud bursts of crazy laughter—my limbs and the various parts of my body violently ridiculing each other in a general atmosphere of caustic and wounding raillery. But when I came to myself completely and started looking at my life, my terror, far from vanishing, increased, though a little laugh which it was impossible to restrain kept turning up to interrupt (or perhaps stimulate) it. Half-way along the path of my life, I found myself in a dark forest; and the worst of it was that the forest was *green*.

For in reality I was as vague and uncoordinated as I was in my dream. I had recently crossed the unavoidable Rubicon of my thirtieth birthday; according to my papers and my appearance, I was grown up. But I was not mature. What was I then? Where was I? I wandered from bar to café, from café to bar, met people, exchanged words and sometimes even thoughts with them, but my situation was by no means clear, and I did not know myself whether I was a man or an adolescent. The result was that in confronting the second half of my life I was neither one nor another, I was nothing at all, and that I was rightly treated with suspicion by those of my generation who had married and had settled positions, if not exactly in relation to life, at any rate in offices of one kind or another. My aunts, those numerous, devoted, clinging, but kind semi-mammas, had been trying for a long time to use their influence to get me to settle down in some suitable occupation, say, as a lawyer or in business, for the prolonged nondescript nature of my life was torture to them. Not really knowing who I was, they did not know what to say to me, and at best their conversation with me was at a level of sad twaddle. 'Johnnie,' they would say to me between one twitter and the next, 'the years are passing, and what will people think? If you don't want to be a doctor, be a *bon viveur* or a collector, but be something, you must be something'; and I would hear one of them whispering to another that I lacked polish; and then, desperate because of the void which thereupon appeared in their heads, they would revert to their twitterings. This situation could not of course be prolonged indefinitely; the hands of nature's clock are inexorable and exact. My last teeth, my wisdom teeth, having come through, I had had to accept the fact that my development was complete, and that the hour had struck for the inevitable murder; the man must slay the youth and take wing like the butterfly, leaving the dead body of the chrysalis on the ground. I had had to enter the grown-up world.

Enter it? But with pleasure. I had made the attempt, and when I looked back on it now I split my sides with laughter. To prepare my entrance into the world of adults I had sat down to write a book, primarily to explain myself and obtain its favours in advance. I had assumed that, if I succeeded in causing a definite idea about my personality to germinate in the minds of others, that idea would itself contribute to my development, with the result that willy-nilly I should attain maturity. But why did my pen betray me? Why did a sanctimonious modesty prevent me from writing a manifestly and tediously mature novel? And why, instead of begetting from my mind and my heart lofty sentiments and noble thoughts, was I able to produce these only from the lower part of my person? Why did I introduce into the text all those extraordinary frogs and legs and things, all that fermenting matter, isolating them on the page only by the style, the cold and disciplined tone, and demonstrating to the reader how completely I dominated the ferment? And why, to the detriment of my own purpose, did I call the book *Memoirs of a Time of Immaturity*? In vain my friends advised me to drop that title, and in general to refrain from all reference to immaturity. 'Don't do it,' they said. 'Immaturity is a very drastic idea. If you yourself don't think yourself mature, how can you expect anybody else to?' But I actually thought it unseemly to pass over in silence the callow youth inside me, and I thought grown-ups far too perspicacious and clear-sighted to be so easily taken in, and, finally, I thought that anyone so closely beset by the callow youth inside him had no right to make a public appearance without him. Perhaps I took serious matters too seriously; perhaps I overestimated the maturity of mature persons.

Memories! My head buried in the pillow and my legs under the blankets, caught between terror and uncontrollable laughter, I looked back at my entrance into the world of grown-ups. I thought of the sad venture of my first book, recalled how instead of giving me the desired stability it had got me more bogged down than ever, while the wave of people's stupid opinions broke over me. What a curse it is that there is no permanent, stable order of things in our life on this planet, that everything in it is in perpetual motion, continual flux, that it is a necessity for everyone to be understood and appreciated by his neighbour, and that what fools and simpletons and oafs think of us is as important as the opinion of the wise, the subtle, the acute! For at heart man depends on the picture of himself formed in the minds of others, even if the others are half-wits. And I protest with all my strength against those of my colleagues who adopt an attitude of aristocratic contempt for the opinions of the ignorant and say: *Odi profanum vulgus*. What a cheap evasion, what a wretched shirking of reality is that high and mighty affectation! I claim, on the contrary, that the more inept and petty criticism is, the more constricting it is, like a tight shoe. Oh! those human opinions, the abyss of views and criticisms of your intelligence, your heart, every detail of your being, which opens up in front of you when you have incautiously clothed your thoughts in words, put them on paper and spread them among men! Oh! paper! paper! Words, words! And I am not talking here of the mild and gentle domestic opinions of our beloved aunts. No, I refer rather to the opinions of our cultural 'aunts', the innumerable author-aunts (I am not here concerned with their morals) who express their opinions in the press. For seated upon the culture of the world are legions of good women, tied and bound to literature, deeply initiated into intellectual values, aesthetically awake, supported by ideas, concepts, and all the rest of it, who are already aware of the fact that Oscar Wilde is out of date and Bernard Shaw a master of paradox. They know very well that you should be independent, simple, and profound, so they are independent, simple, and profound, and full of an entirely domesticated mildness. Aunts, the whole lot of them! Ah! he who has never been taken into the cultural aunts' laboratory and been dissected by their trivial and pettifogging mentalities which dissect the life out of life, he who has not read in the papers what one of these aunts thinks about him, does not know what triviality, what auntiness, really is.

And more; there are the criticisms of country gentlemen, the opinions of pensioners, the petty criticisms of clerks, the bureaucratic opinions of high officials, the criticisms of provincial lawyers, the extremist opinions of young people, the infatuated judgements of old men, to say nothing of the views of doctors' wives, children, female cousins, housemaids and cooks, a whole tidal wave of opinions which describe and portray us as we appear in the minds of others. It is like being born in a thousand rather narrow minds. But my position was even more difficult and painful, because my book, in comparison with conventionally mature writing, seemed drastic and difficult. True, it gained me a handful of picked friends, and if the cultural aunts and other representatives of the vulgar could have heard how I was coddled and saturated with praise in the course of intellectually very elevated conversation in select gatherings of the eminent, the *élite*, inaccessible to them even in dreams, they would probably have fallen on their knees in front of me and kissed my feet. On the other hand there must have been something green, something immature, about my way of writing which attracted the confraternity of the immature and sanctioned their familiarity with me. For it often happened, when I emerged into the street from one of these sacrosanct places in which I was so agreeably treated with lavish respect, that I would run into some engineer or schoolboy who would treat me as if I were his brother in folly, his accomplice in immaturity, and bawl at me, to the accompaniment of hearty and repeated slaps on the back: 'What rubbish you write, old man! How can you write such a lot of tripe!' Thus I was mature to the mature and immature to the immature, with the result that I did not know which side I was on: that of those who treated me with respect or of those who regarded me as half-baked.

But the worst of it was that, though I encountered a fierce and, I imagine, unprecedented hatred on the part of the vulgar, the semi-intelligent, it was with the latter that I sided; I fled from the cordially extended arms of the *élite* into the coarse embrace of those who thought me a fool. A question of primary importance, affecting the whole development of the personality, is that of the reality in relation to which a man fashions himself. Does he, for instance, when he talks, acts, rants, writes, pay attention and take into account only grown-up, fully adult persons? Or is he haunted by the phantom of the vulgar and the immature, the shadow of a dubious and murky half-world, in the green darkness of which you slowly stifle, suffocated by the lianas, the creepers, and other African growths? Never for a moment was I able to forget the sub-world of sub-humanity and, though panic and terror seized me at the mere thought of its swampy verdure, fascinated as I was by it, like a bird by a snake, I could not shake it off. It was as if, in defiance of nature, I sympathized with and even loved the vulgar world, was grateful to it for causing the child in me to survive. Oh! living on the threshold of the lofty, adult world and not being able to go in! Being but one step distant from wisdom, dignity, distinction, ripe judgement, mutual respect, a hierarchy of proper values, and being able to savour these things only through the window, having no access to what was inside, being second-rate! Living among grown-ups and still having the feeling, as at the age of sixteen, of only pretending to be one of them! Playing the writer, the man of letters, mimicking literary style and grown-up expressions! Fighting, as an artist, a grim public battle for one's own 'ego', but at the same time secretly sympathizing with one's mortal enemies!

True, during the first days of my public life I had received a semi-consecration, been generously anointed, by the lower world. But what still further complicated the situation was that my social behaviour left much to be desired; I turned out to be completely helpless and defenceless in the semi-brilliant social world. Some sort of laziness, born of fear and timidity, prevented me from adjusting myself to any kind of maturity whatever, and sometimes, when someone made a flattering intellectual approach to me, I felt like giving him a good, hard pinch. How I envied those men of letters unquestionably predestined to superiority from birth, to sublimity from the cradle, whose minds moved perpetually towards the heights, just as if their backsides had been pricked with a pin! Serious writers who took their souls seriously, had an innate aptitude for creative suffering on the grand scale, and moved freely in a world of ideas so exalted and for ever sanctified that God himself seemed to them vulgar and devoid of majesty! Why is it not given to everybody to write yet another novel about love, or to denounce some social injustice and thus transform himself into a defender of the people? Or to write verse, become a poet, and believe in the 'noble mission of verse'? To have talent and feed the non-talented on it? Ah! How satisfying it must be to suffer and torment oneself, to sacrifice oneself on the altar, to burn oneself alive at the stake, always higher than the heights, in such a sublimated, adult world! How satisfying, to oneself and to others, to launch oneself, with the aid of age-old cultural institutions, with a confidence equal to that with which one puts money in the bank! But I, alas, was an adolescent, and adolescence was my only cultural institution, and I was doubly cornered and trapped, by a childhood which I could not get rid of and by the childishness of the ideas which others formed of me, the caricature of myself which existed in their minds. So I was the slave of greenness, an insect prisoner of the thick foliage.

This situation was not only awkward; it was dangerous too. For nothing horrifies and disgusts the mature so much as immaturity. They have no difficulty in tolerating the most destructive intelligence so long as its field of activity lies within the framework of maturity. They do not fear a revolutionary who opposes one mature ideal to another mature ideal, e.g. overthrows a monarchy in favour of republicanism, or makes mincemeat of republicanism in the interests of royalism. They even look with favour on such a happy, adult, sublimated way of behaving. But if they detect immaturity in someone, discover the youth in him, they fall on him, annihilate him with their sarcasms, peck him to death with their beaks, like swans with a duck.

Where, then, was all this going to end? Where was this road leading me? How, I wondered, had I come to be so subjected to, so fascinated by, the green and the unripe? Perhaps because I was the native of a country rich in individuals at the crude, primitive, transitional stage, a country in which collars do not suit anyone and the countryside is haunted by the lamentations of laziness and incompetence rather than those of Chopinian melancholy. Or perhaps it was because I lived in a period which was itself continually inventing new devices, new grimaces, its face twisting under the influence of a thousand convulsions. . . .

The pale dawn entered the window, and as I lay under the blankets looking back at my life I was seized by an indecent, uncontrollable, embarrassed fit of laughter; it was a helpless, bestial, mechanical laugh, a leg laugh, just as if somebody had tickled the sole of my foot, as if it were not my face but my leg that were laughing. I must make a clean break, put childish things behind me, make up my mind, make a fresh start, do something!

It was then that I had a simple but wonderful idea—to be neither mature nor immature, but simply myself; to express myself in my own proudly sovereign fashion, ignoring everything except my own inner truth. Ah! to shape oneself, express oneself, express not only that part of oneself which had reached clarity and maturity but also that which was still fermenting and obscure. Let my own shape be born of me, let me not owe my formation to anyone. Excitement impelled me towards pen and paper. I took the paper from the drawer, and by now it was full morning. The sun came flooding into the room, the maid brought the coffee and rolls, and I, surrounded by shining and finely modelled forms, started writing the first pages of a book, my book, a book resembling myself, identical with myself, born of myself, a book which was to be the supreme affirmation of myself in the face of everything and everybody. Suddenly the bell rang. The maid opened the door, and there appeared on the threshold T. Pimko, the doctor, the professor, or rather the master, the distinguished Cracow philologist, small, puny, bald, and bespectacled, in striped pants and tailcoat, his yellowish nails projecting under his light-yellow gloves.

'Do you know the professor?'

'The professor?'

Stop! Stop! Panic-stricken at the appearance of this platitudinously dull and dully platitudinous human being, I made hurriedly to hide what I had written. But he sat down, so I had to do the same; and as soon as he was seated he started condoling with me on the death of an aunt who had died some time previously, an aunt whom I had totally forgotten.

'Remembrance of the dead,' he began, 'constitutes a fraternal arch connecting past years with those to come, just like folksong (Mickiewicz). We live the life of the dead (Auguste Comte). Your aunt is dead, so we can, nay must, devote to her some erudite thoughts and lofty ideas. She had her faults (he enumerated them), but she also had her qualities (which he enumerated too), qualities which were useful to society, which enables us to say that we are dealing here with not a bad book, I beg your pardon, aunt; we may even say that the deceased deserved good marks, for, to put it in a nutshell, she was an influence for good, and it follows that the verdict is favourable, and assuring you of that fact is an agreeable duty to me, Pimko, guardian of the cultural values of which your aunt herself formed part, particularly in view of the fact that she is dead. Besides,' he added indulgently, '*de mortuis nil nisi bene.* True, some criticisms might be made here and there, but why discourage a young author, I beg your pardon, nephew? But, good gracious!' he exclaimed, noticing on the table the sheets of paper covered with my scrawl, 'not only nephew, but author as well! I see that we are trying our chances with the Muses. Well! Well! Well! An author! Let me immediately criticize, encourage, advise!' Still seated, he drew the sheets of paper towards him across the table, putting on his spectacles at the same time.

'No!' I muttered. My world collapsed in ruins. Aunt and author had utterly confounded me.

As Pimko spoke he rubbed one of his eyes. Then he took out a cigarette, held it in his left hand while he smoothed it with his right, and started to cough, for the tobacco irritated his nose. Then he sat back and started to read. He sat and read very learnedly. I paled as I watched him, and thought I was going to pass out. I could not use violence on him, because I was seated because he was seated. Heaven knows why the fact that we were seated was fundamental, was the cardinal obstacle. So I shifted in my seat, not knowing what to do; I started moving my legs and biting my finger-nails, while he, composedly and at ease, remained seated, that position following logically from and being completely explained by the fact that he was reading. The reading went on for an eternity. The minutes lasted for hours and the seconds were unnaturally extended, and I was ill at ease, like a sea that somebody was trying to suck up through a straw.

Not the master! I groaned. Not the master! Anything, but not the master!

His masterly composure crushed me; he went on reading in masterly fashion, assimilating my spontaneous outpourings with his typical master's personality, holding the paper up to his eyes. . . . Through the window you could see the block of flats opposite, twelve horizontal windows and twelve vertical. Was it dream or reality? Why had he come here, why was he sitting down, why was I sitting down? By what miracle had all that had been happening previously, dreams, memories, aunts, sufferings, thoughts, work, led to the master's sitting here like this? No! No! It was impossible. As he was reading, he had good reason to be seated, but I had no reason whatever, it was absurd.

I made a convulsive effort to rise to my feet, but at that moment he looked up at me, gazed at me indulgently over his spectacles. And then suddenly I dwindled, my ears grew small, my hands contracted, my body shrank, while he grew

22

enormous and remained still seated, taking in and assimilating what I had written *in saecula saeculorum amen.*

Have you ever had the sensation of dwindling in size inside someone? Ah! Diminishing inside an aunt is most indelicate, but diminishing inside an eminent and famous master is the height of indecency. I could see him feeding on my greenness like a cow. It was an extraordinary sensation: the master grazing in a field, feeding on one's greenness, but at the same time seated in an armchair, and yet grazing, grazing. Something terrible was happening inside and yet outside me, something absurd, something impudently unreal. I muttered that I had a mind of my own, that I was not a mere hack, that I was alive, that I had a mind and a spirit of my own. . . . But he remained seated, so firmly and inexorably seated that the fact of his sitting, though intolerably stupid, was nevertheless all-powerful.

He removed his spectacles, wiped them with his handkerchief, and put them back on his nose . . . and his nose was a thing both indescribable and impregnable. It was a commonplace, pedagogic, rather long, nasal nose, consisting of two parallel tubes, obvious and final.

'What spirit are you talking about, please?'

'Mine!'

'Yours? You refer, no doubt, to the patriotic spirit of the motherland?'

'No! Mine is no patriotic spirit.'

'Yours?' he said benevolently. 'So we think we have a spirit? Do we at least know what the spirit of King Ladislas was?' He remained rooted to his chair.

What King Ladislas? I felt like a train that had been suddenly shunted to King Ladislas's siding. I braked and opened my mouth, realizing that my ignorance of King Ladislas was total and complete. He went on:

'But you must be acquainted with the spirit of history? And the spirit of antiquity? And the spirit of French civilization? And the spirit of the sixteenth-century bucolic writer who used the word "navel" for the first time in literature? And with the spirit of the language in general? Is "meander" masculine or feminine?'

With that question a hundred thousand spirits swept down on mine and I was utterly confounded; stammeringly I admitted that I did not know. He asked what I could tell him about Mickiewicz, and what that poet's attitude had been towards the people. He also asked me about Lelewel's first love affair. I coughed, and glanced furtively at my fingers, but nothing was written on my nails, they were clean. I looked all round, hoping that somebody would prompt me, but nobody was there. Was it dream or reality? Heavens, what was happening? Good Lord! I looked up, but it was not I who looked at Pimko, but a schoolboy darting a stealthy, furtive, look at his master. Anachronistically, I wanted to screw up a sheet of paper and throw it in his face. Feeling that something ghastly was going to happen, I made a desperate effort to control myself and say to him casually, like a man of the world: 'Well? How are you? What's the latest?' but my voice had lost its ordinary tone, had become shrill and raw, as if it were still breaking, so I held my peace. Pimko asked me what I knew about adverbs, made me decline *mensa, mensam, mensae* and conjugate *amo, amas, amat*, pursed his lips disapprovingly, said: 'Well, then, you'll have to revise,' took a notebook from his pocket, and gave me a bad mark. All this while he remained seated, and his sitting had now become immutable, permanent and absolute.

What was all this? I wanted to shout that I wasn't a schoolboy, that it was all a mistake, and I jumped up to run away, but something caught me from behind, a kind of hook which dragged me back, and there I was, caught by my childish, schoolboy's little behind. It was my little behind that stopped me from moving, because of it I could not budge, and the master still sat there, and such an overwhelmingly, schoolmasterly spirit emanated from his posture that instead of crying out I raised my arm like a schoolboy in class. Pimko frowned, and said:

'Keep quiet, Kowalski! Do you want to leave the room again?'

And he remained seated and I remained seated in a situation as absurd and unreal as a dream . . . I, seated on my childish little behind which paralysed me and deprived me of my senses and he seated on his as if on the Acropolis while he noted something in his book.

Eventually he said:

'Come along now, Johnnie, let's go to school.'

'What school?'

'Mr Piorkowski's. It's a first-class establishment. There's still room in the second form. Your knowledge leaves a lot to be desired. The first thing to do is to fill the gaps.'

'But what school?'

'Mr Piorkowski's. He's short of pupils, and, as it happens, has been asking me to find him some. The school has got to be a success, and to be a success it must have pupils. To school then, to school!'

'But what school?'

'That'll do. Come along now!'

He rang for the maid and asked for his overcoat. She started grumbling, not understanding my being taken away like this by a stranger, but Pimko pinched her and she stopped, because when she was pinched she had no choice but to burst out laughing like a servant girl when she has been pinched, showing her teeth. And the schoolmaster took me by the hand and led me out into the street where, in spite of everything, the houses were still standing and people were going and coming.

Help! Police! It was too stupid to be true. It was impossible, because it was impossibly stupid. But it was too stupid for me to be able to stop it. . . . I was powerless against the schoolmaster, paralysed by my childish, idiotic little behind, which hamstrung all possible resistance. The colossus advanced with a giant's stride, I trotted along beside him, and there was nothing I could do against him because of my little behind. Farewell, spirit which was mine, farewell, my work! Off with my true, my real shape, and on with this terrible, puerile, green and grotesque shape!

25

Cruelly dwindled and diminished, I trotted along beside the huge schoolmaster, who muttered:

'Well, well, well, little doggie! Tiny nose, tiny ears, tiny hands! Well, well, well! Little behind, what a pretty little behind!'

In front of us a woman was taking her puppy for a walk. It growled, jumped at Pimko, and tore the bottom of his trousers. Pimko expressed an unfavourable opinion about the puppy, pinned up the tear in his trousers, and led me away by the hand.

* 2 *

Incarceration
and Further Rejuvenescence

AND here—was I to believe my eyes?—was that very ordinary
building, the school to which I was dragged by Pimko in spite
of my tears and protestations. We arrived during the morning
break; young persons varying in age between ten and twenty
were walking about the playground, eating bread and butter or
bread and cheese. Mothers were insatiably gazing at their little
darlings through the gaps in the fence. With his double-barrelled
nasal appendage Pimko voluptuously sniffed the atmosphere of
school.

'Boys, boys, boys!' he exclaimed. 'Boys, boys, boys!'

Meanwhile a member of the staff, a man with a limp, probably
an usher, came towards us, showing every sign of exceptional
and profound respect.

'Here,' Pimko said to him, 'is little Johnnie, whom I want
put in the second form. Johnnie, say good-morning to the
gentleman. I'll leave Johnnie with you to get used to the place
while I have a word with the head.'

I wanted to reply, but instead bowed slightly to the professor.
A slight breeze sprang up and moved the branches of the trees,
as well as a lock of hair on Pimko's head.

'I hope we'll behave ourselves,' the usher said, patting me on
the head.

'And how are all these young people progressing?' Pimko
asked in a low voice. 'I see that they walk very well. They walk,
they talk, and their mothers watch them. There's nothing so

27

effective as a mother strategically placed behind a wall to bring out a pair of fresh young buttocks.'

'All the same, they're still not guileless enough,' the usher started lamenting. 'We still can't get them to be fresh and innocent enough. You will never imagine, my dear colleague, how headstrong and obstinate they are. They just don't want to be as fresh and innocent as spring carrots. They just don't want to be!'

This earned him a sharp rebuke from Pimko, who informed him severely that he was lacking in the schoolmasterly virtues.

'What?' he said, 'they don't want to? They don't want to? We must make them want to! I'll show you how to stimulate innocence straight away. I guarantee that within half an hour the whole atmosphere of the place will be twice as innocent and guileless as it is now. What I shall do is this: I shall spend some time watching the boys, and shall then give them to understand that I consider them innocent and guileless. The effect will be highly provocative; they will immediately try to show that they are the very reverse of innocent, and in so doing will automatically relapse into that innocence and naïveté which is such a delight to us pedagogues.'

Pimko hid behind a big oak tree, while the usher took me by the hand and led me among the schoolboys without giving me a chance to open my mouth.

The boys were walking about in the playground. Some were energetically scrapping or exchanging blows; some had stopped their ears and had buried their heads in their books; others were making faces at each other, or trying to trip each other up, or pushing each other about, and their stupefied, lifeless, sheeplike eyes rested on me without seeing that I was a man of thirty. Believing it was time to put an end to this farce, I went up to the nearest boy, and said:

'Excuse me, but as you see, in view of my age ...'

'Hi, chaps!' he shouted. '*Novum companerum!*'

A group gathered round me. Somebody said:

'*Deo gratias*. What *capricius* of the *tempum* caused your *excellentissimum personus* to arrive so much in *retardus*?'

Somebody else, to the accompaniment of loutish guffaws, improved on this by saying:

'Would our *estimadus colegus* by any chance have been suffering from chronic lymphatic flemingitis, or was it a flame for some damsel that delayed his so eagerly expected arrival?'

This horrible gibberish shut me up like a clam, but they didn't stop, it seemed to be impossible for them to stop; and the more appalled I was, the more pleasure did they take in it, the more exultantly did they wallow in it, the more obstinately and crazily did they persist. Their gestures were half-baked, their faces pasty and callow. The principal subject of conversation of the small boys was sexual organs, and of the big boys sexual intercourse; a horrifying dish served up in their pseudo-archaic, Latinized jargon. They seemed somehow awkward and ill at ease, and they kept looking at the usher and convulsively clutching their behinds, and the feeling that they were under constant observation prevented them from eating their lunch.

The effect on me of this farce to which no end seemed in sight was that my head was swimming and I found it utterly impossible to explain myself. But when they noticed Pimko, who was watching them and missing nothing from his hiding-place behind the oak-tree, they became nervous in the extreme; the news spread quickly that the inspector had arrived, and was spying on them from behind the tree.

'The inspector!' some of the boys said, taking out their books, and moving over towards the tree. But neither they nor the others escaped the eagle eye of Pimko, who started taking notes.

'He's taking notes!' boys muttered all round me. 'He's spying on us and writing everything down!'

Pimko thereupon caused the sheet of paper on which he had been writing to flutter towards them in such a discreet and unobtrusive manner that it seemed to have been blown by the wind. On it he had written: 'On the basis of my observations made at X School during the long break I am able to state that the boys are absolutely innocent—of that I am profoundly convinced. It is demonstrated by their appearance, their innocent chatter, and, finally, their attractive and innocent little backsides. Signed, Pimko, Warsaw, 29th October, 193 . . .'

This put the whole ant-heap in a ferment. 'What! We boys innocent? We who knew everything when we were ten?' There were roars of laughter all round, suppressed, violent, yet secret laughter. What an old fool! What a naïve old fool! But I suddenly realized that the laughter was lasting too long, that it was growing angrier as it grew more violent, that the anger was directed at the laughers themselves, and that the angrier they grew the more hollow and artificial it was. What was happening? Why didn't they stop laughing? It was only later that I understood what sort of poison the diabolical, Machiavellian Pimko had fed them with. For the truth of the matter was that these boys shut up in school away from life were innocent. They were innocent though they were not. They were innocent in their determination not to be. They were innocent when they held a woman in their arms, when they fought, recited poetry, or played billiards. They were innocent when they ate and when they slept. They were innocent when they were innocent. Even when they swore, seduced, tortured, drew blood—all things they did to avoid being innocent—they always had innocence hanging over their heads.

That was why their laughter grew and grew; it was like being on the rack. Some of the boys started using the filthiest language, the language of drunken cabbies. Quickly, feverishly, quietly, they started mouthing oaths and obscenities, some of which they illustrated with chalk on the walls; and the pure air of autumn was filled with language even more appalling than that which had greeted me on my arrival. I thought I must be dreaming, for it is only in a dream that you find yourself in situations more stupid than anything you could imagine awake. I tried to restrain them.

'Why do you say c——?' I asked one of them frantically. 'Why do you use that word?'

'Shut up, you fool!' the brute replied, hitting me. 'It's a whale of a word! Say it! Say it yourself!' he whispered, and stamped on my toes. 'Say it at once! Don't you see that it's our only defence against backside? Don't you see that the inspector's behind the oak-tree, and that he intends to fit us out with little backsides? If you don't start straight away saying all the bad words you know, I'll land you one! Come on! Say them, and we'll say them too! Come on, he wants to give us little backsides!'

This crude individual (known to his intimates as Mientus) thereupon made his way furtively over to the oak-tree and wrote the four-lettered word on it, where neither Pimko nor the mothers could see. This exploit was greeted with a horrible, smug burst of laughter. When they heard it the mothers on the other side of the fence and Pimko behind the tree laughed too—they were delighted that their boys were having such a good time; and the gay laughter of the grown-ups and the sly laughter of the boys, delighted at this successful *coup*, clashed in the quiet autumn air, among the leaves falling from the trees, while the old school porter went on with his sweeping and the sun shone palely and the lawn turned yellow. But Pimko behind his tree, and all these louts convulsed with laughter, and, indeed, the whole situation, were suddenly so terrifyingly naïve that I found myself, with all my unexpected protests, being sucked into the general puerility, and I did not know to whose aid to go to—my own, my comrades', or Pimko's. I went over to the tree and whispered:

'Professor!'.

'What is it?' Pimko replied, also in a whisper.

'Don't stay there, professor! They've written a bad word on the other side of the tree, and that's what they're laughing at. Don't stay there, professor!'

While talking this rubbish I felt myself to be the very high priest of idiocy. I was startled at what I found myself doing—muttering from behind the back of my hand to Pimko standing behind the tree in the school playground.

'What did you say?' the professor asked from behind his tree. 'What did they write?'

There was the sound of a motor-horn in the distance.

31

'A bad word!' I said. 'A bad word! Come out from there!'

'Where did they write it?'

'On the other side of the tree! Come out from there, professor! That's enough! Don't let them make a fool of you! Sir, you tried to make them out to be naïve and innocent, and they've written a four-lettered word.... Don't go on provoking them, professor, it's gone far enough. I can't go on talking into the air like this, professor, I shall go mad! Come out from there, please! I can't stand it any longer!'

While I said this summer declined slowly into autumn and the leaves fell silently.

'What's that?' the professor exclaimed. 'What's that? You expect me to doubt the youthful purity of the youthful generation? Never! In all matters of life and pedagogy I am an old fox.'

He came out from behind the tree, and the boys, seeing him standing there in the flesh, let out a yell.

'My dear young people,' he said after they had calmed down a little. 'I am not ignorant of the fact that among yourselves you use very coarse, indecent, expressions. Don't imagine for a moment that I don't know what goes on. But you have no cause for anxiety. No excess, however lamentable in itself, will ever affect my profound belief that at bottom you are innocent and pure, and that is what you are to me. Your old friend will always believe you to be pure and innocent, and he will always have faith in your decency, your purity, your innocence; and, as for bad words, I know that you use them innocently, without understanding, just for effect—no doubt one of you picked them up from his nurse. That's quite all right, there's no harm in it at all, it's far more innocent than you think!'

He sneezed, blew his nose and, feeling very pleased with himself, went off in the direction of the headmaster's study to talk about me to Mr Piorkowski. Meanwhile the mothers and aunts on the other side of the fence flung themselves into each other's arms and exclaimed with delight:

'What wonderful ideas the professor has! What a wonderful faith in innocence!'

Among the boys, however, Pimko's speech caused consternation. Silently they watched him walk away; and it was not until he was out of sight that the storm broke.

'Did you hear that?' Mientus exclaimed. 'Did you hear that? We're innocent! Innocent! He thinks we're innocent! Whatever we do, we're innocent! Innocent!'

The word was a thorn in his side; it paralysed, tortured, killed him, imposing naïveté and innocence upon him. At this point a boy named Pylaszczkiewicz, but known to his intimates as Siphon, seemed to succumb to what had become the prevailing atmosphere of naïveté; he said to himself, but in a voice which resounded in the pure and limpid air as clearly as a cow-bell:

'Innocent? Why not?'

And he stood there plunged in thought. Why not, indeed, be innocent? He could not have asked a more sensible question. For who is more mature, he who flees from sin, or he who seeks it out? But the thought, though rational and mature, sounded innocent, and Siphon realized this himself, because he flushed.

He tried to slip away, but Mientus had heard what he said, and was not going to allow it to pass.

'What?' he said. 'You admit you're innocent?'

Mientus was so startled by the innocence of what he had just said that he stepped back. But now Siphon was upset too, and was not prepared to allow this remark to pass either.

'Admit it?' he said. 'Why shouldn't I admit it? I'm not a child!'

Mientus laughed sneeringly in the diaphanous air.

'Did you hear him?' he jeered. 'Siphon's innocent! Wah! Wah! Siphon the innocent!'

'*Siphonus innocentus!*' boys started calling out. 'Has our worthy Siphon no knowledge of women?'

Others took up the chorus of this green raillery, and the world became disgusting again. The growing hubbub infuriated Siphon. He glared all round.

'And even if I were innocent, what of it?' he exclaimed. 'What's it got to do with you?'

33

'So it's true, then!' they jeered back at him. 'So it's true!'

And the unhappy lads did not realize that the further they went, the more deeply they engulfed themselves in innocence.

'Would you believe it?' they sneered. 'He doesn't even know the facts of life!'

They started jeering and booing again.

'And even if I didn't, what business is it of yours?' Siphon burst out. 'What business is it of yours, I should like to know?'

There was such a strange, icy tone in his voice that for a moment they were intimidated, and silence prevailed. Then voices started calling out:

'Come off it, Siphon! So it's true that you don't know, is it?'

And they stepped back a pace. Siphon would obviously have liked to have stepped back too, but could not. Then Mientus called out:

'Of course it's true! Look at him! It's obvious!'

And he spat. Bobek called out:

'But that's disgraceful, he ought to be ashamed of himself. I'll tell you everything, Siphon, you really ought to know!'

Siphon: 'But I don't want to!'

Hopek: 'You don't want to?'

Siphon: 'I don't want to, because I don't see the necessity.'

Hopek: 'You don't want to? You don't want to? But it isn't just a matter of what you want or don't want, it's a matter that concerns all of us. It's not a situation we can be expected to tolerate. If we did, how could we ever look girls in the face again?'

'So that's what's getting you, is it?' Siphon burst out angrily. 'Girls! Girls! You want to cut a dash with the girls! I don't give a fig for your girls! So you want to be boys with the girls!'

He had realized that he could no longer retreat, and, moreover, he no longer wanted to.

'Girls!' he exclaimed. 'Girls! And why not decent girls? Why not adolescents and decent, respectable girls? So you want to be boys with the girls! Well, I like being an adolescent for decent girls. Why should I be ashamed of using words which are decent

34

and honourable? Anyway, that's how it is, I want to be an adolescent for decent young women.'

He stopped. But what he said was in reality so true, sensible, and convincing that many of his listeners were left perplexed.

'Doesn't he speak well?' some of them said, and others remarked:

'He's quite right, purity is better than girls!'

'One ought to have some ideals, after all!' another pointed out, and someone else remarked:

'If he wants to be an adolescent, let him!'

'Adolescents!' Siphon announced. 'Up the adolescents! Let us found a society to preserve the purity of youth and oppose everything that soils it! Let us swear never to be ashamed of beauty, purity and nobility! Forward!'

And before anyone could stop him he raised his hand and swore a solemn oath, with a grave, inspired expression on his face. Several juveniles, surprised by his gesture, raised their hand and followed suit. Mientus rushed angrily at Siphon in the pure and transparent air; Siphon's blood was up too, but fortunately they were separated in time.

'Why don't you fellows kick his arse?' said Mientus, struggling with those who were restraining him. 'Have you no blood in your veins? Have you no ambition? Only a good kick in the arse can save you! Just let me get at him!'

He was in an ungovernable rage. Sweating and pale, I looked at him. I had had the shadow of a hope that with Pimko out of the way I might somehow manage to recover my adult personality and explain myself in everybody's eyes. But what chance was there of this while innocence and naïveté were increasing and multiplying in the fresh and limpid air? The backside was split between Boy and Adolescent. The world was being shattered and re-formed on the basis of Boy and Adolescent. I stepped back.

The tension increased. Boys, red-faced and furious, set on one another. Siphon stood motionless, with his arms crossed, while Mientus shook his fists. The mothers and aunts on the other side of the wall were in a highly exalted state too, though they did not have too clear an idea why. But most of the boys remained undecided. They went on stuffing themselves with bread and butter, reciting remorselessly:

'Can the *dignissime* Mientus be a *sensualus luxurius?* Can Siphon be an *idealistus?* Let us work hard, or we shall fail in our exams!'

Others, who did not wish to compromise themselves, talked sport or politics, or pretended to be interested in a game of football. But every now and then one or other, unable to resist the fascination of the heated and piquant controversy, would break away, start listening to it; he would ponder, blush, and join either Mientus's or Siphon's party. Meanwhile the usher sat drowsily on his bench, feasting himself from a distance on the spectacle of youthful naïveté.

'Ah! the pretty little backsides, the innocent little backsides!' he muttered.

In the end only one boy failed to be dragged into the super-heated ideological conflict. He stood aloof, quietly sunning himself, wearing a shirt and white flannel trousers, with a gold chain round his left wrist.

'Kopeida, come over here!'

Everyone seemed to want him, but he took no notice of anybody. He raised one leg and dangled it in the diaphanous air.

Meanwhile Mientus was struggling in the net of his own words.

'But don't you realize that we shall be an object of contempt to every working-class lad, every hall-porter's son and apprentice and agricultural labourer of the same age as ourselves? We must defend the Boy against the Adolescent!' he declared with passion.

'We're not interested in what apprentices, hall-porters' sons and street boys think of us, they've got no education,' replied Gabek, who was one of Siphon's friends.

Mientus went over to Siphon and spoke to him haltingly.

'Siphon, this has gone far enough,' he said. 'If you withdraw what you said, I'll withdraw what I said. That's fair, isn't it?

Let's drop it! I'm ready to withdraw everything I said on condition that you withdraw everything you said ... and agree to be told everything. It's not a matter that concerns you only, after all.'

Pylaszczkiewicz gave him a look that was full of light, dignity, and inner strength. After looking at him in this fashion, it was impossible to reply other than in vigorous fashion. He stepped back.

'There can be no compromising with ideals,' he announced. At this Mientus dashed at him, with clenched fists, shouting: 'Come on! Come on! Death to the Adolescent!'

'Adolescents, rally round me!' cried Pylaszczkiewicz in a penetrating voice. 'Rally round me, rally to the defence of your purity!'

This appeal caused many to feel the Adolescent in themselves rising against the Boy. They formed a thick barrier round Siphon and faced up to the partisans of Mientus. The first blows were exchanged. Siphon leapt on a stone and shouted encouragement to his supporters, but the Mientus party began to gain the upper hand, and Siphon's men beat a disorderly retreat. How dreadful! The Adolescent seemed lost. But Siphon, faced with inevitable defeat, gathered his last strength and struck up the innocent, adolescent song:

> *Youth! Lift the world*
> *On your shoulders . . .*

This made his supporters shudder. Was this a song to sing in this situation? Surely it would have been better not to sing that song. But they could not let Siphon go on singing by himself, so they started joining in, and the song grew, spread, multiplied, became enormous, and took wing. . . . They sang, standing still, their eyes, like those of Siphon, fixed on a distant star; they sang in their assailants' teeth. The latters' arms dropped helplessly to their sides; there seemed no way of getting at the singers, of making any sort of impact on them. Meanwhile the singers went on singing, with a star right in front of their noses, and with gathering strength and piety. Members of the Mientus gang

37

started grumbling, coughing, or muttering, making awkward or idle gestures, and moving away. In the end Mientus had no alternative but to cough and move away himself.

A flight of pigeons shone in the sunlit autumn air, lingered over the roof, came to rest on the oak tree, and flew away. Mientus, who could not stand Siphon's triumphant song, went to the opposite end of the playground, accompanied by Bobek and Hopek. After a time he regained sufficient self-control to be able to speak. He looked down at the ground, and was embarrassed.

'Well, what do we do now?' he said.

'Just the same as we did before,' replied Bobek. 'There's nothing else for it. We go on using the same bad words more vigorously than ever. Our only weapon is the four-lettered word. . . .'

'Go on using that?' Mientus exclaimed. 'It's enough to make you sick, repeating the same thing—playing the same old tune, just because the other fellow goes on playing his!'

He was shaken. He stretched his hands, fell back a few paces, and looked all round. The sky, suspended in the heights, was light, fresh, pale, and sarcastic; the tree, the sturdy oak in the middle of the playground, had turned its back, and the old porter near the gate smiled under his moustache and went away.

'A stable-lad,' Mientus muttered. 'A stable-lad. Suppose a stable-lad overheard the rot we talk!'

And suddenly, terrified by his own idea, he made off; in the diaphanous air of autumn he took flight. His friends stopped him.

'Mientus, what's come over you?' they asked him in the diaphanous air. 'You're the leader! What will become of us without you?'

Mientus, caught and held by all these hands, lowered his head and said bitterly:

'Well, what?'

Bobek and Hopek, shaken, said nothing. Bobek, who was in a state of extreme agitation, picked up a bit of wire, mechanically

38

poked it through a hole in the fence, and injured a mother in the eye. He promptly withdrew the bit of wire, and the woman screamed on the other side of the fence. Finally Hopek, not without diffidence, said:

'Well, what are we to do, Mientus?'

Mientus pulled himself together. 'There's no alternative,' he replied. 'We must fight. Fight to the last round!'

'Bravo!' they exclaimed. 'Bravo! Mientus, that's how we like you!'

But their leader made a gesture of discouragement.

'Oh, you and your shouting!' he said. 'All right. If we have to fight, we shall fight. Fight? But we can't fight. Supposing we did beat him up, what should we gain by it? We should only make a martyr of him, a martyr to innocence, and he'd give us martyred innocence by the ton. Swearing, filth, dirt, are useless, useless I tell you, they're nothing but grist to his mill, milk for his adolescence, and that's what he counts on, you take it from me. But luckily for us,' . . . and strange inflexions of anger crept into his voice . . . 'luckily for us, there's something much more effective we can do, we can rid him for ever of his wish to sing.'

'How?' they asked, not unhopefully.

'Like this,' he said in a peremptory tone. 'If Siphon persists in refusing to be told, we'll force him to hear. We'll tie him up. Fortunately we can still get at him through his ears. We'll tie him up, and we'll enlighten him so thoroughly that afterwards even his mother won't recognize him. We'll do him once and for all, the big baby. But mum's the word. Get some rope.'

I was watching these preparations breathlessly and with beating heart when Pimko appeared at the door and called me to take me in to Piorkowski, the head. The pigeons appeared again. With a flutter of wings they came to rest on the fence behind which all the mothers were standing. As we walked down the long school corridor I frantically searched for words with which to explain myself, without finding them, however, for Pimko spat into every spittoon we passed on the way, and ordered me to do the same. The fact that I was spitting made me unable to

39

protest, and it was thus that we arrived at the headmaster's study.

Piorkowski, a giant of a man, received us seated powerfully and transcendentally on his backside. He pinched my cheek with paternal kindness, stroked my chin, and created a sympathetic impression. Instead of protesting I made a slight bow, and he said to Pimko over my head:

'Pretty little backside, pretty little backside! There's no doubt about it, you can rest assured that the grown-ups whom we artificially reduce to childhood offer an even more productive field for our efforts than children in the natural state. No pupils, no school, and with no school where should we schoolmasters be? I count on you not to forget me in future, for my establishment deserves it, our methods of turning out backsides are unsurpassed, and our teaching body is selected for that purpose with the greatest care. Would you like to see the teaching body?'

'With the greatest of pleasure,' Pimko replied. 'It is well known that nothing has a greater effect on the mind than the body.'

Piorkowski half opened the door of the next room, and the two pedagogues discreetly looked inside; I did the same, and was terrified by what I saw. The staff were seated round a table, having tea. I have never set eyes on such a pathetic collection of little old men. They were all eating noisily. The first was chewing his food, the second bolting it, the third masticating, the fourth munching, the fifth gulping it down, and the sixth looked like a moron.

'There's no doubt about it, professor,' the headmaster said with pride. 'The body is well chosen. Not one of them is agreeable, pleasant, normal, or human, they are no more than pedagogic bodies, as you see. If I am ever faced with the necessity of engaging a new assistant, I take the most scrupulous care to ensure that he is perfectly and completely boring, sterile, docile and abstracted.'

'All the same, the French mistress looks pretty wide awake,' Pimko remarked.

'What an idea! I've never managed to talk to her for a minute without yawning at least twice.'

'Oh, that's different, then. I assume nevertheless that they are all fully experienced people, well aware of their pedagogic mission?'

'They are the best brains in the capital,' the headmaster replied. 'Not one of them has an idea of his own in his head. If such a thing ever happened, I should make it my business immediately to throw out either the originator of the idea or the idea itself. All the members of my staff are perfect pupils, and they teach nothing that they have not been taught. Not a single one has an idea of his own in his head.'

'Backsidikins!' said Pimko. 'I see that I shall be leaving my Johnnie in good hands. Only real teachers are capable of instilling into their pupils that delightful immaturity, that pleasing and ineffectual apathy towards life that will have to prevail, if we, God's own pedagogues, are to have a suitably wide field of action. Only with well-trained staff shall we succeed in reducing everyone to a state of childhood.'

'Sh!' said Piorkowski, taking him by the sleeve. 'Sh! You are perfectly right, but be careful, it's not a thing we want overheard.'

At that moment one body turned towards another body, and said:

'Well, and how are you?'

'How am I?' the second body replied. 'Prices are going up.'

'Going up?' said the first. 'I thought they were going down.'

'Going down?' said the other peevishly. 'My impression is that they are going up.'

'Biscuits are going up,' the first body grumbled, and wrapped the rest of his biscuits in his pocket-handkerchief.

'I keep them on short commons,' said Piorkowski, 'because that is the only way of making them anaemic enough. As you know, there's nothing like anaemia for bringing out the spots and pimples and snuffles of the awkward age.'

41

Suddenly the English teacher noticed the headmaster at the door, accompanied by a learned and impressive-looking stranger. He gulped his tea down the wrong way, and exclaimed:

'The inspector!'

At this all the bodies rose and huddled tremblingly together like partridges; and the headmaster closed the door in order not to startle them further. Pimko kissed me on the brow and said solemnly:

'Well, Johnnie, run along to the classroom, lessons are about to begin. Meanwhile I'll find you lodgings, and I'll come back and fetch you after school.'

I tried to answer, but the sight of the implacable master suddenly so overmastered me that I was unable to utter a word. I bowed slightly, and made for the classroom, my head humming with unspoken protests. The classroom was humming too. The boys were sitting at their desks and yelling, as if they were about to be silenced for ever.

In this hubbub it was impossible to say exactly when the master appeared on his dais. He was the sad, anaemic body who had maintained in the staff-room that biscuits were going down. He took his seat, opened his book, brushed the crumbs from his waistcoat, closed his mouth, pulled down his cuffs to prevent his sleeves from wearing at the elbows, repressed something in himself, and crossed his legs. Then he sighed, and tried to say something. The din redoubled; everyone yelled, with the possible exception of Siphon, who adopted a positive attitude. The master looked at his class, pursed his lips, opened them, and then closed them again. The boys went on yelling. The master frowned and made a gesture of annoyance, adjusted his sleeves, drummed on his desk, thought about something a long, long way away, took out his watch, put it on the desk, sighed, again suppressed something in himself or swallowed something, and devoted a long moment to collecting his energy. Finally he banged the top of his desk with his book and called out:

'That'll do! Silence! The lesson is about to begin!'

At this the whole class like one man (again with the exception of Siphon) expressed the imperious necessity of immediately leaving the room.

The master, who was known to his pupils as Droopy because of his worn and frail appearance, smiled bitterly.

'That'll do!' he said in the acid tone that came naturally to him. 'So you would like to go to the lavatory! So would the soul like to go to paradise, wouldn't it? And why can't I leave the room? Sit down, all of you! Nobody may leave the room!'

No fewer than seven boys thereupon produced certificates testifying to various complaints which had prevented them from doing their homework. Four others complained of violent headache, another had a rash, and yet another convulsions.

'Gracious heavens!' Droopy exclaimed. 'Why doesn't anyone give me a certificate explaining that through no fault of my own it is impossible for me to do my work? Why can't I have convulsions? What I want you to tell me is why I should have to come here every day, except Sundays and public holidays, instead of having convulsions. Quiet! The certificates are faked, and you are nothing but a lot of malingerers. Sit down, I know you!'

Three boys went up to his desk and started telling him a good story about Jews and birds, but he stopped his ears.

'No, no!' he groaned, 'spare me, I mustn't listen to you, spare me, we must get on with the lesson. Supposing the headmaster walked in!'

At this he started trembling, looked towards the door, and paled with fright.

'And supposing the inspector caught us? I warn you, gentlemen, that the inspector is paying a visit to the school at this very moment. It is a fact. I warn you. Enough of this folly, let us be ready in case the inspector walks in. Let me see. Which of you know his lessons best? Tell me, so that I may shine by letting him shine. . . . Well? Doesn't anybody know anything? You'll be the ruin of me! Come, come, somebody must know a little about something, speak up and tell me frankly. Ah! Pylaszczkiewicz! Pylaszczkiewicz, speak up! Thank you, Pylaszczkiewicz,

43

I've always thought you a boy I could rely on. But what are you good at, Pylaszczkiewicz? Which of our glorious poets do you know best?'

Siphon rose and replied:

'Excuse me, sir! If you ask me in front of the inspector, I shall answer, but in the meantime I cannot tell you what I know best, because that would mean betraying myself and my principles.'

'Very well, then,' said the master. 'Pylaszczkiewicz's feelings in the matter are most praiseworthy, and I was only joking. Principles above everything, of course! Let me see, then,' he went on severely, looking at the syllabus, 'what are we in for today? Oh, yes, explain and demonstrate why the great poet Slowacki awakens our love, admiration, and ecstasy. Well, then, gentlemen, first I shall say my piece and then you shall say yours. Quiet!' he called out, and all the boys bent over their desks, holding their heads in their hands, while Droopy surreptitiously opened his text-book, shut his mouth, sighed, suppressed something in himself, and began:

'Hm! Hm! Hm! Well, then, why does Slowacki arouse our admiration, love and ecstasy? Why do we weep with the poet when we read that angelic poem *In Switzerland*? Why does exaltation swell our breasts when we listen to the superb and heroic stanzas of *The Spirit King*? Why is there no escaping the magic and seduction of the *Balladina*? Why do the sorrows of *Lilla Weneda* rend our hearts? Hm! Why? Because, gentlemen, Slowacki was a great poet. Walkiewicz, tell me why! Tell me, Walkiewicz. Why the enchantment, the love, the tears, the exaltation, the magic? Why are our hearts rent? Tell me, Walkiewicz!'

It was like listening to another, but lesser, Pimko, a Pimko of narrower horizons.

'Because he was a great poet, sir,' said Walkiewicz.

The boys were carving up the desk-tops with their pen-knives and screwing up little balls of paper and putting them in the ink-wells. The master sighed, choked, looked at his watch, and continued as follows:

44

'He was a great poet, don't forget that he was a great poet. Why do we feel love, admiration, delight? Because he was a great poet, a great poet. You ignorant dunderheads, get this firmly fixed in your heads and repeat after me: Juliusz Slowacki was a great poet, a great poet, we love Juliusz Slowacki, and his poems delight us because he was a great poet—and because his verses are of an immortal beauty which arouses our deepest admiration.'

This level of exposition got on one boy's nerves and he had an acute attack of the fidgets. When he could stand it no longer he burst out:

'But if he has no effect on me whatever, if he simply doesn't interest me, if I can't read two verses of his without falling asleep . . . Heaven help me, sir, but how am I to be sent into transports of delight if I am not sent into transports of delight?'

His eyes were nearly popping out of his head. He sat down again, as if overwhelmed by what he had said. His naïve confession took the master's breath away.

'For heaven's sake hold your tongue, Kotecki,' he said. 'Kotecki, you're trying to ruin me. No marks for Kotecki. He doesn't realize what he is saying.'

Kotecki: 'But I don't understand, sir. I don't understand how I can be sent into transports of delight if I am not sent into transports of delight.'

The master: 'But Kotecki, how can you not be sent into transports of delight if I have already explained to you a thousand times that you are sent into transports of delight?'

Kotecki: 'You have explained it, sir, but I am not sent into transports of delight.'

The master: 'In that case it's a personal peculiarity. Kotecki seems not to be intelligent. Other people are sent into transports of delight.'

Kotecki: 'No! No! On my word of honour they're not, sir! Nobody can be sent into transports of delight by Slowacki's poetry, because nobody reads him, except at school, when they're forced to.'

The master: 'Kotecki, for heaven's sake sit down and keep quiet. The explanation is that only a limited number of intelligent and cultivated people are capable of appreciating him.'

Kotecki: 'Nothing of the sort, sir, even cultivated people don't read him. Nobody reads him, sir, nobody at all!'

The master: 'Kotecki, I have a wife and a young child. At least have pity on the child, Kotecki. Kotecki, it is a well-known and established fact that great poetry necessarily arouses our admiration. Now, Juliusz Slowacki was a great poet. . . . It may be that Slowacki doesn't move you, my dear Kotecki, but don't tell me, don't tell me that you're not profoundly moved by Mickiewicz, Byron, Pushkin, Shelley, Goethe . . .'

Kotecki: 'He doesn't move anyone, everyone thinks him ridiculous. No one can read more than two verses of him. Heavens, I can't!'

The master: 'Come, come, Kotecki, but that's impossible, absurd. Great poetry, being beautiful, profound, inspired, and great, is bound to move us to the very depths of our souls.'

Kotecki: 'I can't read him. Nobody can.'

The master's brow was wet with perspiration. In an attempt to move Kotecki he produced from his wallet some photographs of his wife and child, but Kotecki's relentless, piercing repetition of *I can't, I can't*, grew, multiplied, and became infectious. It started as a murmur here and there; and it turned out that nearly all of us suffered from the same disability as Kotecki, and the master found himself threatened with it from all sides. He was in a terrible fix; at any moment he might find himself encompassed by a universal disability, the unrestrained proclamation of which might reach the ears of the headmaster and the inspector; at any moment the whole educational edifice might come tumbling about his ears, engulfing his child in the wreckage; and Kotecki obstinately persisted with his *I can't, I can't*. Poor Droopy felt the general inability and helplessness spreading to himself.

'Pylaszczkiewicz!' he exclaimed: 'Pylaszczkiewicz, will you please show me, and Kotecki, and the rest of us, the beauties of a selected passage. Be quick, for delay is dangerous. We must be able to be moved, because otherwise my child is done for.'

Pylaszczkiewicz rose and promptly started declaiming a glorious passage from a great poem, the glorious work of one of the greatest poets.

And Siphon went on declaiming. He had been left totally unaffected by the sudden general helplessness and inability. There was no question of *can't* for him. On the contrary, because of his pure and vigorous principles, he always *could*; and this was due less to his native talents than to the strength of his principles. So he declaimed, with emotion in his voice, meticulous elocution, spiritual fervour, and emphasis. He put into it all the beauty of which he was capable, and the beauty of his recitation multiplied by the beauty of the poem and the greatness of genius and the majesty of art was imperceptibly transformed into a monument of all beauty and all greatness. Moreover, he recited with piety and mystery, inspiration and strength; and he sang the poet's sublime song as the poet's sublime song ought to be sung. Oh, what beauty, what greatness, what genius, what poetry! Fly, wall, finger-nails, roof, blackboard, windows, the threat of impotence were spirited away, wife and child were out of danger, everyone started proclaiming that of course he was fully able to appreciate great poetry, and the only thing that everyone now wanted was that it should stop. At that moment I noticed that my neighbour was smearing my hands with ink —his own were completely smeared with it, and his reason for smearing mine was that his toes were covered by his shoes and socks, and other people's hands are, after all, more or less the same as one's own, so why not? What else was there to do? What could one do with one's legs? Move them; and then what? After a quarter of an hour of this even Kotecki groaned that he had had enough, confessed his appreciation and admiration, apologized, and admitted that he *could*.

'So you see, Kotecki, there's nothing like school for inculcating a love of art. Which of us would have been capable of admiring

47

the great geniuses if the knowledge that they were great geniuses had not been hammered into our heads at school?'

The audience, however, was presenting some very queer symptoms. Everyone's back was bent beneath the weight of the poet, the bard, the master, his child, and the general torpor. The bare partition walls and the bare schoolroom desks with their ink-wells offered not a glimmer of distraction; through the window a small area of wall was visible on which someone had written the simple words: 'He's gone.' So there was nothing for it but to busy oneself either with the pedagogic body or one's own body, and that was why those who did not occupy themselves by counting Droopy's hairs or trying to plumb the mystery of his long nails, tried such things as counting their own hair or unscrewing their necks. Bobek was twisting about, Hopek was grumbling to himself—trying painfully to disarticulate himself, so to speak—some seemed completely immersed in themselves, others had given in to the fatal device of talking to themselves, others were tearing off their buttons and ruining their clothes —in other words, all round there was arising a jungle of absurd reflexes, a desert of senseless actions. The only one to flourish in the midst of this general aridity was Siphon, who was more and more firmly rooted in his principles. The master, who kept remembering his wife and child, endlessly repeated: 'Poet, bard, messianic spirit, the Christ of the nations, the torch of beauty, sacrifice and redemption, hero and symbol.'

The words came in through ears and tormented minds, while faces twitched convulsively, and ceased to be human; fatigued, battered, exhausted, reduced to nullity, they were ready to assume almost any shape—what an exercise for the imagination! And reality, battered and exhausted too, became a world of dreams—oh! escape into dream. . . .

I realized that I must get out of this. Pimko, Droopy, the poetry, school and my school-fellows, in short all my adventures of the morning whirled in my head like a roulette wheel, and the number that came up was that I must escape. How or where I had not the slightest idea, but it was clear that I must get out of this if I were not to be ground to pieces in the fantastic adventures that were befalling me. But instead of running away I put my finger in my shoe, which obviously made it impossible to run away, because you cannot run with one finger at floor-level. It was imperative to escape from Droopy, the boredom, the pretence, the disgust, but, having in my head the poet inserted into it by Droopy and in my shoe the moving finger inserted by myself, I could not run away, and this inability was even more overpowering than that which had affected Kotecki.

In theory nothing could have been easier. All that was needed was to walk out and never come back. Pimko would not have sent for the police, his pedagogic tentacles did not extend as far as that. But I could not make up my mind. Running away presupposes the will to run away, and where are you to get the will from if you are moving your toes with your finger and have lost your face in a grimace of disgust? It was only then that I realized why not one of the boys at the school was able to run away; it was because their faces and their whole personality eliminated the slightest possibility of flight; all of them were the slaves of the faces they were making and, though they should have run away, they did not, because they had ceased to be what they ought to have been. Running away involved more than just running away from the school; it also involved running away from themselves. Oh! to escape, to shake off the callow stripling into which Pimko had turned me, to return to my former adult self! But how can one escape from what one is, where is the leverage to come from? Our shape penetrates and confines us, as much from without as from within. If reality had established its rights for only one single moment, the incredible absurdity of my position would (I felt sure) have been so obvious that everyone would have exclaimed: What on earth is that grown-up doing here? But, against the general extravagance, the extravagance of my own position disappeared. Oh, if I could have seen just one undistorted face to enable me to feel the distortion of my own! But alas! around me were nothing but battered, laundered and ironed faces which reflected my own as in a distorting mirror

—and I was held captive by this facial mirage. Is it dream or is it reality? I said to myself. Suddenly my eyes fell on Kopeida, the boy in flannel trousers, who had smiled aloofly in the playground when the others had talked about girls.

He was sitting at his ease, as indifferent to the schoolmaster as he had been to the row between Mientus and Siphon. His hands were in his pockets, and he looked healthy, clean, normal, pleasant, and self-possessed. He was sitting there aloof from his surroundings, with his legs crossed, and he looked at his legs as if so doing enabled him to escape from school.

Was I dreaming or was this reality? How could this be possible? I said to myself. Neither *boy* nor *adolescent*, but a perfectly ordinary, normal boy at last? Perhaps with his aid I might be able to overcome my impotence.

* 3 *

The Duel

THE master started looking more and more often at his watch; and the boys started looking at their watches more and more often too. At last the bell rang, bringing release. Droopy stopped short in the middle of a sentence and vanished, and his audience awoke and let loose a terrible roar. Only Siphon remained in silent concentration, completely absorbed in himself.

During the lesson the problem of innocence had been stifled by the monotony of the poet, but with Droopy's disappearance it flared up again; and from the aberrations of the official education system the boys plunged headlong into the turbid waters of Boyhood and Adolescence; and reality gradually faded into a dream-world—oh, escape into dream!

And blood once more mounted to cheeks in the heavy and stifling air, for the clash of opinions became colossal; doctrines, views, and systems sallied forth to battle; and theories clashed over the boys' fevered heads. Communism. Fascism. Catholic Youth Movement. Patriotic Youth Movement. Youth Morality Movement. Boy Scouts. Civic Youth Movement. Heroic Youth Movement. More and more far-fetched words and phrases were launched into the fray. It was obvious that each political party stuffed these boys' heads with a different idea of boyhood, that every thinker stuffed them with his own particular tastes and ideals, and that over and above all that their heads were stuffed with films, popular novels, and newspapers. Hence the furious clash of Adolescent, Young Man, Boy, Young Communist, Young Athlete, High-Minded Churchgoer, Juvenile Delinquent, Young Aesthete, Young Philosopher, Young Sceptic, and Young Cynic of every description, who fell upon each other, insulted and expressed bitter contempt for each other, while groans rose from the wounded lying on the ground, and cries were exchanged of: 'How naïve you are!' 'No, how naïve *you* are!' For all the various ideals without exception, far from being made to their protagonists' measure, sat upon them incredibly awkwardly and gauchely, like ill-fitting clothes. Boys flung them into the fray and then retreated, afraid of what they had done, as if they had shot pellets from a catapult which, once launched, were irrecoverable.

Imprisoned as they were in falsehood, having lost all contact with life and reality, having been battered by all the ideologies and all the schools, their concert was a concert of discord, and all they said was foolish. Their pathos was false, their lyricism phoney, their emotionalism hair-raising, their sentimentalism ghastly, their irony and leg-pulling disastrous, their flights of fancy pretentious and their descents to earth disgusting. And that was the way the world was; the world was exactly like this. They were treated artificially, so how could they be anything but artificial? And, being artificial, how could they be expected to express themselves in other than degrading fashion? That was why impotence floated in the oppressive air and reality gradually gave way to a dream-world, and only Kopeida did not allow himself to be carried away by anything, but kept on tearing up bits of paper and gazing at his legs. . . .

Meanwhile Mientus and Bobek had gone into a huddle, and were preparing ropes and things; Bobek even took off his braces.

A shudder went down my spine. If Mientus was going to carry out his plan of violating Siphon's innocence by way of his ears, reality would indeed be such a nightmare and the world so utterly grotesque that I should no longer be able even to dream of escaping from it. I must prevent it at all costs. But how could I face them single-handed, and with my big toe in my shoe into the bargain? No, I could not do it. Oh, for a single, undistorted face! I went over to Kopeida, who was standing by the window, wearing his flannel trousers, looking out at the playground and quietly whistling between his teeth. He at least seemed not to be harbouring any ideal. How was I to begin?

'They want to violate Siphon,' I said simply. 'We've got to stop them. If they do it, the place will become impossible!'

What would Kopeida say? I waited with trepidation. But, instead of replying, he jumped out of the window on to his two feet, and went on quietly whistling between his teeth.

What did this mean? I was left utterly bewildered. Why had he jumped out of the window instead of answering? Why had he avoided me like this? And why were his legs in the foreground? Why were his legs forelegs? I passed my hand across my brow. Forelegs? Was I dreaming, or was this reality? But there was no time to think, because Mientus came up to me. I realized that he had overheard what I said to Kopeida.

'What are you sticking your nose into our affairs for?' he said. 'Who told you to go sneaking about us to Kopeida? It's no business of his. You'd better not talk to him about me again!'

I stepped back. He let out some disgusting oaths.

'Mientus, you mustn't do that to Siphon,' I muttered.

'Why not?'

'Because you mustn't.'

Hardly had I finished the sentence than he burst out again.

'You know what you can do with your Siphon,' he said. 'You can —— him!'

'You mustn't, Mientus, you mustn't,' I implored him. 'Tell me, Mientus, have you imagined Siphon lying tied up on the ground, and you forcibly violating his innocence through his ears? Have you imagined yourself actually doing that, Mientus?'

He twisted his face in an even more repulsive manner.

'I see that you're another noble adolescent,' he sneered. 'You've been influenced by Siphon, haven't you? Do you know what I'll do with your adolescent? I'll —— him!'

And he kicked my shin.

I sought for words, but once more could not find them.

'Stop it, Mientus,' I said. 'Stop turning yourself into . . . into . . . Siphon's innocence is no reason for you to be indecent.'

He looked at me.

'What do you want of me?' he said.

'I want you not to play the fool.'

'Not to play the fool,' he muttered. A cloud came over his eyes. 'Not to play the fool,' he repeated wistfully. 'Obviously there are boys who don't play the fool. Hall-porters' sons, apprentices, stable-lads. They sweep the streets, or work in the fields. They must laugh at Siphon and me, and all our stuff and nonsense.'

For a moment he dropped his deliberate vulgarity and triviality, plunged into a painful private meditation, and his face relaxed. But then he started, as if he had been burnt with a red-hot poker, and let out a volley of fearsome oaths.

'No, I can't allow us to be taken for a lot of innocents!' he said. 'I've got to violate Siphon's innocence through his ears.' Another volley of oaths followed. Once more he twisted his mouth, and his language was so horrible that I stepped back.

'Mientus,' I muttered mechanically and in terror. 'Let's go away from here. Let's get out of this!'

'Get out of this?'

He stopped swearing, listened, looked at me inquiringly, and became more normal. I clutched at his changed attitude like a drowning man clutching at a straw.

'Let's go,' I murmured. 'Let's drop all this and go.'

He hesitated. His face remained in suspense, hesitating. Seeing that the idea of flight was gaining ground in him, fearing that he might once more relapse into monstrosity, I searched for a way of encouraging him.

'Let's get out of this,' I said. 'We might join up with the stable-lads.'

I knew about his passion for the life of the wage-earner and thought he would fall for the stable-lad bait. I no longer cared very much what he said; all I wanted was to keep him from the horrors that made him twist his mouth. His eyes shone; and he gave me a fraternal dig in the ribs with his elbow.

'You'd like that?' he said, softly, in a friendly voice.

He laughed, a low, pure laugh. I laughed in the same way.

'Ah! to get right away from here,' he said. 'To join up with the stable-lads . . . real lads who take the horses down to the river and bathe . . .'

Then I noticed something dreadful. Something new appeared on his face—a kind of wistfulness—a special kind of beauty appropriate to an educated boy on the point of running away in order to take refuge with stable-lads. His brutality was giving way to charm. He felt on terms of trust with me, and dropped his mask; he set his lyricism free.

'Ah!' he said in a low, sing-song voice. 'Ah! to eat black bread with stable-lads, and gallop across the fields . . .'

His lips half-opened in a strange, bitter smile, his body became more supple and more agile, something like a yoke of slavery appeared on his neck and shoulders. He was now a schoolboy yearning for the freedom of the country, and he openly and unreservedly showed me his teeth. I stepped back. I was in a dreadful fix. Ought I to show him my teeth? If I did not, he was capable of letting out another volley of oaths, but if I did, the consequences might be worse. For was not this new beauty that he would offer me in these moments of confidence even more grotesque than his previous hideousness? Why had I tempted him with his stable-lads? What a thing to have done! I ended by not showing him my teeth, but I rounded my lips and whistled; and thus we stood facing each other, one showing his teeth and the other whistling or laughing silently; and the world seemed to be organizing itself on the basis of boy about to leave baring his teeth. But suddenly, from right on top of us, there was a loud, sardonic yell. A general yell. I stepped back. Siphon, Gabek, and a crowd of others were standing there holding their sides with laughter and yelling, with mocking and jeering faces.

'What is it?' said Mientus, startled out of his life.

'Yah! Yah! Yah!' jeered Gabek.

And Siphon said:

'Mientus, let me congratulate you! Now at last we know your

55

secret. We've caught you out! Your ideal is a stable-lad. You dream about galloping through the fields with a stable-lad. You pretend to be hard and cynical, but at bottom you're nothing but a dreamer, a sentimentalist, a stable-boy worshipper!'

'Shut your bloody mouths, you bastards!' Bobek shouted with all the vulgarity of which he was capable, but it was too late. Mientus, caught in the middle of his private dream, was not to be saved by the most fearful oaths. He went scarlet, as if he were on fire, and Siphon went on triumphantly:

'Did you see the fine faces he was making?'

At this Mientus might have been expected to let fly at Siphon, but he didn't; he might have been expected to annihilate him with some piece of super-vulgarity, but he didn't. Having been caught *flagrante delicto*, he could do neither; instead he withdrew behind a tone of cold and caustic friendliness.

'Tell me, Siphon,' he said, assuming an air of apparent casualness in order to gain time. 'So you think I make faces? Tell me, don't you make faces?'

'What, me?' said Siphon. 'No!'

'Oh? . . . Well then, I suggest that you look me straight in the eye for a bit. I suggest, if you wouldn't mind, that we just look each other straight in the eye, like this!'

'Why?' asked Siphon, with a trace of anxiety. He took out his handkerchief, but Mientus snatched it from him and flung it on the ground.

'Why? Because I've had enough of the look of your face, I've had enough of it, I tell you! Stop making that face, will you, or I'll show you a face that . . . you'll see . . . I'll show you . . .'

'What will you show me?'

'I'll show you! I'll show you!' Mientus yelled like a maniac. 'You show me, and I'll show you! That's enough talk, you show me your Adolescent and I'll show you mine! We'll see who sticks it longest. You just show me! You just show me! No more words, and no more delicate and discreet looks, to hell with them! I challenge you to an all-out duel of face-making. You'll see what I'll show you! No more talk! You show me and I'll show you!'

56

Could there be a higher degree of lunacy? Here was Mientus challenging Siphon to a duel of grimaces. Nobody spoke, but everyone stared in amazement at Mientus, as if he had gone off his head, while Siphon thought of a sardonic reply. But there was such fury on Mientus's face that he quickly realized the whole dreadful meaning of the challenge. Grimaces! What an appalling, what an agonizing weapon! No quarter would be given in the struggle. Some of us trembled at the thought of Mientus's bringing out into broad daylight the dreadful weapon which no one had yet dared to use, except after taking precautions to ensure solitude and secrecy. Mientus was proposing to do in public what we had never dared to do, except alone in front of a mirror when nobody could see. I stepped back, for I realized that Mientus intended to debase with his grimaces not only Siphon, but also his stable-lads, the Boy, himself, me, everyone.

'Well, are you afraid?'

'I'm not ashamed of my ideal,' said Siphon without, however, being able to dissemble a trace of anxiety. 'I'm not ashamed.'

But there was a tremor in his voice.

'Very well, then, then that's settled. Here. After school. Choose your seconds. Mine will be Bobek and Hopek. And as umpire (and here Mientus's voice became still more diabolical), as umpire . . . I propose the new boy who has just arrived. He's neutral!'

'What? Me?'

Umpire? Me? Was I dreaming, or was this reality?

'I won't!' I burst out. 'I won't! I don't want to be there at all, I don't want to see it! No, no, no, I won't!'

I dashed forward to make my objections plain, but the general alarm had yielded to general excitement, everyone started shouting, and my appointment as umpire was taken as settled.

At that moment the bell rang, the classroom door opened, and a little man with a beard walked in and took his place at his raised desk.

It was the body who had announced in the staff-room that prices were going up. . . . He was an extremely cordial little old man, a little white dove with a wart on the end of his nasal nose. A death-like silence prevailed when he opened his book. His clear and friendly eyes lingered at the top of the list, and all those whose names began with A trembled; he lowered his eyes to the bottom of the list, and all those whose name began with Z shuddered with apprehension. For no one had done his homework; in the heat of the argument everyone had forgotten all about his Latin preparation, and, apart from Siphon, who always could, could at any time, there was no one, no one at all, who could. The little old man, however, in total ignorance of the fear that he was inspiring, went on calmly casting his eyes up and down the list of names. He hesitated, pondered for a moment, and finally, with confidence and conviction, pronounced the name of Mydlak.

It was immediately obvious that Mydlak was incapable of translating the Caesar of the day, and, still worse, was unaware that *animis oblatis* was an ablative absolute.

'Come, come, Mydlak,' the good old man said reproachfully, 'so you don't know what *animis oblatis* means, or even what kind of grammatical construction it is? How can that be, Mydlak?'

Sincerely grieved, he gave him a nought. But his face promptly lit up again, and in a burst of recovered confidence he called on Koperski to construe. . . . It was evident that in so doing he felt himself to be conferring on him the highest of honours; with look, gesture, his whole person, he encouraged Koperski to enjoy the pleasures of emulation. But Koperski no more knew what *animis oblatis* meant than did Kotecki, Kapusta, or even Kolek; and in the face of this black picture everyone stiffened into mute and hostile silence. Each time the little old man signified his momentary disappointment by rapidly entering a nought in his book, and in a burst of recovered faith promptly called on another boy. The man might have just landed from the moon; he confidently expected each boy he called on to be worthy of the honour, and to respond accordingly. But nobody did so, and soon he had entered ten noughts in his book without realizing that the only effect of his misplaced confidence was to spread fright, and that nobody wanted his confidence. What a confident little old man! His confidence was incurable. Even if boys pretended to be suffering from headache he declared himself to be delighted.

'You have a headache, Bobkowski? Excellent! Here before us we have an interesting maxim *de malis capitis* which most aptly fits the situation. What? You feel an imperious need to leave the room? But, my dear Bobkowski, why? For that too we find a precedent among the ancients. I refer you to the famous passage in Book V in which Caesar's whole army, having eaten bad meat, found itself in the same predicament. The whole army, Bobkowski! Why do you wish to do the same when you have at hand such a classic description? These books, gentlemen, are life, life!'

Siphon, Mientus and their quarrel were dead, buried, and forgotten. Everyone tried to disappear from view, to cease to exist. The boys shrank, sought to make themselves indistinct and indistinguishable, contracted their hands, feet, stomachs. But no one was bored; no, there was not a trace or suspicion of boredom, for everyone was sadly fearful of being fastened on by the claw of the puerile confidence which the Latin text inspired in the old man. And under the pressure of fear faces—as happens to faces—turned into shadows, illusions of faces, and it was no longer possible to say which was the more illusory, chimerical and mad, the faces, the incredible infinitive with subject accusative, or the old maniac's sadistical confidence; and reality turned gradually into a dream world, oh! let me dream, dream!

The master, however, having dismissed Bobkowski with a nought, thought of another grammatical problem. What was the third person plural of the passive periphrastic subjunctive of the verb *colleo, colleare, colleavi, colleatum*? The idea excited him greatly.

'Very curious and instructive, very curious and instructive indeed,' he exclaimed, rubbing his hands. 'Come on, boys, a question to test your shrewdness! An admirable opportunity to show your sharpness of wit! Now if the passive periphrastic subjunctive of *olleare* is *ollandus sim*, what is the passive periphrastic subjunctive of *colleare?* Come, gentlemen!'

The said gentlemen, however, had been frightened out of existence.

'Come, come, come! . . . *Collan . . . collan . . .*'

No answer. But the old man still refused to abandon hope. Again he said:

'Come, come! . . . *Collan . . . collan . . .*'

He praised, he blazed, he goaded, he forgave, implored, encouraged, strove to instil and elicit knowledge, tried to lure his pupils into the pleasure of possessing it. But suddenly he felt that nobody could and nobody wanted to. He collapsed, and in a hollow voice, saddened by the universal ill will, groaned:

'*Collandus sim! Collandus sim!*'

And he went on:

'How, gentlemen, is it possible that you derive no pleasure and satisfaction from that? Do you not see that *collandus sim* sharpens the wits, stimulates the intelligence, forms the character, improves us from every point of view, and puts us on terms of familiarity with the thought of the ancients? For—now follow me carefully, gentlemen—if the gerundive of *olleare* is *ollandus*, the gerundive of *colleare* must be *collandus*, because the future passive ending of the third conjugation is *dus, dus, dus,* with the sole exception of the exceptions when it ends in *us, us, us!* Do you not feel the germ of perfection contained in that termination?'

At this point Kotecki got up and said in desperation:

'But, heaven help us, sir, how can you say that it improves us when it doesn't improve us? How can you say that it stimulates us when it doesn't stimulate us? How can you say that it forms our character when it doesn't form anything? I don't understand, sir!'

The master: 'What are you saying, Mr Kotecki? Do you maintain the termination in *us* does not improve or enrich our minds? Explain yourself, Kotecki!'

Kotecki: 'It doesn't improve or enrich my mind, sir! It does nothing of the sort to me, sir! Heaven help me, sir, but it doesn't!'

The master: 'It does not enrich your mind, Kotecki? But Kotecki, are you not aware that a knowledge of Latin is the foundation of all mental enrichment? Come, Kotecki, what you are suggesting is that thousands of competent teachers have for generations been teaching something entirely devoid of educational value. But Kotecki, surely the fact that we selflessly and unremittingly devote so much effort to instilling Latin into you demonstrates the necessity of learning it? Kotecki, you can take it from me, if you fail to appreciate Latin as you should, the only possible conclusion is that you are not intelligent enough. An intelligence entirely out of the ordinary is required to appreciate the benefits that flow from it, and years of study and application.'

Kotecki: 'But I can't appreciate it, sir, I can't, heaven help me!'

The master: 'I appeal to you, Kotecki. Did we not last year translate the sixty-three lines of Caesar in which he describes how he deployed his legions on the hill? Were those sixty-three lines, plus a page of vocabulary, not a mystic revelation of ancient times? Were they not a revelation to Kotecki of the style, clarity of thought, and correctness of expression, of that military genius Caesar?'

Kotecki: 'No, sir, to me they were not a revelation of anything at all, and I couldn't see any military genius. I didn't want to get a nought, and that was all. I don't like getting noughts. Oh, I can't, I can't!'

The formidable shadow of general impotence once more hovered ominously over the class; and the master felt that he would succumb himself unless he took prompt counteraction by injecting a double dose of faith and confidence.

'Pylaszczkiewicz!' exclaimed the poor man abandoned by everybody, 'do me the favour of immediately recapitulating what we have studied in the course of the term, bringing out all the profundity of thought and felicity of style; and I have confidence, confidence, confidence, because that is what we must have!'

Siphon, who, as has already been mentioned, always could and never suffered from impotence, rose and started reading with perfect fluency and ease:

'Next day Caesar paraded his troops, and reprimanded them for the rashness and impetuosity which they had shown in judging for themselves how far they were to advance and what they were to do, not halting when the signal for withdrawal was given, and refusing to submit to the control of the tribunes and generals. He explained that an unfavourable position made a serious difference; he had experienced this himself at Avaricum, when, though he had the enemy in his grasp without their general and without their cavalry, he had foregone an assured triumph for fear the unfavourable ground should entail a loss, however slight, in the action. He heartily admired their heroic spirit, which entrenched camp and high mountain and walled fortress were powerless to daunt; but just as heartily he reprobated their contempt for discipline and their presumption in imagining that they knew how to win battles and forecast results better than their general. He required from his soldiers obedience and self-control just as much as courage and heroism. Having achieved his purpose, Caesar ordered the withdrawal to be sounded, and immediately halted the Tenth Legion, which he commanded in person. The men of the other legions did not hear the sound of the trumpet, as a considerable valley intervened; still the tribunes and the generals, in obedience to Caesar's command, tried to keep them in hand. Elated, however, by the expectation of a speedy triumph, by the enemy's flight, and by the recollection of past victories, they fancied that nothing was too difficult for their valour to achieve, and pressed on in pursuit till they got close to the wall and gates of the fortress. Then a cry arose from every part of town; and those who were some way off, panic-stricken by the sudden uproar, and believing that the enemy were inside the gates, rushed pell-mell out of the stronghold.'

'*Collandus sim*, gentlemen! *Collandus sim*! What clarity! What style! What thought, what profundity! *Collandus sim*, what a fountain of knowledge! Ah! I breathe, I breathe again! *Collandus sim* for ever and for all eternity, *collandus sim, collandus sim, collandus sim*!'

Suddenly the bell rang, the boys let out a wild yell, and the little old man frowned and walked out.

Simultaneously everybody emerged from the official dream and plunged back into the private dream of Boy *v.* Adolescent! Oh, let me dream, dream! Mientus had made me umpire on purpose, he had done it deliberately, to force me to look on and see it all. The thing had gone to his head; as he was degrading and debasing himself, he wanted to degrade and debase me too; he could not tolerate my having provoked his momentary exhibition of weakness over the stable-lad. But how could I expose my face to such a spectacle? I knew that if it once assimilated such appalling insanity it would never again return to normal, and escape would be impossible. No! No! let them do what they liked, but don't let me be there to see! Moving my toe in my shoe with extreme nervousness, I took Mientus by the sleeve, looked at him imploringly, and said:

'Mientus!'

He shook me off.

'Oh, no, my little adolescent!' he said. 'Nothing doing! You're the umpire, and that's that!'

'Little adolescent!' he called me. What a revolting epithet! It was cruel of him, and I realized that all was lost, and that we were rapidly approaching what I feared most, the reign of insanity, total and complete. Meanwhile even those who normally kept out of things were seized with wild excitement; their nostrils were distended and their cheeks aflame, and it was obvious that the duel of grimaces was to be no mere battle of words, but a matter of life or death. The two principals were surrounded by a mob shouting:

'Come on! Come on! Let him have it! Let him have it!'

Only Kopeida stretched himself with supreme tranquillity and aloofness, picked up his exercise book, and went off home, with his legs.

Siphon was sitting on his Adolescent, as vindictive and alert as a hen on her eggs; it was obvious in spite of everything that he was rather nervous and would have been glad to have been able to back out. But Gabek had been quick to see the enormous advantage he enjoyed by reason of his lofty ideals and noble concepts.

'Don't be afraid, you've got him,' he whispered in his ear to encourage him. 'Think of your principles. You can think up all the grimaces you like because of your principles, while he'll have to invent all his on his own account, because he has no principles.'

Under the influence of this advice Pylaszczkiewicz's face cheered up somewhat and was soon shining again, for his principles gave him the ability to do what was required of him on any occasion and to any extent required. Seeing this, Bobek and Hopek took Mientus aside, and implored him not to expose himself to inevitable defeat.

'He'll get you and us too, he's a better grimacer than you are, Mientus, you'd better call it off,' they said. 'Pretend to be ill, or faint, or do something, and that'll get you out of it. We'll straighten things out in one way or another afterwards.'

'No,' Mientus replied. 'The die is cast. Clear out! You want me to deflate myself. Get rid of all these gaping idiots for me. I want nobody here except the seconds and the umpire!'

But his features were drawn, and he was noticeably ill at ease. This was in such striking contrast to Siphon's self-assurance that Bobek muttered: 'Poor chap!' And everyone, feeling that something dreadful was going to happen, filed quickly and quietly out of the room, carefully shutting the door behind them.

Only seven of us stayed behind in the empty, closed room—

64

Pylaszczkiewicz and Mientus, Bobek, Hopek, and Gabek, a boy named Pyzo, who was Siphon's other second, and myself, the umpire, in the middle. Gabek, looking slightly pale, then read out the rules of combat, in a voice that sounded simultaneously menacing and ironic:

'The two contestants will stand facing each other and will make a series of faces. Each and every constructive and beautiful face made by Siphon will be answered by an ugly and destructive counter-face made by Mientus. The faces made will be as personal and as wounding as possible, and the contestants will continue to make them until a final decision is reached.'

He fell silent. Siphon and Mientus took up their positions. Siphon tapped his cheeks, Mientus rolled his jaw, and Bobek, with his teeth chattering, said:

'You may begin!'

At these words reality burst from its frame, unreality turned into nightmare, the whole improbable adventure became a dream in which I was imprisoned with no possibility of even struggling. It was as if after long training a point had been reached at which one lost one's own face. It would not have been surprising if Mientus and Siphon had taken their faces in their hands and thrown them at each other; nothing would have been surprising. I muttered:

'Take pity on your faces, take pity on my face, for a face is not an object but a subject, a subject, a subject!'

But Siphon had already put his head forward, and he made the first grimace so suddenly that my own face was suddenly as distorted as if it were made of papier mâché.

Siphon blinked, like somebody suddenly emerging from the darkness into broad daylight, looked right and left with an expression of pious astonishment, rolled his eyes, looked up, opened his mouth, made a slight exclamation, as if he had noticed something on the ceiling, assumed an expression of ecstasy, and remained still in that inspired pose; then he put his hand on his heart and sighed.

Mientus collected himself and retorted with an alarming and

derisive counter-grimace. He too rolled his eyes, then raised them to heaven, glared, opened his lips in idiotic fashion, and rotated the face that he had thus composed until a fly fell into his cavernous mouth, whereupon he swallowed it.

Siphon paid no attention to this pantomime, which seemed to make no impact whatever on him (he had the advantage over his opponent of acting for the sake of his principles, not just for his own sake). He burst into tears, pious, bitter tears, floods of tears, that reached the heights of remorse, revelation, and ecstasy. Mientus burst into tears too, and sobbed and sobbed until a tear trickled down to the end of his nose—whereupon he caused it to drop into a spittoon, thus reaching a new level of disgustingness. This assault upon the most sacred feelings was too much for Siphon; it shook him; and, in spite of himself, still sobbing, he looked daggers at his opponent. But this was unwise of him, for it was just what Mientus had been waiting for. Realizing that he had diverted Siphon's attention from the heights, he stuck out his face in such an obscene fashion that Siphon, touched to the quick, groaned. Mientus seemed to be gaining the day, and Bobek and Hopek sighed with relief. But their relief was premature; they sighed too soon.

For Siphon, realizing that he had allowed himself to be excessively distracted by Mientus's face, and that irritation was making him lose control of his own, beat a hasty retreat, recomposed his features, and once more elevated his eyes towards heaven. He advanced one foot slightly, slightly ruffled his hair, caused a lock to droop over his forehead, and froze into a position of unshakeable unity with his principles and ideals; then he raised one hand, and pointed towards the stars. This was a powerful blow.

Mientus thereupon pointed his finger too, spat on it, put it up his nose, scratched himself with it, did everything in his power to debase and ridicule Siphon's noble gesture, thus defending himself by counter-attack. But Siphon went on remorselessly pointing towards the sky. In vain Mientus bit his finger, rubbed his teeth with it, scratched the sole of his foot with it; in vain he did everything he could think of to make his finger odious and contemptible; Siphon stood there remorselessly and impregnably pointing upwards, and yielded not an inch. Mientus's position started becoming untenable; he was using up his stock of insulting gestures, and Siphon's finger still pointed remorselessly towards heaven. The seconds and the umpire were petrified with horror. In a last desperate effort Mientus dipped his finger in the spittoon and waved it at Siphon, covered as it was with sweat and spittle. Not only did Siphon fail to take the slightest notice, but his face became diffused with seven colours, like a rainbow after a storm, and lo! there he stood in seven colours, the Boy Scout, Purity Incarnate, the Innocent Adolescent.

'Victory!' Gabek exclaimed.

Mientus looked dreadful. He retreated to the wall, fuming with rage, took hold of his finger, pulled it as if he were trying to pull it out of its socket, in order to destroy this link that bound him to Siphon, to enable him to recover his independence. But he could not pull out his finger, though he tried with all his strength, in spite of the pain. Impotence hung once more in the air. But there was nothing impotent about Siphon, who stood there as calm as the heavens, with his finger pointing upwards, not for himself, but for the sake of his principles. What a ghastly situation! Here was I, the umpire, between two boys each of whose faces was distorted into a horrible grimace, imprisoned between them no doubt for ever and ever, slave of the faces, the grimaces, of others. My face, the mirror of their faces, was distorted too; terror, disgust, fear, left their ineradicable marks on it. A clown between two other clowns, what could I do except grimace? Sadly my toe accompanied their fingers, and I grimaced and grimaced, well knowing that I was losing myself in my grimaces. Never, never, should I be able to escape from Pimko, never should I be able to return to my old self. What a nightmare! Oh, horror, oh, dreadful silence! For there were moments of dead silence, when the clash of arms was stilled, when there was nothing but silent grimaces and gestures.

Suddenly the silence was broken by a wild yell from Mientus. 'Go for him! Get him!'

What was this? So it wasn't over yet? Mientus dropped his finger, leapt at Siphon and struck him in the face, and Bobek and Hopek did the same to Gabek and Pyzo. A moment later an inextricable heap of bodies was writhing on the floor, with me, the umpire, standing over it.

In a flash Gabek and Pyzo were overpowered and tied up with their braces; and Mientus was sitting on Siphon.

'So, my fine young adolescent, you thought you'd got the better of me, did you?' he boasted. 'So you thought that all you had to do was to stick your finger in the air and the trick was done, did you? So you thought, my fine fellow (here he added some disgusting expressions) that Mientus wouldn't be able to get the better of you, did you? You thought he'd let himself be tied round that little finger of yours, did you? Well, then, for your information, when there's no other way out, fingers have to be brought down by force!'

'Let me go!' Siphon gasped.

'Let you go? I'll let you go! I'll let you go soon, but not in this state! Not till I've dealt with your adolescent in my own way. You'll have cause to remember Mientus. We're going to have a little talk. Come here with your ear. Fortunately it's still possible to get at you through your ears. Come here with your ear, I tell you! Come along, my little innocent, I'm going to tell you some things!'

He bent over and started talking softly. Siphon went green in the face, yelled like a pig in the slaughterhouse, writhed like a fish out of water. Mientus was suffocating him. Siphon turned his head this way and that to move his ears away from Mientus's mouth, and Mientus poured his filth first into one ear and then into the other; and Siphon yelled to prevent himself from hearing Mientus's filth; he yelled gravely, dreadfully, he froze into a quintessential yell. It was difficult to believe that the ideal could yell like this, like a wild beast in the primeval forest. His tormentor started yelling too.

68

'Gag him! Gag him! What are you waiting for, you fool? Stuff a handkerchief in his mouth!'

I was the fool to whom he referred. It was I who was supposed to stuff a handkerchief into Siphon's mouth, for Bobek and Hopek, each of whom were holding down one of Siphon's seconds, obviously could not move. But I would not, I could not, there I stood, rooted to the spot, disgusted with words, gestures, disgusted with every kind of expression. Alas, poor umpire! Where, oh! where were my thirty years? Vanished . . . But, suddenly there was Pimko standing in the doorway, with his yellow buckskin shoes, his brownish overcoat, and his walking-stick, standing there in a manner as definite and absolute as if he were seated.

⋆ 4 ⋆

Introduction to Philifor
Honeycombed with Childishness

BEFORE continuing with these authentic memoirs I desire at
this point to interpose by way of digression a story entitled
Philifor Honeycombed with Childishness. You have seen how the
evil and didactic Pimko endowed me with a childish little backside; you have seen the idealistic convulsions of our youth; its
inability to live, its calamitous lack of proportion and its
cacophony, its tragic artificiality, sad boredom, ridiculous
pretences, and agonizing anachronisms; as well as the follies of
its backsides, faces, and other parts of its body. You have heard
the words it uses, the clash between the lofty and the vulgar, and
those other words, equally empty and unsubstantial, inflicted
on it by its pedagogues; and you have noted how hollow verbiage
ended nastily in absurd facial contortions. Thus is man at the
very outset stuffed full of verbiage and grimaces; such is the
anvil on which our maturity is forged. You will soon be spectators of other grimaces and another duel—the death-struggle
between Professor G. L. Philifor of Leyden and Professor
Momsen of Colombo (better known as Anti-Philifor), in which
words and parts of the body will similarly appear. But it would
be wrong to seek any close connexion between the two parts of
my book; it would be equally wrong to suppose that in inter-
posing the story of Philifor I had any intention other than that of
covering some paper with ink and reducing to some extent the
enormous and intimidating pile of blank pages by which I am
confronted.

If, however, the eminent connoisseurs and men of learning, the Pimkos who specialize in providing us with an intellectual rump with the aid of the critical weapon known as 'faults of construction', object that from their point of view the motivation behind this bit of padding is of too private a nature and is therefore indefensible, and that there is no excuse for introducing into a work of art everything that I may have written in the course of my life, I shall reply that in my humble opinion the separate parts of the body suffice to form a solid and artistically constructed whole, and that this applies still more to words; and I shall demonstrate that my construction yields in no way to the best examples of logical and precise construction. For the fundamental part of the body is the rump, from which, like the trunk of a tree, everything else branches off; and that applies to all the separate parts of the body, including fingers, arms, eyes, teeth, and ears; moreover, some parts subtly and imperceptibly change into others; and at the pinnacle of the human trunk from which the separate parts spread out is the face (also known familiarly as mug or phiz); thus the latter closes the cycle opened by the rump. Having reached this pinnacle, what course is left open to me but that of retracing my steps by way of the various parts of the body to my rumpish starting-point? And that is the purpose of the tale of *Philifor*. *Philifor* is a constructive retrogression serving as a transition, or to state it in more precise terms, a coda, trill, or rather, intestinal lapse, without which it would never be possible for me to reach the left ankle. Is this not cast-iron construction? Does it not meet the most highly specialized requirements? And what will you say when you have discovered other and deeper links between all these parts—connecting, for instance, finger and liver—and when the mystic role of certain privileged parts, and the hidden meaning behind certain articulations will have been revealed to you, and finally, when you have seen the whole of all the parts as well as the parts of all the parts? I maintain that this bit of padding represents construction of the highest order, and would point out that penetrating analysis of this kind will enable you to fill a hundred volumes, to fill more and more space, to occupy an ever higher place, and to sit in it more and more at your ease. But . . . do you like blowing soap-bubbles at daybreak by the lakeside when the fish are darting about and the angler sitting silently by the waterside is gently reflected in the crystalline water?

Moreover, I recommend to you my method of making greater impact by means of repetition; by systematic repetition of a few words, turns of phrase, situations, and parts, I make the impact greater, and thus intensify the effect of stylistic unity, carrying it to the point of mania. It is by repetition that myths are created. Note, however, that this method of construction out of parts is not just construction, but behind the light and frothy form of a superficial newspaper article actually conceals a whole philosophy. Do you not agree that the reader is able to assimilate only one part at a time? He reads, for instance, one part or one passage before breaking off and reading another part or passage later; and he often begins in the middle, or even at the end, and then works his way backwards. Sometimes he reads two or three passages and never returns to the book; and not, mark you, because he is not interested, but because of some totally extraneous circumstance; and, even if he reads the whole thing, do you suppose for one moment that he has a view of it as a whole, appreciates the constructive harmony of the parts, if no specialist gives him the hint? Is it for this that authors spend years cutting, revising, and rearranging, sweating, straining and suffering? All to enable a specialist to tell the reader that the work is well constructed? Let us carry the matter a little further, into the realm of everyday experience. May not a telephone call, or a fly, distract the reader's attention just at the moment when all the parts, themes, threads, are on the point of converging into a supreme unity? Suppose, for instance, that at the critical moment your brother walks in and interrupts? Thus a fly, a telephone call, a brother walking in, can lay an author's noble work in ruins. Cruel flies, why do you persecute a species which has lost its tail and is left with nothing with which to protect itself? Consider, moreover, that that unique and exceptional work of yours on which you have expended so much effort and sweat is just one of the thirty thousand equally unique and exceptional works which will appear during the year. Oh! terrible and accursed parts! So it is for this that we laboriously construct; so that part of a part of a reader may partially assimilate part of a part of a book.

It is difficult not to be frivolous about this. Frivolity is not to be avoided; for we learnt long ago to use humour to evade matters that we find too painful. Will there ever be born a serious genius who will be able to confront the minor contingencies of life without taking refuge in misplaced laughter? Alas! my poor style, my poor, frivolous newspaper style! But (to drain the cup of parts to the lees) let us also note that the laws and principles of construction to which we are so subject are themselves only the product of a part, and an insignificant part into the bargain—a tiny segment of the world, a microcosm scarcely bigger than one's little finger, a minute group of specialists and aesthetes all of whom could be crowded into a teashop, whose relentless pressure on each other results in the distillation of ideas of ever greater subtlety. And the worst of it is that their tastes are not real tastes; your construction can never more than partially please them, for they will always prefer to it their own knowledge of construction. So that if the creative artist tries to excel by his sense of construction, is it only to enable the critic to display his expertise on the subject? . . . Silence . . . hush . . . mystery. Here we have the creative artist kneeling at the altar of art, thinking of a supreme masterpiece, harmony, precision, mind, transcendence; and here the critic, his critical status vouched for by his ability to penetrate to the deepest depths of the creative artist's work; after which the book goes to the reader, and the result of the author's complete and total perspiration is an altogether partial reception between the buzzing of a fly and the ringing of a telephone. The contingencies of life get the better of you. It is you who provoke the monster to a duel, but then a puppy comes along and gives you gooseflesh.

And (to take one more gulp from the cup of parts) I should

also like to ask whether in your opinion a work constructed according to all the canons expresses a whole or only part of a whole. Come, come! Is not form born of elimination, is not construction an impoverishment, can words express more than a part of reality? The rest is silence. In the last resort, is it we who create form, or is it form that creates us? Incidentally, some years ago I knew a writer who at the outset of his literary career gave birth to a book of the purest heroism. With the first few words he put down on paper, quite by chance, he touched the chord of heroism; it might equally well have been that of scepticism or lyricism. But the first sentences that flowed from his pen were heroic, and because of this, and by virtue of the laws of construction, it was impossible for him not to go on concentrating and distilling the spirit of heroism until he got to the end. By painstaking revision, by adjusting the beginning to the end and the end to the beginning, he ended by writing a book that was full of life and stamped with the most profound conviction.

But what about the author's deepest conviction? Could a responsible creative artist confess that heroism had flowed spontaneously from his pen and independently of him, and that his deepest conviction was not his deepest conviction, and that he did not know how it had come from outside and attached itself to him? In vain the unhappy hero of this heroism, feeling ashamed of himself, tried to escape from his part, which, having taken a firm hold on him, refused to let go. He had to adapt himself to the situation; and so thoroughly did he do so that towards the end of his career he had completely identified himself with his part; he was as heroic as it . . . and very much afraid of his heroism. He therefore studiously avoided the friends and companions of his youth, for they never recovered from their surprise at such a thorough adaptation of a whole to a part.

Such are the deep and weighty philosophical reasons which have prompted me to construct the present work on the basis of separate parts—regarding the work as part of a work and man as a conglomeration of physical and mental parts—for humanity as a whole seems to me nothing but a conglomeration of parts.

Now, if anyone objects that a partial concept such as mine is in reality no concept at all, but a joke, a snare and an illusion, and that instead of submitting to the severe rules and canons of art I am making a mock of them by clowning and buffoonery and irresponsible grimaces, I shall reply yes, perfectly true, such indeed is my intention. I am not ashamed to admit it, I have just as strong a desire to escape from your art, gentlemen, as I have to escape from you; and the reason is that I can stand neither you, nor your ideas, nor your aesthetic attitudes, nor your coteries.

For, gentlemen, there exist in the world human groups which are some less, some more, disgraceful, shameful, and humiliating than others—and stupidity is not spread equally everywhere. At first sight, for instance, the world of hairdressers has always seemed to me to be more liable to stupidity than that of shoemakers. But the things that happen in the world's artistic circles beat all records in stupidity and ignominy—to such an extent that it is impossible for a normally constituted and balanced person not to sweat with shame in the presence of their childish and pretentious orgies. Oh! those sublime songs to which nobody listens! Oh! those closed gatherings of initiates, the frenzied excitement of those concerts, those private invitations, those exaltations and arguments, even the faces of those declaiming or listening, celebrating the sacred aesthetic mysteries in a hermetically sealed container! What painful antinomy is it that causes everything you say or do in such an environment to be shameful and ridiculous? If in the course of centuries a social group declines into such convulsions of stupidity, it can be confidently assumed that its ideas are in no sort of correspondence with reality, or simply that the ideas on which it is living are false. For there is no doubt that your ideas are the very pinnacle and summit of conceptional naïveté; and, if you want to know how to change them and in which direction you ought to move, I can tell you straight away. But you must listen.

What in reality is a person aiming at nowadays who feels a vocation for the pen, the paint-brush, or the clarionet? Above all, he wants to be an artist. He wants to create art. He wants to feed on beauty, goodness, and truth, and to feed his fellow-citizens on these things; he wants to be prophet, bard, high priest, to offer himself whole to others, to burn on the altar of the sublime in providing humanity with this so desirable manna. Moreover, he wants to devote his talent to the service of an idea, and perhaps lead mankind or his country towards a better future. What noble aims! What magnificent intentions! Are they not identical with those of Shakespeare, Goethe, Beethoven, or Chopin? But here you run into trouble. The awkward fact is that you are neither Chopin nor Shakespeare, but at most a half-Shakespeare, or a quarter-Chopin (oh! cursed parts!), and consequently the sole result of your attitude is to draw attention to your sad inadequacy and inferiority—and it is as if in the course of your clumsy efforts to leap on to the pedestal you were breaking the most precious parts of your body.

Believe me, there is a big difference between the artist who has fulfilled himself and the infinite multitude of semi-demi-artists and quarter-poets who would desperately like to fulfil themselves—and what is appropriate to genius yields quite a different sound when it comes from you. But you, instead of equipping yourselves with ideas and opinions suited to your measure and in harmony with your situation, adorn yourselves with borrowed plumage—and that is why you transform yourselves into eternal candidates, eternal aspirants to greatness and perfection. Eternally impotent and always mediocre, you become the servants, pupils, and admirers of the art on which you dance attendance. It is indeed dreadful to watch all the efforts you make only to produce a failure, to hear you being told that this time you have not quite managed to pull it off, and to see you never-theless starting out on yet another work—and to watch you trying to put your works across, and consoling yourselves with poor secondary successes, engaging in mutual congratulations, organizing dinners, always seeking out new lies to justify the suspect reason for your existence; and you have not even the consolation of knowing in your bones that your work has real

76

value; because it is all only imitation, repetition of what you learnt from the masters; and all you do is cling to the coat-tails of genius, repeating after it, and in inferior fashion, complaints of obstacles in an area in which there is no room for obstacles. You are in a false situation which, being false, can yield only bitter fruit—and, sure enough, your coteries are the breeding-ground of backbiting, mutual contempt and low esteem; everyone despises everyone else and himself into the bargain, you constitute a mutual contempt society ... and end by despising yourselves to death.

What does the second-rate writer's situation consist of other than a huge repudiation? The first repudiation, and it is a cruel and humiliating one, is that inflicted on him by the average reader, who flatly declines to enjoy his work. The second is self-inflicted, inflicted by the writer's own self, which he has been unable to express, since he is only a copyist and an imitator of the masters. But the third repudiation, the supreme kick in the pants and the most humiliating of all, comes from the art in which he sought refuge, the art which, because of his impotence and inadequacy, treats him with contempt; and that fills the cup of ignominy. The sub-writer comes under the barrage of universal repudiation, becomes an object of general ridicule, and is left stranded. What, after all, can be expected of a man who has been repudiated three times, each time with greater ignominy?

When a man is finished to that extent, should he not vanish, hide himself somewhere out of sight? Is not the sight of inadequacy rising in broad daylight greedy of honours enough to give the universe the hiccups?

But, above all, answer me this: Do you prefer the crab-apple to the custard-apple, or the other way about? Ignominy, gentlemen, ignominy, ignominy, ignominy. No, I am neither a philosopher nor a theorist, it is you I am speaking of, it is your life to which I am referring; you must realize that it is only your personal situation which gives me pain. It is impossible to detach oneself from other people; there is a kind of impotence which prevents one from breaking the umbilical cord which connects one with the refuse of humanity. The unwanted—the unsmelt flower, the untasted sweet, the rejected woman—have always caused me almost physical pain; such frustration is intolerable—and when I meet an artist in the street, and see that the basis of his whole existence is vulgar repudiation, when I note that all his words and gestures, all his faith and his enthusiasm, all his commas and all his transgressions, all his ideas and all his illusions, exude the disagreeable odour of commonplace repudiation, I feel ashamed; ashamed not only because I am sorry for him, but also because I co-exist with him, and his chimerical existence offends my human dignity. Believe me, the attitude of the second-rate writer is in urgent need of reform, for otherwise the whole world will suffer from a grave malaise. It is appalling that persons who profess to be dedicated to the perfection of style, and hence presumably are sensitive to form, should tolerate without protest being placed in such a false and pretentious situation. Do they not understand that nothing could be more disastrous from the point of view of form and style? For he who is placed in a false and artificial situation cannot utter a single word that is not false and artificial, and whatever he says, does, or thinks necessarily turns against him and does him harm.

But then—you will ask—what ideas should we adopt in order to be able to express ourselves in a more reasonable, more sovereign manner, more consonant with our reality? Gentlemen, it is not in your power to become mature artists overnight; it is in your power, however, partially to cure these evils and to recover your lost sovereignty by withdrawing from the art which gives you such an embarrassing rump. Above all, break once and for all with the words 'art' and 'artist'. Cease intoxicating yourselves with those words which you repeat with the monotony of eternity. Is not everyone an artist? Does mankind create art only when seated at a desk in front of a sheet of paper? Is not art continually being created in the course of everyday life? When a girl puts a rose in her hair, when we make a good joke in the course of an agreeable conversation, when we exchange confidences at dusk, is not that art? Why, then, this terrible division between art and everyday life? Why do you say: Oh, I am an artist, I create art—when it would be more appropriate to say simply: Perhaps I take a little more interest in art than other people? Moreover, why this cult, this admiration only for the kind of art that results in so-called works of art? Whence this naïve belief that men so hugely admire works of art and that we go into ecstasy and pass away when we listen to a Beethoven symphony? Have you never considered how impure, adulterated, and formidably immature is that area of culture which you wish to circumscribe with your over-simple terminology? Above all, the boring and commonplace mistake that you make is this: you refer man's contact with art almost exclusively to the aesthetic sense, and consider that contact from an excessively remote and special point of view, as if each individual communed with art in total solitude, hermetically sealed off from his fellows; whereas in reality we are confronted with a large number of different senses, complicated, moreover, by the intermingling of a large number of different individuals, who influence and affect each other and give rise to collective states of mind.

When a concert pianist plays Chopin, for instance, you say: The audience was roused and carried away by a brilliant interpretation of the master's music. But it is possible that not a single member of the audience was carried away; it is perfectly possible that, if they had not known that Chopin was a great master and the virtuoso a great pianist, they might have received the performance with less enthusiasm. It is also possible that the reason why everyone applauded so enthusiastically, their faces distraught with emotion, was that everyone else was doing the same. For each one of them, believing that all the rest were experiencing enormous, super-terrestrial, delight and pleasure, would tend for that very reason to display the same delight and pleasure; and thus it is perfectly possible that nobody in the hall was directly and immediately carried away by the experience, though everyone, adapting his attitude to that of his neighbour, showed all the external signs of it; and it is only when the whole audience has been thus carried away, when every member of it has been encouraged by everyone else to clap, shout, grow red in the face with pleasure and enthusiasm, it is only then, I say, that these demonstrations of pleasure and enthusiasm arise; for we have to adjust our feelings to our behaviour. It is also certain that in listening to the music we are performing something in the nature of a religious, ritual act; and that at a Chopin concert we prostrate ourselves before the god of beauty in a spirit similar to that in which we piously kneel at Mass. In the former case, however, we are merely paying official homage; and who can say what part is played in this tribute to beauty by beauty itself and what part is attributable to the historico-sociological process? Bah! Mankind, as we know, has need of myths; and it picks out one or the other of its numerous creative artists (who will throw light on the reason for its choice?) and lo and behold! it elevates him above his fellows, starts learning his work by heart, discovers its magic and mystery, adapts its way of feeling to it. Now, if we set about exalting some other creative artist with the same persistence and indefatigability, I am convinced that we could make a similarly great genius of him. Do you not see, then, how many different and often non-aesthetic factors (the monotonous enumeration of them could be extended indefinitely) have accumulated in the greatness of our masters and our semi-obscure, troubled, and fragmentary coexistence with the art which you naïvely sum up in the formula: Let the inspired poet sing and let the listener be enchanted? That is why it sometimes happens that a poet is considered great, magnificent, and marvellous by everyone, though no one, perhaps, has ever enjoyed his work; or why sometimes everyone swoons away in the presence of a fine canvas, though no one ever thinks of fainting in the presence of a copy which may resemble it like two drops of water.

Have done, then, with your aesthetic transports, stop being artists, for heaven's sake drop your way of talking about art, its syntheses, analysis, subtleties, profundities, the whole inflated apparatus; and, instead of imposing myths, model yourselves on facts. That alone and by itself should bring you noticeable relief, freeing you from your limitations and opening your mind to reality. Moreover, you must cast off the fear that this broad and healthy way of regarding art will deprive you of any riches and greatness, for reality is richer and greater than naïve illusions and petty lies; let me tell you straight away about the riches that await you along this new path.

Art certainly consists of perfection of form. But you—and here we are faced with another of the cardinal errors of yours—you imagine that art consists of creating perfect works. You apply the immense and universal aspiration to the creation of form to the production of poems and symphonies, but you have never managed properly to appreciate, or to make others appreciate, the role, and the important role, of form in your own lives. Even in pyschology you have not given form the place to which it is entitled. Hitherto we have always considered the feelings, instincts, or ideas which govern our conduct, and regarded form as at the most a harmless, ornamental accessory. When a widow weeps behind her husband's hearse, we think she does so because she is suffering because of her loss. When an engineer, doctor, or lawyer murders his wife, his children, or a friend, we think that he was driven to it by violent and blood-thirsty instincts. When a politician in a public speech expresses himself stupidly, deceitfully, or pettily, we say he is stupid because he expresses himself stupidly. But the real situation is this: a human being does not externalize himself directly and immediately in conformity with his own nature; he invariably does so by way of some definite form; and that form, style, way of speaking and responding, do not derive solely from him, but are imposed on him from without—and the same man can express himself sometimes wisely, sometimes foolishly, blood-thirstily or angelically, maturely or immaturely, according to the form, the style presented to him by the outside world, the pressure put upon him by other men. And just as worms and insects creep and fly all day long in search of food, so we, without a moment's respite or relief, perpetually seek form and expression, struggle with other men for style, for our own way of being; and when we travel in a tram, or eat, or enjoy ourselves, or rest, or engage in business, we are perpetually in search of form, and we delight in it, suffer for it or adapt ourselves to it, we break or violate it, or let ourselves be violated by it, amen.

Oh, the power of form! It causes nations to perish, and it leads to wars. It is the reason why things arise among us which do not come from us. Without it you will never succeed in understanding stupidity, or evil, or crime. It governs our smallest reflexes, and lies at the foundation of the whole of our collective life. But for you form and style are ideas restricted to the field of art; and, just as you have reduced the function of art to the production of works of art, so do you debase the idea of style and form; for you, style is only style on paper, the style of your stories. Who, gentlemen, will chastise the posterior that you present to mankind when you kneel before the altar of art? For you form is not something alive, human, let me say practical and everyday, but a gaudy attribute of art. Bent over your paper, you even forget your own self—and what matters to you is not perfecting yourself in your own personal and concrete style, but perfecting some sort of abstract and imaginary story. Instead of making art your servant, you make yourselves its slave—and that, I imagine, is why in sheep-like fashion you allow it to hamper your development and cast you into perpetual sloth.

See how different would be the attitude of a man who, instead of saturating himself with the phraseology of a million conceptualist metaphysician-aestheticians, looked at the world with new eyes and allowed himself to feel the enormous influence which form has on human life. If he still wanted to use his fountain-pen, he would do so, not in order to become a great writer and create art, but, let us say, the better to express his own personality and draw a clear picture of himself in the eyes of others; or to organize himself, bring order within himself, and by confession to cure any complexes or immaturities; and also, perhaps, to make his contact with others deeper, more intimate,

more creative, more sharply outlined, which could be of great
benefit to his mind and his development; or, for instance, he
might try to combat customs, prejudices, principles which he
found contrary to his nature; or again, he might write simply
to earn a living. He certainly would not spare effort to ensure
that his work possessed an artistically attractive form, but his
principal goal would be, not art, but himself. He would no longer
write pretentiously, to educate, to elevate, to guide, to moralize,
and to edify his fellow-men; his aim would be his own elevation
and his own progress; and he would write, not because he was
mature and had found his form, but because he was still immature
and in his efforts to attain form was humiliating himself, making
a fool of himself, and sweating like a climber still struggling
towards the mountain-top, being a man still on the way to self-
fulfilment. And if he should happen to write a worthless or silly
book, he would say to himself: Well, I have written some rubbish,
but I have signed no contract with anyone to write a clever or
perfect book. I expressed my stupidity, and I am glad of it, for
I am formed and fashioned by the severity of the human
judgements which I have called down on my head, and it is as if
I were being reborn. You see, then, that an artist equipped with
this healthy philosophy is so well rooted in himself that neither
stupidity nor immaturity can frighten or harm him; he can
externalize himself and hold his head high, in spite of his indolence, while you can externalize nothing, for fear makes you
voiceless.

That by itself would be a great alleviation. But, in addition,
only a poet who approached things in this fashion would be
capable of understanding the issue which has hitherto been your
supreme stumbling-block—perhaps the most fundamental, the
most intimidating issue of all. Let me state it in imaginary form.
Let us imagine an adult, mature poet bent over his paper at grips
with his work—and looking over his shoulder an adolescent—
a semi-cultivated, semi-educated individual—an average girl
perhaps, or any other mediocre and obscure young person—and
this person, this adolescent, this girl, this semi·educated or other

obscure product of sub-culture, seizes hold of his mind with a pair of forceps, attacks his soul, clasps and hugs it, refreshes and rejuvenates it, makes it green again, adjusts it to his or her own fashion and reduces it to his or her own level, yes, holding it tenderly in her arms. But the creative artist, instead of facing the intruder, pretends to take no notice, and foolishly imagines that he can avoid the violation by pretending not to have been violated. Is it not that which happens to all of you, from the great genius to the choice little poet of the back row of the chorus? Is it not true that every mature, superior, major and perfected human being depends in a thousand different ways on human beings who are at a less advanced stage of development? And does that dependence not attack the mind right to its very essence? It does so in such a way that we can say that the senior is always the creation of the junior. Do we not, when we write, have to adapt ourselves to the reader? When we speak do we not submit ourselves to the mind of the person to whom our words are addressed? Are we not fatally in love with youth? Are we not constantly forced to seek the favours of inferior persons, to adapt ourselves to them, to bend our necks, bow either to their power or to their spell? And is not this painful violation of ourselves carried out by semi-obscure individuals the most penetrating and most fertile of them all? Now, all that you have hitherto been able to do is to bury your heads in the sand in order not to see the violation; in your concentration on the polishing of your boring verses you have had neither the time nor the inclination to take any interest in it. You act as if nothing had happened, while in reality you have been violated without respite or remission. Oh, why do you enjoy yourselves only among yourselves? Why is your maturity so mature that it can cohabit only with maturity?

But, if you were less preoccupied with art and more with yourselves, you would not keep silent in face of this terrible violation of yourselves; and the poet, instead of writing for other poets, would feel himself penetrated and fertilized from below, by forces which he had hitherto neglected. He would

84

recognize that the only way of freeing himself from the pressure was to recognize it; and in his style, his attitude, his tone, his form—that of his art as well as of his everyday life—he would set himself to displaying this link with a lower level. He would no longer think of himself only as father, but as simultaneously father and son, and he would no longer write as a clever, subtle, and mature man, but as a clever man always reduced to stupidity, as a subtle man reduced to crudity, an adult perpetually reduced to childhood. And if, on leaving his study, he chanced on a child, an adolescent, a girl, or a semi-cultivated person, he would cease to find him or her boring, and no longer pat these people protectively, didactically, and pedagogically on the back while talking down to them in a superior manner; on the contrary, in a holy fit of trembling he would start groaning and roaring, and would perhaps even fall on his knees before them. Instead of shunning immaturity and shutting himself off in what are called coteries, he would realize that a truly universal style is a style born slowly and gradually in contact with human beings of different social conditions, age, education, and stages of development. And that would ultimately lead you to a form of creation so palpitating with life and so full of tremendous poetry that you would all be transformed into sublime geniuses.

So you see what perspectives and what hopes would be opened up to you by these purely personal ideas of mine. But, if you want them to be one hundred per cent creative and categorical, there is still one more step that you must take, and this is such a bold and tremendous step, and its possibilities are so unlimited and its consequences so devastating that it is only softly and from afar that my lips shall mention it. Well, then, this is it. The time has come, the hour has struck on the clock of ages. *Try to set yourself against form, try to shake free of it.* Cease to identify yourself with that which defines you. Try to escape from all expression of yourself. Mistrust your opinions. Mistrust your beliefs, and defend yourself against your feelings. Withdraw from what you seem to be from outside, and flee from all externalization just as the bird flees from the snake.

For—but frankly I do not know whether the time has yet come to tell you this—it is a false assumption that man should be definite, that is to say, unshakeable in his ideas, categorical in his statements, clear in his ideologies, rigid in his tastes, responsible in his speech and actions, crystallized and precise in his way of being. Examine more closely the chimerical nature of the assumption. Our element is eternal immaturity. The things that we think, feel, and say today will necessarily seem foolish to our grandchildren; so it would surely be better to forestall this now, and treat them as if they were foolish already; moreover, the force that impels you to premature finality is not, as you believe, an entirely human force. We shall soon realize that henceforward the most important thing is not to die for ideas, styles, theories, or even to attach oneself to and buttress oneself with them; but to take a step backwards and withdraw in the face of all the things that keep on happening inside us.

Let the cry be backwards! I foresee (though I do not know if the time has yet come to admit it) that the general retreat will soon be sounded. The son of man will realize that he is not expressing himself in harmony with his true nature, but in an artificial manner painfully inflicted on him from outside, either by other men or by circumstances. He will then begin to fear this form that is his own, and to be as ashamed of it as he was previously proud of it and sought stability in it. We shall soon begin to be afraid of ourselves and our personalities, because we shall discover that they do not completely belong to us. And instead of bellowing and shouting: I believe this, I feel that, I am this, I stand for that, we shall say more humbly: In me there is a belief, a feeling, a thought, I am the vehicle for such-and-such an action, production, or whatever it may be. . . . The poet will repudiate his song, the commander will tremble at his own orders, the priest will fear his altar, mothers will no longer be satisfied with teaching their children principles, but will also teach them how to evade them, to prevent them from being stifled by them. And, above all, human beings will one day meet other human beings face to face.

It will be a long and painful path. For nowadays individuals, like nations, can organize their mental life almost at will, and are able to change styles, beliefs, principles, ideals, and feelings as their immediate interests dictate. But they do not yet know how to live and preserve their humanity without style; and we are far from being able to preserve our interior warmth, our freshness, and our human kindness against the Mephistopheles of order. Great discoveries will have to be made, great blows will have to be struck with our poor bare hands against the tough armour-plate of form. Unparalleled cunning, great honesty of thought, and intelligence sharpened to a degree, will be required to enable man to escape from his stiff exterior and succeed in better reconciling order with disorder, form with the formless, maturity with eternal and sacred immaturity. In the meantime tell me which you prefer, red peppers or fresh cucumbers? And do you like enjoying them quietly sitting in the shade of a tree while a sweet and gentle breeze cools the parts of your body? I ask you this question with the greatest seriousness, with the most complete sense of responsibility for what I am saying, and with the greatest respect for all your parts without exception, for I know that you are a part of the humanity of which I too am part, and that you partially participate in something which is in turn a part and of which I too am a part, at any rate in part, like all other particles and parts of parts of parts of parts of parts of parts of parts of parts of parts. Help! Oh, accursed parts! Oh, bloodthirsty and horrifying parts, once more you assault and persecute and stifle and suffocate me from every quarter. Enough, enough! There's nothing that can be done, nothing that can be done about it. Oh, parts with whom I wanted to take refuge, you now rise against me! Enough, enough, let us leave this part of the book, and go on to another, and I swear before God that in the next chapter there will be no more parts, no parts whatever, because I am getting rid of parts, showing them the door, and remaining (at any rate for my part) inside, without parts.

5

Philifor Honeycombed with Childishness

THE prince of synthetists, recognized as the greatest synthetist of all times, was the higher synthetist Dr Philifor, who came from the south of Annam, and was Professor of Synthetisiology in the University of Leyden. He worked according to the pathetic spirit of higher synthesis, generally using the method of adding infinity, though sometimes, when occasion arose, he adopted that of multiplying by infinity. He was a well built, rather corpulent man, with a shaggy beard and the face of a bespectacled prophet. By virtue of Newton's principle of action and equal and opposite reaction, an intellectual phenomenon of such magnitude could not fail to provoke a counter-phenomenon in the bosom of nature; hence the birth at Colombo of an eminent analyst who, after obtaining his doctor's degree and the title of professor of higher analysis at Columbia University, climbed rapidly to the top of the academic tree. He was a dry, slightly built, beardless man, with the face of a bespectacled sceptic, and his sole interior driving force was to pursue and humiliate the distinguished Philifor.

He worked analytically, and his speciality was breaking down individuals into their constituent parts, with the aid of calculation, and more particularly flicks of the finger. With the aid of the latter he was able to invite a nose to enjoy an independent existence of its own and make it move spontaneously this way and that, to the great terror of its owner. When he was bored he used frequently to practise this art on the tram. In response to his deepest vocation he set out in pursuit of Philifor, and in a town somewhere in Spain succeeded in procuring for himself the title of Anti-Philifor, of which he was very proud. Philifor, having discovered that he was being pursued, immediately set out on the heels of his pursuer, and the mutual pursuit of the two men of learning went on for a long time—without result, however, because each was prevented by pride from admitting that he was the pursued as well as the pursuer. Consequently, when Philifor was at Bremen, for instance, Anti-Philifor would hurry there from The Hague, refusing, or perhaps being unable, to take into account the fact that at that very moment Philifor for reasons identical with his own was taking his seat in the Bremen-The Hague express. The collision between the two—a disaster on the scale of the greatest railway accidents—finally took place by pure chance in the first-class restaurant of the Hotel Bristol in Warsaw. Professor Philifor, accompanied by Mrs Philifor, was carefully consulting the indicator when Anti-Philifor, who had just got off the train, entered breathlessly, arm-in-arm with his analytical travelling companion, Fiora Gente of Messina. We who were present, that is to say, Dr Theophilus Poklewski, Dr Theodore Roklewski, and myself, realizing the gravity of the situation, immediately started taking notes.

Anti-Philifor advanced silently and gazed into the eyes of Professor Philifor, who rose to his feet. Each tried to impose the force of his personality on the other. The analyst's eyes travelled coldly from his opponent's feet upwards; those of the stoutly resisting synthetist worked in the opposite direction, from the head downwards. As the outcome of this struggle was a draw, with no advantage accruing to either side, the two contestants resorted to a verbal duel. The doctor and master of analysis said:

'Gnocchi!'

'Gnocchi!' the synthetisiologist retorted.

'Gnocchi, gnocchi, or a mixture of eggs, flour and water,' said Anti-Philifor, and Philifor capped this with:

'Gnocchi means the higher essence, the supreme spirit of gnocchi, the thing-in-itself.'

His eyes flashed fire, he wagged his beard, it was obvious that he had won. The professor of higher analysis recoiled a few paces, seized with impotent rage, but a dreadful idea suddenly flashed into his mind. A sickly and puny man in comparison with Philifor, he decided to attack Mrs Philifor, who was the apple of her worthy professor-husband's eye. The incident, according to the eye-witnesses' report, then developed as follows:

1. Professor Philifor's wife, a stout and majestic woman, was seated, silently absorbed in her thoughts.

2. Professor Anti-Philifor, armed with his cerebral gear, placed himself in front of her, and started undressing her with his eyes, from foot to head. Mrs Philifor trembled with cold and shame. Professor Philifor silently covered her with her travelling rug, casting a look of infinite contempt at the insolent Professor Anti-Philifor, but nevertheless betraying some slight traces of anxiety.

3. Professor Anti-Philifor then calmly said: 'Ear, ear,' and laughed sardonically. At these words the woman's ear appeared in all its nakedness and became indecent, and Professor Philifor ordered her to conceal it beneath her hat. This was not of much use, however, for Anti-Philifor muttered, as if to himself, the words 'two nostrils', thus laying bare in shameful and analytical fashion the nostrils of the professor's highly respectable wife. This aggravated the situation, for there was no way of concealing her nostrils.

4. Professor Philifor threatened to call the police; the tide of battle seemed to be turning distinctly in his opponent's favour. The master of analysis said with intense mental concentration: 'Fingers, the five fingers of each hand.' Mrs Philifor's resistance, unfortunately, was insufficient to conceal a reality which disclosed itself to the eyes of those present in all its stark nakedness, i.e. the five fingers of each of her two hands. There they were, five on each side. Mrs Philifor, utterly profaned, gathered her last strength to try to put on her gloves, but an incredible thing happened. Professor Anti-Philifor fired at her point-blank an

analysis of her urine. With a loud guffaw, he exclaimed victoriously: 'H_2O, C_4, TPS, some leucocytes, and albumen!' Everyone rose, Professor Anti-Philifor withdrew with his mistress, who giggled in a vulgar manner, while Professor Philifor, aided by the undersigned, hurriedly took his wife to hospital. (*Signed*) T. Poklewski, T. Roklewski, Anton Swistak, eye-witnesses.

Next morning Roklewski, Poklewski, and I myself joined the Professor at Mrs Philifor's bedside. Her disintegration, set in train by Anti-Philifor's analytic tooth, was proceeding apace, and she was progressively losing her physiological contexture. From time to time she said with a hollow groan: 'My leg, my eye, my leg, my ear, my finger, my head, my leg,' as if she were bidding farewell to the various parts of her body, which were already moving independently of her. Her personality was in its death-throes. We racked our brains for some way of saving her, but could think of nothing. After further consultations, in which Assistant Professor S. Lopatkin took part—he arrived by the seven-forty plane from Moscow—we were confirmed in our conclusion that the situation called for the application of the most extreme methods of scientific synthetism. But none existed. Philifor thereupon concentrated his mental faculties to such good purpose that we all recoiled a step. He said:

'I've got it! A slap in the face! Only a well-aimed slap in the face can restore my wife's honour and synthesize the scattered elements on a higher level.'

It was no easy task to find the world-famous analyst in the big city; not until nightfall did we succeed in tracking him down to a first-class bar, where he was soberly engaged in drinking. He was emptying bottle after bottle, and the more he drank, the more sober he became; and the same applied to his analytical mistress; the truth of the matter was that both found sobriety more intoxicating than alcohol. When we walked in, the waiters, who had turned as white as their napkins, had timidly taken refuge behind the bar, and the two lovers were silently devoting themselves to an interminable orgy of keeping cool and collected.

We drew up a plan of action. Professor Philifor would first of all feint in the direction of the left cheek and then strike out in earnest at the right, while we witnesses, i.e. Poklewski, Roklewski, and myself, all three holders of doctor's degrees in the University of Warsaw, accompanied by Assistant Professor S. Lopatkin, would proceed forthwith to the drawing up of our report. It was a simple and straightforward plan, calling for no very complicated action, but the professor raised his arm, only to let it drop to his side again. We witnesses were left in a state of stupefaction. The slap in the face did not take place. I repeat, the slap in the face did not take place. All that took place was two little roses and a rough illustration of two doves.

With satanic insight Anti-Philifor had foreseen Philifor's move. The temperate Bacchus had had two little roses tattooed on each cheek, as well as something resembling two doves. Anti-Philifor's cheeks and Philifor's planned blow were thus deprived of meaning; slapping roses and doves would be as idle as casually slapping a piece of painted paper. Thinking it out of the question that our learned and universally respected educator of youth should expose himself to ridicule by striking a piece of painted paper because of his wife's illness, we succeeded in persuading him to abandon a course of action which he might subsequently regret.

'Vile dog!' the professor growled. 'Vile, vile, vile dog!'

'You are an amorphous collection of disparate parts,' the analyst replied, in a burst of analytic pride. 'You are an amorphous collection of disparate parts, and so am I. Kick me in the stomach, if you like; it won't be I whom you kick, but my stomach, and that's all. You wished to provoke my face by slapping it? Well, you can provoke my cheek, but not me. I do not exist! I simply do not exist!'

'I'll provoke your face! As sure as God's in His heaven, I'll provoke your face!'

'My cheeks are impervious to provocation,' Anti-Philifor replied with a sneer.

Fiora Gente, who was sitting by his side, burst out laughing.

The cosmic doctor of double analysis leered sensually at his mistress and walked out. Fiora Gente, however, remained. She was perched on a high stool and looked at us with the relaxed eyes of a completely analysed parrot. A little later, at 8.40 p.m. to be precise, we, that is to say Professor Philifor, the two doctors, Assistant Professor Lopatkin and myself, held a conference. Assistant Professor Lopatkin as usual wielded the fountain-pen. The conference proceeded as follows:

The three doctors of law: 'In view of what has occurred, we see no possibility of settling this quarrel in an honourable manner, and we therefore advise the respected professor to ignore the insult to which he has been subjected, because it came from an individual incapable of giving satisfaction.'

Professor Philifor: 'I propose to ignore it, but my wife is dying.'

Assistant Professor Lopatkin: 'There is no way of saving your wife.'

Professor Philifor: 'Don't say that! Oh, don't say that! A slap in the face is the only hope! But there is no slap in the face, there is no cheek! There is no method of divine synthesis! There is no God! But yes! yes! There are faces! There are slaps! There is a God! Honour! Synthesis!'

Myself: 'I observe that the professor is being illogical. Either there are faces, or there are not.'

Philifor: 'Gentlemen, you forget that I still have my two cheeks. His cheeks do not exist, but mine do. We can still achieve our aim with my two cheeks, which are intact. Gentlemen, what I mean is this: I cannot slap his face, but he can slap mine! It will come to the same thing. A face will have been slapped and synthesis achieved!'

'But how shall we get him to slap the professor's face?'

'How shall we get him to slap the professor's face?'

'How shall we get him to slap the professor?'

'Gentlemen,' the brilliant thinker composedly replied, 'he has cheeks, but I have too. There is an analogy here, and I shall therefore be acting less logically than analogically; that will be much more effective, because nature is governed by the law of analogy. If he is the king of analysis, I am the king of synthesis. If he has cheeks, so have I. If I have a wife, he has a mistress. If he has analysed my wife, I shall synthesize his mistress, and in that fashion I shall get from him the slap that he refuses me.'

Without further delay he beckoned to Fiora Gente. We were left speechless with amazement. She approached, moving all the parts of her body, ogling me with one eye and the professor with the other, smiling with all her teeth at Stephen Lopatkin, projecting her front towards Roklewski and her behind towards Poklewski. The impression she made was such that the assistant professor muttered:

'Are you really proposing to attack those fifty separate parts with your higher synthesis?'

The universal synthetisiologist, however, possessed the virtue of never losing hope. He invited Fiora Gente to sit at the small table, offered her a Cinzano, and by way of preamble, to test the ground, said to her sympathetically:

'Soul, soul.'

She did not reply.

'I!' said the professor impetuously and inquisitorially, desiring to awaken her annihilated ego.

'You? Oh, all right! Five zlotys!'

'Unity!' Philifor exclaimed violently. 'Higher unity! Equality in unity!'

'Boy or old man, it's all the same to me,' she said with the most complete indifference.

We gazed in discouragement at this infernal analyst of the night, whom Anti-Philifor had brought up in his own image, and perhaps trained for himself since earliest childhood.

The father of the synthetic sciences refused, however, to be discouraged. A phase of intense effort and struggle ensued. He read to her the first two cantos of the *Divina Commedia*, for which she charged him ten zlotys. He made her an inspired speech on the higher love which unifies and encompasses everything, and that cost him eleven zlotys. For agreeing to allow him to read to

94

her two superb novels by two well-known women novelists about regeneration by love she asked a hundred and fifty zlotys, and refused to consider a farthing less; and finally, when he got to the point of appealing to her dignity, she insisted on fifty zlotys.

'Fancies have to be paid for, grandpa,' she said. 'For fancies there's no fixed rate.'

Opening and shutting her self-satisfied owl's eyes, she remained entirely untouched by the experience. Her charges kept piling up, and Anti-Philifor, wandering round the town, shook with interior laughter at all these desperate endeavours.

In the course of the subsequent conference, in which Assistant Professor Lopatkin and the three professors took part, the eminent seeker after truth summed up his defeat:

'It has cost me several hundred zlotys already and I really do not see the slightest possibility of any synthesis,' he said. 'In vain I had recourse to the supreme unities such as humanity; she turns everything into money and hands back the change. Meanwhile my wife is steadily losing what remains of her homogeneity. Her leg has already got to the point of walking round the room on its own. When she gets drowsy, she tries to hold it with her hands, but her hands refuse to obey her. It is the most shattering, appalling anarchy.'

Dr T. Poklewski, M.D.: 'And meanwhile Anti-Philifor is spreading the story that the professor is a vicious and depraved old gentleman.'

Assistant Professor Lopatkin: 'But might we not after all be able to catch her with the aid of money? I do not yet see clearly the idea for which I am groping in my mind, but things like that happen in nature. Let me explain. I had a woman patient who suffered from shyness. It was impossible to inject boldness into her, because she was incapable of assimilating it. But I succeeded in injecting into her such an enormous dose of shyness that she could not tolerate it. Finding shyness intolerable, she took courage, and became very bold indeed. The best method is to cure the disease by the disease itself. There must be some way of synthesizing her by means of money, but I confess that I do not...'

Professor Philifor: 'Money ... money ... but money always adds up to a definite sum, a definite amount, which has nothing in common with unity in the true sense of the word. The only sum of money that is indivisible is a farthing, and nobody is impressed by a farthing.... But gentlemen, suppose ... suppose we offered her such a huge sum that she was thunderstruck by it!'

We were left open-mouthed in astonishment. Philifor rose to his feet, his black beard trembling. He was now in one of those hypermanic states which invariably affect genius at seven-year intervals. He sold two houses and a villa in the neighbourhood of Warsaw, and changed the 850,000 zlotys thus realized into one-zloty pieces. Poklewski looked at him in amazement. A simple country doctor, he had never had any understanding of genius, and that was why he failed to understand it now. The philosopher was now sure of himself, however, and sent Anti-Philifor an ironic invitation. The latter sent a sarcastic reply and turned up punctually at nine-thirty in a private room at the Alcazar restaurant, where the decisive test was to take place. The two scholars did not shake hands. The master of analysis laughed, and his laughter was dry and malicious.

'Carry on, sir,' he said. 'Carry on! My woman friend is obviously less liable to composition than is your wife to decomposition. On that my mind is at rest.'

But he too entered progressively into a more and more hypermanic state. Dr Poklewski's fountain-pen was poised and Assistant Professor Lopatkin held the paper at the ready.

Professor Philifor set about things as follows. First of all he laid on the table one zloty. Fiora Gente did not budge. He put down a second zloty; nothing happened. He put down a third; again nothing happened. But when he put down the fourth, she said:

'Oh! Four zlotys!'

At the fifth she yawned, and at the sixth she remarked with an air of indifference:

'What's up, grandpa? Have you gone crackers again?'

Not until after the ninety-seventh zloty did we observe the first symptoms of surprise. At the 115th her eyes, which had been wandering from Dr Poklewski to Assistant Professor Lopatkin and myself, started tending to synthesize somewhat on the money.

At 100,000 zlotys Philifor was gasping painfully for breath. Anti-Philifor was beginning to show signs of alarm, and the hitherto heterogeneous courtesan acquired a certain concentration. She gazed fascinated at the pile, which, to tell the truth was ceasing to be a pile, and tried to count, but she had lost her head for reckoning. The sum had ceased to be a sum, had turned into something impossible to grasp in its entirety, something so tremendous, so inconceivable, that the mind boggled at it, as it does when it considers the dimensions of space. The patient let out a hollow groan. The analyst tried to dash to her assistance, but the two doctors restrained him. In vain he whispered to her to divide the total into hundreds, or five hundreds, but the total refused to yield to this treatment. When the triumphant high priest of synthesis had spent all he had and crowned the pile, or rather the mountain, the Mount Sinai, of money with the last single and indivisible zloty, it was as if some divinity had taken possession of the courtesan. She rose to her feet, showing every symptom of synthesis—tears, sighs, smiles, thoughtfulness—and said:

'Gentlemen, myself. My higher self!'

Philifor uttered a cry of triumph, and with a frantic yell Anti-Philifor broke loose from the two doctors' hold, dashed at Philifor, and struck him in the face.

This synthetic lightning flash snatched from the analytic entrails dispelled the shadows. The assistant professor and the doctors heartily congratulated the gravely dishonoured professor. His sworn enemy writhed and gesticulated in a frenzy against the wall, but no amount of frenzy could now deprive the

97

victorious march of honour of its momentum, and the whole affair, which had hitherto been not very honourable, was now firmly set on an honourable course.

Professor G. L. Philifor of Leyden appointed as his seconds Dr Lopatkin and myself; Professor P. T. Momsen, known by his honorary title of Anti-Philifor, chose the two doctors present. Philifor's seconds honourably challenged Anti-Philifor's seconds, and these in turn challenged Philifor's. Each of these honourable steps created more and more synthesis, and the professor of Columbia University writhed as if he were standing on hot coals, while the sage of Leyden stroked his beard and smiled. At the municipal hospital Mrs Philifor started regaining her unity; in a barely audible whisper she asked for a glass of milk, and hope revived in the doctors' breasts. Honour had made its appearance among the clouds and was smiling down upon mankind. The duel was fixed for Tuesday at 7 a.m.

It was agreed that the fountain-pen should be entrusted to Dr Roklewski, and the pistols to Assistant Professor Lopatkin; and that Dr Poklewski should hold the paper and I the overcoats. The tireless advocate of the cause of synthesis refused to be affected by doubt, dismay or fear. I recall his saying to me on the eve of the duel: 'Young man, I know that I am just as likely to be left on the field of honour as he, but, whatever happens, my spirit will survive and be victorious, for death is essentially synthetic. If he dies, his end will be a tribute paid to synthesis; if he kills me, he will do so synthetically. Hence in any event victory will be mine!' In this state of exaltation, desiring to celebrate more worthily his moment of glory, he invited the womenfolk—his wife and Fiora Gente—to attend in the capacity of simple spectators. I was filled with grim forebodings, I feared . . . what did I fear? I did not know myself. All night I lay a prey to grim anxiety, and not until I reached the appointed duelling ground did I tumble to the reason, which was symmetry; for the situation was symmetrical; hence its strength, but hence also its weakness.

For every move of Philifor led to a similar move by Anti-

Philifor, and the initiative was Philifor's. If Philifor raised his hat, Anti-Philifor must do the same. If Philifor fired, so must he. Moreover, the whole of the action was confined to an imaginary straight line drawn between the two duellists; and this line was the axis of the whole situation. But suppose Anti-Philifor departed from it? Suppose he treacherously wandered from the straight path, basely evaded the iron laws of symmetry and analogy? What vileness, what intellectual depravity might not be hatching in his brain? I was plunged in these thoughts when Professor Philifor raised his arm, aimed at his opponent's heart, fired, and missed. The analyst likewise raised his arm and aimed at his opponent's heart. It seemed almost inevitable that if the former fired synthetically at the heart, the latter must do the same, there seemed to be no possible alternative; no alternative seemed intellectually conceivable. But the analyst made a supreme effort, uttered a savage yell, deflected the barrel of his pistol from the axis of the situation and fired. Where would the bullet strike? Where? Mrs Philifor, accompanied by Fiora Gente, was standing a little to one side, and it struck her little finger. It was a master-shot; the finger was cut clean off and dropped to the ground. Mrs Philifor in astonishment put her hand to her mouth. For a moment we seconds lost all control of ourselves and let out a cry of admiration.

This was too much for the professor of higher synthesis, and something dreadful happened. Fascinated by his opponent's precision of aim, virtuosity and symmetry, and annoyed at our cry of admiration at his marksmanship, he too diverged from the axis, fired, hit Fiora Gente's little finger, and let forth a short, derisive, guttural laugh.

Then the analyst fired again, severing Mrs Philifor's other little finger and causing her to put her other hand to her mouth. Again we exclaimed with admiration. A fraction of a second later the synthetist fired, and with infallible aim deprived Fiora Gente of her other little finger from a distance of six or seven yards. She put her hand to her mouth, and we could not refrain from another exclamation of admiration. And so events took their course. The firing continued, incessant, angry, and as magnificent as magnificence itself; and fingers, ears, noses, and teeth fell like the leaves of a tree in a high wind. We seconds were left with no time to express our admiration at the accuracy of the hail of fire that ensued. The two ladies were soon deprived of all their extremities and natural protuberances; if they did not fall dead it was simply because of lack of time, and I also suspect that they felt greatly flattered at being the target of such consummate marksmanship. With his last round the master from Leyden holed the upper part of Fiora Gente's right lung. Once more we exclaimed with admiration, then silence fell. Life passed from the two women's bodies, they collapsed to the ground, and the two marksmen looked at each other.

And then? They went on looking at each other, without knowing why. And then? And then? They had both run out of ammunition. The dead bodies lay on the ground. There was no more to be done. It was nearly ten o'clock. Strictly speaking, the analyst had won, but what difference did that make? None whatever. If the synthetist had won, it would have made no difference either. Philifor picked up a stone, threw it at a sparrow, and missed; the sparrow flew away. The sun was getting very hot. Anti-Philifor threw a lump of earth at a tree-trunk, and hit it. Philifor threw a stone at a hen which passed across his line of sight; he hit it, and it went and hid behind a bush. The two men of learning then abandoned their positions and went their separate ways.

At dusk Anti-Philifor was at Jeziorno and Philifor at Wawer. The former was shooting rabbits from under the shadow of a windmill; the latter, when he came upon a gas-lamp in an isolated spot, fired at it from fifty paces.

Thus they wandered about the world, firing at what they could with what they could. They sang popular songs and broke windows when they felt like it; and they also enjoyed spitting from balconies at the hats of passers-by. Philifor actually became so skilled that he was able to spit from the roadway at people on first-floor balconies; and Anti-Philifor could put out candles by throwing matchboxes at the flame. Things that they enjoyed even more were shooting frogs with small-calibre rifles and sparrows with bow and arrow; and sometimes they would stand on bridges and throw grass and paper into the stream below. But their greatest pleasure of all was buying a red balloon and chasing it across country, waiting for the thrilling moment when it burst noisily as if struck by an invisible bullet.

And when someone from the academic world recalled their glorious past, their intellectual jousts, analysis, synthesis, and the fame that had now vanished for ever, they would answer rather dreamily:

'Oh, yes, I remember the duel . . . the shooting was excellent!'

'But professor,' I once exclaimed, simultaneously with Roklewski, who had meanwhile married and settled down in Krucza Street, 'you talk like a child!'

And the puerile old man replied:

'Young man, everything is honeycombed with childishness.'

6

Further Inveiglement into Childhood

THUS at the very moment when the appalling psycho-physical violation of Siphon was approaching its climax the classroom door opened and in walked Pimko, clothed in all his infallibility and his exceptional personality.

'How well you young people play ball!' he exclaimed, though it was exceedingly obvious that we were not playing ball—there was no ball in the room.

'So you boys are playing ball,' he continued. 'See how gracefully one boy throws it, how skilfully another catches it!' A flush came over my face, which was pale and contracted with fear, and Pimko noticed it.

'What a healthy colouring you've got already! School is obviously doing you good, and so is playing ball, Johnnie!' he said.

'Come along, then,' he went on. 'Now I'm taking you to Mrs Youthful's, where I've taken a room for you. That's where you'll be living from now on, at Mrs Youthful's.'

And, still talking, he led me away. On the way he talked to me about Mr Youthful, engineer-architect, and his wife.

'You'll find yourself in a very modern environment,' he said. 'Excessively modern, in fact, the Youthfuls' modern ideas are very different from mine. But I detect in you a certain tendency towards posing and affectation, you create the impression that you are still pretending to be grown up. . . . Never mind, the Youthfuls will soon cure you of that and teach you to be yourself. I forgot to tell you that they have a daughter, named Zutka, a young lady who is still at school,' he went on, holding me by the hand and looking at me under his spectacles. 'And a very modern schoolgirl she is too. H'm, she's not ideal company for you, the danger's obvious enough. On the other hand, there's nothing like a modern schoolgirl to attract you towards youthfulness, she'll certainly succeed in converting you to the religion of your age.'

Trams passed. There were flowers in the windows of some of the houses. Someone aimed a plum-stone at Pimko from a top storey, but missed.

A schoolgirl? What was the meaning of this? I saw through Pimko's little plan. He wanted to use her to set the seal on my imprisonment in youthfulness; he thought that if I fell in love with her I should lose all desire to be grown up. I must be allowed not a moment of respite, either at school or at home, I must be allowed no loophole for escape. There was no time to lose. Quickly I bit his finger and ran away. A grown-up woman was just turning the corner. I dashed towards her, dazed, convulsed, my face bruised, in a desperate effort to escape from Pimko and his appalling schoolgirl. But the great reducer to childhood caught up with me in a flash and seized me by the collar.

'To the schoolgirl!' he exclaimed. 'To the schoolgirl! To youth! To the Youthfuls!'

He put me in a cab and took me to the schoolgirl, through streets that were full of people. The sun shone and the sky was full of birds.

'Forward!' he exclaimed. 'Forward! Why do you keep looking back? There's nothing behind you, and there's only me beside you!'

He took my hand and sputtered:

'To the schoolgirl, the modern schoolgirl! She'll make you fall in love with youth! The Youthfuls will reduce you to littleness. They'll give you a little backside. Backsidikins!' he exclaimed so loudly that the horse started lashing out, and the cabby, after reinstalling himself on his seat, turned his back on him with the utmost contempt.

On the point of entering one of those cheap houses which abound in modern suburbs, Pimko seemed to hesitate and, curiously enough, seemed to lose some of his notorious absolutism.

'Johnnie,' he muttered, shaking his head, 'I am making a great sacrifice for you. I am making it for the sake of your youth; it is for the sake of your youth that I am exposing myself to this encounter. H'm, the schoolgirl, the modern schoolgirl!'

He embraced me as if he wanted to seek my favour—but also as if taking leave of me for ever.

Then he started striking the ground with his stick and, in a state of great excitement, declaiming poetry, making quotations, delivering himself of ideas, opinions, aphorisms, all in the very best and most impressive style; but at the same time he seemed to be ill, with a threat pointing like an arrow straight at his pedagogic heart. He quoted the names of writers who were unknown to me but were friends of his, and quietly repeated the flattering things that they had said about him and the flattering things that he had said about them. Moreover, he produced a pencil and wrote the word 'Pimko' three times on the wall—a new Antaeus drawing fresh strength from the mere sight of his own signature. I looked at the master in astonishment. What was the meaning of this? Did he too fear the modern schoolgirl? Or was he merely pretending? How could such a masterly master be afraid of a mere schoolgirl? But the maid came and opened the door. We went in together. The master entered almost humbly, leaving his notorious superiority on the doorstep, and I with my face cruelly crushed and battered, like a crumpled piece of paper. He tapped the floor with his stick and said: 'Is madam in?' At the same moment the schoolgirl emerged from a door at the end of the hall. The modern schoolgirl.

She was sixteen, wore sweater, skirt, and crêpe-soled shoes, was tall, slim, supple, and looked athletic and insolent. I looked at her, and my spirit and my face both trembled. I saw at once that here was a phenomenon perhaps more powerful than

Pimko, as absolute in its way as he. She reminded me of someone, but of whom? Oh, Kopeida of course. You have not forgotten Kopeida? She was like him, but stronger, of the same type, but more intensely, the perfect schoolgirl looking like a modern schoolgirl, perfect in her modernism. She was young twice over —by reason of her age and by reason of her modernity; that was it, she was young because of her youth.

Consequently I was terrified at being confronted with something stronger than myself, and still more terrified when I saw that it was not she who was afraid of the professor, but the professor who was afraid of her. There was shyness in his voice when he addressed her. 'My compliments, young lady,' he said with forced gaiety and courtesy. 'So you are not on the beach? Not on the banks of the Vistula? Is your mother at home? What is the water in the pool like today? Cold, isn't it? But cold water is best. I always used to take cold baths in my time!'

Could I believe my ears? In Pimko's voice I detected old age obsequiously toadying to athletic youth—and I stepped back. The girl did not answer Pimko, she merely looked at him. She put between her teeth the spanner which she had been holding in her right hand, and held him out her left hand with as much indifference as if he had not been Pimko at all. The professor faltered, did not know what to do with the youthful left hand she held out towards him, and ended by taking it between both his hands. I bowed. The girl took the spanner out of her mouth and said:

'Mother's out, but she'll be back soon. Come in!'

She led us into a modern living-room and remained standing while we sat on a divan-bed.

'I suppose your mother is at the committee meeting,' said Pimko, starting a social conversation.

'I don't know,' the modern girl replied.

The walls were painted light blue, and the curtains were cream. There was a wireless set in the corner. The modern furniture was simple, sober, and spotless. There were two built-in cupboards and a small table. The girl stood looking out of the

window as if she were alone in the room, and started removing
bits of blistered skin from her sunburnt face. Our presence
simply did not count so far as she was concerned, she took no
notice whatever of Pimko, and the minutes started ticking away.
Pimko crossed his legs and his fingers, and started twiddling his
thumbs, like a guest who has not been suitably received. He
shifted in his seat, cleared his throat two or three times, coughed,
tried to keep up the conversation, but the girl stood there with
her back turned towards us and went on picking her face. Pimko
ended by falling silent and confined himself to remaining seated,
but there was something imperfect and incomplete about his
silent posture. I rubbed my eyes. What was happening? For
something was happening, that was certain. Pimko's sovereign
sitting incomplete? The master? The master inadequate?
Incompleteness implies that something is lacking. You know the
sensation of discomfort you get when something has finished
and nothing else has started yet? A void formed in my head.
Suddenly I saw age emanating from the master. I had not
realized that he was over fifty, it simply had never occurred to
me, as if the absolute master were eternal, exempt from time.
Old man or master? What a question! Why not simply old
master? No, it wasn't that at all. But what new plot were they
hatching against me? For I was perfectly certain that he and the
girl were hatching some new plot at my expense.

Why in heaven's name was he sitting there like this? Why was
he sitting there next to me opposite the girl? His sitting there
was all the more irritating to me because I was sitting next to
him. It would not have been so bad if I had been able to get up
But the fact of the matter was that it was impossible for me to
get up, there was no reason whatever why I should get up. No,
no, it wasn't that at all, but why was he sitting opposite the girl?
Have pity on me! There was no pity. Why was he sitting there
with the girl? Why was his old age not ordinary old age, but a
schoolgirlish old age? Fear suddenly gripped me, but I could
not move. Schoolgirlish old age, ancestro-juvenile old age,
confused, repulsive, half-formed ideas galloped through my mind.

Suddenly a song re-echoed through the room. I could not believe my ears. The master was singing the girl an aria.

Astonishment brought me back to my senses. No, he wasn't singing, he was humming. In his resentment at the girl's indifference he had started humming some operetta tune, thus drawing attention to her bad manners. The result was that he was singing. She was forcing the little old man to sing! Was this old dodderer sprawling on the divan and forced to sing in the girl's presence, the formidable, the absolute, the forceful, the irresistible Pimko?

I felt very weak. In the course of all my adventures since the morning my face muscles had not been allowed a single moment of relaxation, and my cheeks were burning as if I had spent a whole night in a train. But now it seemed as if the train were about to stop. Pimko was singing. I felt ashamed at having allowed myself to be dominated for so long by a harmless little old man of whom a vulgar little schoolgirl took not the slightest notice. My face started gradually returning to normal, I sat back comfortably, and rapidly started recovering my balance and—oh the joy of it!—my lost thirty years. I got up, intending to walk out quietly, without a word of explanation. But the professor seized my hand. He was different now. He had aged, softened, diminished, and I felt sorry for him.

'Johnnie,' he muttered in my ear, 'don't model yourself on this modern girl, who belongs to the new, post-war generation, the sport-and-jazz age! These barbarous post-war manners! This decay of civilization! The lack of respect! The new generation's passion for enjoying itself, its passion to enjoy life! I am beginning to think that this will not be a healthy environment for you! Give me your word of honour that you will not allow yourself to be influenced by this impudent little hussy! You have something in common with her, you are like her in some ways, I know'—the old man spoke feverishly—'because you are, after all, a modern boy! Oh, what a mistake it was to bring you here, to this modern girl!'

I looked at him as one looks at a lunatic. What had I, a man of thirty, in common with a modern schoolgirl? I decided that

Pimko was raving. But he went on warning me against the modern girl.

'These are new times,' he went on. 'You, the young, the rising generation, scorn your elders, and start calling each other by your Christian names straight away. You have no respect for anything, no respect for the past, dancing, America, *carpe diem*! You young people!'

And he launched into terrible flattery of my alleged youth and modernism, saying more or less that we young people were interested only in legs, and flattering us in other ways, while the girl went on picking her face with the most complete indifference, totally oblivious to what was going on behind her back.

In the end I realized what Pimko was trying to do. He was trying to make me fall in love with the girl; he wanted to hand me straight over to her to prevent me from escaping. He wanted to graft an ideal on me, knowing that if, like Mientus or Siphon, I once succumbed to a definite youthful ideal, I should remain its prisoner for ever. To put it in a nutshell, he cared little what kind of boy I became; all he cared about was preventing my escape from boyhood. If he managed to get me to fall in love straight away, if he got me to succumb to the modern youth ideal, he would be able safely to leave me alone and devote himself to his numerous other activities, which might otherwise prevent him from maintaining me permanently in my diminished state. And the paradox was that Pimko, who evidently set such great store by his own superiority, was, for the sake of pushing me at the girl, actually willing to accept the humiliating role of an antiquated old fossil indignant at the ways of modern youth, thus making me the girl's ally against him and propelling me into modernism and youthfulness. But he also nourished another and no less important design. He did not just want to make me fall in love with her; he wanted to bind me to her in the greatest possible immaturity. He did not want me to fall in love with her in the ordinary way; he wanted to see me consumed by that particularly cheap and nasty kind of modern-ancient passion born of a mixture of pre-war fossil and post-war schoolgirl. All this was very ingenious but really too stupid, and I listened to the old man's clumsy praises feeling completely confident of my total liberation. Too stupid? It was I who was too stupid. I was too stupid, because I did not know that it is only stupid poetry which is really alluring and fascinating.

And out of nothing a terrible whole was born, an appalling poetical constellation. Over there at the window was the modern girl, clothed in complete indifference. Here on the divan was the little old professor. And here was I in between them, assaulted by ancestro-juvenile poetry. Heavens, my thirty years—I must get out of this quickly! But, as if the world had been broken to pieces and put together again on an entirely new basis, my thirty years receded and faded, while the girl at the window grew more and more appetizing. And the accursed Pimko went on.

'Legs!' he said, to stimulate my interest in modernism. 'Legs! I know all about you and your fondness for outdoor games and exercise, I know all about the tastes of the young, Americanized generation. You prefer legs to arms, for you only legs count; and thighs! Outdoor games and exercise! Thighs! Thighs!'—he flattered me terribly—'Thighs! Thighs! Thighs!'

And, just as at school he had injected into us the problem of innocence, which had so dreadfully increased the boys' immaturity, so did he now lure me towards the modern thigh. And it was with pleasure that I heard him associating my thighs with those of the young generation, and sure enough, I started feeling a sense of youthful cruelty towards the thighs of the old. A sort of camaraderie of thighs was established between me and the girl, a kind of secret understanding by way of the thigh, a thigh religion, youthful pride in the thigh, veneration for the thigh. What an infernal part of the body! All this, needless to say, took place in silence behind the girl's back; there she stood at the window, on her thighs, picking her face and taking no notice of anything.

All the same, I should have shaken off this thigh business and fled if the door had not suddenly opened and somebody new appeared. The entry of this new, unknown, person put me off my stroke completely.

The new arrival was Mrs Youthful, a plump but cultivated woman, with the severe and responsible features of a member of the Warsaw Infants Aid Committee or the Society for the Suppression of Juvenile Mendicancy. Pimko rose from the divan, completely oblivious of everything, once more the cordial, distinguished professor of a certain age and with a very nasal nose.

'Ah! my dear lady!' he exclaimed. 'Always busy, always active! No doubt we have come straight from the committee meeting, haven't we? Here is young Johnnie whom I have brought along, Johnnie, of whom you so kindly said that you would take charge. Come along, Johnnie, say good afternoon to the lady!'

What! Pimko had once more assumed his lofty, protective tone. Was I to say good afternoon to this old woman, be polite to her? There was nothing else for it, I did so, and Mrs Youthful held out her short and chubby hand, and looked, not without astonishment, at my face, which was oscillating between the ages of fifteen and thirty.

'How old is the boy?' I heard her ask Pimko in an audible aside.

'Sixteen, my dear lady, sixteen! He was sixteen in April. He looks a little too serious, if such a thing is possible, he is rather inclined to pose in order to appear grown up, but he has a heart of gold.'

'Oh, he's a poseur, is he?'

Instead of protesting, I sat down on the divan and remained glued to it. The incredible stupidity of the suggestion stifled all possibility of explanation. I started suffering the torments of the damned. Pimko and Mrs Youthful moved across towards the window, where the girl was, and started a confidential conversation, glancing in my direction from time to time. Every now and then the famous master raised his voice, and, though it seemed accidental, it was deliberate. An additional torment was that I now heard him allying me with himself against Mrs Youthful, just as previously he had allied me with the girl against himself. But now he allied me with himself. Not content with presenting me as a pretentious poseur who gave himself the airs of a grown-up, he expanded on the depth of my attachment to him, delivered a eulogy of my qualities of heart and mind ('his only failing is his fondness for posing, but that will pass with age'); and he injected into his voice a suggestion of old-worldliness, the typically anachronistic tones of an ageing and old-fashioned schoolmaster, making it appear that I too was old-fashioned and the very reverse of modern. Thus he created a diabolical situation. Here was I sitting on the divan, forced to pretend that I could not hear what was being said; over there by the window was the girl—I could not tell whether she was listening or not; and in the background was Pimko, wagging his head and getting worked up about me, all the time subtly flattering the tastes and inclinations of that progressive female graduate, Mrs Youthful.

Only he who appreciates the full meaning of all that is involved in entering into contact with an unknown person, with all the risks entailed in an enterprise so full of traps and pitfalls, will fully understand my state of utter impotence in the face of Pimko and Mrs Youthful. He was introducing me into the Youthfuls in a deliberately false light, and he was deliberately raising his voice to let me hear his doing so; he was using imposture both in introducing me into the Youthfuls and in introducing the Youthfuls into me.

That was why Mrs Youthful very soon glanced at me with simultaneous pity and impatience.

Pimko's bland conversation obviously got on her nerves. Moreover, the enterprising female graduates of the present day, inflamed by collectivism and emancipation, detest artificiality and pretence in the young, and above all cannot stand their posing to grown-ups. As progressives with their faces turned towards the future, they make a greater cult of youth than it has ever previously enjoyed; and nothing irritates them more than seeing a young person sullying his youth by adopting poses.

And still worse; not only do they dislike it, but they like disliking it, for in disliking it they feel themselves to be modern and progressive; so they are always ready to give rein to this inclination to dislike. So Mrs Youthful—incidentally she was pretty fat—needed no second invitation; she was able to set a seal on her relations with me on the basis of the formula modernism-anachronism. Everything depends on the first chord struck, for that is the only one we are free to choose; all those that follow flow inevitably from the first. But Pimko struck the modern note on his venerable professor's bow, and that immediately set the tone.

'No, I don't like him,' she said irritatedly. 'No, I don't like him. A young, *blasé* old man, obviously with no taste for games or outdoor exercise. I can't stand posing and affectation. Compare him to my Zutka, professor, see how simple, sincere, natural she is, look at what your obsolete methods lead to!'

On hearing this I lost the last shreds of confidence I had left in the effectiveness of any protest I might make. Now it would never be possible to persuade her that I was grown up, because my presence made her appreciate more highly than ever her own charms and those of her daughter. When somebody's presence enhances a mother's pleasure in her daughter, the situation is hopeless, the daughter's charms dictate everything. Could I protest? Who says that I could not protest? At any moment, in spite of all the difficulties, I could have got up and explained that the whole thing was a mistake, that I was not sixteen but thirty. I could have done so, but I could not, because the will was lacking. All I wanted was to show that I was not the fusty youth I was being made out to be. That was all. I was indignant at the idea of the girl's being able to hear all that Pimko was telling her mother about me, and at the pitiful idea she would have of me as a result. This put the question of my thirty years completely out of my head. My true age faded, and this new idea throbbed and burned inside me.

Sitting there on the divan, I could not shout out aloud that Pimko was brazenly lying. So I sat up, tried to pull myself together, to look confident and self-possessed, to sit in a modern manner, in fact, and mutely I shouted with the whole of my body that it wasn't true, that I was not like that, but different. Thigh, thigh, thigh! I leaned forward, put fire into my eyes and, sitting naturally and at ease, denounced Pimko's lies with my whole being. If the girl turned round, she would see. . . . But suddenly I heard Mrs Youthful saying quietly to Pimko:

'It's incredible how affected he is. Look at him, he poses all the time!'

I was petrified. Changing my attitude would have shown that I had heard and plunged me deeper into the artificial; whatever I did was henceforward condemned to artificiality. Meanwhile the girl at the window turned and looked at me, looked me up and down just as I was, sitting there without being able to get rid of my artificially natural attitude . . . and I saw the expression of hostility on her face. This made it still more impossible to escape; and I could feel a sharp, juvenile antipathy arising in the girl, an antipathy as sharp and as clean as a smash on the tennis court. Mrs Youthful interrupted her conversation and asked her daughter, as one friend to another of the same age:

'Why are you looking like that, Zutka?'

The girl, without taking her eyes off me, became—made herself—frank, open and truthful, and said with a pout:

'He's been listening to you the whole time. He has heard everything!'

This was a hard blow. I wanted to protest, but could not, and Mrs Youthful, lowering her voice and enjoying her daughter's sally, said to the professor:

'Nowadays they're terribly sensitive to anything that smacks of slyness and underhandedness; in fact they're crazy about frankness and openness. The new generation. It's the legacy of the Great War. We are all children of the Great War, we and our children.' The woman was visibly exultant. 'The new generation,' she repeated.

'What bright little eye-peeps she has!' the professor said smugly.

'Eye-peeps, professor? Eye-peeps? My daughter hasn't got eye-peeps, but eyes, like the rest of us. Zutka, leave your eyes alone!'

But the girl frowned, and shrugged her shoulders, rejecting her mother. This upset Pimko. He turned to Mrs Youthful and said:

'My dear lady, if you find that way of behaving acceptable . . . In my time a girl would never have dared . . . shrug her shoulders . . . at her mother!'

Mrs Youthful, however, expressed her satisfaction, her delight, her enthusiasm.

'It's the age we live in, professor, the age we live in. You don't know the new generation. Profound transformation, revolution of manners, wind of change, subterranean shocks taking place beneath our feet. It's the age we live in. Everything must be transformed, the old must be swept away and only the new left.'

Meanwhile the girl, who was listening, not without contempt, to what the two old fogeys were saying, chose her moment carefully and gave me a short, sharp, savage, surreptitious kick on the shin, in true gangster fashion, without changing her attitude or her expression. That done, she withdrew her foot and remained impassive and aloof from her mother's and Pimko's conversation. While the mother tried to identify herself with her daughter the latter eluded her . . . as if, being the younger, she was proud . . . of being the younger.

'She kicked him!' the professor exclaimed. 'She kicked him! Did you see? She kicked him, while we were talking she calmly and quietly kicked him! This wild young generation! What barbarism, what impudence, what effrontery! She kicked him!'

'Zutka, keep your legs still. And don't worry about your Johnnie, professor, he won't come to any harm. Far worse things happened at the front during the Great War. I myself, when I was a nurse, often used to get kicks from ordinary soldiers.'

She lit a cigarette.

'In my time,' Pimko said. 'In my time. . . . But what would our great poet Norwid have said?'

'Norwid?' the girl asked. 'Who was he?'

She asked the question perfectly, with the athletic ignorance of the younger generation and the surprise appropriate to the times-we-live-in; she did not engage herself excessively in the question, she just asked it for the sake of making a slight demonstration of her athletic lack of knowledge.

The professor started tearing out his hair.

'She has never heard of Norwid!' he exclaimed.

Mrs Youthful smiled.

'It's the times-we-live-in, professor, it's the times-we-live-in!'

The atmosphere became delightful. The girl, for Pimko's benefit, had never heard of Norwid. Pimko became infuriated at her ignorance, for her benefit. Her mother was in ecstasies about the times-we-live-in. I was the only one left out, and I could not . . . no I could not join in, or understand the change of roles by which the old maniac with his worn-out old thighs allied himself with the girl against me, and why I had to provide the counterpoint to his melody. Oh, diabolical Pimko! But, sitting there like that, silent and nursing my kicked leg, I looked hurt and resentful, and Pimko said benevolently:

'Why are you so quiet, Johnnie? You must speak up for yourself from time to time. . . . Are you angry with the young lady?'

'Of course he is!' the girl said jeeringly.

'Zutka, apologize to the young man,' her mother said firmly. 'You have upset him, but you, young man, must stop being upset, and must show a little less resentment. Of course Zutka will apologize, but on the other hand we must admit that we're a little affected, aren't we? . . . Let's have a little more naturalness, a little more life! Come, come, now, look at Zutka and me! We'll get rid of the young man's affected affairs, you can rely on us, professor. He'll be in good hands with us!'

'From that point of view, I believe that living here will do him a great deal of good,' the professor said. 'Come, come, Johnnie, cheer up!'

Everything they said was definite and final, and seemed to settle matters once and for all. The question of the cost of my board and lodging remained to be disposed of, and when that was over Pimko kissed me on the brow.

'Good-bye, young man,' he said. 'Don't cry, I'll come and see you every Sunday, and I'll keep my eye on you at school. My respects, dear lady, and *au revoir*. Miss Zutka, be kind to Johnnie!'

He took his departure, and could be heard clearing his throat and coughing on the way downstairs, huh! huh! huh! h'm! h'm! h'm! I leapt to my feet to begin my protests and explanations.

But Mrs Youthful took me to a very modern little room just off the hall. The hall (as I subsequently found out) served also as Miss Youthful's bedroom.

'Here you are,' she said. 'The bathroom is next door. Breakfast is at seven o'clock. The maid has brought your things already.'

And before I could say thank-you she was off to the meeting of the Warsaw Committee for the Suppression of Juvenile Mendicancy. I was alone. I sat on the chair. Silence. My head was buzzing. Here I was sitting in my new room, in entirely new conditions. After all the people I had seen that day, I suddenly found myself alone. Only the girl kept moving about outside in the hall. I was not alone, but alone with the girl.

7

Love

ONCE more I started mentally protesting and explaining, I must do something, the situation in which I had been put must not be allowed to consolidate, to become permanent, the longer I put off doing something the harder it would be. I sat stiffly on my chair, not raising a finger to unpack the things the maid had brought at Pimko's orders. Now or never, I said to myself. Pimko had gone, Mrs Youthful was out, the girl was alone. There was not a moment to lose, time bred stiffness, awkwardness, difficulties, I must go now, immediately, this very moment, to explain myself, reveal myself to the girl in my true colours, tomorrow it would be too late.

Reveal myself in my true colours, how violently I wanted to reveal myself to her in my true colours, I was bursting to reveal myself to her in my true colours! But reveal myself as what? As a thirty-year-old adult? Not on your life! I had lost all desire to throw off my youthfulness, to confess to my thirty years, my world was shattered, no world existed other than the fine world of the modern schoolgirl, games, athletics, agility, insolence, thighs, legs, barbarism, boating, canoeing, such was the new heaven of my reality! It was as a modern youth that I wanted to reveal myself. The master, Siphon, Mientus, the duel, all that had previously existed had been pushed aside, and all that I cared about was what the girl thought of me. Had Pimko succeeded in convincing her that I was an anti-modern poseur? The only problem that existed for me was that of walking into her room here and now and making a young, natural, modern appearance before her, making her understand that Pimko had lied, and that in reality I was not like that, but different, a being similar to herself, a companion of her own age and time, related to her by the thigh . . .

But what would my excuse be for walking into her room? How could I explain everything to her if I scarcely knew her? I already existed inside her, but in the social sense I was still a stranger. To reach the depths of her being would be extremely difficult for me, I could only hope to touch the surface, I could hardly do more than knock at the door and ask at what time dinner was served. The kick she had given me favoured my plans in no way whatever; it had been a marginal kick, given by the foot without the slightest collaboration from the face, and what was important to me was the face. Seated in my chair like a caged animal, I wrung my hands. What was my excuse to be, how was I to start the ball rolling between Miss Youthful and myself?

At that moment the telephone rang, and I heard her footsteps. I got up, gingerly half-opened the door, and looked out. There was nobody there, it was beginning to get dark, and she was making an appointment on the telephone with a girl friend, seven o'clock in a bar with Wladys and Wladek (they had their own nicknames and their own private language). You'll come, sure, smashing, yes, no, my leg hurts, I knocked it, idiot, photo, come, you come, I'm coming, O.K., cheerio, bye-bye! These words, softly confided to the mouthpiece by one modern girl to another while nobody else was there, moved me profoundly. Her own language, I said to myself, her own modern, private language! And it seemed to me that the girl, rooted to the spot by the telephone, her mouth glued to the mouthpiece while her eyes were left at liberty, became thereby more accessible, better adapted to my designs. I should be able to reveal myself to her without explanation, make my appearance . . . without comment.

Quickly I straightened my tie, wetted my hair, and combed it to show the parting, for I felt that a straight line across the skull was not without importance in the circumstances; heaven knows why, but it was modern. On my way through the dining-room I helped myself to a tooth-pick, and I made my appearance (the telephone was in the anteroom). I stood in the doorway, cool and impassive, leaning against the embrasure. Silently I presented myself in my entirety, the tooth-pick between my teeth. The tooth-pick was a modern touch. Do not for one moment believe that it was easy to stand there with a tooth-pick in one's mouth pretending complete liberty of movement while inside one felt fatally passive.

Meanwhile the girl was saying to her friend:

'No, you're crazy, the dog, all right then, get on with it, don't go with him, go with her, photo, six, three minutes, wait and see.'

She put down the receiver for a moment and said:

'Do you want to use the telephone?'

She asked the question in a cold, social voice, as if it had not been I whom she had kicked. I shook my head. I wanted her to realize that I was there for no reason whatever except pure companionship, and that I had a perfect right to stand in the doorway while she telephoned, as I was her companion in modernism and her equal in age. Schoolgirl, you must appreciate that between us explanations are superfluous, and that I am perfectly entitled to join you without ado and without formality. I was taking a gigantic risk because, if she asked me for an explanation, I should be unable to supply it, and artificiality, that appalling artificiality, would cause me to beat a hasty retreat. But if she accepted my attitude, tacitly accepted it, I should be able to be modern with her. Mientus, Mientus, I said to myself in alarm, remembering the atrocious grimaces into which he had twisted his face after our first smiles: But with the female sex things were easier. Physical differences helped; they eliminated impotence.

Meanwhile the girl, her ear glued to the receiver, went on talking for a long time without looking at me. Once more the weight of time ominously made itself felt. At last she said:

'O.K., good, the flicks, bye-bye!'

And she put back the receiver.

She went back to her room. I removed the tooth-pick from my mouth, and went back to mine. There was a chair against the wall next to the wardrobe, a chair not meant for sitting but for putting one's clothes on, and I sat on it stiffly and wrung my hands. She had ignored me, she had not even deigned to laugh at me. Never mind, once you have started out on something you must keep on with it, you must settle the matter while her mother is out, you must try again, because otherwise, after that unhappy piece of behaviour, she may once and for all come to the conclusion that you are a poseur, and in any case your pose is taking root, growing, why are you sitting against the wall like this, wringing your hands? Heaven help you, sitting on a chair in your room like this is the very opposite of modernism, it's typically old-fashioned.

I stopped, and listened to what was happening on the other side of the wall.

Miss Youthful was moving about in her room just as all girls move about in their rooms; and while so engaged she was no doubt deciding more definitely than ever that I was an affected poseur. It was a terrible thing to be cast back into my room like this, in isolation, while she moved about next door. But how was I to start, or restart, with her? What was I to do? I had no excuse—even if I had had an excuse, I should have been unable to use it—for the matter was too internal for excuses.

Meanwhile it had grown darker, and the isolation—the illusory isolation of a person who is alone but not alone because mentally he is agonizingly tied to someone on the other side of the wall—and nevertheless sufficiently alone to make the rubbing of hands, the movement of fingers, and other similar phenomena absurd and impossible. The mounting darkness, and the false solitude I was in, went to my head, blinded me, deprived me of my daytime awareness and plunged me into night. How often does night make an irruption into day! Alone in the room in this situation, sitting on my chair, I was deprived of too many senses, it was impossible to remain like this for a moment longer. Things which are not in the least alarming when experienced in company in daylight become intolerable when you are alone. Solitude is aggressive, explosive.

After an endless period of torment I again opened the door and stood in the doorway, still blinded by solitude. I stopped, and realized that I knew no better than before where to start with the girl, how to make contact with her; there was still a barrier all round her, like a closed frontier. What a dreadful thing is that sharp and peremptory demarcation line, form!

She was standing with one foot on a chair, leaning forward, engaged in cleaning her shoe. There was something classic about her position, and I had the impression that she was less interested in making her shoe shine than in privately asserting her type by way of her foot and ankle and maintaining a good modern style. This gave me more courage. I thought that the girl, surprised like this while showing a leg, would be kinder, less stiff.

I went towards her and stood quite close to her, only one or two paces away; I presented myself to her silently, without looking, my eyes withdrawn; I still remember perfectly how I approached her and stopped only a yard away, within the spatial limits in which she began, how I suppressed all my senses in order to approach as close to her as possible, and waited . . . What for? For her to be surprised at nothing. This time I had no tooth-pick and no special attitude. Whether she accepted or rejected me, I tried to be completely passive and neutral. . . .

She removed her foot from the chair and stood upright.

'What do you want?' she asked me without turning her head, hesitantly, like a person who has been approached too closely without good reason. As soon as she stood upright the tension between us increased. I felt that she would have liked to move away, but that I was too close to her for her to be able to do so.

'What do you want?'

'Nothing,' I murmured.

She lowered her hands and looked at me out of the corner of one eye. She was on the defensive.

'Are you trying to be funny?' she said.

'No,' I murmured. 'No.'

Beside me was the table. Farther away there was the stove. On the table were a brush and a penknife. It had grown still darker, everything was a little blurred in the half-light, including the terrible demarcation line. Behind the curtain of darkness I was sincere, sincere with all my strength, propitious to the girl, ready.

I was not pretending. If she accepted the fact that I was not pretending, she would see through the artificiality of my previous behaviour, for which Pimko had been responsible. Did I imagine that a girl could not reject a man who demanded acceptance by her? Did I believe that there, in the dark, the girl would succumb to the temptation of making of me something that suited her? Why should she not like having within her reach someone who was sympathetic and suitable? She would certainly prefer having an American boy-friend in the house to a miserable, old-fashioned, grudge-bearing poseur. So why did she not play her evening tune on me if I lent myself to it? Play, play your tune on me, the modern tune that everyone hums in the big cafés, in the dance halls, and on the beaches, the pure tune of world youth in tennis shorts. Play on me the modernism of white tennis shorts. Won't you?

Miss Youthful, surprised at having me beside her, sat on the table, and put her chin between her hands, not without a trace of physical humour; her face stood out in the dusk, poised between surprise and playfulness . . . and she seemed to have sat down in order to play her tune. . . . That was how American girls sat on the sides of their motor-boats. And the mere fact of her sitting thus established a tacit agreement to prolong the situation. One might have said that she had made herself more comfortable in order to savour . . . with beating heart I noticed that she was setting some of her charms to work. She bent her little head; she moved her leg impatiently; capriciously she pursed her lips, and at the same time turned her big, modern eyes cautiously in the direction of the dining-room, to see if by any chance the maid were spying on us. What would the maid have said if she had discovered us in such a strange situation? Would she have taxed us with an excess of artifice? Or an excess of nature?

But that is just the kind of risk that appeals to these dark young things who can show all that they know only in the dark. I felt that I had conquered the girl by the barbarous naturalness of my artifice. I put my hands in my jacket pockets. Straining towards her, I accompanied her in silence, fervently, with all my strength, putting myself in sympathy with her, putting the whole of my being in sympathy with her. On this occasion time worked in my favour. With each second that passed the artifice grew deeper, but so did the naturalness. I was expecting her suddenly to make some perfectly ordinary remark to me, as if we had known each other for ages, to say something about her leg, for instance, to tell me that it hurt because she had strained a tendon, or to offer me a drink. Martini, whisky, gin?

And she was going to say something of the sort, her lips were actually moving—when the idea suddenly came into her head to say something entirely different. Without wanting to, she said severely:

'What can I do for you?'

I stepped back. She was nettled by what she had said, but did not lose one iota of the attractive, thoroughbred air of a modern girl sitting on a table and swinging her legs; on the contrary, she became more attractive and thoroughbred than ever: and she repeated, with ever greater coldness and severity:

'What can I do for you?'

I turned and walked away, but the back view of myself which I presented to her as I did so nettled her even more, and from the other side of the door I heard her exclaim:

'Completely crackers!'

Repulsed and rejected, I sat down again on the chair by the wall. This is the end, I muttered, she has crushed me. Why did she crush me? Something bit her; she preferred trampling on me to walking by my side. Chair by the wall, I greet you, but I must unpack, the suitcase is in the middle of the room, there's no towel. I sat humbly on my chair and started unpacking and

123

putting my things in the drawers, practically in the dark. I must get everything ready, because tomorrow I go to school—but I didn't turn on the light, no, for my sake it wasn't worth it. How wretched and miserable I felt, but all right, all right, if only I could stay like this, sit down and go on sitting without ever moving again or ever again wanting anything.

However, after a few minutes it became evident that in spite of my lethargy and misery I must become active again. Was there to be no respite? I must go to her room for the third time, show myself to her in the guise of a clown and crackpot, give her to understand that all that had happened previously had been deliberate buffoonery on my part, and that it was I who had been taking the rise out of her, and not the other way about. All is lost except honour, as Francis I remarked. In spite of my depression and exhaustion, I rose, and once more prepared to make my entrance. The preparations took a long time. Eventually I half-opened the door and put my head round it. The light was dazzling—she had turned on the light. I shut my eyes.

'Please knock at the door before coming in,' she said impatiently.

I answered with my eyes closed, moving my head:

'Your humble and obedient servant.'

I completed my entry into the room, creeping in in a humorous manner—oh, that unhappy man's creep! I decided to make her angry, for anger, according to the adage, is detrimental to beauty. I counted on making her nervous, because, if I kept my head behind my clownish mask, I should then have the advantage of her.

'You've got no manners!' she exclaimed.

Coming from a modern girl, these words surprised me. They surprised me all the more because she spoke them as convincingly as if good manners had been the highest aspiration of the wild post-war generation. The modern generation makes use alternately of good manners and bad with the greatest possible virtuosity. She made me feel a fool. It was too late to retreat—

the world exists only because it is always too late to retreat. I collected myself, and bowed.

'I cast myself at your feet,' I said.

She got up and made towards the door. Disaster threatened. If she walked out and left me to my clowning, all would be lost. I leapt forward and barred the way. She stopped.

'What is it you want?' she said.

She was getting frightened.

And I, being unable to retreat, carried away by my own momentum, started advancing upon her—I, fool, crackpot, clown, impossible poseur, clumsy buffoon, started advancing upon her, a gorilla advancing upon a helpless damsel. She retreated behind the table, but I continued remorselessly to advance upon her, pointing the way with my finger with ape-like imbecility, advancing upon her in a drunken, imbecile, evil, threatening manner while she retreated to the wall. But—curse the girl!—I noticed in the midst of this crazy progress that in the face of my imbecility she lost not one iota of her attractiveness—that while I behaved inhumanly she, standing against the wall, small, stooping, pale, breathless, her arms dangling and slightly bent, her eyes popping out of her head and incredibly silent and tense with the danger, was very beautiful—cinematic, modern, poetic, artistic—and that fear, instead of making her ugly, made her more beautiful. Another moment passed. I stepped closer, and new situations were necessarily about to rise—it flashed through my mind that this was the end, that I must take her face in my hand—I was in love, I was in love! At that moment there was a sudden squeal from the anteroom; Mientus was assaulting the maid. We had not heard the bell. He had come to see me at my new address and, finding himself alone with the maid, had tried to violate her.

For the effect on Mientus of his duel with Siphon was that he could no longer escape from his terrible grimaces and was unable to act in other than a disgusting manner. When he saw the maid he did not fail to be as brutal and down-to-earth as he was able. The girl had made a noise, so he had kicked her in the stomach, and now he walked into the room with a bottle of brandy under his arm.

'Hallo, Johnnie, old man!' he exclaimed. 'I just dropped in to see you. I've brought some booze and some grub. Oh! But what's the matter with your face? You look like death warmed up. Bah! mine's not much better!

> 'Clash of faces is our fate,
> Get drunk on your ugly mug!

'Who's the Siphon that gave you a face like that? That tart standing against the wall? My respects, darling!'

'I'm in love, Mientus, I'm in love!'

Mientus replied with a drunkard's wisdom.

'So that's what's given you that face! Shake on it, old man! But what a face she's given you! If you could only see yourself! Well, well, well, mine's not so bad either, shake on it, old man! Come along, it's time to wet your whistle, let's go to your room, get some bread to go with the sausage, I've got a bottle to help wash your troubles away! Don't take it to heart, old chap, we'll cheer ourselves up with the bottle. My respects to the young lady, *bon jour, au revoir, mademoiselle*, come along!'

Once more I advanced towards the girl, I wanted to say something, explain, find some magic formula to save the situation, but Mientus dragged me away and, staggering and lurching, drunk, not with alcohol but with our faces, we reached my room. I burst into tears and told him the whole story about the girl, omitting nothing. He listened to me benevolently, like a father, and sang:

> 'No disgrace
> Like a face
> Out of place . . .

'Come on, why aren't you drinking?' he said. 'Come on, man, drink! Don't make faces at the bottle, the bottle is to give you face!'

His face was still appalling, dreadfully common and vulgar, and he stuffed into the hole in it sausage and grease-paper together.

'Mientus,' I exclaimed. 'I want to free myself . . . I want to free myself!'

'What? From your face?' he said. 'Balls!'

'From the girl,' I said. 'Mientus, I tell you I'm thirty! Thirty!'

He looked at me in amazement, for there was real distress in my voice. Then he burst out laughing.

'Don't rave, man!' he said. 'Thirty? You're bats! You're raving! (He also used other expressions which I shall not repeat.) Thirty? You know (he took a gulp from the bottle, and spat), I don't know where I know her from, but I know that girl. By sight. Kopeida's running after her!'

'Who's he?'

'Kopeida, a chap in our class. He likes her, because she's the same type as he, modern. Come on, man, drink! That's the only thing. D'you think I've freed myself? My face has turned into a rag, but I'm still haunted by the stable-lad.'

'What? Even since you violated Siphon?'

'Yes, but I've still got the same face. Look what a pair we are!' he said in astonishment. 'I and my stable-lad, and you and your schoolgirl! Drink, man, drink!'

He suddenly grew dreamy-eyed.

'Johnnie,' he said, 'if we could only get away to the country, among the stable-lads! If only we could get away to the country, the fields, the open country'—he started becoming incoherent— 'country, stable-lads, stable-lads, country!'

But I didn't care a fig for his stable-lads. All that I cared about was the girl. So Kopeida was running after her. How I envied him. But 'running after' was not the same as 'going with'; evidently they did not know each other. But I did not dare ask any questions. And so we remained with our faces, each plunged in his own thoughts and helping himself to a drink every now and then. Mientus rose lurchingly to his feet.

'I must go,' he said quietly. 'The old woman will be coming

127

back. I'll leave by way of the kitchen (he whispered) and have another look at the maid. . . . She's not a stable-lad, obviously, but she comes from the country. Perhaps she's got a brother who's a stable-lad.'

He went out, and I was left with the girl. The moonlight turned the impalpable dust hanging in the air to silver.

* 8 *

The Fruit Salad

NEXT morning school, Siphon, Mientus, Bobek, Hopek, Kotecki, the infinitive and accusative, Droopy, divine poetry, the daily impotence. Oh, the endless repetition, the excruciating boredom. Oh, the bard and his inspiration, the poet and his muse, the schoolmaster making his living out of the poet, the pupils at their desks suffering from an acute sense of protest, the toe in the shoe, the boredom, boredom, boredom! The gradual transformation of reality under pressure of repulsion, poetry and pedanticism—oh, let me dream—until it became impossible for anyone to distinguish between the real and the unreal, between truth and fiction, between the felt and the unfelt, between the natural and the artificial, the pretentious and the false; until what ought to be inevitable became indistinguishable from what was, each disqualifying tne other and depriving it of all object. Oh, the great school of unreality! The result was that I too for five long hours dreamt uninterruptedly about my ideal, and my face swelled like a balloon, for in this fictitious, unreal world there was nothing to bring it back to normal. The result was that I too had my ideal—the modern schoolgirl. I was in love, a lovelorn, melancholy dreamer. Having failed to conquer the girl, having failed to ridicule her, I was plunged in despair. I knew that all was lost.

I was a prisoner. What can I say about the boredom of those days monotonously divided into two? In the morning I went to school, from school I returned to the Youthful household. I had no more thought of escape, of explaining myself or protesting; on the contrary, I took pleasure in being a schoolboy, because that brought me nearer the girl. I almost forgot my thirty years. The masters were very decent to me, Piorkowski, the head, patted me on the back, and during ideological disputes I too grew red in the face and shouted:

'Modernism for ever! Up with the modern boy! Up with the modern girl!'

That made Kopeida laugh. You remember Kopeida, the most modern boy in the whole school?

I tried to strike up a friendship with him, to discover the secret of his relations with Miss Youthful. But he avoided me, was even more contemptuous of me than he was of the others, as if instinctively aware of my rejection by his spiritual sister, the modern schoolgirl.

In general, the rejection of one type of young person by another type was Draconian and complete. The clean abominated the dirty, the modern regarded the old-fashioned as beneath contempt, and so on *ad infinitum*.

What else is there to say? Siphon died. After being violated through his ears he never became himself again, he was never able to expel what had been injected into him. He spent long hours trying vainly to forget the words of initiation to which he had been forced to listen. He felt a profound aversion for his miscarried personality, and ate his heart out. He grew paler and paler, suffered from obstinate hiccups, spat, choked, puffed and blew, coughed, but no, he could not, and in the end, considering himself unfit to live, one afternoon hanged himself from the hatstand. This caused an enormous sensation; there were even echoes of it in the Press. But Mientus failed to benefit in any way; Siphon's death did nothing to improve the state of his face. Siphon was dead, but what difference did that make? The faces that Mientus had made during the duel had stuck. It is not so easy to get rid of a grimace. A face is not made of india-rubber; once distorted, it does not return to its former shape. The result was that he looked so unpleasant that even his friends Bobek and Hopek avoided him whenever they could; and the more grotesque he became, the more obviously did he indulge in his stable-lad dream, and the more he indulged in his stable-lad dream, the more grotesque did he become. However, unhappiness drew us together; he dreamt about his stable-lads and I about my schoolgirl, and thus we both spent our time dreaming. But reality was still as inaccessible to us as if our faces had been covered all over with spots. He told me that he was thinking of seducing the Youthfuls' maid. That first evening, under the influence of the brandy, he had stolen a kiss from her on his way out through the kitchen, but that had not satisfied him at all.

'What's the good of it?' he said. 'What's the good of stealing a kiss from a maid? She's a girl who walks bare foot, of course, she comes straight from the country, and she has a stable-boy brother, so she tells me, but hell and damnation (he also used other words which I shall not repeat), what's the good of that? A sister's not the same as her brother, a town maid isn't a country stable-boy. I go and see her in the afternoon, when your Mrs Youthful is at her committee meetings, I do the best I can with her. I even go about it peasant-style, but still she won't play!'

Such was the fashion in which he formed his universe—stable-lad filling the foreground and maid occupying a secondary position in the background. School dropped out of my universe; the Youthful household filled it almost completely.

Mrs Youthful, with a mother's perceptiveness, soon realized that I was in love with her daughter. There is no need to specify how stimulated she was by this discovery, coming as it did on top of the stimulation provided by Pimko. An old-fashioned, affected, young man who was unable to conceal his admiration for her daughter's modernism was an instrument she used like a tongue, so to speak, to taste and savour her daughter's charms, and even her own. So I became this fat woman's tongue, and the more old-fashioned, false, and artificial I was, the more both of them enjoyed their modernity, sincerity and simplicity. Two puerile realities—modernity and old-fashionedness—when rubbed together produced electricity and set up thousands of the most fantastic circuits, which twined and coiled to form a world that became ever more fragmentary and green—to such an extent that Mrs Youthful started displaying for my benefit a modernism which in her case simply took the place of youth. At meals and other times there was endless talk of Liberty, Customs, the Times We Live In, Revolutionary Movements, the Post-War Period, etc., etc., and the old woman exulted at being younger, thanks to the Times She Lived In, than a young man who was younger than herself. She made a youth of herself and an old man of me. 'How are you, you little old man?' she used to say. 'How are you, you little rotten egg?'

With the subtlety of a modern female graduate, she inflicted on me the torture of her vital energy and experience and knowledge of life, the kicks she had received while nursing during the Great War, her enthusiasms and her broadmindedness, her liberal woman's bold, progressive, active outlook, her modern ways, her daily hygiene, and the ostentation with which she went to the bathroom. Strange! Strange! Pimko came to see me from time to time. The old professor was delighted at my little backside. 'What an incomparable little rump!' he muttered. And he never missed a chance of still further provoking Mrs Youthful, making the greatest possible play with his old-fashioned schoolmaster act and denouncing the modern schoolgirl with might and main. I noted that in other circumstances, when he was with Piorkowski, for instance, he seemed younger by half, and did not flaunt such antediluvian principles; and I could not make up my mind if it was he who stimulated the Youthfuls' modernity, or if the two phenomena were interdependent and complementary, like the two lines of a rhyming couplet. Which of them created the other? Did the modern schoolgirl create the little old man or did the latter create her? Futile and useless question.

In any case both enjoyed themselves, he as old-fashioned pedagogue, she as unbridled youth, and gradually his visits started becoming longer, and he took less and less interest in me and paid more and more attention to the girl. Must I confess it? I became jealous of Pimko. I died a thousand deaths at seeing these two human beings harmonizing with and completing each other, improvising a piquant old-young ode together, and it was disgusting to see that this old goat, whose thighs were in a hundred times worse condition than mine, nevertheless got on so much better with the modern girl than I. Norwid in particular became the pretext for a positive intrigue between them. The worthy Pimko found her ignorance unpardonable, it offended his deepest feelings. She, however, preferred pole-jumping to poetry, and he grew indignant and she laughed, he lectured her, and she rebelled, he implored, and she went on pole-jumping. I admired the skill with which the Master, without ceasing to be the Master, without for a moment dropping his role as Master, nevertheless managed to get so much pleasure from the girl by means of the contrast of opposites, how he excited her by being the master and how she excited him by being the schoolgirl. My jealousy was horrible, though I too excited the girl by contrast and was excited by her in the same way. But the last thing I wanted was to seem old-fashioned to her, for in her eyes I wanted to be modern.

Oh, the agony of it! I could not get her out of my system. All my efforts to free myself were vain. The sarcasms with which I mentally defended myself against her were useless; what is the good of a cheap, sarcastic remark behind a person's back? The truth of the matter was that my sarcasms were nothing but a tribute to the girl, for they concealed a sad desire to please her. If I used irony, it was only to adorn myself, like a peacock, with the feathers of my irony, and that only because I had been rejected. But my irony turned against me, and gave me a still more horrid and repulsive face. I did not dare give rein to it in her presence; she would have only shrugged her shoulders. For a girl—and in that a girl resembles all other human beings—is never afraid of the irony of someone she has rejected. . . . And the sole consequence of the clownish offensive I had conducted in her room was that henceforward she mistrusted and ignored me—in the fashion which only modern girls know how to ignore a person—though she was perfectly well aware that I was taken with her modern attractions. So with subtle, childish

133

cruelty she increased the latter, carefully avoiding any coquettishness which would have made her dependent on me. It was not for my sake but for her own that she became more and more wild, insolent, bold, shrill, supple, sporting, and thighy. After dinner she would remain seated—oh! how self-assured and mature in her immaturity—impassive and alone for her own sake, while I sat there for her sake, unable even for a single moment not to sit there for her sake, and she absorbed and swallowed me whole, irony included, and her tastes and inclinations were all-important for me and I was able to please myself only to the extent that I pleased her. The agony of it! To be swallowed whole by a modern schoolgirl, and never to be able to find a single fault with her style or detect the slightest chink or cranny which held out the prospect or possibility of flight, liberation, escape.

It was just this which held me under her spell—that maturity and sovereignty of her youthfulness, the assurance of her style. While we at school suffered from acne, were everlastingly plagued with spots and ideals of various kinds, while apathy pursued us in our movements and gaucheness haunted us at every step, her exterior was magnificently finished. Youth for her was not an age of transition; on the contrary, it was the only acceptable phase in human life, the only phase that had value or importance. *She despised maturity or, rather, for her immaturity was maturity.* Beards, moustaches, nurses, mothers with children, were all alike dismissed by her, and it was from that that she derived her magic power. Her youth needed no ideal, because it was an ideal in itself. That I, tormented by idealist youth, should thirst so greatly for this ideal youth should surprise nobody. But she did not like me. She gave me a horrible face, and every day it grew a little more horrible.

Heavens! the aesthetic torment and humiliation she inflicted on me! I know nothing crueller than a person's giving another a new face. Whatever such a person does is enough to make the victim act under false colours, foolishly, ridiculously, grotesquely, for his ugliness nourishes that person's beauty. Believe me, giving somebody a backside is nothing in comparison with giving him

134

a face. In the end I actually reached the state of dreaming of the girl's physical destruction, of disfiguring her pretty little face, injuring her, cutting off her nose. But the example of Mientus and Siphon showed that brute force was not of much use; the mind can free itself only by its own efforts. But what could my mind do, since she contained me within herself? Can you escape from inside a person if you have no point of support, no leverage, nothing whatever to cling to outside that person, if you are completely dominated by that person's style? No, with your own strength it is hopeless, impossible—unless a third party comes to your aid, holds you out at least a little finger. But who was there to come to my aid? Mientus, who was not on visiting terms with the Youthfuls (apart from the kitchen, where he went secretly) and was never present at my struggles with the girl? Mr Youthful, Mrs Youthful, or Pimko, all of whom were the girl's accomplices? Or the maid—a hireling, a person without a voice? Meanwhile my face became more and more horrible; and the more horrible it became, the more mother and daughter entrenched themselves in their modernism, and the more face they manufactured and inflicted on me. Oh, what an instrument of tyranny is style! Hell and damnation! But the two witches were deceiving themselves, for the time came when, by accident, because of Mr Youthful (yes, Mr Youthful) the thraldom of style was relaxed and I recovered a little of my power of action. Thereupon I went over completely to the offensive. Up and at them! Tally ho! Tally ho! After her! After the style and beauty of the modern schoolgirl!

It was strange that I should owe my salvation to the engineer-architect. Without him I should have remained a prisoner for ever. It was he who unwittingly provoked a minor transformation, and brought it about that suddenly it was the girl who was inside me instead of my being inside her; yes, the engineer introduced his daughter into me, and for that I shall be grateful to him till the day of my death. I remember how it started; I remember every detail. I came back from school at lunch-time to find the Youthfuls already at table. The maid served potato soup. The girl was sitting there with her usual perfection, with a tremendous amount of physical culture and in crêpe-soled shoes. She took only a very small helping of soup. However, she drank a glass of water and ate a slice of bread; she avoided that tepid, watery, too easy substance, soup, which must certainly have been detrimental to her style; and it is legitimate also to assume that she wished to preserve her appetite until the meat course, for a hungry modern girl cuts a much more dashing figure than a modern girl replete. Mrs Youthful similarly took very little soup; and she did not ask me what school had been like that morning. Why not? Because she disliked asking such maternal questions. Indeed, she disliked the maternal style in general; she had rather be a sister.

'Victor,' she said in the tone of a loyal comrade and reader of H. G. Wells, passing her husband the salt. Then, looking half into the future and half into space and changing to a tone of humanitarian revolt against social abuses and injustices, she added:

'The death penalty is an anachronism.'

Mr Youthful, that responsible engineer and town-planner who had studied in Paris, from which he had brought back the sun-tanned European style, an easy, informal, way of dressing, yellow suède shoes which were always very conspicuous on him, open-necked shirts, horn-rimmed spectacles, an unprejudiced outlook, a virile pacifism, an admiration for the rational organization of labour, and a stock of scientific anecdotes and cabaret jokes, thereupon took the salt-cellar from his wife and said:

'Thank you, Mary.'

Then, in the accents of a well-informed pacifist tinged with a slight suggestion of those of a graduate of the Ecole Poly-technique, he added:

'In Brazil they are throwing barrels of salt into the sea while here it costs six groschen a gramme. The politicians. We technicians. The world must be reorganized. The League of Nations.'

Mrs Youthful sighed deeply, and, simultaneously glimpsing

a better future, participating in Poland's past struggles and dreaming of the Poland of tomorrow, added intelligently:

'Zutka, who was that boy who brought you home? You needn't tell me if you don't want to, you know we don't want to pry into your affairs!'

Miss Youthful indifferently swallowed a piece of bread.

'I don't know,' she said.

'You don't know?' her mother exclaimed delightedly.

'He picked me up in the street,' the girl explained.

'He picked you up in the street?' said her father.

Actually he asked the question mechanically, but it came out rather ponderously, and might have been interpreted as an old-fashioned paternal rebuke. This caused Mrs Youthful to burst out with a (perhaps) slightly exaggerated matter-of-factness:

'And what is there peculiar about that? He picked her up, and what of it? At most he'll have made a date with you, won't he, Zutka? Splendid! Or perhaps you're planning a whole day's canoeing with him. Or going away with him for the weekend, and spending the night with him. Well, what of it?' she said abjectly, 'spend the night with him, and think no more of it. And perhaps you're thinking of taking no money with you and letting him pay for everything, or perhaps it'll be the other way about, so that you'll have to pay for him; in that case I'll give you the money. But I expect you'll manage without any money between you, won't you?' she exclaimed audaciously, with a movement of her whole body.

She was completely carried away by her excitement, but the daughter neatly eluded her mother, who so obviously wanted to enjoy herself by way of her.

'Of course, Mummy, of course!' she said by way of reply, without taking a second helping or rissoles, because mincemeat was no good to her, I suppose because it was too soft and easy. The girl was very careful of her parents; she never allowed them to get too close to her.

The engineer, however, now took up the subject on which his wife had embarked. As she had implied that he was shocked by his daughter's behaviour, he wanted to demonstrate the opposite.

'Of course there's nothing wrong in all that!' he said. 'Zutka, if you want to have a natural child, go ahead! What's wrong about it? The cult of virginity is dead. We, the engineer-architects of the new social order, refuse to subscribe to the outworn cult of virginity, which is good enough for yokels.'

He took a gulp of water and fell silent, fearing that perhaps he might have gone a little too far. Mrs Youthful then took up the cudgels, and impersonally and indirectly set herself to plant a natural child in her daughter's head. She gave free rein to her liberalism, emphasized the extraordinary freedom that prevailed among young people nowadays, etc., etc. This was the Youthfuls' war-horse. When one of them dismounted, fearing to have gone too far, the other got into the saddle and set off at the gallop. This gallop was the more remarkable in that, as has already been mentioned, neither (not even Mr Youthful) liked mothers or children. But it must be appreciated that they bestrode the theme, not from the mother's point of view, but from the girl's, not from a legitimate child's angle, but from a natural child's. Above all, Mrs Youthful desired by means of her daughter's natural child to place herself in the very forefront of the age, and she would have liked it to be begotten casually, accidentally, insolently, on the grass in the course of a sporting day's outing, by a comrade of the same age, as occurs in modern novels, etc. Moreover, the mere fact of talking about it, of encouraging their daughter in this way, partly satisfied her parents' desire; and they were emboldened in their enjoyment of the idea by their aware-ness of my impotence in the face of it. The truth was that I did not yet know how to protect myself against the spell of a sixteen-year-old on the grass.

But what they did not realize was that that day I was in too wretched a state even for jealousy. They had now been ceaselessly and uninterruptedly making and inflicting a face on me for a whole fortnight, with the result that my face was now so pitiful that I could not manage even to be jealous. I realized that the

boy of whom the girl had spoken could be no other than
Kopeida, but it made no difference—dejection and depression,
depression and dejection, wretchedness, immense fatigue, and
resignation. So, instead of tackling the subject from its proud,
fresh, greeny-blue angle, I tackled it in miserable fashion. A
baby is a baby, I said to myself, imagining the delivery, the nurse,
the childish complaints, the nappies, the expense; and also
imagining that the baby's warmth and the milk would soon do
away with Miss Youthful's girlishness and turn her into a heavy,
commonplace mother. That was why I turned to the girl and
said, pitifully, cerebrally, as if for myself:

'Mamma!'

I said it with great sadness and poverty, and not without the
soft, warm motherliness which they refused to admit into their
sharp, fresh, youthful vision of the world. Why did I say it? It
just came out, that was all. The girl, like all girls, was primarily
an aesthete, beauty was her principal blemish, and I, in applying
to her type the warm, sentimental and somewhat untidy epithet
of 'mamma', had conjured up a grossly maternal and anti-
beautiful idea, and I thought that perhaps she would explode.
But at heart I knew well enough that she would slip away,
leaving the anti-beautiful in me—for the relations between us
were such that whatever I did came back and hit me on the nose
—it was like spitting into the wind.

But suddenly and without warning an uproarious burst of
laughter came from Mr Youthful.

He laughed involuntarily, gutturally, surprised at and ashamed
of himself; he held his napkin to his face, his eyes nearly popped
out of his head, he choked into his napkin, he laughed convulsively, mechanically, against his will, to such an extent that
I was taken utterly aback. What was tickling his nervous system?
The word 'mamma'? He was laughing at the contrast between
his daughter and the word 'mamma', perhaps he associated some
cabaret memory with it, perhaps my sad, plaintive voice brought
him back to the outskirts of humanity. Like all engineers, he was
an habitué of cabarets, and no doubt the word I used was not

139

entirely unknown in cabarets. And he laughed all the more because he had just been singing the praises of having a natural child. His spectacles fell from his nose.

'Victor!' Mrs Youthful exclaimed.

I poured oil on the flames.

'Mamma!' I said. 'Mamma!'

'I'm sorry,' said Mr Youthful, still convulsed with laughter. 'I'm sorry, I can't help it! I'm sorry!'

The girl stuck her nose in her plate, and I felt almost physically that across her father's laughter what I said had struck home—and that, unless I were greatly mistaken, her father's laughter was changing the situation, causing me to emerge from the girl. I was at last able to get at her and strike home. I said no more.

Her parents realized it too, and hurried to her rescue.

'I'm surprised at you, Victor,' Mrs Youthful said. 'Our young old man's remarks are not at all amusing. They're nothing but a pose, that's all!'

The engineer at last recovered himself.

'What? Did you think I was laughing at him? I wasn't doing anything of the sort, I didn't even properly hear what he said, I just remembered something.'

However, his efforts aggravated his daughter's situation. Though I could not manage fully to understand all that was happening, I said 'Mamma! Mamma!' once or twice more in the same apathetic fashion, and repetition must have given additional force to the word, for the engineer once more broke into a short, guttural, broken, strangled, laugh; and this laugh obviously made him laugh again, for he suddenly guffawed unrestrainedly, again holding his napkin to his mouth.

The she-graduate was by now very upset.

'Have the kindness not to intervene in the conversation,' she snapped at me, but her annoyance only plunged her daughter deeper in the mire. In the end the girl shrugged her shoulders.

'Leave him alone, Mummy,' she said with apparent indifference, but this only plunged her deeper still.

Strangely enough, the situation between us was now so altered that everything they said made matters worse for them. Actually I was enjoying the situation; I felt that I was regaining power in relation to the girl. But at heart I was indifferent; and it was precisely because of my indifference that I was regaining power; and I was aware that, if I exchanged depression and apathy, wretchedness and poverty, for success, my power would vanish, for the truth was that it consisted of a magic super-power based on an avowed and acknowledged lack of it. So, to consolidate myself in my pitiful condition and to demonstrate the extent of my utter indifference to everything, my total unworthiness, I started putting breadcrumbs, scraps of lettuce, and so on into my fruit salad, and stirring the mixture with my finger. My face . . . But no matter, it was all the same to me. What does it matter? I said to myself sleepily, adding a little salt, pepper, and two tooth-picks to my fruit salad. It was all the same to me, I didn't mind what I ate—and I felt as if I were lying in my grave while birds circled overhead. I felt at peace.

'What on earth are you doing? What on earth are you doing? What are you putting all that filth in your fruit salad for?' Mrs Youthful asked quietly, but with nervousness in her voice.

Lethargically I raised my eyes from my plate. 'I like it like this. What does it matter?' I murmured dejectedly. I started eating my fruit salad, and in fact failed to find it in any way offensive. The effect on the Youthfuls is difficult to describe; I had not expected such a definite success.

For the third time the engineer burst into a crude, night-clubbish, kitchen sort of laugh. The girl, bent over her plate, ate her fruit salad in a silent, correct, disciplined, even heroic manner. Her graduate mother grew pale—and looked at me as if hypnotized and in evident fear. Fear!

'It's a pose,' she muttered. 'It's a pose! Don't eat it! I won't allow it! Zutka! Victor! Zutka! Victor! Zutka, Zutka, Victor, stop him! Don't allow it! Oh!'

I went on eating, and why shouldn't I? I'd eat anything, a dead rat if you like, it was all the same to me. Bravo Mientus! I said

141

to myself. Bravo! It's all the same, I'd eat anything, what does it matter? It's all the same to me!

'Zutka!' Mrs Youthful exclaimed. She could not bear seeing her daughter's admirer eating with such a total lack of discrimination. At this point the girl, having finished her fruit salad, rose and walked out of the room. Mrs Youthful walked out behind her, and so did Mr Youthful, hiccuping convulsively and holding his handkerchief to his mouth. There was nothing to show whether they had just finished their lunch or were running away. But I knew; they were running away. I bounded behind them in mental pursuit. Victory! Forward, advance, pursue, harry, strike, kill, capture, dominate, surround, crush, strangle, let no quarter be given! Were they frightened? Then frighten them more! Did they flee? Pursue them! But calm, take it easy, keep your head, don't change from beggar to victor, for it was as beggar that you gained the day. Did they fear that I should introduce anarchy into their daughter as I had into the fruit salad? Ah! Now I knew how to smash the schoolgirl's style! I could stuff her mind with anything I liked, mix, stir, mince, scramble, with complete and absolute freedom. But calm, calm!

Who would have believed that Youthful's explosion of subterranean laughter would restore my capacity for resistance? My thoughts and actions recovered their claws. No, the battle was not yet won, but at least I had recovered the power to act. Just as I had made a mess of the fruit salad, reduced it to anarchy and disorder, so could I wreck the schoolgirl's modernism, stuff her with strange and heterogeneous things, and corrupt her by them. Forward against the modern style, against the beauty of the modern schoolgirl! But softly, softly . . .

✴ 9 ✴

Through the Keyhole

I WENT quietly to my room and lay on the divan. I must prepare my plan of action. I was trembling and sweating, for I knew that my pilgrimage was on the point of taking me to the depths of hell. For nothing which is in good taste can be really dreadful (as the word 'taste' indicates); only its opposite, which is 'disgusting', really makes us puke. How delightful, how romantic or classic, are the murders, rapes, blindings, with which prose and poetry abound! Chocolate with garlic is disgusting, but not Shakespeare's magnificent, fascinating crimes. Don't talk to me about your rhymed and mimed sufferings which never offend good taste and go down as easily as oysters. Don't talk to me about the delectable crimes, the atrocities you lap up like strawberries and cream, the appetizing details of poverty, suffering and despair. And why is it that women novelists who do not shrink from heroically dipping their fingers into the most flagrant social abuses, who have no hesitation in describing the agonies of six or a dozen members of a working-class family starving to death, would never dare use those same fingers to pick their noses in public? The answer is that the latter would be much more horrifying. A famine, or the death of a million men in wartime, we can swallow, and even take pleasure in, but that does not alter the fact that some things, in conjunction with each other, are uneatable, disgusting, vomitable, revolting, and intolerable to human sensibilities. The fact of the matter is that our primary duty is to be pleasing to others; our primary duty is to please, to please; you may lose your wife, your husband, your children, your heart may be broken, but it must be broken

143

in accordance with the canons of taste. Now, the operation on which I was about to embark, in the name of maturity, and in order to escape the schoolgirl's spell, was anti-gastronomic, hostile to the stomach and revolting to the palate.

Besides, I nourished no illusions—my success at lunch had been pretty dubious after all; it had been scored principally in relation to the girl's parents; she had extricated herself little the worse for it, she remained remote and inaccessible. How was I to get at her in her modernism? How could I bring her into my operational orbit in spite of the distance between us? For, apart from the mental distance which separated us, there was also the physical distance—we saw each other only at lunch and dinner. How could I spoil her beauty, work on her mind from a distance, when I was not with her, when she was alone? Only, I decided, by keeping a watch on her, by spying on her. This was a task which to a certain extent they had made easier for me, for from my first appearance in the household they had taken me for an eavesdropper and a peeping Tom. Who knows? I said to myself, still apathetically, but with a glimmer of hope. Who knows? If I put my eye to the keyhole, I may see something which will repel me straight away, for many a beauty, alone in her room, behaves in a fantastically revolting manner. On the other hand, I was also taking a grave risk, for some girls who have subjected themselves to the discipline of charm keep just as careful a watch on themselves in private as in public, with the result that instead of ugliness I might see beauty—and beauty in solitude is even more shattering. I remembered that when I had suddenly entered her room I had found the girl polishing her shoe in very stylish fashion. As against this, however, the mere fact of spying on her would serve to a certain extent to detract from her beauty, to diminish her; for when we look at beauty in ugly fashion something sticks.

Such were the thoughts which raced feverishly through my mind. Eventually I rose heavily from the divan and went over towards the keyhole. But, before looking through it, I glanced out of the window; outside in the street, illuminated by the

144

autumn light, it was a magnificent, cool, autumn day. Mientus was just creeping in by the back door, no doubt to see the maid. Pigeons were flying in the clear sky over the house next door, a motor-horn sounded in the distance, a nurse was playing with a child, and the window-panes shone in the light of the declining sun. A beggar was standing outside the house, a bearded and hairy old man, unhappy and desperate. He gave me an idea; heavily and awkwardly I went out into the street and cut a green twig from a tree.

'Here are fifty groschen,' I said to the man. 'If you put this twig in your mouth and keep it there until it gets dark, I'll give you a zloty.'

He put the twig in his mouth and, I don't know why, the sight of the fresh green in his aged mouth gave me a feeling of relief. I went back into the house, thanking heaven for the existence of money, which makes it possible to buy oneself accomplices, and put my eye to the keyhole. The girl was moving about the room in the way in which all girls move about their rooms. She put something away in a drawer, took out an exercise book, put it on the table—and I caught sight of her profile, the profile of a typical schoolgirl bent over her exercise book.

I spied on her miserably and without respite from four o'clock to six (the beggar kept the twig in his mouth the whole time). I waited for her to give herself away, to betray by some nervous movement that the lunch-time defeat had left some trace; I thought that she might bite her lips, for instance, or rub her eyebrows. But I waited in vain. It was as if nothing had happened, as if I did not exist, as if I had never appeared on the scene to disturb her schoolgirlishness. As the time passed the latter grew colder, crueller, more and more aloof and inaccessible, and it seemed possible to doubt the possibility of doing any damage to this girl, who behaved in private exactly as she did in public. One almost got to the point of doubting whether anything whatever had happened at lunch-time. Towards six o'clock the door suddenly opened and the she-graduate walked in.

'Are you working?' she asked with relief in her voice, scrutinizing her daughter closely. 'Are you working?'

'I'm doing my German prep,' the girl replied.

Her mother sighed deeply, several times.

'You're working, good! Good! Work! Work!'

Reassured, she gave the girl a kiss. She too suspected that something in her might have cracked. Zutka moved her little head away. Her mother tried to say something; she opened her mouth, but shut it again without saying it.

'Work!' she said nervously. 'Work! Work! Work! Be active, intense! Go to the dance hall this evening, go dancing! Come back late and sleep like lead . . .'

'Leave my head alone, Mummy!' the girl said unkindly. 'Can't you see I'm busy?'

Her mother looked at her with concealed admiration. Her daughter's hardness reassured her completely; she realized that lunch had left no dent in her armour. But the girl's hardness left me with a lump in my throat; it was directed against herself, and nothing is so moving as to see our beloved behaving hardly and cruelly, not only in our presence but in our absence as well, as if to be ready for any eventuality. Moreover, the girl's cruelty painfully accentuated her poetry. When the mother left the room she bent over her exercise book and, remote and cruel, went on with her homework with supreme composure.

I realized that, if I went on much longer allowing the girl to be poetical in solitude and did not immediately establish contact between her and myself, matters might end disastrously. Instead of making her ugly, I was increasing her attractiveness, instead of my seizing her by the throat, it was she who had a grip on mine. To let her know that I was watching her, I noisily swallowed behind the door. She started, but did not turn her head—which showed that she had realized, and she buried her little head in her shoulders, *touchée*. Simultaneously her profile ceased to exist by itself and for itself alone, with the result that it suddenly and manifestly lost all its poetry. The girl, with me gazing at her profile, went on struggling silently and obstinately for a long time, and the struggle consisted in her not moving even her eyelids. She went on writing, and behaved just as if no one were spying on her.

However, after several minutes the keyhole which was looking at her with my eyes started getting on her nerves. To demonstrate her independence and consolidate her impassivity she deliberately sniffed, a noisy, vulgar, ugly sniff, as if to say: Look at me as much as you like, it's all the same to me! This is how a girl shows her supreme contempt. But her sniff was a tactical error, and I was ready for it. As soon as she sniffed, I sniffed too, quietly but quite distinctly, as if sniffing were contagious and I couldn't help it. She went still and silent like a little bird—a nasal dialogue of this kind was totally unacceptable to her—but her nose, having once started, would not leave her alone. After a moment's hesitation she had to take out her handkerchief and blow it, and after that at long intervals she kept imperceptibly and nervously sniffing again. Every time she sniffed, I sniffed. I congratulated myself on having so easily drawn attention to her nose. Her nose was much less modern than her legs, and much easier to get the better of; accentuating it in this way was a great step forward. If only I had been able to give her a nervous cold, if only it had been possible to give modernism a cold in the head!

After all this sniffing it was impossible for her to get up and block the keyhole, which would have been equivalent to an admission that she had been sniffing nervously and because of me. So let silence and nervous sniffing continue, and let hope be dissembled. However, I underrated the girl's deep cunning; suddenly, with a decisive, energetic gesture, she blew her nose with her hand—with her whole arm—and this daring, primitive, sporting, spontaneous gesture gave charm to the sniffing and changed the situation to her advantage. Once more a lump came into my throat. At that moment—I managed to remove myself from the keyhole only just in time—her mother burst into my room.

'What are you doing?' she exclaimed suspiciously, noting my

indeterminate position in the middle of the room. 'Why . . . are you standing there like that? Why aren't you playing games? You ought to be doing something!' she said angrily. She was afraid because of her daughter; my vague attitude in the middle of the room made her suspect some obscure plot against the girl. I did nothing to explain or enlighten her, but stood my ground, apathetic, unhappy, as if rooted to the spot, until Mrs Youthful could stand it no longer and turned her back on me. Her eyes fell on the beggar standing in front of the house.

'What the . . . What's the matter with him?' she exclaimed. 'Why is he holding that twig in his mouth?'

'Who?'

'The beggar! What does it mean?'

'I don't know. He must have put it in his mouth!'

'You spoke to him. I saw you out of the window.'

'Yes, I spoke to him.'

She looked hard at me. She was swaying like a pendulum. She was obscurely aware that the twig in the man's mouth had some secret implication inimical to her daughter, but she was not to know that for me it was a weapon against modernism. The suspicion that I might have told the beggar to put it in his mouth was too absurd to be put into words. She looked at me with strong suspicion about my state of mind and walked out. At her! After her! Pursue! Strike! Capture! Slave of my imagination, victim of my whim! Quiet! Quiet! I dashed back to the keyhole. The way things were developing made it more and more difficult to preserve my primitive attitude of wretchedness and despair; the struggle was becoming more acute, animal cunning was getting the better of prostration and resignation. However, the girl had disappeared; when she heard voices on the other side of the door, she realized that I was no longer watching her, and this enabled her to emerge from the trap. She had gone out. Had she seen the twig in the beggar's mouth, had she realized for whom he was holding it in his mouth? Even if she had not, the branch grafted on the beard, the green bitterness in the beggar's buccal cavity, must have weakened her, it was in too great a conflict with her modern vision of the world. Night was falling, and the lamps bathed the town in violet. The caretaker's boy came back from the grocer's round the corner. The trees were gradually losing their leaves in the limpid, transparent air. An aircraft hummed in the blue sky. The front-door banged, announcing the departure of Mrs Youthful—anxious, nervous, feeling that there was something evil in the air, she was on the way to her committee meeting, desiring to reassure herself and protect herself against any eventuality by something practical, social, mature.

The lady chairman: 'Ladies, today the first item on the agenda is the terrible social scourge of abandoned children.'

Dr Youthful: 'But where is the money to come from?'

Night was falling, and the beggar was still standing in the street with the bit of fresh verdure in his mouth; a discordant note. I was alone in the house. As I stood there in the darkness, searching in my mind how to continue an operation so auspiciously begun, the atmosphere of some detective novel or other, a whiff of Sherlock Holmes, started percolating into the empty rooms. As both females had fled, I decided to search the house; I might find something which might enable me to get at them. In the Youthfuls' bedroom—it was small, bright, spotless, and austere—there was a lingering odour of soap, the highly cultivated, modern, and civilized post-bath odour, a redolence of nail-files, geysers, and pyjamas. I stood there for a long time, sniffing the atmosphere, analysing its constituent parts, trying to find the clue to the prevalent bad taste, to find a way of fouling the whole environment.

At first sight there was nothing to fasten on. This bedroom, clean, tidy, bright, and austere, was at first sight more pleasing than old-fashioned bedrooms. But I could not tell why the modern engineer's dressing-gown, pyjamas, sponge, shaving cream, slippers, digestive tablets, his wife's gymnastic apparatus, and the bright yellow window curtain on the modern window created such a disagreeable impression. Standardization? Philistinism? Neither provided the answer. Then what was it?

149

I stopped, unable to lay my finger on the key to the bad taste, for lack of the words, gestures, actions which would have enabled me to grasp it, put it in concrete form. My eyes fell on a book on the bedside table. It was Charlie Chaplin's *My Trip Abroad*, lying open at the page where he describes how H. G. Wells danced a solo in his presence. 'Then H. G. Wells did a clog dance and did it very well.' This was the clue I needed; the room was nothing but H. G. Wells dancing a solo in the presence of Charlie Chaplin. What was H. G. Wells when he danced his clog dance? A Utopian. The old modernist believed himself entitled to free expression of his pleasure in dancing. He insisted on his right to joy and harmony, he pirouetted visualizing a future world, a world to come in thousands of years, he danced alone, forestalling the years, he danced in theoretical fashion, believing himself entitled to do so. Now, this bedroom was just as Utopian. Was there room here for the snores and grunts of a sleeping man? Or for his wife's plumpness? Or for his beard, which he removed every morning but nevertheless potentially existed? The engineer undoubtedly had a beard, even if he shaved it off every morning with the aid of his razor and shaving cream—and this room was *shaved*. Once upon a time man's bedroom was the murmuring forest, but where, in this bright bedroom among the towels, was there room for the blackness of the trees? What a poor, constricted thing was this cleanliness, this blue and white paint, incompatible with the colour of the soil and the colour of man! And the Youthfuls in their bedroom seemed to me as dreadful as H. G. Wells dancing a solo jig in the presence of Charlie Chaplin.

But it was only when I started dancing myself that my thoughts took shape and turned into action, ridiculing and deriding my surroundings and throwing the bad taste into relief. I danced, and my dance, partnerless and in silence and solitude, grew so mad-brained that it frightened me. After pirouetting at the Youthfuls' towels, pyjamas, beds, and other hygienic accessories, I quickly walked out, shutting the door behind me. I had injected my dance into their modern interior. Now for the schoolgirl's bedroom, to inject ugliness into that too.

But the room, or rather the entrance hall, in which she slept, was infinitely less well adapted to my distaste. The mere fact that for lack of a proper bedroom she slept in a corner of the hall was sufficient to set off a whole train of fascinating and captivating thoughts. It reflected the contemporary hurry and bustle, the girl's nomadism, a kind of *carpe diem* feeling, connected by secret, underground passages to the free-and-easy, hurrying nature of modern youth in the motor age. You could imagine her dropping off to sleep as soon as she laid her modern head on the pillow, and that again was a reminder of the accelerated rhythm of present-day life. Moreover, the fact that she did not have a proper bedroom inhibited me from carrying out an operation of the kind that I had carried out in her parents' room; for the girl in fact slept, not in private, but in public, she had no real nocturnal life of her own, and that hard state associated her with Europe and America, with work camps, barracks, flags, hotels, and railway stations; it opened vast horizons and ruled out the possibility of a corner of her own. The bedclothes hidden in the divan played a merely marginal role; they did not stand out on their own, they were merely a supplement to sleep. There was no dressing table; to look at herself the girl used the big mirror against the wall. There was no hand mirror. Next to the divan-bed was a little black school-desk, with books and exercise books on it. On top of the exercise books was a nail-file, and on the window-sill a pen-knife, a cheap fountain-pen, an apple, an exam syllabus, a photograph of Fred Astaire and another of Ginger Rogers, a packet of scented cigarettes, a tooth-brush, a tennis shoe, and in the latter a flower, a forgotten carnation. That was all. How little, and yet how much!

I remained silent in the face of the carnation. I could not withhold my admiration from the girl. What subtlety she showed! In dropping the carnation into the shoe she killed two birds with one stone—she spiced love with athleticism and athleticism with love; it was not an ordinary shoe, but a tennis shoe, damp with sweat, for she knew the sweat that comes from playing games is the only kind not damaging to flowers; in associating it with the flower, she made it attractive, added to it something flowery and charming. What a cunning creature!

Ordinary, naïve, old-fashioned girls grew azaleas in pots, but she dropped a flower into a shoe, a sports shoe; what is more, she had certainly done it accidentally, unconsciously, without thinking. What a little virtuoso!

I considered what to do in the face of this. Should I put the flower in the dustbin, or in the bearded beggar's buccal orifice? Any such mechanical, artificial response would merely evade the real difficulty. No, the flower's magic must be neutralized on the spot, and not by physical but by mental means. The beggar, the green twig still projecting from his thick beard, still stood faithfully outside in the street, a fly buzzed against the window-pane, the sound of the monotonous chatter of the maid, whom Mientus was trying to tempt with his stable-boy, floated up from the kitchen, in the distance a tram ground its way round a corner—I stood in the midst of these assorted sounds with a vague smile on my lips. The fly buzzed louder, and I caught it. I tore off its wings and legs, made of it a little ball of terrified, metaphysical suffering, not completely round but certainly pitiful enough, and silently put it in the shoe, next to the flower. The sweat that poured from my brow turned out to be more potent than the flowery tennis sweat; it was as if I had allied myself with the devil against the modern girl. The fly, with its mute, voiceless suffering, soiled and degraded the shoe, the flower, the apple, the cigarettes, the whole of the girl's kingdom, and I, standing there with an evil smile on my lips, listened to what was happening in the room and in myself, sounding the atmosphere as if I had gone mad—and I said to myself that it was not only boys who tortured cats and birds, but that sometimes in the same way grown-up children tortured too—to rid themselves or get their own back on some girl. Did Torquemada torture for such a reason? Who can Torquemada's girl have been? The answer is silence.

The bearded beggar, with the green projecting from his mouth, remained at his post, the fly went on suffering in the shoe, which had now become Chinese, Byzantine, my dance went on in the Youthfuls' bedroom, and I started going through the girl's belongings more thoroughly. I opened the wardrobe, but the contents did not correspond to my expectations. The girl's knickers did not detract from her in any way, they had lost their intimate character, they were more like gym shorts. However, in a drawer which I opened with a knife I found a pile of letters, the girl's accumulated love letters. I pounced on them, while the bearded beggar, the fly, and the dance went ceaselessly on . . .

Oh, the Pandora's box I had hit on, oh, the secrets which that drawer contained! It was only then that I realized the terrible mysteries to which the schoolgirls of today hold the key, and what would happen if one of them betrayed the things confided to her. But these mysteries are swallowed up in them like stones in deep water, they are too pretty, too beautiful, to be able to talk about them—and those who are not gagged by their beauty do not receive such letters. There is something supremely moving in the fact that only human beings bound by their own beauty have access to certain shameful secrets of mankind. Oh, adolescence, that receptacle of shame, locked with the key of beauty! Oh, the things that everyone, young and old, deposited in this temple! Rather than allow them to become public they would unquestionably be willing to die three times in succession, be burnt to death over a slow fire . . . and the face of the century, the face of the twentieth century, the century of the confusion of the ages, appeared as doubtful as that of a Silenus.

There were schoolboys' letters, so unpleasant, infuriating, provocative, gauche, slimy, disgusting and disgraceful, that history had never seen the like, even ancient history, or that of the Middle Ages. The only letters which were tolerable were those which, out of fear, said nothing, such as: 'Zutka, tomorrow at the stadium with Louis and Maritza, confirm, Henry.' Those were the only ones which were not compromising. . . . I found two letters from Bobek and Hopek, vulgar in content and commonplace in form, which tried by excessive crudeness to create an impression of maturity. They allowed themselves to be attracted like moths to a candle, knowing that they would be burnt.

The letters from university students were no less timorous, though this was better concealed. You could tell how frightened each one of them was, how much trouble he took, how he weighed and measured his words, in order to avoid falling into the abyss of his immaturity, his thighs. Their thighs would not leave them in peace. There was an irresoluble conflict between the thigh, unconscious and dormant in its primitive verdure, and all the things that the head dreamt about. But for that very reason there was never any reference to thighs, but a great deal about feelings, social or economic or society events, bridge, racing, and even about changing the structure of the state. The politicians, particularly those who clamoured about 'student life', concealed their thighs with supreme ability, but sent the girl all their programmes, proclamations and ideological statements. 'Zutka, would you like to know what our programme is?' they wrote, but their programmes mentioned thighs no more than their letters did, except occasionally by a slip of the pen, as for instance, when one of them, instead of writing: 'The reputation of our country never stood so high,' wrote: 'The reputation of our country never stood so thigh'; and another, instead of writing: 'The situation can be saved by resolute action, not by sighing over past errors,' wrote: 'The situation can be saved by resolute action, not by thighing over past errors.' Apart from these two instances, thighs were never mentioned. They were similarly carefully concealed in the letters—incidentally distinctly lecherous letters—from the aged aunts who wrote newspaper articles about the jazz age and nudity on the beaches, and tried to enter into spiritual contact with the girl to save her from perdition. Reading them created the impression that the question of thighs never arose at all.

Moreover, at the bottom of the drawer was a pile of books of verse of the kind current today, to the tune of two or three hundred or more, which, it must be confessed, the girl had neither read nor even opened. Each was provided with a dedication written in intimate, sincere, honest language, vigorously exhorting her to read the contents or condemning her in studied and trenchant terms if she should fail to do so, exalting her to the skies for agreeing to read them, or threatening her with expulsion from the *élite* if she did not, or imploring her to read them out of regard for the poet's solitude, or his labour, or his mission, or his status as a pioneer, or his soul, or his inspiration. Curiously enough, they did not mention thighs either, and, still more curiously, the titles of their works did not do so. These were all about dawns and daybreak, and new dawns, and the age of struggle and the struggle of the age, and the difficult age and the youthful age, and youth on guard and the guardianship of youth, and militant youth and youth on the march, and advancing youth and bitter youth, and youthful eyes and youthful mouths and youthful spring and My Spring and Spring and Me and Spring-Time Rhythms and the Rhythm of Machine-Guns, Semaphore Signals, Aerials and Propellers and My Farewells and My Love and My Longing and My Eyes and My Lips, with not a trace of a thigh anywhere; and all this was written in poetical tones with or without studied assonances and with bold metaphors and an intoxication with words. But there was practically nothing which revealed the slightest trace of thigh. Some of the writers, with great skill and much poetic virtuosity, concealed themselves behind beauty, technical perfection, the interior logic of the work, the logical flow of associations, or behind class consciousness, the struggle, the dawn of history, and other similar objectively anti-thigh elements. It was nevertheless obvious at first sight that all this versifying, with its forced and finicky mannerisms useful for nothing and to nobody, amounted to no more than a complicated cipher, and that there must be some good and sufficient reason behind the compulsion which drove these insignificant dreamers to compose such extravagant charades. After a few moments' thought I succeeded in translating into intelligible language the contents of the following:

The horizon bursts like a bottle
The green stain mounts towards the sky
I return to the shade of the pines
And there
I drink the last unassuaging cup
Of my daily Spring.

MY TRANSLATION

Thighs, thighs, thighs,
Thighs, thighs, thighs, thighs,
Thigh.
Thighs, thighs, thighs.

Besides all this—and it was here that the real pandemonium began—there was a pile of intimate letters from judges, lawyers, public prosecutors, chemists, businessmen, landlords, doctors, etc., i.e. the whole tribe of important, respectable people by whom I had always been so much impressed. I was astounded.

Did these men too, in spite of appearances, maintain relations with the modern girl? Incredible, I said to myself, incredible! So they found their maturity so burdensome that, unknown to their wives and children, they addressed long letters to this modern schoolgirl of the top class but one? In their letters, of course, there was less thigh than ever; on the contrary, each one of them explained in detail why he proposed to engage in an 'exchange of ideas' with her, feeling confident that Zutka would understand, would not take it amiss, etc. Then they went on in tortuous but abject terms to pay tribute to the girl, conjuring her between the lines to condescend to dream about them, secretly of course. And each one of them . . . still, however, without any mention of thighs . . . emphasized to the best of his ability the Modern Boy imprisoned in himself.

Here is an extract from a letter from a public prosecutor: 'Though I wear a gown, in reality I am nothing but an errand boy. I am well behaved and disciplined, I do what I am told. I have no opinions of my own. The president of the court can publicly reprimand me, and I have to get up and ask permission to speak, like a schoolboy.'

This from a politician: 'I am a boy, nothing but a boy dedicated to politics.'

A non-commissioned officer wrote this: 'I have to obey orders blindly. I must be prepared to lay down my life in response to a word of command. I am a slave. Our officers always call us "boys", irrespective of our age. Take no notice of my birth certificate, it's a purely external detail, my wife and children are only external accessories. . . . I'm a military boy, with a boy's blind loyalty, and even the soldiers call me a dog, a dog!'

A landed proprietor wrote: 'Now that I have gone bankrupt, my wife will have to go out and cook, my sons will lead a dog's life, and here am I, not a landlord, but a boy in exile, a boy who has lost his way, and I take a secret pleasure in it.'

But thighs were never explicitly mentioned. All the writers wrote postscripts appealing for the most complete secrecy, for if a single word of these confidences became known their careers would be irretrievably ruined. 'Keep this for yourself alone, and don't breathe a word to anyone.' Incredible! These letters revealed to me in a flash the extent of the power wielded by the modern girl. Who was exempt from her charms? What head was immune from her thighs? Under the influence of these thoughts my legs started moving on their own account, and I was on the point of dancing a jig in honour of the old men of the twentieth century, marshalled under the whip like gangs of slaves, when at the bottom of the drawer I noticed a big envelope from the Ministry of Education. I immediately recognized Pimko's handwriting. The letter was dry enough. It said:

I can no longer tolerate your shocking ignorance of things included in the school curriculum.

I invite you to present yourself at my office in the Ministry on Friday at 4.30 p.m. to enable me to explain, comment on, and instruct you in the poetry of Norwid, and thus fill a gap in your education.

I must point out to you that it is in my official capacity that I am inviting you to call here, and that if you fail to appear I shall make written application to your headmistress to have you expelled.

I must reiterate that I can no longer tolerate the gap in your education, and that by reason of my official position I am within my rights in declining to do so.

T. Pimko, PH.D., Hon. Prof., Warsaw.

So things had got to this pitch between them? So he was threatening her, was he? So this was the state of the game, was it? She had made such play with her ignorance that Pimko had ended by showing his teeth. Being unable to make a date with her as Pimko, he summoned her to his presence by virtue of his role as professor of secondary and higher education. Being no longer satisfied with flirting with her under her parents' eyes, he was taking advantage of his position to impose Norwid on her by legal and official means. Being unable to do anything else, he wished at least to penetrate the girl with his Norwid. In my utter astonishment I held the letter in my hand, not knowing whether it boded me good or evil. But another letter lay in the drawer underneath where Pimko's had been; it consisted of a few brief sentences, scrawled in pencil on a crumpled sheet torn from an exercise book—and I immediately recognized Kopeida's handwriting. Yes, Kopeida's, there was no doubt about it. Feverishly I snatched up his laconic, hastily written, crumpled note. There was every indication that it had been thrown in through the window. It said:

I forgot to give you my address (he gave it). If you want to go with me, O.K. Let me know. H.K.

Kopeida! You remember Kopeida? At once I understood everything. My instinct had not deceived me. The boy who had brought the girl home (as they had said at lunch-time) was Kopeida, and Kopeida had thrown this note in through the window. He had picked her up in the street, and now he was making her a complementary proposition—how modern and direct! 'If you want to go with me, O.K.' He had seen her in the street, been struck by her sex appeal, had spoken to her, and later written her a message, devoid of superfluous formalities, in accordance with the new ways of young people among themselves. He had screwed it up into a ball, and thrown it in through the window. Kopeida! And she certainly didn't know his name, for he had not bothered to introduce himself.

All this gave me a lump in the throat. Pimko on the one hand and Kopeida on the other. Pimko, old Pimko, imposing himself, legally, culturally, officially, and severely, with the aid of his professorial role. You must satisfy me about Norwid, schoolgirl, for I am your master and you are my slave. One claimed her as a brother, a companion of the same age, a modern youth; the other as licensed pedagogue and master of secondary education.

Once more they had me by the throat. What did landlords' confidences, lawyers' laments, or poets' ridiculous acrostics matter in the face of these two letters? They announced disaster, catastrophe. The imminent, fatal danger lay in the girl's readiness to yield to Pimko and Kopeida without a trace of sentiment, simply in obedience to her own law, solely because both had rights over her, the one modern and private, the other ancient and public. But then her attractiveness would increase tremendously . . . and neither the dances, nor the flies of my little enterprise would avail me, for she would suffocate me with her attractiveness. If with modern physical a-sentimentality she gave herself to Kopeida . . . or if she went to see Pimko in obedience to his magisterial order . . . girl going to old man because she was a schoolgirl . . . girl giving herself to boy because she was modern. . . .

Oh, the girl's obedience, her enslavement, to the modern schoolgirl pattern! Kopeida and Pimko knew what they were doing in addressing her so crudely and laconically, they knew that it was for that very reason that she would be ready to succumb. Pimko, a man of experience, did not expect her to be frightened by his threat; his calculations were based on the fact that it is pleasing to yield to an old man under threat—almost as pleasing as to yield to a boy for the sole reason that he expresses himself in modern terms. Oh, slavery carried to the point of self-annihilation, oh, slavery to style! Oh, the girl's *obedience*! Yes, yes, it was inevitable . . . and then what should I do, where should I take refuge in the face of this new tide, in the face of this new upsurge? How strange it was! Both, after all, were about to destroy the girl's modern attractiveness; for Pimko was proposing to abolish her athletic ignorance in matters of poetry, and in regard to Kopeida matters were still worse—for they might end in a maternity ward. But the moment of destruction infinitely multiplied her attractiveness. Blessed is ignorance. Why had I stuck my nose into that drawer? If I had not found out—I could have continued the struggle that I had undertaken against the girl. But, now that I knew, I was dreadfully weakened.

Oh, terrible and moving secrets of the private life of an adolescent, oh, diabolical contents of a schoolgirl's drawer! How could I spoil her beauty, abolish its fascination? Holding the two letters in my hand, I wondered what to do, how to thwart the inevitable and potent growth of charms, magic, beauties, and longings.

Finally, in a deep confusion of the senses, I thought of something, a plan so wild and extravagant that it seemed unreal until I started carrying it out. I tore a page out of an exercise book, and on it I wrote in the girl's big, clear handwriting: 'Tomorrow night, Thursday, tap on my window punctually at twelve o'clock. I'll let you in. Z.'

I put it in an envelope and addressed it to Kopeida. I wrote out another note saying: 'Tomorrow night tap at my window just after midnight and I'll let you in. Z.' This one I addressed to Pimko. My calculation was as follows. Pimko, on receiving such an intimate reply to his ceremoniously official letter . . . would cynically do no more or less than lose his head. It would be a real shock to the old man; he would imagine that the girl wanted a *rendezvous* with him in the strict sense of the term. The modern girl's insolence, cynicism, corruption, anarchy, taking into account her age, social class, and education, would completely turn his head. He would be unable to maintain his professorial role, to keep within the framework of strict legality. Secretly and illegally, he would hurry along and tap at the girl's window. There he would meet Kopeida.

What would happen next? I did not know. But I knew that I would raise pandemonium, wake up the family, bring the whole thing into broad daylight, make Pimko look a fool by means of Kopeida and Kopeida look a fool by means of Pimko—and then we should see what all these love affairs would look like, and what remained of the girl's attractiveness.

⋆ 10 ⋆

Escape and Recapture

AFTER a night of torment, I got up at dawn, but not to go to school. I hid behind the curtain of the little hanging cupboard which separated the kitchen from the bathroom. Drawn inexorably into the developing struggle, it was here, in the bathroom, that I must now launch my psychological offensive against the Youthfuls. I must concentrate and reinforce my mind for the decisive battle against Kopeida and Pimko. I was trembling and covered with sweat, but when life and death are at stake there is no room for scruples, and I could not permit myself the luxury of scorning to take this advantage. Try to surprise the enemy in the bath. See him as he really is. Look at him well, and never forget him. When he drops his clothes like the leaves of autumn, and with them all his distinction and elegance, you will be able to fall on him with your whole spirit, like a roaring lion on a sheep. You must neglect nothing helpful to your mobilization, your dynamism, you must assert your superiority over the enemy, the end justifies the means, you must fight, first, last, and all the time. You must concentrate all your energies, use the most modern methods. Such was the wisdom of the nations of the world. The household was still asleep when I took up my strategic position. No sound came from the girl's room, she was sleeping quietly. Youthful, however, was snoring in his bright blue room, just like a foreman or commercial traveller.

But the maid started moving about in the kitchen, sleepy voices made themselves heard, the family started getting out of bed to perform its ablutions and morning rites. I sharpened my senses—in the brutalized state of mind I was in I was like a civilized wild animal of the *Kulturkampf*. The cock crowed. Mrs Youthful appeared in a light grey dressing-gown and an old pair of slippers, her hair half-combed. She walked calmly, with head erect, and her face seemed to reflect a special wisdom, a sanitary convenience wisdom. Before entering the bathroom she walked, head high, in the direction of the lavatory, into which she disappeared, culturally, conscientiously, and intelligently, as a woman well aware that there was nothing to be ashamed of in these natural functions. *She came out even more proudly than she went in*, freed, fortified, and humanized, as if she were emerging from a Greek temple. I realized that she must certainly enter the place in the same way. Could this, then, be the temple from which the modern wives of engineers and lawyers drew their power? Each day she stepped out of it more perfect and more cultivated, holding high the banner of progress, and it was from here that she derived the intelligence and naturalness with which she tormented me so much. But enough. She went into the bathroom. The cock crowed.

Next Youthful trotted in, in his pyjamas, clearing his throat and spitting noisily—hurrying, in order not to be late at the office, bringing the newspaper with him in order to waste no time, wearing his glasses, with a towel round his neck, cleaning his finger-nails with one of his finger-nails, flapping the heels of his bedroom slippers and hopping about capriciously on his bare heels. When his eyes fell on the lavatory door, he let out a little rump laugh, like that of the day before, and went in like a cultivated, gay, mischievous, and particularly humorous engineer-worker. He stayed there for quite a time, smoked a cigarette, sang *Carioca*, and emerged extremely demoralized, a typical stupid little engineer, with a face so cheerfully asinine, so disgustingly lecherous, so revoltingly stupefied, that it was only by exercising all my strength that I was able to refrain from committing an act of violence against it. It was curious that, while the lavatory seemed to have a favourable effect on the wife, its effect on the husband was disastrous, though he was undoubtedly an engineer-builder.

'Hurry up!' he called out frantically to his wife, who was in the bathroom. 'Hurry up! Vicky's got to get to work!'

Under the influence of the lavatory he referred to himself as Vicky, and he walked off with his towel. Through a chink in the glass I peeped cautiously into the bathroom. The she-graduate, naked, was drying her knee, and her face, looking more elevated, intelligent, and pointed than ever, hovered over her big, white, disillusioned thigh like an eagle over a lamb. There seemed to be a dreadful paradox here; the eagle seemed to be hovering impotently, incapable of seizing and carrying the bleating little lamb up into the sky, though it was the she-graduate contemplating her apathetic, female thigh in a hygienic and intelligent manner. When she had finished drying herself she jumped, landed with heels together, put her hands on her hips, and turned her trunk first right and then left, breathing out and breathing in. She raised her leg—her foot was small and pink. Then she raised her other leg. She started doing double-knee bends. She repeated the exercise a dozen times in front of the mirror, breathing through her nose—until her breasts started ringing hollow and my legs started itching to dance an infernal, cultural jig. I leapt back behind the curtain; the girl's light footsteps were approaching, I concealed myself as if in the jungle, ready for the psychological pounce, an inhumanly, superhumanly, bestialized pounce. It was now or never—in surprising her just after she had awoken, untidy and unkempt, I should destroy her beauty in me, her vulgar, schoolgirl charms. We should see if Kopeida and Pimko were able to save her from such annihilation.

She walked in whistling, amusingly, in her pyjamas, with her towel round her neck—every movement precise and supple, all action. In a flash she was in the bathroom, and I dashed over to look at her. Now or never, while she was weakened and relaxed —but she moved so quickly that no relaxation could really affect her. She jumped into the bath and turned on the cold shower. She shook her hair, and her well-proportioned body shivered and shrank under the cold spray. Oh, it was she who seized me by the throat! Without being forced to by anyone, the girl took a cold shower before breakfast, exposing her shivering body to the chilly water to recover her day-time beauty in a youthful renewal.

I could not help admiring the self-discipline of the girl's beauty. Thanks to her speed, precision and virtuosity, she was able to evade that most delicate moment, the passage from night to day; she flew away like a butterfly on the wings of movement. Moreover, she offered her body to the cold water for a sharp, youthful renewal, for her instinct told her that a sharp dose like that neutralized the relaxation. What could harm youth thus whetted and renewed? When she turned the tap to stop the shower and remained naked, wet, and breathless, it was as if she had started living again. Oh, if she had used hot water and soap instead, it would have been useless; only cold water, by renewing her, could impose forgetfulness.

Abjectly and ignominiously I crawled from my hiding-place and went back to my room, convinced of the uselessness of going on spying on her, convinced that on the contrary, it might lead to my perdition. Hell and damnation! Another defeat—at the bottom-most pit of the modern hell I was still suffering defeats. I bit my fingers till the blood flowed, and swore not to admit that I was beaten, but to continue the mobilization of all my forces; and on the bathroom wall I wrote in pencil the words: *Veni, vidi, vici.* Let them at least know that I had seen them. Let them know that they were being watched. Let them know that the enemy did not sleep. Motorization and mobilization. I went to school. At school there was nothing new; Droopy, poetry, Bobek, Hopek, the infinitive and accusative, Kotecki, faces, backsides, finger in shoe, the usual daily impotence, boredom, boredom, and more boredom. As I foresaw, the effect of my note on Kopeida was imperceptible; perhaps he accentuated his leg a little more than usual, perhaps I only imagined it. On the other hand, my school-mates looked at me in horror, and Mientus actually said to me:

'Christ! What on earth have you been up to to get into that state?'

My face, after the motorization and mobilization, was in such a state of agitation that I did not really know what I was sitting on, but what did it matter? I was on tenterhooks, waiting for the night, for tonight was the night of decision. Tonight perhaps victory would be mine. Would Pimko succumb to the temptation? Would the experienced, masterly, double-barrelled master allow himself to be shaken out of his gravity by a childish-sensual letter? Everything depended on that. I prayed to God that Pimko might succumb. I prayed to God that he might lose his head—and all of a sudden I was seized with panic, at the faces and the backsides and the letter, and Pimko, all that had already happened and all that was going to happen, and I got up in the classroom to run away—and then sat down again, for where was I to run to? Backwards, forwards, left or right—could I run away from my own face and my own backside? Sit still, sit still, there's no way out. Tonight will decide. Tonight!

Nothing of note occurred at lunch. The girl and her mother were very laconic, and did not display their usual modernism. They were obviously uneasy; they felt the mobilization and motorization. I realized that the she-graduate was sitting in her chair stiffly, and not without a trace of discomfort, like someone who knows that her posterior has been spied on. The amusing thing was that this gave her a matronly air; this was an effect I had not foreseen. In any case she must certainly have seen my inscription on the bathroom wall. I tried to look at her with all the perspicacity possible, and I said in a pitiful, abject, and absent-minded way that my eyes were sharp and piercing enough to see right through her face. . . . She pretended not to hear, but the engineer exploded with laughter in spite of himself, and he went on laughing, spasmodically and automatically, for some time. Under the influence of recent events Youthful, if my eyes did not deceive me, was developing a certain taste for dirt—he buttered himself enormous slices of bread, stuffed his cheeks full of them, and masticated noisily.

After lunch I tried to spy on the girl through the keyhole, from four to six, but without success, for she did not once come within my field of vision; no doubt she was on her guard. I realized that her mother was spying on me in her turn. She found excuses to come several times into my room, and even naïvely offered to pay for me to go to the cinema. The quarry were becoming more uneasy, they sensed danger in the air without knowing what it was or what I was after—they sensed it, and it was demoralizing them—uncertainty made them uneasy, and there was nothing for their uneasiness to fasten on; they could not even talk about it, for it was so vague that words would only lead them into a bog. The she-graduate gropingly tried to organize some kind of defence and, as I observed, spent the whole afternoon reading Bertrand Russell, and gave H. G. Wells to her husband to read. But he said he preferred his collection of cabaret songs, and every now and then I heard him bursting into a loud guffaw. They were totally unable to pin down their anxiety to anything. In the end Mrs Youthful buried herself in her kitchen accounts, and the engineer started wandering round the house, sitting on one chair after another and humming some pretty lively songs. Knowing that I was in my room and giving no sign of life was getting on their nerves. It was for this reason that I kept completely silent. Silence, silence, silence; sometimes the silence became very intense indeed; the buzzing of a fly sometimes sounded as loud as a trumpet; the vague, the shadowy, the formless came creeping into the silence, and started forming patches of anxiety. Towards seven o'clock I noticed Mientus creeping furtively towards the kitchen and surreptitiously making signs to the maid.

At dusk the she-graduate also started sitting on one chair after another, and the engineer helped himself to a number of drinks in the pantry. They could find neither suitable form nor suitable place for themselves, they could not keep still; when they sat down they jumped up again as if they had been pinched, they moved about restlessly in all directions, as if they were being undermined as if there were an enemy—behind them. Reality, having emerged from its bed as the result of the shoves I had given it, now overflowed and blinded them, shrieked or rumbled obscurely, and darkness, absurd element of ugliness, dejection and depression, more palpably beset them and rose like a ferment on their increasing terror. When the she-graduate sat down to dinner she concentrated entirely on her face and the upper parts of her body. Youthful, however, appeared in his shirt-sleeves, tied his napkin under his chin, started buttering himself huge slices of bread, and told cabaret jokes, interrupted by loud bursts of laughter. He knew that I had seen him in the place in question, and that put him in a state of vulgar childishness; he adapted himself completely to what I had seen of him, and became the childish, smart, amusing little engineer, winning, whimsical, and mischievous. He also tried a few winks of connivance and comic signs of complicity on me, but to these I, sitting there pale-faced and neutral, naturally failed to respond. The girl sat in her place indifferent and tight-lipped, and with true childish heroism tried to ignore everything—oh, how I tremblingly admired this heroism, which further enhanced her beauty! But the night would decide, the night would pronounce its verdict and, if Pimko and Kopeida let me down, the modern girl would certainly be the winner, and then there would be no escape from my bondage.

Night came, and with it the hour of decision. The exact course of events could not be foreseen; all I knew was that I must co-operate with every distorting, disturbing, ridiculous, caricaturish and inharmonious thing that happened, with every destructive thing—and a faint and sorry sense of fear overcame me, a faint sense of fear, in comparison with which, however, the great fear of a murderer would have seemed negligible and ridiculous. Soon after eleven o'clock the girl went to bed. As I had previously made a slit in the door with a pair of scissors, I could now see the part of the room which had previously been outside my field of vision. The girl quickly undressed, got into bed, and turned out the light but, instead of going to sleep, kept tossing restlessly on her hard couch. She switched on the light again, took an English detective novel from the table, and forced herself to read. She sounded space with her eyes as if trying to detect the source of the threatening danger, to divine its form, to see the outline of the bogy, to guess the nature of the plot being hatched against her; she did not know that it had neither sense nor form—was non-sense, in fact something devoid of form or law, that a disturbing, styleless thing was threatening her modern style, and that was all.

I could hear voices from her parents' room, and dashed to the door. The engineer, in his pants, very gay and amusing, was still telling what were evidently cabaret stories.

'That's enough, Victor!'

Mrs Youthful, in her dressing-gown, was nervously rubbing her hands.

'That's enough, Victor, that's enough, stop it!'

'Just a minute, honey, just a minute, let me finish this one.'

'I'm not your honey, my name is Mary. Take off your pants or put on your trousers!'

'Pants, panties, pantaloons!'

'Stop it, will you?'

Abruptly she switched off the light.

'Hi! Turn the light on, Ma!'

'I'm not your ma, and I can't stand looking at you. What's the matter with you, what has come over you, what has come over all of us? Pull yourself together, because we march together towards the New Age. We who are the strugglers for, the builders, of the New Age!'

'That's the spirit, duckie, that's the spirit! My big duckie! My big duckie, always plucky, not so lucky! Wuff, wuff! Waiter, bring the pepper! Wuff, wuff!'

He didn't really want her any more, she had lost her freshness.

'Victor, Victor, what are you saying?'

'Vicky's enjoying himself, Vicky's having a good time, Vicky's being funny.'

'Victor, what on earth are you talking about? Remember the death penalty!' she exclaimed. 'The death penalty must be abolished. The Age We Live In. Civilization. Progress. Our hopes and aspirations. I keep telling you that I wish you wouldn't refer to yourself as Vicky! What's the matter with you? Zutka! Oh, what a nightmare. There's something evil, something horrible in the air. Treason . . .'

'Treasonkins!' said Youthful.

'No, Victor, no diminutives, please!'

'Treasonkins, Vicky said.'

'Victor!'

He started fondling her.

'Turn the light on!' the she-graduate exclaimed. 'Victor, turn the light on! Leave me alone!'

'Just wait!' exclaimed the engineer, laughing and out of breath, 'just wait, or I'll give you a slap! A slappikins on the neckikins!'

'You dare! Let go, or I'll bite you!'

'A slappikins, honeykins . . .'

And suddenly he started coming out with the whole of the vocabulary of the alcove that he had in reserve. . . . I recoiled in horror. Though not lacking in disgustingness myself, this was too much for me. The infernal *diminutive* which for some time had so totally oppressed my destiny started extending its sway to them. The engineer's excesses were appalling; oh, how monstrous is the petty bourgeois when he kicks over the traces, takes the bit between his teeth! What times ours were! There was the sound of a loud smack. Had he applied it to her face, her neck, or her behind?

The girl's room was now in darkness. Had she gone to sleep? Not a sound was to be heard, and I imagined her sleeping with her head on her arm, weary and half-covered by the bed-clothes. Suddenly she groaned; it was not the groan of a person asleep. She tossed violently and nervously on her divan-bed. I knew that she was panic-stricken, that her eyes were popping out of her head trying to pierce the darkness. Had her sensibilities become so acute that she knew I was looking at her in the dark through the slit? The groan, welling up from the dark depths, was exceedingly beautiful, as if her very star had moaned and vainly appealed for help.

She groaned again, quietly and desperately. Could she be aware that at this moment her father, depraved by me, was pawing her mother? Had she made out the horrors that were approaching from all sides? In the dark I seemed to see the girl wringing her hands, biting her arm till the blood flowed, as if she wished to penetrate with her teeth to the beauty enclosed within herself. The ugliness outside that was threatening every hole and corner of her drove her inwards towards her own charms. What a wealth of these she possessed! In the first place, she was a young girl. In the second place, she was a schoolgirl. In the third place, she was a modern girl. All this she had inside her like a nut in its shell; but she was unable to enter her own arsenal, though she felt my infamous eye upon her and knew that her rejected admirer was waiting to destroy, degrade, her beauty, mentally turn it into ugliness.

I was not in the least surprised when the girl, threatened with lurking ugliness like this, suddenly allowed a mad fit to carry her away completely. She jumped out of bed, took off her nightgown, and started dancing round the room. She ceased to care whether I were looking at her or not, it was now she who challenged and provoked me to battle. Her legs carried her lightly, her hands fluttered through the air, her head caressed her shoulders. She wound her arms round her head and shook her hair. She lay on the ground and got up again. She burst into tears, then started laughing and humming. She leapt on to the table, and from the table to the divan. It was as if she were frightened of stopping, as if she were being chased by rats and mice; and in taking wing like this she seemed to be trying to raise herself above the Atrocious Thing. She did not know where to take refuge. Finally she took a leather belt and started whipping her back with it, in order to suffer youthfully, painfully. . . . She gave me a lump in the throat. How she made her beauty suffer! How she degraded it, trampled on it, made it writhe in the dust! Standing with my eye to the keyhole, I nearly died, with my disgraceful, abject face, torn between hatred and admiration. Meanwhile, borne aloft again by her beauty, the girl danced more and more passionately. I adored and hated her, my whole being shuddered, my throat contracted and dilated convulsively, like indiarubber. Heavens, where the love of beauty can lead us!

The dining-room clock struck twelve. There were three almost inaudible taps on the window. I froze. It had begun. Kopeida was coming. Kopeida. The girl stopped dancing. Three more peremptory taps on the window. She went over and peeped out through the curtain.

'Is that you?'

The loud whisper floated up towards her in the night.

She drew aside the curtain, and moonlight flooded the room. I saw her standing in her night-gown, tense, expectant.

'Who is it?' she said.

I could not help admiring the virtuosity of this young creature. Kopeida's appearance at the window must obviously have taken her by surprise. Another girl in her place, an old-fashioned girl, would have got involved in conventional exclamations and questions. What on earth is the meaning of this? What are you doing here at this time of night? But the modern girl knew instinctively that showing surprise could only harm her, that it was much better not to show it. What finesse! She leaned out of the window, confidently, like a good friend and comrade.

'What do you want?' she said under her breath, holding her chin in her hands.

As he had used the familiar second person singular to her, she used it to him. I was filled with admiration for the incredible transformations of her style, the ease with which she passed straight from her crazy dance to this conversation. Who would have supposed that a moment before she had been leaping madly round the room? Kopeida, though modern too, was slightly disconcerted by her extraordinary composure, but he quickly attuned himself to it, and said to her with boyish indifference, his hands in his pockets:

'Let me in!'

'Why?'

He whistled and answered crudely.

'You know perfectly well. Let me in!'

He was excited, and there was a slight tremor in his voice, but he concealed it. I was afraid he might mention the letter, but fortunately the modern code forbade them to talk a great deal, or to be surprised at each other; they had to pretend that everything was straightforward and self-evident. Casualness, crudity, brevity and audacity—see how they struck sparks of poetry from themselves instead of the groans, sighs, and serenades of the lovers of former times. He knew that the only way of getting the girl was by jaunty indifference, and that there was no question of getting her without it. All the same, he added a trace of sensual and modern sentimentalism by saying, in a muffled voice and with his face against the virgin vine which was trained up the wall:

'You want it too!'

She made as if to shut the window. But suddenly, as if the gesture had persuaded her to do the very opposite, she stopped and pursed her lips. For a moment she remained motionless, only her eyes moving cautiously right and left. An expression of ultra-modern cynicism appeared on her face and, excited by this and his eyes and lips in the moonlight, she leant out of the window and stroked his hair with one hand in a way which was not playful.

'Come in!' she said.

Kopeida showed not the slightest surprise; he had no right to be surprised, either at her or at himself. The slightest hesitation would spoil everything. He must behave as if the whole thing were natural and normal, and he behaved accordingly. Oh, the virtuoso! He climbed through the window and jumped down on to the floor just as if he were in the habit every night of entering the bedroom of a schoolgirl whom he had met for the first time the day before. Once inside, he laughed silently, just to be on the safe side. But she took him by the hair, turned his head towards herself, and passionately put her lips to his.

Oh, God! Oh, God! If she were a virgin, if she were a virgin, if she were a virgin—and offered herself without compunction to the first man who knocked at her window—oh, God! Oh, God! A lump came into my throat. If she were a tart, a sensualist, it would not matter in the least but, if she were a virgin, it must be confessed that she knew how to strike a wild beauty out of Kopeida and herself. Taking the boy by the hair so impudently, so crudely, and so naturally, and in complete silence—and taking me by the throat. Oh! she knew I was watching through the slit, and that was why she shrank from nothing in order to crush me with her beauty. I shuddered. If only it had been he who had taken her by the hair! But no, it had been she. Oh, you young ladies, you ordinary young ladies who get married with great pomp and ceremony, you commonplace young ladies who sometimes permit us to steal a kiss, see how a modern girl opens herself to love and to herself! She pushed Kopeida on to the bed. Again I shuddered. The frenzy was beginning. The girl was obviously playing the trump card of her beauty. I prayed for Pimko to arrive; if he did not, I was lost, I should never, never, never be able to escape from the girl's wild spell. I, who had dreamed of throttling her, was being throttled by her, I who had dreamed of victory, was going down to defeat.

Meanwhile the girl, in the supreme blossoming of her youth, lay entwined with Kopeida on the divan, preparing, with his aid to reach the summit of her enchantments—quite simply, never mind how, without love, and sensually, with no respect for herself or anything else, for the sole purpose of throttling me by her wild, schoolgirl's poetry. Oh, God! Oh, God! She was winning, winning, winning, all along the line!

At last I heard the sound which was my salvation. There was a tap on the window. At last! Pimko was coming up in support. The decisive moments were approaching. Would Pimko manage to destroy her? Might he not do the reverse, might he not increase her beauty and her spell? That was what I thought to myself

174

behind the door, preparing my face to intervene. Meanwhile Pimko's taps on the window brought some slight relief, because it forced them to interrupt their transports.

'Somebody's tapping,' Kopeida muttered.

The girl leapt briskly from the divan. They listened hard, to see if it were safe to return to their revels. There was another tap on the window.

'Who is it?' the girl said. An ardent, guttural voice came from outside.

'Zutka!'

She drew aside the curtain, signalling to Kopeida to withdraw, but Pimko came tumbling into the room before she had a chance to speak; he was afraid of being seen from the street.

'My little Zutka!' he muttered passionately. 'My little Zutka! My little Zutka!'

My letter had turned his head. The commonplace professor with the double-barrelled nose had had his mouth painfully distorted by poetry.

'My darling little Zutka! Won't anyone see us? Where is your mother?'

He was intoxicated even more by the danger than by my letter.

'Oh!' he exclaimed. 'Such a child, so young, so impudent . . . to say nothing of the difference in age and position. How could you . . . how did you dare . . . to me? So you felt something for me? So you felt something for me? Say something . . . tell me what it is that attracts you in me!'

Oh! Oh! Oh! the dirty old professor!

'What . . . what do you mean?' the girl stammered.

The affair with Kopeida was over, finished.

'There's somebody here!' Pimko exclaimed in the semi-darkness.

Silence answered him. Kopeida kept mum. The girl stood between them, in her night-gown, void of significance, annihilated.

It was at this point that I shouted from behind the door:

175

'Burglars! Thieves! Burglars!'

Pimko spun round like a top several times and jumped into the wardrobe. Kopeida tried to jump out of the window, but didn't have time, and hid in the other wardrobe. I burst into the room as I was, in trousers and shirt-sleeves. I'd got them! I'd got them! The Youthfuls followed close behind me, he still pawing her, she still pawed by him.

'Burglars?' the engineer, in trousers and bare feet, exclaimed vulgarly, the private property instinct awakening within him.

'Someone came in through the window,' I said. I switched on the light. The girl had gone back to bed and was pretending to be asleep.

'What's the matter, what's happening?' she asked in impeccable style.

'Another intrigue!' exclaimed Mrs Youthful, in her dressing-gown, with red cheeks and dishevelled hair looking at me like a basilisk.

'Intrigue?' I said, picking up Kopeida's braces, which were lying on the ground. 'Intrigue?'

'A pair of braces!' the engineer said with stolid stupidity.

'They're mine!' the girl impudently announced.

Her insolence produced an agreeable effect, though obviously nobody believed her. I kicked open the wardrobe door, exposing to view the lower part of Kopeida's body, that is to say, two legs in a pair of well-creased flannel trousers and two feet in light sports shoes. The rest of him was hidden by the dresses.

'Oh, Zutka!' Mrs Youthful said.

The girl hid her head under the blanket, leaving nothing to be seen but her legs and some of her hair. With what art did she play the game! Another in her place would have started protesting, trying to make excuses. But she merely stretched her bare legs, and in moving them played on the situation as on a flute. Her parents exchanged glances.

'Zutka!' Youthful said.

And he and his wife started laughing. All trace of pawing, vulgarity, disappeared from them, and a strange beauty prevailed.

Her parents, enchanted, delighted, happy, laughed joyously, and looked at the girl, who was still capriciously and wildly hiding her head. Kopeida, seeing that there was nothing to fear from the severe principles of the old days, emerged from the wardrobe, and stood there with a smile on his face, a fair boy with his jacket over his arm, caught by a girl's parents. Youthful looked at me spitefully out of the corner of his eye. He was triumphant. I must still have been under the magic spell; I had wanted to compromise the girl, but the modern boy did not in any way compromise her. To make me feel the full weight of my defeat, Mrs Youthful said:

'What is this young man doing here? It's no affair of his!'

So far I had deliberately refrained from opening the door of Pimko's wardrobe; before I did so I wanted the situation to be consolidated in the plenitude of its modern style. But now I silently opened the wardrobe. Pimko was huddled behind the frocks; only a pair of legs, professorial legs in a pair of crumpled trousers, were standing there, incongruously, improbably, absurdly. The effect was utterly disconcerting. The smile was wiped from the Youthfuls' lips. The whole situation tottered, as if an assassin had stabbed it in the flank. It was ridiculous.

'What's the meaning of this?' exclaimed the girl's mother, growing pale.

From behind the frocks there emerged a slight cough and a forced little laugh, with which Pimko prepared his entrance. Knowing that he must now face ridicule, he forestalled it with a little laugh. The effect of this from behind the dresses was so Rabelaisian that Youthful guffawed and then stopped. . . . Pimko emerged from the wardrobe, outwardly ridiculous, inwardly wretched. I felt wild sadism rising within me, but outwardly I laughed. In that laugh lay my revenge.

The Youthfuls, however, were dumbfounded. Two men in two wardrobes? And one of them an old man into the bargain? Two young men—or even two old men—well, at a pinch. But one young man and one old man? And the old man Pimko of all people? The situation had no axis and no diagonal, and what possible explanation could there be for it? They glanced mechanically at their daughter, but she lay motionless under the blanket.

It was then that Pimko, hemming and hah-ing and with an imploring smile, set about trying to clear up the situation. He started by talking about the letter—which Miss Zutka had written him—that for his part he had wished to use Norwid to—but Miss Zutka had addressed him in the second person singular—he had wished to do the same to her—and that was all. . . .

Never in my life had I heard anything so lame and stupid; the private, secret content of the little old man's ramblings became impossible in a situation clearly illuminated by the electric light in the centre of the ceiling; nobody wanted to understand him, and so nobody understood him. Pimko realized this, but his retreat was cut off. The master, knocked off his perch, was utterly confounded; it seemed impossible that this was the same infallible, double-barrelled professor who not so long before had made me a little backside. His explanation took him deeper and deeper into the mire, and his softness was pitiable; I could easily have gone for him, but instead found myself making a gesture of indifference. His obscure and tangled ramblings drove the engineer to formality—this impulse put in the shade the mistrust with which he regarded my part in the affair. He exclaimed:

'What I want to know is this. What are you doing here at this time of night?'

His peremptoriness set the tone for Pimko. For a moment he recovered his style.

'Please do not raise your voice,' he said.

'What? You permit yourself such observations in my house?' Youthful replied.

At this point Mrs Youthful, who was looking out of the window, let out a little shriek. A bearded face, with a green twig in its mouth, appeared over the railing. I had totally forgotten the beggar. That day, as on the previous day, I had told him to put the twig in his mouth, but I had forgotten to give him his money. He had waited patiently all the evening, and now, seeing us through the window, he came forward to show us his beflowered, hired face, and to remind us of his existence. He turned up like a new dish at a restaurant.

'What does he want?' the she-graduate exclaimed. She could not have been more frightened by a ghost. Pimko and Youthful fell silent.

The wretched man, on whom general attention was now momentarily concentrated, waggled his twig as if it were a moustache. He did not know what to say, so he said:

'Kind ladies and gentlemen, kind ladies and gentlemen!'

'Give him something!'

The she-graduate dropped her hands to her sides and clenched her fists.

'Give him something and tell him to go away!' she shrieked hysterically.

The engineer searched his trouser-pockets, but they were empty. Pimko, clutching convulsively at any change in the situation, hoping perhaps that if in the mounting confusion Youthful accepted money from him his hostility would thereby be somewhat diminished, quickly held out his purse, but Youthful refused it. The question of finding change irrupted through the window and assaulted mankind. As for me, there I was, with my face, observing the course of events, ready to pounce. But in reality I was already looking at it all as if through a pane of glass. Where was my irruption, my revenge, the crash of shattered reality, the collapse of style, and my triumph over the wreckage? This farce was beginning to bore me. Random ideas and questions started passing through my head, such as: Where does Kopeida buy his ties? Does the she-graduate like cats? How much rent do they pay?

Meanwhile Kopeida remained motionless, with his hands in his pockets. He took no notice of me, treated me like a stranger. He was much too angry at being associated with Pimko (from the point of view of the girl) to have any desire to greet a school-fellow in shirt-sleeves; both associations were supremely distasteful to him. When the Youthfuls and Pimko started looking

179

for change he started moving unhurriedly towards the door. I opened my mouth to call out, but Pimko, who had noticed Kopeida's manœuvre, quickly closed his purse and followed his example. The engineer, however, leapt after them like a cat at a mouse.

'One moment, please!' he exclaimed. 'You are not going to leave like this!'

Kopeida and Pimko stopped. Kopeida, furious at Pimko's companionship, moved away from him; but Pimko closed the gap between them again, and so they remained, standing side by side, like two brothers, one old, one young.

The she-graduate, in a dreadful state of nerves, seized her husband's arm.

'Don't make a scene!' she said. 'Don't make a scene!'

This of course provoked him into making a scene.

'Pardon me!' he shouted. 'Pardon me! I am, I believe, the girl's father! I want to know how, and why, you two entered my daughter's room. What is the meaning of it? What is the meaning of it?'

His eyes suddenly fell on me, and he stopped; fear came over his cheeks, he realized that this was grist for my mill, the mill of scandal—and, if he could, he would have fled, abandoned the field. But the words had been spoken, and he could not withdraw them, so he repeated them, but this time more quietly and simply, and merely for the sake of being consistent, inwardly hoping that no one would take up the question:

'What is the meaning of it?'

Silence reigned. No one was able to reply. Everyone present had a good private and personal explanation of his own, but the sum-total of the situation was totally devoid of meaning. Absurdity suffocated in the silence. Then from under the blankets there came the sound of the girl's desperate, muffled sobbing. Oh, the little virtuoso! She sobbed with her naked calves projecting from the blankets, and the louder she sobbed the more conspicuous her calves became, and her sobs united Pimko, Kopeida, and her parents, enveloped them all in a single, desperate, diabolical note. In a flash the affair ceased to be ridiculous and absurd, recovered its meaning, even a modern meaning, though shadowy, sombre, dramatic, and tragic. Kopeida, Pimko and the Youthfuls felt better—and I felt worse, seized by the throat.

'You depraved her,' her mother muttered. 'Don't cry, darling, don't cry!'

'My compliments, professor!' the engineer said angrily. 'You'll give me satisfaction for this!'

Pimko seemed a trifle relieved; this was better than his previous floundering. So they had 'depraved' her. The situation was turning in the girl's favour.

'The police!' I exclaimed. 'Send for the police!'

This was a pretty risky step on my part, seeing that for centuries the police and under-age girls have formed a harmonious, beautiful, and grim combination—that was why the girl's parents both proudly raised their heads; but my object was to terrorize Pimko. He grew pale, gurgled, and coughed.

'The police!' Mrs Youthful repeated, taking pleasure in the thought of the police in the presence of her daughter's bare calves. 'The police, the police!'

'Believe me,' the professor stammered. 'Believe me, you are making a grave mistake, you are accusing me unjustly . . .'

'That is true,' I chimed in. 'I am a witness. I saw everything out of the window. The professor came into the garden because of a necessity of nature. Just at that moment Miss Zutka happened to look out of the window, and the professor had no alternative but to say good evening to her. They got talking, and he popped into the house for a moment.'

Pimko, abject at the thought of the police, seized on this, without realizing its disgusting and repugnant implications.

'That's perfectly true,' he said, 'that's perfectly true, I was in a hurry, and I came into your garden, forgetting that you lived here—and the young lady saw me out of the window—so I had to pretend to be paying a visit—you will understand—

in such a delicate situation—*quid pro quo, quid pro quo,*' he repeated.

This explanation had a disconcerting and shocking effect on all those present. The girl hid her calves. Kopeida pretended not to have heard it. Mrs Youthful turned her back on Pimko but, realizing that it was her back that she was turning on him, turned and faced him again. Youthful's eyelids were flickering. Once more they found themselves in the grip of that infernal part of the body—vulgarity came flooding in over them, and I observed with curiosity how it submerged and overwhelmed them. Was it the same vulgarity as that in which I had recently been sunk? Yes, it seemed to be, but now it was restricted to them alone. No more sign of life came from the girl under the blanket. Youthful guffawed; it was impossible to say what had tickled him; perhaps he associated Pimko's *quid pro quo* with a Warsaw cabaret which once bore that name. He definitely succumbed to the gruesome, buttocky, second-hand laughter of any second-rate little engineer. But this explosion made him lose his temper with Pimko; he leapt at him, and pettily and arrogantly slapped his face. Having done so, he stopped still, his hand still raised, panting for breath. He stiffened and grew serious. I went to my room to get my jacket and shoes, and started slowly dressing, without losing sight of the situation.

Strange rumblings emerged from Pimko as a result of having his face slapped, and he started trembling, but I felt convinced that inwardly he was grateful for the slap, which in some way put him in his place.

'You will give me satisfaction for this,' he said coldly, but with obvious relief. He bowed slightly to the engineer, and the engineer returned the compliment. Pimko took advantage of this to make hurriedly for the door. Kopeida associated himself with the exchange of courtesies, and hastily tried to smuggle himself out in Pimko's wake. At this Youthful started. What! With a question of honour at stake, with a duel in the air, this young puppy proposed to walk quietly out of the house just as if everything were perfectly normal? He had better have his face slapped too. The engineer moved towards him with raised hand, but at the last moment must have decided that it was beneath his dignity to slap the face of a stripling, a schoolboy. His hand hesitated but, being now unable to withdraw, he took the boy by the chin. This indignity infuriated Kopeida more than a slap in the face would have done, and—after the last long quarter of an hour of total absurdity—unleashed his most primitive instincts. Heaven knows what went on in his head; he must have thought that the engineer had done it on purpose, that if you ... I'll ... or something of the sort. In any case, responding to a law that might well be described as that of deviation, he bent down and seized the engineer below the knee. The engineer collapsed, and Kopeida plunged his teeth into his left side and held on like a bull-dog, refusing to let go, glaring round the room with a maniacal look in his eyes.

I was just putting on my jacket and tie, but I stopped, out of sheer curiosity. Never before had I been present at such a scene. The she-graduate hastened to her husband's assistance, seized Kopeida's leg, and pulled with all her might and main. This led to another, more complete, collapse. On top of it all Pimko, who was standing only a foot away from the *mêlée*, did something very curious and almost impossible to describe. Had the master lost all self-confidence? Did he lack the strength to remain on his feet while everyone else was on the floor? Did he think that it could not be worse on the floor than on his feet? Whatever the reason, he deliberately and of his own free will collapsed on to his back and raised his limbs in a gesture of complete subsidence. I was just tying my tie. I did not turn a hair even when the girl, suddenly emerging from under her blanket, started—just like an umpire at a boxing match—jumping round her parents, who were struggling on the ground with Kopeida, and calling out: 'Mummy! Daddy!' between her tears. In the midst of the seething ant-heap the crazed engineer, seeking something to hold on to, grabbed her leg just above the ankle and brought her down too; and there all four of them wallowed—in dead silence, as in church—for shame, after all, had them in its grip. At one point I saw Mrs Youthful biting her daughter, Kopeida clutching Mrs Youthful, the engineer punching Kopeida; a moment later one of the girl's calves appeared over her mother's head.

Meanwhile the professor in his corner started feeling a more and more definite attraction for the fray. Lying on his back with all four hoofs in the air, he imperceptibly but definitely edged towards it. He could not get up, he had no reason to, and he could not go on lying on his back; and the inverted ant-heap had become the only way out for him. When the family, accompanied by Kopeida, brushed against him in the course of the struggle he seized Youthful—I don't know where, but I think not far from the liver—and then he was carried off in the maelstrom. I finished packing my most essential things in an attaché case, and put on my hat. They bored me. Good-bye, modern girl, good-bye, Youthful and Kopeida, good-bye, Pimko—no, you can't say good-bye to something that has ceased to exist. Lightly I took my leave. How delightful to shake the dust from one's feet and go away, leaving nothing behind! Was it really true that that arch-pedagogue Pimko had made me a little behind, that I had been a schoolboy, a modern boy with the modern girl, that I had danced a jig in the room, torn off a fly's wings, spied on them in the bathroom, and all the rest of it? No, it had all vanished, now I was neither young nor old, neither modern nor ancient, nor a schoolboy, neither mature nor immature, I was nothing at all, I was zero. Walking out and taking no memories with me. Oh, sweet indifference, sweet oblivion! When everything is dead inside you and nobody has yet succeeded in begetting you again. Oh, it is worth the agony of having lived for death, just knowing that everything inside you is dead, that nothing exists any longer—emptiness and youth, silence and purity—and as I took my leave it seemed to me that I was not going alone, but with myself, that next to me or inside me or around me—someone the same as myself, someone who was in me and mine was with me—and between us there was neither love nor hate, neither laughter nor parts of the body, nor any feeling nor any mechanism, but nothing, nothing at all—for a millionth of a second. For on making my way through the kitchen, groping in the dark, I heard a voice quietly calling me, coming from the recess where the maid slept.

'Johnnie! Johnnie!'

It was Mientus, who was sitting on the maid, quickly putting on his shoes.

'It's me!' he said. 'Are you going out? Wait a minute, I'll come with you!'

His whisper struck me broadside on, and I stopped as if I had been hit. I couldn't make out his face in the dark, but it must have been dreadful. The maid was snoring heavily.

'Sh! Quiet! Come along!'

He got down off the maid.

'This way, this way . . . careful, mind that basket!'

We reached the street. Dawn was breaking. The little houses, the railings and the bushes, were all arranged tidily in straight lines, and the air, which was clear at ground level, condensed higher up into a desperate mist. Asphalt. Emptiness. Dew. Nothing. Beside me Mientus adjusted his clothing. I tried not to look at him. Behind the open windows of the house the electric light was in its death throes and the puffing and blowing and panting of the *mêlée* continued. The cool air filtered into my bones, the cold of a sleepless night; I started shivering and my teeth started chattering. When Mientus passed the window he noticed the snorting coming from the Youthfuls.

'What's up?' he remarked. 'Is somebody being given a rub-down?'

I didn't answer. Mientus noticed the attaché case I was carrying and said:

'Are you going away?'

I lowered my head. I knew that he would stick to me, that he would follow me, that he would catch me up, for we were both . . .

'Are you going away?' he repeated. 'Then I'll come with you. We'll go together. I've raped the girl. But that's not the reason

. . . it's the stable-lad, the stable-lad. Let's run away to the country! Together! The stable-lad, Johnnie, the stable-lad!' he repeated obstinately.

I held my head straight and stiff, without looking at him.

'Mientus,' I said. 'What do I care about you and your stable-lad?'

But when I walked off he walked with me, and I walked with him, and we walked together.

Introduction to Philimor
Honeycombed with Childishness

ANOTHER preface . . . I must provide a preface, a preface is required of me, without a preface I cannot possibly go on. It is my duty to provide a preface, for the law of symmetry here demands the insertion of *Philimor Honeycombed with Childishness* as balance and counterweight to *Philifor Honeycombed with Childishness*; and similarly the introduction to *Philifor Honeycombed with Childishness* must be balanced by an introduction to *Philimor Honeycombed with Childishness*. Whether I like it or not, I cannot, no I simply cannot, evade the iron laws of symmetry and analogy. Moreover, it is time to interrupt, to make an end of, to emerge, even if only momentarily, from greenness and immaturity, and to look a little more sensibly under the crazy burgeoning of buds and pimples and little leaves, to prevent people from saying that I'm as mad as a hatter, incurable poor chap. And before going farther down the path of inferior, intermediate, sub-human terrors, I must explain, specify, rationalize, classify, bring out the root idea underlying all the other ideas in the book, demonstrate and make plain the essential grief, the great-grandmother of all the other griefs which are here isolated and exposed; and I must establish a hierarchy of griefs and a hierarchy of ideas, comment on the work in an analytic, synthetic and philosophical manner, to enable the reader to find its head, legs, nose, and fingers, and to prevent him from coming and telling me that I don't know what I'm driving at, and that instead of marching forward straight and erect like the great writers of all ages, I am merely revolving ridiculously on my own heels. What, then, shall the fundamental, overriding anguish be? Where art thou, great-grandmother of all griefs? The deeper I dig, the more I explore and analyse, the more clearly do I see that in reality the primary, the fundamental grief is purely and simply, in my opinion, the agony of bad outward form, defective appearance, the agony of phraseology, grimaces, faces . . . yes, that is the origin, the source, the fount from which there flow harmoniously all the other torments, follies, and afflictions without any exceptions whatever. Or perhaps it would be as well to emphasize that the primary and fundamental agony is that born of the constraint of man by man . . . i.e. from the fact that we suffocate and stifle in the narrow and rigid idea of ourselves that others have of us. Or at the basis of the book perhaps there lies the supreme and fatal torment

of sub-human greenness, of spots, pimples, little leaves
or the torment of undeveloped development
or, perhaps, the pain of unformed form
or the burden of being created inside ourselves by others
the agony of physical and psychological violation
the torment of concentrated inter-human tensions
the curving and not yet fully explained torment of psycho-
    logical deviation
the marginal discomfort of psychological dislocation and
    psychological failure
the constant pain of treachery and dishonour
the automatic suffering of mechanization and automatism
the symmetrical torture of analogy and the analogical torture
    of symmetry
the analytic torment of synthesis and the synthetic torment
    of analysis
or, again, the suffering of the parts of the body, and dismay
    about the hierarchy of its various parts
the affliction of benign infantilism
of futile pedagogy and pedanticism

of hopeless innocence and naïveté
of remoteness from reality
of chimaeras, illusions, aberration, pretence
of higher idealism
of lower, crude, petty idealism
second-rate dreams
of being reduced in size, or rather the astonishing torment of
　being reduced in size
the torment of being the eternal candidate
the torment of aspiration
of interminable apprenticeship
or, perhaps, the torment of trying to suppress oneself,
　exceeding one's own strength, and the resulting torment of
　general and particular impotence
the erosion of superiority
the suffering of looking down on people
the suffering of superior and inferior poetry
the dull torment of a psychological *cul-de-sac*
the tortuous torture of the tortuous, of the dirty, underhand
　blow, or, rather the sadness of the age, in the general and
　particular meaning of the word
the torment of anachronism, the torment of modernism
the suffering caused by the formation of new social stratifica-
　tions
the torment of the half-educated
or perhaps simply the torment of micro-educated indecorous-
　ness
the pain of stupidity
wisdom
ugliness
beauties, spells and enchantments
or, perhaps, the deadly pain of logic and consistency in stupidity
the desolation of acting a part
the desperation of imitation
the brutalizing torment of brutalization and of saying the same
　thing over and over again

or, probably, the hypomanic torture of hypomania
the unspeakable sadness of the unspeakable
the sadness of non-sublimation
pain in the finger
nail
tooth
ear

the terrifying torture of mutual interdependence and mutual
barriers, of reciprocal interpenetration of all torments and all
parts, the pain of one hundred and fifty-six thousand three
hundred and twenty-four and a half other pains, not counting
women and children (as a sixteenth-century French writer
would say). Which torture shall we choose as the great-grandmother of all tortures, which part shall we pick on as our point
of departure, where shall we seize hold of the book and which
of the tortures and parts in question shall we choose? Oh
accursed parts, shall I never get rid of you? What a wealth of
parts, and what a multitude of tortures! Where shall we find the
great-grandmother who established the guiding lines, which
torture shall we take as basic? The metaphysical torture? The
physical torture? The sociological torture? Or the psychological
torture? Nevertheless I must attempt the task, I must, I have no
choice, or people would say that I didn't know what I was aiming
at, that I was stupidly revolving on my own heels. Perhaps it
would be wiser not to specify and demonstrate the essence of the
book in terms of tortures at all, but to discuss it in relation to its
subject-matter, show that it was born of

hostility to pedagogues and their charges
the prevalence of besotted scholars
sympathy with devoted and profound minds
involvement with the most prominent figures in our con-
    temporary national literature and the most hallowed and
    representative critics
dislike of schoolgirls

the patronage of mature and distinguished figures
the patronage of distinguished men, connoisseurs, narcissists,
   aesthetes, brilliant intellectuals
dislike of connoisseurs
of being tied to the cultural aunts' apron-strings
dislike of urban overcrowding
the background of the country aristocracy
involvement with small provincial doctors, engineers, and
   clerks with limited horizons
involvement with high officials and leading doctors and lawyers
   with the broadest horizons
involvement with the aristocracy of birth, and other aris-
   tocracies
dislike of the vulgar

Probably, however, the work was to a certain extent born
as a result of co-existence with real persons, the exceedingly
repulsive Mr X, for instance, or Mr Z, whom I detest, or Mr N,
who horrifies and bores me . . . oh, the maddening torment of
being in their company! And perhaps the basic aim and purpose
of the book is merely to demonstrate to these gentlemen the
whole extent of the contempt that I feel for them, to get on their
nerves, to irritate and anger them, and to put me out of their
reach. In that case the purpose of the book would be definite,
concrete, private.

Or, who knows? it might have been written in imitation of
   masterpieces
or out of inability to write an ordinary book?
or as a result of dreams?
Or complexes?
Or childish memories?
Or, perhaps, I just started, and my pen ran away with me?
Or perhaps it was the result of a fear psychosis?
Or some other psychosis?
Or just a blunder?

Or a pinch?
Or a part?
Or a particle?
Or a finger?

Also the task is to evaluate and to assess, and to decide whether the work is a novel, or a book of memoirs, or a parody, or a lampoon, or a variation on imaginative themes, or a psychological study; and to establish its predominant characteristics; whether the whole thing is a joke, or whether its importance lies in its deeper meaning, or whether it is just irony, sarcasm, ridicule, invective, downright stupidity and nonsense, or a piece of pure leg-pulling; and, moreover, to make sure that it is not just a pose, a piece of mystification, a fraud, or the result of a total lack of humour, a total deficiency of feeling or atrophy of the imagination, a collapse of all sense of order, and a total loss of reason. But the sum-total of all these possibilities, torments, descriptions and parts is so vast, so incommensurable, so inconceivable and, what is more, so inexhaustible, that, with the most profound respect for the Word, and after the most scrupulous analysis, it must be admitted that we are no wiser than when we began, cluck! cluck! cluck! as the chicken said. So I invite those who wish to plunge still deeper and get a still better idea of what it is all about to turn to the next page and read my *Philimor Honeycombed with Childishness*, for its mysterious symbolism contains the answer to all tormenting questions. Philimor, then, having definitely been constructed on the basis of analogy with Philifor, conceals in this strange relationship the secret and definitive meaning of the whole work. After the reader has successfully fished this up into the light of day, there will be nothing to prevent him from plunging still deeper into the dense jungle of the monotonous separate parts.

* 12 *

Philimor Honeycombed with Childishness

AT the end of the eighteenth century a Paris peasant had a child; this child eventually had a child too, and so did this latter child; and so child followed child, until one fine afternoon the last child, having become champion of the world, was competing in a tennis tournament at the Racing Club in Paris, in a tense atmosphere and to the accompaniment of thunderous applause.

However (oh, what strange mischances life holds in store for us!) a certain colonel of Zouaves who was sitting in one of the side seats started envying the brilliant and impeccable play of the two champions; and suddenly, to show the six thousand spectators what he was capable of—particularly as his girl-friend was seated by his side—he took out his pistol and fired at the ball as it flew between the two rackets. The ball burst, and fell to the ground. For some time the two champions continued making strokes in the void, but then, exasperated by the folly of such pointless activity, they dashed at each other and started fighting. The audience burst into thunderous applause.

There, no doubt, the matter might have ended. But an unforeseen contingency arose. In his excitement the colonel (oh, how careful one must be in life!) had not taken into account the spectators sitting in the stand opposite. He had assumed, heaven knows why, that after piercing the tennis ball the bullet would go no farther. But, unfortunately, it continued its trajectory, and hit a shipowner in the neck. Blood spurted from the severed artery, and the first impulse of the injured man's wife was to fling herself at the colonel and seize his pistol. This was impossible, however, as she was hemmed in by the crowd, so she contented herself with slapping the face of her right-hand neighbour. She did so because there was no other outlet for her indignation and because, in accordance with her essentially feminine logic, she felt (in the innermost depths of her unconscious) that, being a woman, everything was permitted her.

But obviously things did not turn out as she expected. For the man she slapped (oh, how fallible are our calculations and how unpredictable our destinies!) happened to be suffering from latent epilepsy; under the influence of the shock he had a fit, and started foaming like a geyser. The unhappy woman found herself between a man spitting blood and another foaming at the mouth. The crowd burst into thunderous applause.

At this point a gentleman who was sitting quite near panicked, and jumped on to the head of a lady seated below him. She rose to her feet, bounded forward, and landed on the court, carrying the man on her back with her in her mad career. The crowd burst into thunderous applause. And there, to be sure, the whole thing might have ended, but for the fact (which only goes to show that in this world one should always be ready for anything and never take anything for granted) that a few yards away there happened to be sitting a poor devil, an obscure retired dreamer, who for years past, whenever he attended any public spectacle, had always ardently desired to jump down on to the heads of the people seated below him, and had restrained himself from doing so only with the greatest difficulty. Now, stimulated by this example, without a moment's hesitation he jumped down on to the woman seated immediately in front of him. The latter (she was a badly paid clerk who had arrived only recently from Tangier) assumed this behaviour to be normal and correct, in fact, that this was how people behaved in high society . . . so she too staggered on to the court beneath her burden, taking care that her movements did not betray the slightest sign of nervousness or timidity.

The educated section of the audience started tactfully applauding, in order to conceal the scandal from the eyes of the representatives of foreign embassies and legations. But at this point a misunderstanding occurred; other, less well educated, spectators took the applause as signifying approval, and all the gentlemen started mounting the backs of their ladies. The foreigners looked on with growing astonishment. What could the more distinguished spectators do in these circumstances? They had no alternative but to mount the backs of their ladies too.

And that, certainly or almost certainly, is how the whole thing might have ended. But at this point a certain Marquis de Philimor, who was sitting with his wife and members of her family in the distinguished visitors' seats, suddenly felt his noble blood rising within him; and he appeared in the centre of the court, in his light summer suit and looking pale but determined, and asked in icy tones if anyone, and if so who, desired to insult the Marquise de Philimor, his wife; and he flung into the faces of the crowd a handful of visiting cards on which were inscribed the words 'Philippe de Philimor'. (Oh, how difficult and dangerous life is, how careful we must be!) There was a deathly hush.

Suddenly at least thirty-six gentlemen, riding their thin-ankled, thoroughbred women bareback, approached the *marquise* in order to insult her and feel as blue-blooded as the *marquis*, her husband. She, however (oh, how mad, how crazy, is life!) was so terrified that she had a miscarriage, and the wailing of an infant was heard at the *marquis*'s feet, under the shoes of the prancing women.

The *marquis*, thus suddenly honeycombed and riddled with childishness, doubled and completed by a baby just at the very moment when he was behaving in a particularly adult and gentlemanly fashion, suddenly felt ashamed of himself and went off home, while thunderous applause broke out among the spectators.

* 13 *

Out of the Frying Pan

So off we set, Mientus and I, in search of a stable-boy. We turned the corner, and the villa, and everything else to do with the Youthfuls, vanished from sight. In front of us there stretched the long, shiny ribbon of the Filtrowa road. The sun rose like a yellow ball, we had breakfast at a hairdresser's, the town woke up, it was eight o'clock by now, and off we went again, I with my little attaché case and Mientus with a knotty stick. The birds chirruped and chirped. Onward! Onward! Mientus strode cheerfully, borne along by hope, and his hope infected me, his slave. 'To the outskirts! To the outskirts!' he kept repeating. 'There we'll find a smashing stable-boy, a smashing stable-boy!' The stable-boy painted the morning in bright and pleasing colours; how amusing and agreeable it was to cross the city in search of a stable-boy! Who was I about to become? What would they make of me? What awaited me? I did not know, but trotted along bravely behind my master, Mientus, and I could neither grieve nor suffer, because I was cheerful. The entrances to the houses, which were not very numerous in this district, were infested with hall-porters and their families. Mientus glanced at them all, but what a difference there is between a hall-porter and a stable-boy! Is not a hall-porter merely a potted peasant? Every now and then we saw a hall-porter's son, but not one that satisfied Mientus—is it not also true that a hall-porter's son is a caged, tamed, stable-boy? 'There's no wind here,' Mientus said. 'Between these houses there are nothing but draughts, and I can't conceive of a stable-boy in a draught. For me a stable-boy can exist only in a strong wind.'

We left behind nannies and nursemaids pushing creaky prams. Adorned in finery inherited from their mistresses, and with buckled heels, they cast us coquettish glances. Perfumed, with Greta Garbo hair-dos, two gold teeth, and somebody else's child. We saw managers and clerks on their way to work with briefcases under their arm, all in papier mâché, looking very Slavonic and very clerkish, the husbands of their wives and the boss of the female servants, all cuffs and buttons which they wore as if they were adornments of their ego. Above them was the vastness of the sky. We passed a number of smartly dressed women in fur coats—Warsaw chic—some thin and vivacious, others slower and softer—buried under their hats and so alike that they overtook and passed one another without one's realizing it. Mientus did not think them worthy of a glance, and I was so bored that I started yawning.

'To the outskirts!' he cried. 'To the outskirts! There we shall find the stable-boy. Here there's nothing, everything's cheap and nasty, nothing but the cows and horses of the petty bourgeoisie, doctors' wives and doctors, like old cart-horses. Trash and pestilence! Cows and mules! Look how educated and dumb they are! Distinguished and vulgar!'

At the corner of Wawelska Street we caught sight of some public buildings conceived in the grand style, the impressive sight of which nourishes vast masses of hungry and anaemic taxpayers. These buildings reminded us of school, so we quickened our pace. In Narutowicz Square, where the Students' Hostel is, we came upon the academic fraternity, with threadbare sleeves, short of sleep and ill-shaven, in a hurry to get to their lectures and waiting for the tram. With their noses stuck in their books, they were all munching hard-boiled eggs, stuffing the shells in their pockets and breathing the town dust.

'Nothing but ex-stable-boys,' Mientus exclaimed. 'Peasants' sons working for degrees! To hell with ex-stable-boys! How I hate them! They still pick their noses and study text-books! Book-learning in a stable-boy! Stable-boy lawyer, stable-boy doctor! See how their minds get stuffed with learned jargon!

Look at their great clumsy fingers! It's as disgusting as if they were becoming monks! Some of them would make fine stable-boys, but what's the good of them now? They're travesties of themselves, they've been murdered, liquidated! To the outskirts, to the outskirts, where the air's fresher and the wind blows!'

We turned into Grojecka Street . . . earth, dust, noise, smell —we had left the big houses behind, here there were nothing but little ones. Small and improbable carts, loaded with Jews with all their worldly goods, vehicles loaded with vegetables, feathers, milk, cabbages, wheat, oats, old iron and refuse, filled the streets with noise, clatter and din. In each cart there was either a peasant or a Jew—urbanized peasant or countrified Jew—one hardly knew which to choose. We plunged deeper and deeper into this secondary layer, the immature outlying area of the city, and we saw more and more bad teeth, ears stuffed with cotton-wool, fingers tied up with rags, we came across more and more wavy hair, hiccups, eczemas, cabbages and general decay. Washing was hung out to dry at the windows. The wireless blared continuously, completing the task of public education, and a number of Pimkos, with rather artificially naïve and sincere voices, sometimes gay or cheerful, were cultivating the minds of bakers, instructing them in their civic duties and the love of Kosciuszko.

Tavern keepers revelled in the luxury of high society as described in popular novels, and their wives scratched their backs, deeply affected by Marlene Dietrich. Operation Peda-gogue continued relentlessly, and innumerable specialists worked on the masses, teaching and instructing, influencing and developing, awakening and civilizing them, with simplified grimaces *ad hoc*. Here members of the association of tramway-men's wives dance a round dance, singing with a smile on their lips, and producing *joie de vivre* under the watchful eye of a member of the permanent committee of the Social Gladness organization. There cabmen sang patriotic songs in chorus, producing a singularly naïve effect; while yonder ex-farm-girls were being instructed in how to perceive the beauty of the setting

198

sun; and dozens of idealists, doctrinaires, demagogues, and agitators formed up and reformed and deformed, disseminating their ideas, opinions, doctrines, views, all specially simplified and adapted for the use of simple people. 'Face, face, nothing but face,' said Mientus, with his usual frivolity, 'it's just like school. It's not surprising that they are ravaged by illnesses and ground down by poverty, it would be impossible for such vermin not to be ravaged and ground down. What demon put them in this state? Because I'm convinced that, if they had not been specially prepared and put in that state by somebody, it would be totally impossible for them to produce so much stupidity and muck. Why does it emerge in such abundance from them and not from the peasants, though the peasants never wash? What I want to know is: who transformed the good and worthy proletariat into such a dung factory? Who taught it all that dirt and make-believe? Sodom and Gomorrah! We shan't find our stable-boy here! Onward! Onward! Onward! When will the wind blow? But there's no wind, there's nothing but stagnation, men bathing in humanity like fish in a pond, the stink rises to high heaven, and there's no stable-boy to be seen.

'Unmarried seamstresses grow thin, second-class hairdressers grow fat in cheap comfort, small businessmen suffer from flatulence, servant-girls with nothing to do on their short fat legs come out with awkward, pretentious turns of phrase and false accents, the chemist's wife gives herself airs and holds herself above the washerwoman, who holds herself on high and buckled heels too. Feet . . . in reality bare though shod—feet not meant for shoes, heads not meant for hats, peasant bodies with petty bourgeois embellishments. Nothing but face,' said Mientus, 'nothing sincere or natural, everything false, imitated, and artificial. And not a stable-boy in sight!'

Eventually we chanced on a quite attractive looking young apprentice, a pleasant, well-built, fair-headed young man, but unfortunately he was the possessor of an elevated social conscience and ill-assimilated ideologies.

'Nothing but face,' said Mientus, 'to hell with philosophy!'

Later we came across a typical young gangster, with a knife between his teeth. Though for a moment we took him to be the stable-boy of our dreams, he turned out to be nothing but a suburban braggart in a bowler-hat. A third young man with whom we struck up a conversation at a street-corner seemed at first suitable in every respect, but what is to be done with a person who uses the word 'notwithstanding'?

'Nothing but face,' Mientus muttered furiously. 'It won't do no, it won't do. Onward! Onward!' he repeated feverishly. 'There's nothing here but shit, like at school. The suburbs learn from the town. Hell! The lower classes are obviously nothing but the bottom class at the primary school, and that's surely the reason why they have such snotty noses. By all the spots, pimples and rashes! Are we never to get away from school? Face, face, face! Onward! Onward!'

We pushed on, past little wooden houses, mothers picking fleas from their daughters' heads, daughters picking fleas from their mothers' heads, children wallowing in the gutter, workers coming home from work. From all sides there resounded one single, remarkable word, a key word. It seemed to invade the whole street, it became the proletarian hymn, it smacked of provocation, was trumpeted furiously into space, created at any rate the illusion of strength and life.

'Listen!' said Mientus in astonishment, 'they're giving themselves courage, just as we did at school. For all that, these young puppies won't save themselves from the huge and classic bummery that has been prepared for them. It's a terrible thing, but nowadays there is no one who is not in the maturing stage. Onward! There's no stable-boy here.'

As he said these words a light breeze caressed our cheeks. We had come to the end of houses, streets, canals, drains, hairdressers, windows, workers, wives, mothers and daughters, cant, cabbages, smells, crowds, dust, bosses and apprentices, shoes, blouses, hats, heels, trams, shops, vegetables, gangsters, advertisements, pavements, stomachs, tools, parts of the body, hiccups, knees, elbows, shop-fronts, talk, spitting, blowing of noses, coughing, shouting, children, bustle and din. We had reached the end of the town. Ahead of us lay fields and woods, and an open, asphalt road. Mientus sang:

> *Oh, oh, oh, the green forest!*
> *Oh, oh, oh, the green forest!*

'Get yourself a stick,' he said, 'cut yourself one from a tree. We'll find our stable-boy in the fields. I can see him already. He's O.K.!'
I too started singing:

> *Oh, oh, oh, the green forest!*
> *Oh, oh, oh, the green forest!*

But I could not put one foot in front of another. The song died on my lips. Space. On the horizon . . . a cow. Earth. A duck waddled along in the distance. The immense sky. Blue patches in the haze. At the edge of the town I stopped, and felt that for me life away from the herd, without anything artificial or manufactured, without the human element, humanity, was impossible, and I grabbed Mientus by the arm.

'Let us go back, Mientus,' I said. 'Don't let us leave the town.'

In the midst of the bushes and the unknown vegetation I trembled like a leaf—eliminated from among men. In their absence the distortions that they had inflicted on me seemed absurd and unnecessary.

Mientus hesitated too, but the prospect of the stable-boy got the better of his fear. 'Forward!' he shouted, brandishing his stick. 'I'm not going alone! You've got to come with me! Come on! Come on!'

The wind rose, the trees swayed, the leaves rustled . . . one of them in particular frightened me, right at the very top of a tree, delivered over entirely to space. A bird flew through the air. A dog emerged from the town and made off across the fields. Mientus set off valiantly along the roadside path, and I followed behind him, like a ship debouching into the open sea. The harbour, the towers and chimney-pots, disappeared from view, we were alone. The silence was such that we could almost hear the cold, wet stones sleeping in the earth. I trudged on, with nothing in my mind and the wind whistling in my ears, kept on my feet by the rhythm of walking. Nature. I don't like it, for me nature is man. Mientus, let us turn back, I prefer a crowded cinema to the country wind. Who was it who said that man feels small in the face of nature? I on the contrary, grow, become gigantic, feel utterly fragile, served up naked, so to speak, on the dish of the enormous field of nature in all my human unnaturalness. Oh, where had *my* forest gone, my dense forest of eyes and mouths and words and looks and faces and smiles and twitches? Another forest drew near, a forest of green, silent, tall trees through which the hare picks its way and the caterpillar creeps. As ill luck would have it, not so much as a hamlet was in sight; nothing but fields and woods. I do not know for how long, for how many hours, we trudged on through the fields, apathetically, stiffly, as if on a tightrope. We had no alternative, because standing still was still more tiring, and we could not sit or lie down on the damp earth.

True, we had passed through one or two hamlets, but they seemed dead; hermetically sealed hovels showed nothing but empty sockets. Traffic on the road had ceased entirely. How much longer should we have to go on tramping through the void?

'What's the meaning of this?' said Mientus. 'Have all the peasants been wiped out by the plague? Are they all dead? If things go on like this, we shall never find the stable-boy.'

At last, when we came to another, similarly depopulated hamlet, we decided to knock at one of the hovel doors. The answer was a concert of furious barks; it was as if we were being pursued by a canine pack, ranging from bloodhounds to pugs, all sharpening their fangs for our benefit.

'What's this?' said Mientus. 'Where do all these dogs come from? Why are there no peasants? Pinch me, I must be dreaming!'

The echo of these words had barely died away in the limpid air when a rustic head appeared behind the neighbouring potato clamp and promptly vanished again. We went towards it, and a chorus of furious barking rose from the ditch.

'Good heavens, more dogs?' said Mientus. 'Where has the gaffer gone to?'

Mientus walked round the clamp one way and I walked round the other (to the accompaniment of deafening, frantic barking from the neighbouring hovels), and we found the peasant, as well as his wife and the quadruplets that she was feeding from one anaemic dug (the other had long since become unserviceable). They barked desperately and furiously and tried to run away, but Mientus chased the peasant and caught him. He was so weak that he collapsed to the ground and moaned:

' 'ave pity on me, sorr, 'ave pity! Leave me be, sorr, leave me be!'

'What's the matter with you, man?' said Mientus. 'What's the matter with you? Why did you run away from us?'

At the word 'man' the barking in the huts and behind the fence redoubled, and the yokel went as white as a sheet.

' 'ave pity, sorr, 'ave pity, oi be no man, sorr, leave me be, sorr, please!'

'Citizens,' Mientus then said in friendly fashion, 'citizens, have you gone mad? Why do you and your wife bark like this? We have nothing but good intentions towards you.'

At the sound of the word 'citizens' the barking trebled in intensity, and the woman burst into tears.

'Please, sorr, 'e be no stitizen, 'e be no stitizen, that's the last thing 'e be!' she pleaded. 'Oh 'ow unlucky we be, 'ow unlucky! Here 'ey be, arter us again wi' 'eir intentions!'

'What *is* this about, friend?' said Mientus. 'We have no wish to harm you. We wish you nothing but good.'

'Ow! Ow!' the peasant howled in terror.

' 'e wish us good!' his wife shrieked. ' 'e wish us good! We not 'umans, we dogs, dogs! Wuff! Wuff!'

Suddenly one of the whelps yelped, and the old woman,

realizing that there were only two of us, barked, and bit me in the stomach. I shook her off. By now the whole village had gathered round the fence, barking and giving tongue.

'At 'em! At 'em! Bite the stitizens! Bite 'em and 'eir intentions!' they growled.

While rousing and egging each other on in this fashion they steadily approached us, and the worst of it was that in their fury and resentment, or perhaps to give themselves courage, they brought a lot of real dogs with them, and these, while jumping and bounding about, slavered and barked furiously.

The situation was becoming even more critical from the psychological than from the physical point of view. It was six o'clock in the evening, the sun had vanished behind the clouds, it was starting to drizzle, and there we were, in unfamiliar surroundings, under the fine and freezing rain, facing a large number of yokels who were pretending to be their own dogs in order to evade the omni-rapacious activities of the representatives of urban civilization. Their children had forgotten how to talk, but went about on all fours and yapped, and their parents encouraged them. 'Bark, bark, so 'ey'll leave us be! Bark, bark!' they said. It was the first time in my life that I had had occasion to see a whole troop of human beings hurriedly turning themselves into dogs, as a consequence of the law of imitation, out of fear in the face of over-rapid humanization. But there was no defence against them for, though it is possible to defend yourself against a dog-dog or a peasant-peasant, in the face of men who growl, bark, and try to bite you, you are helpless.

Mientus dropped his stick. I looked gauchely at the damp and mysterious grass on which I was destined shortly to end my life in highly confusing circumstances. Farewell, parts of my body! Farewell, my face, and farewell also my domesticated and tamed posterior! For it seemed certain that we were about to be devoured in an unprecedented manner at this very spot. But suddenly the whole situation changed, a motor-horn sounded, a car drove into the middle of the throng and stopped, and my Aunt Hurlecka, *née* Lin, exclaimed:

'Johnnie, darling! What on earth are you doing here?'

Ignoring the danger, ignoring everything (aunts are like that), she got out of the car, covered in her shawls, and ran forward with outstretched arms to kiss me. My aunt! My aunt! Where could I hide? Better be eaten alive than caught on a main road by an aunt! This aunt had known me since my childhood, the memory of my sailor-suit was engraved in her memory, she had seen me rocked in the cradle. She came up to me and kissed me on the forehead, and the peasants stopped barking and burst out laughing, the whole village split its sides with laughter . . . they realized that I was not an all-powerful clerk, but auntie's little boy. Mientus took off his cap, and my aunt held out her auntish hand for him to kiss.

'Is this your school-friend, Johnnie? Delighted!' she said.

Mientus kissed my aunt's hand. I kissed my aunt's hand. My aunt asked if we weren't cold, where we were going, where we had come from, what for, when, why, and how. I told her that we were on an outing.

'An outing? But children, who let you go in this wet weather? Jump into the car with me. I'll take you home, to Bolimowo. Your uncle will be delighted!'

There was no point in protesting, my aunt put protests out of the question. There we were, with my aunt, on the main road, in the mounting mist under the drizzling drizzly drizzle. We got into the car. The chauffeur sounded his horn and started up; the peasants surreptitiously roared with laughter, and the car, threaded on to the telegraph wires, moved away. We were off.

'Aren't you pleased, Johnnie?' my aunt said. 'I'm your materno-maternal aunt, your mother was the aunt of the aunt of the niece of my aunt on my mother's side. Your poor dead mother! Dear Marie! Let me see, how many years is it since I last saw you? It's four years since Francis's wedding. I still remember how you used to play in the sand—do you remember playing in the sand? What did those people want with you? Oh, what a fright they gave me! I find the people very uninteresting nowadays. There are germs everywhere, don't drink anything but boiled water, and don't eat fruit without peeling it or soaking it in hot water. Please put this shawl round your shoulders if you don't want to upset me, and let your friend put another one round his—please, please, don't be upset with me, there's nothing to be upset about, I could be your mother, your mother must be very worried about you!'

The chauffeur sounded his horn. The car buzzed, the wind buzzed, my aunt buzzed, elms, pines, and oaks, farms and swamps whizzed by; we bumped at speed over the ruts, and bounced in our seats.

'Don't drive so fast, Felix,' my aunt went on. 'Do you remember Uncle Francis? Christine is engaged, Theresa has had the 'flu. Henry is doing his military service. You've grown thinner, if you've got toothache, I've got some aspirin. And how are you getting on at school? Are you doing well? You ought to be good at history, because your poor mother was very good at it, you take after her. You've got your mother's blue eyes, your father's nose, but the real Pifczycki chin. Do you remember how you sobbed when they took the peach-stone away from you, and how you sucked your thumb and cried "Boo! Boo! Boo! Cha! Cha! Cha! Tuff! Tuff! Tuff!" . . . (Oh, accursed aunt!) Let me see, let me see, how many years ago was that? Twenty, twenty-eight, nineteen hundred and . . . of course, of course, I was just leaving for Vichy, I had just bought my green dressing-case, yes, that's it, so you must now be thirty . . . thirty . . . of course, just thirty! Please put the shawl on, darling, you have to be very careful of draughts!'

'Thirty?' said Mientus.

'Thirty!' my aunt said. 'He was thirty on St Peter's and St Paul's day. He's four and a half years younger than Theresa, and Theresa is six weeks older than Sophie, Alfred's daughter. Henry got married in February.'

'But he goes to our school, he's in the second form!'

'Of course! Henry got married in February, five months before I went to Menton—the cold spell—Helen died in June. Thirty—Mother came back from Podolia. Thirty. Just two years after Thomas had the croup. The ball at Modelany—thirty. A sweet? Johnnie, would you like a sweet? (Aunts always have sweets.) Do you remember how you used to hold out your little hands and say: "Sweety, aunty, please! Sweety, aunty, please!" I still have the same sweets, they're very good for coughs, do keep yourself covered, darling!'

The chauffeur sounded his horn. The car sped on. Telegraph poles, trees, huts, bits of fields, bits of forest, and bits of I don't know what parts of the country whizzed by. The open plain. Seven o'clock. Darkness. The chauffeur sent shafts of light ahead of him, my aunt switched on the light in the back of the car and invited us to suck childish sweets. Mientus in astonishment sucked a sweet too, and so did my aunt, holding the bag in her hand. We all sucked sweets. Woman, I'm thirty, I'm thirty, don't you understand? No, she did not understand. She was too good, too kind. Too good and too kind. Goodness and kindness incarnate. I drowned in her goodness, sucking her sticky sweet. To her I was still only two; or, rather, for her did I exist at all? No, I did not. Uncle Edward's hair, my father's nose, my mother's eyes, the Pifczycki chin, parts of the family body. My aunt was drowned in the family, and smothered me with her shawl. A calf leapt on to the roadway and stayed there, stupefied and stubborn. The chauffeur trumpeted like an archangel, but the calf refused to give way. We stopped, and the chauffeur got out and shooed it away, and on we went again, and my aunt described how I used to write big letters on the window with my fingers when I was ten. She remembered things that I did not remember, knew me as I had never known myself, but she was too kind for me to be able to kill her; God, not without good reason, has drowned in kindness all that aunts know about our ridiculous, lamentable, and anonymous past. On we went, we passed through a huge forest. Fragments of trees flashed by illuminated by the headlights, fragments of the past flashed by in our memory, we were in a bad region, a region of ill omen. How far we had gone! Where had we got to? A huge slice of the brutal and obscure provinces surrounded our little box, inside which my aunt went on talking about my fingers, one of which I had once cut—I must still have the scar; while Mientus, with his stable-boy on the brain, sat there dumbfounded at my thirty years. It started raining heavily. The car turned into a secondary road—bumps and ruts—turned again, and dogs, huge mastiffs, dashed furiously at us. A keeper came and chased them away, but they went on growling, barking, and yelping. A flunkey appeared at the gateway, and behind him another flunkey. We got out.

The country. The wind moved the trees and the clouds. The outline of a big house stood out against the night, an outline not unknown to me, obviously because once upon a time I had lived here. My aunt was afraid of the damp, and the servants took her by the arm and deposited her in the antechamber. The chauffeur brought up the rear with the luggage. The side-whiskered old butler helped my aunt off with her wraps. The maid undressed me. The young male servant undressed Mientus. Puppies sniffed at us. I knew all this, without remembering it . . . it was here that I was born and spent the first ten years of my life.

'I've brought some guests!' my aunt exclaimed. 'Edward, this is Stanislas's son. Alfred, your cousin. Isabel, Johnnie, your cousin. This is Johnnie, poor dear Marie's son. Johnnie, your Uncle Edward!'

Handshakes, kisses on the cheek, reciprocal embracing of parts of the body, displays of cheerfulness and hospitality. We were shown into the drawing-room, seated on old Biedermayers, and interrogated about our health, about how we were; and I in turn made inquiries into my interrogators' health; and from health the conversation branched off into illness, caught us, and would not let us go. My aunt had heart trouble, Uncle Edward suffered from rheumatism, Isabel had recently been anaemic and was very subject to colds, the poor girl's tonsils were not in order, but there was no real cure. Alfred was also very liable to colds, and had had serious trouble with his ear, it had swollen a month ago, at the beginning of the damp and windy autumn. Enough—it seemed unhealthy to be acquainted so soon after our arrival with all the family's innumerable complaints but, whenever the conversation showed signs of flagging, my aunt whispered '*Isabelle, parle,*' and Isabel, to revive it, and to the detriment of her own charms, promptly brought up yet another illness. Stiff neck, rheumatism, arthritis, pain in the joints, gout, catarrhs and coughs, sore throats, 'flu, cancer, nettle-rash, toothache, constipation, general anaemia, liver, kidneys, Karlsbad, Professor Kalitowicz and Dr Pistak. It looked as if with Dr Pistak the subject was exhausted, but to keep the conversation going my aunt brought up Dr Wistak, who had a quicker ear than Dr Pistak, and that set them off again—Wistak, Pistak, fevers, nose and throat complaints, affections of the respiratory tract, doctors, stones, chronic indigestion, malaise and red corpuscles. I could not forgive myself for having mentioned the subject of health, though obviously it would have been impossible for me to have done otherwise. It was particularly trying for Isabel, and I realized what it cost her to display her scrofula in public simply to prevent an awkward pause in the conversation; but it was impossible to be silent in the presence of two young people who had just arrived in the house. Did everybody who arrived in the country get caught in this fixed mechanism? Was illness the sole introduction? This was the illness of the country aristocracy: traditional good manners forced them to get into contact with people by way of catarrh, and that, surely was why they looked so pale and seemed to be suffering from such bad colds as they sat there in the lamplight, with their puppies on their knees. The country! The country! Ancient and time-honoured laws! Strange mysteries! What a contrast to urban crowds and streets!

Only my aunt took a really kind and genuine interest in my uncle's fevers and dysentery. The maid, red in her white apron, came in to replenish the lamp. Mientus, who said little, was impressed by the abundance of servants, and by two old sabres hanging on the wall. There was nobility in all this, but I could not tell whether my uncle too remembered all about my childhood. He treated us rather like children, but these people treated themselves rather like children, children with a *Kinderstube* handed down from their ancestors. I dimly remembered playing some sort of game under the broken table, and the fringes of the old sofa standing in the corner came back to me from the past. Had I bitten them or chewed them or plaited them, made them wet or dirty, and if so with what? And when? Or had I stuffed them up my nostrils? My aunt was seated erect on the sofa, in the old school manner, sticking out her chest, her head held a little backwards. Isabel sat with her body bent and sickly from the conversation, with crossed fingers; Alfred, with his elbows on the arms of his easy-chair, gazed at the tips of his shoes, and uncle was teasing the basset-hound and taking interest in an autumn fly which was flying about under the ceiling—the enormous white ceiling. Outside there was a gust of wind, the trees rustled under the burden of their remaining half-dead leaves, the shutters creaked, and a slight draught passed through the room—and I had a sudden premonition of a new and hypertrophied face. The dogs howled. When was I going to howl? For I was certainly going to. For the ways of these squireens, rather quaint and unreal and somehow pampered, inflated in an incredible void . . . delicacy and idleness, refinement, amiability, finesse, distinction, pride, tenderness, potential absurdity, custom reflected in every word . . . filled me with fear and mistrust. But which was more threatening—the solitary fly on the ceiling which had survived into the autumn, my aunt and my childish past, Mientus and his stable-boy, the family complaints, the fringes of the sofa, or the whole lot together, accumulated and concentrated on the point of a needle? In the expectation of an inevitable face I sat silently on the old and patriarchal Biedermayer which had come down from my forebears, while my aunt, sitting on hers, groaned to keep the conversation going, and said that draughts at this time of year were bad for the joints. Isabel, an ordinary, commonplace young woman of the kind one meets in thousands on estates in the country, a young woman who differed in no way from her kind, started laughing to maintain the conversation —and everyone else laughed too—a properly amiable and social imitation of a laugh—and then stopped. For whom, against whom, did they laugh?

But Uncle Edward, who was tall, thin, delicate, rather bald, had a long, pointed nose, long thin fingers, delicate lips, a refined and distinguished manner, an extraordinary ease in his way of behaviour and the negligent elegance of a man of the world, sank back in his armchair and put his yellow-chamois-slippered feet on the table.

'What times we live in!' said he. 'What times we live in!'

The fly buzzed.

'Don't fret, Edward, don't fret!' my aunt said kindly. And gave him a sweet. But Edward did fret, and then he yawned. He opened his mouth so wide that you could see his tobacco-stained molars; and he yawned twice with the greatest non-chalance.

'Ta-ra-ra-boom-te-ay!' he grumbled, 'the dog danced ever so lightly and the cat applauded politely.'

He took out his silver cigarette-case, drummed on it with his fingers, and dropped it on the floor. He did not pick it up, but yawned again. Against whom, for whom, did he yawn like this? The family, sitting on their Biedermayers, followed the performance in silence. Francis, the old servant, came in.

'Dinner is served,' he announced.

'Dinner,' said my aunt.

'Dinner,' said Isabel.

'Dinner,' said Alfred.

'The cigarette-case,' said Uncle Edward.

The flunkey picked it up and handed it to him, and we went into the Henry IV style dining-room, with old portraits hanging on the wall; a samovar was boiling in the corner. We were served with *jambon au gratin* and peas. Conversation was resumed.

'Swallow it down, swallow it down,' said Uncle Edward, helping himself to a little mustard and a pinch of pepper (but against whom did he help himself to mustard and pepper?). 'There's nothing better than *jambon au gratin* when it's properly

211

cooked. The only place where you get good ham nowadays is at Simon's restaurant. Ta-ra-ra-boom-te-ay, you can't get it anywhere else!'

'What about a glass of something?' said Alfred. 'Come on, what about it?'

'Do you remember the ham they used to serve at Bidou's before the war?' Uncle Edward asked.

'Ham is very heavy for the digestion,' my aunt said. 'Why have you taken such a small helping, Isabel? No appetite again?'

Isabel answered, but nobody listened, because everybody knew that she was talking only for talking's sake. Uncle Edward ate noisily, but with delicacy and refinement, though, manœuvring delicately over the plate, he picked up a mouthful of ham with his fingers, seasoned it with mustard or gravy, and slipped it into his buccal orifice. To one mouthful he added a little salt and to the next a little pepper. He buttered himself a slice of toast, and actually spat out a bit that he didn't like. The butler hurriedly caused it to vanish. But against whom did he spit? Against whom did he season his ham? My aunt stowed away abundantly but with subtlety, and not without kindness. Isabel ate dutifully. Alfred absorbed apathetically, and the staff served unobtrusively, 'on tiptoe'. Suddenly Mientus froze, with his fork half-way to his mouth. His eyes darkened, his face turned ashen, his lips half-opened, and a marvellous musical-mandoliny smile flowered on his horrible face—a smile of recognition, of meeting and greeting, so there you are, here am I! He put his hands on the table, leaned forward, and his upper lip curled as if he were about to burst into tears. He did not burst into tears, however, but only leaned forward a little more. He had seen his stable-boy. The young man-servant serving peas in the dining-room was his stable-boy. There was no doubt about it. The stable-boy of his dreams.

The stable-boy. He was about Mientus's age, not more than seventeen, neither big nor small, neither handsome nor ugly, neither dark nor fair, and he waited on us assiduously, barefoot, with a napkin over his left forearm, in his shirt-sleeves and collarless, in the Sunday-best trousers that all country stable-boys have. He had a face, but it had nothing in common with Mientus's disastrous face; it was not a fabricated, but a natural, village face, crudely outlined and rustic. It was not a face that had turned into a mug, but a mug that had never attained the dignity of a face. It was a mug like a leg! Oh, lad unworthy of possessing an honourable face, unworthy of being 'fair' or 'handsome'! Stable-boy unworthy of being a valet! Gloveless and barefoot, he changed his masters' plates—unworthy of a livery, but nobody seemed surprised. Oh! stable-boy! What ill-chance to find him here, at my aunt's and uncle's! Now, it's beginning, I said to myself, chewing my ham as if it were india-rubber, now it's beginning. And now, just to keep the conversation going, they started encouraging us to eat; and I had to sample the stewed pears; and then they offered us some little home-made cakes, for which I had to thank them, and I had to eat some, I had to, and I had to eat some stewed prunes, which stuck in my throat, while my aunt, to keep the conversation going, apologized for the poverty of the repast. 'Ta-ra-ra-boom-te-ay!' Uncle Edward, sprawling over his plate, negligently flung into his wide-open maw a succession of prunes which he held between two fingers.

'Eat! Eat! Fill your bellies, my friends!' he said, swallowing and clicking his tongue. And then he said, as if on purpose, with ostentatious self-satisfaction:

'Tomorrow I'm going to sack five men without paying their wages, because I haven't got any money.'

'Edward!' my aunt expostulated kindly.

'The cheese, please!' Uncle Edward went on.

Against whom did he say that? The staff went on serving on tiptoe. Mientus was engrossed; he devoured with his eyes the lad's undistorted, rustic, village face, drained it as if it were some unique drink. Under his heavy, insistent stare the lad lost countenance, and nearly upset the tea-pot over my aunt's head. Old Francis discreetly boxed his ears.

'Francis!' my aunt exclaimed kindly.

'He only need pay attention to what he is doing,' Uncle Edward grumbled, and helped himself to a cigarette. The servant leapt forward, match in hand. My uncle exhaled a cloud of smoke from between his thin lips, Cousin Alfred did the same through his no less thin lips, and we went back to the drawing-room, where each of us once more sat on his priceless Bieder-mayer. The wind could be heard howling furiously behind the shutters.

'How about a game of bridge?' said Cousin Alfred with a certain briskness.

But Mientus couldn't play, so Alfred remained silent and seated. Isabel said something; she pointed out that it often rained in the autumn, and my aunt asked me for news about Aunt Rosa. The conversation languished, my uncle crossed his legs, leaned back, and contemplated the ceiling, where a fly was desperately flying in all directions; and he yawned, exhibiting his palate and a row of yellow teeth. Alfred silently devoted himself to slowly swinging his leg and contemplating the reflections on his toe-caps. My aunt and Isabel sat with their hands in their laps, the basset-hound, seated on the table, looked at Alfred's foot, and Mientus, sitting in the shadow with his head between his hands, kept desperately silent. My aunt shook herself out of her torpor and ordered the servants to get the guests' room ready, to put hot-water bottles in the beds, and to leave nuts and preserves in the room in case we felt hungry. My uncle thereupon casually remarked that he would like some too, and the menials hastily produced it. We had some too, though we didn't want anything, but we could not refuse the delicacies provided, as there they were on plates all ready to be eaten, and our hosts pressed us to eat them; and they had no alternative but to press us to eat them because there they were on the plates all ready to be eaten. Mientus, however, refused, he absolutely insisted that he didn't want any and I guessed why —the stable-boy was in the room—but my aunt kindly gave him a double portion, and on top of it offered me sweets from the little bag she had. What sweetness, oh what sweetness! I didn't

want anything, the helping of preserves was too much, but with
the plate in front of me I couldn't say no. Everything came up:
my childhood, my aunt, sailor-suit, family, fly, puppy, Mientus,
full belly, suffocation, the wind outside, too much to eat,
saturation, abuse, shocking wealth, the Biedermayer which was
fascinating from underneath. But I couldn't get up and say good-
night without any preamble, it was impossible. In the end we
tried to do so, but we were asked to stay for just a little longer.
Against whom did Uncle Edward put yet one more prune into
his tired and sugary mouth? Isabel suddenly sneezed, and this
precipitated the good-nights. Farewells, salaams, expressions of
gratitude, entwinings of parts of the body. The maid led us to
our room by a staircase that awakened vague memories. A valet
brought up the rear with the nuts and preserves. It was hot and
airless. The preserves came up on me. Mientus had the hiccups
too. The country . . .

As soon as the door shut behind the maid, he said:

'Did you see?'

He sat down and hid his face in his hands.

'You mean the young servant?' I said with feigned unconcern.

I drew the curtains. The light from the window shining out
on to the dark grounds frightened me.

'I must speak to him! I'll go down. No, better ring for him.
He's surely been ordered to attend on us. Ring twice!'

'What for? (I tried to dissuade him.) It may lead to complications. Think of my uncle and aunt, Mientus. Don't ring, first
tell me what you expect to do with him.'

He rang.

'Hell!' he said. 'As if the preserves weren't enough, they've
given us apples and pears as well. Put them in the cupboard. . . .
Hide the hot-water bottles, I don't want him to see them.'

He was in a rage, the kind of rage that conceals fear of what
fate has in store for you, the rage of the most intimate human
affairs.

'Johnnie,' he muttered, trembling, tenderly, sincerely.
'Johnnie, you saw him, he's got an ordinary, normal, untwisted

215

face. A face with no grimaces. We shall never find a better stable-boy, never! Help me! I can't deal with this alone!'

'Take it easy! What do you want to do?'

'I don't know, I don't know! I want to be his friend, I want to fra-fra-ternize with him,' he confessed shamefacedly. 'I want to fra-fra-ternize with him. Be his friend. I must! Help me!'

The servant came in.

'Sir?' he said.

He stood just inside the doorway, awaiting orders. Mientus told him to pour water into the wash-stand basin. He poured water into the wash-stand basin, and waited. Mientus told him to open the wardrobe. He opened it, and waited again. Mientus told him to hang the towel on the towel-horse. He hung the towel on the towel-horse, and Mientus told him to put his jacket away in the wardrobe. All these orders made Mientus suffer cruelly. He gave orders, and the servant obeyed without batting an eyelid—and the orders grew more and more like an ironical dream. Ordering the stable-boy about instead of fraternizing with him! Spending the night ordering him about in accordance with one's sovereign whim! In the end Mientus ran out of orders and, for lack of anything else, ordered the servant to take the hot-water bottles and apples from the wardrobe in which they were hidden, and whispered to me brokenly:

'You try. I can't go on!'

Unhurriedly I took off my jacket and sat down at the head of the bed, swinging my legs—that seemed the most comfortable position in which to begin with the stable-boy.

'What's your name?' I asked.

'Bert,' he replied, and it was obvious that this was his real name and not just short for Albert, as if he were unworthy of the name of Albert or of a whole name to himself. This made Mientus tremble.

'Have you worked here for long?'

'Let me see, just a month, sir.'

'And where did you work before?'

'Before, sir? With the 'orses.'

'Are you happy here?'

'Yes, sir.'

'Bring us some hot water.'

'Very good, sir.'

When he went out Mientus had tears in his eyes. He wept.
Tears streamed down his tortured face.

'Did you hear?' he said. 'Did you hear? His name's Bert. He
hasn't even got a proper name. How that suits him! Did you see
his face? An ordinary face, an ordinary face without a grimace
on it! Johnnie, if he won't fra . . . ternize with me, I don't know
what I shall do!'

He had bursts of anger, reproached me for having ordered
the boy to fetch hot water, could not forgive himself for having
told him, for lack of any other ideas, to take the hot-water
bottles out of the wardrobe.

'He certainly never uses hot water,' he said. 'No doubt he
never washes at all. But in spite of that he isn't dirty. Johnnie,
do you realize that though he never washes he isn't dirty? In him
dirt is not disgusting, he's not disgusting at all. . . . And just
think of our dirt . . . our dirt . . .'

In the guest-room of the old manor house Mientus's passion
broke out. He dried his tears. The stable-boy came back with a
jug of hot water. This time Mientus conducted the attack, taking
up the thread where I had left it.

'How old are you?' he said, looking straight in front of him.

'Good gracious, sir, how should I know?'

This took Mientus's breath away. The stable-boy did not
even know his own age; divine stable-boy, free of the absurd
contingencies of life! On the pretext of being about to wash his
hands he went over towards where the lad was standing and,
forcing himself not to tremble, said:

'We must be about the same age.'

This was a statement, not a question; it left it open to the lad
to reply or not. Fra . . . ternization was about to begin.

'Yes, sir,' he replied.

Mientus unavoidably went back to questions.

'Did you learn to read and write?'

'Good gracious! And where would I do that, sir?'

'Have you got relatives?'

'I've got a sister, sir.'

'And what does she do?'

'She milks the cows, sir.'

The lad was standing and Mientus walking round the room. There seemed to be no getting away from questions and orders, orders and questions. So Mientus sat down, and said:

'Take off my shoes.'

I sat down too. The room was long and narrow, and there was something perverse about the way we moved about it. The house, which was big and austere, stood in a dark and gloomy park. The wind had dropped, which didn't help; a strong wind might have helped the situation. The stable-lad knelt and held his face over Mientus's proffered foot, and Mientus's face hovered feudally over his; Mientus's face was pale and dreadful, hardened by giving orders, powerless to ask more questions. Suddenly he said:

'Does your master ever slap your face?'

The lad's face lit up, and he exclaimed with rustic delight:

'Slap my face? And 'ow, sir, and 'ow!'

This caused me to leap forward like a jack-in-the-box and hit him with all my strength on the left cheek; the blow resounded in the silence like a revolver-shot. The lad put his hand to his face, dropped it, and rose to his feet.

'You certainly know 'ow to 'it too, sir!' he muttered with respect and admiration.

'Get out!' I shouted at him.

He got out.

'What on earth have you done, what on earth have you done?' groaned Mientus, wringing his hands. 'And I wanted to shake hands with him! I wanted to shake hands with him! Then our faces would have been the same, and everything . . . and everything . . . But you slapped his face! And I put my foot in his hands! He took off my shoes!' He groaned. 'He took off my shoes! Why did you do it?'

I had not the slightest idea. My hand had shot out as if it had been on a spring, and I had told the lad to get out. I had struck him, but why? There was a knock on the door, and Cousin Alfred, carrying a candle, came in, in trousers and slippers.

'Has somebody been shooting?' he said. 'I thought I heard a shot. Has somebody been shooting?'

'I slapped your Bert's face.'

'You slapped Bert?'

'He helped himself to my cigarettes.'

I preferred to get in first with my version of the incident before he heard the servant's version. Alfred was rather surprised, but then started laughing agreeably.

'That's fine!' he said, 'that'll cure him of the habit! . . . So you slapped his face,' he went on, rather incredulously.

I laughed, and Mientus cast me a glance that I shall never forget, the glance of a man who has been betrayed . . . and went off to the lavatory. My cousin followed him with his eyes.

'Your friend looks upset,' he remarked. 'Upset with you. A typical bourgeois!'

'Bourgeois,' I said. What else could I say?

'Bourgeois,' said Cousin Alfred. 'It's by treating Bert like that that he'll learn to respect you. You have to know them. They like it.'

'They like it,' I said.

'They like it, they like it! Ha! Ha! Ha! They like it!'

I no longer recognized my cousin, whose attitude towards me had previously been rather reserved. Now all trace of reserve had vanished. His eyes shone, he liked Bert's having had his face slapped, and he liked me; a young aristocrat had emerged from the chrysalis of the listless, morose schoolboy; it was as if Alfred had sniffed the forest and picked up the scent of the plebs. He put the candle on the window-sill and sat at the foot of the bed, a cigarette between his lips.

'They like it!' he said, 'they like it! You can slap 'em, but you must tip 'em too. No tips, no slaps, that's my belief! My father and Uncle Sigismund once slapped the head porter at the Grand Hotel.'

'And,' I said, 'Uncle Eustace once slapped a hairdresser.'

'And Grandmother Evelyn, she knew how to slap! But that was in the good old days. Some time ago Henry Pac got drunk and bashed his chauffeur's face in. D'you know Henry Pac? Very decent fella! And Bob Pitwicki smashed a window at the Cockatoo with a paint merchant's face. And once I gave an engineer a sock in the eye. D'you know the Pipowskis? She shows off a bit, but she's got her head screwed on. Tomorrow we might go partridge shooting.'

Where was Mientus? Where on earth was Mientus? Why hadn't he come back yet? Meanwhile Cousin Alfred showed no signs of wanting to go to bed. Bert's slapped face had drawn us together like a glass of brandy, and he went on breathing out clouds of cigarette smoke and talking about slapped faces and partridges, Mrs Pipowski, very decent little woman, y'know, cabarets and dancing girls, Henry, Lulu, you know what life is, that damned agricultural science, got to mug it up, you know, the lolly, and when would I finish my studies? I answered more or less the same thing, and he answered more or less the same thing, and I answered more or less the same thing. And then he got back to the subject of slaps, you had to know when and whom and how, and I said that it was better to hit a person on the ear than on the jaw. But I didn't really feel so sure, there was something unreal about it all, for nowadays slapping wasn't so common, manners had grown more civilized. I tried to say so, but couldn't, the conversation had become too attractive, and we were intoxicated by the baronial myth, the baronial fiction, and went on talking like two young lords of the manor.

'There's no harm at all in an occasional slap. On the contrary, there's nothing like it!' he said at last. 'It's getting late, we must see each other in Warsaw. I'll introduce you to Henry. Good gracious, it's midnight, and your friend hasn't come back yet, he must have indigestion! Good night!'

He clasped me in his arms.

'Good night, Johnnie!' he said.

'Good night, Alfred,' I said.

But why didn't Mientus come back? I sponged my perspiring brow. Where had that conversation with my cousin come from? I looked through the shutters; it had stopped raining, you couldn't see more than fifty paces, it was only here and there that you could guess the shape of the trees in the dark mass of the night, but their shapes seemed even darker than the night, and vaguer. In the darkness the park was dripping with humidity, penetrated by the sordid, enigmatic, and unknown expanse of fields beyond. Being unable to guess the shape of what I was looking at, looking but seeing nothing but shapes blacker than the night, I closed the shutters, and retreated to the other end of the room. All this was most inopportune. My striking the stable-lad had been inopportune. My conversation with Alfred had been inopportune. It was obvious that in this house slapping a face was like a glass of brandy; how different from a dry and democratic urban slap! The devil take it! What did a servant's face amount to in this feudal domain? By what mischance had it come about that I had drawn attention to it by slapping it, and actually talking to Alfred about it? But where had Mientus got to?

He came back at about one o'clock. He did not walk straight in, but first peeped round the half-open door to see if I were asleep; then he crept in like someone who has been out on the spree. He undressed quickly, and turned down the lamps. I noticed when he bent that his face had undergone a new and exceedingly crude transformation . . . his left cheek was swollen; it looked like a little apple, a little apple in a dish of stewed fruit, a kind of brew in which everything he had been doing was mixed up in miniature. Damn this miniaturization! Once more it had come into my life, this time on the face of a friend. A crazy clown was interfering with it. What brute force had thus transformed him? When I asked he answered in a sharp, strained voice:

'I've been in the kitchen, fra . . . ternizing with the stable-lad. He hit me in the face.'

'He hit you in the face?' I said, unable to believe my ears.

'Yes,' he said with glee—rather thin and artificial glee. 'We are brothers now. In the end I managed to get on good terms with him.'

But he spoke like a Sunday sportsman boasting about his bag, or a townsman boasting of having got drunk at a country wedding. He was in the grip of a crushing, devastating force, but his attitude to that force was not honest. I plied him with questions, and he ended by confessing reluctantly, with his face buried in his hands:

'I ordered him to hit me.'

'What? (My blood ran cold.) You ordered him to hit you? You actually ordered him to hit you in the face? Now he'll take you for a lunatic. (I felt as if I too had been struck in the face.) I congratulate you. If my uncle and aunt find out . . .'

'It's your fault,' he said gloomily. 'You shouldn't have hit him. You started it. You enjoyed playing lord of the manor. I had to let him hit me, because you hit him. . . . Otherwise we could never have met on equal terms and I shouldn't have been able to fra . . . ter . . .'

He turned out the lamp, and in broken phrases described his desperate efforts to achieve this equality. He had found the lad in the kitchen, cleaning the gentry's shoes, and had sat down beside him, whereupon the lad had got up. Again and again he had tried to make contact with him, to gain his confidence, to make him talk, to force his friendship, but all the words that came to his lips had turned to idyllicism, sentimentality, absurdity. The lad had answered as best he could, but it was obvious that all this was starting to bore him, and he could not imagine what this crazy young gentleman wanted of him. In desperation Mientus had fallen back on the cheap verbiage of the French Revolution, explained that all men were equal, and on this pretext had insisted on shaking hands with the youth, but this the latter had vigorously refused to do.

'My 'and's not for the likes of you, sir,' he had said.

It was then that the fantastic idea had come into Mientus's

head that, if he could get the lad to strike him it would break the ice.

'Hit me in the face!' he had begged him, losing all restraint. 'Hit me in the face!'

He had held his face out to be hit, but the lad remained as obstinate as ever.

'Why should I hit you, sir?' he said.

Mientus went on begging and imploring him, and in the end, infuriated by the lad's stubbornness, yelled at him:

'Hit me because I tell you to, you bastard! Hit me, you bastard! What are you waiting for?'

At that the lad hit out in earnest, and Mientus saw stars, and the room reeled round him.

'Again, you bastard, again!'

Once more Mientus saw stars, and again the room reeled. When he opened his eyes he saw the lad standing there, with his hands, waiting for more orders. But a blow in the face delivered by order was not the real thing—it was like having your shoes cleaned or having water poured into your wash-basin, and there was a flush of shame on the face of the giver of the blows.

'Again! Again!' the martyr muttered, in order to force the lad to fra . . . ternize on his face; and again he saw stars, and the room reeled. Oh, being struck in the face in the empty kitchen, among the washing, over a tub of hot water!

Fortunately these gentlemanly extravagances ended by making the son of the people laugh; no doubt he had come to the conclusion that the young gentleman was not quite right in the head (and nothing makes the vulgar more daring than the eccentricity of their masters); and in his rustic fashion he started treating the whole thing as a joke, and this led to familiarity. The lad quickly got to the point of fraternizing to such an extent that he tried to extract a tip from Mientus while still going on hitting him.

'Give me something to buy tobacco with,' he kept repeating.

This rustic, savage mockery, unfraternal and the reverse of friendly, was still not the real thing, however; it led, not to the fraternization of Mientus's dreams, but in the very opposite direction. But he stood his ground, preferring being maltreated by the stable-lad to crushing him beneath his gentlemanly superiority. The kitchen-maid, Maria, came in from the yard with a damp cloth to wash the kitchen floor, and was astonished at the scene. ' 'eavens, what a row!' she exclaimed. The house was asleep, and she and the stable-boy were able with impunity to have a good time at the expense of the young gentleman who was paying them a visit, mocking him with their great rustic guffaws. Mientus himself encouraged them, and joined in the laughter.

But gradually, while still mocking at Mientus, they started mocking at their masters too.

'That's what gennlefolk be loik!' they said, with the heavy, earthy, irony of the farmyard and the scullery. 'That's what gennlefolk be loik! Does nothing but stuffs 'emselves all day long till 'ey burst. Stuffs 'emselves and stuffs 'emselves, and goes to sleep with 'eir bellies sticking up in the air, 'ey walk about their rooms and talks and talks and talks! The amount 'ey puts away! Oi'm only a poor servant, but oi couldn't manage 'alf of it. Lunch, and tea, and chocolate biscuits, and fried eggs for breakfast! 'ey be great guzzlers, the gentry, 'ey be, 'ey does noth'n all day long, and that's what makes 'un ill. And when the gennleman cloimbed Vincent, the gamekeeper, at the boar-hunt! Vincent was stand'n behind 'un with t'other gun. The gennleman, 'e foired at the boar, and the boar went for 'un, and 'e threw away 'is gun and cloimbed Vincent—be quiet, Maria!— yes, 'e cloimbed Vincent! There weren't no tree around, so 'e cloimbed Vincent! Afterwards 'e gave 'un a zloty to keep 'is mouth shut, and told 'un that if 'e didn't keep 'is mouth shut, e'd get the sack!'

'Good 'eavens, the things you be say'n! Stop it, or you'll give me the belly-ache!'

Maria tightened her girdle.

'And the young lady, she goes out walkin', and she walk and she look, and she walk, and she look. The gennlemen goes walkin' too, and 'ey looks too. Mr Alfred, 'e looks at me, though 'e'd a done better not to! Once 'e even tried layin' 'is 'ands on me, but what a 'ope! 'E keep look'n to see if anyone was com'n, and I ended by laugh'n at 'un and runn'n away. Afterwards, Mr Alfred, 'e give me a zloty to keep mi mouth shut, because 'e said 'e'd 'ad a drop too much.'

'Aye, that's it, a drop too much,' the stable-lad chimed in. 'I knows a lot o' girls who won't go with 'un, because 'e always keeps on looking to see if anyone's com'n. Now 'e's got some'un, old Josephine, the widow, down i' the village, 'e meet 'er i' the bushes down by the pond; and 'e make 'er swear not to tell a living soul, 'e do!'

'Ha! Ha! Ha! Will you stop it, Bert! It's 'cos 'ey be so spoilt, the gennlefolk, 'ey be so delicate!'

'So delicate 'ey even 'as to 'ave 'un's noses wiped for 'un, 'cos 'ey can't do it 'emselves. When I first came 'ere, I couldn't get over it. 'and me this, fetch me that, bring me t'other, you even 'as to 'elp 'un on with 'un's overcoats, 'ey can't do it' emselves. If oi 'ad to be coddled like that, oi'd rather be dead, I would! I 'ave to cream the master all over every night!

'And oi 'as to rub the young lady,' the slut chimed in, 'rub 'er all over with me 'ands, she be so delicate, she be!'

'Gennlefolk be soft, 'ey 'as delicate little 'ands, ha! ha! ha! Sweet Jesus, 'ow 'ey goes for walks, and eats, and talks and talks and talks, and bores 'unselves to death.'

'Stop it, Bert, you know the mistress be very koind!'

'Course she be koind, see'n 'ow she suck the blood of the 'ole village . . . course she be koind! We work for 'un and the master, 'e walk about the fields and watch us. The mistress be 'fraid o' cows! Yes, she be 'fraid o' cows, she be! The gennlefolk talks and talks and goes for walks. Ha! Ha! Ha! 'ey be soft!'

The slut was exclaiming and the stable-lad denouncing when Francis walked in.

'What! Francis the butler?'

'The devil himself must have sent him,' Mientus said in desperation. 'Maria's cackling must have woken him. He didn't dare say anything to me, of course, but he started giving Maria and the stable-boy a dressing-down, told them not to make such a row at this time of night, and to get out, it was time they had finished their work, as it was past midnight, and they hadn't cleaned the kitchen yet. They went off at once. Devil take the man!'

'Had he heard?'

'Very likely, I don't know. What a loathsome type! Flunkey in side-whiskers and stiff collar. Peasant with side-whiskers. Traitor to the people. Traitor and spy! If he heard, he'll tell! We were having such a wonderful talk!'

'This will probably cause a shocking scandal,' I said.

'You're a traitor too!' Mientus hissed angrily at me. 'You're a traitor too! You're all traitors! Traitors!'

It was a long time before I got to sleep. Rats and mice danced their saraband in the attic overhead, and I listened to their squeals, their sudden leaps, their scuffles and pursuits, the fearful abortive blows exchanged by the savage animals. Water dripped from the roof. The dogs barked automatically, and our hermetically sealed room was a box of darkness. Mientus lay awake on his bed, and I lay awake on mine. We both lay on our backs, with our hands behind our heads, gazing at the ceiling. Both of us were wide awake, as was indicated by our imperceptible breathing. What was he doing under the cloak of darkness? Yes, what was he doing? For if he was awake he must be doing something . . . and the same applied to me. For a person who is awake must be doing something, he has no alternative. So he was doing something, and I was doing something. What was he thinking about, lying there tense and on edge, as if in the grip of a pair of pincers? I prayed that he would go to sleep, for then, perhaps, he would be less silent, more genuine, less baffling, more relaxed.

I spent the night on the rack. What was I to do? Run away at dawn? I was certain that old Francis would report to my uncle the blows that the stable-lad had struck Mientus and the things that he had said about his betters. And then pandemonium would break out, dissonances and deceptions, a veritable witches' sabbath. Face! Face was about to begin all over again—and arse. Was it for this that we had run away from the Youthfuls? We had awakened the monster, we had unchained the audacity of the lackeys. During that dreadful night, lying sleepless on my bed, I hit on the secret of the manor house, the secret of the rural aristocracy, the numerous and disturbing symptoms of which had from the outset given me a premonition of the approach of facial terror, of face. The secret was the servants. The clue to the gentry was the common people. Against whom did my uncle yawn, against whom did he put an extra sugared plum in his mouth? Against the people, against his lackeys! Why did he not pick up his cigarette-case when he dropped it? In order to have it picked up by the servants. Why had he received us with so much hospitality, lavished so much kindness and attention and delicacy on us? To distinguish himself from the servants and maintain his gentlemanly position against them. Whatever these people did was in some way directed at and against their servants, everything could be traced back to their domestic and farm servants.

Moreover, how could it be otherwise? In town, where we all wore the same clothes, used the same language and made the same gestures, we ceased to be aware that we were landed gentry; we were linked to the proletariat by a multitude of infinitesimal gradations, could descend imperceptibly to the gutter by way of the barber, the fruiterer, and the cabby. But here the gentleman stood out like a solitary poplar in a flat landscape. There was no transition between master and servant, because the bailiff and the village priest each lived in his own house. The roots of my uncle's baronial pride of race plunged straight into the plebeian subsoil; and it was from the plebs that it drew its sap. In towns servitude was of each to all and was exercised indirectly and discreetly, but here the master was in crude and direct control of his people, and held out his foot for them to clean his shoes . . . and my uncle and aunt certainly knew what was said about them below stairs, what they looked like through plebeian eyes. They knew, but the knowledge was unwelcome, they stifled, crushed, repressed it into the deepest depths of their consciousness.

To be waited on by your own plebeian! To be thought of and commented on by him! To be everlastingly refracted in the vulgar prism of the servant who freely enters your rooms, overhears your conversation, looks at your person, and with the breakfast coffee has access to your table and your bed ... to be the daily subject of below-stairs infra-gossip and never be able to explain oneself, never to meet and talk to these people on a level of equality. True, it is only by way of the domestic servants, the valet and the housemaid, that you can penetrate to the marrow of the rural aristocracy. Without the valet you will never understand the master, without the chambermaid you will never grasp the spiritual essence of the country ladies, the inner meaning of their take-offs and flights ... and the young man of the house is a consequence of the strapping farm-girl. Oh! at last I understood the reason for the strange constraint and apprehension which afflict the townsman when he arrives in the country; it is that these people are terrorized by the plebs, the plebs has them in its pocket. That is the reason for the continual sense of discomfort; a perpetual death-struggle into which are distilled all the poisons of subterranean secret struggles, a struggle a thousand times worse than any purely economic dispute. The struggle is imposed by the foreign and the exotic—physical foreignness and mental exoticism. Among the plebeians their minds were as if in a huge forest; their delicate, thoroughbred bodies were surrounded by the bodies of the vulgar as in a jungle. Their hands felt revulsion from the great paws of the plebs, their baronial feet detested those of the people, their faces hated the common faces, their eyes loathed the common eyes, the great round, rustic eyes of the people, their delicate fingers were repelled by the great clumsy fingers of the plebs ... and this was aggravated by being constantly touched ... 'tended' as the stable-lad put it ... by them, pampered by them, rubbed with cream by them. To have close to you, under your own roof, different, strange parts of bodies, and to have none other! For many leagues around there were nothing but vulgar limbs and vulgar language; and perhaps there were only the priest and bailiff who resembled them a little. But the bailiff was an employee, and the priest wore skirts. Did not the eager hospitality which they showed in detaining us for so long after dinner derive from their isolation? With us they felt more at ease. But Mientus had betrayed the baronial faces with the stable-lad's village face.

The lad's perverse gesture in striking Mientus in the face —Mientus was, after all, his master's guest and a master himself— was bound to have equally perverse consequences. The traditional hierarchy depended on the domination of the baronial parts of the body, and it was a tense, feudal hierarchy, in which the master's hand was as good as the servant's face and his foot reached to half the height of the whole rustic body. This hierarchy was long-established, sanctified by immemorial usage. A mystic link, hallowed by the passage of centuries, connected baronial and plebeian parts of the body, and it was only within the hierarchy that the masters could make contact with the people. Hence the magic of the slap in the face. Hence Bert's almost religious awe of a box on the ear. Hence Alfred's baronial fantasies. Certainly nowadays they no longer beat their servants (though Bert had admitted that Alfred sometimes struck him), but the slap in the face still held sway among them, and that maintained their position. But now? Had not a gross plebeian paw permitted itself familiarities with a young master's face?

Now the domestic servants would raise their heads. Below-stairs gossip had already begun. Now the vulgar, demoralized and made more insolent by familiarity between parts of the body, were beginning to mock their masters, plebeian criticism was rising like a tide; and what would happen when my uncle and aunt found out, and the baronial countenance was suddenly brought up against the people's crude mug?

★ 14 ★

Zenith and Culmination

AFTER breakfast next morning my aunt took us aside. It was a fresh, sunny morning, the earth was dark and damp, the bluish foliage of the clumps of trees in the big courtyard rustled in the breeze, and under them the family chickens scratched. In the morning time stood still, and golden rays caressed the smoking-room floor. The family dogs made their way idly from one corner to the other. The family pigeons cooed. My aunt was internally agitated by a wave that came up from the depths.

'Please tell me, Johnnie,' she began. 'Francis told me that . . . it seems that . . . this friend of yours . . . is being familiar with the servants. I hope he's not an agitator.'

'A theorist, mother, nothing but a theorist,' Alfred chimed in. 'Don't take any notice of him, mother, he's a mere theorist who doesn't know the first thing about life. He came to the country with his head stuffed full of theories, he's nothing but a drawing-room democrat!'

He was gay and baronial after the events of the night before.

'But Alfred, the young man doesn't indulge in theories, but in practice. Francis says he saw him shaking hands with Bert!'

Fortunately the old servant had not told everything, and my uncle, as I had occasion to find out, did not know the worst. I pretended to know nothing about anything, and referred vaguely to Mientus's socialist principles. I did so laughingly (how often life imposes laughter on us). Thus the affair was pigeon-holed for the time being. Obviously nobody breathed a word to Mientus. Until lunch-time we played King, because Isabel proposed that fashionable game, and it was impossible to refuse.

So King held us in its net until lunch. Isabel, Alfred, Mientus and I, laughing and bored, threw our cards down on the green felt, big ones on top of little ones, and hearts are trumps, ladies and gentlemen. Alfred played in dry, synthetic, routine fashion; he played his cards dextrously and horizontally, with a cigarette in his mouth, picking them out by the corners with his white fingers. Mientus kept wetting his fingers with saliva, held his cards tight, and I noticed that he was ashamed of playing this game, which was baronial in the extreme; he kept looking towards the door, fearing that the stable-lad would see him; he would have preferred playing cork-penny squatting on the ground. But it was lunch that I was chiefly worried about, because I feared Mientus would not be able to stand the stable-lad's presence; and my fears turned out to be justified.

For lunch there was fish with mayonnaise, tomato soup, *escalopes de veau*, and stewed pears, all prepared by the vulgar fingers of the cook and served on tiptoe by the staff. Francis appeared in white gloves, and the barefooted little lackey with a napkin over his arm. Mientus, pale and with downcast eyes, absorbed the delicate and carefully prepared viands which Bert offered him, and suffered at being fed by the stable-lad on such delicacies. On the other hand my aunt, desiring to give him indirectly to understand the full enormity of the things he had said in the kitchen, spoke to him with exceptional affability and charm, and asked him all about his family and his dead father. Forced to answer in high-flown phrases, he did so, in exasperation and in as low a voice as possible, in order to avoid being overheard by the stable-lad, at whom he did not dare to look. And that is perhaps why it came about, while the sweet was being served, that, instead of answering one of my aunt's questions, oblivious of everything, with his spoon in his hand and a shy and ardent smile on his contracted and grimacing face, he suddenly sank his eyes in those of the stable-lad. I could not jog him with my elbow, as I was sitting on the opposite side of the table. My aunt fell silent, and the little lackey burst into an embarrassed, rustic laugh, as the vulgar do when they are stared at by their masters; then he put his hand over his mouth. The butler tweaked his ear. My uncle lit a cigarette and breathed out a cloud of smoke. Had he seen? It had been so obvious that I feared he was going to order Mientus to leave the table.

Uncle Edward now breathed smoke out through his nose instead of through his mouth.

'Some wine!' he exclaimed. 'Bring a small bottle of wine!'

He was in high spirits. He lolled back in his chair, and drummed on the table with his fingers. 'Wine, Francis,' he said. 'Fetch us a bottle of Dame Thérèse from the cellar. Bert! Coffee and cigars, to hell with cigarettes!'

Raising his glass in honour of Mientus, he embarked on reminiscences. He told us how in his time he had gone pheasant-shooting with Prince Severinus; and, with a special toast for Mientus, ignoring the rest of the company, he went on to talk about the barber at the Hotel Bristol, the best barber he had come across in the whole of his life. He warmed up, grew animated, the servants redoubled their attentions, rapidly refilling the glasses and serving them with their fingers. Mientus, looking cadaverous, drank, not knowing to what to attribute Uncle Edward's unexpected attentions. He died a thousand deaths, but had to swallow the old wine with its delicate bouquet in Bert's presence.

To me too my uncle's reaction was unexpected. After lunch he took me by the arm and led me into the smoking-room.

'Your friend,' he said with aristocratic realism, 'your friend is a queer. Ahem! He's running after Bert. Didn't you notice? Ha! Ha! Ha! Provided the ladies don't notice. Prince Severinus used to like a little of that too sometimes!'

He stretched his long legs. Oh, with what aristocratic virtu-osity did he say those words! With what baronial good breeding, acquired in contact with four hundred waiters, seventy barbers, thirty jockeys, and the same number of butlers ... and with what pleasure did he air his piquant, hotelier's, *bon viveur*'s, *grand seigneur*'s knowledge of life! That is how the genuine aristocracy of birth, when confronted with a case of sexual degeneracy or perversion, displays the virile maturity it has learnt from waiters and barbers. But this highly seasoned wisdom made me suddenly furious with my uncle, like a cat confronted with a dog; his over-facile and lordly interpretation of the situation roused my indignation. I forgot all my fears, and it was I, in order to anger him, who told him the whole truth. May Heaven forgive me! The impact of his hotelier's maturity caused me to relapse into green immaturity, and I decided to give him something to swallow that was less cooked and less elegantly served than the things you get in fashionable restaurants.

'It's not that at all, uncle,' I said naïvely. 'He wants to frater-nize with him, that's all.'

This took Uncle Edward aback.

'He wants to fraternize with him?' he exclaimed in astonish-ment. 'What do you mean, fraternize?'

He looked at me askance.

'He wants to fra . . . ternize,' I said. 'Fra . . . ternize with him.'

'Fra . . . ternize with Bert? Fra . . . ternize? I suppose you mean he's an agitator, stirring up the servants. An agitator, is he? A Bolshevik?'

'No, he wants to fra . . . ternize with him, that's all.'

Uncle Edward rose, and flicked the ash from his cigar. He paused, searching for words.

'So it's fraternizing, is it?' he said. 'Fraternizing with the people, is that it?'

He tried to classify the phenomenon, to find an acceptable formula for it from the worldly and social point of view. Purely boyish fraternization was for him an unassimilable dish, which he knew was not served in good restaurants. What upset him most was that I, in imitation of Mientus, pronounced the word 'fraternize' with a slightly sly and shameful hesitation.

'So he fraternizes with the people,' he said cautiously.

'No, he fraternizes with the boy.'

'What do you mean? Does he want to play ball with him, or what?'

233

'No, they are simply good friends. They just fra . . . ternize like two schoolboys.'

Uncle Edward blushed, perhaps for the first time since he had started frequenting barbers' saloons. Oh, that reluctant blush of a sophisticated adult in the presence of an *ingénu*! He took out his watch, looked at it, and wound it, searching for scientific, political, economic, or medical terms in which to enclose the indelicate subject as in a box.

'It's a perversion, is it? A complex? He fra . . . ternizes? Fra- . . . ternizes? *Mais qu'est-ce que c'est que ça: il fra . . . ternise? Fraternité, égalité, fraternité?*'

He dropped into French, but unaggressively . . . on the contrary, like someone taking refuge in French. Nevertheless he was defenceless against the Boy. He lit a cigarette, put it out, crossed his legs, tugged his little moustache.

'*Il fraternise. Mais qu'est-ce que c'est, fraternise?* Ye gods! Prince Severinus!'

With quiet obstinacy I kept repeating the word 'fraternize', and not for anything in the world would I have abandoned the verdant and soft naïveté with which I was anointing Uncle Edward.

'Edward,' said my aunt kindly, appearing in the doorway with her bag of sweets in her hand, 'don't get excited, dear, no doubt he fraternizes in Jesus Christ, he fraternizes in the spirit of love of one's neighbour.'

'No,' I stubbornly insisted, 'he just fraternizes, pure and simple, and that's all there is to it. It's just schoolboy fraternization!'

'So he is a pervert, then?' Uncle Edward exclaimed.

'Not at all, he just fraternizes, without any perversion. It's nothing but boyish fraternization.'

'Boyish fraternization? Boyish fraternization? *Mais qu'est-ce que c'est* boyish fraternization?' Uncle Edward said idiotically. 'Boyish fraternization with Bert? With Bert, in my house? With my servant under my roof?'

He lost his temper and rang the bell.

234

'I'll show him boyish fraternization!'

The young lackey came in. Uncle Edward went towards him with raised hand. Perhaps he was going to give him a short, sharp slap in the face, but he stopped short, his head reeled, he was unable to hit Bert, make contact with Bert's face—in these circumstances. Hit a boy because he was a boy? Hit him because he 'fraternized'? Impossible. And Uncle Edward who did not mind striking a servant for serving a cup of coffee clumsily, dropped his hand to his side.

'Get out!' he shouted.

'Edward!' exclaimed my aunt kindly. 'Edward!'

'Hitting him won't do any good at all,' I said. 'On the contrary, it will only encourage the fraternization: my friend's crazy about men who get hit.'

Uncle Edward blinked, and made a gesture as if to shake a worm off his waistcoat; this virtuoso of worldly irony, ridiculed from below by my irony, was rather like a fencer attacked by a duck. The most curious thing was that, in spite of his experience of the world, he did not for one moment suspect that I might be on Mientus's and Bert's side against him, and that I might perhaps be enjoying his baronial shudderings. This blind confidence in the members of his own social set, this refusal to admit the slightest possibility of disloyalty on their part, was characteristic of him. Old Francis came in, complete with livery and side-whiskers. He was very upset, and stopped in the middle of the room.

Uncle Edward, who had let himself go somewhat, promptly resumed his normal, rather free-and-easy manner.

'What is it, Francis?' he said loftily, but nevertheless with a trace in his voice of the servility which an old servant, like an old wine, inspires in his master. 'What is it, Francis? (Francis looked at me, but my Uncle made a gesture to him.) Well, Francis, what's the matter?'

'You have spoken to Bert, sir.'

'Yes . . . I've spoken to Bert, Francis, I've spoken to Bert.'

'I only wanted to say, sir, that you did well to speak to him, sir. Sir, I wouldn't keep him here a moment longer, I'd throw him out at once. He has become too familiar, sir. Below stairs, sir, they are starting to talk.'

Three servant-girls ran across the courtyard, showing their bare thighs, and a lame dog chased them, yapping.

'They're starting to talk? What are they talking about?' asked Uncle Edward.

'About their masters, sir.'

'About us?'

Fortunately the old servant did not specify.

'They've started talking about their masters, sir. Bert has become familiar with the young gentleman who arrived yesterday, and now, saving your presence, sir, they have started talking about their masters and against their masters without the slightest respect, sir. Particularly Bert and the kitchen-girls, sir. I heard them myself, sir, talking to the young gentleman late last night, sir. They talked like mad, sir, they stopped at nothing, sir, they said such a lot of things that I couldn't say myself, sir, what they were talking about. But what I do know, sir, is that I'd throw that young rogue out straight away.'

The butler in his magnificent livery went as red as a beetroot. Oh, that old flunkey's blush! A flush spread subtly over his master's face and provided a silent answer. Uncle and aunt went on sitting in silence; it would have been unseemly to ask questions, but perhaps the old butler was going to say something else. They hung on his lips, but he said nothing.

'All right, Francis, you may go,' Uncle Edward said eventually.

And the old servant went as he had come.

'They are talking about their masters.' That was all they had found out. Uncle Edward confined himself to remarking bitterly to my aunt:

'You're too weak with the servants, dear, and they take advantage of it. But what do you suppose they can be talking about?'

They changed the subject, and for quite a time exchanged commonplace remarks and futile questions. 'Where is Isabel, I wonder?' and 'Has the post come?'

They trifled in this way to avoid showing that Francis's reticent story had touched them on the quick. They went on like this for a good quarter of an hour before Uncle Edward stretched, yawned, and started walking slowly in the direction of the drawing-room. I realized what he was doing; he was looking for Mientus. He must find him and talk to him immediately, he was under the imperious necessity of having this thing out with him straight away. Doubt had become insupportable. My aunt went out behind him.

But Mientus was not in the drawing-room; the only person there was Isabel, with a *Manual of Rational Cereal Culture* in her lap She was sitting and watching a fly on the wall. Mientus was not in the dining-room or in the boudoir either. The house was dozing in the quiet of the afternoon snooze. Outside the chickens were prowling about and scratching on the dried-up lawn, and the fox-terrier was playing with and pretending to bite the basset-hound's tail. My uncle and aunt glided into the house again, each by a different door; dignity did not allow them to admit that they were looking for anything. But seeing them like this, apparently casual and unconcerned but in reality on the war-path, was more alarming than the most bloodthirsty chase would have been, and I tried in vain to think of some way of averting the bedlam that was ripening like a boil on the horizon. I could no longer talk to them, I could no longer get at them, they had moved out of my reach, had retreated into themselves. Passing through the dining-room, I saw my aunt stop outside the kitchen door, from which there emerged as usual the voices, the squeals, and broad laughter of the girls engaged in washing up. My aunt stood there thoughtfully, pricking up her ears, in the typical attitude of a mistress spying on her servants, and her usual kind expression had vanished. When she saw me, she coughed and went away. Just at that moment my uncle walked past outside in the garden, in order to be nearer the kitchen, and he stopped under the trees. When the cook looked out of the window, he called out sharply to the gardener:

'Nowak! Nowak! Tell Zielenski to repair this pipe!'

He started walking slowly down the avenue of poplars. Nowak followed him, cap in hand. Alfred appeared. He came up to me, and took me by the arm.

'I don't know if it has ever happened to you to fancy a slightly *passée* old woman, but these peasant women, when they're slightly high, have a terrific effect on me. It was Henry Pac who started the fashion, I love them, *je les aime*. A fat peasant woman just past her prime! Very tasty! Very tasty indeed!'

Oh! Oh! Oh! He was afraid that the servants might have started talking about his old woman, the widow Josephine, with whom he hid himself in the bushes down by the pond; and so he produced the vagaries of fashion as an excuse and invoked the name of Henry Pac. I did not answer, seeing that the family were now well away and that there was no more stopping them; once more the lunatic star was rising over my horizon, and recalled all my adventures since Pimko had made me my arsicule. But this latest adventure threatened to be the worst of all. Alfred and I walked out into the courtyard, where we ran into my uncle emerging from the avenue of poplars, followed by Nowak, the gardener, cap in hand.

'What a magnificent day!' my uncle exclaimed in the diaphanous air. 'Magnificent!'

This was true; it certainly was a magnificent day; the golden-russet foliage of the trees rustled against a background of distant blue, and the fox-terrier was still flirting with the basset-hound. Mientus, however, was nowhere to be seen. My aunt appeared, with two mushrooms in her hand. She held out the mushrooms for us to see, and shot us a sweet, kind smile. We gathered at the front door and, as no one was willing to admit that we were all looking for Mientus, exceptional friendliness and delicacy prevailed among us. My aunt asked kindly if anyone felt cold. Some crows had come to rest on the trees. Some children had stopped at the entrance gate and were wiping their faces with their dirty fingers; they whispered, looking at their masters, until Alfred stamped his foot and sent them scurrying away. A moment later they started staring at us through the fence, and Alfred scattered them again, and Nowak the gardener, threw stones after them. They ran away, but they were soon peeping at us again, this time from the well. Uncle Edward sent for some apples and started ostentatiously eating one, throwing away the peel. He was eating against the children.

'Ta-ra-ra-boom-te-ay,' he grumbled.

There was still no sign of Mientus, a fact to which no one drew attention, though we all felt an urgent need to find him and have a word with him. If this was a chase, it was an incredibly lumbering and lethargic and practically immobile chase, and for that reason an alarming one. The master and mistress of the house were in pursuit of Mientus, but they hardly moved. However, it seemed pointless to remain any longer in the courtyard, particularly as the children were still peeping at us through the fence, and Alfred suggested going round to the back of the house. 'We'll show you the stables,' he said, and there we went, unhurriedly, as if going for a stroll, Uncle Edward still followed by the gardener, cap in hand. The children scampered from the fence to near the barn. After we had passed through the gate, the mud started, and the ducks went for us, but the overseer hurriedly shooed them away; and the dog showed his teeth and growled, but the lodge-keeper quickly silenced him. The mastiffs chained beside the stables started barking and howling, irritated by our exotic clothes—I was wearing a grey town suit, collar, tie, and shoes, my uncle a raglan, my aunt a black, fur-trimmed weeper and a small brimmed hat, and Alfred plus-fours. It was a *via crucis*, and how slow a one, the most agonizing walk I have ever had in my life. One day I shall tell you about my adventures in the desert and among the blacks, but darkest Africa was nothing in comparison with this expedition to the backyard at Bolimowo. Nowhere could there be more concentrated exoticism, more fatal poisons, nowhere a more luxuriant blooming of phantasmagoria and rare flowers, nowhere else were these orchids and super-oriental butterflies to be found, no humming-bird from distant lands could compare in exoticism to a duck our hands had never touched. For nothing here had ever been touched by our hands, neither the stable-lads in the stables nor the farm-girls near the barn, nor the cattle, nor the chickens, nor the hay-forks, nor the harness, nor the chains, nor the sacks. Wild chickens, wild horses, wild girls, and wild pigs! Only the stable-lads' faces were touchable by my uncle's hand; and only my aunt's hand was touchable by the faces of the stable-lads when they planted on it their tamed and rustic kisses. Otherwise it was an expedition into the unknown. While we were thus advancing on our heels, there was an irruption of cows into the yard, and one of them, driven by the children who were spying on our movements, invaded our path, and then we were sur-rounded by the strange and unknown quadrupeds.

'*Attention! Laissez les passer!*' my aunt called out.

'Attansionlessaypa!' the children mimicked her from behind the barn, but the lodge-keeper and overseer hurriedly chased away both children and cows. The wild, native girls in the poultry-yard struck up a country ditty . . . tra-la-la . . . but the words were inaudible. Were they singing about the young master? The most disagreeable thing, however, was the way in which the people seemed to spoil and pamper and make a fuss of their masters. Though the latter reigned over, dominated and economically oppressed them, looked at from the outside it all looked tender and affectionate, as if the plebs were caressing and fondling and making a fuss of them. The overseer in slave-like fashion carried my aunt in his arms over the puddles, but his gesture resembled a caress. Economically they sucked the people's blood, but this economic sucking was accompanied by another kind of sucking—an infantile kind—for they sucked milk as well as blood, and in vain did my uncle sternly and virilely reprimand the farm-hands, and in vain did my aunt allow her hands to be kissed with matronly and matriarchal kindness—neither the latter nor her husband's sternest orders prevented the

240

master from being the people's baby boy and the mistress from being their baby girl.

Not far from the hen-roost the tenant-farmer's wife was stuffing food down the throat of a big turkey, overfeeding it in honour of the baronial palate, preparing it to make a tasty dish for her masters. Outside the farrier's shop a prize filly was having its tail cropped—to give it more distinction—and Alfred patted it and looked at its teeth, for this animal was one of the few things the young master was allowed to touch; at this the unknown and blood-sucked girls sang at him with redoubled vigour—tra-la-la-la-la. But this put him off, the memory of the evening before prevented him from playing the role of the young master; he dropped his hand from the filly's neck, and looked suspiciously in the girls' direction, to see whether by any chance they were mocking him. An old, dried-up peasant, equally unknown and rather blood-sucked too, approached my aunt and kissed the approved part of her body. We came to the end of the buildings. Beyond it was a path and a chequerboard of fields, space. In the distance a blood-sucked labourer noticed us, stopped his plough for a moment, then whipped up his horse again. The wet earth permitted us neither to sit down nor to remain standing. To the masters' right were ditches, corn-fields, fences, patches of woodland; to their left the prickly green of the evergreen forest. There was no sign of Mientus. Wild domestic chickens scratched away among the oats.

Suddenly, not a hundred yards away, Mientus emerged from the wood; and he was not alone, for the little lackey was with him. He did not see us. Spellbound and absorbed by his stable-lad, he was totally oblivious of the world about him. He did not see anyone or anything. He came dawdling and bounding along in a solemn, clownish fashion, and kept taking the lackey's hand and looking him in the eyes. The lackey kept mocking him with his great, rustic laugh, slapping him familiarly on the back. They walked along the edge of the small wood. Mientus with the stable-boy; no, the stable-boy with Mientus accompanying him. Under his spell Mientus kept putting his hand in his pocket and giving something, no doubt small change, to the lad, who kept familiarly slapping him on the back.

'They're drunk!' my aunt muttered.

They were not. The declining sun illuminated everything and left no doubt. The lackey gave Mientus a playful tap on the cheek in the light of the declining sun.

'Bert!' Alfred shouted.

The little lackey vanished into the wood. Mientus, snatched out of his dream, stopped in his tracks. We started walking towards him across the corn-field, because he started walking towards us. But Uncle Edward did not want the confrontation to take place in the open fields, as the urchins were still watching us from the yard and the blood-sucked labourer was labouring.

'Shall we take a turn in the wood?' my uncle said to him with exceptional affability. We walked across the field and entered the dark little wood. Peace and calm. The confrontation took place among the thickly planted pines. We were cramped for space, we all had to stand on top of one another. Uncle Edward was trembling inside, but redoubled his affability.

'I see that you take great pleasure in Bert's company,' he said with subtle irony.

'Yes, I do!' replied Mientus, in a sharp and hate-filled voice.

He was hidden under a prickly pine, his face concealed by the branches, like a fox cornered by the pack. Two yards away from him, among the prickles, were my aunt, Uncle Edward, and Alfred. My uncle said coldly, with barely perceptible sarcasm:

'It seems that you are fra . . . ternizing with Bert.'

'Yes, I am!' came the answer; it was a howl of rage and hatred.

'Edward,' my aunt butted in gently, 'let's go, it's very damp here.'

'This plantation's too thick,' Alfred said to his father. 'We must cut down one tree in three.'

'Yes, I am!' howled Mientus.

He had not expected to be condemned to this torture. So it was for this they had brought him into the little wood, so that they might pretend to be deaf? So it was for this that they had spent such a long time pursuing him, to scorn him after they had found him? What had become of the great confrontation scene, in which everything was going to be explained and made clear? They had treacherously changed roles, they were no longer interested in him; so great was their pride, so all-embracing their contempt, that they had even abandoned their desire to have things out with him. They talked about trifles, they behaved as if everything were normal, they ignored him. Oh, base and villainous masters!

'You climbed the gamekeeper!' he yelled, losing all control of himself. 'You climbed the gamekeeper, because you were afraid of the boar! I know! Everyone knows! Ta-ra-ra-boom-te-ay! Ta-ra-ra-boom-te-ay! And old Mother Josephine!' he added.

Uncle Edward pursed his lips, but said nothing.

'We shall have to get rid of Bert,' Alfred said coldly to his father.

'Yes, we shall have to get rid of him,' Uncle Edward answered coldly. 'I'm sorry, but I'm not in the habit of keeping depraved servants.'

So they were revenging themselves on Bert. Oh, their cold vileness! Not only did they not condescend to answer him, but now they were going to sack Bert, they were going to hurt him by way of Bert. Had not old Francis behaved in the same way in the kitchen when he had given Bert and the girl a dressing-down without saying a word to him? The pine-tree trembled, and Mientus would surely have leapt at them had not a game-keeper suddenly emerged from among the trees at that moment, in his green uniform, with his gun slung over his shoulder, and saluted the company respectfully.

'Climb him!' Mientus shouted. 'Climb him! The boar! The boar!' And, having taken leave completely of his senses, he started running desperately through the wood. I ran after him.

'Mientus! Mientus!' I shouted, but he took no notice, and the pine branches struck me and scratched my face. I didn't want him to be alone in the woods for anything in the world. He fled, leaping the ditches, mounds, roots, and holes. When we emerged from this little plantation and plunged into the wood he redoubled his speed; he ran and ran, like a raging boar.

Suddenly I saw Isabel beguiling her boredom by looking for mushrooms. We were making straight towards her, and I was afraid that in his rage Mientus might do her some harm.

'Look out!' I shouted. 'Look out!'

There must have been urgency in my voice, for Isabel turned and fled, and Mientus saw this and started chasing her. I called on my last strength to catch up with her before he did, but fortunately he tripped over a root and fell, so I caught up with him.

'What is it?' he groaned with his face in the moss. 'What is it?'

'Come back to the house!'

'The masters!' He spat the word out. 'The masters! Go away! Go away! Yer one of 'em yersel'!'

'I'm not!'

'Yer tarred with t'same brush. Yah! Master! Master!'

'Come back to the house, Mientus, that's enough of this, it'll lead to something dreadful. Stop this, make a clean break, we must try again some other way!'

'The masters! The masters! Doan't do this! Doan't do that! Doan't do t'other! And yer sold to 'un too!'

'Stop it Mientus, that's not the way you speak! Why are you speaking like that? Why are you speaking like that to me?'

'Give 'un to me! Give 'un to me! Oi shan't give 'un up! Doan't touch Bert! 'ey wanter throw 'un out! Bert! Moi Bert! Woan't allow that!'

'Come back to the house!'

It was a shameful retreat. Mientus cried, groaned, despaired, burst out into rustic lamentations.

'Oah! Oah! What a loif! What a loif!'

In the yard the girls and the men-servants were dumbfounded to see a master complaining in their rustic fashion. Night was falling by the time we reached the house. I told Mientus to wait in our first-floor room, while I went off to talk to Uncle Edward. In the smoking-room I found Alfred pacing up and down with his hands in his pockets. The young master was outwardly stiff and inwardly furious. I learnt from his dry replies that Isabel had come back from the wood more dead than alive, that she seemed to have caught a cold, and that my aunt was just taking her temperature. Bert, who was back in the kitchen, had been forbidden access to the rest of the house, and was to be sent away next day. Alfred was careful to explain that he did not hold me responsible for 'that gentleman's' excesses, though in his opinion I ought to choose my friends more carefully. He regretted that he would not be able to enjoy my company for a longer period, but did not believe that in the circumstances we would wish to prolong our stay at Bolimowo. The Warsaw train left at 9 a.m., and the chauffeur had already been ordered to take us to the station. As for dinner, no doubt we should prefer to take it in our own room; Francis would see to this. Alfred spoke in a manner which permitted of no reply, he was speaking on his parents' behalf.

'As for myself,' he said, 'I shall react differently. I propose to punish the gentleman for his insulting behaviour towards my parents. I am a member of the Astoria Club.'

And he made the gesture of slapping a face. I saw what was in his mind; he wished to disqualify a face which had been slapped by a common hand, remove it from the list of honourable, gentlemanly faces.

Fortunately Uncle Edward came in and overheard this threat.

'What *gentleman* are you talking about, my boy?' he exclaimed. 'Whose face is it you want to slap? The face of a stripling who's still at school? It's his behind that's in need of correction!'

Alfred blushed, and hesitated in his honourable proposal. After what my uncle said he could no longer slap Mientus's face. At the age of twenty plus he could not honourably strike a boy of seventeen, particularly after the latter's youthfulness had been drawn attention to in this way. The trouble, however, was that

Mientus's age was an age of transition. The masters could regard him as an unlicked cub, but in the eyes of the people, who mature faster, he was already a fully grown gentleman, and in their eyes his face had all the prestige of a gentleman's face. It was a strange position. Mientus's face was mature enough to be a gentleman's when Bert hit it, but not mature enough for a gentleman to be able to obtain satisfaction from it. Alfred looked at his father, furious at this injustice on the part of nature. But Uncle Alfred refused to admit that Mientus was anything but a snuffle-nosed minor, though at lunch he had treated him as man to man, and had sent for a special bottle of old wine to toast his assumed homosexuality. But now he repudiated all affinity with him, treated him with contempt as a minor. His pride, his ancestry, forbade him to do anything else. His ancestral blood was up. The remorseless march of history was robbing him of his wealth and his power, but he still preserved his blood intact, both mentally and physically, and above all physically. He could tolerate agrarian reform and the general levelling in public and political life, but his blood boiled at the idea of private, physical, corporeal equality, at the idea of fra . . . ternization between man and man. Levelling assailed him here in the darkest depths of his personality, in his ancient, ancestral undergrowth, defended by the instinctive reflexes of repulsion, revulsion, detestation, and fear. Let them take his fortune, let them carry out their reforms, but the master's hand must not seek out the hand of the peasant, the master's cheek must not seek out the vulgar paw! How could anyone of his own free will develop a predilection for the vulgar, betray his blood, fawn on a servant, be full of naïve admiration for the limbs, the movements, the awkwardness of a lackey, become enamoured of a farm-hand's inner being? What is the position of a master whose servant is publicly and plainly the object of such attentions by another master?

'No, no,' he said, 'Mientus is not one of us, but the victim of a childish mania influenced by Bolshevik propaganda. I see that young people at school nowadays are being affected by Bolshevik ideas,' he repeated, as if Mientus were an ordinary young man with revolutionary impulses and not a lover of the people.

'What he needs is a good thrashing,' he said with a laugh.

Through the half-open window we suddenly heard noises and giggles from the bushes near the kitchen. It was a warm Saturday afternoon. The farm-hands had joined the kitchen-girls, and things were warming up. . . . Edward leaned out of the window.

'Who's there?' he called out. 'It's not allowed.'

Someone hid in the bushes. There was a loud laugh. A stone, thrown with violence, landed outside the window, and from behind the bushes a disguised voice bawled:

> *A bloody great swoip*
> *On t'gennleman's jaw,*
> *Haw! Haw!*

There was another giggle and more laughter. The news had spread in the village. They knew. The kitchen-girls must have told the farm-hands. That was only to be expected, but the insolence of this singing under his windows was too much for my uncle. He ceased taking the matter lightly, angry red blobs appeared on his cheeks, and he silently took out his revolver. Fortunately my aunt appeared at that moment.

'Edward!' she exclaimed kindly. 'Put that thing down! Put it down at once! I can't stand loaded weapons! If you insist on carrying that thing about with you, unload it!'

And just as he had just previously made light of Alfred, so did she now make light of him. She kissed him, and he, revolver in hand, allowed himself to be kissed; and she straightened his tie, which effectively inhibited his revolver, she shut the window because of the draught, and made a number of other, similar gestures, with an increasingly restricting and diminishing effect. She threw into the balance all the roundness of her person, which exuded a gentle, maternal warmth, wrapping everything in cotton-wool. She took me aside, and surreptitiously gave me some sweets from her bag.

'What have you done, you naughty boys!' she said, in an exceedingly kind rebuke. 'Isabel's ill, and uncle's angry! You and your idylls with the people! You have to know how to handle the servants, you mustn't permit familiarity, you have to under-stand them, they're not educated, they're primitives, they're children! James, Uncle Stanislas's son, had the same mania for the people,' she added, looking at me, 'and you take after him a little, there, round about the nostrils. All right, I'm not angry with you, darling, but don't come down to dinner, Uncle doesn't want you to. I'll send up some preserves to cheer you up. Oh, and do you remember how Ladislas, our old servant, beat you because you said he was crazy? Horrid man! I still shudder to think of it. Beating my little darling, my little angel!'

In a sudden burst of affection she kissed me, and gave me more sweets. I rapidly took my leave, with the taste of the childish sweets still in my mouth, and on my way out I heard my aunt asking Alfred to feel her pulse; and Alfred, looking at his watch, felt his mother's pulse, while she lay on the sofa, staring into the void. With sweets still in my mouth I went back to our room, and felt unreal, but my aunt made everybody unreal, she had the extraordinary gift of dissolving people in kindness, plunging them into all sorts of illnesses, and mingling parts of their bodies with those of other members of the family . . . perhaps out of fear of the servants? She was kind, because she suffocated people. As she suffocated people, how could she be anything but kind?

The situation was getting dangerous. They were each taking things lightly against each other, my uncle out of pride and my aunt out of fear, and it was thanks only to this that no shots had been fired, that Alfred's hand had not struck Mientus's face, that my uncle's ammunition was still in his pistol. I was relieved at the thought that we were leaving next morning.

I found Mientus lying on the floor, his head between his arms—he had got into the habit of surrounding, hiding, enveloping himself with his arms. He did not move when I came in, went on moaning and lamenting in youthful and rustic fashion, with his head buried. 'Oh, lack a day! Oh, lack a day!'

he blubbered disconsolately, and went on incoherently muttering other expressions as grey and crude as the earth, as green as foliage, young, country, peasant expressions. He had lost all sense of shame. When Francis came in with the dinner he did not interrupt his tender complaints and rustic lamentations; he had crossed the threshold beyond which no shame is felt at aspiring to be a servant in a servant's presence, or in sighing for a young lackey in the presence of an old butler. Never before had I seen a member of the educated classes in such a state of degeneration. Francis did not even look in his direction, but when he put the dish on the table his hands were trembling with indignation, and when he went out he slammed the door behind him. Mientus would not eat anything and remained disconsolate—something was murmuring and lamenting, weeping and wailing, inside him, he was sighing for something, grumbling at and wrestling with it, it was impossible to tell exactly what was going on in him; and then again a boorish rage seized him by the throat. He put all the blame for his failure with the stable-boy on my uncle and aunt. It was the masters' fault, the masters'; if they had not put their spoke in the wheel, he would certainly have succeeded in fra . . . ternizing with Bert. Why had they thwarted him? Why were they sacking Bert? In vain I told him that we should have to leave next morning.

'Woan' go!' he said. 'Woan' go! Let 'ey go if 'ey wanna! Oi stay where Bert be! Oi stay wi' Bert! Wi' moi Bert! Moi stable-boy!'

I could not make him see sense, he was totally immersed in his stable-boy, all worldly considerations had ceased to exist for him. When he finally grasped that it was impossible to remain here, he took fright, and started begging me not to abandon the stable-boy.

'Oi woan' go wi'out Bert!' he said. 'Oi woan' leave Bert! We'll take 'un wi' us, oi'll go out an' work an' earn a livin'. Oi'd rather doi than leave 'ere wi'out Bert! Boi all that's 'oly, Johnnie, oi woan' leave wi'out moi Bert! If 'ey turns we out,' he added viciously, 'if 'ey turns we out, oi'll go an' live wi' the widder!

'ey can't turn we out o' the village! Anyone can live i' the village!'

Here was a pretty kettle of fish. I couldn't think what to do. He was perfectly capable of going to live with Alfred's old woman—the 'widow', as the stable-boy called her, compromising my uncle and aunt by denouncing the secrets of the manor-house in the language of the people . . . traitor and spy . . . to make the yokels laugh.

At that moment a monumental smack resounded in the court-yard down below. The windows shook, and the dogs started barking like mad. We looked out. Uncle Edward was silhouetted in the moonlight, gun in hand, trying to pierce the darkness with his eyes. Once more he raised the gun to his cheek and fired— the detonation resounded in the night like a rocket and lost itself in the darkness of space. The dogs broke loose.

' 'ey be foirin' at Bert!'

Mientus gripped me convulsively.

'Bert! 'ey be troyin' to kill 'un!'

Uncle Edward fired to frighten. Had the servants been talking again? Did he fire because he had grown so nervy that he could stand it no longer and had some ammunition in his pocket? Heaven knows what was going on inside him! Was it arrogance and pride that inspired this terroristic gesture? Was the angry master proclaiming far and wide by these detonations that he was awake, on the alert, and armed? My aunt appeared in the doorway, hastily offered him sweets, put a scarf round his neck, and took him inside. But the detonations were beyond recall. When the watch-dogs of the home farm fell silent for a moment I heard the distant answer of the village dogs, and in my mind's eye saw what must be going on in the minds of the villagers —the man-servants, the farm-girls, the labourers all saying to one another:

'What's up there, I wonder? What are they shooting for up at the house? Is that the master shooting? What's he shooting for?'

And the talk about the blows in the face that the young gentleman had taken from Bert spread from mouth to mouth, set free by this fantastic and ostentatious firing. I could no longer control my nerves, I decided to flee immediately; I was afraid of another night in this noxious, feudal house, full of poisonous emanations, I decided to leave instantly, but Mientus refused to go without Bert. So, to save time, I agreed that he should take him with us; he was going to be sacked next morning in any case. We ended by deciding to wait till the whole household was asleep, and that I should then go and find Bert and persuade him to run away with us or, if necessary, order him to. I should bring him back to our room and the three of us should then hold a council of war to decide how best to make our getaway. The dogs knew Bert. We should spend the rest of the night in the fields, and take the train to town next morning. Town! Town! In town man is smaller, better situated among his fellows, more human. Each minute lasted an eternity. We packed our belongings, and tied up in a handkerchief the dinner which we had barely touched.

After midnight, when I had made sure that darkness reigned in the house, I took off my shoes and crept down the little corridor on my bare feet in order to reach the kitchen without making any noise. After Mientus had shut the door behind me, depriving me of the last ray of light, after I had set out on the enterprise and started groping my way about the sleeping house, I saw how senseless and unreasonable was this whole idea of launching myself into space for the purpose of abducting the stable-boy; it is only by action that the full madness of madness is demonstrated. I advanced step by step, every now and then a floor-board creaked under my feet, over the ceiling rats jostled each other and scurried apart. The rustic Mientus was in the room behind me; ahead, on the ground floor, were my uncle and aunt, Alfred and Isabel, whose servant was the objective of all these endeavours. I advanced in death-like stillness and on bare feet. He was straight ahead of me, in the kitchen. I must be very careful. If anyone discovered me like this in the dark corridor, I should be hard put to it for an explanation. What paths lead us to these tortuous and abnormal actions? The normal is a tightrope over the abyss of the abnormal. What lunacies lie hidden behind the daily routine—you can never tell when or how you may be impelled by the course of events to abduct and run away with a stable-boy. It would have been better to abduct Isabel; if anyone was to be abducted, she was the obvious, natural, normal, and obvious choice. Why not abduct Isabel instead of this fatuous and idiotic stable-boy? And in the dark corridor I was tempted by the idea of abducting Isabel, the sensible and rational idea of abducting Isabel. Oh, the sensible and rational idea of abducting Isabel.

Oh, the thought of maturely, nobly, aristocratically abducting Isabel in the manner of so many abductions of the past. I had to fight off the idea, demonstrate to myself how ill-considered it was but the farther I advanced along the treacherous floorboards, the greater the attraction of normality became, the more I was tempted by the idea of a normal and natural abduction as against the involved and complicated abduction of the stable-boy. I tripped over a hole, there was a hole under my feet, a hole in the floor. But where was it? Because I knew it, it was my hole, years before I had made it myself. My uncle had given me a hatchet for my birthday, and I had made the hole with it. My aunt had come hurrying along, and here, standing at this spot, she had scolded me; I still remembered the remonstrations, the tone of severity. Then I had hit her leg with the hatchet. 'Ow!' she had called out. 'Ow!' Her cry still lingered here. I stopped as if the scene had caught me by the foot, though the scene was now non-existent but nevertheless existed at that moment and at that spot. I had hit her leg with the hatchet, and in the darkness I clearly saw myself doing it, without knowing why, without wanting to, and I heard her cry out; she had cried out and jumped. My present and past actions, preterite and pluperfect, were mingled and intertwined; suddenly I started trembling and clenched my teeth. Heavens, if I had been stronger I might have chopped her leg off, thank heaven for my weakness! But now I had strength. Instead of looking for the stable-boy, why not go to my aunt's room and chop off her leg? No, no, what childishness, what childishness! But in heaven's name was not the stable-lad childishness too? One was as childish as the other, so why not chop my aunt's leg off? Oh, childishness, childishness! I felt the floor with my foot, carefully, for a creak might have betrayed me, but it seemed to me that it was a child that was groping his way forward like this. Oh, childishness! I was afflicted with triple childishness—if it had been merely single childishness, I might have been able to to defend myself against it. In the first place there was the childishness of this expedition in search of the stable-boy. Then there was the childishness of my memories of life here years ago; and finally the childishness of this feudal household, and as part of it I was childish too. Oh, there are plenty of more or less puerile places in the world, but a country house is perhaps the most puerile of all. Here both masters and people turned themselves into children, preserved themselves by turning themselves into children, they were children to each other. Advancing barefoot along the corridor under the mask of night, I seemed to re-enter my aristocratic and pre-pubertal past; and the sensuous, physical, incalculable world of childhood absorbed and inveigled me. Blind actions. Irresistible impulses. Atavistic instincts. Puerile baronial fantasies. I succumbed to the anachronistic idea of a gigantic super-slap—an idea at one and the same time infantile and in accordance with immemorial tradition—a gigantic super-slap which should simultaneously liberate both master and child. I felt the banisters down which I had once slid, enjoyed the automatism of the slide from top to bottom. Child, infant, infant-king, Mr Grown-Up Child of the present day, oh, if I struck my aunt with an axe now, she wouldn't get up . . . and I was terrified at the idea of a child's possessing a man's strength. What was I doing here on this staircase, where was I going, and what for? Once more the abduction of Isabel struck me as the only possible excuse for this foray, the only possible manly, mature justification for it. The abduction of Isabel, the manly abduction of Isabel. I fought off the idea, but it tickled my fancy, kept buzzing in my head.

Down below in the lumber-room I stopped. All was quiet, they had all gone to bed at the usual time, just as they did every day, my aunt had undoubtedly packed them all off to bed and tucked them in. But tonight there was the difference that they were not really resting under the bed-clothes, but chewing over the events of the day. Not a sound came from the kitchen either, only a gleam of light showed through the crack of the door, behind which the young manservant was cleaning shoes. I could see no change in his face; everything was normal there too. I went in quietly, with my finger to my lips, closed the door behind me, and with infinite precautions whispered my arguments into his ear. Quick, pick up your cap, drop everything, and come with us to Warsaw, we're going to Warsaw. It was a horrible role to play, I should have preferred almost anything to these idiotic proposals, which had to be whispered into the bargain. Particularly as the lad wouldn't agree to them. I pointed out that he was going to get thrown out next morning in any case, and that from his point of view it would be better to go a long way away, to Warsaw, where Mientus would help him. But he would not, could not understand. 'Woi should oi go?' he replied, with an instinctive mistrust of all upper-class fantasies, and once more I had the impression that Isabel would respond more easily, that midnight whisperings to Isabel would be less inexcusable. But time was pressing, and made it impossible to prolong the argument. I struck the lad in the face and ordered him to follow me, and then he obeyed. But I hit him through a dish-cloth; I held a dish-cloth against his left cheek to deaden the sound of the blow, and oh! oh! oh! it was through a dish-cloth that I slapped him in the middle of the night. But he obeyed, though the dish-cloth must have roused some suspicion in his mind, for the vulgar do not like departures from routine. 'Come along, you son of a bitch!' I ordered him, and went out into the lumber-room, with him behind me. Where was the staircase? Pitch darkness.

A door creaked, and my uncle's voice said:

'Who's there?'

I took the lad's arm and pushed him into the dining-room.

We hid behind the door. Uncle Edward slowly approached, and entered the dining-room too; he glided past quite close to where I was standing.

'Who's there?' he asked cautiously, to avoid looking foolish if nobody was there. After launching this question he advanced a step farther into the room and stopped. He had no matches, and the darkness was impenetrable. He turned, retraced his steps, stopped again and lay doggo, he suddenly lay completely doggo. Had he detected in the darkness the *sui generis* odour of the stable-lad, had the master's delicate skin sensed the presence of paws and mug? He was so close that he could have put out his hands and touched us, but that was why he did not put out his hands, he was too close, proximity held him in its grip. He froze into immobility, and this immobility, which started by being slow, rapidly accelerated and condensed into an expression of fear. I don't think he was a coward, in spite of the story of how he climbed the gamekeeper; no, it wasn't this inability to move that made him afraid, for once he had immobilized himself, for reason of pure form each second that passed made it harder for him to start moving again. But fear entered into him, and now it had started taking shape and suffocating him; his fine, baronial Adam's apple had gone up his throat. The stable-lad did not move, and so all three of us remained standing within a foot of each other. Our skin woke up. I did nothing to interrupt. I waited for Uncle Edward to recover his self-control and go away, which would enable us to resume our flight through the lumber-room to the staircase, but I failed to take into account the paralysing effect on him of fear . . . for now, I could tell, an interior change and transformation was taking place in him, and from being afraid because he could not move, now he could not move because he was afraid. I could divine on his face the grave, concentrated, highly serious expression proper to fear . . . and I in my turn started feeling afraid . . . not of him, but of his fear. If we had retreated or made the slightest movement he would have been able to go for us. If he had had his pistol, he would have been able to pull the trigger, but no, we were too close, it was a physical but not a psychological possibility because, before a man can pull the trigger physically, he has to pull it internally, in his mind, and for that there was no room. True, he might plunge forward with his hands out, but he did not know what was in front of him or what his hands might meet. We knew what he looked like, but he did not know what we looked like. I felt like clearing up the whole situation by saying 'Hello, uncle!' or something of the sort, but after so many seconds perhaps even minutes, it was impossible, it was too late, how was I to explain having kept silent for so long? I felt I was going to laugh, as if someone had tickled me. I had a sense of growing, growing enormous in the dark. Growing enormously in the dark. A sense of becoming enormous, gigantic and simultaneously a sense of growing smaller, shrinking and stiffening, a sense of escape and at the same time a kind of general and particular impoverishment, a sense of paralysing tension and tense paralysis, of being hung by a tense thread, as well as of being converted and changed into something, a sense of transmutation and also of relapse into a kind of accumulating and mounting mechanism, as if on a narrow plank being hoisted to the eighth storey, with all one's sense alerted; and also of sub-tickling. The sound of footsteps came from the lumber-room, but nobody budged. Alfred appeared in his slippers.

'Who's there?' he said. He took a step into the dining-room, said 'Who's there?' again, and then froze into immobility, having sensed something. He knew that his father must be somewhere around, for he had heard him moving about and then asking questions. But why didn't his father answer? Because he was inhibited by ancient fears and terrors, oh he could not, because he was afraid. And the son was inhibited by his father's fear. He was afraid because of the quantity of fear that had already been generated, and fell silent, as if for centuries. Perhaps he felt rather lost at the outset, but the very indefiniteness rapidly assumed a most formidable definition, and grew by itself. The sense of growing, swelling, becoming huge, started all over again, lengthened and broadened, swelled and multiplied itself to the hundredth power, became tense, acute, stretched to bursting point, strain and tension, a sense of stifling monotony, tension, endless, boundless, infinite, a sense of submergence above and below, with Alfred a little further away. A sense of being throttled, yet not throttled; obstacle; hold one's head high, disintegration, explosion, being slowly stripped, repetition, ejection and penetration, transformation and tension, tension, tension. Did this last for minutes or for hours? What was going to happen? Whole worlds flew through my head. I remembered that it was at this spot that I used to lie in wait for my nurse in order to give her a fright—it nearly made me laugh. Hush! Where did that laugh come from? But enough of this, I must stop this, do something, what would happen if my childishness were exposed, if after all this time I were found with the stable-boy, which would be a strange and inexplicable discovery indeed? Oh Isabel, to be with Isabel, to have to hold one's breath with Isabel instead of with the stable-boy! With Isabel it would not be childish. Suddenly I insolently moved and stepped behind the curtain, feeling certain that they would not dare to budge, and sure enough they did not budge. The result was that something like lethargy was superimposed on the fear prevailing in the darkness, for now it was more than just impossible, it was also awkward and embarrassing to break the silence. Perhaps they wanted to, perhaps they thought about it, but they did not know how to set about it. I am referring to their silence, for by my movement I had broken my own silence. Perhaps they were thinking only about the outward formalities of the situation, perhaps they were concerned with appearances, looking for some external pretext or excuse. The worst of it was that the presence of each paralysed the other, and the two thinkers remained standing, powerless to put an end to the situation or to interrupt it, while suspense and repetition still remained ceaselessly at work. Having recovered my own ability to move, I decided to grab the stable-lad and hustle him quickly into the lumber-room, but no sooner had I come to this decision than a gleam of light appeared, casting a slight reflection on the floor, and there was a creaking of floorboards and the sound of footsteps, Francis was coming with a lamp, and the silhouette of my uncle's leg stood out, plain for all to see. Luckily I was behind the curtain. But the old flunkey mercilessly threw a light on the others and all that was going on in the dark—my uncle, his hair slightly dishevelled, standing only a pace away from the stablelad, their noses were almost touching, and Alfred planted like a stick only a little way away.

'Is anyone here?' Francis asked crossly, illuminated by the light of the little petrol lamp. He asked the question belatedly, however, merely in order to justify his appearance, because he could see the three of them as plainly as if they were in his hand.

Uncle Edward moved. What would Francis think, seeing him so close to the young manservant? Why were they together there like that? He could not withdraw altogether, but he moved, and thus broke the link connecting him to Bert; then he stepped to one side.

'What are you doing here?' he shouted, changing the fear inside him to fury.

The lad didn't answer; he couldn't think of anything to say. He stood there with a great deal of naturalness, but his tongue failed him. He was alone with the masters; and the inarticulateness of this child of the people, his lack of education, cast a suspicious shadow. Francis looked at my uncle. . . . What were the masters doing with Bert in the dark? Was the master being familiar with him too? A flush started slowly spreading over the old servant's face as he stood there stiffly with the lamp in his hand, and soon his cheeks were aglow with the brilliance of a sunset. 'Bert!' Alfred exclaimed. All these exclamations were not well placed in time. They were blurted out either too late or too soon, and I cowered behind my curtain.

'I heard someone here,' Alfred started saying, lamely and incoherently, 'I heard someone here . . . Someone. What were you doing here? What were you doing? Speak up, I tell you! What were you doing? Speak up, damn it!'

There were horrible discords in his excitement.

'It's obvious what he was after,' said the flunkey, who was as red as fire, after a long and ghastly silence. 'It's obvious, sir!'

He stroked his moustaches, and went on:

'The silver is in the drawer, and tomorrow you were going to send him packing, sir. So he was going to . . . steal the silver.'

So he had been going to steal the silver! This was the plausible explanation that they wanted, the lad had been caught red-handed while going to steal the silver. Everyone, including Bert, felt a sense of relief. Uncle Edward moved away from the young manservant, and sat down at the table. He resumed his normal, baronial attitude towards the stable-boy, and recovered his self-confidence. So the lad had been going to steal the silver!

'Come here!' said Uncle Edward. 'Come here, I tell you! Come here, quite close to me!'

He was no longer afraid of proximity, and he was obviously enjoying no longer being afraid.

'Nearer!' he said. 'Nearer!'

Bert, heavily and mistrustfully, went nearer him—still nearer—and when he was nearly touching him Uncle Edward raised his arm and struck his face, first forehanded and then back-handed, like Mene, Mene, Tekel and Upharsin.

'I'll teach you to steal!' he shouted.

Oh, the joy of striking out like this in the light after the fear in the dark! Oh the joy of striking the face which has been the cause of the fear, of striking within the limits laid down by the precise, the definite, idea of attempted robbery! Oh, the pleasure of normality after all the abnormality! Alfred, following his father's example, struck the lad in the teeth, like the hanging gardens of Semiramis. He struck the boy hard and repeatedly. Behind the curtain I writhed as if transfixed on a skewer.

'I didn't steal!' the stable-boy said, getting his breath back.

This was what they had been waiting for; it enabled them to exploit the appearance of attempted robbery to the utmost.

'You didn't steal?' said Uncle Edward, leaning back in his chair, and delivering another blow.

'You didn't steal?' said his son, to the accompaniment of a

short, sharp blow. 'You didn't steal?' they kept repeating. 'You didn't steal?' And each time they said the words their hands relentlessly sought and found the lad's face, delivering a shower of blows as if mounted on springs. Mingled with the short sharp blows were broad resounding swipes.

'I'll teach you to steal! I'll teach you to steal!'

Oh, they were well away. Oh, accursed night, oh accursed, treacherous darkness, without this bath in the shadows none of this would have happened! The country nobility was riding high. Under the pretext of attempted robbery it was striking out and getting its own back for its blushes, for the fraternization with Mientus, and for everything that it had suffered.

'This is mine, mine!' Uncle Edward kept repeating. 'Mine, damn it!'

And gradually, the meaning of the word 'mine' changed; you could not tell whether he was referring to the silver, or his body and soul, his hair, his customs, hands, distinction, culture, breeding; it seemed rather that in striking and hitting the lad he was trying to impose on him, not what he owned and possessed, but himself, not his goods and chattels but his own person. He was imposing himself. Terrorize him, terrorize him, use violence upon him, impose yourself on him, so that never again will he dare to fra . . . ternize, or gossip about his masters, or laugh at them, but accept them like gods. With his delicate, gentlemanly hand Edward nailed himself to the lad's face.

Behind the curtain I rubbed my eyes, wanted to scream, shout for help, but could not. And Francis stood there, illuminating the scene with his little lamp. My aunt! My aunt! Did my eyes deceive me, or did I see her for a moment standing in the doorway, with her bag of sweets? I had a flash of hope that perhaps she would save, mollify, neutralize the situation. She raised her hands as if to cry out, but instead smiled senselessly, made an equally meaningless gesture with her arms, and withdrew to the smoking-room. She pretended she hadn't been there, the dose was too strong for her, she couldn't stand it, so she inwardly dissolved herself backwards, or rather spread herself backwards,

260

in such nebulous fashion that I wondered whether she had really been there at all. Uncle Edward started weakening, but once more sprang forward to impose himself—while Alfred sprang forward at his side, and he too imposed himself, imposed himself, imposed himself with all his power and strength. Between their teeth they muttered phrases such as: 'So I climbed the game-keeper, did I? Climbed the gamekeeper, did I?' 'So you wanted to fra . . . ternize, did you?' 'So I've got an old woman, have I?' And to wipe these things out of existence they struck, not the lad's back or his legs, but his face. They did not fight him, oh no, they did not fight him, they just struck him in the face. And this was perfectly permissible. Meanwhile old Francis illuminated the scene with his lamp, and when their hands weakened he said tactfully:

'The masters will teach you, the masters will teach you!'

At last they stopped. They sat down, and the stable-lad got his breath back; his ear was bleeding, his face and head were dreadfully knocked about. The masters offered each other cigarettes, and the old flunkey leapt forward, match in hand. It looked as if it were over. But Alfred blew a smoke ring.

'Bring us brandy!' he said and, helping themselves abundantly to a fine old bottle, they set about breaking in the stable-lad, to make a fine old servant of him. 'We'll teach you! We'll break you in!' And it started all over again . . . to such good purpose that I thought my senses were deceiving me. For nothing is so deceptive as the senses. Hidden behind my curtain, with bare feet, I was not sure whether the scene going on before my eyes was reality or a prolongation of the shadows. Can one see reality with bare feet? Take off your shoes, hide behind a curtain, and try! Look, with your feet bare. What an ignoble scene! 'Bring this! Bring that!' they shouted. 'Small glasses! Napkins! Bread! Rolls! Ham! and be quick about it!' The stable-lad hurried here and there, faithfully doing whatever he was told. And they started eating in front of him, imposing baronial eating on him. 'Your masters drink,' Uncle Edward announced, emptying a small glass of old brandy. 'Your masters eat,' Alfred chimed in, 'I eat my food. I drink my drink. This is my food and my drink. Not yours!' 'Learn to know your masters,' they shouted at him, putting their persons under his nose, imposing all their peculiarities on him, so that to the end of his days he should lose all desire to criticize or have doubts about, or mock at, or be surprised at them, so that he should accept them as a thing in itself, a *Ding an sich*. And they shouted: 'Do what you're told!' and gave him orders, proliferated orders, which he carried out and kept on carrying out. 'Kiss my shoe!' He kissed it. 'Throw yourself at my feet!' He did so, and Francis like a trumpet provided a tactful accompaniment:

'The masters will show you! The masters will teach you!'

Sitting at the brandy-stained table, by the light of the little petrol lamp, they went on teaching him and breaking him in. And this was permitted and permissible, because they were training and breaking in a stable-boy, turning him into a domestic servant. I wanted to shout no, no, stop! But I couldn't. I was ashamed to see what was going on in front of my eyes, I did not know whether I could believe them, whether what I was seeing was true, how much of my own I was putting into the horrible scene; perhaps with my shoes on what I saw might have been different. And I shuddered at the thought that the eye of some third party might be upon me, regarding me as an integral part of the scene. I cringed under the shower of blows on the stable-lad's face, under the blows of my own despair and terror, and at the same time wanted to laugh, I laughed without wanting to, as if my feet were being tickled. Oh, Isabel, if only Isabel were here, oh to carry off Isabel, oh, to run away with Isabel, maturely, like a man! Meanwhile they continued, in baronial fashion from behind their glasses of old brandy, breaking in the immature stable-lad, breaking him in elegantly, even stylishly, sitting in their chairs behind the table and sipping their old brandy. Mientus appeared in the doorway.

'Leave 'un alone! Leave 'un alone!'

He did not shout, but said the words sharply and shrilly, and advanced on my uncle. I suddenly saw that we were not alone, that the whole scene was being observed, that innumerable eyes were on us. Outside the window there was a crowd. Stable-boys, farm-girls, labourers, village men and women, yokels male and female, farm servants and domestic servants, were all watching us. The shutters were not closed, and they had been attracted by the noise in the middle of the night; and they were respectfully watching their masters ordering Bert about, breaking him in, teaching and instructing and training him to become a servant in a smart household. 'Look out, Mientus!' I shouted, but it was too late. Uncle Edward just had time to turn his back on him contemptuously, and to give the stable-boy one more blow in the face. Mientus went and put his arm round the lad and drew him close to him.

'' 'e's moin!' he said. 'Doan't 'it 'un! Doan't 'it 'un! Leave 'un alone! Doan't 'it 'un!'

'You young puppy!' Uncle Edward shouted. 'You young puppy! Just you wait and see what you're going to get on your backside!'

Mientus's juvenile yappings made him and Alfred lose their temper, and they went for him, to ridicule him on his backside, wipe out the value of his fra . . . ternization by chastising him on it in the presence of Bert and of the vulgar outside the window. 'Aow! Aow!' Mientus yelped, cringeing in strange fashion and jumping behind the stable-lad. And the latter, as if his courage in the face of his masters had been restored by Mientus's fra . . . ternization, suddenly fraternized on Uncle Edward's face.

'What does thee think thee's doin'?' he exclaimed vulgarly.

The charm was broken. The servant's hand had fallen on the master's face, and the master saw stars. So unexpected was the blow that he went down like a log. Immaturity spread everywhere. There was the sound of broken glass, and the light went out; a stone thrown from outside shattered the lamp. The windows gave way, and the populace surged in, the darkness was populated with parts of rustic bodies. The atmosphere was as heavy as in the bailiff's office. Paws and hands . . . no, the vulgar have no hands . . . paws, an enormous quantity of big, heavy paws.

The people, roused by the exceptional immaturity of the scene, had lost all sense of respect, and wanted to fra . . . ternize too. I heard Alfred and then Uncle Edward yell . . . they seemed to be holding the two together in some way and to be clumsily and lethargically starting on them, but it all was invisible in the dark ، . . I jumped out from behind the curtain. My aunt, my aunt! I remembered my aunt! I ran on my bare feet to the smoking-room and grabbed her: she was lying on the sofa, pretending not to exist. Into the fray with her, into the fray! 'My child! My child! What are you doing?' She implored, and struggled, and offered me sweets, but like a child I dragged and dragged her towards the fray. Into the fray with her, into the fray. That's it, they've got her! I dashed from room to room . . . not running away, only running, running, running, after myself, sounding the general alarm on my bare feet. I ran to the front gate. The moon was emerging from behind the clouds, but it was not the moon, but a bum, a great bum spreading itself over the top of the trees. A childish bum over the world. Bum and nothing but bum. Behind me they were all wallowing in the *mêlée*, and in front of me was this great bum. The trees trembled in the breeze. And this great bum.

Mortal despair seized and held me in its grip. I had become childish to a degree. Where was I to run? Back to the house? There there was nothing but the wallowing and floundering in the *mêlée*. Where was I to go, what was I to do, how find myself a place in the world? I was alone, almost alone, reduced to childhood. But it was impossible to remain alone, unattached to anything. I ran down the path, jumping like a grasshopper over the dry branches, looking for contact with something, for a new dependence, a new link, even if only a temporary link, in order not to remain in the void. A shadow glided from behind a tree. It was Isabel. She had caught me!

'What's happening?' she asked. 'Have the peasants attacked Mamma and Papa?'

I took her by the arm. 'Let us flee!' I said. We fled together across fields bathed in the remote unknown, and there she was, abducted, and there was I, the abductor. We ran down a path through the fields until we ran out of breath, and spent the rest of the night in a meadow by the waterside, hidden away among the reeds, shivering with cold and with our teeth chattering. The grasshoppers chirred. At dawn another huge bum, red this time and a hundred times more dazzling, appeared in the sky, and flooded the world with its rays, forcing everything to project long shadows.

I did not know what to do. I could not explain and describe to Isabel all that was happening up at the house, because I was ashamed and, moreover, words failed me. No doubt she guessed more or less what was happening, but she too was ashamed and did not know what to say. So she remained seated among the reeds, and coughed, because she was feeling the damp. I counted my money; I had nearly fifty zlotys and some small change.

Theoretically we should have walked to the nearest house and asked for help. But how were we to explain, present the matter? Shame made it impossible. And I felt I should prefer spending the rest of my life among the reeds to telling anyone the whole story. That was something I could never do! Better admit having abducted Isabel, which was much more assimilable, better say that we were running away together from her parents' house, which was far more mature. Once I had made the admission, no more explanations would be necessary, for women are always ready to admit that one is in love with them. This would provide a pretext for us to make our way surreptitiously to the station and take the train to Warsaw, where we would start a new life in secret, the secrecy being attributable to the abduction.

And so I kissed her on the cheek and declared my passion, asking her forgiveness for having abducted her; and I explained that her family would never have consented to the match, because my position was not good enough, but that I had fallen in love with her at first sight, and had felt that she reciprocated my feelings.

'There was nothing for it but to abduct you, Isabel,' I said. 'There was nothing for it but for us to run away together.'

At first she was rather startled, but after half an hour of these declarations she started simpering and looking at me (because I was looking at her) and moving her fingers. She forgot all about the peasants up at the house, and became genuinely convinced that she had been abducted by me. This flattered her inordinately, as hitherto she had done nothing but embroidery, or studied, or had just sat looking at something, or been bored, or gone for walks, or looked out of the window, or played the piano, or busied herself philanthropically with the Solidarity Society, or sat for exams in agriculture, or flirted and danced to music, or gone to the seaside, or made conversation and said something. Hitherto she had lived only in the expectation of meeting someone to whom she could belong. And now, not only had she met such a person, but he had actually abducted her. That was why she called on all her capacity for loving, and loved me—because I loved her.

Meanwhile the super-bum mounted higher in the sky, sending out its dazzling rays by the million over a world which was a kind of imitation of the world, a paper world, painted green and illuminated from on high by blazing light. Following remote paths and avoiding villages, we made our way towards the station, and we had a long way to go . . . about thirteen miles. She walked and I walked, I walked and she walked, we walked together, each supporting the walk of the other, under the rays of the pitiless, shining, glittering, sparkling, puerile and puerilizing super-arch-bum. The grasshoppers hopped, the cicadas stridulated in the fields, the birds flew from tree to tree. But Isabel insisted that she knew the way, for she had passed this way thousands of times by car, landau, or cart. The heat was stifling. Fortunately we were able to refresh ourselves by sucking the milk of a solitary cow. Then we set off again. And the whole time, in view of my declaration of love, I had to go on talking of love and behaving gallantly, helping her over little bridges, for instance, chasing flies away, asking whether she were not tired, and paying her numerous other little attentions and making sentimental demonstrations. She responded by asking me whether

I were not tired too, by chasing flies off me, and by paying me similar attentions. I was dreadfully exhausted. Oh, when I got to Warsaw I should get rid of Isabel and start living again! I only wanted to use her as pretext and cover, to enable me to escape with some appearance of maturity from the *mêlée* at the house and to get to Warsaw, but for the time being I had to take an interest in her and, in a general way, keep up this intimate conversation of two beings who are happy in each other's company. And Isabel as we have seen, subjugated by my demonstration of feeling, grew more and more enterprising. And the super-bum, shining with improbable brightness and elevated to an altitude of a thousand million square miles cubed, flooded the valley of the universe with light.

She was a country young lady, brought up by her mother, my aunt Hurlecka, *née* Lin, and by the servants; and hitherto she had studied a little at the Horticultural College, where she had peeled some fruit, she had cultivated her mind and heart a little, had sat down a little, worked as a supernumerary in an office, played the piano a little, walked a little, and talked a little, but above all, she had waited and waited and waited for a man to turn up and fall in love with her and carry her off. She was a great specialist in waiting, passive and shy, and that is why she suffered from toothache, for she was made for a dentist's waiting-room, and her teeth knew it. So that now, when the object of all this waiting had at last appeared and carried her off, now that the great day had come, she became intensely active, and started showing herself to her best advantage, simpering, smiling and skipping about, making eyes at me, showing me her teeth and her happiness, gesticulating, or humming tunes to me under her breath. Moreover, she made the most of and accentuated the more pleasing parts of her body and did her best to conceal the others. And I had to look at her and pretend to be interested . . . and the arch-bum suspended loftily over the world in the incommensurable blue of the skies shone, gleamed and glowed, and warmed, burned, and dried up the grass and other vegetation. And Isabel, knowing that when one is in love one is happy, was happy; she looked at me with clear and tranquil eyes, forcing me to look back at her; and she said:

'I wish everyone were as happy as we are! If everyone were good, everyone would be happy!'

Or:

'We are young, we are in love. . . . The world is ours!'

And she rubbed herself tenderly against me, and I had to do the same to her.

And then, cónvinced that I was in love with her, she opened up and started telling me her secrets, talking to me sincerely and intimately, which she had never done to anyone before. For hitherto she had been afraid of men and, having been brought up in a certain aristocratic isolation by my Aunt Hurlecka, *née* Lin (now lost in the *mêlée*), and by the servants, she had never confided in anyone, for fear of being criticized or misjudged, and she was undefined, uncrystallized, indeterminate, unsure of herself and uncertain of the impact that she made on others. She had a great need of kindness, couldn't do without it, could talk only to someone whom she knew *a priori* and in advance to be well disposed towards her. And now, seeing that I loved her, seeing that she had managed to secure an ardent admirer *a priori* who would lovingly accept whatever she said because he was in love with her, she started confiding in me and revealing herself, disclosing her joys and sorrows, her tastes and inclinations and enthusiasms, her illusions and disappointments, her hopes and aspirations, her sentimentalism, her memories, and all the trivial details, for at last she had found a man who loved her, a man to whom she could show herself as she was, sure of impunity, sure that everything would be accepted with love and warmth. And I had to fall in with this and accept it, and go into ecstasies about it . . . and she said:

'People should try to perfect their minds and bodies, be always beautiful. In the afternoon I like holding my forehead against the window-pane and shutting my eyes. I like the cinema, but I like music better.'

And I had to acquiesce; and, knowing that her nose could not be an object of indifference to me, she whispered to me that when she awoke in the morning she always had to rub it, and she burst out laughing, and I burst out laughing too. After this she said sadly:

'I know I'm not pretty!'

I had to deny this. And she knew that I denied it, not in the name of reality and truth, but because I was in love with her, and she therefore accepted my denial with delight, enraptured at having found an unconditional, *a priori* admirer who loved and accepted everything with graciousness and warmth.

Oh, the agony through which I went to keep up at least the appearance of maturity along these paths through the fields, while, back at the now-distant house, masters and plebs made shameful play with their hands and the super-arch-bum suspended at the zenith terribly and mercilessly spat forth the lances of its rays, its thousands of arrows . . . oh, insipid charm, oh, deadly tenderness, mutual admiration, love! . . . Oh, the insolence of these females so greedy of love, so eager for amorous harmony, so willing to be the objects of adoration! . . . How dared this soft, empty, and insignificant creature consent to my blandishments and accept my homage, and batten ravenously on it? Does there exist in the world under the ardent and burning rays of the arch-bum anything more appalling than this sweet feminine warmth, idolatry and tender snuggling? And to make matters worse, to requite me and complete the cycle of mutual admiration, she started expressing admiration of me, and asking me questions about myself, not that she was really interested, but as a matter of tit for tat, for she knew that the greater interest she took in me, the greater interest I should take in her. And she in her turn stuffed me with adoration, snuggling amorously against me, whispering that she liked me so much, that I had made such an impression on her at first sight, that I was so bold, so brave . . .

'You carried me off,' she said, intoxicating herself with her own words. 'That's not a thing anybody could do! You fell in love with me, and abducted me without asking anybody's permission, without being afraid of my parents. . . . I love those brave, fearless, feline eyes of yours!'

And I writhed under the blows of her admiration as under Satan's whip, while overhead the huge, infernal super-bum, the great super-arch-bum, the hall-mark of the universe, the key to all problems, the essence and common denominator of all things, shone brilliantly and piercingly. Warmly and shyly she snuggled against me, cajoled and wheedled me, mythologized in her lethargic fashion; and I felt her adoring my qualities and peculiarities, searching and finding, warming up and consuming herself. She took my hand and started stroking it, and I stroked her hand, while the infantile and infernal super-arch-bum reached its zenith and apogee, vertically probing with its fire the very depths down here below.

Suspended at the very tip and summit of space, it launched its rays of gold and silver over the whole of this valley and in all directions. Meanwhile Isabel snuggled more and more tenderly against me, united herself with me more and more, and introduced me more and more into herself. I wanted to go to sleep. I could not go on walking, or listening, or answering. We walked through I know not what fields, and in those fields the grass was greenly green and verdant, abounding in yellow camomiles, but the camomiles were shy, and hid themselves in the grass, which was slightly damp and slippery, steaming under the cruel fire in the sky. Poppies appeared on both sides of the path, but they were rather anaemic poppies. A little farther on, on the hillsides, there were a lot of melons. On the water in the ditches were water lilies, pale, discoloured, blanched and delicate, tranquil under the heat beating down from above. And Isabel snuggled still more tenderly against me, and continued with her confidences. And the arch-bum still transfixed the world. The texture of the dwarf trees was anaemic and rickety, they were more like mushrooms, and they were so timorous that when I touched one it broke. There were a multitude of chirping sparrows. Overhead there were fat little reddish, bluish and whitish clouds, which looked as if they were made of silk paper, sorry and sentimental-looking. Everything was so vague and confused in outline, so silent, so chaste, so full of waiting, so unborn and undefined, that in reality nothing was separate or distinct from anything else; on the contrary, everything was connected with everything else in the bosom of a single, thick, whitish and silent, extinguished mass. Tenuous little brooks murmured, wetted the earth, vaporized or bubbled. And this world dwindled and seemed to shrink, and as it shrank it seemed to tighten, to close round your throat, like a delicate cord strangling you. And the arch-bum still struck down from on high, transcendentally and terribly. I rubbed my brow.

'What is this place?'

She turned her poor, enchanted face towards me, and replied tenderly and blushingly, snuggling against my shoulder:

'*It's my place.*'

This took me by the throat. So this was where she had led me! So this was it, all this was hers. . . . But I wanted to go to sleep, I could hardly hold my head erect, I had no strength left . . . oh, to put some space between us, six inches at any rate, oh, to refuse her, to get angry and strike her, to say something hostile to her, to be nasty, yes nasty to Isabel! I must do it, I said to myself drowsily, my head hanging on my chest, I must do it, I must be nasty to Isabel. Oh, saving and invigorating nastiness, as cold as ice! Time was pressing, I must be nasty! But how was I to be nasty to her if I was so kind, if she kissed me and penetrated me with her kindness and I penetrated her with mine? There was nothing and nobody to help me. In these meadows and fields, among the shy grass, we were together—I with her and she with me—and there was nothing, nobody, to aid me. I was alone, and with Isabel, and the concentrated super-bum was immobilized in his absolute, shining, resplendent domain, puerile and puerilizing, hermetically closed and enigmatic, plunged and buried in itself and at the zenith of its fatal culmination.

Oh, for some third person to come to my aid! Help! Help! Come, third person, come to the two of us, appear, so that I may cling to you, rescue me! May he appear instantly, this third person, a stranger, as fresh and cool and pure as a wave of the sea, may he shatter with his strangeness this vaporizing intimacy,

271

rescue me from Isabel! Come, oh, third person, support me, enable me to resist, let me lean on you, come, living breath, come strength, remove me, take me far away! But Isabel clung to me with redoubled warmth, affection, and tenderness.

'Why are you calling out?' she said. 'Whom are you calling? We're all alone!'

And she put her face near mine. And my strength failed me, sleep submerged wakefulness, and I could not. . . . I had to kiss her face, touch her face with mine, because she touched my face with hers. And now, oh faces! . . . No, I am not bidding you farewell, oh, strange faces of strangers, unknown faces of those who will read me, greetings, greetings, gracious collections of parts of bodies, I am not bidding you farewell, this is only the beginning! Come near, approach, start your work of making me a new face, so that I may run away from you in your turn towards other men, and run, run, and run through the whole of humanity. For there is no shelter from face except in face, and we can escape from men only by taking refuge in other men. And from the arch-bum there is no refuge. I fled, with my face in my hands.

PORNOGRAFIA

Translated from the French by
Alastair Hamilton

____ Preface _____

A Polish author once wrote to me asking about the philosophical meaning of *Pornografia*.

I replied:

"Let us try to express ourselves as simply as possible. Man, as we know, aims at the absolute. At fulfillment. At truth, at God, at total maturity. . . To seize everything, to realize himself entirely—this is his imperative.

"Now, in *Pornografia* it seems to me that another of man's aims appears, a more secret one, undoubtedly, one which is in some way illegal: his need for the unfinished. . . for imperfection. . . for inferiority. . . for youth. . .

"One of the clearest scenes in this sense is the one in church, where the celebration of the Mass collapses under the force of Frederick's strained conscience, and with it God the Absolute, while, from the dark and cosmic void, comes a new, earthly, sensual idol composed of two minor beings who form a closed circle—because they are submitted to a mutual attraction.

"Another important scene is the assembly before Siemian's murder, when the adults feel incapable of killing him because they are aware of the weight of murder. The murder must therefore be committed by adolescents shifted onto a level of frivolity and irresponsibility—this is the only way it can be done.

5

"I have already mentioned this elsewhere, if only in my *Diary*, in a passage about the Retiro in Buenos Aires (1955): 'Youth seemed to me the highest value of life. . . but this "value" has a particularity undoubtedly invented by the devil himself: being youth it is below the level of all values.'

"These last words ('below all values') explained why I have been unable to take root in any contemporary existentialism. Existentialism tries to re-establish value, while for me the 'undervalue,' the 'insufficiency,' the 'underdevelopment' are closer to man than any value. I believe the formula 'Man wants to be God' expresses very well the nostalgia of existentialism, while I set up another immeasurable formula against it: 'Man wants to be young.'

"In my opinion the ages of man serve as a tool for this dialectic between the fulfilled and the unfulfilled, between the value and the undervalue. This is why I give such an enormously dramatic part to youth. And this is why my universe is degraded, as though someone had taken the spirit by the scruff of the neck and immersed it in frivolity and inferiority.

"But remember that for me philosophy has no meaning; it is none of my business. My sole intention is to exploit certain possibilities of a theme. I search for the 'beauties' peculiar to this conflict. . . "

* * *

Is this clear? It is said that a work explains itself, that the author's commentaries are superfluous. On the whole that is true! But contemporary art is not always easily accessible and it is sometimes useful for the author to take the reader by the hand and show him the way.

* * *

Maybe I should say who I am and where I come from.

I am the author of the following works in Polish: *Bakakai* (short stories); *Yvonne, Princess of Burgundy* (comedy); *Ferdydurke* (novel); *The Marriage* (drama); *The Trans-Atlantic* (novel); *Pornografia* (novel). And finally, my *Diary* from 1953 to 1961.

I was almost unknown until 1957. An immigrant in the Argentine.

In 1957 the Polish government, in a moment of fleeting liberalism, allowed my books to be reprinted. The enormous and unexpected success of this enterprise was such that I was banned once more and it became illegal to write about me. (Such is the musical chairs that we writers of certain countries play with our people, even those who, like me, do not meddle in politics.)

* * *

Ferdydurke is undoubtedly my basic work, the best introduction to what I am and what I represent. Written twenty years later, *Pornografia* originates from *Ferdydurke*. I should therefore say a few words about this book.

It is the grotesque story of a gentleman who becomes a child because other people treat him like one. *Ferdydurke* is intended to reveal the Great Immaturity of humanity. Man, as he is described in this book, is an opaque and neutral being who has to express himself by certain means of behavior and therefore becomes, from outside—for others—far more definite and precise than he is for himself. Hence a tragic disproportion between his secret immaturity and the mask he assumes when he deals with other people. All he can do is to adapt himself internally to his mask, as though he really were what he appears to be.

It can therefore be said that the man of *Ferdydurke* is created by others, that men create each other by imposing

forms on each other, or what we would call *façons d'être*.
Ferdydurke was published in 1937 before Sartre formulated his theory of the *regard d'autrui*. But it is owing to the popularization of Sartrean concepts that this aspect of my book has been better understood and assimilated.

And yet *Ferdydurke* ventures on other, lesser known ground, the word "form" is associated with the word "immaturity." How can this Ferdydurkean man be described? Created by form he is created from outside, in other words unauthentic and deformed. To be a man means never to be oneself.

He is also a constant producer of form: he secretes form tirelessly, just as the bee secretes honey.

But he is also at odds with his own form. *Ferdydurke* is the description of the struggle of man with his own expression, of the torture of humanity on the Procrustean bed of form.

Immaturity is not always innate or imposed by others. There is also an immaturity which culture batters us against when it submerges us and we do not manage to hoist ourselves up to its level. We are "infantilized" by all "higher" forms. Man, tortured by his mask, fabricates secretly, for his own usage, a sort of "subculture": a world made out of the refuse of a higher world of culture, a domain of trash, immature myths, inadmissible passions. . . a secondary domain of compensation. That is where a certain shameful poetry is born, a certain compromising beauty. . . .

Are we not close to *Pornografia?*

* * *

Yes, *Pornografia* springs from *Ferdydurke:* it is a particularly irritating case of the Ferdydurkean world: the Younger creating the Older. When the Older creates the Younger everything works very well from a social and cultural point of view. But if the Older is submitted to the Younger—what darkness! What perversity and shame! How many traps! And yet Youth, biologically superior, physically more beautiful, has no trouble in charming and conquering the adult, already poisoned by death. From this point of view *Pornografia* is bolder than *Ferdydurke* which uses, above all, sarcasm and irony—and humor implicates distance. In those days I tackled my themes from above and it could be claimed that in *Ferdydurke* I am struggling proudly against immaturity. And yet you can already perceive an ambiguous note which could imply that this opponent of immaturity is mortally in love with immaturity.

In *Pornografia* I have given up the distance lent by humor. It is not a satire but a noble, a classical novel. . . The novel of two middle-aged men and a couple of adolescents; a sensually metaphysical novel. What a disgrace!

* * *

I quote again from my *Diary*:

"One of my aesthetic and spiritual aims is to discover a more open, more dramatic access to Youth. To reveal its ties with maturity so that they should complete each other."

And:

"I do not believe in a nonerotic philosophy. I do not trust any desexualized idea.

"It is hard to believe that Hegel's *Science of Logic* or Kant's *Critique of Pure Reason* could have been conceived if their authors had not kept a certain distance from their bodies. But pure conscience, when it is hardly realized, must be steeped again in the body, in sex, in Eros; the artist must plunge the philosopher in enchantment, charm, and grace."

One more comment, although I might be suspected of megalomania: "And what if *Pornografia* were an attempt to

renew Polish eroticism? . . . An attempt to revive an eroticism which would bear a stronger relationship to our destiny
and our recent history—composed of rape, slavery, and
boyish squabbles—a descent to the dark limits of the conscience and the body?"

* * *

I am more and more inclined to present what seem to
me the most complex themes in a simple, naive form.
Pornografia is written in the style of a Polish "provincial
novel"; it is as though I were going for a ride in a charabanc,
rendered obsolete by the poison of the *dernier cri* (an old
fashioned cry, of pain, of course). Am I right in thinking
that the more literature is bold and inaccessible the more
it should return to old and easy forms, familiar to the
reader?

K. A. Jelenski, to whom my work owes so many and such
precious suggestions, considered that *Pornografia* presented
itself too definitely; he advised me to cover some of my
traces, like animals and certain painters. But I am already
tired of all the misunderstandings which have accumulated
between me and my reader and if I could I would have
limited his liberty to interpret me still more.

—W. G

PART ONE

1

I shall tell you about another experience I had, undoubtedly the most fatal of all.

In those days, in 1943, I was staying in former Poland, in former Warsaw, at the depths of the *fait accompli*. In silence. The dilapidated group of my old friends and companions from the former cafés, the Zodiak, the Ziemiańska, the Ips, met every Tuesday in a small flat in Krucza Street where we drank and tried to go on living like artists, writers, and thinkers. . . renewing our old conversations, our past discussions about art. . . I can still see them, sitting or lounging on the sofas in the smoky rooms, one or two of them a trifle cadaverous and worn, but all shouting and shrieking. One shouted: "God"; another: "art"; a third: "the people"; a fourth: "the proletariat." We talked ourselves hoarse, and it went on and on—God, art, the people, the proletariat. But one day a middle-aged man appeared, dark and thin, with a hooked nose. He formally introduced himself to everybody, and then hardly spoke a word.

He ceremoniously thanked his host for the glass of vodka he was offered, and equally ceremoniously said: "May I bother you for a match?" . . . He then waited for the match, and waited. . . and when he had been given it, set about lighting his cigarette. In the meantime the discussion raged on—God, art, the people, the proletariat—and the stench

13

began to pervade the air. Someone asked: "What good wind brings you, Frederick?" To which he replied, most explicitly: "Eva told me that Pientak often comes here, so I looked in because I've got four rabbit skins and a leather sole to sell." And, to prove it, he showed us his four rabbit skins wrapped up in a piece of paper.

He was offered some tea, which he drank; a lump of sugar remained on his saucer—he stretched out his hand toward it, but obviously considered his gesture pointless, and withdrew his hand. Since this gesture was even more pointless, however, he stretched out his hand once more, took the lump of sugar, and ate it—not for pleasure but to behave consistently. . . toward the sugar or toward us?. . . Clearly wanting to eradicate this unfavorable impression, he coughed, then, so as the cough should not seem pointless, pulled out his pocket handkerchief—but did not dare blow his nose and simply moved his foot. Moving his foot doubtlessly entailed other complications, so he decided to sit silent and motionless. This strange behavior (because in fact all he ever did was "to behave," he "behaved" the whole time) aroused my curiosity at the first encounter, and, in the course of the following months, I came closer to this man who proved to be by no means uncultured and also had a certain artistic experience (he had once worked in the theater). In short, we collaborated in small deals which earned us a meager living. But that did not last long, because one day I received a letter from Hippo, my friend Hippolytus S., a landowner from the Sandomierz district, inviting us to stay—Hippolytus added that he thought we might be of some assistance in his business affairs in Warsaw and wanted to discuss them with us. "It's quite peaceful down here, of course, except for the occasional raid by one of the gangs—you see, there is hardly any discipline. . . If you both come it will be more enjoyable."

Should we go? Both of us? I had fearful doubts about the journey. . . What, take him so that he could continue his game down there, in the country?. . . And his body which was so. . . so specific?. . . Travel with him regardless of his "obvious but hidden indecency?" . . . Look after somebody so "compromised" and therefore so "compromising?". . . Expose myself to this continual "dialogue" with. . . with whom? And his knowledge, his knowledge of. . . ? And his cunning, his ruses? Yes, it did not seem very enticing, and yet his eternal game made him so different, so alien to our common drama, so detached from our interminable discussions—God, the people, the proletariat, art—that it seemed refreshing, a relief. . . And in spite of it all he was so immaculate, prudent and level-headed! Oh well, come on then! It is so much more enjoyable if we both go! At last we squeezed into the crowded railway carriage, and the train slowly creaked out of the station.

Three o'clock in the afternoon. It was misty. Frederick, standing hunched under the weight of an old woman, a child's foot sticking into his chin, was as formal and well behaved as ever. Neither of us spoke. The train jolted us and hurled us against each other, into a congealed mass. . . through the window I could just see the sleepy, blue fields as we hurtled past. . . it was the same vast plain I had seen hundreds of times, the misty skyline, the checkered earth, trees whizzing by, a house, the figure of a woman. . . always the same, expected thing. . . And yet not the same thing, precisely because it is the same thing! Unexpected, unknown, incomprehensible, almost inconceivable! The child started howling, the old woman sneezed. . .

This bitter smell. . . The eternal sadness of a train journey, this sadness learned by heart, the ascending and descending line of the telegraph wires or the embankment, the sudden appearance of a tree in the window, of a telegraph pole, a signalman's hut, the landscape sliding swiftly past, its incessant retreat. . . as a chimney or a hill on the horizon rush into view. . . before vanishing into nothingness in a slow curve. Frederick was in front of me; his head, separated from me by two or three heads, was very close— he sat in silence, absorbed by the journey. . . and the presence of other bodies, importunate, invasive, and insolent, made my silent tête-à-tête with him so agonizing, so profound that. . . I would rather not have traveled with him and wished our plans had fallen through! For, in a corporal context, he was no more than a body among other bodies. . . but at the same time he existed—on his own, inexorably. . . There was nothing to be done. One could neither elude him, nor neglect him, nor efface him, he was in this crowd of people and existed. . . And his journey, his leap into space, were not comparable to anyone else's—it was a far more important, almost dangerous journey.

From time to time he smiled at me, said something obviously intended to make his presence bearable, less oppressive. I suddenly realized how hazardous it was to remove him from the town, to let him loose in the plains, in the wide-open spaces where his singular inner qualities could come into their own. He too must have realized this because I never saw him so silent, so insignificant. At one point the twilight, that substance which engulfs all forms, began to erase him and he faded away in the jolting, hurtling railway carriage, as it tore into the night, inducing a state of nonexistence. But that did not attenuate his presence, which merely dissolved behind a veil of invisibility. . . he existed just the same. Suddenly the light went on, thrusting him into view, revealing his chin, the lines at the corners of his mouth, his ears. . . but he did not budge and stood staring at the swaying telegraph wire—he was there! The train drew to another halt—from somewhere behind me came

shouts and the sound of boots, the crowd lurched into us—
something was happening, but he remained there! The
train moved off again. It was dark outside, and the engine
spat sparks as the carriage entered the night.—Why had I
brought him with me? Why had I condemned myself to
this presence which, instead of resting me, exhausted me?
The journey lasted for countless sleepy hours, interspersed
with halts and police investigations, gradually becoming an
end in itself, somnolent and obstinate, until we got to
Cmielow and found ourselves with our luggage on a path by
the side of the railway line. The bright quiver of the train in
the abating roar. The silence, a strange breeze and the stars.
A cricket.

Myself, suddenly removed from the bustle of a long
journey, on this path, next to Frederick standing, his coat
over his arm, in silence. Where were we? What was it? And
yet I knew this district, the breeze was familiar—but where
were we? Over there, at an angle, stood the familiar building of the Cmielow railway station and a couple of lamps
swaying in the dark, but. . . where, on which planet had
we disembarked? Frederick stood next to me—he just stood.
And then we walked to the station, myself in front, him behind. There were the break, the horses and the driver—the
break was familiar and familiar, too, was the way the driver
raised his cap—so why did I observe them so closely?

I got into the break, followed by Frederick, and we drove
off. The sandy path in the light of the black sky, on either
side the black shapes of trees or bushes, we went through
the village of Brzustowa, the shimmer of whitewashed
planks, and the bark of a dog—what a strange bark!—in
front of me the driver's back—what a strange back!—and
next to me my silent, polite companion. The invisible
ground rocked and jolted the break, the pits of darkness and

the thick shadows between the trees blocked our view. To hear the sound of my own voice I asked the driver:

"How is it around here? Quiet?"

And I heard him reply:

"It is right now. There are some gangs in the woods. But lately it's been pretty quiet."

The face was invisible and the voice was the same—therefore it was not the same. In front of me nothing but his back, and, for a moment, I wanted to bend forward and have a good look at this back, but I stopped myself. . . because Frederick. . . was there, next to me. And he was curiously silent. With him next to me I preferred not to have a good look at anybody. . . because I suddenly realized that the being sitting next to me was radical in his silence, radical to the point of insanity. Yes, he was an extremist, an extremist to the last degree. No, his was no ordinary existence, it was something infinitely aggressive, exerted to an extent I would never, until that day, have believed possible. I preferred not to have a good look at anybody—not even the driver whose back was crushing us like a mountain, as the invisible ground rocked and jolted the break and the surrounding twilight, pierced by a few shiny stars, blocked our view. The rest of the journey continued in silence. At last we entered a long drive, the horses quickened their pace —the gate, the watchman, the dogs, the heavy creaking of the bolts—Hippo holding a lamp. . .

"Thank God, you're here at last!"

Was it really he? I was struck and, at the same time, repelled by his bloated, red cheeks, bursting out. . . he looked as though he were bloated by a tumor that had distorted his limbs and stretched his flesh in every direction so that his repulsively flourishing body was like an erupting volcano of meat. . . and in his riding boots he flaunted his apocalyptic paws, while his eyes peeped out between lumps of fat. But he drew me to him and embraced me. He whispered shyly:

"I've grown bloated, damn it. I've put on weight. Why? Everything, I suppose."

And looking at his pudgy fingers he repeated with infinite bitterness, softly, to himself:

"I've put on weight. Why? Everything, I suppose."

And he thundered:

"This is my wife!"

And murmured, to himself:

"This is my wife."

And he shouted:

"And this is my darling Henia, my sweet little Henia!"

And whispered to himself, almost inaudibly:

"And this is my darling Henia, my sweet little Henia."

Then, hospitable and flourishing, he turned to us:

"How good of you to come, but please, Witold, introduce your friend. . ." He closed his eyes and repeated. . . his lips went on moving. Frederick gallantly, ceremoniously, kissed his hostess' hand, and a distant smile shone through her melancholy, and her svelte figure trembled. . . We plunged into the turmoil of introductions, our hosts showed us into the house, we sat down, they paid us the customary compliments, we returned them—after that interminable journey—while the paraffin lamp gave out its dreamy light. Dinner was served by a lackey. Our eyes were heavy with sleep. Vodka. Struggling with our exhaustion we strove to hear and to understand what was being said. The conversation was about every sort of difficulty—with the A.K.,* or the Germans, the gangs, the administration, the Polish police, requisitions—about constant fear and violence, evident from the additional iron bars on the shutters, the heavy bolts on the doors, the weapons glinting in the

---

* A.K.—*Armia Krajowa*, the Polish resistance movement.—*Tr. note.*

corner. . . "The Siemiechow's property was burnt down, in Rudniki the overseer's legs were broken, I had the house full of refugees from Poznan. . . the worst of it all is one can't tell what's going to happen next. At Ostrowiec, at Bodzechow, where the factory workers live, they're just waiting for a chance. . . at the moment it's pretty quiet, but if the Front comes any nearer it's going to blow up! It's going to blow up! Then you'll see the slaughter and the fireworks! Then you'll see the fireworks!" he yelled, then whispered to himself, thoughtfully:

"Then you'll see the fireworks."

And he shouted:

"The worst of it is there's nowhere to go!"

And he whispered:

"The worst of it is there's nowhere to go."

The lamp. An interminable dinner. Drowsiness. Hippo's vast figure smeared with the thick sauce of sleep, his wife dissolving into the distance, Frederick, the moths bumping into the lamp, moths in the lamp, moths around the lamp, the steep and narrow staircase, the candle. I collapsed onto a bed and fell asleep. The next morning, a triangle of sun on the wall. A voice below the window. I got up and opened the shutters. The early morning.

2

Clumps of trees between the graceful curves of the paths, the garden sloped gently down to the lime trees behind which could be perceived the hidden surface of a pond—oh! all that green glistening with the dew! And when we went out into the courtyard after breakfast—the house, white, with two floors and its mansard roof, surrounded by firs and thuyas, flower beds and paths, which astonished us like a vision from the past, from the distant days before the war. . . and in its very permanence it seemed more real than the war. . . but at the same time the feeling that it was not true, that it was at odds with reality, transformed it into a theatrical décor. . . finally, the house, the park, the sky, and the fields became both theatrical and real. But here came our host, in all his enormity, a green jacket on his bloated body, and he approached us just as he used to, waving to us from the distance and asking if we had slept well. Chatting idly we went through the gateway into the fields and gazed over the sweep of country, undulating in the wind, and Hippo spoke to Frederick about the harvest and the profits, occasionally crushing little clods of earth with his foot. We came back toward the house. Hippo's wife appeared on the balcony and shouted good morning to us as a little boy ran across the lawn, the son of the cook, perhaps? So we ambled through the morning—the repetition of other mornings—but it was not so simple—because the landscape suddenly seemed somehow withered and again it struck me that everything, although it remained the same, was different. What an absurd idea, what an oppressively disguised thought! Frederick was walking along beside me, illuminated by the bright daylight in such a way that one could perceive the hairs sticking out of his ears and all the pores of his pale, wizened skin, Frederick, I repeat, bent, enfeebled and round-shouldered, in pince-nez, his nervous mouth twitching, his hands in his pockets—the typical city intellectual in the country. . . And yet, in this contrast, the countryside was no longer victorious, the trees lost their assurance, the sky seemed altered, the cow no longer offered the anticipated resistance, the eternity of the countryside now seemed ruffled, uncertain, troubled. . . And Frederick, yes, Frederick now seemed more real than the grass. More real? An exhausting, disquieting, foul idea, even somewhat hysterical, even provocative, invasive, destructive. . . and I did not know whether it was Frederick who had given me this idea, or the war, the revolution, the occupation. . . or both? And yet he behaved impeccably, questioned Hippolytus about the farming, saying the things he was expected to say—and suddenly we saw Henia coming across the lawn. The sun burnt our skin. Our eyes were dry and our lips chapped. She said:

"Mama is ready. I've had the horses harnessed."

"To go to church, to Mass, it's Sunday," explained Hippolytus. And he added softly to himself:

"To go to church, to Mass."

And loudly:

"If you want to join us we'll be delighted, but you're not obliged to. I believe in tolerance, don't I? I'm going, and as long as I'm here I'll go! As long as there's a church I'll go to church! With my wife and daughter, what's more, *and* in a carriage—I don't need to hide—Let people see me—Let them stare to their hearts' content, let them photograph me!"

And he murmured:

"Let them photograph me!"

But Frederick was already stressing our eagerness to go to Mass. We drove along in the carriage, its wheels creaking as they sank into the sandy ruts—and when we reached the top of the hill we saw the vast expanse of low fields, low under the curiously high sky, cowering in an immobilized surge. There, in the distance, was the railway track. I wanted to laugh. The carriage, the horses, the driver, the hot smell of sweat and varnish, the dust, the sun, a fly on my face, and the creak of the wheels on the sand—It was all centuries old and nothing, not one single thing, had changed! But on the hill we caught our breath in the cool waft of the space, of the space which ended in the shimmering skyline of the Mountains of the Holy Cross, and the perversity of this trip almost gave me a start, because it was as though we had stepped out of an oleograph—a dead photograph from an old family album—and the obsolete vehicle on the hill could be seen for miles, thereby making the country-side particularly ironical, cruelly disdainful. The perversity of our deceased journey spread to the bluish landscape, turning and changing imperceptibly as we gradually advanced. Frederick, sitting on the back seat next to Maria, looked around in every direction and admired the color scheme as though he really were going to church. Never, do I think, have I seen him so sociable and polite! We drove around the curve down into the ravine where the village began, and the mud. . . .

I recall (and this is of a certain importance for the events which will subsequently be related) that my dominant feeling was one of vacuity and again, as on the previous night, I wanted to lean out and look the driver in the face. . . But

that was impossible, it was not done. . . so we remained behind his impenetrable back and our journey continued behind his back. We drove into the village of Grocholice, to
our left a stream and to our right scattered houses and
fences, a hen and a goose, a trough and a pond, a man or
a woman in their Sunday clothes hurrying toward the
church. . . the sleepy serenity of a village on a Sunday. But
it was as though our death, leaning over a pool, were presenting its own image, so perfectly was the obsolete antiquity of our entrance reflected in the immemorial existence of the village, and so loudly did it resound in this
insanity—which was, moreover, only a mask used to hide
something. . . But what? Any meaning, every meaning. . .
of the war, the revolution, violence, incontinence, misery,
starvation, despair, a curse or a blessing. . . every meaning, I
repeat, would have been too feeble to pierce the crystal of
this idyll, so that the image we provided, which had long
been antiquated and lacking in substance, remained un-
changeable. Frederick was conversing politely with Maria—
but was it not simply to avoid saying something else that
he sustained this banal conversation? We finally reached
the low wall around the church and started getting out of
the carriage—but I no longer knew what was what—
whether the steps leading to the square were ordinary steps
or whether. . . ? Frederick offered Maria his arm, after having taken off his hat, and ceremoniously led her to the
church, before the eyes of the curious spectators—but
maybe he only did it to avoid doing something else?—and
behind them Hippo, who had managed to clamber out
of the carriage and plunge his enormous frame forward,
through the crowd, determined and impregnable, knowing
that the next day they could slaughter him like a pig, advanced to spite the hatred, looking sinister and resigned.

The landlord! But maybe he was only being a landlord so as not to be something else?

But, as soon as we were engulfed in the twilight where lighted candles were stuck like nails, where a whining chant welled up from the coarse, prostrate throng. . . all the latent ambiguity vanished—as though an invisible hand, more powerful than ours, had re-established the sanctifying order of the Mass. Hippolytus, who had until that moment ardently and passionately acted the role of the landlord to save himself from being devoured, sat, suddenly serene and noble, in the family pew, and nodded to the family of the administrator of Ikania who sat opposite. The Mass had not yet begun, the priest had not yet appeared at the foot of the altar, the congregation was left to its humble, tender, strident, awkward chant, which kept it well under control and made it as harmless as a dog on a leash. What serenity, at last, what a relief: here, in this stone sanctuary, the peasant became the peasant, the master the master, the Mass the Mass, the stone stone and everything returned to itself.

And yet Frederick, who had taken his place next to Hippolytus, knelt down. . . and this troubled me a little for it seemed perhaps slightly exaggerated. . . and I could not help thinking that he had knelt down to avoid doing anything other than kneeling down. . . but the bell rang, the priest came in carrying the chalice and, after placing it on the altar, bowed down before it. The bell rang again. And suddenly I felt so moved, so deeply moved that I dropped to my knees and, in my wild emotion, I almost prayed. . . But Frederick! It seemed to me, and I suspected, that Frederick, on his knees, was "praying" too—I was even sure, yes, knowing his lack of integrity I was certain that he was not pretending but was really "praying" for the benefit of others and for his own benefit, but his prayer was no more than a screen to conceal the enormity of his "non-prayer". . . . it was an act of expulsion, of "eccentricity" which cast us out of this church into the infinite space of absolute disbelief, a negative act, the very act of negation. And what was going on? What was happening? I had never seen anything like it and I had never believed that that could happen. What exactly had happened? Strictly speaking: nothing, strictly speaking it was as though a hand had withdrawn the substance and content from the Mass—and the priest continued—and the priest continued to move, to kneel, to go from one end of the altar to the other, and the acolytes rang the bells and the smoke from the censers rose in spirals, but the whole content was evaporating like gas out of a balloon, and the Mass collapsed in its appalling impotence—limp and sagging—unable to procreate! And this loss of content was a murder committed out on a limb, outside ourselves, outside the Mass, by the mute but lethal commentary of a member of the congregation. And against that the Mass had no means of defense, because it had happened as the result of some subsidiary interpretation; nobody actually in the church could have resisted the Mass and even Frederick was participating as correctly as possible. . . and when he killed it it was only in effigy, one might almost say. But this commentary, this murderous criticism was an act of cruelty—the act of a sharp, cold, penetrating, pitiless consciousness. . . and I suddenly understood that it was insane to have brought this man into a church, for God's sake, that should have been avoided at all costs! For him church was the worst place in the world!

But it was too late! The process taking place before my eyes was revealing reality *in crudo*. . . it began by destroying salvation and in this way nothing could hope to save these repulsive peasant faces, stripped of any style and displayed raw, like scraps of meat on a butcher's stall. They were no longer the "people," they were no longer "peasants," or even "men," they were simple creatures, for what they were worth, and their natural filth was suddenly cut off from grace. But the wild anarchy of this multiheaded, tawny crowd corresponded to the no less arrogant shamelessness of our own faces which ceased being "intelligent" or "cultivated" or "delicate," and became like caricatures without a model, caricatures which had ceased representing anything and which were as bare as behinds! And these two explosions of monstrosity, the lordly and the boorish, blended in the gesture of the priest who was celebrating. . . what? What? Nothing. . . And yet that is not all.

The church was no longer a church. Space had broken in, but it was a cosmic, black space and it was no longer happening on earth, or rather the earth was turning into a planet suspended in the void of the universe, the cosmos was present, we were in the center of it. To a point when the flickering flame of the candles and even the daylight which filtered through the stained-glass windows turned as black as ink. We were no longer in church, nor in this village, nor on earth, but, in accordance with reality—somewhere suspended in the cosmos with our candles and light and it was there, in infinity, that we were playing our curious games with each other, like monkeys grimacing into space. It was a very special game, there, somewhere in the galaxy, a human challenge in darkness, the execution of curious movements and strange grimaces in space. And yet this drowning in space was accompanied by an extraordinary rise of the concrete, we were in the cosmos, but as though we were in something terrifyingly definite, determined in every detail. The bells rang for the elevation. Frederick knelt.

This time, by kneeling down, he dispatched the Mass as one rings the neck of a chicken and the Mass went on, by now mortally wounded and staggering like a drunkard. *Ite, missa est.* And, ah, what a triumph! What a victory over the Mass! What pride! As though this liquidation represented a long-awaited end: alone, at last, all alone, with nobody and nothing except myself, alone in complete darkness. . . I had reached my limit, I had reached darkness. Bitter the end, bitter the taste of victory, and bitter the goal! But it was proud and dizzy, branded by the pitiless immaturity of the at last autonomous mind. It was terrifying, too, and, with no support, I felt in myself as in the hands of a monster, capable of doing everything, of doing anything, anything with me! The aridity of pride. The icy finality. Severity and void. And then? And then? The Mass was ending, I looked around sleepily, I was tired, oh, we had to go out, go back home, to Pogorna, along that sandy path. . . but at a certain moment my gaze. . . my eyes. . . panic-stricken and heavy. . . Yes, something attracted them. . . my eyes. . . Oppressive and seductive. . . Yes. What? What attracted me? What tempted me? The miraculous, like certain veiled spots in our dreams, made more desirable by their inaccessibility and around which we circle with a mute cry, in the confusion of an agonizing longing.

I circled around it thus, still fearful and uncertain. . . but already deliciously abandoned to the sweet violence which seized me—charmed me—enticed me—enchanted me—tempted and subdued me. . . And the contrast between the cosmic ice of this night and this spring bubbling with delight was such that I caught myself thinking vaguely that it was God and a miracle, God and a miracle. . .

But what was it?

It was. . . a fragment of cheek and a piece of neck. . . belonging to someone in the congregation a few steps away from us. . .

Oh, it was unbelievable! It was. . .

(a boy)

(a boy)

And, having understood it was only (a boy) I began to recover from my ecstasy. In fact I had hardly seen him! I had just seen a bit of ordinary skin—on the cheek and the neck. Now he suddenly moved and this meaningless movement cut right through me. What an unlikely attraction!

But it was (a boy).

No more than (a boy).

How awkward! A sixteen-year-old neck, close-cropped hair and the ordinary skin of (the boy) with a few little chaps and a (youthful) bearing—perfectly ordinary—so why was I trembling? Ah. . . now I could see the contour of the nose because he had tilted his head slightly to the left—still perfectly ordinary, and, at an angle, I could see the ordinary face of (the boy)—but perfectly ordinary! He was not a peasant. A student? A probationer? Nothing special about this (youthful) face, untroubled, slightly defiant, a face that would chew the ends of pencils, play football or billiards, and the collar of his jacket concealed his shirt collar, his neck was sunburned. And yet my heart was beating very fast. And he emitted an aura of divinity, marvelously captivating and enchanting in the infinite void of this night, a source of heat and living light. Charm. In vain I wondered why. Why had his insignificance suddenly become so significant?

Frederick? Did he know it, had he seen it, had he noticed it too?. . . But suddenly the congregation moved, the Mass was ended, they were slowly pushing toward the door. And I was among them. Henia was in front of me, her back and her scholarly little neck, and this came before me and, once there, impressed itself so deeply—and blended so harmoniously, so perfectly with that other neck. . . and suddenly I realized, it was easy and entailed no effort, yes: this neck and the other neck. These two necks. These necks were. . .

What? What was it? It was as though her (girl's) neck broke away to join that other (boy's) neck, this neck dragged by the neck and dragging the other neck by the neck! Please excuse the clumsiness of these metaphors. It is not so easy for me to discuss them (and one day I shall have to explain why I put the words *boy* and *girl* in parentheses, yes, this too remains to be explained). Her movements, as they preceded me in the hot, hurrying crowd, seemed to "concern him," in a certain way, and were like the passionate, languid complement of his movements in the same crowd, close by. Really? Was I wrong? Suddenly I saw her hand hanging by her body, crushed into her flesh by the pressure of the crowd, and this crushed hand abandoned her flesh to him in the intimacy and the throng of all these crowded bodies. It is true, all of her was "for him." And he, further on, walking peacefully with the congregation, was straining toward her, for her. This love, this wild desire advanced so calmly with the crowd in affected indifference! Ah, that was it!—I now knew what secret had attracted me to him at the first moment.

We emerged from the church into the sunny square, and the people dispersed—but they—he and she—appeared to me in full. She, wearing a light blouse, a navy blue skirt, a white collar, standing aside, waiting for her parents, was fastening the clasp on her prayer book. He. . . went a few paces toward the wall around the church, and, standing on tiptoe, looked over the other side—I do not know why. Did they know each other? Although they were each on their own, their passionate suitability seemed all the more obvious: they were made for each other. I blinked—the little square was white, green, blue, hot—I blinked. He for her, and she for him, far away from each other, not showing any interest in each other, and the impression was so strong that the (boy's) lips not only seemed made for her lips but for her whole body—and her body seemed supported by his legs!

And yet I think I went too far in this last sentence. . . Would it not have been better to say simply that they were exceptionally well suited to each other. . . and not only sexually? It sometimes happens that we see a couple and say: "They're very well suited," but in this case their suitability, I can call it that, seemed all the more responsive because of its immaturity. . . I really do not know if I am making myself clear. . . and yet this adolescent sensuality had an unusual gleam, like a supernatural treasure, because they represented supreme happiness for each other, the most precious and the most important possession. And there, on that square, under that sun, dazed and baffled, I could not understand why they did not display a greater interest in each other, did not fly toward each other! She stood on her own and he stood on his own!

Sunday, the country, the heat, a sleepy indolence, the church, nobody in a hurry to go home, little groups assembled. Maria touched her face with her finger tip, as though she were examining the texture of the skin, Hippolytus discussed quotas with the administrator of Ikania, next to them, Frederick, courteous, his hands in his jacket pockets, a guest. . . ah, this image deleted the black chasm in which this agonizingly bright flame had just appeared. . . only one thought upset me: had Frederick noticed it? Did he know?

Frederick?

Hippolytus asked the administrator:

"What about the potatoes?"

"Well, we can always deliver half a hundredweight."

The (boy) came up to us.

"This is my son Karol," said the administrator, pushing him toward Frederick, who shook his hand. He greeted everybody, one after the other. Henia said to her mother:

"Look! Mrs. Galecka's better!"

"Well, shall we call on the priest?" asked Hippolytus, and immediately murmured: "What's the use?" and thundered: "Come on, gentlemen, it's time to go back!"

We shook the administrator's hand and got into the carriage together with Karol (well, what does that mean?) who sat next to the driver. We started off, the axles of the rubber wheels creaking in the ruts; the sandy path in the quivering and soporific air, a gilded fly buzzing—and, from the top of the hill, the uneven patches of the fields and the railway track in the distance, there where the forest began. We drove on. Frederick, sitting next to Henia, spoke at length about the golden blue sheen in the air, so typical of the region and due, he explained, to the minute particles of loess. We drove on.

3

The carriage jolted. Karol was sitting next to the driver, on the driver's seat. She was on the front seat and where her head ended he began, as though he were perched on a floor above her, turning his back to us, only visible as a faceless silhouette—his shirt puffed out with the wind—and the combination of her face and his lack of face, her seeing face complementing his blind spine, filled me with a feeling of warm, obscure duplication. . . They were not particularly handsome, neither he nor she—no more than is normal at that age—but they were beauty itself in their magic circle, in their mutual desire and enchantment—something in which nobody had any right to participate. They were for themselves—strictly between themselves. Especially since they were so (young). So I had no right to stare at them and I tried not to see them, but since Frederick was sitting in front of me, next to Henia on the front seat, I again stubbornly wondered: had he seen them? Did he know? And I watched his every glance, glances which feigned indifference but which sneaked across surreptitiously and greedily.

And the others? What did the others know? It was hard to believe that something which seemed so obvious could have escaped (the girl's) parents—so, that afternoon, on my way to the cowshed with Hippolytus, I tried to steer the conversation onto Karol. But it was hard for me to ask straight questions about (the boy) who, what a disgrace! had so excited me, and, as for Hippo, the subject cannot have seemed worth a thought. "Karol, oh yes, a good boy, the administrator's son; he was with the partisans and he was sent near Lublin where he did something silly. . . oh, nothing important, he pinched something, wounded somebody, one of his comrades or his leader, I don't know, anyhow nothing important; but he had to beat it and he came home.—Since he's got it in for his father, the rascal, and they're always going for each other, I'm having him to stay for a bit—He's a good mechanic and there's no harm in having a few more people in the house in case. . . —In case. . ." he repeated as though he were reveling in it and crushed a clod of earth with his foot. And he suddenly changed the subject. Did this sixteen-year-old's biography not seem worth the telling? Or maybe he thought it preferable to play down (the boy's) pranks so as not to make them seem too important? Had he wounded or killed his comrade? I wondered. But even if he had killed that could be excused by his age, which obliterated everything. I asked if he and Henia had known each other long.

"Since they were children," he replied, tapping a cow lightly on the rump, and he added: "She's Dutch! A good milker! Sick, damn it!" That was all I could discover. So neither he nor his wife had noticed anything—anything at all serious, at least, which could have aroused their vigilance. . . How was that possible? I told myself that if the affair had been more adult—slightly less immature—slightly less boyish-and-girlish. . . but it was drowned in the insufficiency of their age.

Frederick? What had he noticed? After the church, after having slaughtered, having throttled the Mass, I simply had to know if he knew—and the idea of his not knowing would have been almost unbearable to me! The worst thing was that I could not in any way connect these two distinct states of mind—the first, the black one, conceived by Frederick, and the other fresh and passionate one caused by Karol and Henia—these two states of mind continued to exist in me, separate and heterogeneous. But how could Frederick be expected to discover anything if there was nothing between them. . . ? and for me it was fantastic, almost inconceivable, that they could both behave as though they were not seducing each other! I waited for them in vain to betray themselves. Their indifference seemed incredible! I watched Karol at lunch. A child, but a corrupt child. An attractive murderer. A smiling slave. A young soldier. A tough softness. A cruel, gory game. But this laughing, or rather, smiling child, had been "taken in hand" by men—he had the silent gravity of an adolescent who had participated at an early age in adult matters, pushed into the war, brought up by the army—and when he buttered his bread, when he ate, he displayed the temperance acquired from hunger. Occasionally his voice became gloomy and dull. He was something like iron. Like a leather thong, a freshly felled tree. At first glance he was perfectly ordinary, serene and friendly, obedient and even eager. Torn between the child and the grown man (and this made him both innocently naive and pitilessly experienced) he was neither the one nor the other, but he was a third term, he was youth, violent and uncontrolled, surrendering him to cruelty, restraint and obedience, and condemning him to slavery and humiliation. He was inferior because he was young. Imperfect because he was young. Sensual because he was young. Carnal because he was young. Destructive because he was young. And, in his very youthfulness, he was despicable. The oddest thing of all was that his smile, the most elegant thing about him, was the very mechanism that dragged him into humiliation, because this child could not defend himself, disarmed as he was by his constant desire to laugh. And all this flung him on Henia like on a bitch in heat, he burned for her and it really had nothing to do with love, no, it was something brutally humiliating which took place on an adolescent level—a childish love, in all its degradation. But at the same time it was not love—he really treated her like a young lady he had known "since he was a child," their conversation was free and familiar. "What's wrong with your hand?" "I scratched it opening a tin." "You know that Roblecki's gone to Warsaw?" And nothing else, not even a glance, just that. Who could suspect from this that there was anything between them? As for her, squeezed by the boy (if I may say so), and under his pressure, she had been violated in advance (if that makes sense), and, without losing her virginity, rendered on the contrary even more virginal by her partner, she was linked with him in the dark corners of his youthful, insufficiently manly compulsion. It could be said about her not that she "knew men" (as it is said about women of loose morals) but that she "knew the boy"—which was both innocent and infinitely more debauched. So it seemed, as they ate their noodles. They ate their noodles like a couple who have known each other since they were children, used to being together, and even a trifle bored. What? How could I hope Frederick would understand this, if the whole story were only a disgraceful illusion of mine? And so the day went by. Twilight. Dinner was served. We gathered once more at table in the dim light of the single oil lamp, the shutters closed, the doors bolted, and we ate curdled milk and potatoes; Henia's mother grazed the ring of her table napkin with her fingertips, Hippo turned his bloated face to the lamp. There was silence—but beyond the walls that protected us was the garden with its furtive and mysterious noises, and beyond the garden stretched the fields fiercely ravaged by the war. . . The conversation came to an end and, sitting motionless, we watched a moth bumping into the glass of the lamp. In a dark corner of the room Karol was taking a lantern to pieces and cleaning it. Suddenly Henia bent over to bite through her thread—she was stitching a blouse—and this brisk movement and the bite were enough to cause Karol to blossom out and light up, in his corner, although he did not flinch. But she put her blouse aside and leaned her arm on the table, and this arm, in full view, correct, modest, even scholarly, belonging to her Mama and Papa—was at the same time bare, completely naked, yes, naked not with the nudity of an arm but of a knee peeping out from under a dress. . . of a leg. . . and, with this shameless and scholarly arm she needled him, teased him in an "idiotically youthful" way (it can hardly be given any other name), but at the same time in a brutal way. And this brutality was joined by a low, fascinating chant, which resounded in them or around them. Karol was cleaning the lantern. Henia did not budge. Frederick was rolling bread crumbs.

The bolted door of the veranda—the shutters reinforced with iron bars—our silence around the lamp, the table, increased by the threat of the outer elements—the objects, the clock, the cupboard, the shelf, seemed to be living a life of their own—in this silence, this heat, their precocious sensuality grew desperate, bloated with instinct and nocturnal, within a closed sphere of excitement and desire, a sort of magic circle. So much so that it looked as though they wanted to stir up through the night that other savage passion which roamed across the fields outside, so thirsty were they for violence. . . although they were serene and even sleepy. Frederick slowly extinguished his cigarette in the glass saucer of the cup of tea he had only half drunk, he extinguished it without hurrying, but a dog suddenly barked in the yard and his hand crushed the stub. Hippolytus' wife passed her slender fingers over her delicate hands, gently, as one picks an autumn leaf, as one smells a faded flower. Henia moved. . . so did Karol, by chance. . . this involuntary movement which bound them to each other sprang up like a flame, set them alight, and her white knees immediately threw (the boy) on his knees, his dark immobile knees, in the dark corner. Hippolytus' large, red, hairy hands, filled with flesh and antediluvian, lay on the tablecloth too, and Hippolytus had to put up with them, since they belonged to him.

"Let's go to bed," he yawned. And he murmured: "Let's go to bed."

No, it was really unbearable! Nothing, absolutely nothing! Nothing but my pornography by which to feast on them! And my fury with their unfathomable stupidity—this little fool, this stupid little goose—because stupidity was the only reason I could give for there being nothing, nothing whatsoever between them! . . . Ah, had they but been two or three years older! But Karol was sitting in his corner, with his lantern, with his childish hands and feet—and had nothing to do but repair his lantern, immersed in his work, turning the screws—and so much the worse if the greatest happiness were concealed in this adolescent god! . . . he turned the screws. And Henia drowsing at the table with bored arms. . . Nothing! It was unbelievable! And Frederick, what did Frederick know about it, extinguishing his cigarette, rolling bread crumbs? Frederick, Frederick, Frederick? Frederick, sitting at the table, at this table, in this house, among those nocturnal fields, in the middle of this knot of passion! With his face which was in itself an immense provocation, so careful was he not to appear provocative. Frederick!

Henia could hardly keep her eyes open. She said good

night. Shortly after Karol did the same thing and, carefully gathering his screws in a piece of paper, he went up to his room on the first floor.

I then tried to slip in guardedly, as I watched the lamp and its kingdom of buzzing satellites: "What a sweet couple!"

Nobody answered. Henia's mother touched her napkin with the tips of her fingers. "If God is willing," she said, "Henia will be getting engaged one of these days."

Frederick, still rolling bread crumbs, asked with polite interest:

"Oh yes? With someone in the neighborhood?"

"Yes, indeed. . . A neighbor. Young Paszkowski from Ruda. Not far from here. He often comes to see us. A very respectable young man. Very respectable. . ." She fluttered her eyelashes.

"A jurist, you know," Hippolytus brightened up. "He was going to buy a practice just before the war broke out. . . Intelligent, serious, a good brain, you know, a well-educated fellow! His mother's a widow, she manages the estate, twelve hundred acres of splendid land, twenty miles away."

"A saintly woman."

"She comes from near Lwow. She's a Trzeszewska, related to the Goluchowskis."

"Henia's still rather young. . . but she'll never make a better match. The boy's responsible, gifted, exceptionally intelligent. When he's here you'll have someone to talk to, that's all I'll say about him."

"But he's really very serious. Honest and upstanding. With a high moral code. The image of his mother. An extraordinary woman, deeply devout and religious. . . a saint. Ruda is a moral sanctuary."

"At least he's a gentleman. We know what he is and who he is."

"At least we know whom we're giving our daughter to."

"Thank God for that!"

"Whatever happens, Henia will make a good marriage. Whatever happens. . ." he added to himself, suddenly deep in thought.

4

The night passed smoothly and imperceptibly. Fortunately
I had a room to myself so I did not have to bear his sleep. . .
The open shutters disclosed a radiant morning with clouds
racing over the bluish garden soaked in dew, and the low
sun cast slanting rays which seemed to implicate everything
in their slant—the horse slanted, the tree slanted! Amusing!
Most amusing and witty! The horizontal surfaces were
vertical and the vertical surfaces slanting! This morning I
was feverish, almost ill as a result of the excitement of the
day before, of that fire and that glow—because it must be
understood that all this suddenly happened to me after
stifling, gray years of horror and exhaustion, or of insane
extravagance. During which I had almost forgotten what
beauty was. During which I had smelt nothing but the rank
stench of death. And now suddenly there appeared before
me the possibility of a warm idyll in a spring I thought
irrevocably ended, and disgust gave way to the marvelous
appetite of these two young people. I wanted nothing more.
I had had enough of this agony. I, a Polish writer, I, Gombrowicz, chased after this will-o'-the-wisp as a fish chases its
bait—but what could Frederick know? The need to ascertain became unbearable, I had to know what he knew, what
he thought, what he imagined. I could no longer do without him, or rather I could no longer bear to be with him,

41

impenetrable as he was. Ask him? But how could I ask him? How could I put it? No, it was better to leave him to himself and watch him—he would soon end up by betraying his excitement. The opportunity presented itself after tea, as we were both sitting on the veranda: I stifled a yawn, I said I was going to have a short rest, and, on my way in, I hid behind the drawing room curtains. For that I required a certain amount of. . . courage. . . no, of audacity. . . because it looked rather like a provocation—but since there was something so provocative about him my act was no more than a way of "provoking the provoker." For me to hide behind the curtains put the first definite strain on our friendship and started a new, slightly illicit phase in our relationship.

What was more, every time I looked at him at moments when, absorbed by something else, he made no response to my gaze, I felt as though I had been caught doing something base. And yet I did not hesitate to hide behind the drawing room curtains. For some time he remained in the position I had left him in, sitting on the bench, his legs outstretched. He was gazing at the trees.

He moved. He stood up. He started to walk slowly around the courtyard, and he must have gone around it at least three times. . . before turning down under an arbor leading from the park to the orchard. I followed him at a distance, keeping him in sight. And I already felt I was on the right track.

Because Henia was in the orchard, peeling potatoes— was that where he was going? No. He went down a side path that led to the pond, and stood by the water, staring into space, his face that of a guest, of a tourist. . . Was his walk no more than a walk? I was on the verge of returning, convinced I had been deceived by my imagination (I had an obscure feeling that this man must sense these things: if he had not noticed anything it meant there was nothing to notice), when I suddenly saw him retrace his steps and come back under the arbor. I followed him.

He walked slowly, stopping from time to time to examine a plant, his intelligent profile bent over the leaves in the most obstinate way. The park was silent. My suspicions evaporated once more, only one remained: was he deceiving himself? He seemed to be making too many moves, to be too agitated as he wandered through the garden.

I was not mistaken. He changed direction twice more, and finally went into the orchard, went a little further, stopped, yawned, looked around... she was there, a hundred yards away, near the cellar, peeling potatoes! Sitting astride a sack! He glanced at her vaguely.

He yawned. Oh, it was incredible. The masquerade! For whose benefit? Why? All these precautions... as though he did not allow himself to participate in what she was doing... while it was obvious that he had been circling around her, getting nearer and nearer to her! There... now he was off toward the house, no, he went into the fields, went further, stopped, looked around, as though he really were going for a walk... but then he set out in a wide arc which led him back to the farmyard, yes, there was no doubt about it, he was going straight to the farmyard. Seeing this I ran as fast as I could through the bushes to get to a comfortable lookout post behind a shed, and, as I hurried over the broken twigs, through the bushes and across the ditch where a dead cat had been thrown and frogs hopped about, I realized that I was drawing the bushes and the ditch into our sinister game. I ran behind the shed. He was there, hidden by a wagon being loaded with manure. The horses suddenly stepped forward and he saw Karol in the opposite corner of the yard, examining a piece of iron near a shed.

It was then that he betrayed himself. Without the wagon

to screen him, unable to bear this open space between himself and the object of his curiosity, instead of remaining where he stood, he rushed to a hedge so that the boy should not see him, jumped over it, and stopped breathlessly. But this sudden move had unmasked him—he was frightened, and walked rapidly to the path leading to the house. Here, he came across me. We were walking toward each other.

There was no way of avoiding the encounter. I had caught him red-handed, and he had caught me. He had seen the voyeur. We were making straight for each other, and I must admit that I was by no means reassured, because now something was bound to change between us. I knew he knew, he knew I knew he knew—this was what went through my mind. We were still fairly far from each other when he shouted:

"Well, my dear Witold, have you come out for a breath of air?"

It was fearfully theatrical; that "Well, my dear Witold" sounded terribly false. He never spoke to me like that. I replied apathetically:

"Yes indeed. . . "

He took me by the arm—something he had never done before—and suggested, just as jovially:

"What a glorious evening, how good the trees smell! May I join you in your evening stroll?"

I replied, joining his contagious minuet:

"But of course, I'd be delighted!"

We went toward the house. But we no longer walked as we walked normally. . . it was as though we had returned to the park in another incarnation, ceremoniously, to the sound of music. . . and I suspected he had taken some decision which held me in its claws. What had happened? For the first time I felt he was hostile, menacing toward me. He still held my arm, but his proximity had something cynical and cold about it. We passed the house (he went on raving about the color scheme of the sunset) and I realized that we were taking the shortest way, straight across the lawn, to her. . . to the girl. . . and indeed the park, filled with rays and shadows, was like an immense bouquet, a blazing lamp bristling with firs and pine trees. We were walking toward her. She looked at us. She was still sitting on the sack, holding a knife. Frederick asked:

"Are we disturbing you?"

"Not at all. I've almost finished the potatoes."

He bent down and asked bluntly:

"May we invite the enchanting young lady to join us in our evening stroll?"

She got up and took off her apron. This eagerness. . . which may only have been politeness. After all, it was just a perfectly ordinary invitation to take a stroll in the garden, maybe said a little too emphatically, with the air of an old bachelor. . . but. . . but in this very approach, in this way of addressing her, I sensed an element of such shameless-ness that I could not help thinking "he's going off to do things to her" or "she's going off with him to let him do things to her."

We took the shortest cut, across the lawn, to the farm-yard, and she asked: "Are we going to see the horses?". . . His goal, his mysterious intent, seemed inscribed in the knowing pattern of the paths and lanes, the trees and the lawn. He did not reply. And this refusal to tell her where we were going filled me with fresh suspicions. A child. . . she was only a sixteen-year-old child. . . But we had almost reached the farmyard, with its floor of trodden earth, sur-rounded by the stables, the barn, the sheds, the watering-trough and a row of maples with the tips of the wagon shafts poking out behind them. . . she was a child, a child. . . but down there, by the shed, was another child, just as young, talking to the cartwright, still holding his piece of iron, standing near a heap of planks, beams, and sawdust, a wagon loaded with sacks, and the smell of chopped straw. We went nearer. Across the slope of trodden earth. When we got there, the three of us stopped.

The sun was setting and there was a curious sort of visibility which both confused and defined the objects—in this lighting a tree trunk, a hole in the bushes, the broken contour of a roof became clear in itself, visible in every detail. The dark-brown earth of the farmyard stretched up to the sheds. Karol was having a leisurely chat with the cartwright, like a peasant, leaning negligently against one of the posts supporting the roof of the shed and he did not interrupt his conversation when he saw us. We both stood there, with Henia between us, and it looked as though we had brought her to him—all the more so since neither of us spoke a word. Henia, too, was silent. . . and her silence expressed her shame. He put down his piece of iron and came up to us, but we did not know whom he was coming up to, to us or to Henia—and this gave him a certain duality, a certain awkwardness which threw him for an instant out of focus, but he joined us with ease, even with a certain gaiety. And yet the silence, because of our common awkwardness, lasted for a few seconds. . . and that was enough for stifling despair, regret, and all the nostalgia of Fate and Destiny to swoop down on them like a oppressive nightmare-ridden dream.

The languor, the beauty of the slim figure before us— what could produce them, apart from the fact that he was no man? Because we brought him Henia as a woman is brought to a man, but he was not one yet. . . he was not a man. He was no lord. No master. And he could not possess. Nothing could belong to him, he had no right to anything, he still had to serve, to obey—his fragility, his flexibility were even more accentuated in this farmyard, among the planks and the beams, and she responded to him in the same way: with fragility and flexibility. They were suddenly united, not like a man and a woman, but in another way, in a common offering to an unknown Moloch, incapable of possessing each other, only capable of offering themselves— and the sexual contract between them grew blurred, giving way to another contract, something undoubtedly more cruel but more beautiful. All that only lasted a few seconds. Nothing happened, either; all four of us just stood there. Frederick pointed to Karol's trousers which were slightly too long and dragged on the ground, and said:

"You ought to turn them up."

"That's true," said Karol. He bent down. Frederick said: "Just a minute."

It was obvious that what he had to say was not easy. He turned away slightly so as not to face them and, looking straight ahead, said in a hoarse but clear voice:

"No, wait. She can do it."

He repeated:

"She can do it."

The shamelessness of this demand—this breach made in their lives—was the admission of the excitement he required: do that, it'll excite me, that's what I want. . . That was how he introduced them to our lust, to the longing we nurtured for them. For half a second their silence quivered. And for half a second I waited for the result of Frederick's audacity. What followed was so simple and easy, yes, "easy," that I felt as dizzy as if an abyss had suddenly appeared before me.

She said nothing. She bent down and turned up his trousers. He had not even moved. Their silence was absolute.

I was suddenly overcome by the strange bareness of this

farmyard, with the shafts of the rack-wagons pointing at the sky, the broken drinking trough, the freshly thatched barn shining like a spark against the black, trodden earth and the woodpiles.

Frederick said: "Come on!" And we went toward the house—he, Henia and I. The audacity seemed still more obvious. Since we left almost immediately our presence near the shed meant one thing only: we had come so that she could turn up his trousers and now we were going away, Frederick, myself, and she. The house came into view with its windows, its double row of windows, below and above, and its veranda. We walked in silence.

We heard someone running across the lawn behind us, Karol caught us up and joined us. . . Still out of breath, he immediately fell into step with us: he walked along next to us, calmly and quietly. This hot race toward us was full of enthusiasm—he enjoyed our games, he wanted to join in— and his sudden change from a run into the calm pace of our return proved that he was aware of the necessity of discretion. All around could be felt the disintegration of being that invariably comes with the night. We gradually entered the dusk—Frederick, myself, Henia, Karol—like a curious erotic combination, a strange, sensual quartet.

5

How did it happen? I wondered, as I lay on a blanket on the cool grass, breathing in the humidity of the earth. How did it happen? She turned up his trousers? Very well. She did it because she could do it, of course, just as a simple favor. . . but she knew what she was doing. She knew it was for Frederick—for his pleasure—so she was prepared to let him extract pleasure from her. . . From her, but not from her alone. . . From her and from Karol. So that was it! She knew that they could both excite and seduce. . . Frederick, at least. . . and Karol knew too, since he had joined in the game. . . In that case they were not as stupid as we thought! They were conscious of their flavor! And if they were conscious of it in spite of their inexperienced youth, it is youth that has far greater intuition for these things than the age of maturity; in a way they were professionals, they possessed the infallible instinct of their premature flesh, their premature blood, their premature tastes. I was the bungler of the piece, not they. But then why did they behave like children in their own relationship? So innocently? If they ceased being innocent the minute a third actor appeared on the stage? If they behaved with such subtlety toward him? What worried me most of all was that this third actor should be none other than Frederick, who was normally so prudent, so level-headed! This sudden march across the park, this defiant advance, like a military maneuver, this march which was to offer the girl to the boy! What was it? What did it mean? Was I not responsible for it all? Having spied on him I had revealed his secret folly, he had been surprised, caught out in his mystery—and now the beast of his secret dream had escaped from its cage and, together with my beast, could rage at will! At the moment the situation was such that all four of us were the mute accomplices in an inadmissible crime, which excluded any explanation in advance, which smothered us with shame.

Her, his—their knees, four knees, in trousers, in a skirt, and (young). . . In the afternoon the famous Albert Paszkowski we had spoken about the day before arrived. A handsome man! Well-built and elegant, no doubt about it! With a prominent but fine nose, very mobile nostrils, eyes like olives and a deep voice—and under his sensitive nose his well-clipped mustache reclined on full, red lips. The sort of manly good looks that appeal to women. . . because women admire a fine figure just as much as the aristocratic delicacy of the details, like the thin veins of the hands with long fingers and well-manicured nails. Who could question his well-bred foot with its high instep, encased in an elegant, yellow shoe, or his small, well-formed ears? Were they not interesting and even, I might say, seductive, those little pits in his forehead which made him seem so intellectual? And was his pale complexion not that of a minstrel? Unquestionably a handsome gentleman! A victorious jurist! A distinguished lawyer! I hated him from the first, with a hatred mingled with disgust of a totally unjustifiable violence which amazed me—because he was charming and *comme il faut*. In fact it was neither loyal nor fair to resent the small imperfections, like, for instance, a slight swelling and fullness which rested lightly on his cheeks and his fingers, which lurked in the region of his stomach, and which was also highly distinguished. Maybe I was annoyed by the excessive and rather sensual subtlety of his features, of his mouth all too eager to eat, of his nose all too ready to smell, of his fingers all too prepared to feel—and yet all this made him a lover! What must have repelled me in him was the impossibility of nakedness—because his body needed a collar, studs, a handkerchief, and even a hat; it was a body in shoes, which called for toilet requisites and garments. . . but the worst thing of all was the transformation of certain defects, like the incipient baldness and the soft corpulence, into attributes of elegance and distinction. The physical appearance of a peasant has the immense advantage that the peasant pays no attention to it, so that it never shocks even if it be anti-aesthetic—but a man who dresses with care emphasizes his physical appearance, enjoys it and revels in it, so that every defect becomes lethal. But why had I suddenly developed such sensitivity about somebody else's body? Why this disgraceful passion for spying on people?

And yet I must admit that the newcomer behaved with intelligence and even with a certain amount of distinction. He did not give himself airs, spoke little and not too loudly. He was very polite. His politeness, his modesty, were the result of a good education, but must also have been innate: his character, by no means frivolous, was reflected in his eyes which seemed to say: I respect you, respect me too. No, he was not at all self-satisfied. He was aware of his faults and would undoubtedly have liked to be different— but he was himself with as much ease, intelligence, and dignity as possible, and although he was soft and fragile looking, he must have been violently obstinate, even determined. His good manners certainly did not stem from his weakness but from a principle, probably a moral one, of duty toward others; at the same time his manners categorically affirmed his class and his highly personal style. He had probably resolved to defend his values: subtlety, delicacy, and sensitivity, and he defended them all the more violently since history was harrowing them pitilessly. His arrival caused a number of changes in our little world. Hippolytus, previously so cautious, seemed to have found a secure track along which to run, he stopped murmuring to himself, ceased his bitter observations, and it was as though he were allowed to take his elegant suits of times gone by out of the closet and wear them once more—he was once again the blustering, ingenuous, jovially hospitable squire. "Well, how's it going? What's new? Have some vodka, it'll do you good!" And his wife pirouetted in her pale languor, and, fluttering her slim fingers, she spread a veil of hospitality.

Frederick responded to the respect Albert displayed for him with an even deeper respect; he allowed him to pass before him into the drawing room, and it was only when Albert insisted that he consented, as a special favor, to enter the room first—it was like Versailles. Then began a real tournament of courtesies—but the strange thing was that each of them seemed to be taking himself into consideration and not the other. After the first words Albert realized that he was dealing with somebody exceptional, but he was far too worldly to show it—and yet the rank he ascribed to Frederick aroused his own self-esteem, he decided his behavior should be à la hauteur and treated himself with exquisite courtesy. Frederick assimilated this aristocratic state of mind with enthusiasm, and became overweeningly arrogant—occasionally condescending to participate in the conversation, but only so as not to inflict an undeserved punishment on his listeners by remaining persistently silent. His fear of being incorrect suddenly turned into superiority and pride! As for Henia (who was the real reason for the visit) and Karol, they were drained of all significance. Sit-ing on a chair near the window she looked like a good little girl, with him, her elder brother, watching his sister's courtship and furtively checking whether his hands were dirty.

What a meal! Pastries and cakes appeared on the table! And then we went into the garden, where there was serenity and sunshine. The young couple, Albert and Henia, preceded us. We followed them at a short distance so as not to disturb them. . . . Hippolytus and his wife, rather moved, joking gently to each other, and next to them myself and Frederick, who was telling me about Venice.

Albert must have been asking her something, explaining something to her, as she tilted her head toward him, attentive and devoted, waving a blade of grass in her hand.

Karol walked across the lawn on his own, like a brother who is bored to tears by his sister's courtship and does not know what to do next.

"It's like a stroll before the war," I told Maria, who replied with a wave of her hand. We were approaching the pond.

But Karol's vagrancy became more nervous and more obvious, he clearly did not know what to do and his movements, imbued with boredom, seemed impatiently restrained. And, at the same time, although we could not hear them, all the things Henia was saying to Albert began to be addressed to Karol—once again her whole existence was surreptitiously united to (the boy), in spite of herself, because she never looked around and could not even have known that Karol was with us. And this tender talk she was having with Albert, as though they really were engaged, underwent, because of (the boy) following them, a sudden devaluation, while she herself began to radiate a kind of perversity. The enamored jurist pulled a branch of hawthorn toward her so she could pick a spray of blossom, and she seemed grateful, even touched; but this emotion did not end with Albert, it continued to Karol and, as it reached him, became obstinately young and adolescent, idiotically undecided and indifferent. . . it was the disparagement of their love, devoid of its real weight, turned into a base and vulgar feeling, taking place on an inferior level, on the level of a sixteen-year-old girl and a seventeen-year-old boy, on the level of their inadequacy and their youth. We came around a clump of hazel trees at the edge of the pond, and there we saw an old woman.

She was doing her washing in the pond and when she saw us she turned and stared at us—an old woman, a broad-bottomed old slut with sagging breasts, hideous, rancid and foully decrepit, with evil little eyes. She watched us, holding her wooden beetle.

Karol broke away from us and walked up to her as though he had something to say to her. And then he suddenly pulled up her skirt. For a second we could see her white belly and the black patch of hair! She bellowed. The boy made an obscene gesture, turned on his heels and came back to us as though nothing had happened, while the old woman yelled at him.

We did not say a word. It was such an unexpected and blatant obscenity, and it had disturbed us brutally. . . But Karol was already ambling along next to us, as serene as ever. Albert and Henia, deep in conversation, had disappeared around a bend in the path—maybe they had not seen anything?—and we followed them in silence, Hippolytus, his wife a trifle disconcerted, Frederick. . . What? What had happened? It was not so much the prank that had upset me, it was the fact that it could be transformed on another level, in another mode, into a perfectly natural gesture, and that Karol should continue to stroll along next to us, as charming as ever, with the strange charm of a scoundrel who assaults old women, a charm that grew on

me without my being able to understand it. How could this
foul gesture crown him with such grace? He literally glowed
with this incomprehensible charm and Frederick patted me
on the shoulder and whispered, almost inaudibly:

"Well, well!"

But he immediately turned his exclamation into a well-
formulated sentence, which he pronounced loudly and
affectedly:

"Well, well, what have you got to say for yourself, my
dear Witold?"

I replied:

"Nothing. Nothing, my dear Frederick."

Maria turned to us.

"I'll show you a fine specimen of American thuya. I
planted it myself."

It was so as not to interrupt the young couple. We examined the thuya until a farm lad came running up, waving his arms. Hippolytus turned sharply: "What is it?"
"The Germans have come from Opatow!" Sure enough
there were some people standing by the stables. He immediately rushed over to them, apoplectically, his wife behind him, Frederick behind them, thinking he could help
them with his good knowledge of German. As for me, I did
not want to get involved with them, I suddenly felt exhausted by the idea of these inevitable, oppressive Germans. . . What a nightmare. . . I went back to the house.

The house was empty, the rooms deserted, the abandoned furniture seemed to exist with greater intensity. . . I
waited for the result of the Germans' visit, taking place
silently by the stables. . . but soon I was waiting for Albert
and Henia who had vanished around the bend in the path. . .
and suddenly the thought of Frederick exploded in this
abandoned house. Where was Frederick? With the Germans? Not so sure. . . Was it not more likely that he would

be elsewhere, by the pond, where he had left the girl? He was there! He must have been there! He had gone back to spy on them. And what did he see? I was jealous of whatever he could see. Cast out of the house by its very emptiness I ran out as though I were going to the farmyard where the Germans were, but in fact I made straight for the pond, through the bushes, along the ditch where the frogs hopped with revolting, fat splashes, I went around the pond and saw them—Albert and Henia—sitting on a bench at the edge of the garden, facing the meadow. Night was falling, it was nearly dark. The air was damp. Where was Frederick? It was impossible for him not to be here. I was not mistaken: down there, among the willows, in a hollow, barely perceptible, he was at his post under the bushes, staring at them. I did not hesitate. I crept up to him and stood next to him. He did not budge and, as I gazed, my silent appearance as a watchman made me a defiant accomplice of his! On the bench two silhouettes could be distinguished, they must have been talking to each other, but so softly that they could not be heard.

That was deceitful of (the girl)—appallingly deceitful—there she was, fawning on the lawyer while (the boy) to whom she should have been faithful had been banished far away from her. . . I could not bear this idea, it was as though the last possibility of beauty were disintegrating in the world that used to be mine, invaded from now on by decomposition, agony, torture, and horror. What a disgrace! Was he embracing her? Or was he holding her hand? What a disgusting and hateful receptacle his hands were for hers! Suddenly I felt, as one feels in a dream, on the point of making a discovery, and, looking around, I saw. . . I saw something astounding.

Frederick was not alone: next to him, a few steps away, hidden in the bushes, was Karol.

Karol there? Next to Frederick? But how had Frederick managed to get him there? On what pretext? Whatever it was, he was there and I knew he was there for Frederick and not for her—he had not come to spy on what was happening on the bench, he had been attracted by Frederick's presence. It was as indistinct as it was subtle, and I do not know how to put it. . . I had the impression that (the boy) had come without being invited, only to arouse us. . . to emphasize. . . to make our feelings more agonizing. No doubt, while the other man, the adult stood staring at the child, shattered by her deceit, he, the little boy, had silently stolen out of the bushes and stood next to him without saying a word. It was bold and savage! But night was falling, we were almost invisible and perfectly silent—none of us could say a thing. The unlikely cynicism of our act foundered in the vacuity of the night and the silence. What was more, the presence of (the boy) effaced it, almost forgave us; his lightness, his slimness absolved us and he, so (youthfully) attractive, could join anybody he liked. . . (later I shall explain the meaning of these parentheses). . . And suddenly he went away as easily as he had arrived.

But the fact that he should have joined us like a shadow now made the sight of the bench pierce us like a dagger. This fantastic, wild apparition of (the boy) while (the girl) deceived him! All situations in the world are figures. The appallingly significant events that had happened here could not be understood or fully deciphered. The world was pitching in an unexpected way. And then, from the stables, we heard a shot. We rushed toward the farmyard, all of us together. Albert running next to me, Henia next to Frederick. Frederick, always level-headed and resourceful in moments of crisis, cut behind the shed, and we followed him. What we saw was by no means so bad. A slightly tipsy German was shooting pigeons with a double-barreled gun. Anyhow, they soon got into their truck and drove off, waving us good-by. Hippolytus looked at us in fury.

"Leave me alone!"

His eyes popped out of him like out of a window, but he closed all the doors and windows immediately. He went into the house.

That evening at dinner, ruddy and serene, he poured us out some vodka.

"Well? Let's drink to Albert and Henia. They're getting engaged."

Frederick and I congratulated them.

6

Alcohol. Vodka. An intoxicating episode. An episode like a large glass of alcohol—and then another glass—but this drunkenness was a steep slope, and at every moment there was the danger of toppling into filth and corruption, into a sensual quagmire. But how could one refrain from drinking? Drink had become a nutriment, everybody drank however he could and whenever he could—and so did I. I simply endeavored to rescue my dignity and retain, in my drunkenness, the appearance of a scholar who continues his researches in spite of everything, who gets drunk in order to study. And so I studied.

Albert left after breakfast. It was agreed that we should all go to Ruda the next day.

Karol drove the break up to the front door. He was off to Ostrowiec to get some paraffin oil. I offered to go with him.

Frederick was opening his mouth to make the same suggestion—when he was suddenly overcome by one of those feelings of embarrassment. . . to which he was liable at any moment. He was opening his mouth, but he shut it, opened it once more and remained in the grip of this agonizing game as Karol and I drove off in the break.

The cruppers of the horses as they trotted, the sandy path, the wide horizons, the slow whirl of the hills rising above each other into the distance. . . The early morning, out in the open, he and I, myself next to him, both of us emerging from the Poworna valley, exposed to view, and my incongruous presence next to him, visible for miles around.

I started off by saying: "Well, Karol, why did you do what you did to that old woman last night by the pond?"

To have a more specific idea of my question he asked, rather suspiciously:

"What?"

"Everybody saw you!"

This was a vague prelude—just a means of beginning a conversation. He laughed, just in case, and also to put what we said in a lighter vein. "Why shouldn't I?" he said, and cracked his whip, indifferently. . . I told him how surprised I was: "If only she'd been pretty! But an old slut like that!" Since he did not answer I went on: "Do you like old women?"

He nonchalantly thrashed his whip at a plant on the side of the road. And as though that were the reply to my questions he lashed out at the horses which plunged forward and almost upset the break. I understood the answer, although it could not be put into words. For a while we drove on at a faster pace. Then the horses slowed down and he grinned, revealing his white teeth, and said:

"What does it matter whether they're young or old?"

And he roared with laughter.

That worried me. I shuddered. I was sitting next to him. What did that mean? To begin with one thing struck me: the extraordinary importance of his white teeth which gleamed and frolicked within him, his inner, purifying whiteness. His teeth were far more important than his words—he seemed to speak for the sole benefit of his teeth —and he could say anything because he spoke for pleasure, devoted to his game and his joy, and he knew that his joyous teeth would be forgiven the foulest obscenities. Who was sitting next to me? Someone like me? Not at all: a being essentially different from myself, an enchanting being from a heavenly realm, endowed with a grace which was gradually turning into charm. A prince and a poem. But why did this prince assault an old woman? That was the question. And why did he enjoy it? Did he enjoy his own lust? Did he enjoy the fact that, being a prince, he was at the mercy of an appetite that made him lust after the most hideous of women? Did this Adonis (Henia's partner) think so little of himself that he did not care who satisfied him, nor whom he mixed with? Here there was something obscure. We went down the hill. In him I found sacrilege resulting from lightheartedness, sacrilege with which the spirit was involved, which contained an element of despair.

(Maybe I only indulged in these speculations so that I could retain the appearance of a scholar at this feast.)

Had he pulled up the old woman's skirt so as to behave like a soldier? Was that not the sort of thing a soldier would do?

Changing the subject—because I began to fear for myself—I inquired: "Why do you have such rows with your father?" He hesitated, puzzled, but realized that I must have found out from Hippolytus. He replied:

"Because he's always pestering my mother. He never leaves her in peace, the swine. If he weren't my father I'd . . ."

A perfectly normal answer—he could confess his love for his mother by admitting he hated his father and avoid any sentimentality—but I decided to pin him down and asked him bluntly: "Do you love your mother very much?"

"Of course! She's my mother. . . ."

Which meant there was nothing strange about it since it is perfectly normal for a boy to love his mother. And yet this intrigued me. At close quarters it seemed odd: a minute ago he had been a pure anarchist who assaulted an old woman, and now he had become conventional, submitting to the law of filial love. Which did he believe in—anarchy or law? If he submitted so passively to convention it was not to increase but to detract from his own value, and to make his love for his mother perfectly commonplace and unimportant. Why did he always underrate himself? This idea was curiously attractive: why did he love to disparage himself? This idea was pure alcohol. . . why, with him, was every idea either fascinating or repulsive, always passionate and intense? We had passed Grocholice and we drove uphill, past a yellow earth wall in which cellars for storing potatoes had been dug. The horses were walking—and there was silence. Karol suddenly brightened up: "Couldn't you get me a job in Warsaw? In the black market, for instance? I'd be able to give my mother a hand if I were earning some money, because she has to take a cure. And now my father's always grumbling because I haven't got a job. I'm fed up with the whole thing!" Now he could really talk, because it was about material and practical matters; it was also perfectly natural for him to talk about them to me. . . or was it so natural? Was it not just an excuse for making contact with me, the adult, for coming closer to me? Of course, at such a difficult time, a boy had to rely on older people, more powerful than himself, and could only hope to gain their good will through personal charm. . . But the coquetry of a young man is infinitely more complicated than that of a girl, who always has the advantage of her sex. . . So, this was probably calculated, however unconsciously, oh, and innocently! He was turning to me for help, but in fact he really did not care about a job in Warsaw, he simply wanted attention, he wanted to break the ice. . . the rest would follow on its own. . . Break the ice? But how? And what was "the rest" that would follow? I only knew, or rather suspected that his adolescence wanted to come into contact with my maturity. I also knew that he was not spoiled and that his appetite, his lust, made him easily accessible. . . I winced when I sensed his secret longing to come closer to me. . . as though that whole world of his were going to invade me. I do not know if I am making myself clear. The relationship between an adult and a boy usually takes place on a level of technical matters, of assistance and collaboration; but the minute it becomes more intimate its faintly improper nature reveals itself. I felt that this individual was going to seduce me with his youth, and it was as though I, the adult, were going to be irrevocably compromised.

But to use the word "youth"—that is to confound him.

We reached the top of the hill and were confronted with the unaltered view: the earth rising in hills, swollen in a motionless surge in the slanting light which here and there pierced the clouds.

"It's better if you stay with your parents. . . " That sounded categorical because I spoke as an adult, and that enabled me to extend our conversation by asking: "Do you like Henia?"

The most difficult question of all had slipped out with no difficulty, and with the same ease he replied:

"Of course I like her."

Pointing with his whip he added: "You see those bushes over there? They're not bushes, they're the tops of trees in the valley of Lisin, which leads to the Bodzechow forests. That's where some of the gangs go and hide, sometimes. . . " He gave me a conspiratorial wink. We drove along the road, past a crucifix on the right, and I went on as though I had not left off. . . . A sudden tranquillity, which I could not account for, enabled me to ignore the time that had elapsed:

"But you're not in love with her?"

This question was far more hazardous, it approached the heart of the matter, and, in its very insistence, could betray my somber emotions, mine and Frederick's, which had been conceived at their feet, at their feet, at their feet. . . I felt as though I were arousing a sleeping tiger. But without reason.

"Nooo. . . we've known each other since we were children! . . . " and it was said without any *arrière-pensée*. . . and yet one would have expected the episode by the shed, in which we had all been accomplices, to have made it slightly more difficult to reply.

Not at all! For him the episode must have been on another level—and now he felt no connection with it—his drawled "Nooo" had the flavor of an irresponsible caprice, even of banter. He spat. By spitting he completed his transformation into a bantering little scamp and he immediately laughed with that disarming laugh which seemed to dispense with the possibility of any other reaction; he looked at me out of the corner of his eye, and leered:

"I'd rather have the mother. . . "

No! It could not be true! Hippolytus' wife with her tearful thinness? Then why did he say it? Because he had pulled up the old woman's skirt? But then why had he pulled it up? How absurd! What an insoluble riddle! And yet I knew (and it was one of the basic principles of my literary science of man) that there are certain human deeds which seem totally senseless, but which are necessary for man because they define him. A simple example of that is the man who is prepared, for no apparent reason, to commit the wildest of follies, simply so as not to feel a coward.

And surely the young, more than anyone else, feel this need
to define themselves in this particular way? . . . It was more
than likely, even certain, that most of the words and deeds
of the adolescent sitting next to me, holding the reins and
the whip, were, precisely, "self-tests"—and even our—Frederick's and my—secretive and enchanted glances must have
encouraged him, without his knowing it, to play this game
with himself. Very well: he went for a walk with us yesterday, was bored and had nothing to do, so he pulled up
the old woman's skirt to do something lewd, which might
at last change him from one who is desired to one who
desires. Quite a little acrobat! All right. But why harp on
it and pretend he would "rather" have the mother? Might
it not conceal some secret, more aggressive intention?

"You're not going to make me believe that!" I said.
"You'd rather the mother than the daughter? What nonsense!" I added. To which he obstinately replied, as the
sun beat down: "But it's true."

Stuff and nonsense! But why, what was the point of it?
We were nearly in Bodzechow and, in the distance, we
could see the blast furnaces of the Ostrowiec steelworks.
Why, why was he dismissing Henia, why did he not want
her? I knew without knowing, I understood without understanding. Would his youth really prefer adults? Did he
want to be "with adults?" What was this idea leading to?
The unlikelihood, the burning keenness, the dramatic character of this idea soon put me on the right track, because
in his strange world, I only believed in intuitions and impulses. Did this brat want to prevail in our maturity? It was
perfectly normal for a boy to fall in love with a beautiful
girl and for their love to take the course of a natural attraction, but maybe he wanted something. . . vaster, more
daring. . . ? He did not want to be merely "a boy with a
girl" but "a boy with adults," a boy who breaks into

maturity. . . What an obscene, perverse idea! Behind him lay the experience of war and anarchy, I did not know him, could not know him, I did not know what had formed him or how, he was as puzzling as the landscape—familiar and yet unfamiliar—there was only one thing I could be sure about: that this scamp had been out of his swaddling clothes for some time! To get involved with what? It was impossible to tell—it was not clear whom or what he preferred. Maybe he wanted to amuse himself with us and not with Henia, and was therefore trying to make me realize that age was no obstacle. . . What? Yes, yes, he was bored, he wanted to amuse himself, to amuse himself with a game which he did not yet know, which he had never even dreamed of—out of boredom, out of laziness, nonchalantly —with us, and not with Henia, because we, in our ugliness, could lead him further, we were more unbounded. And so (recalling what had happened by the shed) he wanted me to know that he was not shocked. All right. I was nauseated by the idea that his beauty could search for my ugliness. I changed the subject.

"Do you go to church? Do you believe in God?"

A question which called him to order, a question designed to shield me from his deceptive lightness.

"In God? Well, you know what the priests say. . ."

"But you do believe in God?"

"Of course. But. . ."

"But what?"

He said nothing.

I should have asked: "Do you go to church?" instead of which I asked: "Do you sleep with women?"

"Sometimes."

"Are you successful with women?"

He laughed.

"No. How could I be? I'm far too young."

Too young. The meaning was humiliating—that was why he could use the word "young" deliberately. But as for me, who had just confused God with women, because of this boy, in some grotesque and almost drunken blunder, I sensed a curious admonition in this "too young." Yes, too young, too young for women, and for God, too young for everything—and what did it matter if he believed in God or not, if he was successful with women or not, because whatever happened he was "too young" and nothing he could do, say, or feel mattered: he was incomplete, he was "too young." He was "too young" for Henia and for all that happened between them, "too young" for Frederick as well, and for me. What was this fragile immaturity? It was meaningless, it did not count! How could I, as an adult, put all my gravity into his lack of gravity, listen to someone of no importance and tremble? I glanced at the countryside. From the top of the hill we could already see the bed of the Kamienna, and even hear the distant rattle of a train coming into Bodzechow; the entire valley lay before us, with the main road winding through it, and right and left the green and yellow chessboard of fields stretching into the distance—a sleepy eternity, but gagged, stifled, throttled. An oppressive smell of iniquity permeated this landscape and, in this iniquity, myself with this boy who was "too young," too light, too flighty, whose insufficiency, whose incompletion were being transformed into an elementary power. . . How could I defend myself against him if I could find no support in anything?

We drove onto the main road and the metal-rimmed wheels of the break clattered over the potholes; the road filled with people and we drove past them as they appeared on the pavement, one in a cap, another in a hat; a little further on we passed a wagon full of bundles, the possessions of an entire family, which a horse dragged along; still further on a woman stopped us; she was standing in the middle of the road and came up to us: I saw a fine face under a rustic kerchief, enormous feet in a man's boots below a rather short, black, silk dress and a low, elegant décolleté like that of an evening gown: she held a parcel wrapped in a newspaper—she had waved to us with it—she wanted to say something, but pursed her lips, then wanted to speak again, but gave a disillusioned wave of her hand, stepped back and stood motionless, watching us move away. Karol sniggered. We finally drove into Ostrowiec, making a terrible din, jolting over the cobbles with our cheeks quivering; we drove past the German sentries in front of the factory; the town had not changed, it was just as it had been, the same squat factory buildings and the blast furnace chimneys, the wall, the bridge on the Kamienna and the crisscross of rails, and the main road leading to the square with the Café Malinowski on the corner. And yet something was missing—there were no Jews. But the streets were crowded, even lively; a woman was sweeping her doorstep, a man was carrying a huge bundle of ropes, a group of people stood in front of a grocery, a street urchin aimed a stone at a sparrow perched on a chimney top. We took a full load of paraffin oil, did some shopping, and left this curiously inhospitable town as quickly as we could. We heaved a sigh of relief as the break drove off the main road, onto the soft soil of the lane. But what was Frederick doing? Was he asleep? Was he sitting down? Was he going for a walk? I knew how scrupulously correct he always was, I was certain that if he were sitting down it would be with all due precautions, and yet I began to suffer from the uncertainty I felt about the way he was spending his time. He was not there when Karol and I returned and sat down to a late lunch; Hippolytus' wife told me he was raking. . . What, for Heaven's sake? He was raking a path in the garden. "I'm afraid he's rather bored here," she said, obviously distressed, as though he were a guest of before the war, and even Hippolytus came up to tell me:

"Your friend is in the garden, you know. . . He's raking."

And something in his voice told me that he was beginning to find this man's company slightly oppressive; he was ashamed, unhappy, and embarrassed. I went to look for Frederick. When he saw me he put down his rake and asked me with his customary politeness how our trip had gone. . . then, looking away, he suggested tentatively that we should return to Warsaw, because, after all, we were perfectly useless down here and, on the other hand, our business interests might suffer considerably if we neglected them for so long, yes, this journey had been undertaken too hastily, it might be better to pack our bags. . . He gradually made his way toward this decision which he had not yet taken, made it gradually more intense, tried to convince himself, to convince me, to convince the trees in the park. What did I think? On the one hand, of course, the country had its advantages. . . but. . . well, we might just as well leave the next day, mightn't we? Suddenly his questions became urgent and I understood: he wanted to know, from my answer, whether I had succeeded in getting anything out of Karol; he realised that I must have tried during the journey to Ostrowiec; he wanted to know if there were still the shadow of a hope that Albert's tender fiancée might end up in Karol's adolescent embrace! At the same time he wanted to tell me secretly that none of the things he knew about the matter entitled us to such an illusion.

It is hard to describe the humiliation of this scene. The true face of an elderly man is concealed by a secret will power, trying to mask the decay, or at least to arrange it in an attractive whole—once disappointment had set in Frederick lost all his charm, all hope and all passion, and his wrinkles spread and crawled over his face like worms on a corpse. He was abject, humbly odious in this submission to his own horror—and his abjection contaminated me to such an extent that my own worms arose, crawled out, climbed up, and polluted my face. But that was not the limit of the humiliation. The sinister comicality of this situation was mainly due to the fact that we were like a couple of lovers deceived and rejected by another couple: our passion, our excitement had nothing on which to feed, and now raged between us. . . We had nothing left except each other. . . and in spite of our revulsion we had to remain together in this sensuality which had been unleashed and was dragging us with it. So we tried not to look at each other. The sun beat down and the bushes smelt of cantharis.

At the end of this secret conference I realized what a blow for me and for him the indifference of those two had been, an indifference which now seemed beyond doubt. The girl—engaged to Albert. The boy—who did not care about it. And all this foundered in their youthful blindness. The ruin of all our dreams!

I told Frederick he was probably right, that our prolonged absence from Warsaw might really injure our business interests. He immediately clung to my agreement. The idea of flight prevailed, and, as we walked up the path, we accustomed ourselves to this decision.

But behind the corner of the house, on the pathway leading to the study, we saw them both. She was holding a bottle. He was standing in front of her. They were talking. Their childishness, their complete childishness was obvious and lethal: she—the schoolgirl, he—the schoolboy, the brat.

Frederick asked them: "What are you doing?"

She: "I've pushed the cork into the bottle."

Karol, holding the bottle up against the light: "I'll get it out with a piece of wire."

Fredcrick: "That's not so easy."

She: "Maybe I ought to get another cork."

Karol: "It's not worth it. . . I'll get it out. . . "

Frederick: "The neck's too narrow."

Karol: "If it went in it must come out."

She: "Or crumble and muck up the fruit juice."

Frederick did not answer. Karol shifted stupidly from one leg to the other. She stood there holding the bottle and said:

"I'll get some corks upstairs. There aren't any in the sideboard."

Karol: "I tell you I can get it out."

Frederick: "It won't be easy to force it through the neck."

She: "He that seeketh findeth."

Karol: "You know what? Those little bottles in the cupboard!"

She: "No. That's medicine."

Frederick: "You can wash them."

A bird flew by.

Frederick: "What sort of bird is that?"

Karol: "An oriole."

Frederick: "Are there many around here?"

She: "Look, what an enormous worm!" .

Karol went on shifting from leg to leg, she raised her foot and scratched her calf—then he raised his shoe, turned it in a semicircle, resting it on the heel, and crushed the worm. . . but only half of it, because his toe did not reach any further and he was too lazy to move his heel; the rest of the worm started to twist and writhe feverishly while the boy gazed at it with interest. It would have been no more horrifying than the death of a fly on a piece of fly-paper, or of a moth on a lamp bulb, had it not been for Frederick's glassy stare, riveted on the worm, revealing its agony to the full. He could have looked indignant but in fact he only wanted to identify himself with the torture, to drain the cup to the dregs. He took the agony on himself, sucked it in, gorged himself on it, and, sluggish and dumb in the grip of the vice, he could no longer move. Karol looked at him out of the corner of his eye, without dispatching the worm; Frederick's horror seemed quite hysterical.

Henia moved her slipper and it was she who crushed the worm.

But only the other end of it, deliberately sparing the middle so it could go on twisting and writhing in pain.

All that was—meaningless. . . as only crushing a worm can be meaningless.

Karol: "There are masses of birds around Lwow."

Henia: "I've got some more potatoes to peel."

Frederick: "I don't envy you. . . it's a terrible bore. . . "

As we returned to the house we continued our conversation, then Frederick disappeared—I do not know where—but I knew what he was doing. He was thinking about what had just happened, about the two innocent legs which had united over the writhing body, in a common act of cruelty. Cruelty? Was it really cruelty? It was more like a trifle: they stepped on a worm, for no reason, casually, just because it was there—how many worms does one kill every day? No, no, it was not cruelty—it was thoughtlessness: gazing childishly at entertaining death throes, without feeling any pain. What did it matter to them? But for Frederick? For a mind accustomed to getting to the heart of a matter? For his extreme sensitivity? For him this act was surely horrifying enough to make his blood run cold? —because suffering is as distressing in the body of a worm as it is in the body of a giant, suffering is "one," in the same way that space is "one," it is indivisible and every-time it appears it is abomination itself. They had caused suffering, created pain, with the soles of their shoes they had transformed the peaceful existence of this worm into something abominable, an inferno—it was impossible to imagine a greater crime, a greater sin. Sin. . . sin. . . Yes, it was a sin, but if it was a sin it was a common sin. . . their legs had united on the writhing body of the worm. . .

I knew what he was thinking, the lunatic! The lunatic! He was thinking about them—he thought they had done it "for him." "Don't deceive yourself. Don't think we haven't got anything in common. . . You saw what hap-pened: one of us crushed a worm. . . And then the other one joined in. We did it for you. To be united—before you and for you—in sin."

That must have been what Frederick was thinking. Or maybe I was only attributing my thoughts to him? And maybe he was attributing his thoughts to me. . . thinking no more about me than I was about him. . . so that each of us was lovingly cultivating his thought, but in the other one's mind. This amused me, I laughed aloud, and I thought that he must be laughing too. . .

"We did it for you. To be united before you and for you in sin. . ."

If this were really the content of the secret message they wanted to transmit to us with their unconsciously cruel legs. . . then they had no need to repeat it! A word to the wise! I smiled again at the idea that Frederick was perhaps smiling at this moment as he thought of what I thought of him, and what I thought was this: that he had given up his assiduously formed plans to leave, and that he was again like a bloodhound on a trail, excited by freshly aroused hopes.

The hopes, the perspectives hidden in this little word "sin," were colossal. If these children were really tempted to sin. . . with each other. . . but also with us. . . Ah, I could almost see Frederick meditating somewhere, his head in his hands, thinking that sin penetrates to our heart of hearts, that it rivets people to each other as firmly as the most passionate caress, that sin, private, secret, and disgraceful, allows us to penetrate as deeply into the existence of others as the sexual act allows us to penetrate their bodies. If this were so. . . it meant that he, Frederick ("that he, Witold," thought Frederick). . . that both of us were not too old for those two—in other words that their youth was accessible. There was this common sin: a sin which was almost created to join in illegal matrimony the flowering of the young couple to somebody—somebody not so attractive. . . somebody older and more serious. In virtue they were hermetically sealed to us. But once in sin they could wallow in it with us. . . that was what Frederick was thinking! And I could almost see him, his finger on his mouth, meditating, searching for the sin that would enable him to penetrate them, reviewing every sin imaginable to find the right one—or else thinking, suspecting that I was searching for a similar sin. What a marvelous system of mirrors: he was reflected in me, I was reflected in him— and so, as we wove dreams for each other we came to conclusions which neither of us wanted to admit were his.

The next morning we were to go to Ruda. Every detail of the trip was discussed at length—which horses, which vehicles, which road—and finally I got into the break with Henia. Since Frederick could not make up his own mind we tossed for it and I turned out to be her companion. The morning shimmered into the distance, the lane wound over the hilly ground, deep paths with yellow walls ran into it, here and there a bush, a tree, a cow, ahead of us jogged the carriage with Karol driving. She—wearing a Sunday dress, a coat white with dust over her shoulders— a fiancée going to join her fiancé. So, no longer able to restrain myself, I said, after a few introductory remarks: "Congratulations! You'll soon be married, with a family. You'll have children!"

She replied: "Yes, I'll have children."

She had replied, but how! Obedient, zealous, like a schoolgirl. Reciting her lesson. Transformed into an obedient child at the thought of her own children. We drove along at a good pace... We could see the tails and the fat cruppers of the horses move rhythmically. Yes! She wanted to marry the lawyer! She wanted children from him! And she had the audacity to say it while the figure of her young lover could be seen silhouetted in the distance.

We passed a heap of rubbish thrown on the side of the road, and soon after, two acacias.

"Do you like Karol?"

"Of course... we've known each other..."

"Since you were children, I know. But I'm asking if you feel anything else for him?"

"Me? I like him very much."

"Very much? Is that all? Then why did you crush that worm together?"

"Which worm?"

"And his trousers? The trousers you turned up by the shed?"

"Which trousers? Oh yes, of course, they were too long. What about it?"

How blinding was this smooth wall of lies, constructed in good faith, of lies which she did not think were lies! But how could I force her to tell the truth? This being sitting next to me, frail, indistinct, and vague, who was not a woman, but was only the embryo of a woman, this provisional entity who only existed so as not to be herself, who was killing herself.

"Karol's in love with you!"

"Him? He's not in love with me or with anyone else. . . all he wants to do is. . . well, to go to bed with somebody. . . " And then she added something which obviously gave her pleasure. "He's just a kid, and what's more. . . well, it's better not to mention it!"

It was clearly an allusion to Karol's rather confused past, but in spite of everything I thought I could detect a certain affection in these words, a shade of "organic" attraction, possibly due to their friendship. At any rate, it was not said reproachfully, but rather as though she liked the idea of it, with a note of familiarity in her voice. As Albert's fiancée she obviously felt that she had to condemn Karol, and yet she seemed to cling to him in the tempestuous destiny common to their generation, born in the shadow of the war. I immediately hung on to this concept, trying to exploit this familiar tone. I told her casually, chummily, that she was no saint and could surely go to bed with him, couldn't she? She took it very well, far better than I had expected, even with a certain eagerness or a strange docility. She immediately agreed with me that "she could, of course," particularly since she had done it once before, last year, with a chap from the A.K. who had hidden in their house. "You won't tell my parents, will you?" Why was she letting me into her secrets so easily? Immediately after her engagement to Albert, too? I asked if her parents suspected anything (about the chap from the A.K.), to which she replied: "They certainly suspect something because they caught us at it. But in actual fact they don't suspect anything."

"In actual fact"—what a brilliant expression! One could say everything, mean everything with it. A magical expression which concealed everything. We were now descending on Brzustowa, across a row of lime trees—the shadows speckled with sunlight, the horses slowing down, the harnesses falling around their necks, the sand squeaking under the wheels. . .

"All right! That's what I mean! Why not? There was the chap from the A.K. What's wrong with this one?"

"No."

The ease with which women say "no!" This capacity for refusing! This "no" which is always at hand—and once they find it in themselves they are pitiless. But. . . could she be in love with Albert? Was this the reason for her continence? I suggested that it would be quite a blow for Albert if he were to find out about her "past"—for him who respected her so deeply, who had such high principles and was so religious. I expressed the hope that she should never tell him about it, no, she really should not put him to that test. . . him who believed so firmly in their spiritual harmony. . . She interrupted me, deeply offended: "But what are you talking about? Don't you think I've got any morals?"

"He's got Catholic morals."

"So have I. I am a Catholic."

"What? Do you go to Communion?"

"Of course."

"Do you believe in God? Literally, like a Catholic?"

"If I didn't believe in God I wouldn't go to confession and Communion. What did you think? Albert's morals suit me very well. And his mother is almost like my mother. You'll see what sort of a woman she is! For me it's an honor to marry into a family like that." And, after a moment's silence, she added, pulling lightly on the reins: "At any rate, if I marry him I won't be sleeping around with everybody."

The sand. The lane. Going uphill.

The vulgarity of her last words—why? "I won't be sleeping around with everybody." She could have put it more delicately. But it was an ambiguous sentence. She expressed her desire for purity and dignity in an undignified, degrading way, in an exciting way, exciting for me, because that made her closer to Karol. And again, as on the day before with Karol, I felt a pang of resentment: it was really impossible to find out anything from them because whatever they felt, said, and thought was only a game to excite each other, to provoke and seduce each other, a narcissistic orgy —and they were the first to suffer from their seduction. This girl?. . . this girl who was nothing but an attraction for herself, a desire to please, molded with coquetry, malleable, flexible, and enchanting—sitting next to me, in her little coat, with her little, far too little, hands. "If I marry him I won't be sleeping around with everybody." This sounded strict, she was regaining control for Albert's sake, through Albert—but it was also a familiar, seductive admission of her own weakness. Even when she was being virtuous she was devilishly exciting. . . but in the distance, going up a slope, was the carriage with Karol driving. . . Karol. . . Karol. . . Driving. Going up a slope. In the distance. Was it because he appeared "in the distance" or "going up a slope?". . . this sudden apparition, this irruption of Karol had something supremely provocative about it, and, in a fury, pointing to him, I said:

"But you love crushing worms with him, don't you?"

"What are you going on about the worm for? He crushed it and I finished it off, that's all."

"You saw how much the beast was suffering!"

"What are you getting at?"

Once again I was foxed. She was sitting next to me. For a moment I thought of giving up, of retreating. . . My position, this way of reveling in their eroticism—no, it could not last! I ought to find some other occupation, something more suitable, more serious! Was it so hard to return to my normal condition, where other problems absorbed my attention and where I tended to despise these little games with the young? But when we are excited we begin to adore our excitement, it excites us and we lose interest in everything else! Pointing once again at Karol with my compromising finger I said insistently, hoping to corner her and extort a confession:

"You're not yours. You're someone else's. And this someone is him. You're his!"

"Me? His? You're crazy!"

She roared with laughter. Their continual, incessant laughter—his and hers—laughter which obscured everything. It made one despair!

She rejected him. . . laughing. . . She rejected him with a laugh. Her laugh was short, and stopped abruptly, it was only the hint of a real laugh—but in this brief instant I saw his laugh in her laugh. The same smiling mouth with beautiful, white teeth. It was "pretty". . . alas, alas! it was "pretty." They were both "pretty." That was why she did not want to!

7

Ruda. We stepped out of the two vehicles before the front door. Albert appeared and ran up to his fiancée to greet her on the threshold—and greeted us with that quiet courtesy which distinguished him. In the hall we kissed the hand of a withered little old lady who smelled of herbs and medicine, and who delicately squeezed our fingers. The house was full, the day before some relatives from near Lwow had arrived unexpectedly. They had been put up on the first floor, but there were beds even in the drawing room; maidservants were hard at work, children were playing on the floor amid bundles and empty suitcases. We therefore decided to go back to Poworna for the night—but Albert's mother, Amelia, protested violently: "You can't do that!" she said. "You'll all be able to fit in somehow." There were other reasons, too, for returning to Poworna. Under a vow of secrecy Albert told us men that there were two fellows from the A.K. spending the night in the house and, according to them, there was going to be some sort of action in the area. All this made the atmosphere rather tense. We sat in the armchairs in the large drawing room, dark in spite of the many windows, and the old lady turned politely to Frederick and me, and asked us about our life in Warsaw. Her incredibly old and withered head hung over her neck like a star; she was undoubtedly a remarkable woman and the air we breathed in this house had a quality of its own. No, it would be impossible to speak too highly of her: we were not dealing with one of those church mice only too common in the provinces, but with an extraordinary personality. It is hard to say how that became apparent. A respect for the human being, not unlike Albert's, but still deeper. A courtesy founded on the subtlest of feelings. An almost inspired tactfulness, imbued with spirituality, and at the same time of incredible simplicity. Immense integrity. Finally the impression of a rigorous, categorical force, of a superior reason dominating the house, of absolute reason, demolishing all doubts. For us, for me and undoubtedly also for Frederick, this highly spiritual house suddenly became a wonderful place of rest, an oasis. A metaphysical principle reigned here, a transcendental principle, in short, the Catholic God, liberated from all corporal bonds, and far too dignified to go chasing after Karol and Henia with us. It was as though the hand of this intelligent mother had given us a slap calling us to order and everything returned to normal instantaneously. Henia with Karol, Henia plus Karol, returned to what they were, to their perfectly normal youth—and Henia with Albert became more important, but only because of their future marriage and their love. But we, we the adults, recovered the sense of our maturity, and we suddenly found ourselves so firmly and so eternally immersed in it that there could no longer be a question of any threat coming from them, from below. In short, we had regained the "lucidity" which Albert had already brought us at Poworna, but not as forcibly as today. The weight of their young knees on our chests became less oppressive.

Frederick came to life. Released from their damnable young feet he believed again in himself—and he breathed again—and he reappeared in his former glory. What he said was by no means dazzling, just ordinary sentences designed to sustain the conversation, but the smallest detail became important when he loaded it with his personality, his emotion, and his lucidity. Even the most commonplace word, "the window," for example, or "the bread," or "thank you" had an entirely different flavor on these lips which knew so well what they were saying. He said casually "one enjoys the little comforts of life," and this immediately became important, if only as an admission of the importance he attached to it. His own particular style, his way of existing became perceptible, was suddenly present in its concrete form. If man could only be judged by the importance he attaches to himself we were confronted by a giant, because he apparently represented an extraordinary phenomenon to himself. Extraordinary not on the scale of social values but as a being, as an existence. And this solitary grandeur was welcomed by Albert and his mother as though the respect they could show for somebody constituted one of their subtlest pleasures. Even Henia, destined to play the leading part in this household, slipped into the background, and there was soon only Frederick.

"Come with me," said Amelia. "I shall show you the view from the terrace before we go in to lunch."

She was so absorbed by him that she spoke to him alone, totally ignoring Henia, her parents, and me. . . We accompanied them to the terrace from where the ground could be seen stretching in gentle hillocks down to the flat, almost invisible surface of the river, which lay there like a corpse. It was pretty. But Frederick blurted out:

"The barrel."

And he was confused. . . because instead of admiring the landscape he had noticed something as insignificant and uninteresting as a barrel lying under a tree. He did not know how he could have said that, or how to extricate himself. And Amelia repeated, like an echo:

"The barrel."

She said it in a whisper, but penetratingly, as though she were confirming what he had said, in total agreement with him—as though she too were used to those fortuitous initiations into a fortuitous object which extracts all its importance from the very importance you attach to it. . . ah, yes, indeed, they both had much in common! We sat down to lunch with the entire family of refugees and their children—but all these guests, this crowd, these children running about, the improvised meal, were most unpleasant. The meal was exhausting. And the "situation" was constantly being discussed, the general one in connection with the German retreat, and the local one; I lost my way in the rustic tone of the conversation, so different from those we had in Warsaw, I did not understand half of what they were saying but I asked no questions, I did not want to ask any, what was the point of it? In all events I would soon understand. Sitting in this din I drank, and all I saw was that Amelia, who supervised the meal from the heights of her withered little head, continued to treat Frederick with special attention, with special concentration, even rather nervously—she looked in love with him. Love? It was more the inexhaustible magic of Frederick's curious lucidity, a magic I had so frequently been aware of myself. He was so penetratingly, irrevocably conscious. Amelia, whose mind must have been stimulated by meditation and spiritual exercises, had immediately sensed the value of her partner. Somebody with immense powers of concentration, never allowing himself to be deceived or distracted from the essence of things, somebody serious to the ultimate degree, who made everyone else seem childish. Having discovered Frederick she wanted to know how this man was going to accept her: whether the truth she had for so long cultivated within herself would meet with approval or refusal.

She realized he was not a believer; that was evident from the precautions she took, from the way she kept her distance. She knew there was an abyss between them and yet it was from him that she wanted recognition and confirmation. All the people she had hitherto known had been believers but they had never delved deep enough—this man however, an unbeliever, was unfathomably deep, and could therefore not fail to recognize her depth, he was an "extremist" and must understand her "extremism"—because he "knew," he "understood," he "felt." Amelia wanted to confront his extremism with hers; I suppose she was like a provincial artist who manages, for the first time in his life, to show his work to a real connoisseur—but her work was herself, it was her life she wanted him to do justice to. She was not of course able to express this, and would probably have been unable to do so even if Frederick's atheism had not restrained her. And yet the sole presence of this alien depth next to her stimulated her to her very depths, and she tried to tell him, to give him to understand through her composure and inner tension, how dependent she was on him and what she expected from him.

As for Frederick, his behavior was, as usual, exquisitely tactful. And yet his contemptibility, the same he had displayed when he was raking the path, when he admitted defeat, gradually began to appear under Amelia's influence. It was the contemptibility of impotence. It was all reminiscent of copulation, spiritual copulation, of course. Amelia wanted him to recognize if not her God, at least her faith, but this man was not capable of such a moral standard, condemned as he was to submit to the eternal terror of the man who exists, a cold mind which nothing could warm—he was as he was—and he simply observed Amelia to ascertain whether she was as she was. This, in the heat of her fervor, seemed lethally impotent. Frederick's atheism increased when confronted by Amelia's victorious theism, the contradiction between them was irreparable and fatal. What was more, under the influence of this extreme spirituality, he affirmed himself physically and I saw his hand, for example, become very, very much a hand, more and more a hand (I do not know why that reminded me of the worm). I also noticed the look with which he undressed her like a Don Juan with a little girl, a look which betrayed the question: what does she look like naked? Not out of any erotic desire, of course, but simply to have a better idea of whom he was talking to. Under this look she wilted and suddenly fell silent—she had just realized that for him she was only what he saw, nothing more.

This took place on the terrace, after lunch. She got up and turned to Frederick:

"May I lean on your arm? Let's go for a walk in the garden."

She took his arm. Maybe, with this physical contact, she wanted to tame him and conquer his "materiality"! They went before us, leaning against one another like a couple of lovers, the six of us following, like a wedding train—it looked like an idyll; was that not how we had escorted Henia and Albert not so long ago?

An idyll, but a tragic one. I presume Amelia experienced a cold shudder as she intercepted the look that undressed her—because nobody had ever treated her like that before, the people who surrounded her had shown nothing but respect and love for her, ever since she was a child. What did he know and what was the nature of his knowledge, that he should dare treat her like that? She was absolutely positive that the value of her spiritual effort, which had earned her the sympathy and respect of everybody, could not be questioned, so she did not fear for herself, she feared for the world—because another concept of the world was being opposed to hers, a concept which was no less serious, also stemming from a similar withdrawal to extreme positions.

These two serious people walked along arm in arm, over the broad meadows; the sun was already setting and was becoming red and swollen; behind us sprang shadows, growing longer and longer. Henia was walking next to Albert. Hippolytus was escorting his wife. I was on my own. And Karol. That couple in front of us deep in conversation. An insignificant conversation. They were talking about. . . Venice.

At a certain moment she stopped:

"Look around you. Isn't it beautiful?"

He replied:

"Yes, it is. Very beautiful."

He just said that to confirm it for her.

She gave a start of impatience. This reply was nonexistent, it simply evaded the real one, although it was said politely and even with a certain emotion, but the emotion of an actor. She, on the other hand, wanted him sincerely to admire this sunset, this work of God, she wanted him to honor the Creator, at least in His works. Her purity transpired from this demand.

"But please look properly. Tell me truthfully. Isn't it beautiful?"

This time, called to order, he pulled himself together, made a genuine effort to sound moved and said, as sincerely as he could:

"But I do think it's very beautiful, I think it's marvelous."

She cannot have expected any more. It was obvious that he was making an effort: as soon as he said something one

felt he was saying it so as not to say something else. . .
What could be done? Amelia decided to put her cards on
the table and said, without any transition:

"You're an atheist?"

Before committing himself to such a deliberate problem
he glanced right and left, as though he wanted to examine
the world. He said, because he had to, because he had nothing else to say, because the reply was already contained in
the question:

"I'm an atheist."

But again, he said that so as not to say something else!
That could be felt. She did not speak, every possibility of
polemic was destroyed. Had he been a real unbeliever she
could have struggled with him, she could have given her
reasons, she could have shown him the depths of her
"extremism," in short, she could have had an equal fight.
But his words only served to hide something else. What?
What? If he were neither a believer nor an unbeliever,
what was he? An abyss of murky darkness opened before
her as she was confronted by this strange "otherness," she
lost her balance, dizzy and dumfounded.

She turned back toward the house, and we followed
her, projecting on the meadows our immense shadows
which reached the distant and unknown border of the field
of stubble. A marvelously limpid evening. Amelia, I could
have sworn, began to be really frightened. She hurried
along, taking no notice of Frederick who paced along beside her—like a faithful dog. She was dumfounded and
disarmed. . . It was no longer her faith that was being attacked, she did not need to defend it—but it was her God
who was becoming useless, confronted by this atheism
which was only a mask, and she felt all alone, without a
God, left to herself, before this elusive existence, based on
an unknown principle. And the fact that this existence

should elude her compromised her irremediably. Because that proved that at every turn Catholic spirituality ran the risk of colliding with something unknown, incomprehensible, uncontrollable. She suddenly felt apprehended by someone in an entirely unknown way—and appeared to herself, in Frederick, as somebody quite incomprehensible.

On this meadow, in the twilight, our wedding train twisted like a snake. A little behind us, at an angle to our left, walked Henia and Albert, both very well behaved and civilized, well anchored in their families, he—the son of his mother, she—the daughter of her parents; and the lawyer's body felt more at ease next to this sixteen-year-old girl, surrounded by two mothers and a father. Karol was on his own, on one side, his hands in his pockets, looking bored, or maybe not; he idly moved his feet on the grass, the left one, then the right one, then the left one, then the right one, then the left one, then the right one, then the left one, in the somnolence of the green meadows, under the setting sun which still gave out some heat in spite of the cool breeze—he moved his feet, this one, that one, slowing down or hurrying up, until he was level with Frederick (who was next to Amelia). They walked a little way in silence. Karol said:

"Would you give me an old jacket?"

"What for?"

"I need one... To sell."

"What's that got to do with me?"

"I need one."

"Well, buy one, then!" said Frederick.

"I haven't got any dough."

"Nor have I."

"Would you give me the jacket?"

Amelia walked faster—so did Frederick—so did Karol.

"Would you give me the jacket?"

"Would you give him the jacket?"

It was Henia. She had left Albert a few yards behind. She was walking next to Karol, talking and moving just like him.

"Would you give him the jacket?"

"Would you give me the jacket?"

Frederick stopped, raised his arms comically: "Leave me in peace, children!" Amelia walked faster and faster, without turning around, so she looked as though she were being pursued by them. Why indeed did she not turn around, once at least? That was a mistake: she now looked as though she were escaping from their adolescent pranks (while her son remained in the background). But who was she escaping from, the two children, or him, Frederick? Or from him with them? Had she sensed the ambiguity of the relationship between the two adolescents? It was unlikely, she cannot have had a nose for that kind of thing and these two did not count in her eyes—Henia only mattered because she was to be Albert's future wife, but Henia and Karol—they were children, they were young. If she was escaping, then, it was from Frederick, from the familiarity with which Karol was treating him—incomprehensible to her—which had grown up here, before her eyes, which was aimed at her. . . because, under the boy's attack, this man lost the seriousness he had acquired before her. . . And this shocking familiarity had just been reinforced by the voice of her son's bride! Amelia's flight was an admission— she had seen all that, she had registered it!

The minute she moved away the two adolescents stopped pestering Frederick. Because she had moved away? Or because they had exhausted their jokes? I need not add that although Frederick was shattered by this youthful assault and looked exactly like somebody who had just escaped a gang of toughs in a suburb at night, he took every precaution to keep up appearances and to let sleeping dogs lie. Without losing any time he joined Hippolytus and Maria and tried to drown these incongruities in a surge of words. What was more, he called Albert and engaged him in a banal but voluble conversation. All evening he remained as quiet as a mouse and did not even so much as glance at Henia and Karol, at Henia with Karol, and made every effort to restore calm and tranquillity. He obviously feared the awakening of the depths that Amelia had tried to provoke in him. He feared the dangerous combination with the superficiality and the youthful lightness of the adolescents, feeling that these two orders could not coexist, and he was afraid of an explosion, of the irruption of. . . Of what? Yes, yes, he was afraid of this explosive mixture of A (Amelia) multiplied by (H plus K). So, ears back, tail between his legs, and silence, hush! And he carried his zeal so far that at dinner (with the family, since the refugees from Lwow were being served in their rooms) he did not hesitate to raise his glass to the health of the betrothed, wishing them his heartfelt congratulations. He could not have behaved better. Unfortunately this strange mechanism was at work once again and made him sink deeper and deeper whenever he tried to retreat—but in this case it happened more violently, more dramatically than ever. Already the fact that he should have stood up, that he should have emerged among us, gave us a thrill of expectation and Hippolytus' wife could not suppress a nervous exclamation—because nobody knew what he was going to say, what he could say. The first words put our minds at rest, conventional and even witty as they were: waving his napkin he thanked the young couple for having illuminated his sad bachelorhood with the glow of their touching engagement, and, in a few well-turned sentences, he paid them a sympathetic tribute. . . It was only gradually, as his speech continued, that what he was not saying began to appear through what he was saying; yes, the same old thing! . . . And soon, to the horror of the orator himself, it appeared that his speech was nothing but an effort to distract our attention from the real speech, the speech without words, beyond words and full of a meaning that words could not convey. Through the well-phrased commonplaces transpired the very essence of this being; nothing could efface this face, these eyes expressing something implacable —and he, feeling he was becoming atrocious, and therefore dangerous to himself, did everything he could to seem kind and inoffensive, and embarked on a conciliating, supernatural, arch-Catholic speech about "the family as a social entity," "the national heritage," and so on. At the same time his disillusioned, implacably present face was a real insult to Amelia and her guests. The destructive force of his speech was inconceivable, and you could see this force, this marginal force, carry away the orator like a bolting horse.

He ended with a felicitation, something like:

"Ladies and gentlemen, they deserve to be happy so they will be happy!"

Which meant:

"I'm talking for the sake of talking."

Amelia thanked him eagerly:

"Thank you, thank you, we are very touched."

The sound of clinking glasses dispelled the anguish. Amelia concentrated on her duties as hostess: "Have some more meat, or some more vodka, perhaps. . . " Everyone started speaking to hear the sound of his own voice, and the din finally erased the feeling of embarrassment. The dessert, a cheesecake, was served. Toward the end of the meal Amelia got up and went into the pantry. But we, stimulated by the alcohol, joked and described to Henia the engagement feasts of the prewar days, when the tables groaned under the weight of the most delicious dishes. Karol roared with laughter and drank. I noticed that when she returned from the pantry Amelia sat down with a curious stiffness—first she stood by her chair, and then she sat down almost mechanically—but before I had time to think twice about it she fell to the ground. Everybody rushed over to her. We saw a red patch on the floor. From the kitchen came a scream, a shot rang out in the courtyard, and someone, I think it was Hippolytus, threw his jacket over the lamp. We were plunged in darkness. There was another shot. The doors were bolted and barred, Amelia was carried to a sofa, amid feverish activity in the dark. . . The jacket on the lamp caught fire, so it had to be stamped out, then there was silence and we stood, listening. Albert slipped a gun into my hands and pushed me over to the drawing room window, whispering: "Keep a lookout!" I could see the calm, silent night and the full moon, and a partly withered leaf on a branch near the window, revealing its silver belly. I gripped my gun and peered out, watching the slightest movement down there, in the shadows of the damp tree trunks. But only a sparrow moved in the scrub. Finally a door slammed, I heard someone raise his voice and other voices joined in—and I realized the moment of panic was over.

Hippolytus' wife appeared next to me: "Do you know anything about medicine? Come along. She's dying. She's been stabbed. . . Do you know anything about medicine?"

Amelia was lying on the sofa, her head on some cushions, and the dining room was full—of the refugees from Lwow, of the servants. . . their immobility maddened me, they exuded impotence. . . the same impotence that sometimes appeared on Frederick's face. . . They all seemed to have withdrawn from her, leaving her to die alone. They just looked on. Her profile stood out, immobile, like a rock out of the sea. Albert, Frederick, Hippolytus stood around her. . . Would she take long to die? On the floor was a bowl full of cotton wool and blood. But Amelia's body was not the only one lying in the room—over there, on the floor, in a corner, there was another one. . . I did not know what it was or how it had got there, I could not even distinguish it. . . I just had the impression there was something erotic about it. . . that an erotic element had intervened. . . Karol? Where was Karol? Leaning against a chair, he was there, with all the rest of them, while Henia knelt down and rested her elbows on an armchair. We were all staring at Amelia, so fixedly that I could not detach my eyes from her to take a more leisurely look at the other body, superfluous and unexpected, lying in the corner of the room. Nobody moved. But everybody gazed at her attentively and seemed to wonder how she was going to die—because one had the right to expect her to die an extraordinary death, and that was what her son, Hippolytus and his wife, Henia, and even Frederick, who did not take his eyes off her, expected. What a paradox! They demanded something from the only person who was incapable of moving, frozen in impotence, and yet the only one who could act. She knew it. Suddenly Maria ran out of the room and returned with a crucifix—it was as though she had given the dying woman the signal to act, and the burden of expectation fell from our hearts— we now knew it would begin at any moment. Hippolytus' wife, holding the cross, stood at the foot of the sofa.

Then something so scandalous happened, despite the extreme subtlety of it, that we all had a shock. . . The dying woman hardly glanced at the cross, turned her eyes to Frederick and would not take them off him—that was what was so incredible! Who could have thought that she would have shown such indifference to the crucifix, now ridiculously

useless in Maria's hands?—and this very indifference gave all
its weight to Amelia's gaze, riveted on Frederick's eyes. She
would not let him out of her sight. The unfortunate Frederick, transfixed by this dying and therefore dangerous look,
stood there turning pale, and drew himself up to attention.
They gazed at each other. Hippolytus' wife went on brandishing the crucifix but the minutes passed and it remained
out of use—a wretched, unemployed crucifix. For this saint
on her deathbed had Frederick really become more important than Christ? Was she really in love with him? No,
it was not love, it was something far more personal, this
woman saw him as her judge—she could not consent to die
before earning his approval, before proving to him that she
was as much of an "extremist" as he was, as fundamental a
phenomenon, as important. So important was his opinion
to her. That she should implore recognition and confirmation of her existence not from Christ, but from him, a
simple mortal, only provided with an exceptional consciousness, was an astonishing heresy for her, a renunciation of
the absolute in favor of life, an admission according to
which it was not God but man who had to judge other men.
At the time I obviously did not see this all so clearly, and
yet I shuddered at the sight of her gaze riveted on the eyes
of a human being, while God passed unnoticed in the hands
of Maria.

Her mortal agony, which did not actually progress under
the weight of our concentration and expectation, became
increasingly tense—we loaded it with all the tension we had
in ourselves. And I knew Frederick well enough to fear that
when confronted by such a special event, such an unusual
event as a human death, he might do something incongruous. But he went on standing at attention, as stiffly as if he
were in church, and behaved impeccably, except for his
eyes which occasionally and uncontrollably slipped from

Amelia's and peered into the room where the other body lay, still mysterious to me since I could not see it properly from where I stood; the increasingly frequent incursions of Frederick's eyes finally made me decide to look for myself. . . I went into the corner. What was my horror, or my emotion, when I saw (a boy), whose slimness was a repetition of (Karol's) slimness, and who lay there alive, and, what was more, was the incarnation of golden, fair-haired beauty, with huge black eyes and dark skin which increased the savagery of his arms and bare feet splayed on the floor!

A savage, feline, fair-haired child, of rustic beauty—a sumptuous idol, covered in dirt, who let his charms gambol on the floor. This body? This body? What was it doing? How had it got there? It was. . . it was a repetition of Karol, but an octave lower. . . and suddenly the youth in the room not only increased in number (because a couple is quite different from three) but also in quality, it was changing, becoming more savage, more base. And at once, as though by repercussion, Karol's body came to life, strengthened and amplified, and Henia, although she was kneeling piously, rushed in all her whiteness into a mysterious and guilty conspiracy with the two of them. At the same time Amelia's agony was tarnished, became suspect—what bond could there be between her and this (boy), what did he want here, at the hour of her death? I realized that the circumstances of this death were proving very ambiguous, far more ambiguous than they seemed at first sight.

Frederick, who had unconsciously put his hands in his pockets, took them out at once and pressed them to the seams of his trousers.

Albert was on his knees.

Maria was brandishing her cross because there was nothing else she could do—to put it down was quite impossible.

Amelia's finger moved, rose and began to beckon. . . to

beckon to Frederick who approached slowly. She continued to beckon until he had lowered his head to her lips, and when he had done that she said, surprisingly loudly:

"Don't go away. You'll see. I want you to see. Everything. To the end."

Frederick bowed and stepped back.

It was only then that she turned to the cross and started to pray, judging from the imperceptible tremor of her lips— finally everything returned to order: the cross, her prayer, our composure—that lasted a very long time, and the passage of time alone gauged the fervor of this prayer which nothing seemed to distract from the cross. This immobile concentration, which was nearly dead already and yet still vibrated from the sheer length of its duration, sanctified the dying woman. Albert, Hippolytus and his wife, Henia, the servants, accompanied it on their knees. Frederick knelt down too. But in vain. Because although the dying woman was totally absorbed in the crucifix, her demand remained just as powerful: she wanted him to see everything, to the end. Why? Did she want to make a final effort to convert him? Did she want to set the example of a Catholic death? Whatever happened, Frederick, not Christ, was the last resort; if she prayed to Christ it was for Frederick and it was in vain that he fell to his knees—he remained, he, not Christ, the supreme arbiter and God, because she was dying for him. What an embarrassing situation—it did not surprise me to see him hide his face in his hands. Still more so since the minutes were passing and we knew that with every one of them her life was fading—but she prolonged her prayer, so she could stretch it as far as it would go, like a string. Again her finger moved and began to beckon, this time to her son. Albert went up to his mother, his arm around Henia. Her finger pointed at them accusingly and she said rapidly:

"Swear to me at once. Love and fidelity. Quick."

They bowed over her hands. Henia burst into tears. But she had already raised her finger and beckoned again, this time to the dark corner, to the body in the corner. . . There was a movement in the room. He was picked up—I saw he was wounded in the thigh, I believe—and he was carried to the dying woman. She moved her lips and I finally thought I would know what he was doing there, this (boy), dripping with blood, what there was between them. But she suddenly gasped, once, twice, and turned white. Maria held up the crucifix. Amelia searched desperately for Frederick and, gazing at him, she died.

_____PART TWO_____

8

Frederick, who had knelt down, rose to his feet and walked into the middle of the room: "Pay your respects to her!" he shouted. "Do homage to her!" He took a bunch of roses out of a vase and cast it by the sofa, then he gave Albert his hand: "A soul worthy of the celestial throng! All we can do is to bow down humbly before her!" These words would have sounded false on the lips of any other of us, not to mention the theatrical gestures that accompanied them, but he pierced us with them as imperiously as a monarch to whom pathos is permitted—who has introduced a new naturalness, far above the norm. A monarch, a master of ceremonies! Albert, carried away by the sovereignty of this pathos, got up and squeezed his hand warmly. It looked as though this intervention of Frederick's were intended to efface the incongruities which had troubled Amelia's death, to restore it to its full glory. He walked a few steps to the right, a few steps to the left—it was as though he were writhing convulsively among us—and went up to the (boy) lying on the floor. "On your knees!" he commanded. "On your knees!" In a way this order was the logical continuation of the preceding order, but on the other hand it was clumsy, because it was given to someone who was wounded and could not move; and it seemed even clumsier when Albert, Hippolytus, and Karol, terrorized by Frederick's authority, rushed up to the (boy) to force him to his knees. Yes, it was too much! And when Karol's hands gripped the (boy) by the shoulders, Frederick flinched, fell silent, and faded away.

I was dazed, exhausted. . . so many emotions. . . and yet I knew him. . . and I knew he had just invented a new game with himself and us. . . ; in the tension created by the presence of the corpse some action was being organized in pursuit of an end known only to his imagination. It was all intentional, although the intention may not have been clear, even to himself. It was undoubtedly better to say that he only knew the beginning of the intention. Did it have anything to do with paying homage to Amelia? No, what he wanted to do was to introduce this wounded (boy), however corrosive and compromising he might be, to make him "stand out," to bring him into the open and "bind" him to Henia and Karol. But what sort of a bond could there be between them? Of course this golden savagery was well suited to our couple, if only on account of age (he too must have been about sixteen), but apart from that I did not see what they could have in common and I do not think Frederick could see it either—but he acted blindly, moved by the same obscure feeling I had, that the wounded (boy) affirmed them as a couple—"demonized" them in some way. And that was why Frederick was trying to pave the path for him to Henia and Karol.

It was only on the next day (which was entirely devoted to the preparations for the funeral) that I was given a detailed account of this fatal accident—which was moreover highly confused, strange, and almost unlikely. To reconstruct the events of the day before was not easy, and there were some desperate gaps made even worse by the fact that the only witnesses, this Olek himself, Olek Skuziak, and the old maid Valerie, were constantly going astray in the confusion of their boorish and ignorant thoughts. At any rate, it appeared that when Amelia was in the pantry she heard a noise on the kitchen stairs and had come across Olek who had slipped into the house hoping to pinch something. Hearing her coming Olck made for the first door he saw and burst into the maid's room, waking up Valerie who immediately lit a match. The rest of the story had been pieced together from her garbled account: "When I'd lit my match and seen there was someone there I had a sort of cramp in my back, so I couldn't move and the match burnt my finger—my finger's still all swollen. Then I saw Madam opposite him over by the door and she didn't move either. My match went out. One couldn't see a thing and the blinds were drawn. So I lay there and looked and I couldn't see a thing—it was pitch-black; if only the floor had creaked, but it didn't, nothing, nothing, as though there wasn't a soul! I held my breath and said a prayer, but nothing happened, it was all quiet, so I looked for the match on the floor which hadn't finished burning, but it didn't light up a thing—it just went out. Not a thing. . . if only one of them had breathed, but they didn't. . . not a thing. And then, all of a sudden. . . " (she choked as though she had swallowed a potato) "all of a sudden. . . I don't know how. . . Madam went for him! I swear it's true! She went for him! Yes, she went for his legs. . . And then they started rolling on the ground! I can't think how—God protect me —but they didn't say a word. I wanted to help, but I felt quite dizzy, then I heard a knife going into some flesh, once, twice, and then I heard it again, then they both made off and I didn't see them any more! And then I passed out proper! I passed out proper, I did!"

"But that's impossible!" said Albert. "It can't have been like that! I'll never believe my mother could. . . behave like that! This old fool's mixed everything up in her thick skull, oh, I'd rather hear a hen clucking," he shouted, "I'd rather hear a hen clucking!"

He mopped his brow.

But little Skuziak's account tallied with the maid's: Madam had gone for him, had gone for his legs and pulled him down. Holding a knife. And he not only showed wounds on his side and thigh, but also tooth marks on his neck and hands. "She bit me," he said. "I tugged her knife away, and then she fell on it. I dashed out, but the bailiff shot at me, I tumbled down and that's how they caught me."

That Amelia could have "fallen" on the knife, as he said, nobody was prepared to believe. "A lie!" said Frederick. "And as for the bites—well, for Heaven's sake, when one's fighting for one's life in a clinch with an armed bandit (because he was the one with the knife, not her). . . well, nerves and all that. . . It's not surprising. You know what instinct is, self-preservation instinct. . . " So said Frederick. Nevertheless it was odd, to say the least. . . and shocking. Amelia biting that. . . As for the knife, the whole matter was pretty obscure, because it turned out to be Valerie's knife, a long, sharp kitchen knife she used for cutting bread. The knife had been on the bed table, right next to where Amelia had stood. So it looked as though Amelia had groped for the knife and rushed at. . .

Amelia's murderer had bare feet with black soles; two fairly vulgar colors prevailed in him—the gold of his hair falling over his black eyes, as mournful as a pond in a deep wood. These colors stood out even more against the pure, almost noble flash of his teeth, their whiteness reminiscent of. . .

Well? Well what? Well, the fact was that Amelia, when she found herself in the dark with this (boy), in the grip of unbearably tense expectation, had not been able to control herself and. . . and. . . had groped for the knife. And when she felt it she became violent. She had rushed at him to kill him, and as they both fell to the ground she had started to bite wildly. Her? This holy woman? At her age? She who set an example, with her God and her principles, of a life of devotion and moral rectitude? This seemed like some fantasy concocted in the obtuse minds of the cook and the little brat, like a savage legend to suit them, the distortion of an obscure and mysterious reality beyond their powers of comprehension. The dark of the maid's room was multiplied by the dark of their imagination—and Albert, totally bewildered by this dark, did not know what to do next; this whole business killed his mother far more definitely than the knife, it poisoned her and disfigured her for him. . . he did not know how he could rescue her image from the fury her teeth had engraved on the sixteen-year-old body, from this knife she had stabbed him with. Such a death tore his life to shreds. Frederick did his best to encourage him: "You can't rely on what they say," he said. "To begin with they couldn't see anything because it was dark. And then it's so unlike your mother, it's totally out of character; the only thing we can be sure of is that it couldn't have happened as they said; something else must have happened in that darkness which was as impenetrable for them as it is for us. That's absolutely definite, there can be no doubt about it. . . although of course. . . it all took place in the dark. . . . " ("Well, what?" asked Albert, seeing him hesitate). . . "You know, the dark. . . the dark. . . can be curiously uninhibiting. . . Man lives on earth, doesn't he? Well, in the dark the earth disappears. You know, nobody's there, one's all alone. You do see that, don't you? We're used to it, of course, we know that every time we turn out the light it gets dark, but nevertheless there are moments when the dark can blind us completely, you see.

but even in that sort of dark your mother must have stayed as she was, she can't have changed, can she? Although in this particular case the dark had something. . ." ("What?" asked Albert. "Go on!") ". . . No. Nothing. That's all nonsense. . . " ("But what?") "Nothing, really, except that this lad, this peasant lad, who's probably even illiterate. . . " ("What does it matter whether he's illiterate or not?") ". . . No, it doesn't matter, of course. . . I only mean that, in this instance, the dark was hiding youth. . . There was a barefooted child. . . it's much easier to do that to someone young. . . that is, if it had been someone more important, more serious, well. . . " ("Well what?") ". . . No, I mean it's always easier with a child, yes, easier, and in the dark, of course. . . it's easier to do that to a boy than to an adult, and. . . You're trying to make me say something I don't mean!" he shouted, and he looked really frightened, little drops of sweat stood out on his forehead. "That's just a supposition, a theory. . . Your mother would never. . . No, that's impossible, insane! Isn't it, Karol? Well, Karol?"

Why did he ask Karol? If he was afraid why did he turn on him? He was one of those people who tries to avert a disaster and only manages to precipitate it—their fear of it attracts disaster, magnifies it and creates it. As soon as he had evoked it he could not help harping on it, inciting it. If his consciousness was so dangerous it was because he associated it not with light but with darkness—for him it was an element as blind as instinct, he did not trust it, he felt he was in its control but did not know where it was taking him. And he was a bad psychologist because he was too intelligent and imaginative—in his vast vision of man there was room for everything. He could even imagine Amelia in an impossible situation. That afternoon Albert went into town "to settle" things with the police, in other words to check any stray impulse of efficiency with a sub-

stantial bribe—if the authorities were also going to start
interfering God only knew where it would end. The funeral
took place the next morning—a brief and obviously rushed
affair. The following day we turned back to Poworna, accompanied by Albert who left the servants in charge of the
house. I was not surprised—I realized he did not want to
leave Henia at such a moment. The carriage went first, with
the ladies, Hippolytus and Albert, and behind, the tilbury,
driven by Karol, with me, Frederick, and somebody else:
Olek.

We had brought him with us because we did not know
what to do with him. Release him? He was a murderer.
Anyhow, Albert would not have released him under any
pretext, this death was far from being over, we could not not
leave it as it was. . . and Albert, above all, hoped he would
succeed in extorting a more suitable and less shocking version of the death. So, on the floor of the tilbury, in front
of the driver's seat, the adolescent murderer lay in the straw
at Karol's feet, while Karol sat at an angle, his feet up on
the splashboard. Frederick and I sat behind. The tilbury
went uphill and downhill, following the motionless surge of
the ground, the landscape opened and closed, the horses
trotted along in the dust and the warm smell of corn. Frederick, sitting on the back seat, could see them both, Karol
and Olek, in that combination and no other—and all four
of us, in this tilbury which climbed from hill to hill, formed
a strange combination, a significant composition, an odd
juxtaposition. . . and the longer our silent journey lasted,
the more obsessive became this figure which we formed.
Karol's timidity was amazing, his frightened adolescence
seemed to have lost some of its assurance under the tragic
impact of the recent events and he was perfectly quiet,
good, and docile. . . he was even wearing a black tie for the
occasion. And yet they were both there, in front of me and

Frederick, half a yard away, on the front seat of the tilbury. The horses trotted along. Frederick, his face toward them. . . what was he trying to see? Those two adolescent figures seemed merged into one figure, so deeply were they bound by the fraternity of their age. But Karol dominated the other, holding the reins and the whip, wearing shoes, his trousers turned high up—and between them there was no sympathy or understanding, nothing but the toughness of one adolescent toward the other, this sort of brutal, hostile malevolence they felt for each other, somewhere down there, between them. And it was quite obvious that Karol belonged to us, to Frederick and me, that he was with us, people of his own class, against this lower-class playmate he had to guard. We had them in front of us for hours of this sandy lane (which occasionally broadened out into a wide road before narrowing abruptly between two chalk walls), there were two of them in front of us and this had a certain effect, created something, set them in something. . . While there in the distance we could occasionally see on the summit of the hills the carriage that bore her—the bride. The carriage came into view and vanished again, but never allowed itself to be forgotten; sometimes it could not be seen for a long time but it inevitably reappeared—and the oblique squares of the fields and the strips of the meadows glided past us, and furled and unfurled around us—in all this tedious geometry, drowned in distant, fleeting perspectives, hung Frederick's face, his profile next to mine. What was he thinking about? What? We were behind the carriage, we were following the carriage; Karol, this other boy lying under his feet, with golden hair, black eyes, and dirty bare feet, seemed gradually to undergo a chemical transformation, he continued to follow the carriage as one star follows another, but he already existed with a playmate—playfully—his whole body in the grip of this mixture of

himself with the other boy, united with him in such a way
that it would not have surprised me suddenly to see them
eating cherries or apples together. The horses trotted along.
Yes, that must have been what Frederick thought about
them—or did he imagine that that was what I was thinking?—and his face was next to mine and I no longer knew
in which of us these thoughts had originated. Anyhow, when
we arrived in Poworna after having driven for hours and
hours, these two playmates were already "together for
Henia," united in connection with her under the effect of
that long journey behind her and before us.

We put the prisoner in a little lumber room with a
barred window. His wounds were superficial and he might
have escaped. Exhausted by the long journey we fell into
bed; I slept deeply all night and part of the morning, and
the next morning I was assailed by imprecise impressions as
irritating as a fly buzzing in one's nose. I could not catch
this buzzing, elusive fly—what sort of a fly was it? Already
before lunch, when I questioned Hippolytus about some
detail to do with the recent events, I detected a change of
tone in his reply—he was not offensive, simply a little
haughty, or disdainful or proud, as though he were bored
with the subject and had other fish to fry. Other fish to
fry when there had just been this murder? I noticed a new
inflection in Albert's voice—how can I put it?—something
dry, and even slightly arrogant. Arrogant? Why arrogant?
The change of tone was as subtle as it was shocking, because how could Albert give himself such airs two days
after this death? My overstrained nerves made me immediately suspect that the center of atmospheric pressure had
moved in our sky and that a fresh wind was blowing—but
what wind? Something had changed. It seemed to be changing direction. My fears only took shape when I caught a
glimpse of Hippolytus going through the dining room and

saying (dropping his voice as he did so): "What a mess, I say, what a mess!" Then he suddenly sat down on a chair, morosely. . . then sprang up, harnessed the horses and drove off. Now I knew something was going on, I was positive, but I did not want to ask anybody and it was only late that afternoon, that, seeing Frederick and Albert deep in conversation, walking around the lawn, I went up to them hoping to discover the cause of this change. Nothing of the kind. They were still discussing the death of two days ago— but in the same tone as the day before—it was an intimate discussion in a whisper. Frederick, his head down, staring at his shoes, continued to dissect this death, deduced, searched, analyzed, reflected. . . until Albert, at the end of his tether, begged to be given time to breathe, even suggesting it was tactless to torment him thus! "What?" said Frederick. "What do you mean by that?" Albert begged for mercy. The events were still too recent, he had not had time to get used to it, it was so unexpected, so appalling! It was then that Frederick swooped onto his soul like an eagle.

Maybe the comparison is too emphatic. But I really did see him dive onto this soul—dive from above. There was neither compassion nor consolation in what he said, on the contrary, there was the desire to see the son drain the cup of his mother's death to the dregs. In the same way, in exactly the same way as Catholics relive Christ's passion, minute by minute. To start with he pointed out that he was not a Catholic. That he had no so-called moral principles. That he was not virtuous. "Then why, you will ask me," he said, "in whose name do I require you to drain this cup to the dregs? I shall reply that it is solely in the name of development. What is man? Who can tell? Man is a mystery." (This commonplace appeared on his lips like something disgraceful and sarcastic, like a pain. . . .) "An angelic and demonic abyss, steeper than a mirror! But we must" (this "must" was confidential and dramatic) "we must get to the heart of the matter. That's inevitable, you know. It's necessary for our development. The law is fulfilled in the history of mankind as it is in the history of every individual. Take a child. A child begins, a child is not, a child is a child, in other words an introduction, an initiation. . . And an adolescent" (he almost spat the word out) "what does he know? What can he feel. . . this embryo? But we?. . . We?" he shouted. "We?"

And he added by the way:

"I communicated with your mother deeply and instantaneously. Not because she was a Catholic. But because she submitted to an inner need for seriousness. . . you know that. . . she was not frivolous. . . "

He looked him in the eye—something he hardly ever did —and this troubled Albert deeply, but he did not dare look away.

"She always went. . . to the heart of the matter."

"What shall I do?" shouted Albert, throwing up his arms. "What shall I do?"

Had he been speaking to anyone else he would not have dared shout like that, or throw up his arms. Frederick took him by the arm and started walking, pointing forward with his other hand: "Live up to it," he said. "Do as you like. But whatever you do, do it like her, scrupulously and seriously."

Seriousness as a basic demand of maturity—no relaxation, nothing that could even momentarily attenuate the severity of his look which persisted in getting to the heart of the matter. . . Albert had no idea how to defend himself from such severity—because it was severity. Otherwise he could have doubted the seriousness of his behavior, the sincerity of this gesticulation. . . but all this performance was being acted under the severe invocation demanding him to assume full consciousness; in Albert's eyes this demand was incontestable. His Catholicism rebelled against the savagery of atheism (for the believer the atheist is a savage) and Frederick's world seemed to him like a chaos deprived of its master, therefore of law, populated solely with the unlimited arbitration of man. And yet as a Catholic he felt he could not neglect the moral order, even if it were from such impious and savage lips. What was more, Albert trembled at the idea of squandering his mother's death— he was afraid of not living up to his drama and of not living up to his love and his respect. And still more than Frederick's impiety he feared his own mediocrity, all that made him an honest, "bourgeois" lawyer. So he clung to Frederick's calm superiority, seeking a support in him. Ah, it did not matter how, it did not matter with whom, but he had to experience this death! Live through it! Suck it dry! For this he needed this savage gaze which got to the heart of the matter, he needed this strange, this fearful, relentless drive into experience.

"But what should I do with young Skuziak?" he shouted. "I ask you: who's to judge him? Have we got the right to keep him prisoner? Very well, we didn't give him up to the police, that was impossible—but we can't keep him in that lumber room indefinitely!"

He brought the matter up next day, when Hippolytus returned, but only succeeded in extracting a shrug of the shoulders: "That's no problem! No use getting worked up about it! Keep him in the lumber room! Give him up to the police! Give him a good hiding! Let him go! Do what you like!" And when Albert tried to make him see reason by saying that, after all, he was his mother's murderer, Hippolytus got annoyed: "Murderer? He's no murderer, he's just a little shit! Do what you like with him, but leave me in peace, I've got other things to do!" He simply did not want to discuss it; he gave the impression that this whole murder only mattered to him from one side, that of Amelia's corpse—and was totally unimportant from the other, that of the murderer. And anyhow he was obviously worried about something else. Frederick, who was leaning against the large porcelain stove, suddenly moved, as though he were going to say something, but just whispered: "Aaah! . . . " He did not say it aloud. He just whispered it. And since we were not expecting the whisper it resounded in the room more forcibly than if Frederick had spoken aloud—and as he whispered he emerged in his whisper while we waited for the rest of what he had to say. He said nothing. Then Albert, who had now learned to detect the slightest change in Frederick's attitude, asked:

"What? Were you going to say something?"

Having been asked a question Frederick glanced around the room.

"Yes, I mean. . . with him, with somebody like that, you can do anything. . . absolutely anything."

"Like that?" Hippolytus burst out in inexplicable anger. "Like what?"

Frederick explained himself, slightly disconcerted:

"Like that, that's obvious, isn't it? You can do anything with him. Whatever you like. Whatever you want."

"The other day you said the same thing about my mother," said Albert suddenly. "That my mother could have. . . with the knife. . . because. . . " He began to stammer. At which Frederick replied, with evident shame:

"No, nothing. I just said it like that. . . Don't let's talk about it."

What an actor! You could see his game quite clearly, he made no attempt to conceal it. But you could also see what it cost him, you could really see him turn pale and tremble as he ended it. As far as I could make out the game consisted in trying to give this murder and this murderer as ambiguous a character as possible—but perhaps he was not trying, perhaps he was submitting to a necessity stronger than himself in his pallor and fear. It was a game, of course, but a game which created him and created the situation. Finally everybody felt slightly uneasy. Hippolytus decided to go out, Albert fell silent. But the blows dealt by the player had hit home, nevertheless, and Olek, in his lumber room, became more and more compromising and it was as though the whole atmosphere were poisoned by a strange and incomprehensible determination. (I knew whom it was aimed at and what the point of it was. . . .) Every evening Olek's wounds had to be washed and dressed, and it was Frederick who did this, since he knew a certain amount about medicine—with Karol's help. And Henia held the lamp. This procedure was as significant as it was compromising, because all three of them stood bowed around him, each one holding something to justify this posture, Frederick the cotton wool, Karol a bowl and a bottle of spirits, Henia the lamp; but this triple bow over the wounded thigh escaped in some way from the objects they were holding and became a pure, gratuitous bow. While the lamp burned. Then Albert shut himself in with him and questioned him —alternately conciliating and threatening—but the inferiority of the boy and his peasant stupidity were impenetrable; he repeated the same thing over and over again: that she had rushed at him and started biting him, and what could he do? And, as he gradually got used to the questions he became familiar with the answers.

"Madam bit as hard as she could. You can still see the marks."

When Albert returned from these interminable interrogations, as exhausted as if he had just recovered from a long illness, Henia came and sat next to him, silent and faithful. . . Karol set the table, or looked through old magazines. . . and when I looked at her, striving to see her "with Karol" I could not believe my eyes, and could not recapture that which had formerly excited me— and I denied my own crazy imagination. There was nothing between them, absolutely nothing! She was only with Albert! But with him she was insatiable. What an appetite! And what impetuous desire! What violent desire! How greedily she approached him, like a man with a little girl! I apologize, I had nothing improper in mind, I only wanted to say that she attacked his soul with unbridled lust: Albert's conscience, his honor, his sense of responsibility, his respectability, and all the sorrows attached to it, were the object of her desire, she was so avid of his maturity that one could have sworn his baldness was more seductive than his mustache! All this, of course, in her peculiar passivity—she simply absorbed his maturity, clinging to him affectionately. And she surrendered herself to the caress of this masculine hand which was nervous, fine and adult, she was so eager for seriousness in the face of this dramatic death (which surpassed her inexperienced precocity), trying to take hold of other people's maturity. The little wretch! Because instead of being brilliant and beautiful, as she could have been with Karol, she chose this lawyer and sought contact with his pampered ugliness! The lawyer was grateful and caressed her gently. While the lamp burned. Several days went by like this. One afternoon Hippolytus told us he was expecting a new guest, Mr. Siemian, who would be paying a visit. . . And he muttered, observing his fingernail: "He'll be paying us a visit." And he closed his eyes.

When we heard this news we did not ask any questions. From the morose resignation in his voice it was clear that he was not even trying to disguise the truth. Behind this "visit" lurked a net which involved us all, which opposed us to each other—a conspiracy. Each of us could only say as much as he was permitted to say—the rest consisted of heavy, oppressive silence and hazardous suppositions. The dull menace that had for some days troubled the unanimity of our feelings born from the tragic events at Ruda, became more evident and the weight that had oppressed us was transported from a recent past into an immediate and dangerous future. That evening, in the rain, a fine, cutting rain of the sort that drizzles all night, a cab drew up in front of the steps and through the half-open door of the hall I saw a tall man in an overcoat, his hat in his hand, follow Hippolytus, who held a lamp, up the stairs to the first floor where a room had been prepared for him—A sudden draft blew through the open door, Hippolytus almost dropped the lamp, and the door slammed. I recognized the man. Yes, I knew him by sight, although he did not know me. . . and I suddenly felt trapped in this house. I happened to know that this man was an important figure in the Resistance, one of the leaders, with a number of daring exploits to his name, and that he was wanted by the Germans. . . There was no doubt about it, it was he and if it was he his arrival heralded the unforeseen, because we were at his mercy: his audacity was no longer his own, by exposing himself he exposed us, too, he could involve us in some murky project—if he asked us something we could not refuse. Because the nation united us, we were comrades and brothers-in-arms—a brotherhood which was as cold as ice, everyone was someone else's tool, everyone could use anyone else pitilessly, for the common cause.

This man, both so close and so dangerously alien, had passed by me like a menacing ghost, and everything was suddenly contracted and stiff in mystery. I was aware of the risk he was making us run and yet I could not control a vague feeling of disgust for all these trappings—action,

Resistance, the leader, conspiracy—like a bad novel, a late incarnation of more or less insane childhood dreams. To destroy our games I would rather have had anything, but not that, not that. The nation and its romanticism constituted for me an undrinkable potion concocted to spite and anger me. But we could not be particular and reject what fate offered us. I met "the leader" when he came down to dinner. He looked like an officer—which, indeed, he was —a cavalry officer, from the Eastern borders, the Ukraine probably, over forty, his face darkened by his close-shaven growth of beard, a thin, elegant, and charming man. He greeted us all—it was obviously not the first time he had been here—and he kissed the ladies' hands. "I know, I've heard the ghastly news! Do you come from Warsaw, gentlemen?. . ." From time to time he closed his eyes and looked like someone who had been traveling for hours by train. . . He sat at the end of the table; he was obviously supposed to be here as a technician, as an expert on cattle-breeding or seed-sowing—a precaution for the benefit of the servants. As for us, his table companions, we clearly knew who he was—and yet the conversation languished and foundered. In the meantime strange things were happening at the end of the table, with Karol. Yes, our (young) Karol, whom the visitor's presence had put into a state of military obedience and servile eagerness—was suddenly intoxicated by loyalty, on edge, toying with death—a soldier, a partisan, a conspirator, a murderous and silent force in his rough hands and brawny arms, ready to obey, awaiting the order, competent in action. And he was not the only one to change. Was it because of Karol? All this romantic mediocrity, so irritating a moment ago, dissolved miraculously and we all communicated in the feeling that force and truth lie in unity. We sat at the table like a military detachment awaiting orders, ready for action. The Resistance, combat, the enemy. . . these words were suddenly imbued with a truth more real than everyday life and burst into the room like a cool wind; impervious to the painful disparity of Henia and Karol we were all brothers-in-arms. And yet this fraternization lacked purity! In reality—this was unbearable, and, in a word, foul. Because, between ourselves, were we adults not slightly repulsive and ridiculous in this battle? as somebody too old to make love is when he makes love? Was this in character with Frederick's slimness, Hippolytus' bloated enormity, Maria's evanescence? The detachment we formed was a reservists' detachment and we were united in decay—melancholy and disgust presided over our fraternization in battle and enthusiasm. At moments it surprised me that enthusiasm and fraternization could still exist. But at other moments I wanted to shout to Henia and Karol: Go away, don't have anything to do with us! Flee from our dirt and our farce! But they (yes, she too) did not want to leave us—they clung to us, stuck to us, offered themselves to us, they were at our command, ready for anything, for our sake, with us, on a signal from the leader! This lasted the whole meal. At least I felt it did. Did I feel that, or did Frederick?

Who knows, maybe it is one of the obscurest mysteries of humanity—and one of the most complex—the mystery of such "communion" between different generations. . . how, and which way does youth suddenly become accessible to maturity and vice versa? In this case the officer held the key to the mystery, because, as an officer, he was bound to the soldier and even more to the young soldier. . . this was evident after dinner when Frederick suggested taking Siemian to the lumber room to show him the murderer. Personally I never believed this proposition to be gratuitous, I knew the presence of Olek-the-young-murderer in the lumber room was becoming more and more urgent, almost unbearable, since Karol had offered himself to the officer. We went up—Siemian, Frederick, myself, Henia, and Karol —with the lamp. In the barred room he lay on some straw —asleep—and when we stood around him he stirred and shielded his eyes with his hand. Childishly. Karol shone the lamp on him. Siemian motioned to Karol not to wake him. In him he saw Amelia's murderer, but Karol was not shining the lamp on him as a murderer but far more as a young soldier—as a comrade. As a recruit for conscription. And Henia stood behind him and watched him shine the lamp on the boy. Karol the soldier shining a lamp on another soldier for the officer, that struck me as singular and worth a great deal of attention—it was a cordial, fraternal gesture, from soldier to soldier, but a cruel one, serving him up. Even more significant was this boy shining a lamp on another boy for an adult—although I did not quite know what it signified.

In this lumber room with its barred window we witnessed a mute explosion of these three children around the lamp and in its light—and their silent explosion released something else, unknown to us, something discreet and eager. Siemian gave them a glance, which only lasted a second, but that was enough for me to realize that he was not unaware of this.

9

Have I already mentioned the four small islands, separated from each other by canals covered with green lichen, which formed the natural prolongation of the pond? Little bridges had been built over the canals. A path, at the end of the garden, wound through the clusters of hazels, syringa, and thuyas, and made it possible to skirt this marshy archipelago of stagnant water by land. As I was going along this path one day it suddenly struck me that one of these islands differed from the others. . . how?. . . why?. . . a fleeting impression, but the garden was too deeply involved in our games for me to be able to overlook it. And yet. . . no, nothing. The corpse of this island, and its few trees with their high foliage, was dead. It was tea-time on a sultry day, and the canal was almost dry, its muddy crust with scattered puddles of green water glinting in the sun, the reeds growing triumphantly on the banks. In our situation every trace of anything unusual would have to be submitted to immediate inspection. So I crossed over to the other bank. The little island inhaled the heat, the grass grew high and thick, invaded by legions of ants, while the treetops led their lofty existences in closed distinction. I made my way through the bushes and. . . Just a minute! . . . What a surprise!

There was a bench. Henia was sitting on the bench, but

her legs looked most peculiar: one of them was encased in a stocking and shoe, while the other was naked to above the knee. . . and, stranger still, he too, lying at her feet in the grass, had uncovered one leg, his trouser rolled up above the knee. Next to him, his shoe with his sock in it. She was looking away. He was not looking at her either, his head in his arm, in the grass. No, no, the whole scene would not have seemed so shocking had it not been so incompatible with their natural rhythm, so set, motionless, and alien. . . and these legs, so curiously naked, one of each pair glistening in its nakedness, in the stifling humidity, interrupted only by the splashes of the frogs! He with a naked leg and she with a naked leg! Maybe they had been paddling in the water. . . no, it was something else, the explanation was not so simple. . . he with a naked leg and she with a naked leg! Her leg stirred and stretched out. She rested her foot on his foot. Nothing else.

I looked on. I was suddenly staggered by my stupidity. Oh! How could I have been so naive—together with Frederick—to think that there was nothing between them. . . to be deceived by appearances! The denial was there, before my eyes, as brutal as a bludgeon stroke. So this was where they met, on the island. . . a long, silent scream of relief rang out—while their contact continued, without a movement, without a sound, without even a look (because they still looked away). He with a naked leg and she with a naked leg.

Very well. . . But. . . No, it was impossible. In all that there was something indubitably false, incomprehensible, perverse. . . What was the origin of this immobility, as though they had been bewitched? And this coldness in their game? For a fraction of a second I had the insane idea that *it must be like that, that it was like that and in no other way that that should take place between them,* that that was more true than if. . . Nonsense! And I immediately had another idea: this was all a show, an act! They must have known, by some miracle, that I was going to go by and they were doing it on purpose—for me. That was all for me, no doubt about it, made for my dreams, for my eyes! For me, for me, for me! Spurred on by this idea that it was for me I threw caution to the winds and left my hiding place behind the bushes. And there the picture was complete: Frederick was sitting on a heap of dried pine needles, under a pine tree. It was for him!

I stopped! . . . As he saw me he said to them:

"You'll have to do it once more."

And at that moment, although I did not understand a thing I felt frozen by the breath of their youthful shamelessness. Their depravity. They still did not move—their youthful freshness was icily cold.

Frederick came up to me, charming. "Well, how are you, my dear Witold?" (A perfectly unnecessary question since we had seen each other less than an hour ago.) "What do you think of their pantomime?" (He gestured toward them with a sweep of his arm.) "They're not bad, are they? Ha, ha, ha!" (This laugh was unnecessary too, but loud.) "Beggars can't be choosers! . . . Did you know about my partiality for stage direction? I was an actor at one point, were you aware of that little biographical detail?"

He took me by the arm and led me around the clearing, gesticulating in a wildly theatrical way. The others looked at us without a word. "I had an idea. . . for a film. . . but some scenes were a little too outspoken, they still have to be adapted and practiced on living material. That'll do for today. You can get dressed."

And without even glancing at them he led me to the bridge, discussing his ideas loudly and volubly. In his opinion the modern method of writing plays and scripts "without taking the actors into consideration" was out of date. You had to start with the actors, "combine them" in some way, and construct the play on the successive combinations. The theater was to "bring out the latent state of living men and deal with their own range of possibilities." The actor "was not to incarnate some imaginary character, to pretend to be what he was not—on the contrary, it was the character who had to be adapted to him and fit the actor like a glove." "I'm trying," he added with a smile, "to do something like this with these children, I've promised them a little present as a reward, because it's hard work! Ah, the country gets pretty boring if one isn't doing anything, one has to do something if only for reasons of health, my dear Witold, if only for reasons of health! I don't want to show off this sort of thing, of course, because—well—it might be a little too daring for Hippo and his better half, I'd rather not risk any gossip! . . ." He spoke loudly, making his voice ring out, and I, next to him, staring at the ground, could not get the flea of that discovery out of my ear, and hardly listened to what he was saying. Ah, the artful dodger! The old fox! The schemer! He made them do things, he thought up little games for them! And all that cynically and perversely! And the flame of his depravity consumed me, I could hardly control myself, at the mercy of pangs of the most sordid jealousy! And the burning reflections of imagination lit up this cold licentiousness, both innocent and diabolic, especially hers, yes, especially hers, because it was, after all, a bit much for this tender and faithful bride to go in for this kind of thing in the bushes. . . all for the promise of a "little present."

"What an interesting theatrical experiment," I replied. "Most interesting! You've got something there!" And I left him as fast as I could so as to be able to think about it at leisure: the licentiousness was by no means one-sided;

Frederick was proving far more effectual than I had imagined, he did not beat about the bush, he took the bull by the horns and carried out his plans ruthlessly. And, what was more, behind my back, all on his own! Nothing got in his way, not even his pathetic discussion with Albert about Amelia's death—he acted. And the problem was to find out whether he had made much progress since then. And how far could one go? As far as he was concerned the problem of limits was particularly tricky—especially since it involved me too. I was afraid. It was evening again, the barely perceptible disappearance of light, the gradual deepening of the dark shades, the sudden expansion of the holes and corners that fills the thick flux of night. . . The sun had disappeared behind the trees. I remembered having left a book on the terrace so I went to get it. . . and in the book I found an unaddressed envelope enclosing a messily scribbled letter in pencil:

I am writing to establish contact. I do not want to be on my own.

If you are alone you can never be quite sure, for example, whether you have gone mad. For two—it is quite different. For two there is a certitude and an objective guarantee. For two there is no insanity!

It is not that I fear it. I could never go mad. Even if I wanted to. It is absolutely impossible for me because I am anti-madness. I want to insure myself against another risk, possibly even more dangerous, that is to say against a certain anomaly, I might say a certain multiplication of possibilities which threatens us as we stray from the only permissible path. . . Do you understand? I have no time to be more precise. If I were to visit other planets, even if it were only the moon, I would rather be with somebody—as a precaution, so that my humanity should have some mirror to look into.

I will write to you again to keep you informed. Strictly confidential—unofficial—concealed from ourselves; please burn this letter and do not mention it to anyone, not even to me. As though nothing had happened. What is the point in provoking—whom? ourselves? It is better to be discreet.

All in all I think it is for the best that you should have seen the incident on the island. Two pairs of eyes are better than one. To hell with the whole thing! Instead of being aroused and excited by this act they play it coldly, like actors. . . for me, on my orders, and if anyone excites them it is me! What rotten luck! You know how it is, you have seen them. But don't worry. We will manage to excite them.

You have seen it, but now you must bring Albert to the show. HE MUST SEE IT! Tell him that: 1) as you were taking a stroll you happened to surprise their meeting in the garden; 2) you consider it your duty to tell him; 3) they do not know you saw them. You must take him to the show tomorrow, and you must arrange for him to see them and not me. I will work it out to the last detail and write to you. You will receive further instructions. Absolutely. That is very important! Tomorrow! He must know, he must see!

You want to know my plans? I have none. I follow the lines of force, you understand? The lines of desire. I now want him to see them and them to know they have been seen. They must be steeped in guilt. We will see about the rest later.

Please do this. Please do not write back. I shall leave the letters on the wall, near the gate, under a brick. Burn them.

And the other one, number 2, Olek, where does he fit

in, how, in what scheme can he be combined with them, for it all to run smoothly? He is made to measure for it, but however much I rack my brains I cannot see how. Little by little it will take shape and I will succeed in fitting him in, but for the moment we must just go ahead! Please obey all my instructions.

This letter scalded me! I began to pace my room and finally took it outside. I was greeted by the torpor of the sleepy earth, the contour of the hills against the fleeting sky, the tension of everything increased, as it does at night-fall. A landscape I well knew, that I was certain was going to be here—but the letter expelled me from every land-scape, yes, that's right, it expelled me and I wondered what to do, what to do? What should I do? Albert, Albert—but no, that was impossible, I would never be able to do that, it could never be done. With horror I saw the nebula of a fantastic desire materialize in a fact, a concrete fact, there in my pocket, this formal demand. What if Frederick had gone mad? Was it not to stand security for his madness that he needed me? It was the ideal moment to desert him—and I already envisaged a very simple solution which I could discuss with Albert and Hippo. . . I already saw myself tell-ing them: "Look, a very awkward thing has happened. . . I'm afraid Frederick. . . is having some psychological disturbance. . . I've been observing him for some time. . . you know, after all we've been through it's not surprising. . . he's not the only one. . . But we ought to look out—I've got a feeling it's some obsession, some erotic obsession con-nected with Henia and Karol. . . " That was what I would tell them. Each word would reject him from the community of normal men and make him into a lunatic—and all this would happen behind his back—he would gradually be-come the object of our discreet care and supervision. He would not know about it—and, not knowing anything, he would be unable to defend himself—and, from a demon he would slowly turn into a lunatic—that was all. While I returned to stability. It was not too late. I had not yet done anything that could have compromised me, this letter was the first sign of our connivance. . . That was why it scalded me. I had to make a decision. Returning to the house, while the trees above me, their foliage lost in the dark, developed a halo of unreality, I bore my decision to render him inoffensive by casting him into the sphere of pure and simple madness. But a brick by the gate attracted my attention—I glanced at it: another letter awaited me.

The worm! You know about it! You understood it! You must have felt it then as I did.

The worm is Albert! They were united over the worm! They will unite over Albert! They will trample on him.

They do not want to go together? They do not want to? You wait and see, we will soon turn Albert into a soft bed on which they will fornicate.

Albert must be dragged in, he must: 1) see them. To be continued.

I took the letter up to my room and did not read it before I got there. The humiliating part was that it was as familiar to me as if I had written it myself. Yes, Albert had to be that worm, trampled on by them both, he had to provide sin for them, make them guilty, precipitate them into the burning night. But what in fact was the obstacle? Why did they NOT WANT to go together? Ah, I knew—no, I did not know—I could not seize that youthful quality which escapes the adult mind. . . it must have been some sort of continence, a morality, a law, yes, some inner prohibition they were obeying. . . so Frederick was probably right

in thinking that it would be enough for them to trample on
Albert, to deprave themselves on Albert, for all the brakes
to be released! When they became lovers for Albert. . . they
would really become lovers. For us, who were too old, it was
the only possibility of an erotic contact with them. . . We
had to precipitate them into this sin! If they were to dive
into it with us we could hope for contact and union! I
realized that! And I knew this sin would not tarnish their
beauty, on the contrary, their youth, their freshness, would
be even more exuberant when they were blackened, dragged
by our withered hands into depravity and united with us!
Yes! I knew it! Enough of this docile, good-natured youth!
We had to create another one, tragically united to us, the
adults.

Enthusiasm! Was I not enthusiastic about this prospect?
Yes, of course. I, who was already excluded from all beauty,
denied entrance to the shimmering net of seduction—un-
seductive, incapable of charming, indifferent to nature. . .
ah, and yet I was still capable of enthusiasm, but I knew
that my enthusiasm would never again fill anyone else with
enthusiasm. . . and I only took part in life like a whipped
and mangy cur. . . But when at that age we are offered the
opportunity of touching that flowering season, of entering
youth even at the price of depravity, and if it appears that
ugliness can still be used and absorbed by beauty, well. . .
A temptation sweeping aside all obstacles, insurmountable!
Enthusiasm, yes, what am I saying? folly, stifling, but on
the other hand. . . No, it was mad! Quite unsuitable! Too
personal, too private, and too unusual—and then it was without a precedent! Take this demonic path, this particular
path with him, with a being whom I fear and whose extremism I knew would take me too far!

And, like Mephistopheles, ruin Albert's love? No, away,
stupid, base fantasy! I do that? For nothing on earth, never!

Then what? Retreat, go to Hippolytus and Albert, make it into a clinical case, turn the devil into a lunatic, hell into an asylum. . . and I was about to proceed and once and for all extirpate this raging iniquity. Raging? Where? What was he doing now? The idea that he should be doing something behind my back pushed me up like a spring and dragged me outside. The dogs bounded up—nobody, nothing but the dark outline of the house came into being before me and stood there like a fact. The lights were on in the kitchen windows. And on the first floor, in the windows of Siemian's room (I had forgotten about him). Myself, before the house, suddenly overwhelmed by the distance of the starry vault, lost among the trees. I hesitated, I trembled. A little further away was the gate, and the loose brick next to it. I went up to it, out of a sense of duty, and when I got there I looked around. . . was he watching me from the bushes? Under the brick, another letter. His inspiration was inexhaustible.

Have you really understood me?
I have already spotted a number of little things.
1) RIDDLE: *Why don't they want to go together?. . . Well? Do you know?*
I know. Because it would be too FULL *for them. Too* COMPLETE.
FULLNESS *and its antithesis! That which is not achieved, that's the key!*
Great God! Thou art fullness! But this is more wonderful than Thou and I hereby deny Thee.
2) RIDDLE: *Why do they stick to us? Why do they flirt with us?*
Because they want to go through us. Through us. And through Albert. Through us, my dear Witold, my dear

friend, yes. They can only go through us. That is why they are so sweet to us.

Have you ever known anything like it? That they should need us to do it?

3) Do you know what the danger is? That I am at the height of my intellectual and moral powers, and find myself in light, inexpert hands which are still growing. Good God! They are still growing. And they are lightly, lightly, superficially introducing me to something which must totally exhaust me intellectually and spiritually. They will hand me this cup lightly, this cup I shall have to drain to the dregs. . .

I have always known something like this was awaiting me. I am Christ crucified on a sixteen-year-old cross. Farewell! We shall see each other in Golgotha. Farewell!

His inspiration was inexhaustible! I was once again sitting in my room by the lamp. Betray him? Give him up? At the same time I would have had to betray myself and give myself up!

Myself!

He was not the only one to have thought of all this. I was involved. Appear as a lunatic myself? Betray in myself the only possibility of entering, of entering. . . what? What? What was that? I heard the dinner gong. When I found myself at the table, in the combination we formed every evening, the everyday problems returned, the war and the Germans, the country and the worries, but I felt they were coming from very far away. . . in short, they were no longer my problems.

Frederick was sitting here too, at his place—and discussed, as he ate his ravioli and cheese, the military situation on the various fronts. On several occasions he turned to me and asked my opinion.

10

Albert's initiation went according to plan. Nothing unforeseen happened to complicate it—it ran without a hitch.

I told him "I had something to show him." I led him to the canal, to the appointed place from where the clearing could be seen between the trees. At this point the water in the canal was quite deep—a necessary precaution to prevent him from crossing over to the island and discovering Frederick.

I pointed to the scene.

This was what Frederick had devised in his honor: Karol under the tree, she behind him, both looking up at something in the tree, a bird, perhaps. He raised his hand. And she raised her hand.

Over their heads their hands touched "accidentally." And as they touched they pulled them down abruptly and violently. For some time they both gazed attentively at their joined hands. Then they suddenly fell down—it was impossible to tell who had been pushed by whom—it looked as though their hands had pushed them down.

They fell down, for a moment they lay next to each other and then jumped up. . . and again they stood there as though they did not know what to do next. Slowly she walked away, with him behind her, and they disappeared into the bushes.

A highly refined scene, despite its apparent simplicity. Because the artlessness with which they joined hands experienced an unexpected shock—this sudden fall to the ground—the naturalness of it was convulsed abruptly, departed so violently from normality that for a split second they looked like puppets at the mercy of an elementary force. But that only lasted a second and the way they got up and walked off calmly and deliberately made one suppose they were used to it. That it was not the first time. That they were accustomed to these falls.

The fumes of the canal. The stifling humidity. The motionless frogs. It was five o'clock. The garden was exhausted. The heat.

"Why did you bring me here?"

He asked me the question on our way back to the house. I replied:

"I considered it my duty."

He pondered.

"Thank you."

As we were already within sight of the house, he added: "I don't think it's of much importance. . . But I'm very grateful to you for having drawn my attention to it. . . I'll mention it to Henia."

That was all. He went up to his room. I remained alone, disappointed as one always is when something is realized—because realization is always indistinct, insufficiently precise, with neither the greatness nor the purity of the intention. Having performed my task I suddenly felt useless—what could I do?—literally drained by the event I had just given birth to. The night was falling. Again the night was falling. I went out to get some air and walk along the edge of the fields, my head down; at my feet the earth was simple, submissive, and silent. On my way back I went to have a look under the brick, but nothing awaited me, only the brick, black with humidity, and cool. I followed the path to the house and I stopped, not having the courage to enter the circle of his sinister intrigues. But at the same time the heat of their embrace, of their precocious, excited blood, of their secret contact, enveloped me in such a glow that I burst into the house almost breaking in the door, to continue to live through my dream! I burst in. But here I was to have one of those surprises that spring on you only too frequently. . .

Hippolytus, Frederick, and Albert were in the study—they called to me.

Thinking that this congress was connected with the events on the island I advanced cautiously. . . but at the last moment I had a sort of premonition that it was to do with something else. Hippolytus was seated morosely at his desk and opened his eyes wide when he saw me. Albert was pacing up and down. Frederick was sprawled in an arm-chair. There was silence. Albert said:

"We must tell Witold."

"They want to liquidate Siemian," said Hippolytus, in a slightly evasive manner.

I still do not understand anything. Explanations followed, which introduced me to the new situation—and again I felt the theatrical quality of patriotic conspiracy—Hippolytus himself must have had this impression too, because his voice became hard and slightly arrogant. And strict. So I discovered that during the night Siemian had had a talk with "some people from Warsaw" in order to establish the details of an action he was supposed to organize in the area. But in the course of the discussion "an odd thing happened, my dear sir," because apparently Siemian said that he was not going to organize this action or any other action, that he had had enough of the whole thing and was withdrawing once and for all from conspiracy, that he was "going home." An odd thing, indeed! There was a row, they started shouting at him and finally, at the end of his tether, he told them he had done what he could and could do no more—"he had lost his nerve"—"his courage had turned to fear" and: "Leave me alone, something's snapped inside me, I'm scared, I don't even know why." He did not feel he could do it any more, it would be the height of irresponsibility to entrust him with anything in these circumstances, he was giving them a loyal warning and asked to be relieved of his duties. That was the last straw! After a violent argument an initially vague suspicion began to take shape: either Siemian had gone mad or he was on the verge of a nervous breakdown. Then they were panic-stricken by the idea that a certain secret they had disclosed to him was no longer in safe hands, that he might well reveal it. . . And, for various reasons, this took on the aspect of a catastrophe, a defeat, a universal disaster, and it was like this, in this tension and excitement, that the terrified and terrifying decision to liquidate him burst into being. Hippo said that they had wanted to follow Siemian into his room at once and "do him in"—but that he had succeeded in extorting a reprieve until the next night, persuading them of the necessity of working out a technical plan so as not to endanger the inhabitants of the home. They agreed on a reprieve, but only for twenty-four hours. They were afraid he might get wind of their plan and escape. Poworna was the best place for them to execute this deed because Siemian had come here in dead secrecy and it would not occur to anybody to look for him here. They finally agreed to return that night to "settle it."

Why did the truth of our struggle against the enemy and the aggressor have to appear in this ridiculous guise—how humiliating and unbearable!—like something out of an old melodrama, but stained with blood and death, a real death!

In order to have a better idea of the new situation and to get used to it I asked: "What's he doing now?" Hippolytus replied:

"He's upstairs. In his room. He's locked himself in. He asked me for horses to go home. But I can't let him have any horses."

And he whispered to himself:

"I can't let him have any horses."

Of course he could not. And yet we could not do something like this—we could not just liquidate somebody, kill a man without leaving any traces, without a verdict, without formalities, without any document! But that was none of our business. We spoke like people stricken by misfortune. But when I asked them what they intended to do the reply lashed out, almost insolently: "What d'you think? The only thing! Obey!"

Hippolytus' tone of voice showed up the sinister change in our relationship. I was no longer his guest, I was on duty, united with them in the severity and cruelty which was aimed at us just as much as at Siemian. What had he done to us? Suddenly, from one day to the other, we had to kill him, risking our own necks!

"Right now there's nothing to be done. They're coming back at half-past twelve at night. I've sent the night watchman to Ostrowicc on a supposedly urgent errand. I'll keep the dogs chained up. All I'm going to do is to show them up and then it's up to them. I've made one condition—no noise, or they'll wake the whole house. As for the body, it'll be removed. . . I've already worked that out. . . in the barn. Tomorrow one of us will pretend to take Siemian to the station, and that'll be that. If they don't make a noise it can all go quite smoothly and not a living soul will suspect a thing. . . "

Frederick asked: "In the old barn, behind the shed?"

He asked the question bluntly, like a conspirator, an agent. And in spite of everything I felt relieved that he should have been mobilized like that, like a conscripted drunkard. But would he have another drink? And suddenly this new adventure struck me as being infinitely more healthy, more decent than what we had been doing until then. But this feeling of relief did not last long.

Immediately after dinner (eaten in the absence of Siemian who had been "indisposed" for a few days and who ate his meals in his room) I went to the gate, just to be sure, and, sure enough, a piece of paper shimmered under the brick.

A complication. What a bore the whole business is! We shall have to wait. Quiet, hush!

We shall have to see how and what. How things are going to turn out. If there's a row and we have to clear off to Warsaw, for instance, and they have to go somewhere else, well, nothing doing. The whole thing will be messed up.

But this may not happen.

You have to know the old whore. You know who I mean? Nature. When she creeps up alongside with something unexpected you must not protest, you must not resist, you must obey, make the best of it, faire bonne mine... but in our heart of hearts we must not let go, we must not lose sight of our end, so she can know that we are pursuing our own end. To start with, her attacks are very direct and determined, but afterward it is as though she were to lose interest, she releases her grip and you can return secretly to your own work and even reckon on her being fairly indulgent... Look out! Copy my behavior. So there will not be any discrepancies. I shall write to you. This letter must be burned.

This letter! . . . this letter which was even more insane than the ones before it—and yet I understood this insanity so well! It was so legible! These *tactics* he used in his dealings with Nature—they were not unfamiliar to me. And it was obvious that he never let his end out of sight for a minute; this letter showed that he would not give way, that he was faithful to the plan he had conceived and, under the appearance of submission, it concealed an appeal to resistance and obstinacy. And who knows whether it was written for me or for Her—so that she should know that we were not going to give up—and I was only a go-between? I suddenly thought about it: how strange that every word, every movement of Frederick's only seemed to refer to whomever they were addressed, while he continued his inexhaustible dialogue with the Power. . . a cunning dialogue where the truth seemed the lie, and the lie the truth. Oh, how hard he pretended in this letter to act behind Nature's back, while in fact he was writing it to keep her informed! He obviously thought this strategy would disarm her, amuse her perhaps. . . We spent the rest of the evening waiting. From time to time somebody surreptitiously glanced at the clock. The lamp hardly lit the room. Henia, as usual, was huddled next to Albert; he, as he did every evening, had put his arm around her shoulders and I discovered that the "island" had in no way changed his behavior toward her. He was impenetrable and I wondered how much he was worrying about Siemian and if he noticed the noise Karol was making as he shifted and arranged some large crates. Maria was sewing (like the "children," she had not been let into the secret). Frederick, his legs outstretched, his arms resting on the arms of the chair. Hippolytus sitting gazing into space. Our tension began to be enveloped by exhaustion.

United by Siemian, by this secret mission which had

been assigned to us, we, the men, formed a group apart. Henia asked: "What are you doing with those crates, Karol?" "Don't you get in my way!" he replied. Their voices rang out in the silence and we could not understand what they meant, what they were trying to do—we did not say a word.

At eleven they went to bed, as did Maria, and we, the men, began to make the necessary preparations. Hippolytus brought out some shovels, a large sack, and a coil of rope. Frederick cleaned the gun as a precaution, Albert and I made a tour of inspection around the house. All the lights were out except in one window on the first floor—Siemian's —where it shone through a thin curtain in a pale halo of light and fear, fear and light. What could have happened to make his courage turn to fear so suddenly? What could have happened to make him lose his nerve overnight? A Resistance leader turn into a coward! What an odd thing! Suddenly the house seemed to me to contain two forms of insanity, with Siemian on the first floor and Frederick on the ground floor (playing his game with Nature). . . they were both cornered, driven to their limit. On my way back to the house I almost burst out laughing at the sight of Hippo examining two kitchen knives and testing their blades. Good God! This poor old fat man, transformed into a murderer preparing for the slaughter, was a buffoonery. And suddenly the absurdity of our situation, so clumsily immersed in this murder, made these preparations look like a play acted by a group of amateurs, far more comic than dangerous. Anyhow, all this was only being done *as a precaution*, there was nothing decisive about it. But at the same time the glint of the knife seemed to have something irrevocable: the die was cast, the knife had already appeared!

Olek. . . Frederick's eyes, staring at the knife, showed

that he was thinking about it too, there could be no doubt. Olek. . . A knife. . . Identical to the other, the one which stabbed Amelia, almost the same, here, among us—ah, this knife connected us to the other crime, it evoked it inexorably, it marked its beginning in some way—hanging here, now, over our heads. A strange analogy, a curious repetition! The knife. Albert was also staring at it attentively—and so both of them, Frederick and Albert, had taken a mental grip on this knife, each one in view of his own ends. But since they were on duty, in action, they withdrew into themselves—and we continued our preparations and waited.

We had to perform this task fully—but we were so exhausted, so fed up with this melodrama of history, we thirsted for fresh air! After midnight Hippo left the house on tiptoe to meet the fellows from the A.K. Albert went up to the first floor to guard Siemian's door—I remained downstairs with Frederick and never have I found a tête-à-tête so oppressive. I knew he had something to say to me, but we were not allowed to speak—so he remained silent—and although nobody was there to overhear us we behaved like strangers; it was these precautions that evoked out of thin air a third mysterious presence, inexplicable and obstinate. And opposite me his face—so familiar, that of an accomplice—walled in and inaccessible. . . Next to one another we existed, that was all, we just existed and nothing else, but we soon heard the heavy steps and hard breathing of Hippo on his way back to the house. He was alone. What had happened? More complications! Something had gone wrong. Panic. The people he had arranged to meet had not come to the appointment. Somebody else had turned up instead of them and left almost immediately. As for Siemian, Hippo said:

"It's up to us. They can't do it, they've had to clear off in a hurry. That's the order."

In Hippo's voice was complete determination; it was an order not to let him escape on any account, the lives of several people depended on it and we had no right to take any risks; it was an order, no, not a written one, there was no time for that, there was no time anyhow, that was all, he just had to be liquidated! We had been assigned that task. Such was the order, brutal, panic-stricken, the product of a tense situation we could not know about. Doubt it? That would have been to assume the responsibility for all consequences, and that could be catastrophic. After all, we would not have resorted to such drastic expedients without good reason. And any resistance on our side would have looked like flight—at a moment when we wanted to be ready for action. In these circumstances we could not allow ourselves to be in any way weak, and, if Hippo had led us straight to Siemian's room we would very probably have settled it in one go. But these unexpected complications gave us the excuse for putting off the operation until the next night. Because the parts had to be distributed, because we had to get ready and take the necessary precautions. . . and it turned out to be preferable if we could do it the next night. . . I was told to guard Siemian's door until dawn, when I was to be relieved by Albert, and we wished one another good night, because, in spite of everything, we retained our good manners. Hippolytus went off to his bedroom carrying the lamp and we were still on the staircase when a figure moved in the dark suite of rooms. Albert had a torch and flashed a ray of white light. Karol. In his shirt.

"Where have you been? What are you doing at this time of night?" shouted Albert, unable to control his nervous agitation.

"I was in the bathroom."

That could have been true. And Albert would certainly not have let out such a groan of anguish if he himself had not shown up the boy with the ray of his own torch. But as he showed him up he groaned aloud. This groan astounded us. And we were no less astonished by the almost vulgar and provocative tone of Karol's:

"What d'you want?"

He was prepared to hit him. Henia's fiancé switched off his torch at once. "I'm sorry," we heard in the dark, "I just wondered."

And he walked away rapidly, in the dark.

I did not have to leave my room to guard Siemian's door—our rooms were adjoining. He made no noise, but he had left the light on. I did not lie down for fear of falling asleep. I sat at my table and in my head I could still feel the frantic rush of the recent events which I could neither control nor understand because, over the material course of things, spread a mystical sphere of accents and meanings, like the gleam of the sun on troubled waters. I sat for over an hour, lost in the contemplation of this glittering flow, before I noticed a piece of paper that had been slipped under my door.

Apropos of the last short circuit A.—K. Did you see how his fury exploded? K. wanted to hit him.

They already know he has seen them. That is why.

They already know because I told them. I told them you told me Albert told you—that he had surprised them on the island. That he had seen them (but not me) quite by chance as he was going for a walk in the garden.

As you can well believe they laughed, that is they laughed together because I told them both and, being together, they could do nothing but laugh. . . because they were together and, what is more, in front of me! Now they are already ESTABLISHED *as* A.'*s laughing executioners. Only as long as they are together, of course, as long as they form a couple, as long as they are a couple—because, you saw what happened at dinner, she, as far as she is she, that is, on her own, is faithful to her fiancé. But together they laugh at him.*

And now the KNIFE.

The knife creates a new formula, s. *(Siemian)*—s¹ *(Skuziak).*

Which makes: (ss¹)—A., *through* A., *through Amelia's murder.*

But at the same time there is A.—KH. *Or* (KH.)—(ss¹).

What chemistry! It is all connected. As yet the connections are obscure, but you can already spot a TENDENCY *in this direction. . . And to think that I did not know how to fit Skuziak into the game—and he enters it on his own via the* KNIFE. *But be careful! Do not upset anything. We must not force. . . we must not impose ourselves. . . let us drift with the tide as though nothing had happened and just take every chance to get nearer to our end.*

We must collaborate in Hippo's underground action. Without revealing that our underground action has another aim. Pretend to be up to your neck in the national struggle, in the A.K., in the Poland-Germany dilemma, as though that were what it was about. . . while in fact it is only about making:

HENIA WITH KAROL.

But we cannot let that be seen. We cannot let that be seen by anyone. We must not give ourselves away. Not a word to anyone. Not even between ourselves, we are not allowed to mention it. Above all no alarm. Quiet. It must work itself out. . .

We need courage and determination to proceed with our venture even if it should look like a licentious obscenity.

Obscenity ceases being obscene if we persevere! We must push on because if we give way the obscenity will crush us. Do not be discouraged, do not betray! There is no return. Best wishes. Your obedient servant. Burn this letter, huh!

"Burn this letter, huh!" he ordered. But he had already said. "IT IS ONLY ABOUT MAKING: HENIA WITH KAROL." Who was this letter written to? To me? Or to Her, to Nature? There was a knock at my door.

"Come in."

It was Albert.

"May I speak to you?"

I offered him my chair, and he sat down. I sat on the bed.

"I do apologize and I know you're tired. But I've just realized that I won't be able to sleep a wink tonight before I've had a talk with you. Different from the other ones. More frank, I hope you won't be annoyed. You can imagine why I'm here. It's about. . . the business on the island."

"I don't think I can be of much use to you. . ."

"I know. I know. Forgive me for interrupting you. I know you don't know anything. But I'd like to know what you think. I can't put my ideas straight. What do you think about it? What do you think about it?"

"Me? What can I think about it? I pointed it out to you because I considered it my du. . ."

"Of course. And I'm most grateful to you. I really don't know how to thank you. But I'd like to know your point of view. In my opinion it's of no importance, because they've known each other since they were children. . . It's more childish than anything else. . . And at that age! There was probably something between them some time ago. . . most likely. . . you know, those infantile jokes and caresses— strange, isn't it? And now they occasionally do it again. A sort of sprouting, budding sensuality. And then it could also have been an optical illusion, since we were quite far away, behind the bushes. I can't doubt Henia's feelings for me. I have no right, no reason to do so. I know she loves me. Anyhow, how could I compare our love to these—childish pranks? Ridiculous!"

His body! He was sitting opposite me. His body! He was in a dressing gown—with his corpulent, pampered, chubby, pale, clean, and dressing-gowned body! He was sitting with this body as if with a bag or a travel kit. His body! Infuriated by this body and become carnal in my turn, I looked at him mockingly, I mocked him outright, almost with a whistle. Not an atom of pity. His body!

"Believe me if you can, but I assure you I would never have thought twice about it. . . But one thing worries me. I don't know, I may have been deceived. . . That's why I wanted to ask you. I apologize at the start if this were to seem. . . at all fanciful. I admit I don't even know how to put it. What they were doing. . . you know, when they suddenly fell down and then got up. . . you'll agree it was rather. . . peculiar. One doesn't do it *like that!*"

He stopped, swallowed and seemed ashamed of having swallowed.

"Is that the impression you had?"

"No, it didn't seem normal. You see, they could have kissed, but normally. . . If, for instance, he had pushed her over—normally. Even if he had had her in front of me. . . it wouldn't have upset me. . . so much. . . as those odd movements. . . "

He took my hand. He looked me in the eyes. I felt sick. I started to hate him.

."Please tell me frankly, am I right? Maybe I didn't see it as I should have seen it? Maybe this strangeness is something in myself? I don't know any more. Tell me, please!"

His body!

Skillfully concealing my quivering but pitiless malice I said—hardly anything—but hardly anything was enough to add fuel to the fire: "How should I know?. . . But I suppose. . . Maybe, up to a point. . ."

"But I don't know how much importance I should attribute to it! Is it serious? And how far? First of all, tell me: do you think that he and she. . ."

"What?"

"Forgive me. I was thinking of sex appeal. What we call sex appeal. When I saw them together for the first time I noticed it at once. Sex appeal. Attraction. Sexual attraction. Him and her. But then, when I started feeling something for her, it faded into the background, compared with what I felt it was meaningless. I stopped thinking about it. It was so childish! It's only now. . ."

He sighed.

"Now I'm afraid it might be—still worse than I could ever have imagined."

He got up.

"They fell onto the ground. . . but not as they should have fallen. They got up almost immediately—not as they should have got up, either. And then they walked away, and that wasn't as they should have walked away! What is it? What is it hiding? One doesn't do it *like that!*"

He sat down again.

"Well? Well? What can that mean?"

He looked at me.

"You have no idea how this is torturing me! Say something! Say something, for heaven's sake! Don't leave me all alone—with that!" He gave me a pale smile. "Please forgive me."

So he too was after my company and preferred not to "be alone with it"—I was decidedly in fashion! But unlike Frederick he implored me not to confirm his folly and waited with his heart in his mouth for my denial which would reduce everything to a chimera. He depended on me to calm him. . . His body! And my prodigious lightness! To sentence him to hell I hardly had to make any effort, all I had to do, as I had just done, was to mumble a few vague phrases: "To tell the truth. . . It could be. . . I must admit. . . Perhaps. . . " I said them. He replied:

"She loves me, I know she loves me, I'm certain she loves me!"

He was defending himself in spite of everything.

"She loves you? No doubt. But don't you think that between them love is superfluous? Love is necessary with you, not with him."

His body!

For a long time he said nothing. He sat in silence. I too sat in silence. Silence enveloped us. Frederick? Was he asleep? And Siemian? And Olek in the lumber room? What was he doing? Was he asleep? The house seemed harnessed to masses of horses, each one charging in a different direction.

He smiled awkwardly:

"It really is distressing," he said. "I've just lost my mother. And now. . . "

He mused.

"I really don't know how to apologize for this nocturnal visit. Alone, it was unbearable. I'd like to say something else to you, if you don't mind. Look. Sometimes I myself am amazed. . . that she should feel something for me. What I feel for her is another matter. I feel what I feel for her because she's made for love, to be loved. But what can she love in me? My feeling, my love for her? No, not only that, she loves *me too*—but why? What does she love in me? You see what I'm like. I'm under no illusions. I don't particularly like myself, and I really can't conceive, can't begin to understand what she can see in me, and I must admit I'm rather shocked by it. If I had to reproach her for something it would be precisely. . . for accepting me so eagerly. Will you believe me if I tell you that in the moment of most violent ecstasy I resent her for this ecstasy, for giving in to it with me? And I've never felt at ease with her, I always had the impression of a favor, of a concession granted to me, I even had to resort to cynicism to benefit from these "facilities," this astonishing favor of nature. Very well. But apart from this—she loves me. It's a fact. Deserved or undeserved, favor or not, she loves me."

"She loves you. No doubt about it."

"Wait! I know what you're going to say: that the other business is beyond love, in another sphere. Quite right! And this is why my position is so. . . barbarous and immoral, so refined in its cruelty—One wonders how it could have gone so far. If she were to be unfaithful to me. . .

"My bride is doing it with. . . with. . . someone like that," he suddenly said in another tone, and looked at me. "What does that mean? And how can I defend myself? What can I do?

"She's doing it with. . . " he went on, "and in a strange. . . exclusive. . . unknown way, which hurts me, which stabs me to the bone, because you know, I can feel this taste, I'm catching it. . . Will you believe it, but on the basis of the sample we saw I've reconstructed *every* possibility between them, the totality of their mutual behavior. And it is so. . . ingeniously erotic that I can't imagine who can have thought it up! It's like a dream! Who invented it? He or she? If she did—she's an artist!"

After a moment:

"And do you know what I think? That he's never had her. And that that's far more terrible than if they were sleeping together. An idea like that is sheer lunacy, isn't it? And yet! Because if he'd had her I would at least have been able to defend myself, while there. . . I can't. . . and I don't know if she belongs more to him simply because he never had her. Because everything happens differently in them! It's different! It's different!"

Ha! He did not know the most important part. That what he had seen on the island existed *for* Frederick and *through* Frederick—it was a sort of bastard born from them and Frederick. And how satisfying to be able to keep him in ignorance, that he should never for a moment suspect that I, his confidant, was on the side of his persecutors, of the element that was destroying him! Although it was not my element (they were too young). Although I was his comrade and not theirs—and as I destroyed him I destroyed myself. But. . . this extraordinary lightness.

"It's the war that does that," he said. "It's the war. But why must I be at war with brats! One of them murdered my mother and the other. . . It's too much, this time it's too much. It's really gone too far. Do you want to know what I'm going to do?"

Since I did not reply, he repeated emphatically:

"Do you know what I intend to do?"

"I'm listening. Tell me."

"I won't surrender an inch of ground."

"Really?"

"I won't allow her to be seduced—and I won't allow myself to be seduced."

"What do you mean by that?"

"I'll be able to defend and look after my own interests. I love her. She loves me. That's all that matters. The rest must yield, the rest must be meaningless, because that's how I want it. Because I'll be able to want it. You know, I don't actually believe in God. My mother did, but not I. But I want God to exist. In this case too I'll be able to want, and will impose my rights and my morals. . . I shall call Henia to order. I haven't spoken to her yet, but I'll do so tomorrow and I'll bring her to her senses."

"What will you say to her?"

"I shall behave decently and force her to behave decently. I shall behave respectfully—I'll respect her and make her respect me. I shall treat her in such a way that she won't be able to deny me her love or her fidelity. I firmly believe, you know, that respect and consideration create reciprocal obligations. And I shall behave correctly toward this brat, too. Just now he almost made me fly off the handle—but this won't happen again."

"You want to behave. . . responsibly?"

"That's just what I meant! Responsibly! I'll make them behave responsibly!"

"Yes, but 'responsibly' implies seriousness, 'importance.' Someone who's responsible only thinks about what's important. And what is the most important thing? It might be one thing for you and another for them. Everyone chooses in accordance with his taste and opinion."

"How do you mean? I'm responsible, not they. How could they be responsible? If it's all a lot of childish nonsense. Nonsense!"

"And what if—for them—childishness were to be more important?"

"What? What's important for me must be important for them. What do they know? I know more. I'll force them! I'm more important than they, you can't deny that; my common sense must prevail!"

"Just a minute. I thought you considered yourself more important because of your principles. . . but it now seems that your principles are more important because you yourself are more important. Personally. As a man. As an adult."

"Whichever way you look at it!" he shouted. "It's six of one and half a dozen of the other! Please excuse me again.

These confidences so late at night. . . Thank you so much."

He went out. I wanted to roar with laughter. Well! He had swallowed the bait—and was now writhing like a fish out of water!

That was a fine trick our little couple had played!

·He was suffering. Was he suffering? Of course he was suffering, but a chubby—tired—bald suffering. . .

Charm was on the other bank. So I too was on the other bank. Everything that came from over there had something seductive, enchanting, voluptuous. . . His body!

This lout who pretended to defend morals and was in fact crushing them with his own weight! He wanted to crush them. He forced his morals on them for the sole reason that they were "his"—that they were heavier, older, and more developed. . . the morals of an adult. He forced them on them.

A real lout! I hated him. Only. . . was I not a little like him? I, an adult. . . That was what I was thinking about when there was another knock on the door. I was sure it was Albert who had forgotten to say something—but it was Siemian! I almost choked in his face with surprise—he was the last person I expected!

"I'm sorry to disturb you, but I heard voices and knew you weren't asleep. May I have a glass of water?"

He drank it slowly, in little sips, without looking at me. He had no tie, his shirt was open and creased, he had put on some brilliantine but his hair was on end and he kept on passing his fingers through it. He drank the water but did not leave. He stood in the middle of the room passing his hand through his hair.

"What an arabesque!" he muttered. "Unbelievable. . . "

He stood there, as though he were alone. Intentionally I said nothing. He murmured, not to me:

"I need help."

"What can I do for you?"

"You realize I'm at the end of my tether, don't you?" he asked me indifferently, as though he were talking about somebody else.

"I must admit. . . I don't quite understand. . . "

"You must be *au courant!*" he laughed. "You know who I am. And that I've lost my nerve."

He ruffled his hair, waiting for an answer. He was in no hurry because he looked thoughtful, or rather as though he were concentrating on some thought without really thinking about it. I decided to discover what he wanted—I told him I was *au courant*. . .

"You're a nice man. . . I couldn't stay in my room next door. . . shut in. . . " He pointed to the room next door. "How can I put it? I decided to appeal to someone. I decided to appeal to you. Maybe because I like you, maybe because our rooms are adjoining. . . I can't be alone any more. I can't stand it. May I sit down?"

He sat down gingerly as though he had just recovered from a long illness, had difficulty in controlling his limbs, and had to work out every movement in advance. "I would like you to tell me something," he said, "is there some sort of plot against me?"

"Why?" I asked.

He decided to laugh, and went on: "I'm sorry, I wanted to talk openly and frankly. . . but first I must tell you in what state of mind I've come to you. I must tell you a few things about my life. Please listen to me as benevolently as you can. Anyhow, you must have heard about me. You heard of me as a brave man, as a dangerous man, I dare say. . . Yes. . . But a short time ago something went wrong. . . I'm in a funk, you see. A little weakness in the pit of my stomach. It's been like that for about a week. I was sitting by the lamp when I suddenly thought: so far you've been lucky. What would happen if something were to go wrong tomorrow and they caught you?"

"You must have thought that before?"

"Of course! Frequently! But this time it was worse—because I suddenly thought of something else—that I shouldn't be thinking this because it could weaken me, make me pervious, or what do you call it?—and attract danger. I told myself it was better not to think about it. And no sooner had I said that than it was too late, I couldn't put the idea out of my head, it took a hold of me, and now I can't think about anything else—something's going to go wrong and I mustn't think about it because then something really will go wrong, and so on, in a vicious circle. What do you think? I'm trapped!"

"Nerves."

"It isn't nerves. Do you know what it is? It's courage turning to fear. There's nothing one can do about it."

He lit a cigarette. He inhaled deeply and blew the smoke out. "Look. Three weeks ago I still had an aim in life, an assignment, a struggle, such and such an objective. . . Now I have nothing. Everything has suddenly slipped down, like my trousers, if you don't mind my saying so. Now I only think of one thing: keeping out of harm's way. And I'm right. Whoever fears for himself is always right! The worst of it is that I am right, for the first time in my life! But what do you want to do to me? I've been here for five days. I ask for horses and they won't let me have any. It's as though you were keeping me in prison. What do you want to do to me? I'm going crazy in my room. Is that what you want?"

"Calm yourself. It's nerves."

"Do you want to finish me off?"

"You're overdoing it."

"I'm not that stupid. I lost my nerve. The trouble is I

was in such a funk I gave myself away. Now they know. As long as I wasn't afraid they weren't afraid of me. Now I'm afraid, I'm dangerous. I understand that. I can't be trusted any more. But I'm appealing to you as a man. I took this decision: to get up and talk to you, man to man. It's my last chance. I've come straight to you because a man in my position has no choice. Listen to me. It's a vicious circle. You're afraid of me because I'm afraid of you, I'm afraid of you because you're afraid of me. I can only get out by taking a leap and that's why I've come to you in the middle of the night, although we don't know each other. . . You're an intelligent man, a writer, try to understand, give me a hand, help me out."

"What can I do?"

"They must let me leave. Get away. That's my only dream. To get away. To withdraw. I could go on foot—but you could catch me in a field, and there. . . Persuade them to let me live, tell them I won't hurt anyone, I've had enough of it, I can't go on. I want to be left in peace. In peace. Once I've got away—it'll be all right. Please, I beg of you, tell them, I can't stand it any more. . . Or help me to escape. I appeal to you because I can't be alone against you all, like an outcast, give me a hand, don't leave me like that. We don't know each other, but I chose you. I came to you. Why do you want to go on persecuting me since I'm already harmless—for good. It's all over!"

I struck the most unexpected rock in the person of this man who had started to tremble. What could I say to him? I was still full of Albert—and I was confronted by this vomiting man—enough, enough, enough!—who begged for pity. In a flash I saw the whole problem that faced me. I could not reject him because his death took shape from his quivering life before me. He had come to me, confided in me, had become, from that alone, close and therefore immense, his life and his death towered high above me. At the same time his appearance—wrenching me from Albert —led me back to duty, to our cause, to our common action under Hippolytus' command and he, Siemian, was nothing but the objective of our action. . . and, as an objective, he was rejected from the sphere of the living. I could neither recognize him nor agree with him, nor speak to him frankly, I had to keep my distance, not let him come too near, maneuver him politically. . . and for a moment my spirit rebelled, like a horse before an insurmountable obstacle. . . because he was appealing to the man in me, wanted to approach me as a man, and I had no right to see a man in him. What could I say to him? The most important thing was not to let him get any closer—not to let him guess what was going on inside me.

"Look," I said, "there is a war on. The country is under occupation. In these circumstances desertion is a luxury we cannot indulge in. Each of us has to watch the other. You know that."

"That means you don't. . . really want to talk to me."

He paused, as though he were savoring the silence that separated us more and more.

"Tell me," he said, "have you ever lost your trousers?"

Once again I did not reply, increasing the distance. "You know," he said patiently, "I've lost everything. . . I've lost my pants. . . I'm stark naked. Let's speak to the point. I've come to see you in the middle of the night like one stranger to another, can't we talk more openly? You don't want to?"

He stopped and waited for me to answer. I said nothing.

"I couldn't care less what you think of me," he added apathetically. "But I've chosen you—as my savior or my murderer. Which do you prefer?"

I then resorted to a blatant lie—as blatant to me as it

was to him—and so I finally rejected him from the sphere of men: "I'm not aware of your being in any danger. You're exaggerating. It's your nerves."

This cut the ground from under his feet. He did not say anything—but he made no attempt to leave, did not move, stood there—passively. As though I had destroyed all means of retreat. And I thought this could last forever, he would not budge, why should he budge? He would stay there. . . crushing me. I did not know what to do with him and he could not help me because I had rejected him, cast him out, and I was without him, facing him—alone. . . He was at my mercy. But between us there was nothing but indifference, a cold hostility. He was alien to me, he disgusted me! A dog, a horse, a chicken, even a maggot would have appealed to me more than this adult, worn man, with his life history written on his face—an adult hates adults! Nothing more disgusting for a man than another man—I mean, of course, elderly men with their life history written on their faces. He did not attract me, no! He could not seduce me. He could not please me! He repelled me like Albert, and even more—he repelled me as I repelled him and we almost clashed antlers like two stags—and that I should repel him in my deterioration simply increased my animosity. First Albert, now him—both of them horrible! And myself with them! An adult can only be bearable for another adult as a renunciation, when he renounces himself to incarnate something else—horror, virtue, the people, the fight. . . But a man who is nothing but a man—how ghastly!

But he had chosen me. He had chosen me and now would not leave. He stood motionless before me. I coughed and this little cough informed me that the situation was getting worse. His death—however revolting—loomed up like an inevitable reef.

I had one desire—that he should leave. I would have

plenty of time to think about it afterward, but first he had to leave. Why not tell him I was prepared to help him? I would not be committing myself, I could always turn this promise into a ruse, into a maneuver—if I were to decide to kill him and disclose everything to Hippolytus—; it was in the interest of our own action, of our group, that I should gain his confidence and be able to do what I liked with him. If I were to decide to kill him. . . What harm was there in lying to a man you were going to kill?

"Listen to me. The first thing to do is to control your nerves. That's vital. Come down to lunch tomorrow. Say you've had a nervous breakdown and that it's over. That you'll gradually return to normal. Pretend. As for me I'll talk to Hippolytus and try to arrange for you to leave. Now go back to your room, somebody might come in and find you here. . . "

As I spoke I had no idea what I was saying. Truth or lies? Help or betrayal? We would soon see—in the meantime he had to go! He got to his feet and drew himself up, I did not see a glimmer of hope in his face, nothing flickered, he made no attempt to thank me, even with a glance— knowing there was nothing he could do, that he could only be, be what he was, be this ungrateful, unpleasant existence —whose suppression would be even more revolting. He was blackmailing me with his existence. . . ah, how different it all was from Karol!

Karol!

When he had gone out I started to write to Frederick. It was a report. I told him about my two visits. And it was also a document which confirmed my clear acceptance of our common action. Confirmed it in writing. I established a dialogue.

11

The next day Siemian appeared for lunch.

I had got up late and when I came downstairs they were just about to go in to lunch and that was when Siemian appeared, freshly shaved, his hair oiled and scented, a handkerchief peeping out of his breast pocket. It was the appearance of a corpse—had we not been killing him uninterruptedly for two days? And yet the corpse kissed his hostess' hand with the grace and manners of a cavalry officer and, after having greeted everybody, started to explain that "the indisposition which had kept him in his room was almost over," that he was feeling better and that he was sick of rotting away upstairs in his room "while the entire family was reunited down here." Hippolytus himself drew up a chair for him, another place was laid, our respect for him returned unaltered and he sat down at the table—as superior and oppressive as on the evening he arrived. The soup was brought in. He asked for a glass of vodka. He must have been making a considerable effort: he spoke like a corpse, ate like a corpse, and drank like a corpse—and these activities must have been extorted by fear from the power of his apathy. "I haven't quite recovered my appetite but. . . maybe a little soup. I'd like another vodka too, if I may."

This meal. . . confused, based on a latent force full of uncontrollable crescendos and contradictory meanings, as blurred as one text typed over another. . . ! Albert sitting at his place next to Henia—and he must have spoken to her and "conquered her with respect" because they both treated each other with special consideration and politeness, she was ennobled, he was ennobled—they were both noble. As for Frederick, he was as voluble and sociable as ever, but he was clearly pushed into the background by Siemian, who had imperceptibly seized control. . . Yes, far more than at his first appearance we felt obliged to obey and accept with a sort of inner tension the smallest desire which rose in him like a plea but struck us like an order. For me, who knew that it was his misery disguised, out of fear, in his former superiority which was now dead and buried, the whole thing seemed a good farce! To start with he concealed his state of mind under the affability of an officer, a braggart Cossack, but his bitterness soon began to ooze from every pore together with the cold indifference composed of apathy which I had noticed the day before. He became visibly more morose and ugly. He felt confronted by an unbearable contradiction when, out of fear, he tried to embody for us the former Siemian, the Siemian he was no more, whom he feared more than we did, whom he no longer had a right to be—the former Siemian, the dangerous Siemian, accustomed to giving orders, to using men, to making them kill each other. "I'd like a little salt. . . oh, thank you!" That sounded familiar and good-natured, but it was aggressive and somewhere, in its essence, it was filled with scorn for other people's existence, and Siemian felt his fear turn into something terrifying. Frederick, I knew, must have been particularly receptive to this increase of horror and terror. But Siemian's game would never have become so impetuous if Karol had not joined him from the other end of the table, and had not supported his power with his whole person.

Karol ate his soup, buttered his bread—but Siemian had instantly assumed control over him as he had on the first evening. The boy had a leader once again. His hands became military and efficient. His whole incomplete being was surrendered to the leader, surrendered and offered up—and if he ate it was to serve him, if he buttered his bread it was with his consent and his head was suddenly submitted to Siemian with his close-cropped hair which curled slightly over his brow. He had no need for words—he had just become like that—as one changes in different lighting. Maybe Siemian had not realized it at once but a special relationship developed between him and the boy and this dark cloud of aggression filled with sovereignty (which was only simulated) began to search for Karol and to concentrate its force on him. Albert looked on, sitting next to Henia, as noble as one could wish. . . Albert imbued with justice, demanding love and virtue. . . watched the leader clouded by the boy, the boy by the leader.

He must have felt this—Albert—that this alliance full of animosity was directed chiefly against the respect which he defended and which defended him because what was being formed between the boy and the leader was nothing but disdain and, above all, disdain for death. If the boy was offering his body and soul to his leader, his life and death, was it not because the leader was not afraid either to die or to kill and could therefore dominate others? This disdain for life and death entailed all the other possibilities of devaluation, whole oceans of devaluation. And the adolescent's capacity for disdain joined the superior nonchalance of the leader—they affirmed each other, fearing neither pain nor death, one because he was a boy, the other because he was the leader. The situation became more tense and vast because it rested on artificial assumptions which are always hard to control—it was only from fear and desire to survive that Siemian was playing the part of a leader. And this part, confirmed by the adolescent, suffocated him, terrified him. Frederick must (I was sure) have been aware of the violent increase of tension among these three people, Siemian, Karol and Albert—an increase which heralded an explosion. . . while Henia was bending calmly over her plate.

Siemian ate. . . to prove he was capable of eating like everyone else. . . and tried to exert his Slavonic charm which was poisoned by his cadaverous coldness, and which, in contact with Karol, was instantly turned to violence and blood. Frederick was all eyes and ears. But it then happened that Karol asked for a glass and Henia handed it to him— and it was just possible that the moment when the glass passed from one hand to the other lasted slightly, very slightly, too long, that Henia had hesitated for a split second before withdrawing her hand. It was possible. But was it true? This insignificant suspicion struck Albert like a mallet —he turned ashen—and Frederick cast a glance at them— an indifferent glance.

The fruit was served. Siemian fell silent. He sat there, becoming more and more disagreeable, as though his store of politeness were exhausted, as though he were from now on determined not to please, as though the doors of horror were now wide open before him. He was cold. Henia started toying with her fork and it happened that Karol touched her fork with his—it was impossible to tell for sure whether he was playing with it or had touched it by chance, and it could have been quite accidental, because the fork was by his hand—but Albert turned ashen again: was it possible that it was by chance? Of course it was possible, and anyhow the matter was so insignificant that it was not worth thinking twice about. But on the other hand it was not impossible. . . yes, maybe this very insignificance allowed them to play this game which was oh! so innocent, so light, so microscopic that (the girl) could play it with (the boy) under the eyes of her fiancé without compromising her virtue—such an inoffensive game. . . And was it not this lightness that tempted them—the fact that the faintest movement of their hands struck Albert a violent blow— maybe they had not been able to resist the temptation of this game, so harmless in itself but so disastrous for Albert. Siemian finished eating his fruit. Even if Karol liked, un- consciously, to torment Albert, the game did not in any way affect his fidelity to Siemian: he played it like a soldier ready to die lightheartedly and blindly. But that too seemed to me curiously uncontrolled, artificial: the game with the forks was an obvious continuation of the fictitious game on the island and this flirtation of theirs was "theatrical." So I found myself at this table between two mystifications, but far more tense than any real situation could have been. An artificial leader and an artificial love.

We got up. Lunch was over.

Siemian went over to Karol.

"Hey there, you little rascal. . . " he said.

"Well?" asked Karol, thrilled.

The officer turned his pale eyes to Hippolytus, cold and disagreeable: "What about having a word together?" he proposed between his teeth.

I wanted to listen to their conversation, but he stopped me with a short: "Not you." What was that? An order? Had he forgotten our talk last night? But I complied with his wish and stayed on the veranda while he went off with Hippolytus into the garden. Henia stood next to Albert and had even taken his arm, as though nothing had happened between them, once again faithful and pure; but Karol who was standing by the open door had also put his hand on it (his hand on the door—Henia's hand on Albert's arm). And the fiancé said to the young lady: "Let us go for a walk." To which she replied, like an echo: "Let us go for a walk." They went down a path and Karol stayed with us, like a bawdy and incomprehensible joke. . . Frederick, looking at the couple and then at Karol, could not help murmuring: "You don't say!" I replied with a furtive smile, addressed to him alone.

Hippolytus came back after a quarter of an hour and called us into the study.

"We must finish him off," he said. "We must do it tonight. He's insisting!"

And sinking into the sofa, he repeated to himself, closing his eyes voluptuously: "He's insisting!"

It transpired that Siemian had again asked for horses— not as a plea but in such terms that Hippolytus could not get over it. "Gentlemen, he's a gangster! He's a murderer! He wanted horses, I told him today was impossible but maybe tomorrow. . . Then he gripped my hand and squeezed it, I tell you, like a real murderer. . . and he said that if the horses weren't ready tomorrow morning at ten o'clock he would. . . He's insisting, I tell you!" he concluded excitedly. "We must get rid of him tonight because tomorrow I'll be *forced* to give him the horses."

And he added softly:

"I'll be forced to. . ."

That was a surprise for me. Obviously Siemian had not been able to sustain the role we had agreed on the night before; instead of talking calmly, conciliatingly, he had threatened. . . he must have been possessed, terrorized by the dangerous ex-Siemian whom he had resuscitated during the meal, hence the threats, the order, the insistence, the cruelty (he could not control this ex-Siemian since he feared him more than anyone else). In short, he had become dangerous again. But at least I no longer felt exclusively responsible for him at present as I had the night before in my room—because I had shifted the matter onto Frederick.

Hippolytus got up: "Well, gentlemen, how are we going to do it? Who?" He produced four matches and broke one of them. I watched Frederick—I expected him to give some sign, should I reveal last night's conversation with Siemian? But he was terribly pale. He swallowed.

"I'm sorry," he said. "I don't know if. . . "

"What?" asked Hippolytus.

"Death," said Frederick briefly. He avoided his eyes. "Mur-der him?"

"What do you mean? It's an order."

"Mur-der him?" he repeated. He did not look at anyone. He was alone with this word. Nobody but him and mur-der. His chalky pallor betrayed him, because he *knew what it was to murder*. At that moment, he knew to the depths of his soul.

"I will. . . not. . . do this," he said, and gestured with his fingers to the side, to the side, backward. . . He suddenly turned to Albert.

And it was as though a clear image had appeared on his pallor, before he spoke I already knew for sure that he had not collapsed but continued to direct events, to maneuver them. . . without letting Henia and Karol out of his sight. . . in their direction! So what? Was he afraid? Or was he running after them?

"Not you either," he said straight out to Albert.

"Me?"

"How are you going to do it? . . . with a knife? Because it'll have to be a knife, not a revolver, that's too noisy—how could you with a knife, when your mother was. . . a few days ago with a knife too? You? You, with your mother and your Catholicism? I ask you, how would you do it?"

His words were confused but they were sincere, supported by this face which provoked Albert's face, crying "no!" No doubt—"he knew what he was saying." He knew what was meant by "murder" and was at the end of his tether, could no longer stand it. No, it was no longer a game, or tactics, it was true at this moment!

"Are you deserting?" asked Hippolytus coldly.

In answer he smiled, dazed and disarmed.

Albert gulped as though he were being forced to swallow something inedible. Up till now he must have thought about the problem as I had, on a military level: this murder was just another death, for him, one of many—repellent but usual and even necessary, inevitable. But now it was being extracted from its anonymity and presented to him on its own, like the act of killing himself, immense and terrible! He too turned pale. And his mother, into the bargain! And the knife! The same knife as the one that killed his mother. . . So he would murder with the knife that had just been pulled out of his mother, he would deal the same blow, repeat the same movement on Siemian's body. . . But behind his furrowed brow was his mother not suddenly merging into Henia? At any rate it was Henia, not his mother, who proved decisive. He must have seen himself acting Skuziak's role as he dealt the blow. . . But how would he then behave toward Henia and Karol, how would he resist their union, Henia in Karol's arms, adolescent Henia in his adolescent arms, Henia brazenly "boyified?". . . Murder Siemian as Skuziak had murdered?—but what would he become? Another Skuziak? What would he oppose to this adolescent force? If only Frederick had not magnified and exalted the act of murdering—but now it was the act of himself killing and this knife thrust struck his own dignity, his honor, his virtue, everything with which he defended his mother from Skuziak and Henia from Karol.

That was obviously why he turned to Hippolytus and muttered, as though he were stating a fact:

"Me... No, I couldn't do it..."

Frederick questioned me, with an almost triumphant look which anticipated the answer:

"And you? Would you murder him?"

Well? What? Was it only tactics? He operated by simulating fear, by forcing us to refuse. Inconceivable: this fear of his, pallid and trembling, drenched in sweat, was nothing but a horse on which he galloped... toward those young knees and hands! He put his fear to an erotic use. The height of imposture, a disgrace! Unheard of, intolerable! He treated himself like a horse! But his force took me with it and I felt I must gallop with him. What was more, I naturally did not want to murder. I was happy to be able to get out of it—our collective discipline had already been destroyed. I replied:

"No."

"What a bloody mess," said Hippolytus vulgarly. "All right, that'll do. I'll do it myself. Without any help."

"You?" said Frederick. "You?"

"Me."

"No."

"Why not?"

"Nooo..."

"Look," said Hippolytus, "think it over. We can't be pigs. You must have a sense of duty. This is duty! We're obeying orders!"

"Do you want to murder an innocent man out of a sense of duty?"

"It's an order. We've received an order. This is an action. I won't neglect my duty and I hope I can say the same of you. We must do it! We're responsible! What do you want? To let him escape alive?"

"That's impossible," admitted Frederick. "I know. . ."

Hippolytus opened his eyes wide. Had he expected Frederick to reply: "Yes, let him escape alive"? Did he count on it? If that were his secret hope, Frederick's reply had put an end to it.

"Well, what do you want?"

"I know, of course. . . necessity. . . duty. . . orders. . . We can't. . . But you. . . no. . . You can't slaughter him. . . Not you. . . You can't! Nooo. . ."

Hippolytus, confronted by this humble, modest, whispered "nooo," sat down. This "nooo" knew what it was to murder and—all this knowledge turned against him and crushed him. Enclosed in his puffy body he watched us through a sort of window, with bulging eyes. A "straightforward" liquidation of Siemian was now out of the question, after our three refusals. It had turned foul under the pressure of our horror. He could no longer allow himself to be superficial. By nature he was neither profound nor particularly sensitive, but he belonged to a certain social class, a certain elite, and when we became profound he could no longer remain superficial, if only for social reasons. In certain situations it is not permissible to be "less profound" or "less subtle," this disqualifies you socially. So good manners required him to be profound, required him to join us in sounding the meaning of the word "murder," to see, as we had seen, its full horror. Like us he felt powerless. Slaughter someone with his bare hands? No, no, he could not do that. But in this case the only alternative was "not to murder"—"not to murder" was tantamount to betraying, deserting! He spread out his arms, overtaken by the course of events. He was trapped between two nightmares —one of which was to become his.

"What shall we do then?"

"Leave it to Karol."

Karol? So that was what he had been driving at—the fox! The old rake! Spurring himself on like a horse.

"Karol?"

"Of course. He'll do it. You just have to tell him."

He spoke of it as though it were the easiest thing in the world—all difficulty had vanished miraculously. As though Karol were to do some shopping in Ostrowiec. I don't know why, but this sudden change of tone seemed quite justifiable. Hippolytus hesitated.

"Must we leave it to him?"

"Who else? We can't do it, it's not for us. . . But it must be done. You tell him. He'll do it if you tell him. It won't be any problem for him. Why shouldn't he do it? Order him."

"If I order him he'll do it, of course. . . But. . . How shall I put it?. . . He'd be doing. . . our job?"

Albert joined in nervously:

"You don't seem to realize the risk involved. . . It's a responsibility. We can't shift it onto him, make him run this risk, that's impossible. It isn't done."

"We'll take the risk. If it ever comes to light we can say we did it. What's the matter? Take a knife. . . and wham! It'll be easier for him than for any of us."

"But I tell you we have no right to use him. . . Just because he's sixteen. . . we can't put him in this. . . let a child replace us. . ."

He was panic-stricken. Make Karol commit a murder which he, Albert, was incapable of committing, exploit his youth, Karol's, just because he was a child. . . no, it was dishonest, and it weakened him before the boy. . . and he must be strong before the boy! He started pacing up and down the room. "It would be immoral!" he burst out in fury and turned purple, as humiliated as though his innermost thoughts had been revealed. Hippo, on the other hand, was gradually getting used to the idea.

"Maybe, after all. . . Actually, it's the easiest way. . . Nobody's evading responsibility. We're just keeping our hands clean. . . It's no job for us. It's for him."

And he calmed down as though he had been charmed— at last the only natural solution to the problem had been found. He realized it was in accordance with the order of things and calmed down. He did not withdraw. He was there to give orders—Karol to obey them.

He turned to calm and reason. . . He became aristocratic.

"And to think it didn't occur to me! . . . Of course!"

It was a curious spectacle: two men, one ashamed of what had returned dignity to the other. This exploitation of an adolescent filled one with pride and the other with shame, it was as though one of them had suddenly become less masculine and the other more so. But Frederick— what genius! To have brought Karol in. . . to make it all slant toward him. . . thanks to this the intended death suddenly heated up and glowed not only with Karol but with Henia, with their arms and legs—and the future corpse bloomed with all their adolescent, clumsy, rough sensuality. The heat burst inside me: this death was in love. And all this—this death, our fear, our horror, our helplessness—so that this young, this too young hand should be able to seize the girl. . . I already plunged into the event as though it were not a murder but the marvelous adventure of their untried, secret bodies. Exquisite!

And at the same time this decision revealed a cruel irony and something resembling a taste of defeat—because we adults were obliged to resort to this child who was alone capable of accomplishing what was beyond us. Was this murder to be like a cherry on a fragile branch, only accessible to the lightest of us?. . . Lightness! Suddenly everything began to turn in this direction, Frederick, Hippolytus, and I turned toward the adolescent as one turns to a soothing ointment.

Suddenly Albert too came out in favor of Karol. If he had refused he would have had to act on his own because we were already *hors concours*. And then something must have made him change his mind—his Catholicism clearly convinced him that Karol as a murderer would revolt Henia just as much as he, Albert, would as a murderer: an error due to the fact that he sniffed flowers with his spirit instead of using his nose, he believed too firmly in the ugliness of sin and the beauty of virtue. He had forgotten that crime could have a certain taste in Karol's body and a different one in his. And, clinging to this illusion, he agreed to our plan—in fact he had no alternative if he did not want to break away from us and find himself all alone in such a difficult situation.

Frederick, fearing he might change his mind, rushed off to look for Karol; I went with him. He was not in the house. We found Henia hanging up linen in the pantry; but it was not she we wanted. We grew more nervous. Where was Karol? We searched for him feverishly, without saying a word, as though we were strangers.

He was in the stable grooming the horses; we called him and he came up to us, smiling. I well remember that smile because at the moment we called him I realized the folly of our plan. He adored Siemian. He was wholly devoted to him. How could we force him to do such a thing? But his smile immediately transported us to another world where everything was easy and friendly. This child already knew his assets. He knew that if we expected anything from him it was his youth—so he came up to us slightly mockingly, prepared to be amused. And the way he came up to us put us at our ease, it showed how familiar he had become. And

it was strange: this smiling lightness was the best introduction to the brutality that was to follow.

"Siemian's a betrayer," explained Frederick briefly. "It's
been proved."

"Aha!" said Karol.

"He has to be done in today, tonight. Can you do it?"

"Me?"

"Are you scared?"

"No."

He was standing by a shaft with a saddle girth hanging
on it. His fidelity to Siemian did not reveal itself in any
way. When he heard about killing him he became taciturn,
almost ashamed. He shut himself up in his shell. He did
not look as though he were going to protest. I told myself
that for him to kill Siemian or to kill on Siemian's orders
was more or less the same thing—what bound him to
Siemian was death, it did not matter which death. Blindly
obedient and soldierly to Siemian—but obedient and soldierly too when he had to turn against Siemian on our
orders. His blindness toward his leader had turned into the
immediate and silent capacity to kill him. He showed no
surprise.

And yet (the boy) stole a glance at us. There was a
secret in that glance (as though he were asking us: are you
doing this for Siemian. . . or me?). But he said nothing.
He had become discreet.

Slightly stunned by this incredible facility (which seemed
to introduce us to another dimension) we led him to Hippolytus who gave him further instructions: to go there at
night with a knife and above all make no noise. Hippo had
already regained complete self-control and gave orders like
an officer—he was in his place.

"And what if he doesn't open his door? He locks himself
in at night."

"We'll find a way of making him open it."

Karol went off.

That he should go off like that made me wild. Where had he gone? Home? What was his home? What was that world of his where people died as easily as they murdered? In him we had found an obedience and eagerness which proved that he was indeed just the man we needed—it had all gone so smoothly! Oh, he had left so superbly, silent and docile. . . and I could not doubt that it was she, Henia, he had gone to join, with his hands into which we had put a knife. Henia! There was no doubt. Now, as a boy with a knife, a murderer, he was closer than ever to conquering and possessing Henia—and if Hippolytus had not detained us a few moments in the study we would have rushed after him, to spy on him. So it was only some time later that we left the study and made for the garden in search of him, of her. We were already in the hall when we heard Albert's stifled voice break off—something was going on! We retraced our steps. A scene like the ones on the island. Albert two steps away from Henia. . . We had no idea what, but something must have just happened.

Karol was standing further off, by the sideboard.

When he saw us Albert said:

"I've just slapped her."

He went out. Then she said:

"He's pretty tough!"

"He's pretty tough," repeated Karol.

They were laughing. They were mocking. Malicious but amused. Not so much, though—not too much—they were just joking. But with what elegance! And then they enjoyed it, this "he's pretty tough," they looked as though they were reveling in it.

"What got into him?" asked Frederick. "What was he driving at?"

"What do you think?" answered Henia. She turned up her eyes comically, coquettishly, and we immediately realized it was because of Karol. The marvelous part of it was that she did not even have to look at him, knowing that it was useless, that it was enough for her to be coquettish—she knew she could only attract us "with" Karol. How easy it was for us to communicate with them—and I could see they both reckoned on our good will. Cunning, discreetly amused, and fully aware that they enchanted us. That was quite clear.

Evidently Albert must have lost his self-control—they must have wounded him again by an imperceptible glance, a touch. . . ah, these childish provocations! Frederick suddenly asked Henia:

"Has Karol told you anything?"

"What about?"

"That tonight. . . Siemian. . . "

He drew his hand across his throat—a gesture that would have been amusing had the game not had such serious consequences for him. He was having fun in earnest. He sat down. No, she knew nothing, Karol had not mentioned it. He told her briefly what they intended to do that night and that Karol was going to do it. He talked about it as though it were quite unimportant. Both of them (Karol too) listened—they could listen to us because they had to attract us and this slowed down their reactions. Only, when he had finished, she did not say a word—any more than Karol—and we felt the silence rise in them. We did not quite know what they meant. But (the boy) leaning on the sideboard looked sullen and she became sullen too.

Frederick explained: "The only problem is that Siemian might refuse to open the door. He'll be frightened. You could go together. Henia, you could knock for some reason or other. He'll open to you. It wouldn't even occur to him

not to open. You could say you've got a letter for him, or
something like that. And when he opens you step back
and let Karol in. . . I think that's the best plan, don't
you?"

He suggested it casually, "like that," and he was right
because this plan of attack was pretty dubious; he was by
no means sure that Siemian would open his door without
any difficulty, and Frederick barely concealed the real
meaning of the suggestion, which was to involve Henia. . .
to put them in it together. He organized it like a scene on
the island. It was not so much the idea that dazzled me as
the way in which it was executed: he had suddenly presented the plan, casually, taking advantage of a moment
when they were both prepared to be kind to us, to join us,
or simply to charm us—both of them! Frederick counted
on their "good will," hoping they would easily be persuaded
to satisfy him—once again he was reckoning on the "facility," that same facility of which Karol had given proof.
He simply wanted them to crush this worm "together". . .
From now on the erotic, sensual, amorous sense of the enterprise came into the open—it was quite obvious. For the
fraction of a second I thought the two sides of the matter
were struggling before us, because on the one hand the
proposition was fairly ghastly (were we not plunging this
girl too into sin and crime?) but on the other it was "intoxicating and exciting," because they had to perform this
act "together."

Which of them would win? I had time to ask myself
the question because they did not reply at once. I was well
aware, from the way they stood before us, that they always
remained reserved, unaffectionate and dry *toward each
other*—and yet they were so upset by our amazement, the
intoxication we secretly demanded from them, that they
were submissive. They could no longer struggle against the

beauty we discovered in them. And in fact this submissiveness suited them—were they not made for submission? It was another of these acts committed "on oneself," so characteristic of youth, thanks to which it affirms itself, of these acts the power of which is so intoxicating, that their objective and exterior meaning almost vanishes. For them the most important thing was neither Siemian nor his death—but themselves. The girl just answered:

"Why not? We can do it."

Karol suddenly laughed, rather stupidly:

"If it works we can do it, if it doesn't work we can't."

At that moment I felt this stupidity was necessary for them.

"Very well," he said. "So you knock at the door, and then you slip back and I'll bump him off. It'll work provided he opens the door."

She laughed and said: "Don't worry. If I knock he'll open it."

She too looked rather stupid, just then.

"This is all between ourselves, of course," said Frederick.

"Don't worry!"

Thereupon our conversation ended—conversations of this sort cannot be prolonged indefinitely. I went onto the veranda and then into the garden; I wanted a breath of air —it was hurtling along too fast for my liking. The light was fading. The colors had lost their sheen, the greens and the reds were no longer so dazzling—it was the shady repose of colors before night. What did the night conceal? Ah, yes. . . crushing the worm. . . but the worm was now Siemian, not Albert. . . I was no longer sure whether it was all such a good idea, at moments a dark fire enflamed me, and at others I grew feeble, gloomy, even desperate, because it was all too fantastic, too arbitrary and not real enough— it was always a game, yes, we were "playing with fire."

Wandering into the garden, among the bushes, I lost my train of thought. It was then that I saw Albert striding up to me.

"I want to explain! Please try to see my point! I'd never have slapped her, but she did something revolting—that's all I can say—something revolting!"

"What?"

"She did something revolting. Really revolting, however insignificant. . . no, I know I'm right. . . Something insignificant but really revolting! We were talking in the dining room. He came in—the lover. I felt at once that she was talking to me, but saying everything to him."

"She was saying it to him?"

"Yes, to him. Not in words, of course. . . but with everything. Entirely. She pretended to be talking to me but at the same time she caught him and gave herself up to him. In front of me. Talking to me. Can you believe it? It was quite something. . . I saw she was talking to me and at the same time was with him. . . giving herself up to him! As though I weren't there! I slapped her. And now what can I do? Tell me what I can do?"

"Can't you make it up?"

"But I hit her! I've committed myself. I hit her! Now it's all over and done with. I hit her! I don't know how I managed it. . . You know what? I believe that if I hadn't consented to his being appointed for this. . . liquidation. . . I wouldn't have hit her."

"Why?"

He looked at me sharply.

"Because I'm no longer behaving correctly—toward him. I've let him replace me. I've lost my moral right and that's why I hit her. I hit her because my misery no longer matters. It's no longer respectable. It's been dishonored. That's

why I hit her, hit her, hit her. . . and I won't stop at hitting
him, I'll kill him!"

"What are you talking about?"

"I'll kill him, and with no difficulty. . . It's of no importance! To kill. . . someone like that? It's like crushing a
worm. Less than nothing! But on the other hand to kill
someone like that. . . would be scandalous! And disgraceful! It's far harder than killing an adult. It's impossible!
Only adults can kill each other. And if I cut her throat. . .
Just imagine it! Don't worry. I'm joking. I'm only joking.
They're making fun of me. Why shouldn't I make fun of
them? Oh God, save me from this joke! Oh God, oh God,
you're my only hope! What was I going to say? Oh yes,
I'm the only one who has to kill. . . but kill Siemian. . . I
should do it while there's still time, I shall have to hurry. . .
I can still do it instead of that brat. . . As long as he does
it I'm not behaving correctly!"

He pondered.

"It's too late. You've talked me out of it. How can I do
this job instead of him, now? If I want to do it so much,
it's not out of a sense of duty, but simply so as not to give
her to him—not to lose my moral advantage over her. All
my morals—just to possess her!"

He stretched out his arms helplessly.

"I don't see what I can do. I don't think there's anything
I can do."

He said several more things which left me thinking.

"I'm naked! I feel naked! Oh God! They've undressed
me! . . . At my age I should no longer feel naked! Nakedness
—it's all right for the young!"

And then:

"She's not only deceiving me. She's deceiving men. Men
in general. Because she's not deceiving me with one man.
Is she really a woman? Aha, look, she's exploiting the fact

that she isn't a woman yet. They're taking advantage of a certain particularity of theirs, a certain spe-ci-fi-ci-ty, which I do not even suspect. . ."

And then:

"I just wonder where they got it from? I've already told you: they can't have thought it out on their own. The island. What they're doing to me now. . . This continual provocation. . . It's too sophisticated. I hope you see what I mean: they can't have thought it out because it's too sophisticated. Where did they get it from, then? From books? How can I tell?"

* * *

Growing blacker and blacker the ink of night leaked out, confusing everything, and while the crowns of the trees still bathed in a light, joyful sky of feathers, the trunks were indistinct and imperceptible. I looked under the brick. A letter.

You must talk to Siemian.

Tell him that tonight you will take him out of the house with Henia and that Karol will be waiting with the horses. That Henia will knock on his door tonight when everything is ready. He will believe you. He knows Karol is his and that Henia is Karol's! He will believe you passionately! It's the best way to make him open his door when she knocks. This is very important. Please do not forget.

And do not forget that we are past the point of no return. We could only return to disgrace.

What about Skuziak? How does he come in? I'm racking my brains about it. He cannot be left out, all three of them must do it. . . But how?

Take care! We must not force things. Proceed gingerly and subtly, so as not to arouse anything and not to run any unnecessary risks. Until now, thank God, luck is on our side—but we must not spoil it. Look after yourself. Very carefully!

* * *

I went to see Siemian.

I knocked—he opened when he realized it was I, but immediately fell back onto his bed. How long had he been lying there? In his socks—his highly polished riding boots glistened on the ground in a heap of cigarette stubs. He was smoking one cigarette after the other. His long, slender hand with a ring on his finger. He obviously had no desire to talk. He lay on his back and stared at the ceiling. I told him I had come to warn him: he should have no illusions, Hippolytus was not going to let him have any horses.

He made no reply.

"Neither tomorrow nor the next day. What's more, your fear of not leaving this house alive may prove justified."

Silence.

"So I've come to suggest a means of escape."

Silence.

"I want to help you."

He made no reply.

He lay like a log. I thought he was afraid—but it was not fear, it was anger. Rage. He lay there fuming—that was all. Full of venom. That is because (I thought) I have seen into his shame. I knew his weakness, which is why it turned to anger.

I revealed my plan. I told him Henia would knock at his door and that we would take him outside.

"Ff. . ."

"Have you got any money?"

"Yes."

"So much the better. Be prepared—soon after midnight."

"Ff. . ."

"Cursing won't do you any good."

"Ff. . ."

"Don't be too vulgar. We might still change our minds."

"Ff. . ."

I did not go on. He accepted our aid, allowed us to rescue him—but would not say thank you. Lying on his bed, long, muscular, he still expressed force and power— he was the lord and master—but he could no longer use force. It was over. And he knew I knew it. A short time ago he still had no need to beg anyone for help, since he was dangerous and could impose himself by violence, now he lay before me, seething with aggression and rage, but without his claws, compelled to seek compassion. . . and he knew he was unpleasant and unattractive in his emasculated masculinity. . . So he scratched his thigh with his stockinged foot. . . then raised his leg and moved his toes— it was a supremely selfish movement—he did not care whether I liked him or not. . . he did not like me. . . and he was drowning in an ocean of disgust, he wanted to vomit. . . so did I. I went out. This cynicism peculiar to the male sex poisoned me like cigarette smoke. In the dining room I bumped into Hippolytus and I felt sick, I was a hairsbreadth from vomiting, yes, a hairsbreadth, one of those little hairs that grew on our hands! At that moment I could not stand the sight of a man!

There were five of them—men—in the house. Hippolytus, Siemian, Albert, Frederick and I. Ugh. . . Nothing in the animal world attains such deformity—what dog, what horse can compete with this incontinence, with this cynicism of form? Alas! After the age of thirty men lapse into monstrosity. *In their youth the whole beauty of the world was on their side.* I, an adult, could find no refuge with my comrades, the adults, because they repelled me. They pushed me over to the other side.

*   *   *

Hippolytus' wife stood on the veranda.

"Where have they gone?" she asked. "They've all vanished."

"I don't know... I was upstairs."

"And Henia? Haven't you seen Henia?"

"Maybe she's in the orchard?"

She fluttered her fingers. "Don't you feel... Albert seems so nervous, so depressed. Has something gone wrong between them? It's as though something had snapped. I'm beginning to worry, I'll have to have a word with Albert... or maybe with Henia... I don't know... Oh God..."

She was worried.

"I don't know. But if he's depressed... well, after all, he's just lost his mother."

"Do you think it's because of his mother?"

"Of course! We only have one mother."

"Yes. That's what I thought. He's lost his mother, poor thing. Not even Henia will ever replace her for him. We only have one mother! One mother!" Her fingers quivered. And this really calmed her, as though the word "mother" were so powerful that it even removed the meaning from the word "Henia," as though it were the most sacred thing imaginable! ... A mother! Surely she was one too? Who could claim she was nothing, since she was a mother? This obsolete being who was only a mother and nothing but a mother looked at me with her eyes swimming in perfection and walked away with her cult for the Mother—I knew there was no risk of her getting in our way. Being essentially a mother she could no longer accomplish anything...

As she moved away her former charms pranced around her.

* * *

As the night crept on with all its heralds—the lighting of the lamps, the closing of the shutters, the laying of the table for dinner—I felt more and more uncomfortable, and I went from one place to another without being able to keep still. Our treason, Frederick's and mine, seemed clearer and clearer: we had betrayed masculinity for (a boy plus a girl). Wandering through the house I glanced into the drawing room, where it was almost dark, and I saw Albert sitting on a sofa. I came in and sat in an armchair some distance from him, against the opposite wall. My plans were fairly vague. Confused. A desperate attempt: to try to overcome my disgust by a supreme effort and come into contact with his maturity. But my disgust increased immeasurably, aroused by my presence here and the position of my body so close to his—increased by his aversion for me. . . an aversion which made me repulsive and made my repulsion for him repulsive too. And vice versa. I knew that in these circumstances it was out of the question for one of us to make use of any of the luxuries available to us—I mean the luxuries of virtue, common sense, devotion, heroism, magnanimity, which we could have manifested and of which we were the potential heirs—but the repulsion was too strong. Could we not overcome it by force? Force? Rape? What were we men for? It is the man who reigns supreme. A man does not ask whether he pleases; he is only concerned with his own pleasure. His pleasure decides what is beautiful and what is ugly—for him, and him alone! Man is for himself alone, not for anyone else!

This was the force I wanted to produce. . . In the present situation both he and I were impotent, since we were not ourselves, we were not for ourselves, we were for that other, younger sensitivity—and this plunged us into ugliness. But if only I could succeed, even for a second, in this drawing room, in existing for him, for Albert, and he for me—if only we could succeed in being a man for a man! How immense our masculinity would be! We would have to force each other to masculinity. This was the calculation on which I based the remnants of a desperate, unconscious hope. Because force, which is the essence of man, must spring from masculinity, from men. . . and maybe my presence alone would suffice to enclose us in this hermetically sealed circle. . . I attached immense importance to the fact that the dark modified our Achilles' heel, the body. I thought that maybe, taking advantage of its enfeeblement, we could succeed in joining each other, affirming each other, that we could become men with enough power no longer to be disgusted by ourselves—because one is never disgusted by oneself, because it is enough to be oneself not to be disgusted! These were my intentions, admittedly already tarnished with despair. But he did not budge, nor did I. . . we could not begin like that, we did not know how to begin. . .

Suddenly Henia slipped into the drawing room.

She did not see me, but went up to Albert and sat next to him in silence. She looked as though she wanted to make everything up. She must have been sweet and gentle (I could hardly see her face). Conciliating. Good. Submissive. Maybe disarmed. Lost. What was happening? Had she had enough of the other one. . . or was she afraid, did she want to withdraw, to find some support or refuge in her fiancé? Anyhow, she sat down sweetly, without a word, leaving the initiative to him. That meant: "I'm at your mercy, do what you like with us." Albert did not budge—not even his little finger.

As motionless as a frog. I wondered what was going on inside him. Pride? Jealousy? Bitterness? Or maybe he just felt guilty and did not know how to behave—and I wanted to shout to him that he should at least embrace her, lay his hands on her, our safety depended on it! Our last chance! On her his hands would regain their sovereignty, I would just have to hop over to them with my hands and it would work! Force—force in this drawing room! But no. Nothing. The time passed. He did not move. And it was like suicide—a failure—a failure—the girl stood up and went out. . . I followed her.

* * *

Dinner was served. Out of regard for our hostess we only spoke about insignificant matters. After dinner I could not think what to do. There would appear to be plenty to do in the few hours before a murder, but nobody looked as though he were doing anything—we all dispersed. . . maybe on account of the excessively intimate and disreputable nature of the plan. Frederick? Where was Frederick? He too had disappeared and this disappearance suddenly blinded me as though my eyes had been bandaged, I no longer knew where I was, I had to find him immediately— so I went to look for him. I went into the garden. It was about to rain, there was a warm moisture in the air, one could feel the clouds gathering in the black starless sky, the wind rose in gusts, weaved through the garden; guessing at the alleys rather than seeing them, treading them with the audacity of unconsciousness, and only the occasional familiar silhouette of a tree or a bush told me all was in order and that I really was where I thought I was. At the same time I realized that I was not expecting this im- mutability of the garden and that it amazed me. . . I would not have been surprised if the garden had been turned upside down in the dark. This thought made me pitch like a skiff on the high seas, and I realized land was already out of sight. Frederick was not there. I went as far as the islands in a sort of daze and every tree, every bush appearing on my path was an assault of fantasy—because although they were as they were, they *could have been* different. Frederick? Frederick? I needed him urgently. Without him it was all incomplete. Where was he hiding? What was he doing? I came back to the house to look for him again, when I suddenly came upon him in the bushes near the kitchen. He whistled like a street urchin. He did not seem very pleased to see me, and looked almost ashamed.

"What are you doing here?" I asked.

"I'm racking my brains."

"What about?"

"About that."

He pointed to the barred window of the lumber room. At the same time he showed me something in his left hand. The key to the lumber room. "Now we can talk," he said easily, aloud. "Letters are superfluous. She can no longer. . . you know—Nature. . . upset our plans because things have gone too far, the position is too secure. . . We won't have to reckon with her any more! . . . " He said that in a strange way. Something odd emanated from him. Innocence? Holiness? Purity? Anyhow, he was no longer afraid, that was for sure. He tore off a branch and threw it on the ground— before he would have thought twice about it: whether to throw it or not to throw it. . .

"I've brought this key with me," he added, "to force myself to think of a solution to this problem. This problem. This problem of. . . Skuziak."

"Well? Have you thought of one?"

"Yes."

"May I know what?"

"Not yet. . . not now. . . You'll know when the time comes. Or no. I'll tell you now. Look!"

He held out his other hand—in it a knife, a large kitchen knife. "Well, I must say!" I exclaimed, unpleasantly surprised. For the first time I suddenly realized I was dealing with a lunatic.

"I couldn't think of anything better," he said almost apologetically. "But this'll do. *When the young kill the old up there, the old will kill the young down here*—you see? It will close the circle. It will reunite them—him, Henia, and Karol, all three of them. The knife. I've known for a long time that what united them was blood and the knife. Of course it must be simultaneous," he added. "When Karol sticks his knife into Siemian, I'll stick mine into Olek. . . oooh!"

What an idea! A lunatic! A madman! What did he mean—he was going to murder him? And yet on another level this lunacy seemed to be in the order of things and explained itself. This lunatic was right, it could be done, it would reunite them "in a whole". . . The more bloody and horrible this madness was, the more firmly they would be united. . . And as though this were not enough, this raving thought which stank of the lunatic asylum, degenerate and wild, this nauseating, intellectual idea suddenly gave out the divine, intoxicating scent of a shrub in flower, yes, it was truly sublime! I marveled at it! On another level, on "their" level. This bloody intensification of youth and death, and this union through the knife (of the boy with the girl). It did not actually matter what crime was committed on them—or by them—every cruelty heightened their taste, like a spicy sauce.

The indivisible garden swelled up and gorged itself with charm—although it was damp and misty—around the deformed lunatic. I had to take a deep breath of fresh air, I had just had a bath of marvelous bitterness, of searing seduction. Again everything, everything became young and sensual, even ourselves! And yet. . . no, no, no. I could not agree to it, it was impossible! It had decidedly gone too far! It was out of the question, impossible, this sinister murder of the boy in the lumber room—no, no, no. . . He laughed.

"Don't worry! I just wanted to check whether you still thought I was in my right mind. What an idea! No, not that! It was just a dream. . . from sheer annoyance at not having thought anything up for this Skuziak. It would be monstrous!"

Monstrous. Certainly. When he himself agreed about it the full horror of the plan struck me, as obvious as a plate of roast beef, and I was amazed that I could have been deceived. We went back to the house.

12

There is not much left to tell. In fact everything went very well, better and better, until the finale which, I must admit, exceeded our wildest expectations. And with such ease! . . . I almost had to laugh at the idea of so oppressive a difficulty being solved with such disconcerting facility.

Once again I had to guard Siemian's room. From my bed, lying on my back, I strained my ears—we had entered the night and the house seemed to have fallen asleep. I waited for the stairs to creak under the tread of the two youthful murderers, but it was still too early, there was a good quarter of an hour to go. Silence. Hippo was on guard in the courtyard. Frederick was on the ground floor, by the front door. Finally, at half-past twelve precisely, somewhere below me, the stairs creaked under their feet, which were undoubtedly bare. Bare? Or in socks?

Unforgettable moments! The stairs creaked once more: why were they taking such care?—It would have been far more natural for her to climb the stairs as though there were nothing afoot, and only he would have had to hide, but it was not surprising that the conspiratorial atmosphere had affected them. . . and their nerves must have been on edge. I could almost see them following each other up the stairs, she in front, he behind, groping for the steps with their feet so as to make as little noise as possible. I felt intensely bitter. This furtive approach together was surely nothing but a ridiculous substitute for another approach, a thousand times more desirable, where she would be the object of his furtive steps. . . and yet in this moment their object—not Siemian but his execution—was no less sensual, no less guilty, no less ardent than love, and their furtive approach no less strained. Ah, the stairs creaked again! Youth was approaching! It was infinitely voluptuous, because, under their steps, a horrible act was turning into a triumphant and therefore refreshing act. . . Only. . . only what was this youth that was creeping up, was it pure and really fresh, simple, natural and innocent? No. It was. . . for the adults —if those two were indulging in this venture it was just for us, submissively, to please us, to flirt with us. . . And my maturity "reaching toward" youth had to encounter their youth, "reaching toward maturity," over Siemian's body— this was the appointment.

But there was joy and pride—but what pride?—and something else, like pure alcohol, in the fact that they were conniving with us. At our instigation and also out of a certain necessity to serve us they were running this risk— and creeping up—prepared to commit such a crime! It was divine. It was incredible! It contained the most fascinating beauty in the world! Lying on my bed I literally jumped for joy at the idea that we, Frederick and I, were the inspiration of these legs—ah, the stairs creaked again, but much closer this time, and then nothing, there was silence and I thought that maybe they had given way, that maybe, tempted by this approach together, they had veered from their goal, turned toward each other, and, in a warm embrace had forgotten everything, to depart in discovery of their forbidden bodies! In the dark! On the stairs. Panting. It was not impossible. Was that what had happened? Was it?. . . No, another creak informed me that my hopes were vain, nothing had happened, they went on—and I realized my wish was quite out of the question, absolutely out of the question, not even conceivable, incompatible with their style. Too young. They were too young. Too young for that! They had to reach Siemian and kill him! I thought again (because there was another pause on the stairs) that they had lost heart, she may have pulled his hand to hold him back, they may suddenly have realized the immense weight of their task, its overpowering volume, the horror of the word "murder." Had they discovered that, been stricken with panic? No, never! That was out, too. For the same reason. If that precipice attracted them it was precisely because they could jump over it—their lightness tended toward bloody acts because they could immediately transform them into something else—and their approach to crime was already an annihilation of crime: as they committed it they annihilated it.

A creak. Marvelous, their illegality, this light, furtive (boyish-girlish) sin. . . and I could almost see their legs united in mystery, their half-open lips, I could almost hear them holding their breath. I thought of Frederick, listening to the same furtive noises downstairs, near the front door where he was posted. I thought of Albert, I saw them all, Hippolytus, his wife, and Siemian who must, like me, have been lying on his bed—and I reveled in the exquisite taste of this virginal crime, this youthful sin. . . Tap, tap, tap.

Tap, tap, tap!

A knock. She was knocking at Siemian's door.

It is really here that my story ends. The finale was too. . . smooth and too. . . fast, too. . . light and easy for me to be able to recount it realistically enough. I shall stick to the facts.

I heard Henia: "It's me." The key turned in the lock, the door opened, there followed the noise of a knife thrust and the crash of a body which must have fallen headlong into the corridor. I believe the boy stabbed him two more times as a precaution. I rushed into the corridor. Karol had already switched on his torch. Siemian lay on the floor. When we turned him over we saw some blood.

"That's that," said Karol.

But the face was curiously bandaged by a handkerchief as though he had a toothache. . . It was not Siemian. . . And then, a few seconds later, the truth dawned on us: Albert.

Albert instead of Siemian dead on the ground. But Siemian was dead too—the only difference was that he was on his bed—he lay on his bed, a knife wound in his side, his nose in the pillow.

We turned on the light. I gazed at the scene, filled with a strange doubt. It. . . it did not seem quite true. Too convenient—too easy! I felt vaguely that it could not be like that, like the end of a fairy tale—that Albert had been killed by them and not Siemian! I suddenly realized. This is what happened: immediately after dinner Albert succeeded in getting into Siemian's room through the communicating door between their two rooms. He killed him. Then he waited for Henia and Karol to arrive, and opened the door. He had worked it all out so that they should kill him. To make doubly sure he had switched off the light and wound a handkerchief around his face—so they should not recognize him at once.

The horror of my duality: because the tragic brutality of those bodies, their bloody truth, was the heavy fruit of a supple tree! Those two bodies, those two murderers! As though a fatally definite idea had been pierced right through by lightness.

We went back into the corridor. They looked at him. They said nothing.

We heard someone run up the stairs. Frederick. He stopped, seeing Albert's body. He waved to us—what could he want? He took a knife out of his pocket, held it up in the air for a moment, and threw it on the floor. . . The knife was steeped in blood.

"Olek," he said. "Olek. Here he is."

He was innocent! He was innocent! He exuded innocent naïveté! I looked at our couple. They smiled. As the young always do when they are trying to get out of a scrape. And for a split second, all four of us smiled.

COSMOS

English Version by Eric Mosbacher

NOTE

Title of the Polish original *Kosmos*. This version by Eric Mosbacher made from the French translation by Georges Sedir and the German translation (*Indizien*) by Walter Tiel.

I

But let me tell you about another, even more curious adventure.

It was sweltering. Fuchs tramped on ahead and I followed behind. Trouser-legs. Heels. Sand. On we plodded. Earth. Ruts. The road was vile. Gleams from shiny pebbles, the air shimmering and buzzing with heat, everything black with sunlight. Houses, fences, fields and woods. What a road. What a tramp. Where we were coming from and why . . . but that would be a long story. The fact of the matter was that I was sick of my parents, and indeed the whole family, and also I wanted to pass at least one exam and get right away from it all. So I took off to Zakopane and was walking through Krupowki, wondering where to find a good cheap pension, when whom should I run into but Fuchs. Fuchs had carroty hair, fading into blond, and dead, protruding, fish-like eyes, but he was pleased to see me and I was pleased to see him, how are you, what are you doing here, I'm looking for a room, so am I, I've got an address (he said), a little place right out in the country where it's cheaper because it's a long way out, right outside the village. So off we went. Trouser-legs, heels in the sand, the road, the heat. I stared at my feet. Earth and sand, glistening pebbles, one foot after the other, trouser-legs, heels, sweat, my eyes kept blinking with fatigue, I had slept badly in the train, and on we plodded in the sweltering heat. There was nothing but this endless, ground-level plodding.

He stopped.

'Shall we stop and have a rest?'

'How far do we still have to go?'

'Not very far now'.

I looked round at what was to be seen, though I had no desire to see it, because I had seen it so often already—pines and hedges, firs and houses, grass and weeds, a ditch, footpaths and flower-beds, fields and a chimney. The air was shimmering with sunlight, but black, the trees were black, the earth was grey, the vegetation at ground-level was green, but everything was pretty black. A dog barked. Fuchs strode off towards a roadside thicket.

'It'll be cooler,' he said.

'No, let's go on.'

'Let's have a short rest first.'

He plunged deeper into the thicket, where there were shady nooks and corners under the mingling branches of hazel-trees and pines. I gazed into the maze of leaves and branches, dappled light, dense vegetation, gaps and recesses and windings and slopes and yawning chasms and heaven knows what else besides that advanced on us and receded, forced us aside and yielded to us, jostled us and made way for us. . . . Lost and dripping with sweat, I felt the bare, black earth under my feet. But there, among the branches, was something peculiar and strange, though at first I could not make out exactly what it was. My companion had seen it and was staring at it too.

'It's a sparrow.'

'Good heavens alive.'

Yes, it was a sparrow. A sparrow hanging from a bit of wire. It had been hanged. Its little head was bent and its mouth wide open. It was hanging by a bit of wire attached to a branch of a tree.

Extraordinary. A hanged bird. A hanged sparrow. This shrieking eccentricity indicated that a human hand had penetrated this fastness. Who on earth could have done such a thing, and why? I wondered, standing in the midst of this chaos, this proliferating vegetation with its endless complications, my head full of the rattle and clatter of the night-long train journey, insufficient sleep, the air and the sun and the tramp through the heat with this man Fuchs, and Jesia and my mother, the row about the letter and my rudeness to the old man, and Julius, and also Fuchs's troubles with his chief at the office (about which he had told me), and the bad road, and the ruts and lumps of earth and heels, trouser-legs, stones, and all this vegetation, all culminating like a crowd genuflecting before this hanged sparrow—reigning triumphant and eccentric over this outlandish spot.

'Who on earth could have done a thing like that?'

"Some boy or other.'

'No, it's too high.'

'Let's go.'

But he didn't budge. The sparrow went on hanging. Except for some grassy patches, the earth was bare. A lot of things were lying about: a strip of galvanised iron, a twig, another twig, a torn cardboard box, a broken off branch. There were also a beetle and an ant, and another ant, an unknown worm, a log, and so on and so forth, all the way to the undergrowth at the foot of the trees. He stared at all this, just as I did. 'Let's go,' he said, but he stayed where he was and went on staring, and the sparrow went on hanging, and I stayed there and went on staring too. 'Come on,' he said, but we didn't move, perhaps because we had already stayed there too long and had missed the right moment for going, and now, with that sparrow hanging in the trees, the situation grew graver and more unmanageable every moment, and I had the feeling that there was something disproportionate, untactful or unmannerly about us. I was sleepy.

'Come on,' I said, and off we went, leaving the sparrow in the trees behind us, alone.

But plodding on down that road in the heat of the sun made us sweat again, it was too much, and after going a short way we stopped, exhausted and miserable, and again I asked if we still had a long way to go. Fuchs replied by pointing to a notice on a fence.

'Look,' he said, 'they've got rooms to let there.'

I looked. Behind the fence there was a garden, and a sad, cheap, tedious house, lacking in ornamentation and balconies, with a gimcrack flight of steps leading up to the front door. It was built of wood in the Zakopane fashion, with two rows of windows, five on the ground floor and five on the first floor. As for the garden, there were some dwarf trees, and some pansies withering in the flower-beds, and some gravel paths. But Fuchs was in favour of trying the place, we had nothing to lose, after all, sometimes in joints like that the cooking was first class, he said, and also it might be very cheap. I too was willing to go in and see what the place was like, though we had previously walked past several houses with rooms to let without taking any notice of them. But it was sweltering, and the sweat was pouring from us. Fuchs opened the little gate, and we walked up the gravel path towards the shining window-panes. He rang the bell, we waited for a few moments on the top step, the door opened, and a woman appeared. She was past her first youth, about forty, perhaps, she was buxom, and seemed to be the maid.

'We should like to see the rooms you have to let.'

'Just a moment, please, I'll go and fetch madam.'

We waited on the top step, my head was still buzzing with the journey, the clatter of the train, the events of the day before, the crowds, the fumes, the din. The noise in my head was deafening. I was startled by a strange deformity in the decent, domesticated, blue-eyed face of the woman who opened the door. Her mouth seemed to be excessively prolonged to one side, though only to an infinitesimal extent, perhaps about a millimetre, but when she spoke this imparted a darting or gliding, almost reptilian, motion to her upper lip. There was a repellent coldness, like that of a frog or snake, about those lateral movements of her mouth, but in spite of that the woman warmed and excited me, for there was a kind of obscure transition leading straight to her bed, to gliding, creeping sin. Also her voice surprised me. I don't know what I expected to come from that mouth of hers, but the voice with which she spoke was that of the ordinary, stoutish, middle-aged, domestic servant that she was. Next I heard it from inside the house.

'Aunt. Here are some gentlemen to see the rooms.'

A few moments later the individual so addressed advanced towards us on her short legs, as if on a roller. She was completely round. We exchanged a few phrases. Yes, certainly, a room for two with full pension, come this way please. There was a smell of freshly-ground coffee. A short corridor, a wooden staircase, a small landing. Will you be staying for long? I see, working for exams, it's very quiet indeed here, you'll be completely undisturbed. Upstairs another corridor and several doors, the house was small and poky. She opened the last door at the end of the corridor, and I saw at a glance the kind of room it was. Like all rooms to let, it was rather dark. The roller-blind was down, there were two beds and a wardrobe, a hat-stand, a jug on a tray, two bed-side lamps without bulbs and a mirror in an ugly, stained frame. A ray of sunlight coming in through the blind illuminated a patch of floor, and a smell of ivy and the buzzing of an insect also came in from outside. All the same there was a surprise, for one of the beds was occupied. A woman was lying on it, and I had the feeling that there was something slightly abnormal about the way she was doing so, though I had no idea what it was, whether it was because there was nothing on the bed but the mattress, or because one of her legs was lying on the metal springs, as the mattress had slipped a bit. At all events the combination of leg and metal springs struck me on that hot, buzzing, harassing day. Had she been asleep? When she saw us she sat up and tidied her hair.

'Lena, what are you doing, darling? . . . Let me introduce you to my daughter.'

She bowed her head in reply to our greeting, got up, and walked out. Her silence made me forget the idea that something unusual had been going on here.

We were also shown the neighbouring room, which was similar but a little cheaper, because it did not have direct access to the bathroom. Fuchs sat on the bed, Mrs Wojtys sat on a small chair, and the result was that we took this cheaper room, with full board. In regard to the cooking, Mrs Wojtys said: 'Gentlemen, you will see for yourselves.' It was arranged that we should have breakfast and lunch in our room and dinner with the family downstairs.

'Fetch your things and Katasia and I will get the room ready.'

We went down and collected our things and then we came back with them.

We unpacked, and Fuchs expressed his satisfaction. The room was cheap, the place he had been recommended would certainly have been dearer, besides which it was much farther out. And we were going to be fed like turkey-cocks, just you wait and see.

I was getting more and more tired of his fish-face, and all

I wanted was sleep. I went over to the window and looked out. The miserable little garden lay stewing in the hot sunshine, and on the other side of the fence lay the road, and beyond it two pine-trees marked the spot where the sparrow was hanging in the thicket.

Feeling quite dizzy, I flung myself on the bed and dozed off. There was a mouth emerging from another mouth, there were lips with more lips round them, the lips were more like lips because they were less . . . but I fell fast asleep. Then I was awakened. The maid was standing over me.

It was early morning, a morning as black as night. No, it wasn't. 'Dinner's ready,' she said. I got up. Fuchs was already putting on his shoes. Dinner in the poky dining-room. Sideboard equipped with mirror. Yoghourt, radishes, and the eloquence of Mr Wojtys, a retired bank manager, complete with signet ring and gold cuff-links.

'Allow me to inform you, my dear sir, that I have now put myself entirely at the disposal of my better half and am now used by her for special services such as repairing the radio or fitting a new washer when a tap drips. Let me advise you, if I may be so bold, to take a little more butter with your radishes, the butter is first rate.'

'Thank you.'

'This heat will end in a thunderstorm, I'll be bound. In fact I'd be prepared to take a solemn oath on it by all that I consider most holy.'

'Didn't you hear the thunder in the distance behind the wood, papa?' (This was Lena, whom I hadn't seen properly yet, I couldn't really see anything at all distinctly, but at all events the retired bank manager had a picturesque way of expressing himself.)

'Why don't you have just a teeny-weeny bit more yoghourt? My wife is a quite outstanding specialist in the art of preparing yoghourt. And where do you suppose the secret lies, my dear sir? In the jug. The degree of perfection of the end-product in this case is directly related to the lactic qualities of the jug.'

'What do you know about it, Leo?' (This was an interruption by Mrs Wojtys.)

'I am a bridge player, gentlemen, a retired bank manager who by special permission of his wife now devotes himself every afternoon and on Sunday evenings to bridge. And so you two gentlemen are working for exams. Well, my humble abode is just the place for that, there's complete peace and quiet here, it's so quiet that you can go to sleep standing on your two legs, if I may be permitted to say so. . . .'

But I was hardly listening. Leo Wojtys was like a gnome. His head was like a gourd, and his bald pate, reinforced by the sarcastic flashing of his pince-nez, dominated the whole table. Lena, sitting next to him, was as gentle as a sleeping pool. Mrs Wojtys sat ensconced in her plumpness, from which she emerged to preside over the progress of the meal with a kind of self-sacrificing devotion which I had not expected, and every now and then Fuchs said something in a pale, white, phlegmatic voice. I ate a tart, oh, how sleepy I still felt, and there was talk about how dusty it was, and someone said the season hadn't started yet, and I asked whether the nights were cooler here. We finished the pastry, stewed fruit appeared, and when that was finished Katasia came in again and planted on the table next to Lena an ash-tray covered with a criss-cross wire mesh which acted as a reminder, a pale reminder, of that other mesh (that of the springs of the bed) on which Lena had been lying when I went into the bedroom and saw her foot and a short length of her calf, etc., etc. Katasia's gliding lip moved quite close to Lena's mouth.

I was hooked. I had fled from Warsaw to get away from things, and here I was, starting all over again, getting mixed up in things here. For a brief moment I was hooked. But Katasia went away again, Lena pushed the ashtray towards the middle of the table, I lit a cigarette, and someone switched on the radio. Mr Wojtys drummed on the table with his finger-tips and hummed a little tune, something like tri-li-li-lee, but stopped, drummed on the table again, started humming again, and then stopped again. The room was too small, it was cramped. Lena kept her mouth either closed or half open, she was very timid and reserved. And that was all. Good night, we're going up to bed.

While we were undressing Fuchs resumed his complaints

15

about Drozdowski, his chief at the office. He complained in a pale, white voice, standing there with his red hair and holding his shirt in his hand.

'At first we got on splendidly, but then somehow everything went wrong, I started getting on his nerves and I still do, I can't lift my little finger without getting on his nerves. Do you realize what it's like to get on your chief's nerves seven hours a day every day of the week? He can't stand me, he spends seven hours a day obviously trying not to look at me, and if he does by any chance catch sight of me a look comes into his eyes as if he had touched a red-hot poker. And that goes on for seven hours a day.

'I'm at my wit's end,' he went on, staring at his shoes, 'sometimes I feel like going down on bended knee and imploring him to forgive me. But he hasn't got anything to forgive me for. I don't believe he really bears me any ill will, I just get on his nerves and that's all there is to it. My colleagues tell me the only thing to do is to keep as quiet as possible and avoid attracting his attention as much as possible, but'—he looked at me wide-eyed, like a melancholy fish—'what can I do about attracting or not attracting his attention since we are cooped up in the same office for seven hours a day and I only have to cough or move my hand for him to come out in a rash? Do I stink, by any chance?'

These lamentations of the rejected Fuchs linked up in my mind with my own discontented, resentful departure from Warsaw robbed of . . . and in that rented room in a strange house we had hit upon by pure chance the two of us undressed like men rejected and repulsed. We went on talking for a bit about the Wojtyses and the family environment, and I dropped off to sleep. Then I woke up. It was dark. It took me some time to realize where I was, lying in bed between the wardrobe, the table and the water-jug, and I had to make an intense and prolonged intellectual effort to realize my position in relation to the windows and the door. I spent a long time wondering whether to go to sleep again or not. As I had no desire either to go to sleep or to get up, I spent quite a time racking my brains whether to do either or just to stay there lying awake. Eventually I put out one leg and sat up in bed, and as I did so caught sight of the whitish patch of the window. I tiptoed over to it and lifted the blind. Beyond the garden, on the other side of the fence and the road, was the place where the sparrow was hanging in a maze of branches, and underneath it was black earth, and an old cardboard box and a sheet of corrugated iron and other junk were lying about, over there where the tips of the pine-trees were bathed in the light of the starry night. I dropped .the blind again and stopped still, for it struck me that Fuchs might have been watching me.

Actually I couldn't hear him breathing. If he wasn't asleep he must have seen me looking out of the window. There would have been nothing out of the way about this but for the sparrow and the night, the sparrow in the night, the combination of the sparrow and the night. If I had looked out of the window it could only have been because of the sparrow, and this made me feel ashamed. But the silence was so complete and protracted that it suddenly dawned on me that he was not in the room; and indeed he was not, his bed was empty. Once more I pulled up the blind, and the gleam from the star-filled sky revealed the place where he ought to have been. Where could he have gone?

To the bathroom? No, the slight sound of water that came from it showed that it was empty. But in that case. . . . Supposing he had gone to see the sparrow? I don't know where I got the idea from, but it struck me that it was by no means impossible, he might very well have gone to have a look at it, he was very interested in it, perhaps he was searching the bushes for an explanation, that reddish, expressionless face of his was well suited to a search of that kind, it was very like him to be racking his brains and working out theories about who could have hanged the sparrow and why. And one of the reasons for his picking on this house might well have been the sparrow (this idea struck me as being rather exaggerated, I kept it in the background, in reserve, so to speak), but at all events he had woken up, or perhaps he had not gone to sleep, curiosity had got the better of him, he had got up and gone out, perhaps to check some detail and have a look round in the middle of the night. Was he playing the detective? I felt inclined to think so. I grew more and more inclined to think so. There was no real objection

17

to this, of course, but I should have preferred our stay with the Wojtyses not to have started with such nocturnal adventures, and another thing was that I was slightly annoyed at the sparrow's coming back and haunting us like this, flaunting itself in front of us as if it were swelling and inflating itself and making itself out to be more important and interesting than it really was. If the fool had really gone to see it, it was becoming a personality who received visitors. I smiled. But what was I to do? I didn't know what to do. As I hadn't the slightest desire to go back to bed, I slipped on my trousers, opened the door and peeped out into the corridor. It was empty and rather chilly. It was a trifle less dark on the left, where the staircase was, there was a small window there. I listened, but there was not a sound to be heard, so I crept out into the corridor, feeling mildly irritated that he should have crept out furtively and that I was now doing the same. . . . The fact of the matter was that two of us behaving like this didn't look very innocent. Outside the room I reconstructed in my mind the plan of the house, the arrangement of the rooms, walls, landings, corridors, furniture, and also its occupants, who were still strangers to me, I had scarcely even begun to get to know them yet.

Here I was in the middle of the night in the corridor of a strange house, wearing only shirt and trousers. This suggested sensuality, a creeping and gliding like that of Katasia's lip, perhaps creeping towards her room. Where was her room? Was she asleep? Asking myself this question promptly turned me into a sensualist in shirt and trousers creeping barefoot down the corridor towards her; and that gliding, darting, reptilian, lip disfigurement, reinforced to some extent by my setback in Warsaw, where my family had coldly and disagreeably rejected me, impelled me coldly in that sleeping house towards her indecency. . . . Where was her room? I advanced a few paces, reached the staircase, and looked out of the window, the only one in the corridor. It was on the other side of the house, the side opposite the road and the sparrow, and I looked out on to a big open space enclosed by a wall and lit by clouds and swarms of stars. Immediately below the small garden was exactly like the one in the front, with gravel paths and meagre young trees, and beyond it the ground was bare, with nothing to see but a pile of bricks and a hut. On the left, right up against the house, there was a kind of outhouse, no doubt that was where the kitchen or the wash-house was, and perhaps it was there too that Katasia was lying asleep, nursing that sinister mouth of hers.

There was an incredible profusion of stars in the moonless sky, and the constellations stood out. I picked out and identified some of them, the Great Bear and the Scales, for instance, but others unknown to me were also glowering and waiting to be identified, as if they were inscribed on the map of the night sky by the positioning of the most important stars, and I tried to work out the lines that made the various shapes. But trying to decipher the map suddenly exhausted me, so I turned my attention to the garden, though here too I was quickly exhausted by the profusion of things, such as the chimney, a pipe, the bends in the gutter, or a young tree, and the moulding on the wall, as well as more difficult because more complicated things such as the bending and disappearance of the path or the rhythm of the shadows. But in spite of myself I started working out shapes and relationships, I felt tired, impatient, and irritated, until I realized that what attracted or perhaps captivated me about these things was one thing's being behind another; the pipe was behind the chimney, for instance, and the wall behind the angle formed by the kitchen . . . just as Katasia's mouth had been behind Lena's when she put the ashtray with the mesh lid on the table and bent over her and put that darting, gliding lip near hers. . . . I was more surprised by this than was right and proper, I rather tended to exaggeration in general, and also the constellations, the Great Bear, etc., superimposed something painfully cerebral upon me. Their mouths together? I said to myself, and a detail that particularly surprised me was that in retrospect and imagination the two women's mouths seemed to be in closer relationship now than they had at dinner. I actually shook my head as if to pull myself together, but the connection between Lena's lips and Katasia's only became the plainer. But then I smiled, because there was really nothing whatever in common be-

19

tween Katasia's dissolute perverseness, that indecent, gliding mouth movement, and Lena's fresh, virginal, half-open lips, except that they were 'related' to each other as on a map, just as one town on a map is related to another—I could not get the idea of maps out of my head, maps of the night sky or ordinary geographical maps showing towns, etc. In reality there was no link whatever between those two mouths, I had merely seen one in relation to the other, it had been an accident of distance, angle and position, and there was no more to it than that. But the fact remained that I, considering that Katasia's mouth must certainly be somewhere in the neighbourhood of the kitchen (where she slept), kept asking myself where, in which direction and at what distance from that spot Lena's little mouth might be; and the cold sensuality that drove me down the corridor towards Katasia was deflected by Lena's accidental intrusion.

A growing distraction was associated with this, and there was nothing surprising about that, for excessive concentration leads to distraction, looking at one thing masks everything else—when we stare at a single point on a map we are quite well aware that the others elude us. With my mind fixed on the garden, the sky, and that pair of mouths, I was perfectly well aware that something was eluding me, something important. . . . Oh, Fuchs, of course. Where on earth was he and what was he doing? Playing the sleuth? If only it didn't lead to trouble. It was depressing to be sharing a room with that fish-like individual whom I hardly knew. In front of me the garden, the little trees, the paths that ended in an open space extending to a surprisingly white wall with a pile of bricks in the middle of it, the whole scene, now struck me as a visible reminder of what I could not see: that is, the other side of the house, where there was also a bit of garden bounded by a fence, and beyond it the road and then that thicket . . . and the tension of the light of the stars fused inside me with that of the hanged sparrow. Was that where Fuchs was, with the sparrow?

The sparrow, the sparrow. The truth of the matter was that I was not really interested either in the sparrow or in Fuchs. What I was much more interested in was that mouth, or so it seemed to me in my distraction. So I dropped the sparrow to concentrate on the mouth, and a kind of exhausting game of tennis set in, for the sparrow returned me to the mouth and the mouth returned me to the sparrow, I was the ball in the middle, and each was hidden by the other. As soon as I caught the mouth, really caught it, as if I had lost it, I was aware that besides this side of the house there was the other, and that besides the mouth there was the lonely, hanged sparrow. And the worst of it was that it was impossible to place the sparrow on the same map as the mouth, it belonged to an entirely different one, a different area altogether, a fortuitous and entirely absurd and irrelevant area, so why did it keep on haunting me, it had no right to. No, it had no right to. No right to? The less excuse there was for it, the more it obsessed me, the more difficult it was to shake off; the less right it had, the closer it clung and the more significant it became.

I stayed in the corridor a little longer, torn between the sparrow and the mouth. Then I went back to the room, got back into bed, and went to sleep more quickly than might have been expected.

Next morning Fuchs and I took out our books and papers and settled down to work. I did not ask him what he had been doing during the night, and I recalled my own nocturnal adventures in the corridor with no pleasure whatever. I felt like someone who knows he has gone too far and consequently feels ill at ease, yes, that was it, I felt ill at ease, but there was an equivocal air about Fuchs too. He set about his calculations in silence. These were very difficult and complicated, covered sheet after sheet of paper, and were embellished with logarithms; his object was to discover a system for winning at roulette, and he was perfectly well aware that this was a crackpot enterprise, a complete and total waste of time, but he devoted all his energy to the task because he had nothing, absolutely nothing, better to do, he was in a hopeless situation, in a fortnight his leave would be over and he would have to go back to the office and to Drozdowski, who would make superhuman efforts to avoid looking in his direction, and there was absolutely no way out of his plight, because even if he outdid himself in conscientiousness and efficiency Drozdowski would find that intolerable too. . . . He yawned and his eyes contracted to two slits, and he no longer even complained. He relapsed into apathy, which was his real state, and at most tried sympathizing with me about my troubles with my family. We've all got our own troubles, haven't we? They've got their knife into you too, to hell with the lot of them.

In the afternoon we took the bus to Krupowki to do some shopping. Dinner-time approached. I waited for it impatiently, because after the previous night's adventures I was very curious to see Lena and Katasia, Katasia with Lena. In the meantime I avoided thinking about them; I wanted to have another look at them first.

But a totally unexpected factor changed the whole set up. Lena was married. Her husband appeared after we had started dinner. I scrutinized her sexual partner with distasteful curiosity while he bent his long nose over his plate. I was utterly taken aback. Not that I felt jealousy for the man, but Lena had changed completely in my eyes, she had been utterly transformed by this stranger who was so completely initiated into all the secrets of her mouth. They had obviously been married only recently, he rested his hand on hers and looked into her eyes. What was he like? He was tall, well-built, inclined to stoutness and very intelligent. By profession he was an architect, and he was now engaged on building a hotel. He did not talk very much and helped himself to a radish. But what was he like? What was he like? And what were they like when they were alone together, what was he like with her and what was she like with him? When a man suddenly comes between you and a woman in whom you are interested there's nothing agreeable about it, but it's worse still if, though a complete stranger, he suddenly becomes the subject of your enforced curiosity and you have to guess his most secret tastes and inclinations and, in spite of your repugnance, you have to divine these through the woman. Attractive in herself as she was, I don't know whether I wanted her to turn out to be repugnant to him or to be even more attractive to the man of her choice. Both alternatives were equally appalling.

Were they in love? Passionately? Rationally? Romantically? Were their relations easy or difficult? Or were they not in love at all? Here, at table, in the presence of the family, they displayed the normal affection of a young couple, but it was impossible to scrutinize them closely, one could do no more than glance casually at them every now and then, resort to borderline manœuvres without infringing the border. I could not very well stare into the man's eyes, so my passionate and pretty revolting conjectures had to be based exclusively on inspection of his hand resting on the table opposite me, near hers. The hand was long and well cared-for, and his fingers and short-cut nails were not displeasing. I examined it, with growing fury at having to try to discover its erotic possibilities as if I had been Lena.

I discovered nothing at all. It appeared to be a perfectly decent hand, but what did appearances signify? Everything depended on the way he touched her, and I could very well imagine his touching her decently, or indecently, or passionately, brutally and furiously, or simply conjugally. But I discovered nothing at all, absolutely nothing whatever, for why should not ordinary, well shaped hands touch each other in abnormal or even disgusting fashion, how could one tell? It was hard to believe that a healthy, decent hand could commit extreme indecencies, but it was sufficient to imagine that it *might*, and that *might* made the indecency the greater. And if I was totally unable to find out anything whatever from their hands, what was I to think about individuals farther in the background, where I was afraid even of looking? I knew that if he so much as secretly and surreptitiously linked his little finger with hers it would be sufficient to turn both of them into supremely dissolute personalities, though he, Louis, at that moment was merely remarking that he had brought the photos, that they had come out excellently, and that he would show them to us after dinner.

Fuchs told the story of how we had found the sparrow. 'What an extraordinary thing,' he said in conclusion. 'Can you imagine anybody actually hanging a sparrow? That's really going too far.'

'Yes, it really is,' Leo said politely, only too happy to be able to agree. 'But what sadism.'

'It must have been juvenile delinquents,' his wife Kulka announced sharply and conclusively, removing a thread from his sleeve. Again he was only too pleased to be able to agree.

'Yes, delinquents,' he said approvingly, whereupon Kulka rounded on him and exclaimed:

'Why do you always have to contradict?'

'But I didn't contradict, darling, I agreed completely with what you said.'

'But I said it was delinquents,' she announced as if he had said something different.

'But that's exactly what I said.'

'You don't know what you're talking about.'

She adjusted the handkerchief in his breast-pocket.

Katasia advanced from the sideboard to clear the table, and her deformed, gliding, darting mouth approached the mouth opposite me. This was the moment I had been impatiently awaiting, but I controlled myself and looked away, in order not to interfere or intervene in any way, because I wanted the experience to be completely objective. One mouth 'came into relationship' with the other, and I simultaneously saw Lena's husband saying something to her, Leo intervening in the conversation, Katasia moving busily round the table and one mouth coming into relationship with the other, like one star with another, and this oral constellation confirmed the reality of my nocturnal adventure that I wished to reject. Those two mouths together, the gliding, darting horror of the one in conjunction with the pure, gentle, half closing and half opening of the other. . . . I succumbed to a kind of quivering astonishment at the fact that two mouths that had nothing in common could nevertheless have something in common, it bewildered me, and more particularly it plunged me into a state of incredible distraction—a gloomy distraction impregnated with night and saturated, so to speak, with the events of the day before.

Louis wiped his mouth with his napkin, folded it neatly (he seemed very clean and respectable, but might there not be something pretty dirty about that?) and said in his deep baritone voice that just about a week previously he had himself seen a chicken hanging from a pine-tree at the edge of the road, but he had not taken any particular notice of it, and in any case a few days later it had disappeared.

'But what an extraordinary thing,' Fuchs exclaimed. 'Hanging sparrows, and now hanging chickens. Do you suppose it presages the end of the world? How high was the chicken hanging? How far was it from the road?'

He asked these questions because Drozdowski could not stand him and he hated Drozdowski and did not know what to do about it. He helped himself to a radish.

'Delinquents,' Kulka repeated. Like a good housewife, she rearranged the bread left in the bread-basket and removed some crumbs. 'Juvenile delinquents. Nowadays young people are allowed to do whatever they like.'

'That's true,' Leo agreed.

'But the point,' Fuchs said in his white voice, 'the point is that both the sparrow and the chicken were too high up for it to have been done by anyone but an adult.'

'If it wasn't done by juvenile delinquents, who could it have been?' said Leo. 'Are you suggesting, my dear sir, that it might have been a lunatic? I have not heard of any lunatics in the neighbourhood.'

He hummed tri-li-li-lee again, concentrated on making some little bread-pellets, carefully arranged them in a straight line on the table-cloth, and then contemplated them. Katasia placed the ashtray with the meshwork lid in front of Lena, who dropped the ash from her cigarette in it. The meshwork reminded me of her leg on the springs of the bed, but I was distracted, what with one mouth over another mouth, the hanged sparrow and the hanged chicken, Lena's husband and Lena, the chimney behind the gutter, lips behind lips, mouth behind mouth, shrubs and paths, trees and road. There was too much of it, wave upon wave without rhyme or reason, I was plunged in a bottomless pit of distraction and bewilderment, I was lost and astray. A bottle was standing on a shelf over in the corner, and something, perhaps a bit of cork, was stuck to the neck.

I concentrated on that bit of cork, took refuge with it until it was time to go to bed, I was sleepy and soon dropped off to sleep, and during the next few days nothing happened at all, they were a hotch-potch of words and happenings and meals and going downstairs and coming up again, though I discovered (1) that Lena was a language teacher and had been married to Louis for barely two months, and that they had spent their honeymoon at Hela on the Baltic and were living here until their house was ready (Katasia told me this while conscientiously going about her business, duster in hand); and (2) that (in Kulka's words) 'the scar ought to be reopened and sewn up again, the surgeon, he's an old friend of Leo's, told me so himself, how many times have I told her I would pay for the operation myself, because, even though she's a peasant girl from Grojec, she's a niece of mine, but I don't disown my poor relations, and in any case it's un-aesthetic, it offends the aesthetic sense, it's quite revolting in fact, and how many times have I hold her so during all these years, because do you realize that it's already five years since it happened? It was an accident, you know, a bus ran into a tree, it might have been far worse, how many times have I told her not to put it off any longer but to go and see the surgeon and have it done, because she looks so dreadful, but it's no good, she's afraid of the operation, she always says she's going to do something about it, but she never does, and so it goes on. We've got used to it, and nowadays it's only when someone calls attention to it that we notice it, I'm very sensitive in aesthetic matters of course, but there's all the housework to be done as you can see for yourself, the washing and the cleaning and one thing after another for Leo and Lena and Louis, what with one thing and another I'm busy from morning to night, I never have a free moment, but perhaps when Louis and Lena move into their house, and how lucky it is that Lena has found a good husband, if he made her unhappy I swear to you that I'd kill him, I'd take a kitchen knife and kill him, but thank heaven everything's all right so far, the only thing is they won't do anything for themselves, neither of them, she's just like Leo, she takes after her father, I have to see to everything, the hot water, the coffee, the laundry, darning their socks and mending and sewing on their buttons and the ironing and the shoe-cleaning and the clean handkerchiefs and the bread-cutting, and they won't lift a finger to do anything for themselves, and, what with the cooking and everything, so it goes on from morning to night, and on top of it there are the lodgers, you see what it's like, I don't complain, of course, they take the rooms and pay for them, but there are always things that you have to remember to do for them, and they all have their own little ways and own little wants, and so it goes on from morning to night. . . .'

There were also many other happenings that occupied and absorbed one during the day, and every evening, as inevitable as sunset, there was dinner, at which I sat facing Lena, with Katasia's mouth circulating in the background. Leo manufactured little bread-pellets, carefully arranged them in a straight line, examined them closely and then, after a moment's thought, picked one of them up and transfixed it with a toothpick. Sometimes, after a prolonged period of meditation, he would take a pinch of salt on his knife and sprinkle it on the pellet, scrutinizing it doubtfully through his pince-nez.

'Tri-li-li-lee.' he would hum.

'Pray papass to your papakins a radiculous radicle, my precious bulbul.'

That meant that he wanted Lena to pass the radishes. His jargon was not always easy to understand. 'My honeysuckling, my meadowsweetipie,' he would call Lena, or if he wanted the sugar he would say to Kulka: 'Don't you see that popopkins wants to sweetify the pillikins?'

He was not always able to coin these verbal monstrosities at will, but sometimes started off in crazy fashion and ended up normally, or the other way about. His round, shiny bald pate with face appended underneath, to which in turn his pince-nez was appended, loomed over the table like a balloon. He often had fits of good humour and told us jokes. 'Do you know the one about the bicycle? When an icicle is mounted on a bicycle it results in a tricycle. Ha-ha!' His wife would adjust his tie or remove a speck of dust from his lapel. Then he would grow thoughtful and tie the corner of his napkin into a knot or stick his tooth-pick into the tablecloth, not at random but only at certain definite spots to which he invariably returned after prolonged

27

meditation with knitted brows. Then he would hum: 'Tri-li-li-lee.'

All this got on my nerves because of Fuchs, because I knew that it was grist to the Drozdowski mill that haunted him from morning to night; for in a fortnight he would have to go back to his office, where Drozdowski would gaze at the stove with an air of martyrdom when he appeared. 'Even my jacket's enough to give him the creeps, he just can't stand me, and there's nothing whatever I can do about it.' Somehow or other Leo's flow of talk helped him as he sat there watching him in his pale, yellow, red-headed way, and that somehow increased my resentment against my parents and reinforced my revolt against Warsaw and everything connected with it. There I sat, feeling miserable and hostile, reluctantly examining Louis's hand, which was no affair of mine but repelled and fascinated me and whose erotic potentialities obsessed me, and my mind reverted to Kulka, who was always working, washing, sweeping, mending, darning, dusting, tidying, ironing, etc., etc. I was in a state of total distraction, my ears buzzed and my head swam, the bit of cork on the bottle caught my eye again, and I looked at it, perhaps to avoid looking at anything else I used it as my life-line as I floundered in the ocean, though the only sound that reached me from the latter was too faint and distant and diffuse to be really audible. Otherwise nothing at all. A few days filled with a bit of everything.

The heat persisted. The summer was exhausting, and everything just dragged on. Lena's husband, his hands, those mouths, Fuchs and Leo, it was like tramping along in the heat, they just dragged on. On the fourth or fifth day my eyes strayed, not for the first time, to the end of the room. I was drinking tea and smoking a cigarette, and my eyes abandoned the cork and fell on a nail on the wall near the shelf, and from there they wandered to the cupboard, counted the mouldings on it, and then, sleepy and exhausted, started examining less accessible places over the wardrobe, where the wall-paper was frayed, and then reached the white desert of the ceiling. But a little farther away, near the window, the tedious whiteness changed into a darker, wrinkled zone which had been affected by damp, and inspection revealed a complicated geography of continents, gulfs, islands, peninsulas, strange concentric circles like moon craters, and other oblique, fugitive lines. In places it looked unhealthy, like a skin disease, here raging wild and unbridled, there adorned haphazardly with curves and arabesques; it contained the menace of finality and vanished into a giddy distance. Also there were a lot of dots that I could not explain. Almost certainly they were not flies, and their origin remained obscure. Totally absorbed as I was by these things and my own internal complications, I gazed at them, persistently and yet without any particular concentration, until I ended by crossing a threshhold, as it were, and finding myself on the other side. I sipped some tea, and Fuchs said:

'What on earth are you gazing at like that?'

It was stifling and, what with that and the tea, I had no desire to speak.

'Do you see that line there, in the corner, behind the island . . . and that kind of triangle near the isthmus?' I said.

'What about it?'

'Nothing.'

'But what about?'

'Oh, nothing at all.'

After a long pause I said:

'What does it remind you of?'

'Do you mean that shape there?' he replied eagerly (I knew why, it took his mind off Drozdowski). 'Just a minute, yes, it's a rake.'

'Yes, perhaps it is a rake.'

Lena intervened, because we had started playing a guessing game, a not very demanding social pastime well-suited to her modest nature.

'It's not a rake, it's an arrow,' she said.

Fuchs vigorously contested this.

'But how can it be an arrow?' he exclaimed.

The next few minutes were occupied with other things. Louis asked his father-in-law if he would like a game of chess, I had a broken finger-nail that annoyed me, a newspaper dropped to the floor, the dogs barked outside the window (they were two quite young dogs which were let out at night, and there was also a cat), Leo said 'one game only,' and Fuchs admitted that perhaps it was an arrow after all.

'It may be an arrow or may not,' I remarked. I picked up the newspaper, Louis rose to his feet, a bus passed, and Kulka said:

'Did you remember to telephone?'

II

As I am telling this story in retrospect, I cannot tell it as it really happened. Take that arrow, for instance. That evening it was no more important than Leo's game of chess, the newspaper or my cup of tea; everything happened at the same level, combined into a kind of concert, like the buzzing of a swarm of bees. But now I know in retrospect that the most important thing that evening was the arrow, so I am giving it a prominent place in the story, shaping the future out of a mass of undifferentiated facts.

But how can one avoid telling a story *ex post facto*? Can nothing ever be described as it really was, reconstituted in its anonymous actuality? Will no one ever be able to reproduce the incoherence of the living moment at its moment of birth? Born as we are out of chaos, why can we never establish contact with it? No sooner do we look at it than order, pattern, shape is born under our eyes. Never mind. Let it pass. Every morning Katasia brought me my breakfast in bed, and the first thing I saw when I woke was that disfigurement over my head, that darting, gliding movement superimposed on her honest, rustic, blue-eyed face. Could she not have stayed in that position for a quarter of a second less? Did she not spend a fraction of a second too long bending over me? Perhaps she did or perhaps she did not. I could not be sure, but the possibility penetrated inside me together with the memory of my nocturnal imaginings about her. On the other hand, might she not stay leaning over me like that for perfectly innocent reasons? I had great difficulty in seeing anything clearly. Only things can be properly seen; there are far more obstacles in the way of seeing persons. At all events, that early morning scene in which I lay in bed with her mouth right over me engraved itself daily on my mind and stayed with me all day long, thus keeping alive the obsession with her mouth to which I clung so tenaciously.

The heat did not help my work or Fuchs's, we were both tired, and he was bored and embittered and he grew pathetic, he was like a howling dog, though he didn't howl, he was only bored. The ceiling. One afternoon we were lying on our beds, the venetian blinds were drawn, the air was buzzing with flies, and I heard his voice.

'Majziewicz might perhaps offer me a job, but I can't give up my present job, it's impossible, what I'm doing now counts as a qualifying period, and I can't afford to waste eighteen months, it's no use even thinking about it, it's out of the question. . . . Look up there at the ceiling.'

'Where? What at?'

'Up there on the ceiling, over there just by the stove.'

'What is it?'

'What do you see there?'

'Nothing at all.'

'If only I could spit in his face, but I can't. And in any case it wouldn't do any good. It's not as if there was any real ill will on his part, I just get on his nerves, his jaw just drops at the mere sight of me. . . . But have another look at the ceiling. Can't you see anything?'

'No. What is there to see?'

'Something like the arrow on the ceiling in the dining-room, but more distinct.'

I did not answer. A minute or two passed.

'The point is that it wasn't there yesterday,' he said.

Silence. Heat. My head weighed heavily on the pillow. I felt weak. He went on again, as if he were fascinated by the sound of his own voice floating in the gravy of the afternoon.

'It wasn't there yesterday. Yesterday afternoon a spider was letting itself down there, I watched it, and if the arrow had been there then I should have seen it. I tell you it wasn't there yesterday. Look at the line that forms the shaft, I tell you it wasn't there; I grant you the rest of it, the tip of the arrow and the other lines are old cracks, I admit, but the main thing, the shaft of the arrow, wasn't there.'

He paused for breath, raised himself, leaned on one elbow, and the dust danced in a ray of sunshine coming in through a crack in the blinds.

'I tell you the shaft wasn't there yesterday.'

I heard him creeping out of bed, and then watched him standing there in his underpants with raised head, staring at the ceiling. His zeal and his staring eyes, which remained fixed on the ceiling, took me aback.

'It's fifty-fifty,' he said. 'How can one be sure? The devil alone knows.'

He went back to bed, but I knew that he was still staring at the ceiling, which bored me.

After a time I heard him get up again and resume his inspection of the ceiling. He would have stopped if he could, but he couldn't.

'Look at the line that forms the shaft of the arrow. I can make out a faint smell, as if it had only just been traced with a larding pin. It stands out from all the rest. If it had been there yesterday I should have noticed it. And it's pointing in exactly the same direction as the one in the dining-room.'

I didn't move.

'If it's an arrow, it's pointing to something.'

'And if it isn't an arrow it isn't pointing to anything,' I replied.

The evening before, while I was again examining Louis's hand with that rather disgusting curiosity of mine, I had glanced at Lena's little hand, which was also resting on the table, and had had the impression that it was quivering, or was slightly contracted. I was not sure, it was fifty-fifty either way. As for Fuchs, I was displeased, and even angry, at the thought that everything he said or did was because of Drozdowski and their mutual loathing. As for myself, but for that row with my parents in Warsaw . . . but one thing fed on another, the result was cumulative. Fuchs started talking again.

He stood in his underpants in the middle of the room and went on talking. He suggested that we should find out whether the arrow was really pointing to something. Finding out one way or another would cost us nothing, after all, and if it turned out to be an illusion at least our minds would be at rest, we should know that no one had traced any arrow on purpose and that the whole thing was nothing but a mare's nest. How else could we make sure whether it was

33

an arrow or not? I listened in silence, wondering how I could refuse to take part in this project on which he insisted only very weakly, but then I was weak too—weakness had in fact permeated everything. I told him to do it himself if he had set his heart on it, but he pointed out that my co-operation was indispensable if the exact direction in which the arrow was pointing was to be fixed, because it would be necessary to follow it outside in the corridor and in the garden, and that required both of us. His final argument was that two heads were better than one, and suddenly I got off my bed and agreed with him, because the prospect of following a definite line, doing something positive for a definite purpose, seemed more refreshing at that moment than a glass of cold water.

We pulled on our trousers.

The room immediately became full of rational and purposeful action. But, as this was undertaken out of boredom, caprice and having nothing better to do, a certain amount of imbecility was concealed behind it. . . . Besides, our task was no easy one.

It was obvious that whatever the arrow was pointing at was not in our room. So the direction in which it was pointing had to be extended as accurately as possible through the wall into the corridor and from there outside into the garden. This involved some pretty complicated manœuvres, which Fuchs would certainly not have been able to carry out without my aid. I went out into the garden with a rake; the object was to lay it on the grass in line with a broomhandle manipulated by my companion standing at the staircase window.

It was nearly five o'clock. The gravel lay hot in the sunshine and the grass had dried up round the young trees, which cast no shadow. Overhead great white clouds drifted in the pitiless blue. The house looked at me through its two rows of windows on the ground floor, and the glass glittered in the sun.

Wasn't there something human about the way in which one of those windows was looking at me? To judge by the quiet, the family were still taking their afternoon nap, but it was by no means impossible that someone—Leo? Kulka?

Katasia?—was watching from behind that window, and that the observer, whoever it might be, might be the person who had slipped into our room, no doubt during the morning, and traced the line that made the arrow. Why? Was somebody trying to make fools of us? Was it a practical joke? Or was the object to communicate a message? Stuff and nonsense, the whole thing was absurd. The sheer absurdity of it was a double-edged weapon; Fuchs and I were using one edge and acting in a fashion that was by no means absurd, so that I, while engaged in these laborious manœuvres, had, unless I were willing to deny my own actions, to count on the possibility that someone might be looking at us from behind those windows that shone in such dazzling and exhausting fashion.

So I took the possibility into account, and Fuch's watching me from the upstairs window helped. I advanced cautiously to avoid rousing suspicion, raked the grass a little, and then, as if exhausted by the heat, dropped the rake, and pushed it imperceptibly in the desired direction with my foot. These precautions made my co-operation with Fuchs closer than I desired, I behaved almost as if I were his slave. Eventually we established the direction of the arrow; the line led to a spot behind the tool shed near the boundary wall, where the property ended in a plot of ough ground, scattered with rubbish and bricks, beyond the garden. We strolled slowly in that direction, taking occasional detours and talking and pausing every now and then as if to look at the flowers or plants, sometimes making expansive gestures and keeping an eye open for any significant features. So we advanced from bed to bed, from bit of stone to bit of wood, with eyes downcast and mind absorbed by the ashen, yellowy, rust-coloured, boring, complicated, sleepy, monotonous, empty but hard earth.

I wiped the sweat from my face. The whole thing was a waste of time.

When we got near the wall we stopped in embarrassment. The last ten paces seemed impossible, they would give us away completely. So far our stroll through the garden under the watchful windows had been easy enough—a few dozen yards of level ground, after all—though we had been in-

hibited by a kind of secret difficulty that made it equivalent
to a steep climb. But now the slope became steeper and
giddier, and the difficulty of the climb accordingly increased,
as if we were approaching the summit. What a height we
had reached. Fuchs squatted on his heels and pretended to
be examining a beetle and advanced to the wall in the same
squatting position, as if he were following it, and I strolled
off in a different direction, taking a circular route so as to
join up with him again; and so eventually we reached the
wall right at the end of the garden in the corner formed
by the hut.

It was hot. Some long grasses swayed in the breeze, a
beetle was making its way along the ground, and there were
some bird droppings on the wall. But the heat was different
here, and so was the smell, it suggested urine, and I had a
sense of remoteness, as if we had been walking for months
and months and were thousands of miles away at the other
end of the world. The smell was of warm, decomposing
vegetable matter, not far away there was a compost heap,
and rain had worn a little channel along the wall. Stalks,
stems, bits of brick and plaster, stones, clumps of earth,
yellowy things. Again the heat changed and became strange
and unfamiliar. . . . But no, there was a link between this
isolated corner living a life of its own and the cool, dark
thicket where the cardboard box and corrugated iron were
and we had found the sparrow, and this seemed to put new
life into our quest.

It was a hard task. Even if something were concealed here
to which the arrow on our bedroom ceiling pointed, what
hope was there of identifying it in this chaos of weeds and
refuse, which in quantity far exceeded anything that could
be done on walls and ceilings? There was an oppressive profusion of possible links and clues. How many sentences can
be composed with the twenty-six letters of the alphabet?
How many meanings could be deduced from these hundreds
of weeds, clumps of earth, and other details? The wall and
the boards of the wooden hut similarly offered innumerable
possibilities. I had had enough. I stood up and looked at the
house and garden. The big, artificial shapes, huge mastodons
of the world of things, re-established a sense of order, in

which I rested. I decided to go back. I was just going to say so to Fuchs, but the expression on his face made me stop short. He was gazing at something.

In the crumbling wall just above our heads there was a sort of niche, consisting of three little hollows each smaller than the last, and in one of them something was hanging— a bit of wood, less than half an inch long. It was hanging by a bit of white thread of about the same length tied to a piece of brick.

That was all. Again we looked carefully all around, but that was all. I turned and looked at the house and its shining windows. A cooler breeze was now blowing, announcing the evening and restoring life to the foliage that had been petrified by the heat. It shook the leaves of the carefully aligned, staked and whitewashed young trees.

We went back to our room. Fuchs flung himself on his bed.

'At any rate it led to something,' he cautiously announced.

'Yes, but what?' I replied slightly less cautiously.

But it was hard to pretend not to know. First the hanging sparrow and then the hanging bit of wood. A strange repetition that gave increased significance to the former (and revealed how greatly we were concerned with it, though we pretended not to think about it). It was difficult to resist the assumption that someone had used the arrow to guide us to the bit of wood and so establish a link with the sparrow. But why? What for? Was it a joke? Was someone pulling our leg? Someone was playing a trick on us, making fools of us, enjoying himself at our expense. I felt uncertain, and so did he, and that made us cautious.

'I bet someone's trying to take us for a ride.'

'Yes, but who?'

'One of them. One of them who was there when I told them about the sparrow and we found the arrow on the dining-room ceiling. Whoever it was drew another arrow here in our bedroom pointing towards the bit of wood. Someone's playing a trick, trying to make fools of us.'

But this theory didn't stand up. Who would want to play such a complicated joke, and what for? How could he have known that we would discover the arrow and take such interest in it? No, the whole thing was pure coincidence. True, you don't see a bit of wood hanging from a string every day, but, after all, it might have been done for a thousand reasons having nothing whatever to do with the sparrow, we exaggerated its significance simply because we had found it at the end of our search and had jumped to a conclusion. But it wasn't a conclusion, it was merely a bit of wood hanging from a string. The whole thing was pure coincidence. But was it? A sort of pattern, a kind of confused message could be divined in the series of events. The hanged sparrow, the hanged chicken, the arrow in the dining-room, the arrow in our bedroom, the bit of wood hanging from a string, all pointed to a hidden meaning, as in a game of charades, when the letters start combining to try to form a word. But what word? It did seem as if an attempt was being made to convey an idea. But what idea?

And from whom did it come? If it was an idea, then there must be someone behind it. But who? Who would want to do such a thing? Suppose it was Fuchs who was playing this trick on me, out of sheer boredom, perhaps? But no, it was impossible. Was he likely to go to so much trouble to play such a stupid joke? That theory simply did not stand up. Was it just a series of coincidences, then? That would, perhaps, have been my final conclusion if there had not been yet another abnormality that I could not help associating with the whole abnormal business, if the anomaly of that bit of wood hanging by a string had not been backed by another that I preferred not to discuss with Fuchs.

'Katasia,' he said.

So he too had noted at least one of the faces of the sphinx. He was sitting on his bed with lowered head, slowly dangling his legs.

'What about her?' I said.

'A person with a facial affliction like that . . . ' he said thoughtfully. Then he added with a wily air: 'One is what one is, after all.'

He liked this idea, for he repeated it with greater emphasis. 'You take it from me. In the last resort one is what one is.'

Indeed it seemed plausible, if only because of the uncanniness of that lip of hers, that she might have had something to do with the sparrow. But what conclusion could be drawn from that? Was one to assume that she had resorted to such subtle plotting? It seemed out of the question. All the same, some sort of link remained, and these links and associations opened in front of me like a dark, yawning, pit—dark but alluring and fascinating, because behind Katasia's lip there was the vision of Lena's half-closed, half-open lips. I actually felt a violent shock, for the bit of wood linked with the sparrow in the thicket was the first definite sign in the real, objective world (however faint and vague it might be) that to some extent confirmed my imaginings about Lena's mouth 'in relation' to Katasia's; it was only an analogy, a slender and fantastic one, but it constituted a 'relationship', provided a basis for reading some sort of order into the chaos. Did Fuchs know anything about this buccal link or association between Lena and Katasia? Had he noticed it too, or did it come purely from myself? Nothing in the world would have persuaded me to mention the subject to him, and my reluctance was not based only on shame. Nothing in the world would have made me expose the matter to that voice and those protruding, fish-like eyes of his that exasperated Drozdowski. I felt weakened, exasperated and oppressed by his being here with that Drozdowski of his and at my being here with my parents, I wanted him neither as a confidant nor as a fellow-sufferer, and this double rejection was the clue to our relationship. But it did me good to hear him mention Katasia. I felt almost pleased that someone else had seen the possibility of there being something in common between her lip, the bit of wood, and the bird.

'Katasia,' he said slowly and reflectively. 'Katasia.'

But after a short period of euphoria the toneless pallor came back into his eyes, Drozdowski reappeared on the horizon, and it was solely to kill time that he produced a series of clumsy arguments.

'It struck me right away that . . . the disfigurement of her mouth seemed to me . . . but . . . on the other hand . . . in either case. What do you think?'

III

THE vagueness and triviality of all this forced us to beat
a retreat. We went back to work, but my distraction, so far
from leaving me, increased as evening fell, and the light of
our lamp was obscured for me by the growing darkness of
that spot at the end of the garden. I was haunted by another
possibility. Apart from the arrow we had discovered, there
was no knowing what other signs might be concealed on the
walls or elsewhere. Might there not be a link, for instance,
between the stain over the wash-stand and the peg of the
wardrobe or the scratches on the floor? We might have
spotted one sign, but how many more that we had not
spotted might be concealed in the natural order of things?
Every now and then I raised my eyes from my papers and
stared at the end of the room (taking care that Fuchs, whose
eyes were no doubt wandering too, should not notice what
I was doing). But I was not greatly perturbed; the baffling,
fantastic nature of the whole thing, which kept dissolving
into nothing, could lead only to conclusions equally unsubstantial.

However, surrounding reality was now contaminated, so
to speak, by the possibility of innumerable hidden meanings,
and this continually distracted me, though it seemed absurd
that an ordinary bit of wood should be capable of upsetting
me so much. Dinner came as inevitably as sunset, and again
I found myself sitting opposite Lena. Before we went downstairs Fuchs remarked that 'all that isn't worth mentioning,'
and he was perfectly right, of course; discretion was called
for if we were not to be taken for a pair of lunatics or half-
wits. Well, the dinner. Leo, munching radishes, described
how many years before he had learned from his chief at the
bank, Director Krysinski, the art of what he called incongruence or contrariety which, he maintained, every candidate for high position must have at his finger-tips.

He imitated the strangled, guttural voice of the late

Director Krysinski. 'Pay close attention to what I'm saying, my dear Leo, because it is absolutely vital to your career. If you have to reprimand a member of your staff, for instance, in the middle of it you must take out your cigarette case and offer him a cigarette. For the sake of the incongruence, you understand. If you have to be hard and disagreeable to a customer, you must smile, if not at him, at any rate at your secretary, otherwise you risk antagonising him too much. On the other hand, if you wish to be obliging or conciliatory to him, every now and then you must say something quite rude or disagreeable, to startle him out of his torpor, otherwise you won't get anywhere with him.'

Leo went on talking, with his napkin tucked under his chin and with finger outstretched. 'Well, gentlemen,' he went on, 'one day the president of the bank arrived on a visit of inspection to the branch of which I was manager at the time. I turned out the guard, of course, and received him ceremoniously and with full honours, but at lunch I tripped and spilled half a carafe of red wine over him. "I see you were trained in the school of Director Krysinski," he said.'

He laughed. He was carefully buttering and salting a radish, after cutting off its tail. When he had finished his handiwork he spent a moment carefully examining it before popping it in his mouth.

'Oh dear, oh dear, oh dear,' he went on, 'I could go on talking about the bank for a whole year on end, but it's difficult to explain, it's difficult to know where to begin, when I think about it I don't know where to begin myself, there were so many hours and days and years, oh dear, oh dear, oh dear, all those months and years and minutes and seconds. I used to squabble like mad with the president's secretary, God Almighty, what a fool that woman was, and she was a tell-tale into the bargain, once she went and told the director I'd spat into the wastepaper basket. "Are you mad?" I told her. But how could I possibly explain how things gradually boiled up to that little episode, it had been boiling up for months and years, and how could I possibly explain the hows and the whys and the whos and the wherefores? How could I possibly remember all the details after all this time? And what's the good of talking about it anyway?'

He relapsed into silent meditation, and then went on in a low voice:

'And which blouse was she wearing that day? I simply can't remember. Which one was it? The one with the embroidery?'

He emerged from his reverie and said cheerfully to his wife:

'Well, Kulka, my chick, my chuck, my mopsy, how are we, then?'

'Your collar's sticking up,' she said, putting down the jampot she had in her hand and straightening his collar.

'Thirty-seven years of married life, young gentlemen, just think of that. The past has gone, gone never to return, but memories, sweet memories remain. Kulka and I, the two of us on the Vistula together, the blue Vistula, and once it rained, oh dear, dear me, how many years ago was that? I bought some sweets, yes, I bought them from the concierge, and the rain came in through the roof, good gracious me, how many years ago was that in the little café? What a café it was, but it's dead and past and gone and can't be stuck together again. Thirty-seven years. Great heavens alive.'

He fell silent, looking pleased with himself, then withdrew into himself again, took some bread and started slowly manufacturing a pellet. He looked at it with wrapt concentration and hummed tri-li-li-lee.

Then he cut himself a slice of bread, removed the crust to make it square, put a lump of butter on it, spread it, patted it with his knife, examined it carefully, sprinkled some salt on it, popped it in his mouth, and ate it, as if solemnly noting the fact that he was eating it. I looked at the arrow on the ceiling, which now looked vague and indistinct. What? That an arrow? How could we possibly have taken it to be an arrow? I also looked at the table and the tablecloth—it must be admitted that the number of things one can look at is very limited—and at Lena's hand which was resting on it, small, relaxed, the colour of white coffee, warm and yet cool and attached by the wrist to the whiteness of her arm (which I imagined rather than saw, for I did not look as far as that). Her hand was still and inactive, but when you looked more closely you discovered some slight tremors, for instance, of the skin at the bottom of her fourth finger, and sometimes her third and fourth fingers touched; sometimes such embryonic movements developed into real ones, as when she touched the tablecloth with her forefinger or passed her nail along the fold. These things seemed so remote from Lena herself that she might have been a great country full of internal movements that it was impossible to apprehend, except statistically, no doubt. One of these movements consisted of a slow closing of the hand and folding of the fingers, a chaste, fugitive movement that I had noticed before. Had it really no relation to me? Who could tell? It was curious that it generally coincided with a lowering of her eyes (which I hardly ever saw), she never raised her eyes when she did it. Her husband's hand, that erotically non-erotic abomination, that remarkable object that was charged with eroticism 'through' her and in connection with her little hand, also rested on the tablecloth near hers, and it looked a very decent, respectable, sort of hand. Of course, the contractions of her hand might be related to his hand, but it was also possible that they might not be completely unrelated to the way I was looking at them through my half-closed eyes, though the chances of this were remote, I had to confess, about a million to one against. But the possibility, minimal though it was, was as explosive as the spark that causes a fire or the puff that rouses the whirlwind. For —who knows?—she *might* hate this man at whom I did not wish to look more closely because I was afraid—I merely looked all round him, he was an unknown quantity, just as she was. Supposing it was true that, while sitting at her husband's side, she was closing her little hand like that partly because I was looking at it? It was perfectly possible, after all, that slight sin might be superimposed on her modesty and innocence, which would make the latter far more perverse. Oh, the explosive power of a slender hypothesis. Dinner was in full swing, Louis had suddenly remembered something and taken out his notebook, Fuchs was boring us to death and was saying to Leo: 'So that's the sort of

43

dragon she was, was she?' Or 'just imagine all those years at the bank,' and Leo, with wrinkled brow, bald head and flashing pince-nez, was describing in detail this, that and the other, and how, when and why, and saying 'just imagine', and 'no, she didn't use the blotting paper' and 'the table was over there', and Fuchs was listening to him only to avoid having to think about Drozdowski. I was thinking that if it was because of me that that little hand was opening and shutting, though I was perfectly well aware that the idea was totally frivolous and absurd . . . when suddenly there was a commotion, an upheaval, a cataclysm. What on earth could be happening? Kulka's plump form leapt from her seat like a jack-in-the-box, dived headlong under the table, disappeared beneath it. Total chaos ensued. What on earth could it be? It was the cat. Kulka withdrew it from under the table with a mouse in its mouth.

After a due amount of verbal seething and boiling, the froth subsided, the agitation melted away, the cataract returned to its ordinary dinner-time bed, the cat was ejected, and the table, the tablecloth, the lamp and the glasses returned to normal. Kulka smoothed out some unevennesses in her napkin, Leo raised his forefinger to announce the imminence of a joke, Fuchs shifted in his chair, the door opened, Katasia came in, and Kulka asked Lena to pass her the salad bowl. Nothingness, eternity, peace. She loves him, she loves him not, I started saying to myself all over again, she's disillusioned with him, she hates him, she's happy, she's unhappy. She might have been all these things, but most probably she was none of them, for the simple reason that that hand of hers was too small, it was hardly a real hand at all. With a hand as small as that what could she amount to? Nothing at all. But how could she be nothing at all if she made such an impact? No, in herself she was nothing at all, but she made a tremendous impact all the same. Gloom, gloom, gloom. Matches, spectacles, snapshots of her, the bread-basket, onions, ginger-bread. Why could I not look at her directly? Why could I look only at her hands, sleeves, arms, neck, the periphery only? Why could I look her in the face only when a special occasion presented itself? How could I discover anything about her in these conditions?

But even if I had been able to look at her freely I should not have found out any more. Ha, ha, ha! Laughter, in which I joined, at one of Leo's stories. Kulka cheeped like a chicken, Fuchs had the hiccups, and Leo, with finger outstretched, said: 'I assure you it's true, on my word of honour.' She laughed too, but only to adorn the general laughter with her own laugh, which was why she did everything, only for the sake of adornment, and if I had been able to scrutinize her to my heart's content I should have discovered no more about her, because between her and her husband anything was possible.

'I need some string and a piece of wood.'

What was this? Fuchs was talking to me.

'What for?' I said.

'I forgot to bring my compass, and I've got to draw a circle, I need it for my calculations. I can manage perfectly well with some string and a piece of wood.'

Louis said politely that he thought he had a compass upstairs which he would be very willing to lend him. (The cork and the bottle, the cork on the neck of that bottle over there.) Fuchs thanked him. Oh, I see, he said to himself. You're a sly one, aren't you?

Fuchs's motive was to indicate to the possible practical joker in our midst that he had detected the arrow on our bedroom ceiling and discovered the bit of wood hanging by a string. Just in case someone present was amusing himself by confronting us with mysterious signs, he would realize that we had seen them and were waiting for the next move. It was only an outside chance, but what harm could it do? I looked at the company in the light of the strange possibility that the perpetrator might be among us, and at once the bit of wood and the dead bird in the thicket returned to my mind, the bit of wood hanging in its little niche at the end of the garden. I felt myself to be suspended between these two poles, so to speak, and our sitting together at the table under the lamp here seemed to have a special significance 'in relation to' the bird and the bit of wood; and this was not displeasing to me, for this strange situation opened the way to another that tormented and fascinated me. After all, if I found out about the bird and the bit of wood, one day

I might find out the truth that lay behind those mouths. (But how? Why? How absurd.)

Concentration led to distraction, but I accepted that, it enabled me to be both here and elsewhere, it helped relaxation. I accepted the sight of Katasia's disfigurement moving this way and that, approaching and receding, appearing behind Lena's head and over it, with a kind of stifled grunt, like someone who has swallowed something the wrong way. Again its almost imperceptible perversity became associated in my mind with the normal and charming half opening and half closing of the little mouth opposite me, and this association, which grew stronger or weaker according to circumstances, led to anomalies in my mind such as debauched timidity, shameless modesty, cold heat or sober drunkenness.

'But you don't understand, father.'

'What? What don't I understand?'

'Organization.'

'What sort of organization?'

'Rational organization of society and of the world.'

Leo with his bald pate was launching an assault on Louis across the table.

'What are you trying to organize and how are you going to organize it?'

'I mean scientific organization.'

'Scientific organization?'

Leo's eyes, his pince-nez, his wrinkles, and his bald pate gleamed with commiseration, and his voice dropped to a murmur.

'But my poor young man,' he said confidentially, 'have you gone out of your mind, by any chance? Organization? So you suppose that all you've got to do is stretch out your hand and take the world and reorganize it, just like that?'

He splayed his fingers like the claws of a beast of prey, advanced them across the tablecloth, and then opened his hand and blew on it. 'One puff and it's gone, don't you see?' he said. 'Gone, just like that.' Then he relapsed into contemplation of the salad bowl.

'I can't discuss these things with you, I'm afraid, father,' said Louis.

'Can't discuss them with me? Why not?'

46

'Because you haven't had the right training.'

'Training? What training?'

'Scientific training.'

'Scientific fiddlesticks,' he said slowly. 'Explain to the immaculate *tabula rasa* of my mind just how you with your scientific training are going to set about organizing the world, what your objectives and methods are going to be, how you are going to tackle the problem, what model you are going to follow, where and how you are going to begin. . . .'

He ran out of steam and sat there gazing in silence. Louis helped himself to some potatoes, and that set Leo off again.

'What do you know about the world?' he exclaimed bitterly. 'I never went to the university, but I have spent years thinking. Thinking. Since leaving the bank I've done nothing but think, my head's bursting with it, and what are you trying . . . what are you trying to . . . what's the good . . . leave me in peace with all that.'

But Louis was eating a lettuce leaf, Leo subsided and calmed down, everything calmed down, Katasia closed the sideboard door, Fuchs asked what the thermometer reading was because it was so hot, Kulka passed some plates to Katasia, somebody said something about the King of Sweden, the conversation shifted to Scandinavia, and from there to T.B. and injections. The table was now much emptier, nothing was on it but tea or coffee cups, the bread-basket, and folded napkins, only Leo had not folded his napkin yet. I sleepily drank tea, nobody moved, the chairs had been pushed back a bit and we had arranged ourselves more comfortably on them, Leo picked up a newspaper, and Kulka sat as still as a statue. She did that every so often, sitting perfectly still, empty and expressionless, only to wake up as suddenly as the plop of a stone falling into the water. Leo had a wart with some hairs on it on his hand. He examined it, took a toothpick, stroked the hairs with it, examined it again, sprinkled some salt on the hairs and went on looking at it. A smile appeared on his face, and he hummed tri-li-li-lee.

Lena's hand appeared on the tablecloth near her cup. A continuous, uninterrupted flow of minuscule events, like the croaking of frogs in a pond, a swarm of flies, a swarm of stars, in which I floated as in a cloud that enclosed and obliterated me and carried me along in its course. The ceiling was full of archipelagos and peninsulas, dots and damp-stains, all the way to the white desert over the venetian blind ... a countless multitude of trivialities perhaps related to those that interested Fuchs and me, with our little lumps of earth, sticks, etc., and perhaps also related in some way to Leo's trivialities. How could one tell? Perhaps I supposed all this only because I was reduced to triviality myself. I felt so trivial.

Katasia put the ashtray in front of Lena.

That mouth, the cold, hideous, darting and gliding movement of that mouth. Stop, don't, take it away, and the ashtray and the springs of the bed and the leg on it. . . . Silence, a black abyss, a turbulent void. And in the midst of the turbulence (Katasia having withdrawn) there suddenly loomed an irresistible, shining constellation of mouths, with two mouths unquestionably related to each other.

I lowered my eyes, and again saw nothing but a little hand on the tablecloth, a double mouth with double lips, innocent and yet corrupt, pure and yet evil and darting, I gazed at it intently, gasping for breath, whereupon the whole place suddenly started swarming with hands, Leo's and Fuchs's and Kulka's and Louis's, a whole multitude of hands were being agitated in the air. What on earth could this be? It was a wasp. A wasp had flown into the room. It flew out again, and the hands subsided. The wave receded and calm returned, leaving my mind full of all those hands, and Leo said to Lena:

'Multiple adventure, pray papass the inflammable phosphorus to your papa.' He wanted the matches.

'Multiple adventure' was one of the many strange things he called his daughter; others were 'dear donkins' or 'dallying darling'; Kulka made some camomile tea, Louis read the newspaper, Fuchs finished his tea, Louis laid the newspaper aside, Leo stared straight ahead of him, and I sat there wondering whether all that agitation of hands had been because of the wasp or because of that hand on the table. Strictly speaking, of course, there was no doubt that it had been because of the wasp. But what guarantee was there that the wasp had not been merely a pretext for a general raising of hands in connivance with Lena's? Ambiguity lay everywhere, and (who could tell) perhaps extended also to Katasia's and Lena's mouths, as well as to the hanged sparrow and the bit of wood. I was wandering on the periphery. Under the light of the dining-room lamp the trees lay dark on the other side of the road. Sleep. The cork on the bottle. The bit of cork stuck to the mouth of the bottle detached itself and advanced towards me. . . .

IV

NEXT day turned out to be dry, bright, sparkling, but distracted; small, round, chubby, immaculate white clouds kept floating along out of the blue of the sky, and it was impossible to concentrate. I plunged into my work; after the excesses of the previous evening I felt ascetic, severe with myself, hostile to any form of eccentricity. Was I to go and have another look at the bit of wood and see whether there was anything new, particularly after Fuchs's discreet hint at dinner that we had spotted it? I was prevented from doing so by a sense of revulsion against the whole vaguely abnormal business, it was as distasteful as the result of an abortion. So, with my head in my hands, I concentrated on my books—particularly as I felt certain that Fuchs would be going to have a look for me. His interior void was bound to take him there, though he refrained from mentioning the subject which, so far as we were concerned, was exhausted. So I sat there bending over my books while he fussed and fidgeted round the room. But finally off he went. In due course he came back, and as usual Katasia brought up our lunch. But he did not touch on the subject until nearly four o'clock, after his afternoon nap. Then, lying on his bed, he said:

'Come along, there's something I want to show you.'

I did not answer. I wanted to humiliate him, and the best way of doing so was just to ignore him. This worked, he fell silent and dared not insist, but the minutes passed and I started shaving, and eventually I said:

'Is there anything new?'

'Yes and no,' he replied.

When I had finished shaving he said:

'Come along and I'll show you.'

We went out and made our way to the wall, taking precautions as before in relation to the house, which again gazed at us out of all its windows, and we looked at the bit of

50

wood. You could feel the heat coming off the wall, as well as a smell of urine or apples, and just to one side there was a drainage ditch and some yellowed grasses. . . . Remoteness, detachment, life apart in a hot, buzzing silence. The bit of wood was hanging from its string exactly as before.

'Look at that,' Fuchs said, pointing to a pile of rubbish behind the open door of the hut. 'Do you see?'

'No, I don't. I can't see anything.'

'You can't see anything?'

'No.'

There he stood, boring both himself and me.

'Look at that pole,' he said.

'What about it?'

'Did you notice it yesterday?'

'I may have done.'

'Was it exactly like that yesterday? Is it still in the same position?'

He was bored, and had no illusions about it. There he stood, exuding the fatalism of a man irrevocably self-condemned to boredom, and the situation could not have been more insane and futile.

'Try and remember,' he insisted, and I knew he did so only out of boredom, which bored me. A yellow ant advanced along the broken pole. The stalks of a weed growing in a crevice on top of the wall formed a very elegant design against the open sky. No, I did not remember, how could I possibly remember? The pole might be in the same position as the day before or it might not. My attention was caught by a small yellow flower.

Fuchs stood there in front of me and refused to give up. The worst of it was that the futility of our boredom at that isolated spot was superimposed on the futility of those so-called signs which were not signs. The whole thing was too stupid for words. There were two futilities, and we were in between them. I yawned. Fuchs said:

'Look what it's pointing to.'

'What is it pointing to?'

'Katasia's room.'

It was indeed pointing directly to her little bedroom next to the kitchen in the outhouse.

'Good heavens alive.'

'Exactly. If it hasn't been moved since yesterday, it means nothing at all, it's completely immaterial, but if it has been moved, it must have been to guide us towards Katasia. Someone must have taken my hint at dinner that we were on the trail and come here during the night and pointed the pole towards her room. It's like another arrow. He knew we would come back to see whether there was some new sign.'

'But what makes you sure the pole has been moved?'

'I can't be sure, but it rather looks to me as if it has. There's a mark in the sawdust that suggests it was in a different position yesterday. And look at those three stones—and those three pegs, and those three grass stalks that have been pulled out, and those three buttons that must have come from a saddle. Don't you see?'

'What?'

'They form a sort of series of triangles pointing towards the pole, as if someone were trying to draw our attention to it. Don't you see that they form a kind of pattern leading to the pole? Surely that means. . . . But what do you think?'

I tore my eyes away from the yellow ant which was appearing and disappearing among the harness, going now right and now left, now forward and now back. I was hardly listening, I was listening with only one ear, how foolish, pitiful and humiliating was all this excitement about a lot of odds and ends lying under a wall, to say nothing of poor Fuchs's red, rejected face and fish-like eyes. I started arguing. Who on earth would have taken the trouble to leave clues so tenuous as to be practically invisible? How could we have been expected to notice that the pole had been moved? Only a person not quite right in the head could have. . . . He interrupted.

'And what,' he said, 'leads you to suppose that it was someone who was not quite right in the head? And how do you know how many clues he may have left for us? We may have discovered only about one per cent.'

He made a gesture embracing the house and garden.

'The place may be swarming with clues.'

We stood there motionless. I noticed a wrinkled patch of earth, and a cobweb. It was obvious that we were not going to leave things where they stood. What else were we to do but follow the trail? I picked up a piece of broken brick, examined it, put it back again, and said:

'Well, what are we going to do about it? Explore where the pole is pointing to?'

He smiled, embarrassed.

'We've got to. You realize that yourself. To set our minds at rest. Tomorrow's Sunday, it's her day off. We must search her room and see if there's anything there. If there isn't, at least we shall be able to stop bothering our heads about it.'

I stared at the rubbish (and so did he) as if scrutinizing the slight but repulsive disfigurement of a gliding lip, and indeed the rubbish, the swing-bar, the harness, straps and other odds and ends lying about seemed to be vibrating and exuding a sinister atmosphere of perversion . . . also there were the ashtray and the springs of the bed and the half closing and half opening of Lena's mouth and, as she was involved, everything vibrated and boiled and seethed, which frightened me, for, I said to myself, here we are about to act, and by acting we shall create reality . . . and we are going to bring this pole into it, all this rubbish here will bring me nearer to that mouth . . . and I felt pleased, for now, I said to myself, we are going to act, get to the bottom of the mystery, search Katasia's room, solve the enigma, clear it up for good, or banish it to the chimaeras of the night.

In spite of everything I felt better. We walked back along the gravel path like two detectives. Working out all the details of our project would enable me to hold out honourably till next day. Dinner passed off quietly, my field of vision was more than ever restricted to the tablecloth, I had greater and greater difficulty in raising my eyes and looking at the company, I just gazed at the tablecloth and Lena's little hand. Today it was calmer and more relaxed, it hardly trembled at all (though that might point to her having moved the pole). As for the other hands, Leo's, for instance, was asleep, Louis's was erotically non-erotic, and Kulka's was as red as a beetroot. The small red hand at the end of her fat, witch's arm made me more and more uneasy, and my uneasiness was further increased by the sight of the area of her elbow, where redness changed to blue and violet gulfs that gave warning of other concealed zones. Involved, complicated patterns of hands, similar to the involved, complicated patterns on the ceiling, the walls, everywhere. Leo stopped tapping the table, he took one finger of his left hand in two of his right and carefully examined it while a dreamy smile spread over his face. Meanwhile conversation continued at a higher level, higher than that of the hands, though I picked up only a few snatches every now and then. Several different subjects were discussed, and at one point Louis, addressing himself to his father-in-law, asked him to assume that ten soldiers were drawn up in single file. How long did he think it would take to exhaust all the possible permutations and combinations of their marching order, supposing, for instance, that No. 3 took the place of No. 1, and so on and so forth, and assuming that only one change was made a day?

Leo considered the problem.

'About three months?' he suggested.

'No, 10,000 years,' Louis replied. 'It has been calculated.'

'Good gracious me,' said Leo. 'Good gracious me.'

He fell silent, motionless and bristling. The word 'permutations' used by Louis suggested all the permutations and combinations going on in my own mind, in fact I was drowning in them at that moment, and Louis's use of the phrase could be regarded as a strange coincidence—did it not 'almost' amount to an open expression of my uneasiness? How many 'almosts' had I not come across like that? I also had to take into account the circumstance that the reason why this soldier business made such an impact on me was that it seemed to be connected with what was going on in my own mind, and that thus the coincidence was partly (oh, that partly) created by myself, and that that was why I had picked on it instead of on a lot of other things which had been said on which I might equally well have picked. Thus the dreadful, baffling, bewildering thing was that I could never be sure to what extent I was myself the creator of the permutations and combinations taking place all round me. How quickly the thief feels the policeman's eye upon him. When one considers the fantastic quantity of sounds and shapes that impinge upon one at each and every moment of one's life, what is easier than to combine two and two into a pattern where none exists? For a moment the thought surprised me like a wild beast in a dark forest, but then it was swallowed up again in the chaos of seven people talking and eating. Dinner was still going on, and Katasia put the ashtray in front of Lena.

'Clear it all up and get to the bottom of it all.' But I did not believe that an inspection of Katasia's bedroom would throw light on anything whatever. All the same, our plan for next day made the strange relationship between two mouths, two towns, two stars, more tolerable. And was it really so strange, after all, for one mouth to lead to another since everything always led to something else? There was always something behind everything, behind Lena's hand there was Louis's, behind that cup there was a glass, behind that line on the ceiling there was an island, the world was like a moving screen that led you on from one partial revelation to another, it was playing with me as if with a balloon.

Suddenly there was a sharp crack, as if someone had hit something with a stick. It wasn't a loud noise, but it was strange enough to stand out from the other noises. What could it have been? A kind of 'now it's coming' feeling flashed through my head. I froze and held my breath. 'Phantom, show thyself.' But the sound vanished into time, nothing happened, perhaps only a chair had creaked, it had been nothing at all.

Nothing at all. Next day was a Sunday, the day that disturbs the ordinary course of our lives. Katasia woke me as usual, and stayed leaning over me for a moment out of pure good will, but it was Kulka who made the bed and did the room. Moving around with duster in hand, she told me that they had used to have a very attractive ground-floor flat in a comfortable villa at Drohobycz, and that she had used to let rooms there with or without full board, and then they had had a comfortable third-floor flat at Pultusk for six years, where in addition to her lodgers she sometimes had as many as six regular customers for meals, generally more or less elderly gentlemen, each with his own little complaints and fads, one always had to have his special bottle and another his special soup, and another could eat nothing acid, in the end she had had to give it up, it got too much for her, and she told the old gentlemen so, and you should have seen the state of despair they were in, 'My dear good lady,' they had said, 'who will look after us now?' and 'that's just it,' she had replied, 'I put too much of myself into it, do you want me to work myself to death?' Particularly as she had had to look after Leo all her life, and you have no idea what that means, there's always something he needs, I don't know what he'd do without me, I've always given him his breakfast in bed, always, but fortunately that's what I'm like, I can't stand having nothing to do, I'm busy from morning to night, and being busy doesn't mean you have no pleasure in life, every now and then I go and see friends or they come and see me, and do you know, Leo's cousin on his mother's side is married to a Count Koziebrodzki, yes, a Count Koziebrodzki, and when Leo married me his family turned up their noses, and Leo was so afraid of the countess that for two years he didn't introduce me, but I said to him 'Don't be afraid, Leo, I'll stand up to her,' and one day I read in the paper that there was going to be a charity ball and that Countess Koziebrodzka was on the organizing committee, but I didn't say anything about that to Leo, I just told him we were going to a ball, and I spent a whole fortnight secretly getting ready for it—two tailors, a hairdresser, a masseuse and a chiropodist, and Tela lent me some jewellery, and when Leo saw me it took his breath away, but I was as cool as a cucumber, and when we went in the band was playing and I took him by the arm and marched him straight up to the countess. And what do you think happened then? Just imagine it, she turned her back on me. How insulting can one be? 'Leo,' I said, 'your cousin is an arrogant so-and-so,' and spat. But he didn't say a word, that's what he's like, he talks and talks, but when it comes to the point he either does nothing or he's just evasive. But then, when we moved to Kielce and I went in for jam-making, people used to

56

come from miles around and order my jam months in advance.

She stopped, and went on with her dusting as silently as if she had never opened her mouth. So deep was the silence that Fuchs got embarrassed and asked her what had happened next.

She said that one of her lodgers at Pultusk had had T.B. and had to be given cream three times a day. 'In the end it made you feel quite sick,' she said, and walked straight out of the room.

What did this mean? What lay behind it? And what lay behind that glass I had noticed the evening before on the table near the window in the drawing-room, with two reels of cotton beside it? Why had it caught my eye as I passed? Was there really anything curious about it? Should I go down and have a look and make sure? Fuchs also must have been secretly watching, examining, pondering, for he too was very dispersed, stupidly dispersed, but he did not have even one per cent as much excuse as I had, for Lena was going round inside me like my bloodstream.

I could not help feeling that it was she who was behind all this, that she was aiming it all at me, that she was making shy, surreptitious advances. I could almost imagine her wandering about the house, drawing shapes on the ceiling, altering the position of the pole, hanging up the little bit of wood, arranging things in symbolic patterns, creeping along the walls and in the corners. Lena, Lena, making her way towards me and perhaps imploring my aid. . . . What absolute rubbish! Yes, of course it was absolute rubbish, but on the other hand was it conceivable that there was nothing whatever in common between those two anomalies, the mouths on the one hand and all those strange signs on the other? Could it be a pure figment of the imagination? It was absurd, of course, but could the tension caused in me by the contamination of Lena's mouth by Katasia's be nothing but a chimaera?

Fuchs and I dined alone with Kulka, for Lena had gone out with her husband to see some friends, Leo was out playing bridge, and Katasia, whose day off it was, had disappeared immediately after lunch.

57

Dinner was spiced with an endless flow of talk from Kulka (a phenomenon evidently connected with Leo's absence). The lodgers this and the lodgers that and the lodgers the other, all her life, you have no idea, and what with getting meals and making beds and one thing after another all day long, and one day somebody had to have an enema, and something went wrong with the stove in one of the rooms, can you imagine it. I was hardly listening, but I heard her telling a story about a lodger who evidently tried to take a woman to his room, and there was another who stacked empty bottles behind his bed almost to the day of his death . . . 'I told her not to be silly, she knew quite well where the shawl was. . . . I'm made of flesh and blood, after all, I had worked myself to the bone, I couldn't stand it any longer, and ended by making myself ill. . . . Would you suppose such behaviour possible? Such dirtiness is really too much to put up with. . . .' Her little eyes followed all that we ate, she leant with her bust against the table, the rough skin near her elbow turned a pinky violet just as the patches or warts on the principal gulf on the ceiling turned into a pale, yellowish island. . . . 'But for me they would have died . . . sometimes when he groaned during the night . . . then Leo was transferred and we took. . . .' She was like the ceiling, behind her ear there was a kind of big wart, and there the forest of her hair began, first two or three little ringlets and then the forest proper, thick, greyish-black, twisting and coiling, with wisps here and curls there, and farther on a smooth, sloping area. The skin at the back of the neck was very white and delicate, and there was a mark that looked as if it might have been made by a finger-nail and a kind of reddish patch, and under the shoulder at the edge of the blouse a kind of faded, used-up area began but promptly disappeared under her clothes, continuing underneath that blouse of hers to other indentations and protuberances below. She was like the ceiling. . . . 'When we lived at Drohobycz . . . tonsillitis, then rheumatism and stones in the bladder'. . . . She was like the ceiling, with its zones, islands and archipelagos, elusive, incalculable and inexhaustible. After dinner we waited for her to go to bed, and at about ten o'clock we got to work.

58

The phenomena ensuing from our activity?

We had no trouble opening the door of Katasia's little room. We knew that she always left the key on the ivy-covered window-sill. Our difficulty was of another kind. We could not be sure that whoever it was who was pulling our leg—assuming that someone was pulling our leg—was not watching us from some secret hiding-place, waiting to pounce on us and denounce our nefarious activities when he caught us red-handed. So we could not be too careful. We spent a long time wandering about trying to find out if anyone was spying on us, but the house, the windows, the garden, lay quietly in the night, which had been invaded by thick, woolly clouds between which a sickle moon darted rapidly. The dogs chased each other in the bushes. We were terrified of making fools of ourselves. Fuchs showed me a small box which he was carrying.

'What's in it?'

'A frog. A live frog. I caught it today.'

'What for?'

'If we're caught we can say it was a practical joke, we were going to put it in her bed.'

His red and white fish-face that Drozdowski couldn't stand. But the frog was a bright idea. I had to admit that its damp slipperiness went well with Katasia's mouth, so much so that it made me feel uneasy, particularly as the frog was not so very far in my mind from the sparrow. Sparrow and frog, frog and sparrow. Didn't something lay behind that? Didn't it mean something?

'Let's go and have a look at the sparrow. It's too early to start yet in any case,' Fuchs said.

Off we went. Among the bushes and the trees there was the same shadow, the same smell. We approached the spot, but our eyes were defeated by the darkness, or rather the innumerable varieties of darkness, that confused everything; there were black, yawning caverns as well as all sorts of other cavities and spheres and different levels all contaminated by a kind of half life, and the whole was plunged into a sort of resistant, inhibiting, viscous fluid. I had a pocket lamp with me, but felt I must not use it. The sparrow could not have been more than six feet away straight in front of our noses, we could see the place but could not make it out, for it was absorbed by the overriding sense of inhibition as well as by the darkness, but finally it emerged, a dark blob no bigger than a pear, hanging from its string.

'There it is.'

In the silent darkness the frog that was with us drew attention to itself. Not that it croaked, but its existence, revealed by that of the sparrow, made itself felt. We were with it and it was with us, communing and fraternising with the sparrow in the avian-batrachian realm, and that reminded me of a darting and gliding lip. The frog-sparrow-Katasia trio impelled me towards the latter and transformed the dark cavern of the bushes into a mouth equipped with that odd, convulsive lateral movement. It was both exciting and repugnant. I stayed there motionless. Fuchs muttered: 'There's nothing new,' and began moving away, and when we got back to the road the night sky was overhead, and the moon suddenly shone out brightly from the midst of a mass of silvery-edged clouds. I felt a crazy need for action, the clean wind of purifying action. I was ready for anything.

The action on which we embarked, alas, could hardly have been more pitiable and pathetic—two petty conspirators with a frog, following the direction in which a pole was pointing. Once more we took in the scene, the house, the slender, white-washed tree-trunks, the deeper shadow of the bigger trees in the background, and the open space of the garden. I groped for the key under the ivy on the window-sill and found it. We inserted it in the lock and lifted the door on its hinges slightly to prevent it from creaking. At this point the frog in the box lost importance and receded into the wings. But as soon as the door was open the cavity of the low little room, from which there emerged a musty, stale smell, combined with that of washing, bread and dried herbs—this cavity belonging to Katasia excited me, her disfigured mouth loomed alluringly before me, and I had to be careful not to let Fuchs notice how hard I was breathing.

He went in with the frog and the pocket lamp while I stayed on guard by the half-open door.

The dim light of the pocket lamp, which Fuchs had

wrapped in a cloth, ran along a bed, a cupboard, a small table, a big basket, and a shelf, revealing in its course new places, things, corners, articles of clothing, dusters and bits of rag, a broken comb, a small mirror, a plate with some coins on it, a bar of soap; a whole succession of things appeared one after the other as if in a film, while the clouds followed each other outside—I, standing in the doorway, was in between the two processions. Though every single thing in the room separately and individually belonged to her, it was only collectively that they created Katasia's presence, a kind of secondary or *ersatz* presence, that I was violating, slowly violating, through Fuchs with his pocket lamp. I was myself laterally displaced standing there on guard at the door. The wandering patch of light sometimes darted about and sometimes rested thoughtfully on something for a moment, only to set off again on its meddlesome, leering, indecent quest for dirt—because that is what we expected and what we were looking for. Dirt, dirt. And the frog was still in its box on the table, where Fuchs had put it.

The dirty comb with teeth missing, the broken pocket mirror, the thin, damp towel, were the worldly possessions of a poor, ingenuous, innocent, decent, domestic servant, partly urbanised but still a peasant at heart, whom we were subjecting to an inquisition in search of some lurking, perverse guilt, of which there was no trace in this mouth-like cavity. We were groping for a corruption, a perversity, a wickedness that must be somewhere here. Fuchs's pocket lamp revealed a big photograph behind the cupboard with Katasia emerging from the frame. Katasia, oh, wonder of wonders, with a perfectly normal mouth, a decent, honest, peasant mouth.

The face was much younger and more rounded, and Katasia was in her Sunday best, a smart, low-necked dress, sitting on a bench under a palm tree behind which you could see one end of a ship, and she was holding the hand of an honest, moustached working man wearing a stiff collar, and there was a pleasant smile on her face.

Sometimes, when we wake suddenly in the night, we could swear that the window was on the right and the door behind our head, but a single clue, a gleam of light from the window or the ticking of a watch, is sufficient to make everything fall back into its proper place. What now? Reality imposed itself on us like a flash, everything returned to normal as on a call to order. Katasia was an honest respectable servant girl who had suffered an injury to her upper lip in a road accident. And we were a couple of lunatics.

I looked at Fuchs, feeling utterly abashed. In spite of everything he was still searching, the pocket lamp was still nosing about, and it revealed an open account book on the table, some stockings and some pious pictures, Christ and the Virgin Mary holding a bunch of flowers. But what was the point? Why be obstinate? Why not admit our total defeat?

'Come on,' I muttered. 'Let's get out of here.'

All suggestion of indecency had fled from the things on which the lamp rested; it was the light that it cast on them that was indecent now. By our searching and probing we were sullying only ourselves. In that little room we were like two lascivious apes. Fuchs looked at me with a mechanical little smile and went on flashing his torch about at random. Obviously his mind was a blank, he was as empty as a man who has lost everything but his shirt and trousers and nevertheless continues on his way, and his failure with Drozdowski doubled up on his present failure, and the two combined into a single failure of unique proportions. With a smile that had become a brothel smile, the smile of a voyeur, he inspected Katasia's clothes, her suspenders, her reel of cotton, her dirty stockings, her knick-knacks, and I, standing in the shadow, watched him; he was only face-saving, getting his own back by his own indecency on what had ceased to be indecent. He went on with his probing, the patch of light flitted round the comb, and then round the heel of a shoe, but it was useless, there was nothing, nothing whatever, to be discovered, the whole thing was utterly pointless and slowly collapsed like a parcel after the string has been cut. The things on which the torch alighted were neutral and our sensuality died. The disastrous moment was rapidly approaching when we should have no idea what to do next.

But then I noticed something.

It might have been nothing at all, but it might equally well have been something. Most likely it was nothing at all, but. . . .

The light of the torch was resting on a needle. The only strange thing about it was that it was stuck into the middle of the table.

This would have been hardly worthy of notice if I had not previously spotted a slightly more surprising thing, a nib stuck into a lemon-rind. When Fuchs spotted the needle I took his hand and directed the torch to the nib, for the sole purpose of justifying our continued presence here by the semblance of a search.

Then the patch of light darted about in lively fashion again and a few moments later revealed something else: a nail-file stuck into a cardboard box on the chest of drawers. I had not previously noticed it, and the ray of light held it as if asking: What do you say to that?

The nail-file, the nib, and now the needle. The lamp was now like a dog that had picked up a scent, it sprang from object to object, and we discovered two similar phenomena: two safety-pins stuck into a cardboard box. That didn't amount to very much either, but nevertheless in our sad plight it provided a pretext for further action. The lamp got to work again, flitting about and probing. Then we discovered something else, a nail stuck in the wall; the only strange thing about it was that it was stuck into the wall only about an inch or so above the floor. But this was not really strange enough, and illuminating it by the light of the torch really seemed going too far. After that we found nothing at all. We went on looking, but a sort of decomposition set in in the stuffy little hole of a room. Our search petered out, and the lamp stopped flitting about.

Fuchs opened the door, and we began our withdrawal. But just before we left he once more directed the lamp at Katasia's mouth. I was leaning against the window-ledge and felt a hammer under my hand, and I muttered 'a hammer', no doubt associating it with the nail stuck in the wall. But so what? Let's be off. We carefully closed the door behind us and put the key back in its place. 'How windy it is up there,' Fuchs muttered under the vault of scurrying clouds. He was a useless, irritating idiot, and what was I doing with him here? But I had only myself to blame. The house rose in front of us, the pine-trees on the other side of the road did the same, the young trees in the garden were drawn up in ranks—it reminded me of a dance when the music suddenly stops and the couples are left standing, it was stupid.

What was I to do next? Go up to bed? I felt finished, afflicted by a kind of total exhaustion, plunged into a universal debility. I did not even have any feelings left.

Fuchs turned towards me and was just going to say something when the silence was shattered by the sound of violent, sonorous blows.

I froze. The noise was coming from the other side of the house, the road side. It sounded as if somebody were striking something with a big hammer. The blows were heavy, rhythmical, delivered with a maximum of effort and fury—so startling in the silence of the night that they seemed not to belong to this world. Was this aimed at us? We dashed towards the wall as if these hammer-blows, which fitted in with nothing around us, were aimed at us.

On they went. I crept round the corner and had a look, and then seized Fuchs by the sleeve. It was Kulka.

She was in her dressing-gown. Between the long, flapping sleeves she was raising a big hammer or axe and bringing it down on a tree-stump or block of wood. There was a frenzied expression on her face. What was she doing? Was she knocking something in? But what? What was the meaning of this desperate, crazy knocking in of things . . . that we had just left behind in Katasia's room and was now raging here unbridled?

The small hammer that I had touched with my elbow just before leaving Katasia's room had grown enormous, the pins, needles, nibs and nails stuck into things suddenly assumed gigantic proportions. I rejected this idea as absurd almost as soon as it struck me, but at that very moment the sound of other blows came from inside the house, from somewhere upstairs, from the first floor, they were quicker and sharper, providing a corroboratory accompaniment and making my head burst. Panic raged in the night, madness, it was like an earthquake. Wasn't this knocking coming from Lena's room? I tore myself away from Fuchs and rushed into the house and up the stairs. Was it Lena?

But while I was dashing up the stairs the noise abruptly stopped. I stopped on the first floor, panting for breath. The din was over and all was quiet. It actually occurred to me that it would be a good idea for us to calm down and go quietly back to our room. But Lena's door, the third along the corridor, was facing me, and inside me the din was still going on. Hammering, needles, nails, hammering, hammering, hammering, hammering on the door of Lena's room and battering my way in. I started hammering on the door with my fist with all my strength.

Silence.

It struck me like a flash that if the door opened I should start shouting 'Burglar!' at the top of my voice to justify my behaviour. But nothing happened and everything remained quiet, there was nothing to be heard. I hurriedly tiptoed away and went downstairs again. Here all was quiet too, and nobody was around. There was no sign of Fuchs or Kulka. That nothing had happened when I hammered at Lena's door was easy to explain, they must still be out, the noise cannot have been coming from their room. But what had happened to Fuchs? And Kulka? I walked round the house, keeping close to the wall so as to be invisible from the windows, but the madness had disappeared without trace. The trees and the gravel paths lay under the scurrying moon, and that was all. But where was Fuchs? It would not have taken very much to make me sit down and weep.

Then I noticed a light from a room on the first floor, and it was their room, Lena's and Louis's.

So they had been there all the time and had heard my hammering. Why hadn't they opened the door? What was I to do? Once more I was at a total loss, at a dead end. Was I to go back to our room, undress and go to bed? Hide somewhere and watch? Burst into tears? The curtains of their room were not drawn, the light streamed out . . . and . . .

right opposite on the other side of the fence there was a big pine-tree . . . with closely growing branches. If I climbed it I should be able to see inside. This was a rather eccentric idea, but its eccentricity fitted in with what had been going on before. And what else was there for me to do?

The din and confusion of it all made the idea obvious to me, as obvious as the tree that was straight in front of my nose, and there was nothing else there. So I went out on to the road, made my way to the tree, and started shinning up the rough and prickly trunk. Advancing on Lena, making my way to Lena . . . the echo of my hammering on her door was still inside me, and here I was advancing on her again . . . and everything else—Katasia's room, her photograph, the needles and the nails, Kulka's hammering, faded in the face of battering my way through to Lena. Cautiously I climbed higher and higher, from branch to branch.

It wasn't easy, it took a long time, and my curiosity grew frantic. I wanted to see her . . . her with him. . . . What was I going to see? After the din, the hammering, what was I going to see? The trembling that had overcome me outside her door revived again inside me. What was I going to see? At last I could see the ceiling, the upper part of the wall, and the lamp.

And then at last I saw them.

I was staggered.

He was showing her a teapot. Yes, a teapot.

She was sitting on a small chair by the table, with a bath towel round her shoulders like a shawl. He was standing in his waistcoat and shirtsleeves, holding a teapot in his hands and showing it to her, and she was looking at it. She said something, and then he did.

A teapot.

I had been ready for anything, but not for a teapot. Enough is enough, and this was the last straw. There is a sort of excess about reality, and after a certain point it can become intolerable. After so many things that I could no longer enumerate, the nails, the frog, the sparrow, the bit of wood, the pole, the nib, the lemon peel, the cardboard box, etc., the chimney, the cork, the arrow on the ceiling, the gutter, the hand, the hands, etc., etc., the lumps of earth, the bed springs, the ashtray, bits of wire, toothpicks, pebbles, the chicken, warts, gulfs, islands, needles, etc., etc. *ad nauseam,* here was this teapot popping up like a jack-in-the-box without rhyme or reason, extra, gratis, and for nothing, like a fifth wheel on a coach, an ornament of chaos. I had had enough. My throat contracted. This teapot was too much, and I could not swallow it. I had had enough. There was nothing for it but to pack up and go home.

She removed the towel from her shoulders, and I received the shock of her nudity, her breasts and shoulders. She started taking off one of her stockings, her husband spoke again and she answered, she took off the other stocking, and he put his foot on a chair to unlace his shoe. I stayed there, thinking that now I was going to find out what she was like when she was with him in the nude, whether she was vile, sensual, elusive, saint-like, sensitive, pure, faithful, fresh, alluring, or perhaps coquettish. Or perhaps only easy. Or deep. Or perhaps merely resigned and disillusioned, or bored and indifferent, or ardent and full of wiles, or angelic, shy or shameless. At last I was going to find out. Her thighs appeared, first one and then the other, I was going to find out, at last I was going to find out something, at last something definite was going to be revealed to me.

The teapot.

He picked it up from the table, put it on a shelf, and then walked towards the door.

The light went out.

I went on looking though I could not see, I went on gazing blindly into the pitch-black darkness. What were they doing? What were they doing and how were they doing it? Anything whatever might be going on. There was nothing on their part that was inconceivable, the darkness was impenetrable, she might be timid or reluctant or amorous or shameless or perhaps none of these things, indeed abomination and horror might be taking place, but I should never know. I climbed down and dropped gently to the ground, thinking that, though she was a blue-eyed child, she might also be a monster—a childlike, blue-eyed monster. How was one to tell?

I should never know anything about her, never.

67

I brushed myself down and walked slowly back towards the house. Tremendous activity was going on in the sky, great herds were chasing each other across it, black in the middle and shining white at the edges. The moon was hurrying too. It glided, was obscured and extinguished and then emerged immaculate again, the sky was traversed by those two silent, contrary motions. Walking along I wondered whether I should not dismiss the whole thing, shake off the burden, because, as the photograph proved, Katasia's lip defect was due to a purely material cause. So what was the point of it all?

And on top of it there was that teapot.

What was the point of associating Katasia's mouth with Lena's? No, I should not do it again. I should drop the whole thing.

I reached the top step outside the front door. Lena's cat, Dawidek, was sitting on the balustrade. When it saw me it got up and stretched out its back to be stroked. I grabbed it by the throat and started throttling it, wondering why, but it was too late, it happened to me in a flash and I could not help it, I put all my strength into throttling it. Its body hung limp.

Now what was I to do? There I was on the doorstep with a strangled cat in my hands. I had to do something with it, get rid of it, hide it somewhere, but I did not know where. Was I to bury it? Dig a hole in the ground in the middle of the night? Sling it on the road, to make it look as if it had been run over? Dump it in the bushes where the sparrow was? I thought it over, the cat weighed heavily on me, I could not make up my mind, all was quiet. I noticed a young tree tied to a stake by a strong piece of string, it was one of those with whitewashed trunks, I untied the string, made a slip-knot, and looked cautiously all round to make sure I was unobserved (the house had gone to sleep, no one would have believed what a din had been coming from it such a short time before). I remembered that there was a hook on the wall, perhaps for hanging out the laundry. I took the cat there, it was not very far, only about twenty paces, and hung it from the hook. It hung there, like the sparrow and the bit of wood, completing the series. What was I to do now? I was dead-beat, I could hardly stand up, and I was rather afraid of going back to our room, perhaps Fuchs would be there, still awake, and he would ask me questions. But when I quietly opened the door and crept in I saw at once that he was fast asleep. I went to sleep too.

V

KATASIA'S horrified voice, her horrified face right over my head. Just think of it, she was saying, Dawidek has been hanged, hanged from a hook in the garden. Who on earth could have done it? Who on earth could have done such a thing to Lena's cat? This woke me with a start. The cat had been hanged, and I had hanged it. I glanced uneasily at Fuchs's bed, but it was empty. He must already have gone down to see, which would allow me some time to think.

I was as taken aback as if I had not been the strangler. Imagine waking up suddenly and finding yourself in such a situation. Why on earth had I done it? I had had the same feeling of battering my way through to Lena as I had had while hammering on her door. Yes, that was it, strangling her beloved cat had brought me closer to her—though while doing it I had cursed myself for not being able to help it. But why had I hung it from that hook? What idiocy, what blind folly. And to make matters worse, thinking about it while getting dressed and seeing the vague smile on my distorted face in the mirror, I found myself feeling pleasure as well as dismay, pleasure at having brought off a coup. I actually caught myself complacently whispering 'I hanged it'. But what was I to do now? How was I to get out of it? Downstairs they must already be discussing all the possible perpetrators of the deed. Had no one seen me?

It was I who had done it. This shattered me. I had strangled the cat and hung it from a hook, and all I could do was to have breakfast, go downstairs, and pretend to know nothing about it. But why had I done it? There had been such an accumulation of things, so many intertwining threads, Lena, Katasia, the arrows, the hammerings and all the rest of it, the frog or the ashtray would have been enough by themselves, I had been floundering in the chaos, it even occurred to me that the teapot had made me do it, and that I had acted out of sheer excess and superfluity, in other words, that killing the cat had been an extra, one thing too much, just like the teapot. But no, it wasn't true, it had not been connected with the teapot. Then what had it been connected with? I had no time to consider the question further, I had to go downstairs and face the situation which, being still chock-full of the extravagances of the night, was strange enough without that.

So downstairs I went. There was no one around, so they must all be in the garden. Before showing myself on the verandah I looked out of the window from behind the curtain. There was the wall, and the dead cat hanging from the hook, with several people, including Lena, standing round it. Seen from a distance, in perspective like this, there seemed to be something symbolic about the scene. Showing myself on the verandah was no light task, it had all the characteristics of a leap into the dark. If someone had seen me, in a moment or two I should be paralysed with shame, reduced to helpless incoherence. Slowly I walked down the gravel path, the sky was like a vast expanse of white sauce in which the sun was dissolved, it was going to be terribly hot again; what a summer it was. I walked closer, and made out the dead cat more clearly; its tongue was hanging obliquely out of its mouth and its eyes were starting out of their sockets. It would have been better if it had not been a cat, I said to myself, cats are horrible creatures, soft and downy but also liable to howl and scratch and scream, they like being stroked but they also like torturing, they are sweet but they are also monstrous. To gain time, I walked slowly, for I was surprised by the day-time result of my nocturnal deed, which at the time had been hardly visible or distinct from the extravagances of the night. Everybody seemed to be affected by the same slowness, for they were hardly moving. Fuchs was bending forward, scrutinizing the wall and the ground in front of it, which amused me. Lena's sudden and extraordinary beauty took me aback. How beautiful she has got since last night's events, I said to myself in terror.

'Well, what do you make of it?' said Leo, with his hands in his pockets. A wisp of brilliantined hair stood out on his bald head like the pilot of a ship.

I breathed a sigh of relief. No one had seen me. They did not know I had done it.

I spoke to Lena.

'What a nasty shock for you,' I said. 'I'm so sorry.'

I looked at her. She wore a coffee-coloured blouse and a navy blue skirt, and there she stood, withdrawn into herself. Her mouth was soft, and she held her arms close to her sides like a recruit . . . and her feet, nose and ears were too small and too delicate. For a moment this annoyed me. I had savagely and brutally killed her cat, and her little feet were as small as ever.

But my annoyance turned to pleasure, for she herself, if you see what I mean, was too small and delicate in relation to the cat, and she felt ashamed of it for that reason, I could tell. She was too small and delicate for everything, she was just a trifle smaller than she ought to have been, she was useless for anything but love, she was no good for anything else at all, and that was why she felt ashamed of the cat, for she knew that everything connected with her must have an amorous meaning and, though she could not imagine who had killed the cat, she nevertheless felt ashamed of it, for it belonged to her, it was hers.

But it was also mine, because I had strangled it, so it belonged to both of us.

Was I to feel delighted or was I to be sick?

'Do you know anything about this?' Leo asked. 'Did you hear or see anything?'

No, I knew nothing, I had gone out for a walk late last night and when I came back it was well after midnight, I had gone in through the verandah, but could not say whether or not the cat had been hanged at that time. While telling these lies I felt pleasure mounting inside me, pleasure at leading them astray, at being no longer with them but against them, on being on the opposite side to them. As if the cat had put me on the obverse side of the medal and I was now in a realm of hieroglyphics, where occult and mysterious things took place. No, I was no longer with them. The sight of Fuchs, who stopped his laborious search for clues to listen to my lies, made me want to laugh.

It was I who knew the truth, for it was I who had killed the creature.

'Just imagine hanging a cat,' Kulka exclaimed indignantly, and then stopped as if something had happened to her.

Katasia emerged from the kitchen and made her way towards us through the flower beds. Her distorted mouth was approaching the mouth of the cat. As she drew nearer I sensed that she felt she had inside her something related to the cat's mouth, and that gave me a sudden feeling of pleasure, as if it put my cat too on the opposite side. Her lip approached the cat's lip, and dissipated all the doubts her so innocent photograph had put in my mind. She approached with that creepy disfigurement of hers, a strange similarity in lewdness presented itself, and a kind of obscure nocturnal shudder went up my spine. All the time I did not let Lena out of my sight, and oh, my astonishment, my secret emotion, I don't know whether it was pleasure or not, at feeling her shame increase as that distorted mouth approached the cat. Shame is a strange and humbling thing, in fighting off something it draws it down into its own most secret depths, and thus it was that Lena, feeling ashamed of the cat and of the relationship between the lip and the cat, absorbed them into the realm of her most intimate secrets; and thanks to her shame the cat linked up with Katasia's lip like a cog-wheel engaging with another. But my silent cry of triumph was mingled with a groan. By what diabolical miracle could this fresh and innocent beauty absorb such horror and by its shame confirm my imaginings?

Katasia had a box in her hand, the box with the frog.

Good heavens alive, Fuchs must have left it in her room.

'I found this in my room, on the window-ledge,' she announced.

'What is it?' Leo asked.

Katasia removed the lid.

'A frog.'

Leo raised his arms to heaven, but Fuchs intervened with unexpected energy.

'Excuse me,' he said, taking the box from Katasia. 'We'll deal with this later, we'll find the explanation. Now I suggest that we all go to the dining-room. I want to say a few words.

Let us leave the cat as it is, I'll come back and have another look at it later.'

Did the idiot want to go on playing the sleuth?

We walked slowly back towards the house, myself, Kulka, who looked disagreeable and upset and said nothing, and Leo, with his crumpled suit and protruding lock of hair. Louis was at his office and would not be back till the evening. Katasia returned to the kitchen.

'Ladies and gentlemen,' Fuchs began in the dining-room. 'Let us be frank. It's obvious that something is up here.'

All this to forget Drozdowski. It was obvious that he had got his teeth into this now and had no intention of letting go.

'Something is up here,' he went on. 'Witold and I noticed it as soon as we arrived, but it was only an impression, there was nothing positive, only a lot of vague signs and hints, so we couldn't mention it to anybody. But now the time has come for frankness.'

'I was just going to . . .' said Leo, but Fuchs did not let him finish his sentence.

'Excuse me,' he said, and went on to recall the discovery of the hanged sparrow on the day of our arrival. Definitely a thought-provoking phenomenon. He went on to describe the discovery of a kind of arrow on the ceiling of our room. It might have been an arrow and might not. It was impossible to exclude the possibility that it had been an illusion, particularly as the evening before, as we would all remember, we had thought we saw an arrow here on the dining-room ceiling. An arrow or perhaps a rake, self-deception was of course always possible. At all events Witold and he, just for the fun of the thing and out of sheer curiosity, had decided to follow the trail.

He described how it had led us to the bit of wood, described the exact location of the crevice in the wall, and shut his eyes . . . we would all agree . . . the hanging sparrow . . . the hanging bit of wood . . . it was just as if . . . there must be something in it . . . if it had not been exactly in the direction in which the arrow was pointing. . . .

I suddenly felt delighted at the idea of the cat's hanging just like the bit of wood and the sparrow and continuing

74

the series. Leo rose to his feet, he wanted to go and see the bit of wood straight away, but Fuchs would not let him.

'Wait a few minutes,' he said. 'First let me tell you the whole story.'

But it was a pitiful story, he got tangled in a cobweb of suppositions and conjectures and analogies, he visibly weakened, at one point he actually laughed at himself and me. Then he grew serious again and, looking as weary as an aged pilgrim, embarked on a long diatribe about the pole and the direction in which it was pointing. 'What reason was there for us not to follow it up?' he said. 'What harm could it do? Having followed up the direction of the arrow, there was no reason why we should not do the same in the case of the pole. Our aim was no more and no less than to establish facts, and what harm could there be in that? Not that we had the slightest suspicion of Katasia, our aim was merely to establish facts. And, to provide against all eventualities, I took with me a frog in a box, so that if we were caught I could say it was a joke. When we left I forgot it, and that's why Katasia found it there.'

'A frog,' Kulka exclaimed.

He described how we had searched Katasia's room, searched and searched and found nothing. But right at the end, just when we were on the point of giving up and leaving, we had noticed something peculiar. True, it was utterly trivial, utterly trivial, he agreed, but when something was repeated more often than it ought to be, well, we knew what it was like when something was repeated more often than it ought to be. But we must decide for ourselves, he would content himself with a mere enumeration. And he began his enumeration, but oh, so weakly and unconvincingly.

A needle stuck into the table.

A nib stuck into some lemon-rind.

A nail file stuck into a cardboard box.

A safety pin stuck into another cardboard box.

A nail knocked into the wall just above floor-level.

Oh, how this recitation weakened and exhausted him. He breathed deeply, rubbed the corners of his protruding eyes, and stopped, like a pilgrim who has lost his faith. Leo put one leg over another, a gesture that implied impatience. This terrified Fuchs, whose self-confidence, in which he was in any case deficient, had been totally destroyed by Drozdowski. I felt furious at being associated with him in front of all these people. As if my own trouble with my family in Warsaw was not enough. What a kettle of fish. But what could I do about it?

'Needles and lemon rind . . .' Leo grunted.

He had no need to say any more to make us feel like a couple of pitiful beggars scratching about on a refuse heap.

'But wait a moment,' said Fuchs. 'The point is that just when we were coming away you, madam, (he addressed himself to Kulka) were knocking something in. With a hammer. On that tree stump near the little door. Hammering it in with all your strength.'

He looked aside and adjusted his tie.

'I was knocking something in?'

'Yes, you, madam.'

'And what of it?'

'But how can you say that, madam? Don't you see the point I am making? Katasia's room is full of things that have been stuck or knocked into other things, and you too were knocking something into something else.'

'I was doing nothing of the sort, I was only hitting the tree stump.'

Kulka extracted these words from a vast, an infinite, store of patience, the patience of a martyr.

'Lena, darling, please tell them why I was hitting the tree stump.'

Her voice had grown stony and impersonal, and the look in her eyes indicated that she was flying the banner of 'I shall see it through to the end.' Lena withdrew into herself; it was less a movement than the semblance of a movement, she was like a snail or certain kinds of plant, anything that withdraws or rolls itself up to protect itself from contact. She swallowed.

'Lena, tell them the truth.'

'Every now and then . . . mother has a sort of crisis. A sort of nervous crisis . . . it happens every now and then. She

76

picks up anything handy . . . to work it off. If it's glass, she smashes it.'

She was lying. No, she was not. It was both truth and falsehood. Truth because it accorded with the facts, falsehood because the significance of what she said—as I already knew—depended not on its truth but on the fact that it came from her, like the look in her eyes or her perfume. What she said was incomplete, compromised by her charm, it was nervous and, so to speak, remained hanging in the air. Who but her mother could understand the embarrassment of this? So she hastened to translate what Lena had said into the more concrete language of an old woman.

'I'm at it all day long from morning to night all the year round, as you know. You know me, and you know that I'm quiet and patient and well behaved. But sometimes my quietness and patience cracks, and I pick up anything handy.'

She thought for a moment, and then said seriously:

'Anything.'

She could not leave it at that, but shrieked:

'Anything,'

'Darling,' said Leo.

'Anything!' she screamed back at him.

'Yes, anything,' Leo repeated, whereupon she shouted:

'No, not anything. Anything!'

Then she quietened down.

I too sat quietly in my chair.

'But that's very understandable, very understandable indeed,' said Fuchs, falling over himself with politeness. 'It's very understandable indeed with all that work and worry. Nerves, of course, that explains everything. But wasn't there another noise immediately afterwards that seemed to be coming from inside the house, from the first floor?'

'That was me,' Lena announced.

'Yes,' said Kulka with infinite patience. 'As soon as she hears it coming over me, she either comes and holds my arm or bangs things too. It helps to calm me down.'

So everything was being cleared up. Lena added some supplementary details. She had just come home with Louis, and when she heard the noise her mother was making she picked up one of her husband's shoes (he was in the bathroom) and started hitting the table with it, and then a suit-case. So that was that. One after the other the baffling riddles of the night were being stranded on the dry sand of explanation. That did not surprise me, I had been expecting it, but it was very sad all the same. The events through which we had been living dropped from our hands and lay at our feet like sweepings—needles, hammers, and all. I looked at the table and saw a jug on a tray, a crescent-shaped crumb brush, Leo's reading spectacles, and a few other in-different objects, lying there as if they had given up the ghost.

The indifference of these objects was associated with the indifference of these people, which was turning to hostility, as if we were beginning to get on their nerves. But then I remembered the cat, and that strengthened my morale, for in spite of everything a bit of horror remained, with its big open mouth. Also I reflected that, though two noises were now lying helpless on the ground, explained away and im-potent, I had a third up my sleeve, a really alarming and em-barrassing one that was less easy to explain. What would Lena make of my battering on her door?

I interrogated her on the subject. There had been two series of bangs coming from the first floor, had there not? One had followed the other. 'I'm quite sure of what I'm saying because I was near the front door when the second series began. And it was different from the first.'

Battering my way through to her, as I had tried to do during the night. Had I touched a sensitive spot? What would she say? It was like being outside her door and hammering at it all over again. Did she guess who it was? Why had she said nothing about it yet?

'Another noise? Oh, yes, a little later I started knocking again, with my fist on the shutters. My nerves were on edge. I wasn't sure that mother had quietened down.'

She was lying.

Out of shame, suspecting that it had been me? All right, but what about Louis? He had been with her, he must have heard the hammering, why hadn't he opened the door?

'And your husband? Wasn't he with you?'

'No, he was in the bathroom.'

So she had been alone when I started knocking, and she had not opened the door. Perhaps she had guessed that it was I or perhaps she had not, but in any case she knew that the knocking had been meant for her. She had not opened the door because she had been afraid to. And now she was lying, pretending she had done it herself. Oh, triumph, my lie had broken through to hers and we were united in a common lie, and by my lie I had implanted myself in hers.

However, Leo returned to the point.

'But who hanged the cat?' he said.

He pointed out politely that, the noises having been completely explained, there was no point in discussing them further, and in any case he could contribute nothing to the subject as his bridge party had lasted until three a.m. But who had hanged the cat, and why? His insistence was not directed at anyone in particular, but it was ominous and threatening. There was a stubborn expression of his face under the crown of his bald patch. In all good faith and with good reason he wanted to know who had killed the cat. His persistence began to worry me. Kulka quietly interrupted him.

'Leo,' she said.

Supposing she had done it? Supposing she had done it? Of course I was very well aware that I had done it myself, but by saying 'Leo' like that she attracted everyone's attention to herself and Leo's persistence seemed to have attained its object and alighted on her. I had the feeling that in spite of everything she *could* have done it, that if she was capable of battering a tree stump with a hammer in a nervous crisis she was equally capable of a murderous onslaught on a cat. With those short limbs and thick wrists and ankles of hers and that short, thickset body, rich in maternal bounties, she would have been perfectly capable of throttling the cat and then hanging it. It would have been just like her.

'Tri-li-li-lee!'

There was concealed satisfaction in the tune that Leo started humming, but he quickly broke it off. There was something malicious about it.

Had he been pleased that his Kulka had not been able to stand up to the question, that his insistence had struck home, and that she had therefore attracted general attention to herself? So . . . the culprit might have been Leo himself. Of course, why not, he would have been perfectly capable of it. . . . With those bread pellets he made and enjoyed himself so much with, transfixing them with a toothpick, moving them about and arranging them, and the way he hummed and cut apple peelings with his finger nail and spent his time 'thinking' and scheming, why should he be incapable of throttling a cat and hanging it? Of course it was I who had done it, but he *could* have done it. He was perfectly capable of it, just as he was perfectly capable now of taking malicious pleasure in seeing his wife under suspicion. Though he had actually not done it (since I had done it myself), he might very well have hanged the sparrow and the bit of wood.

The mystery of the latter had not been in any way diminished by my killing the cat. They were still hanging as before, like two centres of darkness.

Darkness. I needed it myself, to prolong the night during which I had battered at Lena's door. And Leo perhaps inserted himself into this darkness of mine, for his behaviour hinted at the possibility of licentious sybaritism, secret orgies, haunting the confines of this respectable home—a hypothesis that would not have been so plausible but for the way he quickly cut short his little tune for fear of giving himself away. That tri-li-li-lee of his had been like a whoop of pleasure at his wife's downfall. . . . Was it dawning on Fuchs too that this respectable retired bank manager, this sterling husband and father who never went out except for a game of bridge, was capable of enjoying private pleasures of his own under his wife's eye at the family dining table? If he enjoyed himself playing with bread pellets, why should he not also enjoy himself tracing arrows on the ceiling? To say nothing of other secret vices. He was a thinker, he thought and thought, and he was capable of thinking up a lot of things.

There was a noise, a clatter, a terrible din outside, the whole place shook, it was a passing lorry, a big one with a trailer, the noise faded away again, vanished, the windows stopped rattling and we looked away from them again, but the incident was sufficient to recall the outside world, the world beyond our little group, and I heard the barking of the dogs in the next-door garden, noticed the jug of water on the little table, nothing of the slightest consequence, of course, but this intrusion of the outside world somehow changed the situation and the talk became more disorderly. Somebody said it could not have been a stranger because the dogs would have gone for him, and somebody else remembered that last year there had been thieves in the neighbourhood, and so on and so forth, and so it went on for a long time, but I kept on picking out distant sounds, as if someone were tapping or hitting something somewhere, and a sort of coppery echo like that of a samovar. The dogs barked again, I felt tired and depressed, and then I had the feeling that something was coming up again.

'Who did this to you, darling? Who can it have been?'

It was Kulka with her arms round Lena, they were locked in a firm embrace. This struck me as unpleasant, as if it were aimed at me, and put me on the alert again. But what really put me on my guard was the prolongation of the embrace for a fraction of a second longer than was strictly necessary (which made it excessive and exaggerated).

'Who can have done this to you?' said Kulka, releasing Lena from between her two short arms. 'Who can have done this to you?'

What was she after? Was she aiming at anyone? She was not aiming at Leo, so perhaps she was aiming at me. Yes, at Fuchs and at me. By hugging Lena she was dragging into the light of day all the dark passion that underlay that cat morning. When she said 'who did this to you?' what she meant was 'these two young men who arrived here recently are the obvious suspects.' The implication that the cat was an object of passion gave me pleasure, but danger loomed, I must be on my guard. What was I to say? I hesitated, I was at a loss, my mind was blank, I was at a dead end, at the bottom of a deep, dark pit, but at last I heard Fuchs's voice.

He spoke quite calmly, as if he were thinking aloud, as if what he was saying had no connection with Kulka.

'First the chicken was hanged, then the sparrow, and then the bit of wood,' he said. 'It's always the same act of hanging, though the object changes. And it has been going on for some time, the sparrow stank pretty badly when we found it on the day we arrived.'

Good for Fuchs, he was not such a fool after all. It was a good point, the hangings had begun well before our arrival, so we were beyond suspicion. But what a pity.

'That's perfectly true,' said Leo, and I realized that he too must have suspected us for a time. Conversation sprang to life again. 'Katasia?' said Kulka. 'How could it possibly have been Katasia? What an idea! She's going round like a soul in torment, she's beside herself with grief, she was terribly fond of the cat, she was devoted to it, and I've known her from childhood, and but for all I've done for her. . . .' She went on talking, but she talked much too much and exaggerated as landladies do, and I wondered if she wasn't overdoing it. But I heard the sound of water running from a tap, and what might have been a car starting up.

'Someone must have crept in,' Leo said. 'But to hang a cat? Who on earth would creep in to hang a cat? Who on earth would creep in to hang a cat? And the dogs next door wouldn't have let him.'

My arm ached. I looked out of the window. The young trees, the pines, the sky, the heat. The moulding of the window-frame was made of a different kind of wood. A leaf was sticking to one of the panes. Leo announced that he was going to have a look at the bit of wood and the other clues.

'But perhaps you can see some from here,' said Fuchs.

'I beg your pardon?'

'How can we be sure that there are not other clues in this room that we haven't spotted yet?'

I turned to Lena and said:

'And do you suspect anyone?' She withdrew into her shell.

'I don't think anyone wishes me ill,' she replied.

(This made me realize that I did not wish her ill myself. Oh, to stop living, to die, not to have to go on with it all. What a burden. Death would have been welcome at that moment.)

Leo launched into a pathetic lament.

'How disagreeable, how distasteful, all this is,' he said. 'If only we knew where to begin, but we don't know even that. We haven't got a single hard fact to work on. Whoever it was cannot have come in over the fence, and it cannot have been someone from inside the house either. So who can it have been? It cannot have been either the one or the other, so who can it have been? I feel like sending for the police, but what would be the good of that, the only result would be to set tongues wagging, we should make ourselves a laughing-stock. So we can't even send for the police. But, gentlemen, the point is this, it's not just the matter of the cat. Cat or no cat, there's something strange and abnormal at work, there's a kind of aberration or something in the air, it opens a field for speculation, unlimited speculation, and we are entitled to trust no one and suspect everyone, for who could take an oath that it was not one of us who are quietly sitting here? It's a case of madness, perversion, aberration, the sort of thing that could happen to anyone, me, my wife, Katasia, you gentlemen, my daughter, for if it's an aberration there's no telling, *aberratio fiat ubi vult*, ha, ha, ha, as the saying is, it can happen to anyone anywhere and take any form. But all the same, what a mean and disgusting thing. To think that in my old age, in my own home and in the bosom of my family, I am not able even to be sure of the ground under my feet or in what sort of company I am. To think that I am reduced to being like a lost dog in my own home. To think that I can't trust anyone, that my house has become a lunatic asylum. And to think that all the work and worry of a lifetime, the millions of things I can't count or remember any more, all those years and months and weeks and days and minutes and seconds, that vast inconceivable number of hours, that whole great mountain of hours, each marked by work and worry . . . to think that it should all end in my no longer being able to trust anyone. And I should like to know why. I admit, of course, that it could be said that I am dramatising the whole thing and that a cat is not very important but, gentlemen, it's very disagreeable, very disagreeable indeed, for how can we be sure that the cat is the end of the story and that next time it won't be bigger game? If there's a lunatic in the house, how can we be sure what will happen next? Now, the last thing I want to do is to exaggerate, but how can one's mind be at rest until it has been cleared up? At the mercy of . . . at the mercy of . . . in one's own home at the mercy of. . . .'

'Leo, stop it.'

He looked at Kulka, sadly.

'Stop it,' he said. 'All right, I'll stop it. But I shan't stop thinking. No, I shan't stop thinking.'

'If only you would,' Lena whispered under her breath, and I thought I detected something new in her in the way she did this, something that had not been there before. But how could one tell? How could one tell? I wondered. A car full of people rumbled past, I only caught sight of their heads behind the last bush, the dogs barked, a shutter creaked on the first floor, a child whimpered, there was a general, collective, orchestrated noise from the depths, and on the sideboard there was a bottle and a cork. Would she be capable of killing a child? With that gentle expression of hers? If she did such a thing, it would promptly merge into and harmonize with that expression of hers, and it would be demonstrated that a child murderer could have a gentle expression. How could one tell? The cork and the bottle.

'What's the matter with you?' Leo said irritably. Then he turned to Fuchs and said to him humbly:

'Perhaps you will be able to give us some advice. Let us go and have a look at the arrow and the bit of wood.'

It was hot, the little rooms on the ground floor were stifling at that time of day, you could see the dust in the air, I felt tired and my feet ached, all the doors and windows were open, things kept happening, a bird flew past, there was a universal buzzing and humming, and I heard Fuchs saying: '. . . there I entirely agree with you. At any rate it has been useful to speak out frankly. If anyone sees anything new, he must let us know at once. . . .' Drozdowski, Drozdowski. Everything was struggling slowly out of a glue-pot. It was like someone who has got half his body out of a bog and has struggled to his knees but is going to slide back again at any moment. There were so many details to take into account. . . . I remembered that I had not had breakfast yet. My head ached. I wanted to light a cigarette, and rummaged in my pockets for my matches, but I had forgotten them. There were some at the other end of the table next to Leo. Should I ask him for them or not? I ended by showing him my cigarette, he nodded, stretched out his hand and pushed the box towards me, and I stretched out my hand and took it.

VI

THE CAT was buried on the other side of the fence, in the ditch by the roadside. The job was done by Louis after he came back from his office and had been told everything. He looked disgusted, muttered 'barbarism', put his arms round Lena, hugged her, and went off and buried the creature. It was impossible to settle down to work, of course, so I wandered about. I walked a little way down the road but came back and paced up and down the garden. From a distance, and cautiously, so that nobody should notice, I inspected the pine-tree I had climbed, the tree stump that Kulka had battered, the door of Katasia's room, and the place behind the corner of the house where I had been standing when I heard the knocking coming from the first floor. Hidden somewhere in all these places and things, in the totality of these places and things, lay the path that had led me to strangle the cat. If I could discover the thread running through all these things, I might perhaps find out what had made me do it.

I even found an excuse to go to the kitchen and have another look at Katasia's mouth. But the labyrinth was growing, there was such a proliferation, such a multitude of things and places and events. Is not every pulsation of our lives made up of thousands of millions of tiny fragments? So what can one do? I had absolutely nothing to do. I was unemployed.

I even went to the empty room where I had first seen Lena and her foot on the springs of the bed. On the way back I stopped in the corridor to recall the way a floor-board had creaked during that first night when I went to look for Fuchs. I looked at the arrow on the ceiling, the ashtray, the bit of cork on the neck of the bottle, but idly, with no thoughts in my head, I just looked, feeling weak among all those insignificant trifles, rather like an invalid after a severe illness whose world has shrunk to a beetle or a patch of sunlight; and at the same time I felt like someone trying to re-create his own strange and inexplicable past life (this reminded me of Leo, with his myriads of hours and minutes and seconds, and made me smile).

What was I looking for? What was I looking for? A basic theme, a *Leitmotiv*, an axis, something of which I could take firm hold and use as a basis for reconstructing my personality here? But distraction, not only my own personal, inner distraction, but also that coming from without, from the chaos, profusion and excess of things, preventing me from concentrating. One trifle distracted me from another, everything was equally important and unimportant, I kept approaching things and stepping back again.

The cat. Why had I killed that cat of hers? Gazing at some clumps of earth in the garden, some of those that Fuchs and I had examined while following the direction of the arrow (which I had established with the aid of the broom-handle), I decided that the question would have been easier to answer if my feelings towards her had been less obscure. What were they? I kept asking myself, trampling the grass as I had done on that other occasion. What were they? Love? But what sort of love? Passion? But what sort of passion? How had it come about without my knowing what she was like, what sort of person she was? I still did not know. Looking at the continents, the archipelagos and the nebulae on the bedroom ceiling, I told myself she was obscure, illegible, undecipherable and tantalizing, I could imagine her so many different ways in so many different situations depending on which way I looked at her, I kept losing her and finding her again, turning her this way and that. But (I went on, continuing to spin my thread as I looked carefully at the ground between the house and the kitchen and inspected the young trees tied firmly to their stakes) there could be no denying that I had been sucked into and swallowed up by the vacuum that she was, that it was she and she only. . . . And (I said to myself, gazing at the pattern formed by the bent gutter, the broken one) what did I want of her? Did I want to caress her? Torment her? Humiliate her? Worship her? Did I want to be an angel with her or a brute? Did I want to assault her or take her in

87

my arms? Did I know what I wanted? That was the agony, I did not. I could have raised her chin and gazed into her eyes, or I could have spat in her mouth, I did not know what I wanted. But she weighed on my conscience, she emerged as out of a dream, heavy with a despair that followed her as her long hair would if she let it down. And that made the cat more horrible than ever.

In the course of my wanderings I strolled in the direction of the sparrow, I was plagued by the disproportionate role it played in my mind. It remained perpetually on the side-lines and kept on obtruding itself, though it was impossible to connect it with anything. All the same (I said to myself, sauntering down the baking road and trampling on the dried up grass), it could not be denied that there were certain analogies, even if it was only that there was a certain relation-ship between cats and sparrows, cats ate sparrows, after all. Why was there no escape from the cobweb of relationships?

But all that was secondary. What mattered was that some-thing was advancing steadily into the foreground, assuming greater and greater importance and more insistently obtrud-ing itself. It derived from the fact of the cat that I had not just strangled but hanged.

I had of course hanged it for lack of anything else to do with it. After our multiple adventures with the sparrow and the bit of wood the idea of hanging it had come mechanic-ally. I had acted out of rage and fury at having let myself be drawn into a stupid adventure; in other words, I had wanted to get my own back. I had wanted to play a trick on them, so that I could have a good laugh, and I had also wanted to divert suspicion elsewhere. Yes, yes, but the fact remained that I had done it and, though the deed was my own, it associated itself with the hanging of the sparrow and the bit of wood. Now, three hangings were different from two, they amounted to something. The fact of hanging be-gan swelling and growing, assuming tremendous proportions in the torrid, cloudless heat, with the result that there was nothing eccentric about my plunging into the thicket to go and see the sparrow. As I wandered about waiting for something finally to prevail inside me, the necessity of going and having a look at it imposed itself on me by itself. Going and having a look at it? Just before plunging into the thicket I stopped dead, with one foot in the air. No, better not, I said to myself, if you do, hanging will impose itself still more powerfully on you, you had better be careful. If we had not chanced on the sparrow, perhaps . . . or rather it's practically certain. Better be careful. I stayed where I was, knowing perfectly well that the only result of this hesitation would be to magnify the importance of my advance into the thicket, which duly followed. In the shade I felt better. A butterfly suddenly appeared and flew away. I reached the spot, foliage formed a vault of deeper shadow, and there it was, hanging from a wire.

It was still hanging, just as it had been when Fuchs and I found it. I examined the little dried-up ball, which was becoming less and less like a sparrow every day. Strange, I wanted to laugh, but better not. But I didn't really know what I wanted to do, because after all I had not come here only to look at it. I could not think what the right thing to do was, perhaps I ought to greet it with an appropriate gesture, or say something, but no, better not, that would be exaggerating, going too far. . . . How dappled with sunshine the black earth was. And look at that worm there. The round trunk of a pine-tree. If I came here bringing my hanging of the cat with me, it's certainly no trivial matter, but something I have done to myself. Amen, amen, amen. The edges of the leaves were curling, that was the effect of the heat. Who had dropped that old tin here, and what was inside it? Oh, ants, of course, I hadn't noticed them. Oh, that's enough, let's be off. What a good thing you've associated your hanging of the cat with the hanging of the sparrow, that has made something quite different of it. Why different? Don't ask. Let's be off. What's that bit of paper over there?

A few moments later I was opening the little garden gate, scorched by the sun shining in the tremulous sky. Dinner was exactly the same as usual, complete with Leo's usual little jokes and play with words, but all the same the artificiality and feline tension were catching and, though everyone tried to behave with complete naturalness, there was an element of theatricality about their naturalness. Not that anyone suspected anyone else, good gracious no, but everyone was tangled in a net of clues that led nowhere and questions to which there were no answers. Bafflement hung almost tangibly in the air. True, no one suspected anyone else, but no one could be certain that others did not suspect him, so everyone behaved with slightly exaggerated charm and courtesy and felt slightly ashamed of not being completely himself however hard he tried, and of having to make an effort to be what ought to be the easiest thing in the world. The whole of everyone's behaviour being thus to some extent distorted, everything started being related to the cat and all the revelations associated with the creature. Kulka, for instance, complained that Leo or Lena, or perhaps both, had forgotten to remind her of something, and that somehow made her cat-like, as if it were all because of the cat; there was the same element of morbid distortion in Leo's conversation, which kept casting side-long glances in the same direction. . . . I was already familiar with these symptoms, they were on my trail, my eyes grew busy, avoiding the eyes of others, began rummaging in the corners, plunging into the depths, searching and examining the shelf and behind the cupboard; and the so familiar carpet or curtain turned into a desert or achieved the giddy distances of the archipelagos and continents on the ceiling. And supposing. . . . And of course they did not keep off the subject of the cat altogether. No, here they were actually talking about it, because not talking about it would have been worse.

Lena's hand. There it was on the table-cloth, as usual, next to her fork, in the light of the lamp. I looked at it as I had previously looked at the sparrow, it was resting on the table just as the sparrow had been hanging in the thicket. The sparrow was there, and the hand was here. It approached the fork, picked it up—no, the fingers merely rested on it. My fingers approached my fork and did the same. I was plunged into silent ecstasy by this understanding between us, though it was a phoney, one-sided one, existing in myself alone. Next to my hand, almost touching it, there was a spoon, and there was an exactly similar spoon next to hers. Should I rest the edge of my hand on the spoon? The distance was so slight that nobody would notice. My hand moved, touched the spoon, and her hand moved too and touched her spoon.

This happened during a period of time that sounded like a gong and was filled over the brim with cascades, whirlwinds, swarms of locusts, clouds, the Milky Way, dust and noise, events and one thing and another. Had it been a coincidence or not? How could one tell? It might and it might not, her hand had moved, perhaps deliberately, perhaps half deliberately, or perhaps not deliberately at all. There was no knowing. Kulka removed some plates and Fuchs tugged at his sleeve.

Early next morning we went off on an excursion into the mountains.

This was an old idea of Leo's, he had been boring us with it for a long time. He had promised us a treat in a thousand, a really outstanding experience in our own, familiar mountains. Famous beauty-spots such as Tornic and Koscieliska and Morskie Oke had nothing to offer in comparison, nothing but stale picture postcard stuff, commonplace, second-rate tourist attractions, while the mountain panorama that he proposed to lay before us was a song of songs, a marvel of marvels, an unforgettable, an ecstatic experience we would dream about for the rest of our lives. Did we want to know how he had discovered it? He had lost his way and had hit on it completely by chance. How many years ago? Twenty-seven, it would be twenty-seven in July, he remembered it as if it were yesterday, he had been in the Koscielisko valley and had lost his way and had wandered and wandered, and there, three miles off the road, he had come across a panorama that . . . one could go there by carriage, there was even a mountain refuge there, though an abandoned one, he had found out that it had been bought by the bank, who were going to develop it. It was really a sight to be seen, a garland of natural beauty, a dark green dream world of grass and trees and flowers and streams with a poetical whisper everywhere, set in a superb amphitheatre of mountains, it was magnificent, it was breath-taking, it was unique, the mere thought of it was enough to make you smack your lips and lick your fingers, and we could make a one-day or two-day excursion of it by carriage, taking provisions and bed-ding, we could take his word for it, to anyone who had once been there it was an experience he would remember for the rest of his life. He had been living on it ever since and had sworn to go back. The years were passing, but he would keep his oath.

After the cat incident the prospect of distraction and getting some fresh air into our lungs was the more tempting as we were all stifling in the house. Kulka, after repeatedly saying what absurd ideas Leo had and telling him to be quiet, ended by falling in with the project, particularly after he pointed out that it would be an excellent opportunity of returning the hospitality of two friends of Lena's who were staying at Zakopane. Thus Leo's insistence yielded to intense culinary and other activity on Kulka's part directed to ensuring the success of a social event.

The consequence was that, though the cat-mouth-hand-bit of wood, etc., constellation still survived with all its offshoots, ramifications and tentacles, a new and healthier trend set in, and we all fell in with the idea. In a fit of benevolence Kulka informed Fuchs and me that it would be an exceptionally delightful occasion, as both Lena's friends had only just got married, so there would be three honeymoon couples, so to speak, which would make it a far more interesting social event than ordinary outings to 'commonplace' spots. This too, of course, was related to the cat. The cat was the moving spirit behind the whole thing, for without it none of us would have agreed to Leo's project so readily. But it also served to distract us from the cat, and so it was a relief. However, the last few days beforehand were imbued with a kind of immobility, as if nothing wanted to happen. One evening meal was exactly like another, just like the nightly moon, and the signs and constellations seemed gradually to be fading away. I began to feel afraid that things were settling down for good like this, like a chronic illness or permanent complications, so it was better that something should happen, if only this excursion; and at the same time I was rather surprised at Leo's enthusiasm; he kept reverting to that distant day twenty-seven years before when he had lost his way and discovered that magnificent view. ('In spite of all my efforts I can't remember all the details distinctly. I remember I was wearing a coffee-coloured shirt, the one in that photo, but I can't remember which pair of trousers I had on. And good gracious me, I remember washing my legs, a lot of things I've completely forgotten, I rack my brains but can't remember them no matter how hard I try, but it's a funny thing, I remember washing my legs, though how or where I've forgotten completely.') This surprised me, and I found myself getting more and more interested in the coincidence that both of us, each in his own way, seemed similarly deeply involved in something, he in the past and I in all those trivialities.

To say nothing of the fact that my suspicions started settling on him. Might he not have had a finger in hanging the sparrow and the bit of wood? How often I had previously told myself that the idea was absurd. All the same, there was something about him. That bald, dome-like head and those pince-nez of his twitched with lewdness as well as with unhappiness, and it was a sly lewdness. He suddenly rose from the table and came back with a dried-up stick.

'It comes from there,' he announced. 'I've kept it all these years. Yes, it comes from that miraculous spot, though I'm damned if I remember where I picked it up, whether in the fields or at the side of the road.'

There he stood with his bald pate, holding the stick in his hand, and I vaguely said to myself: Stick, bit of wood, stick, bit of wood?

And that was all.

Two or three days passed like that. At last, when we took our seats in the two carriages at seven o'clock one morning, it seemed as if we were really saying good-bye. The house already looked abandoned, with the mark of approaching solitude upon it; it was to be left in charge of Katasia, who was given detailed instructions. She must take care of everything, never leave the door open, and call the neighbours if anything happened. But all these precautions applied to a situation we were about to leave behind. And so indeed we did. The two piebald horses set off down the sandy road under the indifferent dawn, the house vanished, the horses trotted, and the carriage jolted and creaked. A peasant was sitting up on the box and Louis, Lena and I were sitting on the padded seats (Leo, his wife and Fuchs were in the first carriage), and we were all still sleepy-eyed. After the house had vanished nothing was left but the motion of the carriage, rattling and creaking and jolting, and the displacement of everything all round us. But the excursion had not yet really begun. First we had to pick up one of the two young couples from their pension. The carriage jolted on. We stopped at the pension, the young couple climbed in with a lot of parcels, there was laughter and sleepy kisses were exchanged with Lena, and there was some awkward and trivial conversation.

We emerged on to the main road, the country opened out before us, and on we went. The jog-trot continued. A tree approached, passed, and disappeared behind us. A fence and a house. A small field planted with something. Sloping meadows and rounded hills. There was a break. A barrel with an advertisement on it. A car overtook us and left us behind. Our progress consisted of jolting, creaking and swaying, trotting horses, their backsides and tails, the peasant on the box and his whip, and overhead the early morning sky and the sun, which had already got boring and was beginning to burn the back of our necks. Lena jolted and swayed with the carriage, but that was unimportant, nothing was important in the slow disappearance of things that carriage travel consists of. I was absorbed by something else, something non-corporeal, that is to say the relationship between the speed with which close objects passed by and the far slower displacement of things that were not so close, to say nothing of those in the distance that seemed to be practically motionless. When one travels like this, I reflected, things appear only to disappear again, they are unimportant, and so is the landscape; there is nothing but appearance and disappearance. A tree. A field. Another tree. They passed.

I was absent. Because of our fragmentary, chaotic, casual and superficial contact with our environment we are nearly

94

always absent, I reflected—or at any rate not entirely present. People taking part in a social occasion (such as this excursion, for instance) are about ten per cent absent, I calculated. In our case the insistent flood of things and yet more things, sights and yet more sights, this vast horizon separated by such a short distance from the restricted space in which we had been cooped up only the day before, with its involvement in clumps of earth, dust, dried-up leaves, cracks, etc. etc., warts, glasses, bottles, bits of thread, corks, etc. etc., and the configurations etc. etc., that resulted from them, became a great, dissolving stream, a deluge without end. I sank in it, and so did Lena beside me. Jolting and trotting. Snatches of sleepy conversation with the new young couple. Nothing, nothingness. Except that I was leaving the house, and Lena was with me, and Katasia had stayed behind in the house, which we were leaving farther and farther behind every moment. It, and the garden-gate and the staked and whitewashed young trees, were still there, but we were moving farther and farther away from them.

Gradually things livened up in the carriage. The newly-weds, who were called Lolo and Lola, grew more animated, and after a bout of preliminary exchanges such as 'Oh, Lolo, have I forgotten the thermos?' and 'Lola, take this bag, it's in my way,' they gave themselves up completely to lolery. Lola, who was younger than Lena, was soft and pink, had pretty dimples and pretty little fingers, a pretty little handbag and a pretty little handkerchief, as well as a pretty little sunshade, a lipstick and a lighter, and all these things kept her perpetually busy while she giggled and chatted away. 'This is the road to the Koscielisko valley, isn't it? I know it, it jolts you, doesn't it? I like it, it's a long time since I've been jolted. And you like being jolted too, don't you, Lolo? Oh, look, Lena darling. Look at that funny verandah over there, I'd have a little room for myself there, and I'd put Lolo there, where the big window is, that's where I'd give him his work room, only I'd get rid of all those little dwarfs, I can't stand little dwarfs, do you like little dwarfs, Lena? You haven't forgotten the film, have you, Lolo? Or the field-glasses? Oh, how this seat keeps sticking into my sit-upon, ow, oh dear, what are you doing, Lolo? What's the name of that mountain over there?'

Lolo was exactly like Lola, though more solid, with big calves. He was chubby and round at the hips and had a small, up-tilted nose, a small Tyrolean hat, a camera, small blue eyes, a dressing-case, plump hands, plus-fours and chequered woollen socks. They were thrilled by the practical identity of their names, and encouraged and outdid each other in their lolery. When Lola, seeing a pretty villa, for instance, announced that her mother was used to her comforts, Lolo countered by informing the world that his mother went abroad every year to take the waters, and added for good measure that she had a collection of Chinese lampshades, to which Lola replied that her mother had seven ivory elephants. It was impossible not to smile at this chatter, and our smiling encouraged them, and the chatter combined with the unreality slipping monotonously by in step with the trotting horses. Our motion resolved the landscape into concentric circles revolving at different rates depending on the distance. Louis took out his watch.

'It's half past nine.'

The sun was hot, but the air was still cool.

'Let's have a snack.'

So I was going away with Lena. This was a striking, astonishing, important fact. How on earth had I failed to realize its importance before? Everything had been left behind in the house, or outside it, such a quantity of things, from the bed to the tree and even the way we touched the spoons. And now we were here, wanderers with no fixed abode. The house with all those constellations and configurations and the rest of it was receding, was no longer 'here' but 'there', together with the sparrow in the thicket and the dappled sunshine on the black earth—a highly important fact, except that my thoughts on the subject were continually receding too—and growing weaker in the process under the impact of the surrounding landscape (though at the same time I coolly noted through half-closed eyes the curious fact that, though the sparrow was receding, its existence was by no means undermined by the process of recession, it was merely receding, and that was all).

'Where's the bread and butter?' 'Where on earth did you put the thermos?' 'Pass the paper, please.' 'Leave me alone, Lolo.' 'Where are the cups mama gave us?' 'Be careful, Lolo, don't be silly.' 'It's you that's silly, Lola.' 'Ha, ha, ha!'

What we had left behind was no longer real, but its unreality was still real. Lena's little face was small to the point of insignificance, but Louis also looked diminished, lifeless, as if annihilated by the space that extended over the barrier of a range of mountains and was terminated by another unknown range in the ultimate distance. I was ignorant of the names of most of the things around me. Those of at least half the mountains, trees, bushes, vegetables, agricultural implements, villages, etc., were completely unknown to me.

We were on a plateau.

And what was Katasia doing? Was she in the kitchen with that lip of hers? I looked at Lena's little mouth to see what it was like when freed from the intervention of that other mouth, I scrutinized its behaviour when separated from it. But there was nothing to see, it was merely a mouth on an excursion in a carriage. I ate some turkey; Kulka's provisions were delicious.

Gradually a new life established itself in the carriage, as on a new planet. Under the influence of the Lolos, Lena and even Louis began loloing too. 'What on earth are you doing, Louis?' Lena exclaimed, and he said: 'I'm not doing anything, my dear.' I watched them discreetly. It was extraordinary. So they could be like this too? A strange and incredible journey. We started dropping down from the plateau, the spaces diminished, eminences crept up on us on either side, Lena wagged her finger at Louis, and he frowned. Their gaiety was superficial and frivolous, but at any rate they were capable of it. This was interesting. But distance has its own laws and these ended by prevailing, and I ended by making a few jokes myself. After all, we were on an excursion.

Mountains which had long since been approaching were suddenly on top of us, we entered a valley where it was deliciously shady, though the foliage on the upper slopes was was still bathed in sunlight. We plunged into a quiet that

97

came from everywhere and nowhere, a delightful river of coolness. We turned a corner, and came to towering walls and pinnacles, contorted piles of rock and deep chasms, peaceful rounded eminences, summits or peaks, craggy crests and vertical precipices to which the bushes clung, then rocks on the heights and below them meadows descending into silence, an incomprehensible, motionless, universal silence, such a powerful silence that the noise of our minute, advancing carriage seemed to exist quite apart from it. This landscape continued for some time, and then a new element imposed itself, a nude or chaotic or shining, sometimes heroic, element, made up of chasms and abysses, solid rock, variations on the theme of overhanging cliffs, ascending and descending rhythms of trees and vegetation, wounds and scars and landslides; idylls floated towards us, sometimes soft and gentle and sometimes hard and crystalline. There were all sorts of different things—marvellous distances, enchanting convolutions, space captured and stretched, aggressive or yielding space, space twisting or bending, striking up or down. Gigantic, motionless movement.

'Tremendous, isn't it, Lola?'

'Oh, Lolo, I'm frightened. I shall be frightened of sleeping alone tonight.'

Giddiness, confusion, excess. Too much, too much, too much. Weight, mass, piles rising into the sky, piles collapsed, general chaos, huge, swelling mastodons that appeared and a moment later vanished in unruly confusion into a thousand details and then suddenly reassembled again into majestic edifices. It was just as in the thicket or looking at the wall or the eeiling or the rubbish where the pole was, or in Katasia's room, or looking at the walls and cupboards and shelves and curtains where things also formed themselves into shapes and configurations. But there they had been only little things, here there was a mighty storm of matter. And I had become such a decipherer of still life that I could not help scrutinizing and examining as if there were something to be deciphered here, and I seized on the continually changing patterns that our little carriage joltingly extracted from the bosom of the mountains. But it amounted to nothing, nothing at all. A bird appeared, hovering high and motionless in the sky. Was it a vulture, an eagle, a hawk? At any rate it was not a sparrow, but its not being a sparrow made it a non-sparrow, and it was connected with the sparrow by virtue of this.

Heavens, how refreshed I was by the sight of that solitary bird hovering supremely and royally over everything, dominating the scene. It showed me how exhausted I had been by the disorder and confusion in the house down below, the chaos of mouths, the hangings, the cat, the teapot, Louis, the bit of wood, the gutter, Leo, the knockings and hammerings, the hands and the needles, Lena, the pole, Fuchs's eyes, etc., etc. I had been living in a fog. But here, heaven be praised, there was this royal bird. And by what miracle, though a mere dot in the sky, had it imposed itself like the discharge of a gun, scattering the confusion and chaos? I looked at Lena. She too was looking at the dot in the sky.

It described an arc and disappeared, plunging us back into the unbridled spectacle of the mountains, behind which there were more mountains, each consisting of spaces where stones abounded (how many stones could there be?) and thus the rear rank of that great army moved into the foreground and advanced to the assault in a strange silence, partially explained by the motionlessness of universal motion. 'Oh, Lolo, look at that rock.' 'Look over there, Lola, isn't it just like a nose?' 'Look at that old man smoking a pipe, Lolo darling.' 'Look, over there on the left, look at that top-boot, he's kicking something with it. What is it he's kicking? Oh, look, it's a chimney.' Another bend in the road restricted our vision, a balcony advanced towards us, and then a triangle, and then a tree clinging to the rock-face attracted our attention, but it promptly decomposed and disappeared. Then we saw a priest.

A priest, sitting on a stone at the roadside, wearing a cassock. A priest in a cassock sitting on a stone at the roadside in the mountains? I was reminded of the teapot, this priest was just like the teapot. His cassock was a superfluity too.

We stopped.

'Can we give you a lift, father?'

He was young and plump and had a nose like a duckling, his round, peasant's face emerged from his stiff ecclesiastical collar, and he dropped his eyes.

'May the Lord reward you,' he said.

But he did not move. His hair was clinging to his brow with perspiration. Louis asked him how far we could take him and where he would like to be dropped, but he climbed in as if he had not heard the question, muttering how grateful he was. The horses resumed their trot and we jolted on.

'I was in the mountains and lost my way,' he said.

'You're tired, father.'

'Oh, yes, I live at Zakopane.'

The bottom of his cassock was dirty, his shoes were worn, and his eyes reddish. Had he spent the night in the mountains? He explained slowly that he had been on an excursion and had got lost. An excursion in a cassock? Lost his way in an area cut through by a valley? When had he set out on this excursion? The previous afternoon. Setting out on a mountain excursion in the afternoon? We did not ask him too many questions, but invited him to help himself from our provisions, which he did. He ate with embarrassment, and when he had finished he was still embarrassed, and the carriage jolted him, the sun was scorching, there was no more shade, we were thirsty but had no desire to stop and take out the bottles, we just wanted to go on. Overhanging cliffs cast vertical shadows, and the sound of a waterfall became audible. On we went. Previously I had never taken any interest in the nevertheless remarkable fact that for centuries past a certain proportion of mankind had been set apart by wearing cassocks and being earmarked for the service of God—a whole category of specialists in the divine, servants of the spiritual, officers of the transcendental. But here in the mountains this black-clothed guest who had got involved in our trip and felt out of place in this mountain chaos was a nuisance because he was a superfluity. Rather like the teapot?

This depressed me. Curiously enough, the eagle or hawk flying high in the sky had revived my spirits, perhaps (I thought) because, being a bird, it was related to the sparrow, but also, and perhaps chiefly, because, being suspended in the sky and thus associating the sparrow with hanging, the hanged cat and the hanged sparrow . . . yes (I saw it more clearly every moment) . . . it conferred a regal, transcendental quality on the idea of hanging; and if I managed to plumb the mystery of this idea, succeeded in grasping or even suspecting what lay at the bottom of it, even if only in relation to the sparrow, the bit of wood and the cat, it would be easier for me to clear up the question of the mouths and all its ramifications. For (I went on, trying to solve the riddle, which was a difficult and painful one) there was no doubt that the secret of the link between those two mouths lay in myself, for it had arisen in me and I alone had created it. But (and here I had to watch my step, be very careful) by hanging the cat I had (completely or perhaps only to a certain extent?) associated myself with the sparrow-bit of wood configuration. Thus I belonged to both configurations. Did it not follow that the link between Lena and Katasia on the one hand and the sparrow and the bit of wood on the other existed only by virtue of my own intervention? By hanging the cat had I not in a way myself constructed a bridge connecting the whole?

No, nothing at all was very clear, but all the same something had started germinating and taking shape, and behold, a huge bird had suspended itself—had been hanging—in the sky overhead. But what the devil was this priest doing here, this totally extraneous, unexpected, superfluous, stupid priest?

He was as irrelevant, as extraneous, as the teapot had been, and I felt just as furious as when the teapot had made me kill the cat (quite right, I was by no means sure that the teapot had not been the last straw that had made me do it; also, perhaps, I had wanted to force reality to declare itself, like throwing something at a bush when you suspect something has moved in it). Yes, strangling the cat had been my furious reaction to the provocation of that senseless teapot. . . . But in that case, priest, you had better look out. For what guarantee is there that I might not fling something, do something to you . . .

He sat there quite unsuspicious of my state of mind, and on we went. Mountains and more mountains, the horses trotted on, it was stifling. A detail struck me; he was fidgeting with his fat fingers.

He was mechanically spreading them between his knees and interlocking them; the persistence with which he kept doing this was disagreeable.

Conversation.

'Is this the first time you have been in this area?'

Lola answered like a shy schoolgirl.

'Yes, father, we're still on our honeymoon, we only got married last month.'

Lolo picked up the thread, looking just as shy and delighted.

'We're a couple of newly-weds.'

The priest coughed in embarrassment. Lola, speaking up just like a schoolgirl telling a teacher something about another girl, pointed to Lena and Louis and said:

'And so are they, father, they've just got married too.'

'They've only just had permission to . . .' Lolo announced.

Louis said 'hmm,' in a deep voice, Lena smiled, the priest remained silent, oh, those Lolos, what a way of talking they had invented especially for the priest's benefit. He went on playing miserably with his fat fingers, he was ungainly, rustic, pitiful, and it looked to me as if he perhaps had something on his conscience. What was he doing with those fat fingers of his? Oh those fingers moving between his knees . . . and mine and Lena's on the tablecloth. The fork. The spoon.

'Lolo, leave me alone, what will the reverend father think?'

'Don't be silly, Lola, he won't think there's anything wrong in it at all.'

We suddenly turned, cut across the valley and started climbing the mountain, following a poor, ill-marked road. We had been in a ravine that had been growing closer and closer, and now entered another lateral ravine, and drove on surrounded by new summits and new mountainsides, and we were now completely isolated and cut off. The trees, the grass, the rocks were the same and yet quite different, marked by the obliquity and deviation that had led us away from the main road. Yes, I said to myself, he must have been up to something, he's got something on his conscience.

But what? A sin? What kind of sin? He may have strangled a cat. But how stupid can one be, since when has it been sinful to kill a cat? But this man in a cassock, this man of prayer, of the church, of the confessional, appears by the roadside and climbs into your carriage, and the immediate consequence is sinfulness, conscience, guilt and retribution, tra-la-la-la-, tra-la-la-la (which is just like tri-li-li-lee). He climbs into your carriage and you are confronted with sin.

Sinfulness, that is to say, this colleague of yours, this priest-colleague of yours, is fidgeting with his fat fingers because he has something on his conscience. Just like you. Fraternally he keeps fidgeting with his fingers. Have they too by chance strangled anything? New rock piles and chasms assaulted us, new displays of green, sombre larches and pines, a blue-green world of marvellous peace and quiet, and Lena sitting opposite me, with those hands of hers, and the whole constellation of hands—mine, hers, Louis's—had been given a shot in the arm by this fat-fingered priest's hands, which I was unable to concentrate on properly because of the motion, the mountains, the isolation. Oh, merciful, almighty God, why was it impossible to concentrate on anything? The world was a hundred million times too rich, and what could I do in my distracted state? 'Driver do you know the dance of the mountaineers?' 'Leave him alone, Lola.' 'Leave her alone, Lolo.' 'Oh, Lola, I've got pins and needles in my leg.' On we drove. One thing was clear, that bird had been too high up, and it was just as well that this priest-colleague of mine was bumbling about down here below. On we drove, the motion was monotonous, a big stream approached and passed by, the horses trotted, the carriage rattled and jolted, it was hot, we perspired, and here we were, we were just arriving.

It was two o'clock. We had reached a kind of open valley, with meadows, birds and pines. A lot of rocks were dotted about, and there was a house. A wooden house with a verandah. In the shade behind it was the gate through which Lena's parents had preceded us with Fuchs and the other young married couple. They appeared at the door, there was a babble of words, greetings and exclamations, out you get, what a delightful trip, how long have you been here, let's have lunch straight away, hand out the bags, it's ready already, Leo, fetch the bottles.

They came from another planet, and so did we. Our presence here was a presence 'elsewhere', and this house was simply a house that was not the other house that we had left behind.

VII

Everything was happening at a distance. It was not the other house that had left us, but we who had left it. This new house here in its terrible isolation that our cries and exclamations combated in vain had no existence of its own; it existed only to the extent that it was not the one we had left. This revelation came to me as soon as I got out of the carriage.

'We're completely on our own here, there's not a soul for miles, we're left entirely to our own resources, it's a long way to Tipperary, and we've got to fend for ourselves. What a treat you've got coming to you, all you lucky people, you'll soon see I wasn't leading you up the garden path. But the first thing to do is to stave off the pangs of hunger. Into the breach, dear friends. . . .'

'Leo, the spoons are in the rucksack. Lena, pass round the napkins, make yourselves comfortable, everyone, you, father, sit here, please.'

To which there was a chorus of replies, such as: 'We'll do as we're told,' 'good, let's sit down then,' 'we need another two chairs,' 'what a feast!' 'sit here, next to me,' 'please pass the napkins.'

The table at which we took our places was in the hall. There were a number of doors leading to the various rooms, and a staircase up to the first floor. The doors were open and the rooms more or less bare, with nothing in them but beds and chairs, a great many chairs. The table groaned with food, cheerfulness prevailed, and the wine circulated. But the cheerfulness was of the kind that prevails at parties, at which everyone behaves cheerfully in order not to spoil the pleasure of others, while the truth is that everyone feels slightly absent, as when seeing someone off at the station; and this sensation was also associated with the bareness of the house, the absence of curtains and cupboards and bedclothes or shelves and pictures on the walls; there was nothing but windows, beds and chairs.

In the emptiness not only words but personalities seemed louder, and in particular Leo and Kulka seemed to expand. Their fortissimo buzz was accompanied by the noisy voices of their guests as they ate, the giggling of the Lolos and the buffoonery of Fuchs, who was already pretty tipsy and was drinking, I knew, to drown his troubles with Drozdowski and the feeling of being unwanted, which I knew so well from my own experiences at home. He was a Jonah, poor fellow, and the only thing you could do was to shut your eyes or look away. Kulka ruled the roost, dispensing salads and cold meats, encouraging us to try just a little more of this and just a little more of that, assuring us that there was plenty to go round and that no one would have to go hungry. She had made tremendous efforts to ensure that everything was perfect and in the best of taste, she was determined to make this original excursion a social success, and she had made quite certain that there should be no excuse for anyone to complain later that there hadn't been enough to eat or drink. Leo seemed doubled or trebled in size; he was Amphitryon, guide and leader, the initiator of the whole thing, and his enthusiasm knew no bounds. 'Come children, enjoy yourselves, *carpe diem*, gather ye roses while ye may,' etc., etc. Nevertheless, in spite of all the talk and the noise, the whole thing was somehow hollow, incomplete, lacking in conviction, to such an extent that for a time I had the feeling that I was looking at my companions and myself through the wrong end of a telescope or from a great distance, as if the whole thing were happening on the moon. In other words, this excursion-evasion was useless, the world we had left was all the more present because of our attempt to get away from it. Never mind, it couldn't be helped, the only thing to do was to take things as they came. I actually had the feeling that something new was coagulating, and I began to notice little things, and in particular the peculiar excitement that overcame the Lolos in the presence of the third honeymoon couple who had arrived with Leo and Kulka.

The brand new husband was named Tolo, and was also known as the cavalry captain. Tall and broad-shouldered, with a face that was pink almost to the point of naiveté and a light moustache, he was every inch the cavalryman, and

Leo started humming a song about a dashing hussar, but broke off short, because it went on to speak of a girl who was as fresh as a rose, and the cavalry captain's bride Jadeczka was one of those resigned women who have renounced giving pleasure, having decided that such a thing is not for them, though heaven knows why. She was not unattractive, though her figure was rather uninteresting, monotonous, as it were. True, she had 'everything in the right place', as Fuchs whispered, nudging me with his elbow, but the mere thought of putting one's arm round her was unpleasing, so unsuitable was she for the purpose. Was it a kind of physical self-centredness? You felt that her hands, feet, nose, ears, were organs existing for herself alone and nothing else, she totally lacked the generosity that suggests to a woman that her hand might be a tempting and exciting gift. Was it prudishness? No, it was rather a curious kind of physical isolationism. Lola, trying hard to suppress her giggles, whispered to Lolo: 'When she smells herself she doesn't mind.' Lola was quite right, she had put her finger on why Jadeczka was so unpleasing; she was rather like those bodily smells that are tolerable only to the person who produces them.

But neither Lolo nor Lola would have been so startled, or would have had to make such efforts to suppress their giggles, if her husband had not been such a handsome, rakish-looking man with that little moustache of his. No one who saw them together could help wondering why he had married her. The answer (whispered to me with a suppressed giggle by Lola) was that she was the daughter of a rich industrialist, which of course provided further ammunition for wagging tongues. Nor was this the end of the story, indeed it was only the beginning, for (as was also evident at first sight) they had no illusions about the impression they made, and tried to counter human malice with nothing but the purity of their intentions and their perfect right to do as they pleased. Have I not a perfect right to him? she seemed to say. Of course I have. I know he is good-looking and I am not, but have I not a perfect right to be in love with him? Of course I have, and you cannot forbid me to be in love with him, for it is my unassailable human right. I love him, and my love is pure and beautiful, there is no reason why I should be bashful about it, and look, I am not. Isolated from the rest of the party and not taking part in the general hilarity, she watched over this feeling as over a treasure, concentrated and silent, her eyes fixed on her husband or lost in contemplation of the green beauty of the meadows outside the window, and from time to time her bosom heaved with a sigh that was almost a prayer. And, as was her perfect right, every now and then she quietly said something like 'Tolo', with that mouth of hers that belonged to herself alone.

Lolo said to Lola that his sides were bursting and he wouldn't be able to hold out much longer. Leo, with the leg of a turkey at the end of his fork and his pince-nez perched on his nose, held forth as usual, the priest sat in his corner, Fuchs looked for something, Kulka brought in cherries for dessert, but all the noise failed to stifle the total, singular, solitary, inhuman silence. I drank red wine.

Tolo, the cavalry captain, drank too, holding his head high. He always held his head high, to show that no one had any right to cast doubts on the genuineness of his love for this woman, as if he did not have a perfect right to be in love with her, as if his love for her was not as good as any other love. He was assiduous in his attentions to her. 'You're not tired, darling, are you?' he said, and he tried hard to be at the same level of ecstasy as she. But there was a slight air of martyrdom about him. 'Lolo, hold me, I can't stand it any longer.' The Lolos, wearing an air of seraphic innocence, watched and waited to pounce on the slightest sign of tenderness between them, like a couple of prowling tigers thirsty for blood. If the poor priest had given them so much pleasure in the carriage, imagine the delight they now derived from this couple, newly-weds like themselves, who seemed specially made to let them lolo to their hearts' content.

Kulka arrived with a tart. 'Oh please have some, do, it melts in your mouth, please try it. You will try it, won't you?' But the cat, oh, the cat, buried at the foot of a tree after being hanged. All this was because of the cat, the whole object of this outing was to get rid of the cat, that was why she and Leo were being so sociable. But the cat was still present, this outing was a disastrous mistake, they could not possibly have thought of anything worse. Distance wiped out nothing, on the contrary, it reinforced and strengthened it, to such an extent that it seemed as if we had spent years and years living with the sparrow and the cat and had arrived here years afterwards. I ate a slice of tart. The only thing to do was to get into the carriage and drive back, there was nothing else for it. Because if we stayed here still linked with all the things that had happened in the house. . . .

I ate my slice of tart and talked to Louis and Tolo. I was distracted. How exhausting was this superabundance and excess from which new persons, events and things constantly emerged. If only the flood would stop for a moment. Lena was sitting on the other side of the table, perhaps she was exhausted too, though she was smiling with her eyes and mouth at Lola (both of them being brides of recent date); the Lena here was a faithful reflection of the Lena there, she was 'related' to the other by a 'relationship' which now shattered me just as the hammer blows had; Fuchs was drowning Drozdowski in alcohol and was red and yellow with bloated resentment; Louis, sitting next to Lena, was quiet, agreeable and polite, and the priest in the corner. . . . Lena's hand was on the table, next to a fork, just as before, and I could have rested my hand on the table too, but I didn't want to. All the same, in spite of everything, new threads were beginning to be spun, and a new, local dynamism independent of the old was coming into being, though it seemed sickly and weak. The presence of the three young couples gave weight and significance to the priest, and the cassock in turn bestowed a marital quality on them, and the result was the creation of a sort of marital pressure; yes, marriage was dominant, the whole thing might have been a wedding reception. And then there was the priest. He kept playing with his fat fingers (which he kept under the table, withdrawing them only to take food to his lips), but nevertheless he was a priest, and as such constituted a natural bastion against the drolleries of the Lolos. Also his cassock exercised a powerful effect on Kulka, who (since the cat episode) had laid marked emphasis on the importance of correct social behaviour. Rapidly diminishing benevolence became evident in the glances she cast at the Lolos, and her disapproving little coughs became more and more expressive as Leo's outbursts of laughter grew louder and more frequent, supported as they were by Fuchs's tipsy laugh (the consequence of Drozdowski) and by our own silly jokes in the void, the distance, the deathly quiet of the mountains, in which it again seemed as if something were forming and coming into being, though it was still so vague and formless that there was nothing to fasten on yet. Meanwhile I fastened on this and that, followed whatever presented itself, neglecting all the rest, the immense, menacing rest—while all that we had left behind down in the house still existed as it had done before.

And suddenly there was a scene that connected me with the cat, through the priest.

Like the first flash of light through the dark clouds when night is over, it showed us up plainly in relation to the house below. It was preceded by remarks by Kulka of the following type. To Tolo, for instance, she said, very politely: 'Won't you remove that little bit of sugar from Jadeczka's blouse?' To Leo, in a voice intended to be heard by everyone, she said: 'It's as I said, Leo, the road isn't so bad after all, I told you we should have come by car, you should have asked Talek, he's always saying his car's at your disposal.' To Lola she said rather acidly: 'You're giggling and laughing instead of eating your tart.' Meanwhile Fuchs was removing the plates. Not being sure that he did not get on our nerves as he got on Drozdowski's, he helped with the clearing up in order to ingratiate himself. But at one point he got up, distorted his fishy, tipsy face with a yawn, and said:

'How I should love to have a bath.'

Now, baths and washing were one of Lolo's favourite topics, and Lola rated them even more highly, indeed she liked talking about them almost as much as she liked talking about her 'mama', and on the way here she had already made such statements as 'I wouldn't be able to live without a shower', and 'I don't know how anyone can live in a town without having two baths a day', and 'my mama puts lemon juice in her bath' and 'my mama goes to Karlsbad every year'. So, when Fuchs mentioned the subject, it immediately set Lola loloing. She said that if she were in the Sahara she would use her last glass of water to wash, 'because water for washing is more important than water for drinking, and wouldn't you do the same, Lolo?' etc. In the midst of all this chatter she must have noticed, as I did, that the word 'bath' was unpleasantly related to Jadeczka. Not that Jadeczka was not clean. But she had a special kind of physical self-centredness that reminded me of Fuchs's statement on another occasion that 'one is what one is.' In relationship to her own body she behaved as if (like certain smells) it were tolerable only to its owner, and consequently she created the impression of being a person uninterested in baths. Lola, after sticking out her little nose and behaving as if she could sniff something from that quarter, continued harping on the theme. 'If I miss my bath for any reason, I feel ill,' etc., etc., she said, and Lolo followed suit, and so did Leo, Fuchs, Louis, and Lena, as is usual in such circumstances, in order not to be suspected of indifference in relation to water. Jadeczka and Tolo, however, remained silent.

The result of the talkativeness on the one hand and the silence on the other was a tacit implication that Jadeczka did not take baths. Hence the feeling that 'one is what one is.'

There was a whiff coming from her direction, not a physical smell, but the whiff of an unpleasing personality; and Lola, backed up by Lolo, with the most innocent air in the world was like a bloodhound on the trail. Jadeczka, however, behaved exactly as before, that is, she remained silent and did not take part—except that her withdrawal into herself now became associated with insufficient familiarity with water; and Tolo's silence was even worse, because he was obviously a perfect swimmer and was in his element in water, so why did he not open his mouth? Did he not want to leave her alone in her silence?

'And all that business about the. . . .'

The speaker of these words moved as if he felt uncomfortable in his chair and promptly returned to his silent immobility. But this totally unexpected intervention of his had an extraordinary effect. It cut right through the loloing of the Lolos, and everyone looked at him. I don't know if we all had the same impression, but those fat fingers of his, the skin of his neck reddened by his hard collar, his physical clumsiness, the worries that he evidently had on mind and his moroseness—everything about him, in fact, including the wart at the root of his nose—connected him with Jadeczka and Jadeczka with him. His black cassock and the way he played with his fingers, her staring eyes, her self-confidence, her right to love, his awkwardness, her anguish and his suffering, combined to create a unity between them, a perfectly clear but totally unclear unity that was completely intelligible and at the same totally unintelligible. Each was stewing in his own juice and both were stewing in the same juice. 'One is what one is. . . .'

I ate some tart, but suddenly stopped with my mouth full. My throat contracted. What was I to call what was happening to me? Was it a return to the interior? A return to my own horribleness, my own dirt, my crime, my imprisonment in myself, my self-condemnation? In a flash I saw that this must lead straight back to the cat. Yes, there it was, it came creeping up, it came quite close, I could feel it. I could feel the buried, strangled cat, hanged between the sparrow and the bit of wood, all three motionless where we had left them and made significant by their very immobility. Oh, the persistent horror of it. The farther away you were the nearer they came. The more insignificant and meaningless they were, the greater their power and oppressiveness. What a diabolical noose I had put round my neck.

The cat that I had strangled and hanged.

VIII

Lou is remarked sleepily to Lena that it would be a good idea to have a snooze. He was perfectly right; we needed it after starting out at dawn. We got up, and began looking around for blankets.

'Tri-li-li-lee!'

Leo's refrain was louder than usual, and sounded provocative.

'Are you all right, Leo? Is there anything you want?' Kulka asked in surprise.

He was sitting alone at the table, which was still loaded with the remnants of the feast, his bald pate and pince-nez were gleaming, and there was a drop of sweat on his brow.

'Berg!' he said.

'I beg your pardon?'

'Berg!'

'What do you mean by berg, may I ask?'

'Berg!'

There was not a shadow of benevolence about him. He was a faun, Caesar, Bacchus, Heliogabalus, Attila. Then he smiled mildly behind his pince-nez.

'*Nichevo*, darling, I was just going to tell a story about two Jews who were having an argument. Never mind, I'll tell you another time.'

It was over, disintegration had set in. The table was left forlorn and abandoned, chairs were carried indoors, blankets were produced, the beds in the empty rooms were occupied, somnolence set in, the effect of the wine. . . .

At about five o'clock, when I had finished my snooze, I walked out in front of the house.

Most of them were still asleep and no one was around. A field with firs and pines and rocks scattered about, bathed in sunshine and hot. Behind me the house, full of somnolence and flies. In front of me the field, and beyond it the mountains, so many mountains, steep and wooded mountains were all round. Incredible how wooded these remote places were. This was not my place, what was the point of being here? I might just as well be somewhere else, it made no difference. I knew that behind that range of mountains there were other places unknown but no more strange to me than this. A kind of indifference had interposed itself between me and the landscape, the kind of indifference that can change into rigidity or even something worse. Into what? The isolated slumber of those remote, unknown, uninteresting, rising and falling meadows and woods concealed the possibility of suddenly seizing, twisting, strangling and hanging. But the possibility was 'behind' and 'beyond', in the distance. I stood in the shadow among the trees immediately in front of the house, picking my teeth with a twig. It was still hot, but the air was fresh.

I looked round. Lena was standing five yards away.

There she was. Seeing her suddenly like this, she struck me as being small and childlike, and my eyes were attracted by her sleeveless green blouse. This lasted only for a moment. I turned my head and looked elsewhere.

'Beautiful, isn't it?'

She said this because, being only five yards away, she had to say something. I went on not looking at her, and not looking at her killed me. She had come to me, she had come to me. Did she want to start something with me? The thought terrified me, I did not look at her, and I did not know what to do, there was nothing I could do, I just stayed there not looking at her.

'So you're dumb, are you? With admiration?'

She spoke in the slightly loloish way she had picked up from them.

'Where is your father's view?' I said, for the sake of saying something. She laughed that soft, gentle laugh of hers.

'How should I know?'

Another silence, this time less embarrassing, because everything was taking place in slow motion. Heat, evening approaching, a small stone, a cockchafer, a fly, the earth. After the maximum of delay consistent with normal politeness, I said:

'Well, we shall soon find out.'

'Yes, papa's taking us after dinner,' she replied immediately. I said nothing, but looked at the earth—at my feet. The earth and I, and she beside me. I felt uncomfortable, even bored, I should have been happier if she had gone away. Again it was time for me to break the silence, but before doing so I stole a quick glance at her, just long enough to see that she was not looking at me either, but was looking elsewhere, just as I was, and there was a touch of weakness about this exchange of non-looks, a touch of the weakness that derives from distance. Neither of us were sufficiently here, we were like projections from somewhere else, from the house we had left behind, we were weak and sickly phantoms not really here at all, like non-seeing figures in dreams who are bound up with something else. Was her mouth still 'related' to the horrible, disfigured mouth now in the kitchen or the little bedroom in that house? I wanted to find out. I took a quick glance and saw at once that her mouth and the other were related like two towns on a map or two stars in a constellation; more than ever, in fact, at this distant spot.

'What time shall we be leaving?'

'At about half past eleven, perhaps. I don't know.'

Why had I done that to her?

Why had I had to soil her like that? Why on that first night in the corridor had I first associated her mouth with Katasia's? (Alas, the things we do are as capricious and un-predictable as butterflies; it is only slowly, as one returns to them in retrospect, that they assume a convulsive quality, grip you as with pincers and do not let go.) That night it had been a fleeting idea, a caprice, a fantasy, a trifle. But now? What in the name of heaven could I do now? Now I had spoiled her for myself, spoiled her so thoroughly inside myself that I wanted to seize her and spit in her mouth. Why had I corrupted her so utterly for myself? It was worse than violating a little girl, I had violated her for myself. It was the priest's presence that suggested this to me, sinfulness was in the air, I felt I was in a state of mortal sin, which brought me back to the cat, and the cat returned.

Earth . . . clumps of earth, two clumps separated by a few

tenths of an inch. How many tenths of an inch? Two or three. I ought to go for a walk. It must be admitted that the air. . . . Another clump of earth. How many tenths of an inch?

'I had a snooze after lunch,' she said with that mouth of hers that I knew, could not fail to know, was corrupted by that other mouth.

'So did I.'

It was not she. She was down below in the house, in the garden where the little white-washed trees were tied to their stakes. I was not here either. But that made us a hundred times more significant here. As if we were symbols of ourselves. Earth. Clumps. Grass. I knew that *because of the distance* I ought to go for a walk. What was I doing standing here? I knew that *because of the distance* the significance of the here and now was immense and decisive. And this immensity. . . . Oh, that's enough, let's be off. Immensity, what sort of animal is that? The sun is setting already, what about a stroll? If I strangled and hanged the cat I ought to strangle and hang her too. It was incumbent upon me.

The sparrow was hanging in the thicket by the roadside, and the bit of wood was hanging in the crevice in the wall, they were both hanging motionless, but in the immobility here their immobility exceeded all the limits of immobility, the first limit, the second limit, the third, the fourth and fifth, and the sixth stone and seventh stone and the grass. It was getting cooler now.

I looked round, but she had gone. She had gone with that corrupt mouth of hers, and she was over there somewhere with it. I went away too, that is, I went away from the place where I was and walked across the meadow in the calm bosom of the mountains in the sunshine that was less troublesome now. My attention was absorbed by small unevennesses in the ground, but chiefly by stones lying in the grass that got in the way of my feet. What a pity that she put up no resistance to me, but how can somebody whose words serve only as an excuse for her voice put up any resistance? The way she said her piece after the killing of the cat. Ha, ha, ha. Very well, then, she doesn't put up any resistance, there will be no resistance. How painful that meeting had been, we had stood sideways without looking at each other, as if we were blind. There were more and more flowers in the grass, blue ones and yellow ones, and groups of pines and firs, the ground fell away and I was going downhill, I had gone quite a long way already, everything was inconceivably different and remote, butterflies flew about in the silence, there was a caressing breeze. Earth and grass and wooded slopes that transformed themselves into peaks. And there, under a tree, a bald patch and a pair of pince-nez. Leo.

He was sitting on a tree-trunk, smoking a cigarette.

'What are you doing here?'

'Nothing, nothing, nothing, nothing, nothing, nothing at all,' he replied, smiling happily.

'What is amusing you so much?'

'What is amusing me? Why, nothing. That's just the point. What amuses me, gentle sir and travelling companion, is precisely nothing, the nothing one does the whole of one's life. You get up, sit down, speak, write, and it's all nothing. You buy, sell, marry, don't marry, and it's all nothing. You sit on a tree-trunk and it's nothing. Like bubbles in a glass of soda water.'

He spoke slowly, casually, almost graciously.

'You speak as if you had never done any work,' I said.

'Work? And how I worked. The bank, the great big bank that keeps rumbling in my belly like a whale. Good gracious me. Thirty-two years inside the whale. And what did it all amount to? Nothing, nothing at all.'

He grew pensive and blew on his hand.

'Gone with the wind,' he said.

'What has gone with the wind?'

He replied in a nasal, monotonous voice:

'Years are divided into months, months into days, days into hours, hours into minutes and minutes into seconds, and the seconds go with the wind. They fly away and you can't catch them. What am I? An accumulation of seconds that have gone with the wind. They add up to nothing, nothing at all.

'It's downright robbery,' he exclaimed.

He removed his pince-nez and trembled with indignation. He suddenly looked old, and reminded me of the old gentlemen who sometimes make speeches of protest at street corners or in the tram or outside cinemas. Ought I to say something? But what? I was lost, did not know which way to go, there were so many threads, associations, implications. Supposing I counted them all up from the beginning, the cork, the tray, the trembling hand, the chimney, no, I should get lost in a cloud of meaningless objects and other imperfectly and vaguely defined matters, one little thing kept fitting in perfectly with another like a couple of cog-wheels, and then other links leading in other directions arose, and that was what I lived on, it wasn't living at all. It was chaos, like putting my hand into a ragbag and seeing what came out and whether it was suitable . . . for building my house with, and my house assumed pretty fantastic forms. And so on *ad infinitum*. . . . And this Leo. For some time I had noted the perplexing fact that he seemed to be circling round me and sometimes even accompanying and imitating me. So there was a resemblance between us, even if it was only that he lost himself in his seconds as I did in my trivialities, and there were also other little things that provided food for thought, those bread pellets he made at dinner, for instance, and that tri-li-li-lee of his; also it occurred to me, I don't know why, that that unpleasant whiff of egocentricity ('one is what one is') that was given off by the Tolos and the priest also somehow applied to him. What harm could it do if I mentioned the sparrow and all the strange goings-on in the house? Why not mention them and see what turned up? I felt like a clairvoyant concentrating on a crystal ball.

'You're in a bit of a nervous state, and it's not surprising after all the things that have been happening during the last few days. The cat, and so on and so forth. Little things, but puzzling and difficult to shake off, like a plague of vermin.'

'The cat?' he exclaimed. 'Who gives a damn for a dead cat? Who gives a damn for a dead cat? Look at that bumblebee, old chap, what a noise it's making. Yesterday the cat tickled my nervous system, that I admit, but today, in the face of all these mountains, my divine mountains? Of course my nerves are a bit on edge, but in solemn, festival fashion. Have you not noticed, my very dear friend, have you really not noticed anything?'

'What?'

He pointed to a flower in his buttonhole.

'And please advance your honourable nose and sniff.'

Sniff? This alarmed me, perhaps more than was necessary.

'Why?' I asked.

'I am slightly perfumed.'

'You perfumed yourself for your guests?'

I sat on another tree-trunk. His baldness and pince-nez produced a glass dome effect. I asked him if he knew the names of the mountains, but no, he did not, so I asked him the name of this valley, but he said he had forgotten it.

'What do you care about the names of the mountains?' he said. 'As if that mattered.'

I was on the point of asking him what mattered, but refrained. Better let it come up of its own accord. Let the mountains do their work. When Fuchs and I reached the end of the wall and found the bit of wood we also felt as if we were at the end of the world, what with the smells, including the whiff of urine, and the heat. So what was the point of asking questions here? It would be much better to let it come up by itself, because things were undoubtedly working up to something. So I kept quiet and behaved as if I were not there.

'Tri-li-li-lee.'

I stayed perfectly still.

'Tri-li-li-lee.'

Silence, the meadow, the blue sky, the sun, which was lower now, and the lengthening shadows.

'Tri-li-li-lee.'

Each time he repeated his little refrain it came out more vigorously. By now it was positively aggressive, like the signal for an attack.

'Berg,' he then exclaimed, loudly and distinctly, in a way that made it impossible for me not to inquire what it meant.

'I beg your pardon?'

'Berg.'

'What do you mean, berg?'

'Berg.'

'Oh yes, I remember, that Jewish story. You were going to tell us a story about two Jews.'

'What story? Fiddlesticks. Berging with the berg in the berg. Don't you see? Bamberging with the bamberg. Tri-li-li-lee,' he went on in a sly tone of voice

He moved his arms, and even his legs, as if he were dancing joyfully. Mechanically he repeated 'berg, berg,' which seemed to come up from almost unfathomable depths. Then he calmed down and waited.

'Well, I think I'll stroll on,' I said.

'No, stay where you are, why walk in the sun? It's pleasanter in the shade, much pleasanter. Such little pleasures are the best.'

'I've noticed that you like little pleasures.'

'I beg your pardon?' he said, and then he laughed with a kind of interior laugh.

'Well, I'll be damned,' he went on. 'You're perfectly right, I bet you're thinking of my little personal amusements on the tablecloth, under the eyes of my better half. My discreet little personal amusements, discreet, as is only fitting in polite society, giving no cause for comment. But she doesn't know. . . .'

'What doesn't she know?'

'That it's berging. Berging with my bamberg with all the bambergity of my bamberg.'

'Oh, I see. You have a rest here while I stroll on.'

'What's the point of dashing off like that? Wait a moment, perhaps I'll tell you. . . .'

'What?'

'What you're curious about.'

'You're a swine,' I said. 'A swine.'

Silence. Trees and shadows. A clearing. Silence. I had spoken quietly, but I had nothing to fear. At worst he would take offence and throw me out. Very well, that would be the end of that, it would cut things short, I would move to another pension or even go back to Warsaw and get on my father's nerves again and reduce my mother to despair at my insufferable character. Oh, rubbish, he would not take offence.

'You're a filthy swine,' I added.

The clearing. Silence. The only thing I was worried about was that he might be mad. For there seemed reason to fear that he might not be quite right in the head, in which case he or any possible actions or statements of his would be deprived of all significance, and this story of mine would turn out to be based on the futile and gratuitous extravagances of a poor lunatic. But by touching on this little matter of swinishness I might be able to make use of him, he might supply me with a link to Jadeczka, the priest, the cat, Katasia. He might supply another brick for the house I was laboriously building on the frontiers.

'What are you getting excited about?' he said casually.

'I'm not getting excited.'

All round us lay the peace of nature. Even if I had offended him, the whole thing was hazy and distant, as seen through a telescope.

'I might ask you by what right. . . .'

'You are utterly depraved.'

'That's enough. My lord and gentlemen of the jury, I crave your indulgence. I, Leo Wojtys, exemplary husband and father, with no police record or stain on my character, after a life-time of drudgery and toil all day and every day except Sundays and public holidays, a life-time of shuttling between my bank and my home, my home and my bank, have now retired on pension, and continue to live a no less exemplary life. Every morning I get up at 6.15 and every evening I go to bed at 11.30 (except when, by permission of my better half, I go to a little bridge party). In twenty-seven years of married life, my dear sir, I have never had another woman. In all that time I have never deceived my wife. Not once. I am an affectionate husband, kind, understanding, cheerful and polite, and I am the best of fathers. To my fellow men I am full of good will, courteous, obliging and helpful. Please tell me, my dear sir, what there is in my record that justifies you in making such . . . an insinuation, implying that I . . . surreptitiously and outside and apart from my immaculate married life . . . visit night clubs, indulge in drink, orgies, lechery, debauchery with women, bacchanalia with odalisques by lamplight. But you see for yourself that I am sitting quietly and talking and (he shouted triumphantly in my face) that I am correct in every particular and *tutti frutti*.'

Tutti frutti! The old rogue.

'You are a masturbator.'

'What? I beg your pardon? What am I to understand by that?'

. 'One is what one is.'

'What do you mean?'

I moved my face quite close to his and said:

'Berg.'

This worked. For a moment he swayed with astonishment at hearing this private word of his coming to him from outside. He was taken aback, and looked at me indignantly. Then he said:

'What on earth are you saying?'

But then he started shaking with inner laughter, he seemed to swell with it.

'Ha, ha, ha,' he went on. 'Berging the berg, doubly and trebly berging the berg, discreetly and surreptitiously berging the berg every moment of the night and day, and for choice at the family table in the dining-room, discreet and solitary bamberging under my wife's and daughter's eye! Berg! Berg! You have a very sharp eye, my dear sir. Nevertheless, if you will permit me. . . .'

He grew serious and thoughtful again, and then, as if he had remembered something, rummaged in his pocket and produced in the hollow of his hand a piece of sugar wrapped in paper, two or three sweets, the broken end of a fork, two indecent photographs and a lighter.

Trifles, trifles, just like the clumps of earth, the arrows, the bit of wood, the sparrow. I promptly felt positive that it had been he.

'What's all that?'

'Bergtitbits and bergpenalties awarded by the High Court. Bergpunishments inflicted by the local penal authorities and bergtitbits awarded by the department of caresses and delights. Rewards and punishments.'

'Whom do you punish and reward?'

'Whom?'

He sat there stiffly with outstretched hand, looking at it 'for himself alone', just as the priest had played with his fingers and Jadeczka found pleasure in her love . . . and just as I had corrupted my love. My fear that he would turn out to be a lunatic disappeared, it now seemed to me that we were both working together at something, working hard. Working hard at a long-term job. I wiped my brow which, incidentally, was dry.

It was hot, but by no means disagreeably so.

He moistened his fingers, carefully wiped his hand with it, and then thoughtfully scrutinized his finger-nail.

'You're cocking a snook at the world,' I said.

He made the welkin ring with his laughter, and almost started dancing without moving from his seat.

'Ha, ha, ha! Yes, you're quite right, yes, that's what I'm doing, cocking a snook at the world.'

'Did you hang the sparrow?'

'What? Hang the sparrow? Good gracious no, of course not.'

'Then who did?'

'How should I know?'

The conversation stopped short, and I did not know whether or not to revive it in this petrified landscape. I scratched off a bit of earth which was sticking to my trousers. We sat on our tree-trunks like two wise men taking counsel, though we did not know what we were taking counsel about. I again said 'berg' to him, this time more softly and quietly, and my expectations were not deceived, for he looked at me appreciatively, flicked his fingers, and murmured:

'I see that you're a berger, a bamberger, too.'

Then, in an objective, factual tone of voice, he said:

'Are you a bamberger?'

He burst out laughing and went on:

'My dear fellow, my dear fellow, do you realize why I have admitted you to the secret of my bambergery? Do you suppose I am stupid enough to admit all comers? Of course you don't. I admitted you because. . . .'

'Because of what?'

'How inquisitive you are. But I'll tell you.'

He gently took my ear and blew in it.

'I'll tell you. Why shouldn't I tell you? Well, it's because you berg, you bamberg, my own daughter, my own child and the child of my loins, by name Helena, known familiarly as Lena. You secretly and surreptitiously bamberg her. Do you suppose I have no eyes to see? You're a rogue.'

'What?'

'You're a rogue.'

'What are you getting at?'

'Still waters run deep. My dear young man, you secretly and surreptitiously bamberg my daughter, you would greatly like to creep under her skirts as berger No. 1 in her marriage. Tri-li-li-lee, tri-li-li-lee!'

The bark of a tree. Knots and veins. So he knew, or rather guessed. So my secret was out. But how much did he know? How was I to talk to him? Normally or . . . confidentially?

'Berg,' I said.

He looked at me appreciatively. A swarm, a kind of whirling bundle, of white butterflies flew across the field and disappeared behind the larches near the mountain stream. Yes, there was a mountain stream.

'So you are a bamberger, then. You're a sly one. I'm a bamberger too. We shall bamberg happily together. But all this, my dear fellow, is on the strict understanding that you keep your mouth shut, locked with a triple lock, and don't breath a word to any living soul. Because if you breathed a word to my beloved wife I'd throw you straight out of the house, head over heels, because of your evil designs on my darling daughter's marriage. I assume you accept that condition? Very well, then, in recognition of the fact that you have shown yourself to be a person worthy of confidence, it is hereby resolved that in accordance with the terms of decree . . . let us say decree No. 12,137 . . . you shall be admitted to my strictly private and secret bambergal ceremony due to take place this very day, complete with buttonhole and perfume. In other words, do you suppose, my dear sir, that I brought you all this long way just to admire the view?'

'Then why did you do it?'

'I brought you here for a celebration.'

'A celebration? Of what?'

'An anniversary.'

'Of what?'

He looked at me, and said reverently, with a kind of strange solicitude:

'Of the greatest occasion in my life. Twenty-seven years ago.'

He looked at me again, with the mystical look of a saint or martyr.

'With a cook,' he said.

'What cook?'

'The cook that was here then. The only time in my life. I carry it about inside me like the Holy Sacrament. The only time in my life.'

He relapsed into silence while I looked at the surrounding mountains. Mountains and still more mountains, rocks and still more rocks, forest and still more forest, trees and still more trees. Again he licked his finger, stroked his hand with it, and scrutinized it. Then he went on again, normally and seriously:

'You must understand that my youth was very mediocre. We lived in a small town, Sokolov, where my father was the head of a co-operative, you know what it's like in a small town, you have to watch your step all the time, everybody knows everything straight away, you know what it's like, it's like living in a glass-case, every step you take, everything you do, is public, and that's how I grew up, feeling I was being watched all the time, and on top of it, I admit, I have never been noted for outstanding courage, on the contrary, I was very shy and reserved. Of course I took a few little chances when they came my way, one does the best one can, but they didn't amount to very much. No, they amounted to very little, I was always under observation. And then, you know, as soon as I joined the bank I got married, and then there weren't many chances either, we nearly always lived in small towns, where it's like living in a glass-case with people watching you all the time and, I might even say, in those circumstances you do even more

125

watching yourself, because in marriage, you know, you watch each other from morning to night and from night to morning, and you can imagine what it was like under my wife's watchful eye, and later my daughter's. And of course at the bank you're watched all the time too. I devised a small entertainment for myself during office hours. I made a long scratch on my desk with my finger-nail, but one day the head of the department came in and said: "What on earth are you doing with your nail?" and what was I to say? The consequence was that I had increasingly to resort to minor and almost invisible little pleasures. Once, while we were living at Drohobycz, an actress came to the town on tour, she was a superb creature, absolutely superb, and one day I happened by pure chance to touch her hand in the bus, oh, what heaven, what ecstasy, oh, to be able to start life all over again, but it's no good, you can't put the clock back. I felt bitter and resentful, but I ended by pulling myself together and deciding that there was no point in wasting time thinking about touching somebody else's hand when you had two hands of your own. Believe it or not, after a certain amount of practice you can get quite expert in touching one hand with the other, under the table, for instance, where nobody can see, and even if they could see there would be nothing in it, there's nothing wrong in your hands touching or even your thighs, for example, or in touching your ear with your finger, because pleasure, it seems to me, is a question of setting your mind to it, and if you persist you can get pleasure from your own body, not a great deal of course, but it's better than nothing. I should prefer a houri or an odalisque, of course, but in the absence of a houri or an odalisque. . . .'

He rose to his feet, bowed, and sang:

> *If you can't get what you want*
> *You must want what you've got.*

He bowed again, resumed his seat, and continued:

'So I can't complain, I have managed to get something out of life. If others have managed to get more, well, good luck to them. And in any case, how can one tell? They brag and boast about the women they have had, though in reality they have had a pretty thin time. They come home, sit down, take their shoes off, and go to bed alone. So why make such a song and dance about it? At any rate I. . . . But if you concentrate on seeking out quite small and insignificant pleasures for yourself, and I do not mean only sexual pleasures, you can enjoy yourself like a pasha making little bread pellets, for instance. Or wiping your pince-nez, which I have practised for two years, because family troubles and office worries and arguing about politics are enough to drive you round the bend. I let them get on with it and just wipe my pince-nez. . . . What was I saying? Oh yes, you have no idea how these little things can help you to grow and get big. If your heel itches, it can make you feel as if you were in Volhynia at the other end of Poland, and incidentally you can get a certain amount of pleasure even from an itching heel, it all depends on your setting your mind to it. When you come to think about it, if a corn can be painful, why can it not also be pleasurable? And the same applies to sticking your tongue in the holes between your teeth. What was I going to say? Epicurism, or voluptuousness, can be of two kinds, it can be like a wild boar, a buffalo or a lion, or it can be like a flea or a mosquito, that is, it can be either large-scale or small-scale and, if the latter, it must be capable of microscopical treatment, of being divided and sub-divided and appreciated in small doses. Eating a sweet, for instance, can be divided into quite a large number of phases. First you can sniff it, then you can lick it, then you can pop it in your mouth, then you can play with it with your tongue and your saliva, then you can spit it out on to your hand and examine it, and you can burst it open with a tooth, and so on and so forth. At all events, as I have tried to make clear, you can manage without dancing, champagne, caviare, low-necked evening dress, bustling skirts, stockings, knickers, busts, ticklings, hee-hee-hee, oh, what are you doing? how do you dare? leave me alone, hee-hee-hee, ha-ha-ha, etc. I take my place quietly at the family dinner table, talk to the family and the lodgers, and nevertheless manage surreptitiously to enjoy some of the pleasures of Paris. And no one will ever find me out. No one will ever find me out. It all depends on one's creating for oneself a kind of comfortable, luxurious, voluptuous interior throne with fans and ostrich feathers in the style of Suleiman the Magnificent. Artillery salutes are important. And so is the ringing of bells.'

He rose to his feet, bowed, and again sang:

> *If you can't get what you want*
> *You must want what you've got.*

Again he bowed and resumed his seat.

'You certainly suspect me of being slightly cracked?'

'Slightly.'

'That's fine, you may assume that your suspicion is correct, it makes life easier. I play the madman to some extent to make life easier. Otherwise it would be too difficult. You like enjoying yourself?'

'Yes.'

'And you are a voluptuary?'

'Yes.'

'Well, my young friend, we are beginning to understand each other, as you see. It's really very simple. Men like . . . men like . . . what? They like love-making. They like berg.'

'Berg.'

'I beg your pardon?'

'Berg.'

'What do you mean?'

'Berg.'

'Oh, no, that's enough. Stop it.'

'Berg.'

'Ha, ha, ha, ha! So you've bamberged me. You're a deep one. You're a sly one. Who would have imagined that? You're a double, triple, superberger. That's the spirit. That's the spirit. Three cheers for berg.'

I looked at the ground. Again I found myself absorbed in the ground, the grass, and little clumps of earth. How many thousands of millions of them were there?

'Lick.'

'What?'

'Lick, I say, lickberg or spitberg.'

'*What* did you say?' I exclaimed. '*What* did you say?'

'I said lickberg or spitberg.'

The meadow, the trees, the tree-trunk. A pure chance. A pure coincidence. I must not lose my head. It was by pure chance that he had said 'spitberg', and he had said nothing about spitting in the mouth. No, I must not lose my head. He was not talking about me.

'Tonight is the great occasion.'

'What sort of occasion?'

'A pilgrimage.'

'You're very pious,' I remarked, and he looked at me with the same strange solicitude as before, and said earnestly and shyly:

'How could I not be pious? Of course I'm pious. Piety is essential, indispensable, the *sine qua non*. Not even the slightest of little pleasures can be enjoyed without piety. Oh, what am I saying? Personally I know nothing about it, and sometimes I'm lost as in a vast cloister, but you must appreciate that piety is the secret rule of the order, the holy mass on which the whole thing depends. Amen, amen, amen.'

He rose, bowed, and said:

'*Ite missa est.*'

Then he bowed again and sat down.

'The whole point,' he went on in an objective, matter-of-fact way, 'is that Leo Wojtys enjoyed pleasure, that is to say, absolute, perfect pleasure, only once in the course of his grey life, and that was twenty-seven years ago with the cook who worked in this mountain refuge. That was twenty-seven years ago. Today is the anniversary. Actually it is not the real anniversary, it's a month and three days short. And they (he leaned towards me as he said this) think I brought them here to admire the view. Actually I brought them here on a pilgrimage to the spot where twenty-seven years ago less one month and three days, I . . . that cook. I brought them here on a pilgrimage. My wife, my daughter, my son-in-law, the priest, the Lolos and the Tolos, are all here on a pilgrimage in honour of my supreme experience, my super-berg, and at midnight I shall emberg them to the place below the rock where she and I. . . . Let them commemorate the occasion. Unknowing pilgrims to the voluptaberg. But *you* will be in the secret.'

He smiled.

'But you will not tell.'

He smiled again.

'Do you bamberg?' he said. 'So do I. We shall bamberg together.'

Again he smiled.

'Now go,' he went on. 'I want to be alone, to concentrate my mind and prepare myself with due reverence for my solemn mass, my celebration, my greatest celebration. I want to be alone, so that in fasting and prayer I may purify and prepare myself to celebrate the memory of the most divine bamberg of my life on that unforgettable day. Now go, *arrivederci*.'

The fields, the trees, the mountains, the sky and the declining sun.

'And don't imagine that I'm gaga. I merely play the fool to make things easier. In reality I am a monk and a bishop. What is the time?'

'It's past six.'

His mention of spitting had of course been sheer coincidence. How could he possibly know anything about Lena's mouth that I carried about inside me? But these curious coincidences were more frequent than one would have expected, things kept popping up and sticking together as if they were glued, events and happenings were like those magnetized particles that sought each other out and joined up with one another as soon as they got close enough, never mind how. There was nothing surprising in his having discovered my secret passion for Lena, he was certainly a specialist in these things. And was it he who had hanged the sparrow and was responsible for the arrow and the bit of wood, as well as the pole, perhaps? Probably. No, certainly. But it was immaterial, it made not the slightest difference whether it was he or another. The really curious and interesting thing was that the sparrow and the bit of wood were still present and had not lost one iota of their power. Was there no salvation anywhere? It was also very curious and interesting that there should be this resemblance between us that made us click like two cog-wheels. In some things it was very obvious, as in his worship of details. Did we really have something in common? But what? Could it not be said that he was escorting me, guiding me, leading me astray? Sometimes I had the feeling that I was co-operating with him in a difficult birth—as if both of us were giving birth to something. Oh, come, come. Alternatively (how many alternatives can there be?) there was the consideration that 'one is what one is' that could not be overlooked. Might not that be the clue to the riddle of what was cooking here? A kind of growing wave approached me from that quarter, that of the priest and the Tolos, and it contained a menace, and the menace approached me like a forest, yes a forest—we say 'forest', but think what it means, think how many little details and particles go to make up a single leaf of a single tree, we say 'forest', but the word implies the unknown, the inconceivable, the unknowable. Earth and stones. You rest in broad daylight among ordinary, every day things that have been familiar since childhood; grass, trees, a dog (or cat), a chair, but only so long as you do not realize that each and every object is a huge army, an inexhaustible host. I was sitting on my tree-trunk as on a suit-case, waiting for a train.

'Tonight's pilgrimage will be to the place of my unique and supreme bliss experienced twenty-seven years ago, less one month and three days.'

I rose to my feet, but he was obviously unwilling to let me go without more definite information, he started talking more quickly, the words came pouring out of him.

'Tonight the secret and occult celebration of the great bambergus is taking place,' he said. 'The view? What view? You are all here to celebrate the anniversary of my supreme bambergus with the cook I told you about who used to work at the house,' he called out as I walked away. Fields, trees, mountains, vulture-like shadows.

I walked on. The grass was yellow and fragrant, flowers were dotted about, the fragrance was not like that by the wall which Fuchs and I had reached by following the direction of the broom-handle after crossing the area of whitewashed trees tied to their stakes and the waste area covered with weeds and rubbish. There had been a smell of urine, or whatever it was in that urine-like warmth, and the bit of wood had been waiting for us in that warm and disagreeable fragrance, waiting to be associated, not immediately, but later, with the pole lying in the rubbish in the hut, the harness and other odds and ends, and the door had been open.

The pole had led us to Katasia's room—the kitchen, the key, the window, the ivy—and all the things hidden all over the place had reached a climax in Kulka's hammering and Lena's knocking, which had led me to the big, prickly pine-tree I had climbed, and then I had seen the teapot, which had led to my murderous assault on the cat. The cat, the cat. How disgusting, it's enough to make you sick, I said to myself drowsily, the field was drowsy, and I walked on slowly, staring at the ground beneath my feet and looking at the flowers, and suddenly I fell into a trap.

It was a stupid, trivial trap. In front of me were two small stones, one to the right and the other to the left. On the left a little farther on there was a brown patch of earth that had been loosened by ants, and beyond that, also on the left, there was a big, black, rotten root, and these three things were in a straight line, hidden in the sunshine, sewn up in it, concealed in the luminous air. Just when I was on the point of walking between the two stones I made a small diversion to pass between one of them and the little patch of earth that the ants had turned over, it was a minimal diversion amounting to nothing at all, but there was no real reason for it, and that, I think, disconcerted me. So I mechanically made another minor diversion to pass between the two stones as I had originally intended, but I experienced a certain difficulty about this, a very slight difficulty, it is true, deriving from the fact that in view of these two successive diversions my intention to pass between the stones had assumed the quality of a decision, a trivial decision, needless to say, but nevertheless a decision. There was no excuse for this, of course, for the total neutrality of the objects lying in the grass justified no decision. What difference did it make which way I went? Also the valley, sleeping in its covering of trees, dazed by the buzzing of flies, seemed petrified, embalmed. Silence, drowsiness, sleep, dreams. In these circumstances I decided to pass between the two stones. But the few moments that had passed made the decision more of a decision than ever, and how was one to decide since it made no difference either way? So I stopped again. Furious at this, I again put my foot forward to pass between the stone and the patch of earth, as I had now decided, but realized that if I did so after two false starts it would not be ordinary walking, but something more important. So I decided to take the route between the patch of earth and the root. But then I realized that if I did this I should be acting as if I were afraid, so again I decided to pass between the stone and the patch of earth. Good heavens alive, what was happening, what was the matter with me, I could not allow myself to be held up like this on a level path while I struggled with such phantoms. What was the matter with me? The vegetation, the flowers, the mountains were enveloped in a warm, gentle drowsiness, and not even a blade of grass moved. I did not move either, I just stood. This position became more and more irresponsible and actually crazy. I had no right to stand there like this, it was impossible, I must go on, but I stayed rooted to the spot. And then, in the general immobility my own immobility became identified with that of the sparrow in the thicket and all the things that were immobile down there below, the sparrow, the bit of wood, the cat, and the death-like immobility that was accumulating here. At this I moved, thereby immediately destroying all the impossibility inside me, and I moved forward quite easily, without even realizing which way I was going, because it was completely immaterial, thinking about something else as I did so, namely, that the sun disappeared earlier here, because of the mountains. Yes, the sun was already pretty low. I walked on towards the house, whistling to myself, I lit a cigarette, and all that was left in my mind was a vague residue, a pale memory.

There was the house. No one was around. The windows and doors were wide open, the place was empty. I lay on a bed and rested. Later, when I went downstairs again, Kulka was in the hall.

'Where are they all?' I said.

'They've gone for a walk. Would you like some punch?'

IX

SHE gave me the drink and silence fell. It was a sad, or tired, or resigned silence. Neither of us concealed from the other that we had no wish to speak, or could not. I drank slowly, in long gulps, and she leaned out of the window, looking exhausted, as if after a route march.

'Mr Witol,' she said, without pronouncing the final 'd', as she did when she was nervy. 'Have you ever seen such a hussy? She can't even leave a priest alone. What does she take me for? A brothel madam?' (she suddenly shrieked, completely beside herself). 'I won't stand for it. I'll teach them to behave themselves when they are in polite society. And that husband of hers, that little whippersnapper in plus-fours, is even worse. If she were the only one to behave like that it would be bad enough, but he carries on just like she does. Have you ever seen one man provoking another with his own wife? It's absolutely incredible, making her sit on his knees, just imagine a husband flinging his wife at another man, and on his honeymoon, too. I should never have believed that a daughter of mine would have such immoral and mannerless friends. And it's all aimed at Jadeczka, they're trying to spoil her honeymoon. I've seen a great many things in my life, Mr Witol, but I've never seen anything like that, and I won't stand for it.' Then she said:

'Have you seen Leo?'

'Yes, I met him, he was sitting on a tree-trunk.'

I slowly emptied my glass and waited for her to go on, and I wanted to say something myself. But she didn't want to go on, and I ended by not wanting to say anything either. Impotence. What was the good of talking? We were too far away, over the hills and valleys, we were elsewhere.

But even this was an absent feeling, not really felt, so to speak. I put down my glass, said something, and walked out.

This time I strolled off in the opposite direction. I was

looking for them. With my hands in my pockets and bent head, thinking with the deepest part of my being but without a real thought in my head—as if all my thoughts had been stolen from me. The valley, with its plumes of trees, its mantles of forests, the mountainous humps all round, attracted my attention, but in the background, so to speak, like a noise, the sound of a distant waterfall, an incident from the Old Testament, or the light of a star. In front of me were millions of blades of grass. I raised my head, for loloish laughter and giggles reached my ears, and they emerged from behind the trees. 'Lolo, stop it at once.' 'Lola, let go or I'll bite.' Blouses, shawls, handkerchiefs, plus-fours. They were advancing in disorderly fashion, and when they saw me they waved, and I waved too.

'Where have you been? What have you been up to? We've been all the way to that hill over there.'

I joined them, and walked straight in the direction of the sun, which had now vanished. All it had left behind was a solar void, a kind of sunny emptiness exposed by the tense brilliance coming from behind a mountain as from a hidden source and inflaming the lilac sky that was now shining as if for itself and was no longer in communication with the earth. I looked round. Down below everything had changed, though it was still daylight. But the beginnings of a kind of indifference had set in, a kind of condensation and a sense of abandonment, as if a key had been turned in a lock. The mountains, hills, stones, trees, now existed only for themselves and were approaching their end. The gaiety of our little party was cacophonous, like the sound of a breaking window-pane. Nobody walked with anyone else, everyone was on his own. The Lolos were on the flank, she in front and he behind, looking cheerful, though you could tell that all was not so gay within. The main body consisted of Lena, Louis and Fuchs. Tolo and Jadeczka were on the other flank, with the priest behind them. But they were scattered all over the pace. There are too many, what am I to do with them? I said to myself in alarm.

I was amazed to see Fuchs skipping about in a state of huge delight and calling out:

'Help! Help! Help me, Miss Wojtys, please!'

'Don't you dare help him, Lena, he isn't on his honeymoon,' said Lola.

'I'm always on honeymoon, I'm on permanent honeymoon,' said Fuchs.

'It happens to him every month,' said Lolo. 'He's always going on about what happens to him monthly.'

Lena laughed softly.

Oh, the honey, the sticky honey of that triple honeymoon. In Jadeczka's case it turned into a private and peculiar honey of her own, because when she smelled herself she didn't mind and she did not take baths, why should she, or if she did it was only for hygienic reasons, for herself alone and not for anyone else. The Lolos were going for Fuchs, but of course Jadeczka was their real target, Fuchs was only the cushion off which the billiard balls bounced, and he knew it, but he was delighted at being bombarded with their jokes; he, Drozdowski's victim, was tickled to death and was almost dancing with red-haired ecstasy. While he thus danced for himself alone in close proximity to the Lolos a deep and rather repellent silence prevailed on the part of the Tolos. At my feet there was grass and yet more grass, made up of stalks and leaves in various positions and at various angles, twisted or broken, crushed or dried up; this fleetingly caught my attention, which was chiefly engaged by the whole of the vegetation which extended uninterruptedly to the mountains but was already locked up and condemned to itself.

We advanced slowly. Fuchs's laughter was even more stupid than the Lolos' giggles. I was taken aback by his idiocy, the surprising crescendo of his idiocy, but even more by the honey which was increasing and multiplying. It had started with the talk about honeymooning, but now, thanks to Jadeczka, it became more and more 'private' and disgusting. And the priest contributed to this by his insistent twiddling with his fingers. This amorous and disgusting honey was also connected in some way with me. Oh, these connections. I must stop connecting and associating.

Our slow, wandering footsteps led us to an idyllic little stream. Fuchs hurried forward, sought out the easiest place to cross, and called out 'this way'. Lack of light increasingly impinged on the light framed by the trees on the mountain-side. Lola called out:

'Lolo, please carry me across. Take pity on my shoes, Lolo, please. Please carry me across, darling.'

'Tolo, you carry her across,' Lolo said impudently.

Tolo's reply took the form of a cough, whereupon Lolo wriggled his hips and said with an innocent, schoolboy air:

'You will oblige me, won't you, Tolo, I'm dead beat, I've no strength left.'

The subsequent course of events was as follows. Lola called Lolo a weakling and a coward and dashed over to Tolo and started what was almost a little dance in front of him.

'Please take pity on me, Mr Tolo,' she said. 'Look, my husband has let me down, please take pity on my poor shoes.' And she held out her little foot.

'Come on, Tolo, one, two, three and it's done. Where's your courage, man?' said Lolo, and Lola said 'one, two, three,' and tried to put herself in his arms.

'Come on, one, two, three and it's done,' said Lolo.

I did not take too much notice of all this, for I was more or less absorbed by the scene that enveloped us, the surrounding mountains that from a distance embraced and enclosed us. There was a certain severity about them now, for their covering of forests made them grimmer as darkness fell (high above us there was still bright light, though it was separated from us). But I distinctly saw the Lolos dancing a war dance, the cavalry captain not doing so, Fuchs in the seventh heaven of delight, Louis not in the seventh heaven of delight, the priest standing still, and Lena. . . . Oh, why had I contaminated her with Katasia's lip on that first night in the corridor, and why, instead of forgetting it next day, had I returned to it and made the contamination permanent? There was one thing I was curious about: had that association been pure caprice on my part, or had I divined a real link between that mouth and that lip? But what link? What link?

Had it been pure caprice and fantasy? No. I felt no guilt in the matter. It had come to me, not from me. And why should I have deliberately made her repulsive to me, since without her my life would henceforth be meaningless and grey, spoilt and disfigured? There she stood, looking so attractive that I looked the other way, preferring to stare at the grass and have the valley in my head. No, the situation was not that that filthy association with Katasia prevented me from loving her, it was far worse than that. I did not want to love her, I simply did not want to, and the reason was that if my body had been covered all over with spots and in that state I had set eyes on Venus herself, I should not have wanted her either. I should not have looked at her. I felt ill, so I did not want her. But have a care, have a care. So it was I who was disgusting and not she? So I was the source of the disgust, it was my fault? I could not make head or tail of it and never would. But look.

'Come on, man, be bold.' Lolo's calves covered with chequered socks. 'Come on, carry her across, you're on honeymoon too.'

Then came Jadeczka's deep, confident, generous voice: 'Please carry the lady across, Tolo,' she said.

I looked. By this time Tolo was depositing Lola on the grass on the other side of the stream, and the farce was over. We resumed our progress, our slow progress over the grass. Honey, why honey, why honey? Why did I connect honey with the priest's fingers? I walked on as if in the middle of a wood at night, when noises, shadows and fugitive, intangible shapes surround and oppress you, always on the point of assaulting you. . . . And Leo with his bamberging in the berg? When and from where would the prowling wild beast pounce? The mountain-ringed meadows led straight to silence, abandonment and isolation, to pockets of non-existence and invisibility, to citadels of blindness and dumbness, and behind some trees in their midst there appeared the house that was not a house, the house that existed only to the extent that it did not exist, was not that other house with its self-contained system of hanged sparrow, bit of wood, and cat, the whole supervised by the disfigured mouth of Katasia, who was in the kitchen—or the garden—or perhaps out on the verandah.

The penetration of this house by the other was not only troublesome, it was also morbid, completely and horribly morbid, and not only morbid but also imperious, and I said to myself oh well, it can't be helped, there's nothing that can be done about it, the whole constellation can no longer be destroyed or got rid of, there's no getting away from it, it's too well established by now and there's too much of it. And I walked on mechanically, and Louis asked me if I could lend him a razor-blade (but of course, with pleasure), and I said to myself that nothing could be done about it, because any attempt to fight it off or run away from it only embroiled you further, as in one of those traps in which the slightest movement only ensnares you more deeply. And who knows, perhaps this had happened to me only because I had defended myself against it. Perhaps I had been too frightened when Katasia's lip first mingled in my mind with Lena's, and perhaps that had caused the seizure with which it had all begun. Might my defence have preceded the attack? I could not tell. In any case it was too late now. A polyp had formed somewhere on the surface of my being, and the more I destroyed it the more obstinately it survived.

The house in front of us seemed already to have been ravaged by the dusk, and its very substance had been weakened. The whole valley was filled with helplessness, the sky was vanishing, curtains of mist were being drawn across it, things were refusing to communicate and were creeping back into their lairs. They were disappearing, disintegrating, coming to an end. It was still fairly light, but the power of sight itself seemed to be dangerously diminishing. I smiled, saying to myself that darkness was propitious, in the dark one could approach, touch, seize, embrace, make love to the point of madness, but what was the use, I did not want to, I was ill, I had a rash, I was ill. All I wanted was to spit in her mouth.

I did not want to.

'Look.'

I heard the woman say this quietly but fervently to her loved one (and without looking at them I was sure she was referring to the lilac-coloured horizon). 'Look,' she said in a sincere and elevated tone with her buccal orifice, and I also heard him reply 'yes' in a deep voice that was no less sincere. And what about the priest? What was he up to with those fingers of his?

When we got close to the house Fuchs and Lolo ran a race to the front door.

We went in. Kulka was in the kitchen. Leo emerged from one of the other rooms with a towel in his hands.

'Get ready for supper, children,' he said. 'Make yourselves neat and tidy, all nice and shiny like a packet of new pins. A bite will do you good after your walk.'

Louis again asked me to lend him a razor-blade, and immediately afterwards Leo nudged me and asked if he could borrow my watch, because he could not rely on his own. I gave it to him, and asked him whether punctuality was so important, and he whispered that it had to be exact to the very minute. Soon afterwards Louis came back and this time asked me if I could lend him a piece of string, but I had none. A watch, a razor-blade and a piece of string, I said to myself. They kept asking for things, what was cooking now? How many plots were hatching simultaneously with my own? How many non-apparent, rudimentary, distorted or concealed configurations were maturing independently of my own? And what was that priest up to, for instance?

The table was already half laid, the shadows in the house were growing blacker, night prevailed on the staircase, but in our room on the first floor, where Fuchs was combing his hair in front of a pocket mirror on the window-ledge some light still remained. Nevertheless the darkness of the forests covering the slopes about a mile away crept in through the window in hostile fashion, and two trees near the house started rustling, for a breeze had sprung up.

'It was absolutely fantastic, old man.' Fuchs was talking. 'It was absolutely fantastic, I tell you. You saw for yourself how they had it in for those two, but you can't imagine what it was like during the walk. It was enough to make you split your sides, when once they get their knives into someone, heaven preserve him. But I must admit I'm not surprised. The worst of it is that Lola is so . . . inspired, that's the only word for it. Would you mind holding the comb for me? Thank you. Actually I can't blame Lola. Jadeczka's buying herself a husband with her father's money is provoking enough, but running after another man on top of it. . . . Of course it's embarrassing for Lena, because they are her guests and both of them are friends of hers, and she hasn't enough savoir-faire to handle the situation, she's too weak, and Louis is a strange fellow, he's nothing but a well-dressed office work-horse, he doesn't amount to anything at all, I wonder why Lena picked on a man like that, it's extraordinary the choices people make. Of course it's a difficult situation with three honeymoon couples, and trouble was to be expected, after all. But I must admit that going too far is going too far, and I can't blame Lola for wanting to get her own back. She actually caught her in the act with Lolo.'

'What do you mean, caught her in the act?'

'I saw it with my own eyes. At lunch, when I bent down to pick up a box of matches. His hand was on his knee under the table, and Jadeczka's was just beside it, only a fraction of an inch away, and not in a very natural position either. You can guess the rest.'

'You must have imagined it.'

'Imagined it? I certainly did not imagine it. I've got a nose for that sort of thing. And Lola must have noticed it too, I could tell from her behaviour. Now both she and Lolo have got their knives into Jadeczka.'

I did not want to argue, it was too much for me. Was it possible? Why should it not be possible? Jadeczka might be like that, why should she not be like that? If she were, thousands of reasons could be found to explain it. But why should Fuchs not have been mistaken? Perhaps he had not seen properly, he might have been mistaken, or he might even have invented the whole thing for reasons of his own. I was ill, ill, ill; and the fact that *hands* had turned up again alarmed and oppressed me and made me clench my fingers. How many dangers threatened. Meanwhile Fuchs went on talking, changed his shirt, showed his red face, talked red-facedly, the sky faded into nothing, Leo could be heard singing *She's just the girl for dad*, and I said cruelly:

'And how about Drozdowski?'

He flushed.

'Good God, man, how brutal can one be?' he exclaimed. 'Do you have to remind me of him now? When I think that in a few days' time I'll be cooped up with him again for seven hours a day . . . he makes me sick, I tell you, it's incredible the knack he has for getting on my nerves. If you could only see the way he has of sticking out his leg. It's enough to make you feel sick. But to hell with him, *carpe diem*, gather ye rosebuds while ye may, as Leo says, I'm going to enjoy myself while I can, am I right or not?'

From down below Kulka could be heard announcing in a wooden, if not actually stony, voice that supper was ready. The wall beside the window facing me was rich in distractions, as all walls are; there were veins, a round red patch, two scratches, the paper was peeling in one or two places and some of the fibre was in a bad state, it was the accumulation of years. In fact not much of the paper was left, but it was still there, and as I found my way about it I said I wondered what the latest news of Katasia was and whether anything had happened down at the house, what did he think? I stopped for a moment listening to my own question.

'What on earth do you expect to have happened? Do you really want to know what I think? Well, I'll tell you. If we hadn't been so bored there, nothing at all would have happened. Boredom, my dear fellow, makes you imagine even more things than fear does. Heaven alone knows what you're capable of imagining when you're bored. Come on.'

Down below it was dark, and above all it was cramped. The hall was uncomfortable, and the table had had to be put in a corner because of two benches that were fixed into the wall. Several persons were engaged in taking their seats on them, to the accompaniment of jokes and laughter, of course. 'A squeeze in the dark. What could be more ideal for honeymoon couples?' somebody said, whereupon Kulka brought in two petrol lamps that spread a sort of foggy light.

A moment later, when one had been put on a shelf and the other on a cupboard, they burned better, and the oblique light they cast magnified our bodies ranged round the table and made them fantastic; vast shadows swept along the wall, the light cruelly revealed fragments of faces and busts while the rest was invisible, more people took their seats, making it more cramped than ever, it was like being in a dense forest, and the enlargement of hands, sleeves and necks made it denser still. Meat was served, vodka was poured out, and the whole thing was like a phantasmagoria of mastodons and hippopotami. The lamps made the darkness outside denser and wilder than before. I sat next to Lola. Lena was rather a long way away between Jadeczka and Fuchs on the other side of the table. In this fantastic scene heads joined up with each other and hands outstretched towards dishes projected complicated shadows that mingled with each other on the walls. There was no lack of appetite, people helped themselves to ham, veal and beef, and the mustard circulated. I had a good appetite myself, but the thought of spitting in her mouth . . . the food in my mouth got covered with spittle. And honey. My appetite was poisoned and so was I. Jadeczka, in ecstasy, let Tolo give her a second helping of salad and I wondered whether it was possible that she might be not only what I thought she was, but also what Fuchs said she was. It was by no means impossible, with that buccal orifice of hers and the state of ecstasy she was in she might really be like that, for everything was always possible, and among the thousands of millions of possible reasons for everything you could always find one to explain anything. And the priest? What was the truth about this silent priest who was swallowing something just as if it were noodles or porridge? He ate awkwardly, his way of ingesting food was peasant-like, poor and pinched, somehow downtrodden like a worm (though I couldn't really say for certain, I wasn't sure about anything, I was staring at the ceiling). But what was the matter with him? Was something cooking in that quarter? I too did the meal pretty good justice, though I was nauseated. But it was I who was nauseating, not the cold veal, what a pity to have to spoil . . . everything by my own corruption. But I was not too upset by this, for what could really upset me at this distance? Leo was also eating at a distance. He was sitting right in the corner, where the two fixed benches joined, the protruding lenses of his pince-nez shone like drops of water under the dome of his bald pate, his face was suspended over his plate, and he cut some bread and ham into small pieces, and then proceeded as follows: he stuck his fork into each morsel, raised it to his mouth, popped it in, tasted it, masticated it, and finally swallowed it; consequently he took a long time over each. Strangely enough, he was silent, and perhaps for that reason there was little conversation, everyone just ate. Leo obtained satisfaction by eating like that, it was a kind of masturbation, and I found this pretty wearing, particularly as the way Jadeczka was satisfying her appetite next to the cavalry captain, though dissimilar, was similar ('one is what one is'); and, apart from the way she ate, there was also the way the priest ate, which was rustic. And 'eating' was connected with 'mouths', and in spite of everything mouths started haunting me again. Spitting in her mouth. Spitting in her mouth. I went on eating, not without appetite, which disgustingly enough testified to the fact that I had got used to my own spit, but I was not disgusted by my disgust, for it was distant.

I went on eating cold veal and salad. There was also vodka.

'The eleventh.'

'The eleventh is a Tuesday.'

'. . . with silver plate at the bottom it's all right.'

'. . . to the Red Cross, but they said that. . . .'

Snatches of conversation. '. . . or nuts, the salted ones.' 'I won't take no thank you for an answer. Take some more and don't argue.' 'He sticks to the right and won't let anyone pass.' 'Whose?' 'Last night.' The forest grew thicker, and seemed to be going round and round. I was in the middle of a cloud that was also going round and round and was always bringing up something new, so much of it that it was impossible to remember and grasp it all. It had all begun with the iron bed on which she had been lying when I first saw her and noticed her foot, but in the meantime that bed seemed to have got lost somewhere on the way. And the bit of cork in the dining-room had also vanished. And then there had been the knocking noise and the chicken Louis had talked about, and the ashtray, and the staircase, yes, the staircase, and the little window, the chimney and the gutter, and all the rubbish lying under and round the pole, and of course the fork, the knife and the hand, the hands, her hand, my hand, Leo's tri-li-li-lee, to say nothing of Fuchs and all the rest of it, for instance the ray of sunshine coming in through a crack in the blind, and our following the direction indicated by the broom-handle, and the staked trees, and our tramp along the road in the heat. Oh Lord, oh Lord, the exhaustion, the smells, the cup of tea . . . and the way Kulka said 'my daughter' and, oh Lord in heaven above, the hole behind that root and so on and so forth, and that bit of soap in Katasia's room, and the teapot, and her fugitive glances as modest as a sprig of mimosa, the garden gate and all its details, including the padlock, oh almighty and merciful God, all the things on the window-sill and under the ivy, and when the light went out in their room, the branches of the pine-tree when I climbed down, and the priest on the road, and the prolongation of those imaginary lines, oh Lord, oh Lord, the bird hanging in the sky, Fuchs taking off his shoes and conducting his stupid inquest in the dining-room, and the way we had left the house in Katasia's charge, the verandah and the door when we first set eyes on it, the heat, the fact of Louis's going to his office and the situation of the kitchen in relation to the house, one particular stone, a yellowish one, and the key to Katasia's room, the frog—what on earth had happened to that frog?—a bit of ceiling that was peeling, and the ants near the second tree along the path, and the corner of the house behind which we were standing when . . . oh Lord, oh Lord, oh Lord, *Kyrie eleison, Christe eleison*, the tree on the height over there, and that place behind the cupboard, and my father and my rows with him, the wire on that hot fence, *Kyrie eleison.* . . .

Leo put a bit of salt on his finger, raised it to his mouth, put it on his tongue, and then withdrew it.

'. . . they were forced sideways on top of them'. . . . 'somewhere in the Bystra neighbourhood'. . . . 'on the second floor, I wonder if anyone'. . . . Words accumulating as on a dirty carpet . . . or ceiling.

Leo finished eating and sat there with his face concealed under his dome-like head. His face seemed to be suspended from his bald pate. . . . No doubt the reason why they were talking so much was that he was silent. His silence created a gap.

He dabbed his finger on a little pile of salt to make some stick to it, inspected his finger, put out his tongue, put the salt on it, closed his mouth and savoured it.

Jadeczka took some slices of cucumber with her fork. She was silent.

The priest leaned forward with his hands under the table. His cassock.

Lena, who had been sitting there quietly, suddenly engaged in a whole series of minor activities. She folded her napkin, moved a glass, removed a speck of dust, put a glass in front of Fuchs, and smiled.

Lolo jumped to his feet and called out: 'Bang!'

Kulka came in, stood there stolidly for a moment, looked at the table, and withdrew to the kitchen again.

Why did I notice these things and not others? Why? I looked at the walls. Dots and stains. Something emerged from them, a kind of shape, but it vanished, leaving chaos and excess behind. What was the matter with the priest? And with Fuchs, Jadeczka and honey. And where was Louis (he wasn't there, he had not come down to supper, I assumed he was shaving, I wanted to ask Lena where he was, but didn't). And what had become of the peasants who had driven us here? Chaos and confusion. What can one know? Suddenly I was struck by the landscape outside, the landscape with all its variations stretching to the mountains and beyond, the main road winding through the night, which was painful and oppressive. Why had I strangled the cat? Why had I strangled the cat?

Leo raised his eyes and looked at me very thoughtfully and attentively and even laboriously—and helped himself to a glass of wine and raised it to his mouth.

His attentiveness and laboriousness communicated themselves to me. I raised my glass to my mouth and drank.

His eyebrows were quivering. I dropped my eyes.

'Ladies and gentlemen, I ask you to rise and drink to the health of the bachelors'. . . . 'Shame on you, how dare you propose that toast on your honeymoon!'. . . . 'Well then, the ex-bachelors'. . . . 'Leave him alone, let him drown his sorrows'. . . . 'What *are* you doing, Lolo?'. . . . 'What are *you* doing, Lola?'

Leo, with pince-nez gleaming under his bald pate, stretched out his finger, took a pinch of salt, popped it in his mouth and kept it there.

Jadeczka raised her glass to her lips.

The priest produced a very strange sound indeed, a kind of glug-glug. He shifted in his seat.

A small window, with a little hook.

I took a long drink.

Leo's eyelids were quivering.

I dropped my eyes.

'Why are you so thoughtful, Mr Wojtys?'

'Mr Wojtys, what are you thinking about?'

This was the Lolos. Then Kulka said:

'Leo, what are you thinking about?'

She asked the question fiercely, standing in the kitchen doorway with dangling hands, and she made no attempt to conceal her anxiety; she spoke as if she were injecting anxiety into us with a syringe, and I thought hard and deeply and at the same time my mind was a blank.

'She asks what I'm thinking about,' said Leo casually, as if the question had nothing to do with him.

Honey.

The tip of his tongue appeared between the slit of his thin, pink lips and stayed there, it was the tongue of an old gentleman in pince-nez. Tongue, spitting in her mouth, then suddenly a scene of chaos and confusion that was like thunder and lightning, and Lena's mouth and Katasia's came to the surface for a moment, I caught a fleeting glimpse of them, as one might catch sight of a bit of paper being whirled about in the seething cauldron under a waterfall before it vanished.

I gripped the leg of my chair to avoid being carried away myself. But the gesture came too late. In any case it was a rhetorical gesture. Absurd.

The priest.

Kulka. Nothingness. Leo. Lola said plaintively:

'What about this expedition of yours, Mr Wojtys? In the middle of the night, in the dark? But we shan't be able to see a thing.'

'We certainly shan't be able to see much in the dark,' Fuchs said impatiently and not very politely.

'My wife,' Leo said (he actually said that, with the bird and the bit of wood still hanging down there below). 'My wife,' he said (oh Holy Mother of God), 'my wife' (I clasped my fingers hard) . . . 'but do not let us get excited,' he said cheerfully. 'There's nothing whatever to get excited about, nothing whatever. Everything is in order, we are all sitting here very comfortably, thanks be to God. We are all sitting here on our little sit-upons gratefully enjoying God's gifts, glug, glug, glug, with wine and vodka, and in a short time a little expedition will set out under my guidance to that unique spot where a most marvellous view is to be obtained, thanks, as I was saying, to the marvellous moon dancing tra-la-la in the midst of the mountains, the hills and the vales, tra-la, as I myself saw it twenty-seven years ago minus one month and three days, ladies and gentlemen, when for the first time at the same bewitching hour I went to that remarkable spot and saw. . . .

'Sucking,' he said, and went pale and gasped for breath.

'But's it's getting cloudy,' Lolo said indignantly and rather impolitely. 'It'll be pitch dark and we shan't be able to see a thing.'

'So it's cloudy,' Leo muttered. 'So it's cloudy. That's fine. It was cloudy then too, I remember. I noticed it on the way back, I remember distinctly,' he said impatiently, as if he were in a great hurry. Then he relapsed into thoughtfulness again.

I was thoughtful too. I was thinking all the time, as hard as I could. Kulka, who had withdrawn into the kitchen, reappeared in the doorway.

'Mind your sleeve.'

These words of Leo's made me start. But he was talking to Fuchs, whose sleeve was touching the sauceboat which had contained mayonnaise. Nothing important, take it easy. But why wasn't Louis here, where was he, why wasn't he with her?

The sparrow.

The bit of wood.

The cat.

'My wife doesn't trust me,' Leo announced.

One by one he examined the first three fingers of his right hand, beginning with the forefinger.

'My wife wants to know what I am thinking about, ladies and gentlemen.'

He waved three fingers of his right hand in the air, and I clasped my hands together firmly.

'Ladies and gentlemen, after twenty-seven years of unblemished married life it is a slight . . . er, disappointment to me that my wife should so nervously enquire what I am thinking about.'

The priest interrupted.

'The cheese, please,' he said. Everyone looked at him, he repeated 'the cheese, please,' Lolo passed him the cheese, but instead of cutting himself a slice he said: 'We might perhaps push the table back a bit, we're rather cramped here.'

'Yes, we might push the table back a bit,' Leo said. 'What was I saying? Oh yes, after all those years of irreproachable, unimpeachable and exemplary married life that was something I felt I did not deserve. After all those years, months, weeks, days, hours, minutes and seconds. Do you realize, ladies and gentlemen, that I sat down with paper and pencil and worked out how many seconds of married life I had enjoyed up to 7.30 this evening? The result, not forgetting to take the leap years into account, was 140,912,984. And since eight o'clock several thousands more have to be added.'

He rose to his feet and sang:

> *If you can't get what you want*
> *You must want what you've got.*

He sat down and grew thoughtful again.

'If you would like to push the table back a little, please do,' he said. 'What was I saying? Oh yes. All those seconds under my wife's and my daughter's eye. Who would ever have supposed that my wife would be suspicious about what I was thinking?'

Again he broke off and grew thoughtful. These repeated relapses into thoughtfulness were untimely, and a strong sense of dismay or disorder or something of the sort became discernible, not perhaps in his speech, but in general, in the whole atmosphere. And this was his celebration. The sparrow. The bit of wood. The cat. It was not about that. So it was about that. But it was not about that. So it was about that.

He was conducting a kind of religious service, and he seemed to be trying to say: See how attentively I am devoting myself to inattention.

Then he went on again.

'So my wife does not trust my thoughts. Tell me, ladies and gentlemen, do I deserve that? It seems to me that I do not. Except that, if we are to tell the truth (yes, do push the table back a bit, I'm cramped too, and these seats are hard, but that can't be helped), except that, as I was saying, if we are to tell the truth, it must be admitted that it is impossible to tell what is going on in someone else's mind. Let me illustrate what I mean. Let us say that I, for example, an exemplary husband and father, pick up this egg-shell.'

He suited the action to the word and went on:

'Supposing I twist it between my fingers like this, quite slowly, in full sight of everybody. It is impossible to imagine anything more innocent, more innocuous, more inoffensive. Nothing but an utterly harmless little pastime, in fact. But let us go a little more closely into the question of how I twist it between my fingers. Because, you see, I can twist it perfectly virtuously and innocently. But, if I want to, I can also . . . Eh? If I want to, I can also twist it in a slightly more . . . Eh? Yes. This is only an example, of course, to show that even the most admirable of husbands might be capable of twisting an egg-shell in his wife's presence in a manner. . . .'

He flushed. He grew purple. It was astonishing. He realized what was happening and half closed his eyes, but made no attempt to dissimulate his shame. On the contrary, he displayed it to everybody like a monstrance.

Still twisting the egg-shell in his fingers, he waited for the flush to pass. Then he opened his eyes again and said:

'Well, that's all, it's nothing.'

The tension relaxed, though in our corner under the lantern they still felt slightly nervous and oppressed. They looked at him, obviously thinking he was a bit off his head. At all events, nobody spoke.

There was a thump from somewhere outside, as if something had fallen. What could it have been? It was a sound apart, an extra, superadded sound, and it engaged my attention and I thought about it for a long time. But I could make nothing of it.

Then Leo quietly and very politely and distinctly said: 'Berg.'

And I, no less politely and distinctly, responded: 'Berg.'

He looked at me briefly and dropped his eyes. We both sat there quietly, listening to the echoes of the word 'berg', as if it were a subterranean monster, one of those that never appear in daylight but was now here, in front of us. They all looked at it, I presume. Suddenly I felt that everything was on the move, like a flood or an avalanche, or an army marching with banners; I felt as if something decisive had happened, and everything was now moving forward in a definite direction. Quick march. Into the breach, dear friends. If Leo alone had said 'berg' it would not have amounted to anything, but I had said it too. My 'berg' coming on top of his had deprived it of its private and confidential character, it was no longer the private expression of a crackpot, but was something that really existed and was here before us, in our presence. It immediately advanced, invaded and took possession.

For a moment I saw the sparrow, the bit of wood, and the cat, and at the same time the mouths also, whirling away and sinking like scraps of paper in a mountain torrent. I was waiting for everything to march off in the berg direction. I was an officer on the general staff, a choir boy helping at mass, an acolyte, the loyal and disciplined servant of a cause. Quick march.

But Lola called out:

'Bravo, Mr Wojtys!'

She ignored me, but I felt certain that she did this for the simple reason that she was afraid, afraid of cooperating with him. The whole thing suddenly collapsed and disintegrated, there was some quiet laughter, everyone started talking, Leo broke into a loud guffaw. It was time for everyone to whet his whistle, ha, ha, ha, ha! How disappointing that such a disastrous collapse should follow such a solemn moment, when everything had been poised for a great leap forward. Once more there was a buzzing as if of a swarm of bees, yes, I'll have a little vodka, aren't you drinking, father? have just a drop of cognac. Jadeczka, Tolo, Lolo, Lola, Fuchs and Lena with that fresh, pretty little mouth of hers, a party on an outing. Everything had collapsed. Nothingness. Once more everything was like a dirty wall. Chaos and confusion.

The sparrow.

The bit of wood.

The cat.

I remembered them just because I was forgetting them. They came back to me because they had been moving away. They were sinking and disappearing. I had to look into myself for the sparrow, the bit of wood and the cat that were sinking and disappearing from sight, I had to look for them, find them and keep them. And I had to make an effort to return in thought to the thicket on the other side of the road and the wall. The priest got up and clumsily extricated himself from between the table and the bench, muttering excuses. He opened the door, and he and his cassock crept out of the room.

In the absence of berg I felt foolish and at a loss. I decided that I too must go outside for a breath of fresh air.

I rose, walked towards the door, and went out.

It was cool on the verandah. The moon. A swelling, towering cloud, solid and luminous. Lower down, and much darker, there was a fountain of petrified mountains. And all round there were fairy-like meadows carpeted with trees and flowers and processions, as in a park where dancing and singing were taking place. The whole was submerged at the bottom of the moonlight.

Near the steps the priest was leaning over the balustrade.

He was motionless, and was doing something strange with his mouth.

X

I SHALL find it difficult to tell the rest of this story. Incidentally, I am not sure that it is one. Such a continual accumulation and disintegration of things can hardly be called a story.

Outside on the verandah, when I saw the priest doing something strange with his mouth, I was taken utterly aback. I should not have been more taken aback if the earth's crust had suddenly burst open and subterranean monsters emerged. Could what I was seeing be true? I alone knew the secret of the mouths. No one but me had been initiated into the mystery of Lena's mouth. It was my secret, and this priest had no right to it. What right had he to put it in his own mouth?

Then I realized that he was vomiting. Yes, vomiting. His wretched, hideous, pitiful vomiting was easy to explain. He had drunk too much.

So much for that. It was insignificant.

He saw me, and produced a shame-faced smile. I was just going to tell him to go to bed and sleep it off when someone else came out on the verandah. It was Jadeczka. She swept past me into the meadow, stopped, put her hand to her mouth, and then by the light of the moon I saw that she was vomiting too.

If the priest vomited, why should she not do the same? Of course. Certainly. But if the priest vomited, that did not excuse her. And her mouth after the priest's mouth. It was like the hanging of the bit of wood than reinforced the hanging of the sparrow, the hanging of the cat that reinforced the hanging of the bit of wood, the knocking that reinforced Kulka's hammering, my berg that reinforced Leo's.

Why did those vomiting mouths grip me like this? What did they know of the mouths concealed inside me? Whence this oral monstrosity? Perhaps the best thing for me to do would be to go away, and I did so. I did not go back into the house, but walked out into the meadow. I had had enough. The night and the moon floating through it were poisoned. There was a halo behind the tops of the trees, and innumerable groupings, processions, conversations, murmurings and whisperings, gay parties and games, were taking place all round. It really was a magical night. I would not go back to them, if I had my way I would never go back to them, probably the thing to do was get into one of the carriages, whip up the horses, and drive away for ever. But no. It was a magnificent night. In spite of everything I was enjoying myself. It was a wonderful night. But I must not prolong it, because I was really ill. It was a wonderful night. No, I was not so ill as all that. The house disappeared behind a hill, and as I approached the stream the turf beneath my feet was very soft. But what was the matter with that tree there, there was something unusual about it.

I stopped. There was a clump of trees, but one of them was different from the others, or rather it was exactly like the others, but there must have been something different about it for it to have attracted my attention. It was concealed by the other trees and it was hard to make it out in the dark, but all the same it somehow attracted my attention —by its unusual density or weight or a sense of strain or something. I walked past it with the feeling that it was terribly heavy, too heavy. I stopped and went back.

I walked into the clump of trees, sure now that there was something there. There were some scattered birches, and then a denser, darker, group of pines. I had a distinct feeling of advancing towards a crushing weight.

I looked round.

A shoe.

A leg hanging from one of the pine-trees. A leg, I said to myself, but was not sure. Another leg. It was a man . . . hanged. I looked again. Yes, it was a man. Legs, shoes, higher up a head all askew. In the darkness of the branches the rest of him was indistinguishable from the tree-trunk.

I looked all round. Nothing, nobody, silence. Then I looked again. A hanged man. There was something familiar about that yellow shoe, it reminded me of Louis's. I moved aside the branches, and saw Louis's jacket and Louis's face.

Louis. Louis, hanging by a belt. His own trouser-belt.

Was it Louis? Yes, it was Louis. I tried to get used to the idea. I could not get used to the idea. If he had hanged himself, he must have had his reasons, and slowly I tried seeking for them and imagining them. Who had hanged him? Had he done it himself? And when had it happened? I remembered that just before supper he had asked me to lend him a razor-blade, he had been quite calm, and during the walk he had seemed perfectly normal. And now, not much more than an hour later, here he was, hanged; and it must somehow have been inevitable, there must have been an accumulation of causes, though I had not the slightest clue to what they might have been. Yet an eddy of which I knew nothing must have disturbed the river that carries everything along, there must have been a blockage of some sort, links and connections and interlocking wheels. But Louis. Why Louis? If it had been Leo, or the priest, or Jadeczka, or even Lena, it would have been less unintelligible. But Louis? Nevertheless here it was, this fact, this hanging fact, the fact of Louis hanged, an enormous, brutal, heavy, aggressive fact, Louis hanging from a pine-tree with his shoes on.

One day I went to the dentist to have a tooth extracted, but for some reason or other the dentist could not grasp it properly with his pincers, which kept slipping, I don't know why, and it was the same with this heavily hanging, inaccessible and ungraspable fact which kept eluding me. If it had happened, in some way or other of course it must have been bound to happen. Cautiously I looked all round. I grew calmer. No doubt because I had understood.

Louis.

The sparrow.

I looked at him exactly as I had looked at the hanged sparrow.

This made four. The sparrow, the bit of wood, the cat, and now Louis. What consistency, what logic. This absurd corpse promptly turned into a rational corpse. But it was a clumsy sort of logic, a rather too personal and private logic of my own.

There was nothing I could do but think, and so I thought. I tried hard to make sense of it. Had he perhaps hanged the sparrow? Had he drawn the arrows, hanged the bit of wood, thought up all those feeble jokes? He must have had a sort of mania, a mania for hanging, which had ended up in his hanging himself here. He must have been mad. I remembered Leo sitting on the tree-trunk and denying, no doubt with complete truthfulness, that he had had anything to do with all that. So it must have been Louis. An obsession, a mania, a kind of madness.

There was also another possibility, this one on the lines of ordinary, normal logic. He might have been the victim of blackmail, someone might have been persecuting him, seeking revenge, perhaps, and might have surrounded him with those warning signs, which might have suggested to him the idea of hanging himself. But who could that have been? A member of the household? Kulka? Leo? Lena? Katasia?

Another, no less 'normal' possibility was that he might not have hanged himself but might have been murdered. Perhaps he had been strangled before being hanged. The maniac who amused himself by hanging things of no significance might have ended by wanting to hang something heavier than the bit of wood. Who might that have been? Leo? Katasia? But Katasia had stayed behind. But what did that prove? She *might* have made her way here secretly, for a thousand reasons and in a thousand ways, there was no limit to the theoretical possibilities. And what about Fuchs? Might he not have succumbed to the hanging contagion? Yes, he might. But he had been with us the whole time. But what of that? If it turned out that it had been he, a gap would certainly be found in his alibi, you could always find anything in the bottomless pit of things that happened. And the priest? There *might* be millions and millions of threads connecting his fat fingers with this hanged man.

It was perfectly conceivable. And what about the peasants who had driven us here? I smiled in the moonlight at the impotence of reason in the face of overflowing, destroying, enveloping reality. Everything was possible and nothing was impossible.

Yes, but the threads were slender, and here was this brutally hanging corpse, fitting so neatly into the sparrow—bit of wood—cat series like a, b, c, d or 1, 2, 3, 4. What consistency, what subterranean logic. It leapt to the eye.

Yet for all its self-evidence it dissolved into nothingness, into a mist, as soon as you tried to include it in the framework of ordinary logic. What arguments Fuchs and I had had. Could one speak of a logical thread connecting the sparrow and the bit of wood, linked as they were by a barely visible arrow on our bedroom ceiling, an arrow so indistinct that we had noticed it only by chance? So indistinct that we had had to complete it in our imagination? Discovering it, and then finding the bit of wood, had been like finding a needle in a haystack. Who, whether Louis or anyone else, would have taken the trouble to devise a whole system of practically invisible clues?

And in any case, what was the connection between the sparrow, the bit of wood and the cat if the cat had been hanged by me? True, the sparrow, the bit of wood and the cat made three hangings, but the third had been done by me, it was I who had added the third rhyme.

The whole thing was illusion, chimaera, moonshine. Yes, but here was this man hanging, and he was the fourth in the series. I wanted to go close and perhaps touch him, but I recoiled. The slight movement I made frightened me, as if it were indecent to move in the presence of a corpse. My horror—for it was horror—derived from the repetition, for the sparrow had been hanging just like this among the trees. I looked all round. What a spectacle. Mountains projecting themselves blindly into the expanse of the sky, on which centaurs, swans, ships, lions with shining manes, were navigating, and below a ballet of hills and woods enveloped in tremulous whiteness. Oh, the moon, a dead sphere shining with borrowed light; its second-hand, weakened, nocturnal glow was as contaminating and poisonous as an illness. And the constellations were unreal, artificial, imposed; they were the obsessions of the luminous sky.

But the important corpse was not the moon's, but Louis's, hanging from a tree just as the cat had been hanging from the wall. One, two, three, four (my counting merged into the distant pulsation of the night). I moved as if to go away, but it was not so easy. The time had not yet come.

What was I to do? The best thing . . . would be to act as if I had seen nothing, let things take their course. Why should I get involved? I was thinking about this when mouths returned to my mind, not very insistently, but they returned: Leo's mouth chewing, the priest's and Jadeczka's mouths vomiting, Katasia's and Lena's mouths, all of them. They imposed themselves on me, not very insistently, but mildly.

I moved my mouth, as if to defend myself, and at the same time the vague thought was at the back of my mind that I must not do that here. In fact what was the point of moving my lips in the presence of this corpse? Doing things in the presence of a corpse is not the same as doing them elsewhere. I felt alarmed and decided to go away.

Simultaneously something else happened that for the past minute I had been afraid was going to happen; I decided that I wanted to look this corpse in the mouth. It was not so much that this thought frightened me as that I more or less guessed that my desire to leave the corpse and go away would make me want to provoke it.

It was that that I was frightened of, and of course it made me want to do it all the more.

But it was not so easy. I should have to move the branches, turn the face towards the moon, look at it. I was not sure whether I should be able to do it without climbing the tree. A complicated and difficult task. Better not touch it.

I touched it, turned the head, looked.

The lips looked blackened, the upper lip was raised and the teeth were visible. A hole, a cavity. For a long time, of course, I had been faced with the possibility, the hypothesis, that one day I should have . . . to hang either myself or her. Hanging had presented itself to me under many aspects, and other theoretical possibilities, many of them very far-fetched, were connected with it. I had already hanged a cat, after all. But a cat is only a cat. Now, for the first time in my life, I was looking human death straight in the mouth. I was looking into a human buccal orifice, the buccal orifice of a hanged man.

Go away and leave it alone.

Go away and leave it alone. It was no business of mine, it had nothing to do with me. I was not under the slightest obligation to find out how or why it had happened. You took a little sand in the hollow of your hand and got hopelessly lost in the infinite, the inconceivable, the immeasurable. How could I hope to discover all the links and connections? He might, for instance, have hanged himself because Lena slept with Leo. How could one tell? One could never tell, one knew nothing. I would go away and leave it alone. But I stayed rooted to the spot, and the thought that passed through my mind was something like: What a pity I've looked him in the mouth, now I shan't be able to go.

This thought surprised me in the brightness of the night, but it was not without good reason. If I had behaved normally with this corpse I should have been able to leave, but after what I had done with my mouth and his mouth I could not. Or rather I could, but if I did I should no longer be able to say that I was not personally involved.

I pondered deeply, very deeply and breathlessly, but without any real thoughts in my mind, and then I started feeling afraid, really afraid, for I was with the corpse and the corpse was with me, and here we were together, and after looking it in the mouth I should not be able to detach myself from it.

I stretched out my hand and put my finger in its mouth.

It was not so easy, the jaws had already begun to stiffen, but I managed to insert my finger and met a strange, unknown tongue and a palate, which struck me as being cold and low, like the ceiling of a low room.

I withdrew my finger and wiped it on my handkerchief. I looked all round. Had no one seen me? No, no one had seen me. I turned the corpse round into its previous position, concealed it as much as possible behind the branches, obliterated my footprints in the grass, quickly, quickly, I was afraid, my nerves, I was afraid, I must get out of this. I made my way through the clump of trees and, seeing there was nothing but tremulous moonlight, I started walking away. I walked faster and faster in the direction of the house, but I did not run. Then I slowed down. What was I to tell them? How was I to tell them? Things were getting difficult. I had not hanged him. I had not hanged him. But, after putting my finger in his mouth, this hanged man was partly mine.

At the same time I felt a deep satisfaction that at last a link had been established between 'mouth' and 'hanging'. It was I who had done it. At last. I felt as if I had fulfilled my mission.

And now I must go and hang Lena.

I was astonished at this, genuinely astonished, for hitherto the idea of hanging had been purely gratuitous and hypothetical, and after putting my finger in his mouth its nature, so far from changing in any way, had been as eccentric, extravagant or even rhetorical as ever. But the force with which that corpse had entered me and I had entered it had broken down all the barriers. The sparrow had been hanged, and so had the bit of wood and the cat (before it was buried), and so had Louis. Hanged. Hanging and I were one. I stopped and stood still, reflecting that everyone wanted to be himself, and it followed that I too wanted to be myself. Who wanted syphilis, for instance? No one, of course, and yet the syphilitic wanted to be himself, *i.e.*, a syphilitic; it was easy to say he wanted to get well again, but it was like saying 'I don't want to be what I am', it didn't ring true.

The sparrow.

The bit of wood.

The cat.

Louis.

And now I should have to hang Lena.

Her mouth.

Katasia's mouth.

(The priest's and Jadeczka's mouths vomiting).

Louis's mouth.

And now I should have to hang Lena.

Strange. On the one hand, in this remote spot, with the mountains and forests bathed in the moonlight, all this seemed futile, insignificant, unreal, and on the other the tension of the hanging and the tension of the mouths must necessarily lead to. . . . Too bad. It was inevitable.

I walked on with my hands in my pockets.

I reached the top of a slope overlooking the house. I heard the sound of voices and singing. I saw lanterns about half a mile away on a hill opposite. It was they. Leo was showing them the way, and they were keeping up each other's spirits by singing and joking. Lena was with them.

From where I was standing the landscape stretching out before me trembled as if it had been chloroformed. Lena's sudden appearance on the scene had exactly the same effect on me as if I had been out shooting with a double-barrelled shot-gun and had spotted a hare in the distance. I could not help actually laughing. I struck out across country to join them. The sparrow was hanging and on I went. The bit of wood was hanging and on I went. I had hanged the cat and on I went. Louis was hanging and on I went.

I caught up with them just when they were leaving a barely visible path and going down into a wood. There was a lot of undergrowth and sharp stones, and they were advancing cautiously, and Leo, carrying a lantern, was acting as guide. They were joking and calling out to one another. 'Guide us, guide!' they shouted or 'why are we going down instead of up?' Somebody wanted to know how there could be a magnificent view right at the bottom of a dip, and somebody else announced a determination to sit down and not walk another step.

'Patience, patience,' said Leo, 'we haven't got far to go now, we'll soon be there, keep behind me, it's not much farther now.'

They had not noticed me, and I followed them. Lena was walking slightly apart from the others, and there would have been no difficulty in approaching her. I approached her in my role of strangler and hangman, and it would not have been difficult to take her aside (for we were in love, she was just as much in love with me as I was with her, there could be no doubt about that, because if I wanted to kill her it followed that she must be in love with me). And if I took her aside it would be easy to strangle her and hang her. I started realizing what it is like to be a murderer. You murder when murder is easy, when there is nothing else for you to do; the other possibilities have merely been exhausted. The sparrow was hanging, the bit of wood was hanging, Louis was hanging, and I was going to hang her as I had hanged the cat. Of course I might not hang her, but what a let-down, what a fiasco, that would be. Was I to disturb the natural order of things? After all that striving and scheming hanging had been plainly revealed to me and I had connected it with 'mouth'. Was I to give up and become a renegade now?

Out of the question.

I followed them. They played with their lanterns. Sometimes at the cinema you see a comic sequence in which a hunter cautiously advances with his gun at the ready while just behind him, following in his tracks, a fearsome wild beast, a huge bear or gigantic gorilla, is stalking him. The wild beast stalking me in this instance was the priest. He was walking close behind me and a little to one side, and obviously he was trailing in the rear without knowing where he was going or why. Perhaps he had been afraid of being left alone in the house. At first I had not noticed him, and I had no idea how long he had been at my heels with those big, peasant fingers of his which he kept fidgeting. And in his cassock. Heaven and hell. Sin. Our mother, the Holy Catholic Church. The cold of the confessional. The Church and the Pope. Damnation. The cassock. Heaven and hell. *Ite missa est.* Sin. Virtue. The cold of the confessional. *Sequentia sancti.* . . . The Church. Hell. The cassock. Sin. The cold of the confessional.

I gave him a violent push that made him stagger. Terror overcame me as I did so. What on earth had come over me? Had I gone mad? Now he would make a scene.

He did not. My hand met such a pathetic passivity that I felt totally reassured. He stood still without even looking at me. We stayed like that. I could see his face plainly. And his mouth. I raised my hand, wanting to stick a finger in his mouth, but he was gritting his teeth. I took his chin in my left hand, opened his mouth, and put my finger in.

I withdrew it and wiped it with my handkerchief.

I had to hasten my stride to catch up with the others. Sticking my finger in this priest's mouth had done me good, it was quite different from doing it to a corpse, and it was like introducing my chimaeras into the real world. I felt bolder and more cheerful. It struck me that all this had momentarily distracted me from the sparrow, etc., so I resumed awareness of the fact that down below some twenty-five miles away it was still there, with the bit of wood and the cat. Katasia was there too.

'Ladies and gentlemen,' Leo announced, 'let us pause here for a short rest.'

He was standing under a huge rock overhanging a gully rank with vegetation. Immediately in front of the rock there was a small clearing; it must have been a much frequented place, I thought I could make out wheel-tracks. There were some bushes and some grass. 'Lolo, I don't like it here, what a funny place he has chosen.' 'But colonel, there isn't anywhere to sit down.' 'My dear president, are we to sit on the bare earth?'

'All right, all right,' said Leo plaintively. 'But papa has lost a button from his sleeve. Ye gods, a button. Won't somebody bring a lantern?'

The sparrow.

The bit of wood.

The cat.

Louis.

The priest.

Leo bent up double looking for his button while Lolo held the lantern for him. I remembered Katasia's room, and Fuchs and me searching it with a pocket lamp. How long ago that had been. The room was still there, and so was Katasia. He went on searching, and ended by taking the lantern from Lolo's hands. But soon I noticed that, instead of using it to illuminate the ground, he was surreptitiously shining it on the big rock and other rocks that were lying around, reminding me of the way the pocket torch had flitted about when Fuchs and I examined the walls of Katasia's room. Was he really looking for a lost button? Perhaps he was doing nothing of the sort, perhaps this was the place to which he had been leading us, the place where twenty-seven years before . . . but he was not sure. He could not recognize it for certain. Since then new trees had grown, the ground had sunk, the rock might have shifted. He searched more and more feverishly, just as we had done. Seeing him wavering thus, lost and uncertain, almost drowning, with the water up to his chin, I could not help remembering how lost Fuchs and I had been in those ceilings, walls, and flower-beds. But that was the past. Meanwhile everybody waited and nobody spoke, perhaps because everyone was curious to see what was going to happen. I caught sight of Lena. She was delicate, like lace, and she was there with the sparrow, the cat, Katasia, Louis and the priest.

Leo was lost, bewildered and at his wit's end. He leaned over and examined the base of the rock. Silence.

Then he stood erect again.

'It's here,' he announced.

'But what is here, Mr Wojtys?' Lola said plaintively. 'We can't see anything.'

Leo faced us modestly, calmly and confidently.

'What an amazing coincidence, my friends,' he said. 'What a truly amazing coincidence. The odds against must have been about a million to one. Here was I looking for a shirt button when I realized that this rock . . . that I had been here before. It was here that I, twenty-seven years ago . . . it was here.'

He relapsed into thoughtfulness as suddenly if on a word of command, and remained like that. This went on and on. No one moved or spoke, and not till several minutes had passed did Lola say quietly and anxiously:

'What is the matter with you, Mr Wojtys?'

'Nothing,' he replied.

I noticed that Kulka was not present. Had she been left behind? Had she hanged Louis, perhaps? What nonsense, he had hanged himself. Why? Nobody knew yet. What would happen when they found out?

The sparrow.

The bit of wood.

The cat.

Louis.

It was exceedingly difficult to realize that what was happening here and now was related to other things that had happened in that house more than twenty miles away. I resented the fact that Leo was playing first violin and that everyone (myself included) had turned into an audience for him. We had been brought here to. . . .

He indistinctly muttered:

'Here. With a. . . .'

164

Several more minutes passed in silence. They were long minutes that reeked of lewdness, but they had their own eloquence, for if nobody spoke it meant that we were here for the sole purpose of enabling him to obtain his satisfaction in our presence. 'One is what one is.' We waited for him to finish. Time passed.

Suddenly he shone the lantern on his own face. His pincenez, his bald pate, his mouth, everything. His eyes were shut. Voluptuary and martyr. Then he said: 'That's all there is to see,' and put out the lantern.

The darkness leapt at me, it was much darker than one would have expected, clouds must have gathered overhead. Under the great rock he was almost invisible. What was he doing? He must have been surrendering to I don't know what lewd thoughts, concentrating on the memory of that one and only woman of his, celebrating his own lubricity. But . . . supposing he were not absolutely sure that this was the right spot? Supposing he had just picked on it at random?

I was surprised to see that nobody moved, though they must all have realized why they had been brought here—to be in attendance·on him, look at him, excite him by watching him. It would have been so easy to get up and go, but nobody moved. Lena, for instance, could have gone, but did not. She did not move. He began panting rhythmically. No one could see what he was doing, but he did not move. He groaned. He groaned aloud. It was a licentious groan but also a laborious one, to increase his lubricity. He groaned and whimpered. It was a stifled, guttural whimper. How he worked at it, struggled and strained, concentrated and celebrated. He worked and we waited. Then he said:

'Berg.'

'Berg,' I replied.

'Bamberging in the berg,' he shouted, and I replied:

'Bamberging in the berg.'

He quietened down completely and total silence prevailed. I thought sparrow Lena bit of wood cat in the mouth honey disfigured lip little clump of earth tear in the wallpaper finger Louis young trees hanging Lena lonely there teapot cat bit of wood fence road Louis priest wall cat bit of wood sparrow cat Louis hanged bit of wood hanged sparrow hanged Louis cat I'm going to hang. . . .

Suddenly it started raining. First big, isolated drops made us raise our heads, and then the heavens opened. A wind arose, universal panic broke out, everyone dashed for shelter to the nearest tree. But the big pines offered no protection, they dripped and dripped, water, water, everywhere, wet hair, wet shoulders, wet thighs, facing us in the darkness a vertical wall of water penetrated only by the pathetic light of the lanterns, by the light of which I saw rain falling and water flowing, forming rivulets and waterfalls and lakes, pouring and splashing everywhere, with gurgling torrents in which leaves and bits of straw or wood were carried away and disappeared. Torrents united into rivers, islands and blockages and obstacles appeared, streams flowed round them in complicated patterns, above the deluge continued and below a leaf was carried away or a bit of bark vanished in the flood. It all ended up in shivers and colds and fever. Lena had tonsillitis, and a taxi had to be sent for from Zakopane. Illness, doctors, in short everything changed.

I went back to Warsaw and my parents—warfare with my father was resumed—and to other things, problems, difficulties and complications. Today we had chicken and rice for lunch.